WHEN THE STORM BREAKS

EMERY ROSE

WHEN THE STORM BREAKS

by Emery Rose

Copyright © 2021 Emery Rose

All rights reserved.

Branding: Lori Jackson

Cover Design: Najla Qamber

Photographer: Michelle Lancaster

Editors: Jennifer Mirabelli (Content Edits); Ellie McLove, My Brother's Editor

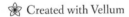 Created with Vellum

Dedication

For my readers. Thank you so much to each and every one of you who has ever picked up one of my books. With so many amazing books to choose from, I'm honored and grateful that you chose to read mine. It's because of you that I'm able to live out my dreams and write the stories of my heart. xoxo

PLAYLIST

"everything i wanted" – Billie Eilish
"Dreams" – Fleetwood Mac
"Down South" – Kings of Leon
"Comeback Story" – Kings of Leon
"I Got You" – Amy Shark
"Iris" – The Goo Goo Dolls
"Fire Away" – Chris Stapleton
"Sometimes I Cry" – Chris Stapleton
"Dust to Dust" – The Civil Wars
"My Soul I" – Anna Leone
"Shallow" – Lewis Capaldi
"Forever" – Lewis Capaldi
"With or Without You" – U2
"What Have I Done" – Dermot Kennedy
"Who Am I" – NEEDTOBREATHE
"I'm Still Here" – Sia
"Stand By Me" – Skylar Grey

PROLOGUE

Shiloh

"PLEASE, MAW MAW, YOU PROMISED," I pleaded. She tugged on the thick rope, pulling in the crawfish trap tied to our dock and emptied the haul into an old blue and white cooler. "It's the *only* thing I want for my birthday."

"Aw, cher t'bebe." She threw her hands up in the air and turned to face me. Maw Maw's face was weathered like old leather and lined with wrinkles, but her eyes were the clearest gray. Like an Arctic lake. Mine were gray too but instead of being clear, they were stormy.

I gave her my best puppy dog eyes and a sweet smile. She pinched my cheek, none too gently. Her hands smelled like crawfish. "How can I say no to this face?"

She was going to do it. This was really happening. I was so excited, I nearly threw up. A swarm of hornets had invaded my belly. Today was the day I would finally know what my future had in store for me.

"I want to know everything." The wood underneath my

feet creaked with every step, the cooler we were carrying banging against my leg as we walked to the side of the house. She turned on the hose and I helped her purge the muddy crawfish. My brother Landry should have been doing this, but he'd taken off with his friends, leaving me behind. As usual. This wasn't my favorite job but complaining about it wouldn't get the job done quicker. When the water ran clear and the crawfish were clean, I carried the cooler to the house by myself, eager to hurry this up before Landry came home with his idiot friends and ruined everything.

Lanterns strung from the wood rafters danced in the winter breeze and a ceramic gator greeted me at the front door. We lived in a swamp shack, the turquoise paint peeling to expose the gray underneath, the tin roof weathered and rusted with age. I side-stepped the drum kit, keyboard, and guitars crowding the front room where we held our practice sessions and carried the cooler to the kitchen, setting it on the avocado green linoleum floor.

Maw Maw and I took turns washing our hands at the kitchen sink with lemon-scented dish soap. Pale sunlight filtered through the bald cypresses outside the kitchen window and cast a honey glow on the kitchen, making it look warm and inviting instead of shabby. I wiped my wet hands on my Saints hoodie to dry them, my mind racing with possibilities. "I want to know if I'll be famous. If I'll fall in love... who will he be? Will he be handsome? Rich? A musician?"

Maw Maw held up her hand to silence me. "Hush, child. You have to be still. Quiet your mind."

I took a deep breath and nodded, then took my seat in one of the mismatched wood chairs across from her at the orange Formica kitchen table. "You're not using the cards?" I asked, my eyes roaming the room for her deck of Tarot cards she used for readings.

"No. Your vibrations are strong. Now no more talking. Close your eyes," she said softly.

I did as she asked, and she took both my hands in her gnarled ones. It was so quiet, I could hear my own heart beating and the hum of the refrigerator. I waited, and I waited, and I waited. Losing patience, I cracked one eye open. Maw Maw was staring straight ahead, but I could tell she was somewhere else. In a trance.

Her breathing sounded raspy and she squeezed my hands so tightly it hurt. But I didn't pull away. When she finally spoke, she didn't even sound like herself.

"I see a boy." I sucked in a breath. *A boy.* "Your paths will cross many times."

I wanted to ask what he looked like and how I would know him when I met him. Was he Dean Bouchon? Dean was my brother's best friend and the lead guitarist in the rock band we started over the summer. I wanted to ask a million questions, but I stayed quiet, not wanting to ruin her concentration.

"They've already crossed once before but ..."

My eyes flew open. Her face looked troubled.

"No." She shook her head vigorously, her long silver hair flying out around her. "It wasn't him. It was someone else... someone who took something precious away from you."

Something precious? Like what? My guitar? I didn't have much in the way of material possessions. Maw Maw and Landry were the most precious... oh, my mother? Did he take my mother away from me?

"The boy is a man now. He will save you more than once. And then it will be your turn to save him."

Save him from what?

"There will be many storms in your life, cher. The path you choose will not be an easy one, but it will bring you to the place you've always desired. Don't mistake it for where you really need to be." I heard the warning in her tone. A chill raced up my spine.

I waited for more, but her eyes cleared, and she slumped in her seat, exhausted. Disappointment settled in my gut. She hadn't told me *anything*. And what she had told me made zero sense.

After a few long moments of silence, her gray eyes locked onto mine. Spooky eyes, people said. A lot of folks called her crazy, but they were the non-believers. Like the horrible lady who put a gris-gris on us. After that, we couldn't use the front door for an entire year. "Shiloh, what is the one thing you want most in the world?"

I thought about it for a minute. "I want to find my one true love. And I want to be a rock star."

"That's two things. Two very different things. What if you had to choose?"

I didn't want to choose but my answer was automatic. "I'd choose music."

The corners of her mouth turned down in disappointment. "I was afraid you'd say that."

"Why does that make you afraid?"

A shadow crossed over her face. "Because it's what your momma chose."

"Music didn't kill her though. It wasn't music—"

"I know," Maw Maw cut me off. She didn't like to talk about what happened to my mom. She didn't really like to talk about my mom at all. I wish I'd gotten a chance to know her, but she'd been taken away from us when I was six months old and Landry was three and a half. And neither of us would ever, *not in a million years*, forgive the man who had killed her.

"Just promise me one thing."

I nodded.

"Don't chase fame. It's too fickle and the cost is too great."

"I don't care about being famous. I just want to play my guitar and sing for a living."

She pressed her lips together but didn't comment. Then she abruptly stood up from the table and stuck her head in the refrigerator, blocking my view. She came out with celery, carrots, chicken, and Andouille sausage and set them on the counter. "Come. Help me with the gumbo."

It might be my thirteenth birthday, but it was also a game day. When the Saints played, we always had a crawfish boil and gumbo with one chicken heart and a gizzard thrown in the pot for luck.

"Okay." I eyed the onions and the stainless-steel knife on the counter. "But it's my birthday, so I'm not chopping the onions."

Maw Maw smiled. "Tears are a good thing. They cleanse the soul."

I pulled a face. I hated chopping onions. I hated crying too. By now, I probably had the cleanest soul in all of Louisiana. While I chopped the hateful onions, my tears fell freely, cleansing my soul.

Raucous laughter alerted me to my brother's presence, and I hastily wiped away the tears on the sleeve of my hoodie before the boys caught me crying.

"Hey little sister." Dean tugged the end of my braid. The scent of weed clung to his clothes, and he moved his lips a hair's breadth from the shell of my ear. "I have a birthday surprise for you."

I gave him a little shove to give myself some space then turned my head to look at him, my curiosity piqued. Hazel-green eyes danced with mischief and he wore a smirk. The boy was trouble. Always had been. Everyone said he'd end up just like his Pops. A drunk and a gambler. I suspected the black eye he was sporting was compliments of Virgil Bouchon. His Pops was a nasty drunk.

But I knew Dean had a different destiny. Music would save him. Landry and I would make sure of it. I arched a brow, not wanting him to know that I cared. About his well-being. Or about his stupid surprise. Knowing him, he was lying about it. If he'd even gotten me a gift, it was probably stolen. "Oh yeah? What kind of surprise?"

"Keep your hands off my sister," Landry growled from the doorway. Dean laughed and sauntered out of the kitchen. Seconds later, he was playing the chords of Happy Birthday on the Stratocaster he'd gotten at a pawn shop. Gus set the rhythm on the bass guitar and Landry kept the beat on the drums. All three of them sang Happy Birthday, even Gus who barely ever opened his mouth to speak let alone sing.

Someday we'd make all our dreams come true. Me and the band. I'd do what my mom hadn't gotten a chance to. I'd go out to L.A. and dance among the stars. Write my lyrics in the sky. Blaze a trail straight up to the heavens. I wouldn't chase the stars like she had. I'd *be* a star. I didn't even need Maw Maw to confirm it.

In my heart of hearts, I *knew* it was my destiny. *Our* destiny. Acadian Storm. That was our band's name, and someday we'd be playing sold-out stadium concerts in front of thousands of screaming fans.

I'd do whatever it took to make it happen. I'd sacrifice anything and everything to make our dreams come true.

At thirteen, I had no idea how true that would be.

CHAPTER ONE

Shiloh

I FINISHED PACKING up the last of my things and zipped the case. It felt like I spent most of my life living out of a suitcase. Dragging it down the curved staircase, I held onto the wrought iron banister for support.

When I reached the bottom of the stairs, I glided my bag across the Italian marble foyer and left it by the front door then went in search of Bastian. There were twenty-two rooms in this house and he only used one—the "Blue Room." It looked like a cross between a boudoir and a French nightclub. I opened the carved oak door and stepped inside. French doors opened to the terrace and the pool, affording a view of the Hollywood Hills but heavy midnight blue curtains were drawn to ward off the sunlight. A jewel-toned chandelier cast light on the man who preferred the darkness to the light.

"Those cigarettes are going to kill you," I observed as I moved farther into the room, past the low-slung, midnight blue velvet sofas, my boots soundless on the Aubusson rug.

Bastian was sitting at the black baby grand, a lit cigarette dangling from his lips, eyes squinted against the smoke. He was wearing a purple velvet robe and a gray fedora, the ends of his dark hair curling where they hit his collar. "L.A. is sucking the soul out of me." His hands—insured for millions—played a jaunty medley of the bubblegum pop tunes he claimed to detest. "Through a pixie stick. It's a slow, arduous process. But the City of Angels won't rest until it's consumed every last drop of my liquid black soul."

I rolled my eyes—what a drama queen—and leaned my hip against the piano.

Bastian Cox was a British rock god. A gifted poet. A living legend who was notoriously difficult to interview. He was also my best friend. He'd been there for me through all the ups and downs of the past few years. I adored him. He was so talented. An unhinged genius with madness running through his veins. "You need fresh air and sunshine, Liberace."

He shuddered. "I need gray skies and thunderstorms." He switched gears and played a jazzy, sultry ballad I didn't recognize. A torch song. It sounded like something that would have been sung in a Parisian nightclub in the 1920s. "Sing for me, my little chanteuse."

I shook my head and laughed. "I can't. I'm leaving. Hayden's bringing the car around." Hayden was Bastian's driver, bodyguard, and closest male friend. Bastian rarely went anywhere without him. Hayden was the yang to Bastian's yin. If you asked me, they belonged together.

Bastian's hands paused on the keys and the last lonesome note echoed in the room. I grabbed a crystal ashtray from the black lacquer Chinoiserie sideboard under the antique mirror and walked it over to the piano then held the ashtray under his cigarette to catch the ash. He took it from me, ground out his cigarette, and set the ashtray on the piano bench next to him. "You're going through with it."

I nodded.

Bastian was the only one who knew why I was going to Texas. He was the only person I completely trusted. Not even Landry knew. My brother and I weren't on the best terms right now.

"Be careful, yeah?"

"Careful in what way?"

"Don't get too attached. Your life isn't in Texas." I could hear the worry in his tone. It had taken me a few years to wrap my head around the fact that Bastian Cox actually cared. Not about everyone. But about a chosen few. I was lucky to be one of them. After I broke up with Dean and left Acadian Storm last year, he not only offered me a place to stay, he produced my solo album and released it under the record label he set up five years ago.

"By all means, find yourself a hot cowboy. Ride him hard and put him away wet." He lit another cigarette and took a drag, his dark eyes studying my face through the blue haze of smoke. "But whatever you do, don't fall in love."

For Bastian, love was a dirty word. He was still dealing with the fallout of a nasty divorce after his Brazilian super-model wife of six months sold an exclusive story to the tabloids, pleading poverty even though the prenup left her six million dollars richer. And as for me? Falling in love was the last thing I wanted or needed. History had proven that I had lousy taste in men. Give me a bad boy, preferably one with a tragic backstory and a penchant for self-destruction, and I was all over him like flies on shit. Which was exactly what I always ended up with. A shit sandwich and enough heartache and misery to last a lifetime.

"I have no intention of falling in love."

"Good. But if you do fall madly and irrevocably in love, I want to hear the whole tragic tale. I could use some new material."

"I have to save all the best stuff for myself."

"Greedy."

"Why do you always assume love will be tragic?" I was contradicting myself. It always ended tragically.

"You can't have it all, Shiloh. Never make the mistake of believing you can. It will only end in heartbreak."

"Did Gia break your heart?" I asked, even though I knew she hadn't.

"I'd have to have a heart to break."

"You do have a heart. A big one."

"My soul has proven worthier than my heart. If forced to choose..." His eyes narrowed on my face. "Which would it be? Love or your music career?"

"Why should I have to choose? Some people make it work. With the right person, it's possible." I didn't know why I was insisting it was possible when I had no reason to believe it.

"When you find that unicorn, I'll dance the tango at your wedding. But until that tarnished prince who's willing to fall on the sword for you comes along... protect your battered heart. Trust no one. The world is filled with bloodsuckers and wankers and you, my little chanteuse, are a wanker magnet. Case in point. Cunt Dracula, the blood-sucking Bouchon," he said with a flourish of his hand. Ash fell from his cigarette to the parquet floor.

You could always count on Bastian to give you the cynical, jaded view of life. Too bad he was right.

If I was forced to choose, my career would always win. There was no man on earth worth giving up everything I'd worked so hard for. Luckily, I didn't have to worry about that.

Falling in love wasn't in the cards for me. My reason for going to Cypress Springs was something entirely different.

All I had to do was ingratiate myself into the McCallister family's lives. More specifically, Brody McCallister.

Thanks to the private investigator I'd hired, I knew Brody was the key to getting me closer to what I wanted.

I looked over at the doorway as Hayden strode into the room. All six foot four inches of sheer male perfection. He was a former rugby player and so ridiculously handsome it should be illegal. "How's his Highness feeling today?" he asked wryly.

"Apparently L.A. is sucking the soul out of him."

"Nothing new then." Hayden plucked the cigarette out of Bastian's mouth, crushed it in the ashtray and pocketed the pack of Marlboro Lights. He was always trying to get Bastian to give up cigarettes and eat healthier. A futile effort.

"Off you go." Bastian waved him away. "You wouldn't want her to miss her flight, would you?"

"I'll be back in time for dinner." He pointed at Bastian. "We're sitting outside."

"Do you live for the sole purpose of torturing me?"

"So it seems."

I smirked. They acted like a married couple. I wish they'd get together already. The only hitch was that Bastian, who had been with both men and women, never slept with anyone he truly cared about. Which was how I knew his marriage had been a sham.

"I'll see you at Glastonbury, yeah?" Bastian asked.

"I'll be there with bells on."

I grabbed my '63 Gibson acoustic, already packed in the hard case and said my goodbyes to Bastian before Hayden and I walked out the front door of the 1920s Hollywood Hills mansion into the eternal L.A. sunshine. I slid into the passenger seat of the silver Aston Martin, put on my sunglasses and pulled down the brim of my ball cap as Hayden navigated the curves in the road, "This Charming Man" by The Smiths blasting from the speakers.

I was Texas-bound, and I had exactly six weeks to find closure. To make peace with something I'd done when I was eighteen.

On the eve of my twenty-fifth birthday, Maw Maw visited me in a dream and told me I needed to go to Texas. Even though she was gone, she was still looking out for me. Still guiding me through this crazy thing called life. Dean was safely out of the way, serving sixty days in court-mandated rehab after his DUI and the stash of drugs they found in his glove compartment, so the timing couldn't be more perfect.

CHAPTER TWO

Brody

"Not only did you talk me into renting the guesthouse to a total stranger, you promised I'd pick her up at the airport?" I'd been informed of this plan via text from my aunt Kate. Now, thanks to an accident blocking the exit, I'd been sitting in bumper-to-bumper traffic for the past hour.

"She's flying in from California. She doesn't have a car."

"And how's that my problem? Hasn't she ever heard of Budget rental cars?"

Kate sighed. "Be nice. Be that charming Brody McCallister I know you're capable of and show her some good old-fashioned Southern hospitality."

"If she wants hospitality, she should have checked into a Comfort Inn. She'd better stay out of my way, that's all I've got to say."

My aunt sighed again. I didn't know why I was giving her shit. She didn't deserve it. But I didn't like the idea of a total stranger staying on my property. Unfortunately, I had a shitload of bills to pay and money was tight, so I had to do what I had to do.

"The grant hasn't come through yet?"

"No." My cousin Gideon, who worked for a venture capital firm in New York, had come up with a way for me to purchase more land and rescue more horses. Unfortunately, the US government was not so quick to fork over the cash. Even when the money hit my bank account, I'd only be breaking even. But as long as I could pay my bills and provide for my son, that was good enough for me.

"If you weren't so stubborn, you could let us give you the money. We're your family, Brody," she reminded me, her voice softer now. "When will you ever learn to accept our help?"

"I'm not taking handouts from anyone. Not even family." We'd been down this road before and she knew where I stood on the topic. There was no point discussing it again. Nothing she said would change my mind and Kate was smart enough to drop the subject.

"Once she's here, you won't even have to deal with her. She's all paid up for six weeks. And from what she said in her email, she's looking for peace and quiet. You won't even know she's there."

"Meanwhile, I have to act like a goddamn chauffeur," I grumbled. Another flaw in this plan was that the woman I was picking up—Vivienne Shaw—had my cell number but I didn't have hers. I didn't trust websites. Anyone could book a stay at my ranch with a credit card and some details that may or may not be the truth.

"You know I would have picked her up—"

"I sure as hell wasn't about to let you pick up a stranger at the airport." I wiped the sweat off my forehead with the back of my arm and took a few deep breaths. I needed fresh air, not exhaust fumes. And I needed the traffic to start moving before I lost my shit. I was hemmed in with nowhere to go.

"Well, there you go. And that's one of the many reasons I love you. You have a protective streak a mile long. Now be nice. She's your guest and she's paid a lot of money that you are sorely in need of. When you get to the airport, wait in your truck until she messages you and everything will be just fine. Goodbye Brody," Kate sing-songed.

I tossed my phone in the console then leaned back in my seat, crossed my arms over my chest, and waited for the traffic to start moving again.

It had been Kate's idea to renovate the guesthouse so I could rent it out. She'd been trying to help me out and I should have shown my appreciation instead of bitching and moaning like a little pussy. I'd apologize. Find a way to make it up to her. Not her fault I was drowning in bills. Not her fault I kept rescuing horses or that I'd bought another thirty acres for my mustangs. The more land I acquired, the fewer neighbors I'd have to deal with. The man who had owned those thirty acres had always been a thorn in my side.

Because of him, one of my rescue horses had ended up tangled in barbed wire. Call me ungracious but when his property went into foreclosure, I drank my finest bourbon and toasted his misfortune.

Finally, the traffic started moving and I heaved a sigh of relief.

As I drove past the scene of the accident—a fender bender—my cell rang with a number I didn't recognize. *Charming Brody*, I reminded myself before I said hello in my most pleasant voice.

"I was told there would be a car picking me up," she said without preamble. "I'm at the baggage claim. Are you my driver?" Her voice sounded like she smoked two packs a day.

Are you my driver? The fuck?

"Yes, ma'am. I'm on my way."

"Are you saying you're not at the airport yet?" she asked incredulously.

"I'm about fifteen minutes out. Got caught in a traffic—"

"*Fifteen minutes?* You mean I have to wait? Dammit. This is the last thing I need right now."

I clenched my jaw. It was her tone. The air of entitlement that pissed me off. "You think I don't have better things to do with my time? I'm doing eighty. But if you keep it up, I'll slow the fuck down." So much for charming Brody. Kate put way too much faith in me. Always had.

She sighed loudly. "Fine. Guess I'll have to make the best of it. But call me as soon as you get here."

There she went again, making demands. I already knew Vivienne Shaw was going to be a pain in my ass. I'd be willing to bet she was the type who complained about every little fucking thing. The bed's too soft. There's too much nature. My allergies are acting up.

How the hell was she going to get around without a car? Her problem, not mine. After I picked her up and dropped her off at the guesthouse, she was on her own.

"Will do." I cut the call and eased off the accelerator, taking my own sweet time. No need to risk a speeding ticket for this woman. She could wait.

Thirty minutes later, I pulled up in front of the arrivals area at the Austin airport and parked at the curb. Then I called my new best friend, Vivienne.

"I'm here."

"Thank God. I'm on my way out. How will I find you?"

"Look for the black stretch limo parked by the pillar marked D."

"A limo? You're in a limo?" I chuckled under my breath.

"I'm outside now and I don't see... can you stop playing games," she huffed. "Where are you?"

"I'm in a black pickup." I climbed out of my truck and rounded the hood so she could see me. The sooner she got in the truck, the sooner I'd get this over with. I scanned the passengers exiting the glass doors and the ones milling around out front but didn't see anyone who sounded like the name or the voice on the phone.

"Can you see me now?" I asked.

"Dirty blond hair, jeans, and a T-shirt?"

"That's me."

She cut the call and I watched a girl in a black ball cap with the gold New Orleans Saints logo, her head ducked as she walked toward me. *This* was Vivienne Shaw? She was wearing an oversized black hoodie and ripped black jeans, pulling a roller bag behind her, a guitar case strapped to her back.

Black leather combat boots stopped in front of me. She glanced over her shoulder before she pulled the guitar off her back and set the hard case at my feet. "Can we get out of here now?"

"In a hurry?"

She blew out an exasperated breath. "I need to get out of here. Can we go now?"

"All depends." I crossed my arms over my chest. "What's your name?"

She lifted her chin and gray eyes met mine. Stormy grays. Like the sky just before a thunderstorm. Ever feel like you've just got struck by lightning? A jolt of white heat shot through my body and I visibly shuddered.

The fuck?

I'd never had this kind of physical reaction to a girl before. I'd been attracted to plenty of women, had been with my fair share. But never once had I looked into someone's eyes and felt like I was looking at someone who would have the power to wreck me.

It wasn't just a physical attraction either. This was something altogether different. Like a deja vu moment. As if we'd been here before. In a dream or another lifetime.

Where have you been all my life? That was the question on the tip of my tongue as we stood on the sidewalk outside the airport and stared at each other in the fading light.

My eyes flitted over her face, partially hidden by the ball cap pulled down low over her forehead. I caught a glint of silver from the thin hoop piercing her left nostril. Her lips were full, naturally pink, stormy eyes fringed by thick black lashes, her cheekbones high and sharp. No two ways around it, she was beautiful. But she had an edge to her.

I took a step back and raked my hand through my hair. Averting my gaze, I sucked in a deep breath of muggy air. This couldn't be good.

"Vivienne Shaw," she said, finally answering a question I'd forgotten I asked, in that same throaty voice from the phone. Sexy. Gravelly. It reached deep inside and rattled my bones. Not what you'd expect to hear coming out of this girl's mouth. She was all of five foot three or four and underneath the baggy sweatshirt I suspected she was small and thin. She was young, early twenties if I had to guess, but her eyes looked older. Like they'd seen the world and it hadn't always done right by her.

"Hey, wait!" a guy shouted. "Can you give me a smile?" She looked over her shoulder as the flash from his camera went off.

What the hell?

"We need to go." She jostled my arm. That spurred me into action.

I opened the passenger door of my truck and quickly

ushered her inside like I really was a chauffeur. Or a gentleman. Not that anyone had ever accused me of that before.

Once she was safely inside, I stowed her bag and guitar case in the back and slammed the door, turning to face the guy who was right in my face now. I blocked his view of the girl with my body and widened my stance, crossing my arms over my chest. Motherfucker would have to get through me first. Good luck with that.

"Take another step closer and I'll smash your camera on the sidewalk then break your fucking hand for good measure."

Dickwad held up his hands like he was innocent but the smirk on his face suggested otherwise. I glared at him. I had half a mind to smash his camera anyway just for that stupid smirk. "If you know what's good for you, you'll back off. Right. The. Fuck. Now."

"What are you, her bodyguard? New boyfriend? What's your name?"

"I'm about to become your worst fucking nightmare if you don't do as I say." I hadn't lifted a finger to touch him. Not looking for an assault charge tonight. But I stared him down until his confidence faltered. I could kick his ass from here to Sunday and the little weasel in his skinny jeans damn well knew it.

"Jesus, man. calm down. I just want a photo."

"You're not getting jack shit."

"Get in the truck," she hissed, tugging on the hem of my T-shirt through the open window. "Let's go."

The guy was still there, so I didn't budge. I bared my teeth and growled like a wild animal until he finally scurried away. I waited until he was gone before I left her side and climbed into the truck then hit the gas and pulled away from the curb.

"Did you know that guy?" I asked when we got onto the 290, headed west.

"No."

"Why was he trying to take your photo?" I side-eyed her. "Was he hassling you?"

She shook her head. "It's fine. No big deal. But if you'd smashed his camera, it would have turned into a big deal."

"Did you want him taking your photo?"

"No."

"Well, there you go. What else was I supposed to do?"

"You were supposed to get in the truck and get us out of there."

"Duly noted. Next time I see a pervert taking photos of a girl he doesn't know, a girl who clearly doesn't want her photo taken, I'll just walk away and leave her to deal with it on her own."

"You wouldn't do that though, would you?"

"If it's someone other than you, hell no. But for you, I'll make an exception."

She laughed. "Good to know. Look, I'm sorry I gave you a hard time. I'm not usually such a diva." She sighed. "I was tired and irritable."

Her apology sounded sincere. "Sorry I was late. There was an accident."

"Was anyone hurt?" She sounded as if she really cared.

"No."

She exhaled. "That's good. I never caught your name."

"Brody."

"Brody? *You're* Brody?"

"Were you expecting someone different?"

"I ... didn't know what to expect." She cleared her throat. "Thanks for picking me up."

"No problem." I nearly laughed at myself. What a dumb shit. *No problem.* Funny how my tune had changed. But I had a bad feeling this girl would be a problem and more trouble was the last thing I needed. "What do you plan to do in Cypress Springs for six weeks?"

"I heard it's a good spot for drug dealers and fugitives to lay low," she deadpanned.

Smart ass. A smart ass who had no intention of telling me what had brought her to Texas. Her accent was Southern, but it wasn't Texan. Judging by the hat, I'd say she was a Louisiana girl. "Did you stash your drugs in the case?"

"Nah. That's where I stashed my semi-automatic. A girl's gotta protect herself." She shot me a finger gun and blew the smoke off it. Cute. Not that you'd call her cute. Lethal, more like it.

"I forgot how hot it gets down South." It was the beginning of May, not even summer yet, but we were having a heatwave. She eyed the A/C but didn't ask me to turn it on. I always drove with the windows down. Summer. Winter. Spring. Didn't matter. I hated being cooped up in an enclosed space. She didn't ask me to roll up the windows and maybe I should have offered but I didn't. Kate had tried to instill good manners in me since the age of ten but they'd never fully sunk in.

I side-eyed her as she unzipped the hoodie and slid her arms out of the sleeves. A tattoo wrapped around her left bicep and disappeared under the strap of her black tank top. Her black hair was braided into a thick coil that hung over one shoulder and reached the top of her breast. Round, full tits. More than a handful. Bigger than you'd expect on her small frame.

"Keep your eyes on the road, cowboy."

I returned my eyes to the road. "What makes you think I'm a cowboy?"

"Your truck smells like leather and horses, I'm guessing you live on the ranch and you have that cowboy swagger."

"Cowboy swagger, huh?"

"You look, act and talk like a cowboy. I know trouble when I see it."

"Funny. I was thinking the same about you."

"I'm not looking to cause any trouble."

"People never are. But sometimes it just finds you."

"Sounds like you know something about that. Do you attract a lot of trouble?"

"More than my fair share. You're in my passenger seat, aren't you?"

She laughed. "Kate said she'd be happy to send a car to pick me up. In fact, she insisted on it."

That sounded like Kate so it didn't surprise me. Kate was the contact person on the website. She didn't mind using her own name and photo whereas I had balked at the idea. I liked my privacy and guarded it fiercely.

"Do you work on the ranch?" she asked.

"Yeah, I work there." It was the truth. I worked my ass off. "How about you? What's your line of work? Drug dealer? Assassin?"

"Those are my side gigs. They fund my music addiction."

"As far as addictions go, that's a good one."

"I guess it is," she said thoughtfully, her voice tinged with sadness. "Music is my life. My salvation. The one thing that's always there for me in good times and bad."

I wanted to hear about her bad times and what she'd needed to find salvation from. That's what told you what a person was truly made of. Anyone could get by in the good times when life was easy and ran smoothly. But all the bad shit that went along with being human? That's where you found your strength. That's what made you who you are. But she was a total stranger, and I wasn't in the habit of digging too deep. If you got too personal, people expected you to reciprocate.

"How long have you been playing the guitar?" Not sure

why but I wanted to keep her talking. More for the sound of her voice than the actual words coming out of her mouth.

"Since I was old enough to hold my first one. Guess I was around five or six." I heard the smile in her voice. "I used to play until my fingers were raw and bleeding. Until I built up so many calluses it didn't hurt to play anymore." I glanced at her hands as her tattooed fingers spun the chunky silver ring around her thumb.

"Do you have something like that in your life, Brody? Do you have something that's your salvation?"

"What makes you think I'm in need of saving?"

"We're all in need of saving. But some of us more than others. What's your thing? What's your salvation?"

Strange questions from a strange girl. "Working with horses, I guess."

"I'm glad you have that. Everyone needs something."

After that, she was quiet. When I looked over at her, her eyes were closed.

We lapsed into silence and I drove like I did when I had my son in the car. I took it slow and easy, keeping my eyes on the road, hyper-vigilant for threats to her safety. Like I was transporting precious cargo and I'd sooner die before letting anything happen to her. I couldn't say what it was about her that made me feel like she needed my protection, but I thought she did.

It was only when I was two miles from home that I realized what a dumb shit I'd been. I laughed under my breath. How could I not have figured it out sooner? I glanced at her again to confirm my suspicions. Her cheek was pressed against the leather seat, her body tucked underneath her, eyes closed, the hat discarded.

What were the fucking chances Shiloh Leroux would end up in my truck, staying at the guesthouse on my horse ranch?

One in a million. Yet here she was, curled up in the passenger seat, sound asleep.

I'd been right about her. She was trouble with a capital T. I never went looking for it, but it always managed to find me.

This was the second time we'd met, although I doubt she remembered the first.

CHAPTER THREE

Brody

HEADLIGHTS ILLUMINATING THE WAY, my tires crunched over the gravel as I followed the dirt lane that led to the timber-framed cottage nestled in a grove of trees.

I parked and cut the engine, plunging us into silence. Someone had left the porch light on. Probably Kate. She'd always been big on giving everyone a warm welcome, whether they deserved it or not.

Shiloh was still sound asleep. Something stopped me from waking her. Instead, I sat back in my seat, folded my arms over my chest, and waited for her to wake up. Like I had all the time in the world and this was no inconvenience.

I'd seen Shiloh once before. About nine years ago. Back when I was on the rodeo circuit and living in an Airstream on Austin Armacost's ranch. Years before she'd hit the big time. She and her band were playing on a makeshift stage in a dive bar in Lafayette, Louisiana. I usually tried to steer clear of Louisiana, especially Lafayette. Too many bad memories associated with the place. But that time, I'd agreed to ride in Lafayette and was well on my way to getting drunk before she showed up.

Shiloh couldn't have been older than fifteen or sixteen at the time. When she stepped up to the mic, cradling her guitar, nobody had been expecting much. The crowd had been rowdy, talking and laughing over the music blasting from the speakers.

But when the music had cut out and she'd started playing and singing, I stopped whatever I was doing to listen. She sang a cover version of "Iris" by The Goo Goo Dolls that made me feel like I'd never heard the song before.

I don't remember the girl I was with that night, barely glanced at the guys in her band, but I remember Shiloh Leroux and the sound of her voice that would go on to make her one of the hottest stars in the music industry. I remember the look on her face that night when she played and sang. Like she was in another world far away from that dive bar with sawdust on the floor and the scent of sweat and stale beer in the air.

I had no idea what had brought her to Cypress Springs. Maybe it was just peace and quiet she was after, but I had a feeling it was something more.

I'd been sitting in silence for an hour, my thoughts wandering from the night I met Shiloh to the endless list of jobs that needed to be done on the ranch, when I heard her stir. I turned my head to look at her as she sat up and tried to get her bearings. Except for the glow of the porch light, the night was pitch black.

"Hey," she said, her voice sleep-groggy as she pulled the hat down over her head again. "You should have woken me up."

"You're awake now."

I grabbed her bag and the guitar case from the back. She followed me to the porch and waited while I entered the code in the keypad then pushed open the door.

Once inside, I flicked on the lights and was almost surprised to find the cabin was empty. Even though Walt was gone, I still expected to see his craggy face peering back at me from the leather sofa, sharing words of wisdom he'd gathered during his eighty-odd years on earth. But he wasn't here, and the place had been renovated after he died so it no longer smelled like Camel cigarettes and the medicinal plants and herbs he used to brew into teas.

Kate had left a peach pie on the kitchen counter and wildflowers in mason jars sat on the windowsill, compliments of Lila. According to Kate's write-up on the website, the cottage was charming and rustic with a spectacular view of the spring-fed lake and rolling green hills. A home away from home, she'd called it.

I didn't think Shiloh Leroux really gave a shit what the place looked like or the view, so I saved the speech and carried her bags up the wooden staircase to the bigger of the two bedrooms. It was a nice enough room—light and airy with rustic wood walls, furnished with a bed, dresser, and bedside tables, a patchwork quilt on the bed—but probably not the glitz and glamor she'd become accustomed to. I set her suitcase on the long stool at the bottom of the bed and turned around to find her right in front of me.

"Thanks for the lift, Brody."

"Yeah, sure." I raked my hand through my hair, trying to shake off the strange feeling I got whenever I was near her. Edging out of the bedroom, I took the stairs down to the main level with her following on my heels.

"You've got my number if you need anything." I was halfway out the door when she called my name. I looked over my shoulder, my brow cocked in question.

"I'm going to need a car. I can pay cash. Nothing fancy. Just something to get me around town while I'm here. A pickup would be good," she added. "Do you know of anyone who might be looking to sell?"

She could walk onto a lot and drive away in any damn car she wanted. Which confirmed my suspicion. She was looking to lay low and fly under the radar. Couldn't blame her. Who in their right mind would want to be hounded by the paparazzi and crazed fans? "I'll see what I can do."

She tipped her chin in thanks and I closed the door behind me, her secret safe for now.

Five minutes later, I walked through the front door of my house and called Ridge's name. No response. The TV was blaring in the living room and I stopped in the doorway. Muttering a curse, I scrubbed my hand over my face, wishing I could unsee the sight before me. Ridge's gaze was focused on the TV, remote in hand as he flicked channels just as if some chick didn't have his dick in her mouth.

Jesus Christ.

"Ridge. Put your dick back in your pants. And you can go." I pointed to the blonde who released him with a pop and scrambled to her feet while he tucked himself back into his jeans and zipped them up, propping his feet on the coffee table. So far, I hadn't managed to find anything that Ridge truly cared about, and he sure as hell didn't give a shit about this girl who was giving him the eye and waiting for him to defend her. He kept flicking through the channels, not even sparing her a glance.

Had I been this much of an asshole at seventeen? I'd turned thirty-three a few weeks ago and depending who you asked, I was *still* an asshole. So there you go.

"Have you got a ride home?" I asked the girl when Ridge made no move to get his lazy ass off the sofa.

"Um yeah, I'm good," she mumbled, keeping her eyes down, unable to look at me as she gathered her books and stuffed them in her backpack. "So... I'll just... I'll go now. See you at school, I guess," she told Ridge, her smile hopeful.

I wanted to shake some sense into her, tell her not to waste her time or her smile on guys like Ridge. It never ceased to amaze me that there were girls out there who fell for the bad boys. The worse you treated them, the more they knocked themselves out. I knew this because there had been a time I'd been just like Ridge.

He winked at her. "See you around, babe."

"Walk her to the door, Ridge," I said through clenched teeth.

His feet hit the ground and he stood up slowly, yawning and stretching, taking his sweet time before he walked the girl to the front door. Their voices were low, and I had no interest in eavesdropping but I waited for him to return which took at least five more minutes.

"Catch you in the morning, bro." He swaggered to the doorway, ready to make his exit.

"Hold up."

He turned, a bored look on his face, and roughed a hand through his hair. It was a few shades darker than mine and reached the collar of his T-shirt. We were of similar height and build and according to my cousin Jesse, Ridge looked like a male stripper. He relied on his looks to get him whatever he wanted. Which meant he'd been intent on seducing every woman in a ten-mile radius, including his female teachers. In the past four months, I'd been called into the principal's and guidance counselor's office almost as many times as I had been in my four years of high school.

"Did you finish your English essay?"

He smirked. "Sure did." He grabbed a notebook from the coffee table. "Pretty sure it's gonna get me an A."

"Let's see it."

"I need to re-copy it. It's still messy."

I stifled the laughter that threatened to burst free. This shit wasn't funny. I was looking at my worst nightmare. Brody McCallister 2.0.

I jerked my chin at the notebook. "Let me read it."

"Nah. You don't wanna do that. This shit's boring."

I grabbed the notebook out of his hand and flicked through the loose-leaf pages until I got to an essay about *Of Mice and Men*. The handwriting was neat, the cursive loopy and decidedly feminine. Not his chicken scratch. Color me surprised.

"Let me get this straight. You got the girl to write your essay and to thank her, you let her give you a blowjob?"

He snickered. So fucking proud of himself and too stupid to hide it. "Good deal, right?"

I ripped the pages out of the notebook, crumpled them into a ball and stuffed it in my pocket before I slapped the notebook against his chest. "Sit down and write your own goddamn essay."

"Fuck that. I'm outta here." He headed for the front door. Ridge was always on the verge of running away but considering he had nowhere to go, he never got far. He might be failing school, but the kid wasn't stupid. He was street smart. A survivor who knew that staying with me meant he'd have food, clothes, and shelter. As long as he was under my roof, he was mine to protect and to fight for. Which was exactly what I intended to do.

I grabbed the collar of his T-shirt and hauled him back then shoved him onto the sofa. "You're not going anywhere until this essay is done."

His eyes narrowed. I crossed my arms over my chest and stared him down. He rolled his eyes, a reminder that he was only seventeen. Still a kid. A fucked-up kid who needed guidance and love and the reassurance that I wasn't going to quit on him no matter what he did or said or how hard he pushed me. This was what Kate had told me and she was the best fucking mother on the planet, so I took her advice on board.

"What are you gonna do?" He smirked. "Kick me out if I don't write a stupid ass essay?"

"Nah. Not looking to take the easy way out. We're not leaving this room until it's written."

He groaned. "Come on, man." His head hit the back of the sofa and he stared at the ceiling. "I'm not good at this shit."

Well, that makes two of us. "Did you read the book?"

He shrugged one shoulder. "Couldn't get past the first page. Total snooze-fest."

I picked up the book and checked the page count. Just over a hundred pages. Not *War and Peace*, thank fuck. "Then I guess I'd better make a pot of coffee. It's gonna be a long-ass night." I tossed the book into his lap. "Start reading. Out loud so I can listen too."

"Why are you being such a hard-ass about this? It's just a stupid English essay. I've got better shit to do with my time."

"So do I. But we're doing this."

"*We?*"

"Start reading," I commanded as I strode into the kitchen to put on a pot of coffee. Like this was what I wanted to be doing on a Tuesday night. I sure as hell hadn't been the best student. But this kid would finish high school if it fucking killed me.

The first time I met Ridge was New Year's Day. Before the cops called and told me he'd been found alongside the road about fourteen miles from here and was asking for me by name, I had no idea my baby brother even existed. He'd taken a bus and hitchhiked across four state lines to get to me. By the time he showed up, he was beaten and bloody. A long-haul trucker had dumped his ass on the side of the road after he was informed over the radio that someone matching

Ridge's description had stolen another trucker's wallet at the truck stop in the next county. I was sure he'd done worse things.

Ridge had been raised by a junkie who would go for years of being clean only to lapse again. Until finally the drugs had killed her. Instead of calling the authorities when he found her dead in their apartment, Ridge had packed his bags and high-tailed it out of there. He said he'd only found out about me six months before our mother died. She'd let it slip that she had another son named Brody who lived in Cypress Springs, Texas. She'd claimed I had deserted her, turned my back on her and told lies that had resulted in her losing custody of me.

I hadn't lied. I hadn't told the whole truth either. If I had, she would have lost me years before that.

Like me, Ridge had been dealt a shit hand but unlike me, he hadn't been lucky enough to be taken in by family at the age of ten. Kate and Patrick had offered to take him in but the way I saw it, he had come here looking for me. He was my responsibility, not theirs, and I had no intention of failing him the way our mother had. I'd do whatever I could to help him move on from his past and make a good life for himself.

More living, less dwelling. That was my motto and it had served me well. Hell knows I'd done a lot of living.

Booted feet propped on the coffee table, mug of coffee in my hand, I pulled out my phone and texted my buddy Austin while Ridge grudgingly read *Of Mice and Men*.

You still got that old pickup you use for hayrides?

Message sent, I pocketed my phone and listened to the story. It had probably been assigned reading back when I was in high school, but hell knows I hadn't read it either. Turns out I'd missed out on some good shit.

"Well, damn, that was harsh," Ridge said when he reached

the end, and tossed the book on the coffee table. "That's the trouble with having big dreams."

I side-eyed him. "You have to have big dreams, Ridge. It's what gives you hope. Gives you something worth fighting for."

He snorted. "That was cheesy as hell."

"Yeah. Guess it was." I chuckled under my breath. I'd never felt as old as I did right now, trying to straddle the line between parent and older brother. It was easier with a six-year-old. Noah still believed I walked on water whereas Ridge saw through all my bullshit and called me out on it. It wasn't just their age difference though. It was their circumstances. Noah's life had always been good. From the minute he was born, he never had to worry about being loved or taken care of. Had never had to question or doubt that the adults in his life would always be there for him. With no reason not to, Noah's first instinct was to put his trust in people, believing they'd always do right by him. I don't think I'd ever been that innocent or trusting, not even at six.

Ridge was more like me. Took more convincing to believe that people's intentions were good, and they'd have your back if you should ever need them. No doubt he'd been looking after himself for a long time, never trusting that our mother would be there when he needed her. Because she never fucking was.

You would think that finding out my mother was dead would have made me feel something. But I hadn't felt a damn thing. She'd been dead to me for a long time. But Ridge was a different story. He'd spent seventeen years of his life with her.

Now he stared at the blank sheet of paper in front of him, his shoulders slumped. "What the fuck am I supposed to write?"

"Write your own truth."

He looked at me like I was crazy but a few seconds later he started writing.

I didn't give a shit if he got an A or a D. What mattered was that he didn't take the easy way out and have someone do his work for him. Because guess what? That ain't how life works. Nobody can carry your load except for you. And sometimes that shit got heavy.

While he wrote his essay, I Googled Shiloh Leroux and justified the intrusion on her privacy by telling myself it was because she was staying on my property. Bullshit.

I read about the Louisiana girl's meteoric rise to fame with the indie rock band, Acadian Storm. It was your typical rock and roll story—sex, drugs, stints in rehab, lawsuits settled out of court. One year ago, Shiloh left Acadian Storm to pursue a solo career. She won a Grammy for "Damage", the lead track on her self-titled debut album featuring Bastian Cox, the British rock star.

My eye caught on a photo of Shiloh with Dean Bouchon, her ex-boyfriend and lead guitarist for Acadian Storm, coming out of a club in L.A. Her hair was silver, eyes smoky, lips red. She was wearing a black leather mini dress and ankle boots with sky-high heels and looked nothing like the girl who had fallen asleep in my truck. Dean Bouchon looked like a douche, wearing sunglasses at night.

The headline read: ***The TRUTH About Dean & Shiloh's Breakup***

I didn't read the story. I didn't read the one about how Shiloh broke up the band or the rumors that she left Dean for Bastian Cox either.

Shiloh was currently in the midst of a world tour. It had started in Singapore at the end of January, with dates still being added well into next year, the tickets selling out as soon as they were released.

All of which begged the question: *Why are you here, Shiloh? And why should I even care?*

I pocketed my phone. Never should have looked her up in the first place. None of my damn business.

"Done," Ridge said, closing his notebook, a satisfied smile on his face. "Turns out I had a lot to say."

In retrospect, I should have questioned that or at the very least, read the damn thing. Instead, I took the easy way out and went to bed.

CHAPTER FOUR

Shiloh

A KNOCK on the front door woke me. I pushed the black cashmere eye mask on top of my head and squinted at the bright sunlight streaming through the windows. Where was I? Not in a hotel. The sheets were soft and smelled like lavender. Outside my open windows, the sky was glaringly blue, and the air smelled fresh and sweet.

I was in Cypress Springs, Texas and someone was still banging on the door. Dragging myself out of bed, I ran my fingers through my tangled hair as I walked down the stairs. Padding across the braided rug covering the hardwood floor, I stopped in front of the locked door.

"Who is it?" I'd had too many groupies and creepers showing up outside my door to open it to just anyone and there was no peephole to tell me who my caller was.

"Brody."

Brody. My lips curved into a small smile as I opened the door. He wore faded denim, dusty work boots, and a sweat-stained gray T-shirt tight enough to show the ripples and dips of his chiseled abs. I was mesmerized by his broad shoulders, bulging biceps and the sheen of sweat on his suntanned skin. He was so deliciously masculine.

"Hey Cowboy."

"Viv."

Viv. He'd already shortened my alias.

His gaze roamed from my face and down, slow as you like, taking in my silky pearl-gray camisole and matching short set trimmed in black lace. When his whiskey browns finally returned to my face, it felt like he'd branded every inch of my skin and left a trail of heat in its wake.

"Enjoying the view?"

"It'll do." He chuckled at my raised brows. *It'll do?* What a charmer. "Didn't mean to wake you..." There was no hint of an apology in his voice. "But it is two in the afternoon."

"I didn't fall asleep until six this morning."

He tilted his head, studying my face like I was a riddle he wanted to solve. "Why couldn't you sleep?"

"Jet lag."

"California is only two hours behind Texas."

"Guess I'm sensitive to time changes." Four days ago, I'd flown back from Australia and had gone directly into meetings with the record label followed by interviews, a feature story in Vanity Fair, and an appearance on *Jimmy Kimmel Live.* Before I hopped my flight from L.A., I'd made the mistake of answering my phone and had yet another argument with Landry. When I'd stopped to take a breath, the stress and exhaustion had caught up to me. I leaned my hip against the doorframe and crossed my arms over my chest. "Did you need something, Brody?"

"No. But you did. Got you that pickup you asked for."

I looked over his shoulder at a faded blue Chevy. It looked

like the one Maw Maw used to drive. The thought of her and that old truck put a big smile on my face.

"There it is," he said softly.

My gaze swung back to his face. "There what is?"

"Your smile. You should do it more often."

"Give me a reason and I just might."

"I thought me standing in your doorway would be enough reason."

I laughed at his response, but my laughter faded under the intensity of his gaze. I wanted to know what his story was. From the moment we first laid eyes on each other, I knew he had one and that parts of it were tragic. It was just a feeling I got. Maybe that was why I'd been drawn to him in the first place. But he looked as if he'd ridden out the storm and had come out on the other side of it. Or maybe he was really good at pretending.

Maw Maw always told me I'd inherited her psychic powers. Whether it was a blessing or a curse, I was never quite sure. Either way, I'd never really believed I had her gift.

Right now, though, something was taking hold of me. A strong vibration that told me something big was headed our way. I didn't know if the outcome would be good or bad, but I knew one thing with absolute certainty. Neither of us would come out of it unscathed. All the more reason to keep my distance.

I dragged my gaze away from his to the pickup truck parked right in front. "How much do you want for it?"

"I don't want your money. Just use it while you're here and leave it with a full tank when you're done."

"I need to pay you for it. I can't just take your truck."

"It's not mine. Friend owed me a favor. It's a crap truck but it should get you around just fine. So take the damn truck." He ran his hand through his longish dirty blond hair, his voice gruff. "I can't be playing chauffeur every time you need to go somewhere."

With that, Brody handed me the keys and strode away.

"I never asked you to play chauffeur," I called after him. "I never asked you for anything."

"Well, that just ain't true now, is it? You asked me to find you a ride and I did." He patted the hood of the pickup and turned around to face me as I moved to the edge of the porch. "And if you need me to keep your secret and protect you from assholes, I'll do that too, Shi-loh," he said, dragging out the syllables of my real name in his smooth Texas drawl. "All you gotta do is ask nicely."

I didn't bother telling him I'd never asked for his protection last night. I was too fixated on the fact that he knew my name. "Dammit. How long did it take you to figure out who I am?"

He chuckled and shook his head. "Longer than it should've. Never claimed to be all that bright. But I've got plenty of other attributes to make up for it."

As if to prove his point, he gave me a slow, lazy grin that was completely disarming. That smile of his got to me every time. But the last thing I needed was more trouble in my life.

Damn you, Brody McCallister. Falling for you is not part of my plan.

I needed to get close to him without getting fucked five ways from Sunday. Been there. Done that. Still had the battle wounds to show for it.

"Do you think..." I didn't want anyone to recognize me. The last thing I needed was to have the media hounding me. That would ruin everything. "I don't want anyone to know I'm here."

"I don't think everyone in town will know who you are. Now, if you were Carrie Underwood, you might have a problem."

"And why's that?" I was no Carrie Underwood. Nobody would ever call me America's sweetheart. But I bristled at his words all the same. Which was stupid. Hadn't I just said I wanted to go unnoticed?

"This is Texas Hill Country. Lot of folks around here listen to country music."

"How about you? Do you listen to a lot of country music?"

"Nah. Not my thing."

"What kind of cowboy are you?" I scoffed.

"Never claimed to be a cowboy. You said it, not me."

"And now you're going to deny it?"

He shrugged. "There's no rulebook that says I have to listen to country music."

"Even if there was, you'd probably break every rule in that book."

"Feels like you already know everything about me. Or at least you *think* you do."

"Well, all you have to do is Google me and you can find out anything you want." That wasn't true. There was plenty that you wouldn't find by Googling me. But he could learn more than I'd ever want him to. Had he already Googled me? "Seems like you have me at an unfair advantage."

"Them's the breaks of reaching for the stars, Sugar Lips."

"How many girls have you called by that name?"

He grinned. "More than I can count. Now if you'll excuse me, I've got a shitload of work to do."

"Nobody's keeping you."

"I'd beg to differ." He tilted his chin down to prove his point. My hand was on his chest and I swear to God I had no idea how it had gotten there or when my feet had carried me this close but here I was, my hand over his heart, the hard muscles of his chest taut under my palm.

I removed my hand and let it fall to my side, so he was free to go. Which was exactly what he did. "See you around, *Shy*," he called over his shoulder and I heard him laughing as he strode away, headed into the sun. Maybe I should have offered him a ride to wherever he was going but I didn't.

I had a shitload of things to do too and I'd already slept half my day away.

The first thing I had to do was shower and then I could get my stalking game on.

It had been a stroke of luck when this cottage showed up on the website. I'd taken it as a sign that this was exactly where I was supposed to be. On this very ranch owned by none other than Brody McCallister. Former rodeo bare bronc rider. Rescuer of wild horses. Horse breeder and trainer.

But most importantly, Noah's daddy.

I'D BEEN SITTING in the truck for twenty minutes, slumped down in the seat, music blasting in my ears when a silver SUV pulled into the parking lot. I cut the music and stared out the windshield, my heart hammering against my rib cage as the SUV pulled into a space farther up the row and across from me. Perfect. They'd have to walk past my truck to get to the dance studio.

Thanks to the private investigator I'd hired, I knew their daily routine.

A slim brunette got out of the driver's seat. Meredith Peterson. She was in her late thirties, dressed in khaki capris, a short-sleeve blouse and ballet flats. She looked nice. Approachable. Sensible. Like a soccer mom. The opposite of me in every way. I held my breath as she rounded the back of the car and opened the passenger door. Seconds later, the little girl emerged, and Meredith took her hand and led her away from the car.

I studied the girl's face, searching for some resemblance. Her brown hair, lighter than mine was the same shade as Dean's and it was smoothed back into a high ponytail. She was small-boned and delicate, wearing a lilac leotard with an attached skirt that looked like petals. My little bird. She walked with a bounce in her step and passed right in front of my truck, without even noticing me.

There goes my baby girl.

She looked happy. And that was what I'd wanted for her. A loving family. A good life.

Everything I couldn't give her at eighteen when I was dirt poor and left to do it all on my own.

I watched her through the windshield until she disappeared behind the closed door of the dance studio and then I sagged against the seat and closed my eyes.

The last time I saw her, she was so tiny, her face all red and scrunched up, but she'd still been the most beautiful thing I'd ever laid eyes on. She was born on October seventh at two in the morning and weighed six pounds, seven ounces. Now she was six and a half years old and was walking and talking, wishing on stars and dreaming big dreams. Did she want to be a dancer? Did she sing all the time? Was she anything like me?

My forehead dropped to the steering wheel. Tears streamed down my cheeks.

Fuck you, Dean.

He'd always been trouble, so I should have known better. But when you fall in love with the wrong boy at seventeen, you're not always thinking clearly. After Maw Maw died, it was just Landry and me, and I'd clung to Dean like a lifeline. As if he could save me from sinking. Ha. What a joke.

"I'll take care of you and the baby, Shy. I've got this."

His idea of taking care of me had landed him in prison.

Why I'd ever believed a single word out of that liar's mouth was a question I'd never been able to answer.

While Dean was serving his stint in prison, Landry talked me into giving up the baby. I understood why he did it. We were barely scraping by as it was, and I wasn't in the right place in my life to be a good mother. In my heart, I knew it was for the best, but I couldn't help thinking that he hadn't been thinking of me or the baby at all. He didn't want anything to get in the way of the band.

Music had brought us all together. It was why I'd stayed in that toxic relationship for all those years. When we sang and played together, it was like magic, and it made me forget all the shit we'd gone through.

That magic took us all the way to L.A. Me, Dean, Landry, and Gus. Forever tied together by the secrets and lies we locked in a vault and hid from the media. We were on top of the world, all our dreams were coming true, but Dean was spiraling down and trying to drag me down with him.

Unlike me, Dean had never mourned the loss of our baby. Had never even brought it up. Nobody in the band ever breathed a word of it. Just as if it had never happened. Now I had living proof that it had.

Forty-five minutes later, I was still parked in the same spot when the little girl and her mom walked out of the dance studio. I pretended to be on the phone, not paying any attention, but watched from beneath the brim of my ball cap. Like a bonafide creeper.

When they were gone, I drove aimlessly on winding roads that cut through a carpet of bluebonnets and wildflowers. I hadn't come here with a solid plan. All I'd wanted was to see her, to be around her, spend some time getting to know her. Did I even deserve that much after the way I'd abandoned her?

How had I thought this would play out? Would I knock on their front door and announce who I was and the reason for my visit? Somehow, I didn't think that would go over too well.

Brody was my best bet. I needed to earn his trust, so he'd let me hang out with him and his son. I knew better than to think it would be easy. Brody's grin might be charming, but his walls were high. I had six weeks to knock them down. Then I'd go back to my regularly scheduled life.

CHAPTER FIVE

Shiloh

IT HAD BEEN two days since I last saw Brody. Since he wasn't interested in seeking me out it was up to me to pursue him. Tomorrow was Saturday and I'd need an invitation or an excuse to hang out with him. There were only so many times I could sit in the school parking lot or lurk outside the Petersons' house, hoping to catch a glimpse of my little girl before her parents noticed and slapped a restraining order on me. Her name was Hayley. I'd called her Ophelia, after my mom.

When I was pregnant, I knew I was having a girl. Not because of a scan. I hadn't gotten one. But in my heart, I just knew. I used to play music for her. Talk to her. Tell her my hopes and dreams and plans. When she was born, Dean was still in prison and Landry and Gus wanted nothing to do with her.

Don't get too attached, Landry had warned me, as if I could turn my emotions on and off like a faucet.

I loved my brother but sometimes he could be so cold. As it

turned out, I was even worse. A horrible mother and an even more horrible person. I'd traded my baby girl for those big dreams of mine but not a day went by when I didn't think about her wrapped in a soft pink blanket, so innocent and trusting.

I set off across the field, following the line of the stained wood fence, the trees providing shade from the morning sun. A few horses were grazing in the pasture and I stopped to watch a sleek black horse running with a chestnut horse before I set off again, my sights on the timber barn with a tin roof where I thought I might find Brody.

About an acre of land separated the barn from a two-story wood-shingled farmhouse with dark green trim and a wrap-around porch. Instead of a tire swing in the backyard, a saddle hung from two ropes tied to the thick branch of an oak tree. Guess Noah was being raised to be a cowboy too. It made me smile.

A white star, the paint peeling to expose the stained wood underneath, was painted above the open barn doors. I leaned down to pet a black and white border collie with a red bandana tied around his neck. He wagged his tail in greeting. "Who's a good boy?" I asked, rubbing behind the dog's ears before I strode into the barn.

Dust motes floated in the sunlight, the air scented with hay, manure and dry cedar. My black leather high tops moved soundlessly across the wide wood planks as I passed the stalls, all of them empty, the dog following close at my heels. When I reached the end of the row, the dog barked twice as if in warning. I peered over the top of a double stall that opened to a small paddock, home to one chestnut horse. She was munching on her breakfast, so I left her to eat in peace and walked back the way I'd come.

I poked my head in the doorway of the tack room that

doubled as an office and inhaled the scent of leather, running my hand over an intricately carved western saddle. My eye caught on a row of gold belt buckles and trophies collecting dust on a shelf, but Brody was nowhere to be found.

I looked down at the dog sitting next to my feet. "Where's Brody?"

"Brody's in the round pen," a male voice answered.

I lifted my head. A guy, in his late teens or early twenties, carrying a bale of hay on his back, grinned at me, one dimple appearing in his cheek. He set down his load and took off his backward ball cap, ran his hand through his sweaty brown hair and replaced the cap. "I'm Chris. Work for Brody."

"I'm Viv. I'm staying at the guesthouse."

His gaze lowered to my black Japanese Ramen Noodles T-shirt. "Cool T-shirt."

"Thanks." He was staring. I cleared my throat. "Where's the round pen?"

"Just on the other side of the barn. But tread carefully. He's in one of his moods."

"What kind of mood?"

He chuckled. "A Brody McCallister mood."

That was all he said before he lifted his load again and left me standing there.

I followed the dog past a flatbed truck loaded with hay to a round pen where Brody was working with a gray horse. Two older men stood a few feet back from the metal tube fencing, their eyes on Brody. One wore a cowboy hat with a short-sleeved plaid shirt, cowboy boots, and Wranglers. The other one was in a dark green polo shirt and khakis. They both saw me, so I had no other choice but to walk over and introduce myself.

"Hi." I gave them a smile. "I'm Viv. I'm staying at the guest-house." I was starting to sound like a broken record.

The man in the polo shirt with salt and pepper hair and a powerful build raised his brows. "So you're Viv. Huh. You don't say." He held out his hand to me with a smile. "I'm Patrick. Brody's uncle." We shook hands, his grip firm. There was no sign of recognition in his blue eyes and I sighed in relief.

"Nice to meet you."

"You too."

"Wade Kimball," the other man said, shaking my hand. "See you made a new friend."

I smiled at the dog who was sitting right next to me, his ears perked up. "What's his name?"

"Buster," Patrick said with a chuckle.

With the introductions out of the way, I watched Brody working with a horse in the round pen.

"What's he doing?" I asked, my voice hushed so as not to disturb him.

"Starting a colt," Wade gestured in Brody's direction. "A wild mustang. Never been saddled or ridden. Brody's breaking him for me... sorry." He held up his hands, eyeing Brody who scowled at him, although I couldn't imagine how he could have heard us when we were keeping our voices low. "He don't like that term. He's *gentling* him. Brody's the only trainer I trust to get the job done right."

"He's always had a way with horses." Patrick's voice was filled with pride. "Ever since he was a boy."

Wade nodded and stroked his ginger beard. "He's one of the best in the business. I'm always telling him he should do some videos. Make some money off his training methods. But he don't wanna hear it."

"Boy's always been stubborn," Patrick said with a shake of his head.

Even knowing Brody as little as I did, it didn't surprise me that he had no interest in doing videos or that he was stubborn.

I focused my attention on Brody whose sole focus was on the horse, his posture so calm and relaxed, and he never once raised his voice.

The colt was running in circles around the perimeter while Brody stood in the middle, turning in a slow circle to follow the horse's movements. Then the colt stopped abruptly, turned around and started running in the opposite direction. My gaze moved to Brody to see what he'd done to make the horse change direction. He took a few steps forward, crossing an imaginary line and flicked the coiled rope in his hand against his thigh, causing the horse to change direction again.

When Brody clucked, the horse stopped and looked at Brody. For a few seconds, neither of them moved a muscle. Brody approached the horse slowly, not making any sudden movements until he was standing close enough to touch him. He was talking to the horse and although I couldn't hear what he was saying, the horse appeared to be listening to his every word.

Then Brody had the colt follow him around the enclosure and into the middle. He turned to face the horse. Brody moved forward, and the horse backed up, accomplishing all of this without even touching the horse.

"You gonna try putting a saddle on him?" Wade asked.

Brody was standing right in front of us, his back turned, giving me a view of his broad shoulders tapering down to a narrow waist, his black T-shirt fitted, and his faded jeans slung low on his narrow hips. Not a bad view. Not bad at all.

"Nope. Not today. Need to do more groundwork. You only get one chance to do it right and he ain't ready yet."

Just then, Buster started barking and tore off toward the woods that bordered the property. I held my hand over my forehead like a visor and searched the trees for whatever distracted him. Two whitetail deer ran past with Buster in hot pursuit.

"Buster! Get back here," Patrick shouted.

I'd been so distracted I hadn't even noticed what was going on inside the pen until Wade said, "Oh shit."

The colt was bucking, its ears pinned to its head. This didn't look good. I wasn't even standing close to the fence, but I backed up all the same and wiped my sweaty hands on my jeans as the horse kicked up its back legs.

"Brody. Get out of there," I warned. That horse might only be a colt, but he was big and strong and could easily kill Brody with one of those powerful kicks.

But Brody ignored my warning.

"Stop showing off," Brody chided, unfazed by the horse's rebellion. "We're done for the day."

"How the hell you gonna get him out of the round pen now?" Wade asked, his voice low. The colt snorted, eyeballing Brody as he backed away then spun around and ran in the opposite direction as if to prove he wasn't about to get caught or told what to do.

Brody was quiet for a few minutes, his gaze calmly following the horse who was running right for the fence and looked like he was about to jump it. Brody snapped the rope against the ground, and the colt stopped dead in its tracks. Brody approached the colt and lay the rope over its shoulders, sliding it back and forth and pushing his body against the horse's side until he had him up against the fence.

What was he doing?

Seconds later, I exhaled a breath of relief when Brody clipped the lead rope onto the horse's bridle and led him through the gate like nothing had happened. He set him free in a paddock behind the round pen where a few other horses had gathered to watch and closed the gate, leaning on the fence to watch the wild mustang canter away with the other horses.

"Hey Cowboy," I said when he joined us.

"Viv." His eyes narrowed with suspicion and he crossed his arms over his chest. His dirty blond hair was matted down with sweat and curled up a little where it met the collar of his T-shirt. Despite the sweat and his surly attitude, I still found him downright edible. "What're you doing here?"

"Just looking for you."

"I'm busy," he said brusquely. "If you need something, call Kate."

O-kay. Looked as if I wouldn't be getting charming Brody today.

Dismissing me, Brody talked to Wade about the colt for a few minutes, then Wade said his goodbyes and left, and Brody turned his attention to Patrick.

"You want the bad news or the good news?" Patrick asked him.

"Don't tell me. My house needs a new roof."

"Afraid so."

Brody muttered a curse and ran both hands through his hair, holding the back of his head. "What's the good news?"

"I've got a good crew that can start next month. Thought I'd put Ridge on one of my crews. It'll do him some good to do some honest work."

Brody's eyes narrowed. "You wanna put Ridge on a construction crew?"

"School will be out."

"Unless he's in summer school," Brody muttered.

"Summer school? What the hell? How could you let him fail—"

"He's not going to fail," Brody said through clenched teeth.

"I told you you should have let him live with us." Patrick crossed his arms over his broad chest. "That boy needs discipline and a firm hand."

"I've got it. Don't worry about Ridge. He's my responsibility. And take it easy, you hear me? You're working too hard. We don't want you having another heart attack."

Patrick scowled. "My ticker's just fine. Work keeps me going. Retirement would have driven me to an early grave."

Brody snorted. "Your retirement lasted all of three months."

"Four. And it nearly killed me having all that free time on my hands." With that, Patrick said his goodbyes then strode away, leaving me alone with grumpy Brody.

"Do you need some help?" I had to jog a little to keep up with him as he strode to the barn.

"Nope." I waited for him outside the tack room where he grabbed a handful of bridles and some lead ropes then stepped aside to let Chris pass with another bale of hay. "I'm moving the horses to the back pasture," Brody told him. "When you're done unloading, I'll need you to clean up the manure then mow it to three inches... second thought, make it four inches."

"You got it, boss man."

"Stop calling me that," Brody grumbled before he stalked away.

Chris winked at me and we shared a smile before I trailed Brody to the last double stall at the end.

"Are you still here?" He wouldn't even look at me.

"Put me to work. I don't mind getting my hands dirty."

He took my hand in one of his, not to hold it but to inspect it. When we touched, did he feel the same electric charge I did? My nails were painted midnight blue, a tiny tattoo on each finger, each one holding a special meaning to me. After studying my hand for a moment, he released it quickly as if my touch burned him. "Your hands were made for playing a guitar, not for manual labor. Why would you wanna help me?"

"Since you won't take any money for the truck, I want to find a way to repay you."

He blew out an exasperated breath like I was annoying him just by breathing the same air. A smarter girl would leave him be, but I'd never been one to back down from a challenge and this was starting to feel like one. If there was one thing I'd learned in life, it was that you had to go after the things you wanted. And I wanted Brody. Scratch that. I *needed* him.

"What do you really want, Shiloh?"

"I just told you what I want." I planted my hands on my hips. "I don't take handouts. Put me to work."

"Why do I get the feeling you'll be more trouble than you're worth?"

I grinned. "I don't know. I feel the opposite about you. I have a feeling you're worth *all* the trouble."

He ran his hand over the stubble on his jaw. "What's your angle?"

I sighed loudly. "Why are you so suspicious?"

"It's my nature."

I tucked my hands in the back pockets of my ripped jeans and rocked back on my heels. "What if I told you there's nothing I'd rather be doing than spending time with you?"

"I'd hand you a shovel and tell you to clean up your bullshit."

I laughed. I got the feeling Brody's bark was worse than his bite. He handed me the bridles and lead ropes, stepped inside the stall, and ran his hands over the horse's sides and belly. "How are you doing today, Cayenne?" The horse nickered softly in response. This guy was nicer to horses than he was to people.

"Why isn't she out with the other horses?"

"Expecting a foal any day now." He stroked the horse a few times then joined me, and we walked out the open back doors of the barn to the pasture where the horses were grazing.

He held the gate open for me and closed it when we were

inside, instructing Buster to sit and wait outside the gate. Obediently, he did as he was told. "Have you ever spent time around horses?"

"Not really. They're beautiful animals though."

"All animals are beautiful. But yeah, horses are special." He put two fingers in his mouth and whistled. I watched in amazement as the horses trotted over to him and gathered at the gate, jostling for position like they all wanted Brody to pay them special attention. I knew the feeling.

"Do they all just come to you when you whistle?"

"Nope." He jerked his chin at the black horse trotting in the opposite direction as if to prove he wasn't a follower. "They're herd animals, but you always get the ones who won't come when they're called."

He slipped a bridle on a reddish-brown horse with a black mane, clipped the lead rope to its bridle and handed off the rope to me, our hands brushing in the exchange.

I reached up a tentative hand to pet the horse. She nickered softly, and I took it as a positive sign that she liked it when I stroked her neck. I kept petting the horse while Brody slipped a bridle on a brown and white painted horse with one blue eye and one brown and led him out of the gate, beckoning me to follow.

"Just walk next to her. Loosen your grip. Relax. She'll follow me."

I took a deep breath and did as he said, adjusting my steps to the horse's gait as we walked up a dirt and grass trail under a canopy of trees that protected us from the heat of the Texas sun. Brody's land was beautiful. Lush and green with rolling hills and tall grasses swaying in the warm May breeze. I took deep breaths of the fresh air, feeling like it had been forever since I'd been able to breathe properly. I spent so much time on the road, living out of suitcases and sleeping in a different hotel room every night. Sometimes I forgot what it was like to be around nature. L.A. was home now, but it had never really felt like home.

Brody looked over his shoulder to make sure I was okay. "You good?"

I nodded. "Yep."

When we reached the other pasture, I walked my horse into the enclosure and waited while Brody removed the bridles. Then we walked back down the path to get the other horses. "Why are you moving them?"

"Gives the pasture a chance to grow back."

After we'd moved four more horses, there was still one that stubbornly refused to come to Brody. Instead of chasing after the black horse with the white star on its forehead, Brody closed the gate and walked away.

"You're just going to leave him there?"

"Nah. She'll come around eventually." I wasn't so sure of that. The horse seemed stubborn and not interested in following the pack. I decided she was my favorite horse.

"What's her name?"

"Rebel," he said with a chuckle and I got the feeling I was missing an inside joke. "Her name is Rebel."

"Now that I know she's a girl, I like her even better."

"Figured you would."

I helped Brody fill the salt buckets hanging in the shelters in the pasture and clean and refill the water in the troughs. When that was done, Brody said he had to fix the fence in the first pasture, so I waited outside the shed that housed a John Deere tractor and farm equipment while he gathered his tools and planks of cedar then trailed along beside him. I wasn't surprised when he refused my offer to help.

Leaning my back against the fence inside the paddock, I watched Rebel displaying her independent spirit. From the corner of my eye, I also watched Brody as he used a crowbar to rip off the damaged fence panels, the muscles in his arms bulging and flexing, the veins in his forearms pronounced. This was vein porn at its finest and try as I might, I couldn't drag my eyes away.

I had a thing for a man's hands and his were big and strong and capable looking.

How would it feel to have those calloused, suntanned hands touching my skin? Would he be rough? Or gentle? I thought Brody was capable of both.

"Enjoying the view?"

"It'll do."

His lips tugged up at the corners. I smiled to myself when he finally asked for my help after having denied he needed it.

CHAPTER SIX

Shiloh

I HELD the cedar fence panel steady at the opposite post while he used a screw gun to secure it, his other hand bearing the brunt of the weight. I wasn't used to being around men who worked with their hands and had the ability to fix things. The men in my life were better at breaking things than fixing them.

"Did someone die in the guesthouse?" I blurted when he rose to his feet and moved around me to screw the wood to the other post.

"Why do you ask?"

"Just a feeling I get."

He side-eyed me. "What kind of feeling exactly?"

"I can't describe it. But I sense someone else's presence."

"Like a ghost?"

"More like a strong vibration. But his spirit is good. Whenever he shows up, a feeling of peace and calm washes over me." Wow. I was flying my freak flag. Not sure why I'd felt the need to share. You would think by now, after years of having my words twisted by reporters and quotes taken out of context, I'd have learned to use filters. Apparently not.

Brody was quiet for a beat while he used the screw gun. I waited for him to laugh or call me crazy. I wasn't really expecting an answer, so it surprised me when I got one. "His name was Walt. Guess you could say he was my mentor. Best horse handler I've ever had the privilege of knowing. I met him about twelve years ago when I was on the rodeo circuit. When I bought this place, he asked if I needed help. Came out for two weeks, took a liking to the place, and ended up staying."

"Can't say I blame him. I can see how this place would make you want to stay. It's special." Brody glanced at me, as if to check whether I was being sincere. I smiled, remembering how he told me I should do it more often.

"Yeah, it is." He stood back to assess his work then lined up another fence panel. Without being told, I held it in place for him.

"What happened to Walt? How did he die?"

"Doc said he went peacefully. In his sleep. Best you could hope for anyone."

I nodded. "It was the same with my Maw Maw. My grand-mother," I added in case he wasn't familiar with the Cajun term.

"I know what a Maw Maw is. You were close?"

"Yeah." I smiled. "She's the one who raised me and my brother. Some people thought she was crazy. Others were true believers."

"Believers of what?"

"She was a psychic." I watched his face for signs of disbelief but there were none. He accepted it as if it was perfectly natural that some people had those powers.

"You got the gift too?"

"So she said."

"But you don't believe it?"

"Sometimes I do. Some things can't be explained. And sometimes I know things that people don't tell me." He looked wary and I hastened to reassure him. "Not specifics. I'm not a mind reader. Just... I get a feeling about people. Kind of like a vibe. I don't get it with everyone. Only certain people." *Like you.* "But some people have an aura and give off strong vibrations."

"Some people... like me?"

Noting the wariness in his tone, I hesitated before answering. Sounded to me like Brody had a lot to hide. "Would it scare you if I said yes? Would it send you running?"

"Running from what exactly?"

"Me."

"If this is your idea of hitting on me, you get points for originality."

"I'm not hitting on you. I'm just making conversation. Thought you might be interested. Considering you're obviously some kind of horse whisperer."

He snorted. "I'm not a horse whisperer."

"Okay. Whatever you say."

"Here she comes," he said quietly as he rose to his feet and tested the fence panels to make sure they were strong.

I turned around and watched Rebel as she crept closer to us then stopped. *How had he even seen her with his back turned?*

I stood statue-still and waited to see what she'd do. After about a minute of this stand-off, she took a few more hesitant steps closer and then a few more until she was standing right in front of me.

"Aren't you a pretty girl?" I reached out a tentative hand and when she didn't back off, I rubbed the side of her neck. She nickered softly, so I kept doing it, my strokes growing bolder until she nudged my thigh with her nose, a playful gesture that made me smile.

"She likes you."

He sounded surprised. I should have been insulted, really. "Maybe she's trying to tell you something."

"And what would that be?" he asked, packing up his tools.

"Be nicer to Shiloh."

"How much nicer do you want me to be?" he scoffed, slipping a bridle onto Rebel and clipping on the lead rope.

I shrugged one shoulder. "I could use a friend."

"You want to be friends?" he asked skeptically.

"Sure. Why not?" He was standing next to me now, close enough that I could smell his singular scent and feel the warmth radiating from his skin. "I'm not looking for a relationship."

"Good thing. Because I don't do relationships."

"What do you do?" I asked as I led Rebel out of the pasture while Brody carried his tools.

"Casual hookups. How about you?"

Just bad relationships, apparently. "I'm taking a hiatus from men. I packed extra batteries."

A laugh burst out of him. "That's just sad."

"My big boy takes good care of me. I can change the settings. Speed up. Slow down."

"Your big boy." Another laugh burst out of him. "Holy shit. That's pathetic." After a beat he said, "Bet it's not as big as me."

"Are you seriously competing with a sex toy? Size isn't everything."

"Does that big boy of yours have a tongue and hands too? Can your big boy take you from behind and whisper dirty things in your ear while he—"

"Stop!" I smacked his arm. Not that I was a prude, but now

he'd gotten me thinking about what he could do with his tongue and hands and his big dick.

My eyes lowered to his crotch and he laughed. "You're considering it, aren't you?"

"Nope." Admittedly, I couldn't stop thinking about it, but he didn't need to know that. "I just want to be friends." I wasn't even thinking about using him to get to Hayley. It was the truth. Even though he was moody, I liked hanging out with him. "I meet a lot of fake people. And a lot of users. People who... just want something from me. It's hard to know who to trust sometimes. But you're different. You're real."

He set Rebel loose inside the pasture and closed the gate, turning to face me. The sun on his face made his eyes appear lighter, like golden honey. "And how about you? Are you real, Shiloh?"

"Not always," I admitted. "But right now? With you? Yes. You're getting the real Shiloh."

He studied my face for a moment, searching for the truth in my words. Could he read people as well as he read horses? As if he'd made up his mind about me, he nodded. "Come on. I'll introduce you to Dakota."

We walked to another paddock, smaller than the first two, with only one horse in it. I didn't know the first thing about horses, but this horse didn't look like the others. She looked depressed. Sad. She was standing near the fence with her head down. Brody clucked, and she lifted her head and looked over at him.

"Why is Dakota alone?"

"She's not ready to be put with the others yet. She was abused."

"What happened to her?" This time I stayed outside the gate while Brody went inside, and Dakota slowly walked toward him. I leaned my forearms on the top of the fence and rested my chin on my hands.

"She was found in a stall standing in four feet of manure. Skinny. Malnourished. Neglected." He rubbed the horse's neck with firm but gentle strokes. "Not sure what all had happened to her but none of it was good."

"And what do you do with a horse like that?"

"Start from the ground up. Take it nice and slow. You can't rush it, or you'll undo any of the good you try to do. For now, I'm just trying to get her healthy and get her used to human touch. I spend time with her, just talking and stroking her. She's come a long way in the past few months."

We spent about twenty minutes with Dakota and all Brody did was stroke her and talk to her. But I could have watched him doing that all day long. It made me feel so calm and peaceful, the warm sun on my face, the soft swish of Dakota's tail that made me think was her way of showing appreciation. She trusted Brody to be kind to her.

These horses were so damn lucky to have a Brody in their lives. Even though he could be grouchy and sometimes rude, I knew deep down he was a good person. I'd been around enough bad ones to know the difference.

"Wish I could rescue them all," he said when he joined me by the fence.

I wished he could too.

"The Paint was a rescue horse. The first one I led out of the pasture," he clarified as we walked back down the trail toward the barn.

"With one blue eye?"

"That's the one. When he came to me a few years ago, he was in bad shape. We suspected he'd been beaten and whipped. His owners had left his saddle on for weeks and tied his head to the stall." Brody shook his head in disgust.

"And look at him now. You gave him a good life."

"Doesn't always work out. Some of them don't make it. But yeah, when I can rehabilitate them, there's no better feeling in the world."

"You have a gift, Cowboy."

He glanced at me. "So do you, Shy. So do you."

"I might have to write a song about you."

He snorted. "A rock song about an asshole cowboy. Sounds like a chart-topper."

"I get the feeling there are a lot of layers to you."

"Lucky for me, you won't be here long enough to peel back all the layers."

"Don't underestimate my psychic powers." I nudged his arm with my shoulder. "For all you know, I'm reading your mind right now."

We stopped outside the barn and he turned to face me, his eyes roaming down my body before returning to my face. "Nah. If you could read my mind, you'd be blushing like a schoolgirl."

"Doubt it. I'm not an innocent little virgin."

He spun the rope in his hand. "Too bad you've given up men."

"Yeah. Too bad."

"You hungry?"

"Starving."

Brody's pickup bounced over a rutted dirt lane that cut through his property, the sunshine pouring in through the windshield, and the warm breeze whipping my hair around. I'd tuned into the oldies station and Aretha was singing about a woman who demanded respect from her man. Something I should have done years ago.

I had no idea where he was taking me. Earlier, we'd made sandwiches in his farmhouse kitchen with terracotta floors and oak cabinets. His house had surprised me. I wasn't sure what I'd expected—maybe a bachelor pad—but it looked like a well-loved home, the paneled walls painted off-white, braided rugs scattered on the wide-plank hardwood floors and a brown suede sectional in the living room that looked worn but comfortable.

He'd packed up our lunch, grabbed bottles of water and hustled me into the truck, claiming he preferred to eat outside and wanted to show me something. A few minutes later, he backed the truck under a tree and cut the engine.

We sat on the tailgate to eat, the valley spread out below us, sitting close but not so close that we were touching.

"What did you want to show me?" I asked after I'd eaten half of my turkey and swiss on rye and he'd almost finished a second sandwich.

I followed his finger to where he was pointing and leaned forward, straining my eyes for a better look. "Hang on," he said. He hopped off the tailgate and came back a few seconds later with a pair of binoculars. I took them from his hand and held them up to my eyes, bringing the horses into focus. There were about a dozen horses, maybe more, clouds of dust kicking up behind them as they ran. They looked so wild and free.

"God, they're so beautiful."

"They are," he said quietly. "America's living legends."

After a few minutes, I lowered the binoculars and set them next to me then picked up the other half of my sandwich and took a bite. Now that I knew what I was looking for, I could watch them from here. "Why aren't they with the other horses?"

"They're wild horses. Mustangs. I wanted them to be free to roam the land but still be able to take care of them." He bit into his green apple, his gaze focused on the valley. "If I could, I'd rescue hundreds of them, but I don't have enough land."

"How much would you need?" I wrapped my crusts in saran wrap, tossed it in the paper sack and plucked a grape off the stem, popping it into my mouth.

"Thousands of acres. I've got eighty now. Forty are for them. I've got eighteen mustangs and can't take on any more. As it is, that's not enough land for them." He finished his apple and tossed the core into the grass. "So yeah, that's never gonna happen."

"You never know. Sometimes dreams come true."

"Are you living the dream, Shy?"

I unscrewed the lid off my water bottle and took a long drink of cool water before I answered. "Sometimes it feels like a dream. Sometimes it's a nightmare. But it's the only thing I've ever wanted. I feel most at home on a stage or in a recording studio. Without music, my life would be so empty."

He studied my face. "Why are you here?"

The way he was looking at me, searching my face as if he'd know a lie if I told it, I couldn't form a response. Until finally, I answered as truthfully as possible. "I have my reasons but they're personal. And I guess..." I let out a breath. "I'm just looking for some calm in the storm."

Brody nodded like that was something he understood and respected. "Okay."

"What's the deal with Ridge?"

He let out a weary sigh. "My seventeen-year-old brother is doing his damnedest to get kicked out of school. I have no intention of letting that happen. I just need to find a way to get through to him."

"Does he like working with horses?"

"Nope. Not interested."

"What were you like at seventeen?"

Brody laughed to himself and scrubbed a hand over his face. "I was a train wreck. Spent most of my time getting drunk and stoned, fighting, and screwing."

Somehow, that didn't surprise me but right now he seemed so calm and at peace with himself. "And now?"

"Now I'm older but none the wiser. How about you? What were you like at seventeen?"

"Train wreck is pretty accurate. My Maw Maw died a few months before I turned seventeen and it really hit me hard. My brother Landry is three years older and it was left to him to look after me."

"You didn't have any other family?"

I shook my head. "My mom died when I was a baby, so I never really knew her. My dad checked out after... she died," I finished. "He just up and left, never to be heard from again. Until our band hit it big."

"He looked you up?"

I huffed out a laugh. "Yeah. Came to us with a whole sob story about how his manager screwed him out of money and his record label dropped him. Tried to hit us up for money. He's a washed-up country singer. Hasn't had a hit song in over fifteen years. I guess he thought we were the answer to his prayers and could help him revive his career." It still stung that he'd had no interest in his kids beyond what we could do for him.

"Asshole. I hope you kicked him to the curb. Deadbeat dads don't deserve the time of day. You don't owe him your loyalty or your money."

"I know. I just... I wanted to believe that he actually cared, you know? That he wasn't using us. But if he ever cared, he wouldn't have left us in the first place." When Landry was thirteen, he told Maw Maw he wanted to change our last name to Leroux, our mom's maiden name. Six months later, we went to a lawyer and had our name legally changed from Holloway to

Leroux, officially cutting ties with Rhett Holloway, the man who had no interest in being a father.

"What about your parents?" I asked Brody. "Are you close?"

"They're both dead." His voice was flat.

"I'm sorry."

He shook his head. "Don't be. My aunt and uncle raised me like one of their own. And I've got three cousins who are like brothers to me."

"And Ridge..."

"Turned up a few months ago. I didn't even know he existed. I hadn't seen my mom since I was thirteen."

"How old are you now?"

"Thirty-tree last month. How old are you?"

"I was twenty-five in December."

He nodded and squinted into the distance. Brody had these little lines around his eyes from squinting into the sun that I found ridiculously sexy.

"I saw you once. You must have been sixteen. You were playing in a dive bar in Lafayette." His jaw clenched, and he flexed his right hand. "Saw you after the show when I was coming out of the men's room and some asshole was all over you." He turned his head to look at me. "You remember that?"

My breath caught. "That was you..."

"That was me alright."

"You pack a mean punch, Cowboy." I gave him a little slug on the arm, trying to make light of it, to ease some of the tension I felt coming off him.

"Did that kind of thing happen a lot?"

I shrugged, not meeting his eye. "The guy was just drunk. I could have handled it on my own."

"Why did you have to handle it on your own when you had three guys in the band who should have had your back? Where the hell were they when you needed them?" His voice held so much accusation that I instinctively rushed to the defense of my boys. Even when they didn't deserve my loyalty or return the favor, defending them was a habit I'd never outgrown.

"They were outside packing up the equipment. I had to run back inside to use the ladies' room." I shrugged, once again trying to make light of it. "It was no big deal."

"You were sixteen years old and some drunk asshole had you up against the wall," he said, his voice low and angry. "You don't think that's a big fucking deal?"

I never told anyone what happened that night. We couldn't afford to lose that gig, so I hadn't wanted to cause any trouble. When Brody pulled that guy off me, slammed him against the opposite wall and punched him, I didn't stick around long enough to thank him. I ran out the back door and hopped in the truck, my body shaking and my knees knocking the whole way home. If I had told the guys, Landry, Dean, and Gus would have gone back in there and taken care of the situation. We'd lost plenty of gigs back then, but I never wanted it to be because of me.

"It had shaken me up a bit," I admitted, downplaying it. "But I was fine. Thanks for stepping in. Were you okay?"

He huffed out a laugh. "Not my first bar fight. Not my last. I was just fine. Can't say the same about the other guy. Pretty sure he had trouble walking out of there on his own."

"You sound mighty proud of yourself."

"Some things justify getting the shit kicked out of you. Never been one to stand back and let bad shit happen if I can stop it. So yeah, I'm always gonna fight for the things I believe in. Sometimes that requires a gentle touch and patience. And sometimes it requires a punch in the face and a swift kick to the balls."

I studied his profile. Square jaw, straight nose, his dirty

blond hair disheveled from running his hand through it, and I thought he was beautiful. Strong and tough but not the kind of guy who was looking to break you into submission. "When is a gentle touch and patience required?"

He turned his head, his brown eyes locking onto mine and in that moment, I thought that maybe he could read my mind. "When you're dealing with wild, broken things."

We gravitated toward each other, our movements almost imperceptible. We were thigh to thigh, and I was leaning into him, the muscles in his arm tensing, and I was desperate to feel his touch on my skin. He lifted his hand to my face, cupped my cheekbone in one of his big hands, and brushed his thumb over my lips. His touch was gentle, but it sent shivers up and down my spine and reached straight into my core.

I lifted my eyes to his and stared into their brown depths. The man who could knock a guy out but gentle a wild horse. Maybe he had the power to fix all the broken pieces inside me. To heal the wounds left by the men I'd loved who had abandoned me. And the one who tried to break me. To cleanse my soul of the sins I'd committed.

Kiss me. Kiss me. Kiss me.

As if he heard my silent plea, his hand slid around the back of my head and he pulled me closer until our mouths were so close, I felt his soft breath on my lips. Just when I thought he would kiss me, his phone alarm went off, interrupting our moment of intimacy. He released me abruptly and slid his phone out of his pocket, silencing it.

"I need to go." And just like that, I'd lost him.

We were quiet on the drive back and I stared out the windshield, wondering if Brody was the man Maw Maw had told me about on my thirteenth birthday. I used to think it was Dean. But it couldn't have been him. He'd never once saved me from anything. If it was Brody, he'd already saved me once. But what could he possibly need saving from?

Minutes later, Brody pulled up outside the guesthouse and I hopped out of the truck, not ready to let him go yet. Before he had a chance to drive away, I poked my head in the open window, a plan formulating.

"Do you like Cajun food?"

"Why?"

This guy. One minute you could be sharing deep and emotional things, sharing a moment that almost turned into a kiss, and five minutes later he was all suspicious again. "You don't make things easy on a girl, do you?"

"You're not just any girl, Shy."

I'd like to think he meant it as a compliment, but it didn't sound like one. "With you, I feel like I am. With you, I feel like I have to work for every smile and word."

"If you wanted five-star treatment you should have checked into the Ritz."

"Funny. I don't see a Ritz around here."

"Exactly."

I rolled my eyes. "Come over for dinner. Around seven. I'll cook."

He gave me a skeptical look. "You're gonna cook me dinner?"

"Ye of little faith. I happen to be a girl of many talents."

"Don't doubt that for a minute."

"Don't keep me waiting," I called after him as he backed out and swung the truck around.

"Or what will you do, Shi-loh?"

I moved to his open window. "If you keep me waiting, I'll just have to hunt you down."

He grinned. "Catch me if you can."

"So you want me to chase you?"

"All depends. Do you think you're up to the task? I'm more than a handful. Not sure you can handle me."

"Challenge accepted. Tonight, we'll see if you're all talk or if you can handle the *heat* I'll be bringing. Just as friends, of course," I added.

He was laughing as he drove away, his tires kicking up a cloud of dust, his left hand tapping out the beat of the music on the window frame.

Now that I'd invited him to dinner, I'd have to brave the grocery store. Oh joy.

CHAPTER SEVEN

Brody

I SHOULD HAVE SHOWERED before my meeting with Ridge's English teacher. But if I'd stopped to shower, I would have been late. So here I was in my sweat-stained T-shirt and dirty work boots. I rapped my knuckles against the door then strolled into the classroom to face Chloe Whitman. She was used to my sweat and grime. But it had been a while since I'd last seen her—six months, to be exact—and I'd never met her at the school before. She stood up from her desk where she was marking papers and tucked her blond hair behind her ear.

"Thanks for coming in today, Brody."

"No problem."

"Let's sit at the table." I nodded and followed her to a round table, her heels clicking across the floor. She was wearing one of those pencil skirts that hugged her curves and stopped at the knee and a short-sleeved blouse with puffy sleeves. Chloe was every high school boy's wet dream. Twenty-six, single, and more adventurous in bed than her buttoned-up appearance would lead you to believe.

I pulled up a chair across from her. Had she applied fresh lipstick for me? Her nails were painted to match her rose-tinted lips and her cheeks were flushed against her creamy skin.

I leaned back in my chair and waited for her to speak. She stared at the folder she'd placed on the table in front of her. Was I supposed to make small talk now? Not my forte. "How's the teaching gig going?"

She lifted her head, her doe eyes meeting mine, and licked her lips. "It's been a challenge. I've almost survived my second year." She fingered the silver heart medallion on her silver necklace. Next to the heart was a small silver key. "How've you been, Brody?"

"Yeah, it's all good."

She nodded and forced a smile. This was the reason I didn't do relationships. I sucked at them. And now, as bad luck would have it, I was sitting across the table from someone I'd fucked. Not just once or twice either. Nope. I'd dated Chloe for seven months, a record for me. Last April, one week after Jude and Lila's wedding Lila's friend Sophie, the town matchmaker, had set us up on a blind date. I hadn't even known it was a date or I wouldn't have gone.

"I know you're here to discuss Ridge but before we get into that, I was kind of hoping you could tell me where I went wrong. I really liked you, Brody."

Oh shit, here we go. I rubbed the back of my neck. She told me she loved me. Not a crime. But I couldn't say it back. I'd *never* been able to say it to any woman. Not only that, but after seven months of 'casual' dating she was already talking about marriage and kids. Why she would ever think I was a good candidate for marriage was beyond me. I didn't even believe in the institution of marriage. If you asked me, it wasn't natural to make vows to love and honor only one person, until death do you part.

"It wasn't anything you did. It was all on me."

"I guess I should have known better. You never even introduced me to your son." She laughed but she didn't sound happy. "You warned me, but I didn't listen. Shame on me."

She looked at me expectantly, waiting for me to speak. To explain myself. This was awkward as fuck. But I had warned her from the start. Told her I didn't want anything more than a casual relationship. Guess I'd stayed too long, and she'd taken it as a sign that I'd changed my mind.

I shifted in my seat, an orange plastic chair on thin metal legs, and crossed my ankle over my thigh. "Let's talk about Ridge."

Her face fell but she quickly rearranged her features and squared her shoulders. "Yes. Of course. I'm sorry. I shouldn't have mentioned it."

And now I felt like shit. I looked over my shoulder at the door. Where the fuck was Ridge anyway?

"Ridge will be joining us soon. He's in Chemistry. His last period."

So she'd asked me to meet her early to discuss the reason I dumped her, not to talk about Ridge.

After the awkward start, the meeting went about as well as could be expected, given the circumstances. It didn't take a rocket scientist to figure out that Ridge had been cheating all semester. Chloe was willing to give him another chance and I got the distinct impression she was doing this for me as much as for Ridge. I was going to kick his ass.

This school year couldn't end fast enough.

W<small>HEN</small> I <small>ENTERED</small> the kitchen after my shower, Ridge tossed something at me. I caught it in one hand and opened my fist, staring at the strip of foil packets. I should never have told him my plans for the evening.

"Four enough?" he asked. "I've got more if you need 'em."

The little shit. "Why are you giving me condoms?"

"Didn't anyone ever teach you to practice safe sex?"

"Always do."

"Well, now who's lying? You knocked up your cousin's fiancée. That's just bad form, bro." He shook his head and tsked. "How low will you go?"

He was lucky I didn't plant my fist in his face. There was so much about him that reminded me of myself. Same cocky grin. Same surly look. Same defiance for authority figures. But this smug bullshit? The judgment? That had Jude written all over it. I would have loved to hear Jude's side of the story. Had he talked about this with Ridge?

Must have. Why else would Ridge be calling me out on something he knew nothing about? I tossed the condoms in the kitchen junk drawer and shut it, then leaned against the counter to face my brother.

Ridge was sitting at the chopping block island shoveling leftover lasagna into his mouth with one hand and playing on his phone with the other.

"What did Jude tell you?"

"Jude didn't tell me jack shit. He thinks of you as a brother. I'm just calling it the way I see it. Your girl Lila's crazy in love with the dude," he taunted, like he was telling me something I didn't already know.

Lila wasn't my girl. Never had been. But my smart-ass brother obviously knew that too, and he wasn't the only one who thought I was low for getting Lila pregnant. When the family found out, Patrick called me every name in the book then refused to speak to me for an entire year. My cousin Jesse, the baby of the family who had a blind loyalty to his brother Jude, just shook his head and told me he was 'disappointed in me.' Strong words for Jesse who was the most easygoing and forgiving McCallister. And Gideon, well, he hated Jude at the time, so he was Team Brody.

Payback is a bitch, Gideon had said, a sly smile on his face like he was reveling in Jude's downfall.

"So who's the chick staying in the guesthouse?" Ridge asked.

"Nobody."

He looked up from his phone. "Is nobody hot?"

Was a five-alarm fire hot? I shrugged, not wanting to give him any more ammunition. "She's okay."

He set down his phone and studied my face. "Why are you still here? You don't have to stay home and babysit me every night. I'm not Noah. I'm used to looking out for myself."

But he didn't have to do that anymore and I wanted to say as much but I didn't. "I know that."

He shook his head. "I don't get you. Is it because of Lila?"

"Is what because of Lila?"

"Is she the reason you don't have a girlfriend? You're not exactly ugly."

"Thanks for that. And Lila has nothing to do with it."

"From where I'm sitting, she has *everything* to do with it." He shoveled another bite of food in his mouth. "But, hey. It's none of my business. You do you."

Good thing because I had no intention of explaining my actions to Ridge. In order to understand what happened between me and Lila, you would have had to be there. Me, Jude, and Lila had a lot of history. Going back to when we were ten years old.

I checked my phone for the time. Quarter past seven. I was

already late for dinner. Shiloh was another problem I really didn't need right now. I *should* steer clear of her. But I'd never been very good at doing what I should. And even though I'd tried my damnedest to dissuade her from helping me today, I'd be lying if I said I wasn't happy she'd stubbornly refused to listen.

Trouble was I liked hanging out with her. Shiloh intrigued me in a way that very few women did. She was tough and tenacious, two traits you needed if you wanted to get to the top of any profession, with a brand of crazy that made for some interesting conversation.

Ridge finished every bite on his plate, the lasagna courtesy of Kate who felt the need to 'take care of her boys' even though we were fully capable of cooking for ourselves. He wiped his mouth on the back of his arm like the true gentleman he was and got to his feet. "But hey, if you're looking to get laid, pretty sure my English teacher is up for it." I kept my face neutral, but Ridge obviously read something on it. "Holy shit," he crowed. "You've already tapped that, haven't you? No wonder she went easy on me. I'd do her though. She's hot in that sexy librarian way."

I pinched the bridge of my nose. Give me patience. "Stay away from your English teacher. You're in enough trouble as it is."

He was laughing as he walked past me and right out of the kitchen. I grabbed him and hauled him back. "Clean up after yourself. I'm going out. If you need me, call me."

"I won't need you. I have a fun-packed evening ahead of me."

"Don't screw things up with Delaney. You need her help so you don't fail English. That's the only reason she's coming over. To tutor you. She's not—"

"Dude. Save your breath. I'm not interested in screwing

Delaney. You met her." I'd met her this afternoon when she was called into our cozy meeting. Delaney had volunteered to tutor him in English.

"Little Goody Two Shoes is way too uptight. Not to mention she treats me like a charity case. Guess it'll look good on her college applications to say she tutored some white trash loser."

I heard the bitterness in his tone and couldn't entirely blame him for it. Under the circumstances, I would have felt the same way. Even I had sensed Delaney's air of superiority. But Chloe was willing to give him another chance and he couldn't afford to blow it. Not after she figured out he'd been cheating for the entire semester. Not after that joke of an essay he'd handed in. Soft porn, Chloe had called it.

Now he had two choices. Accept help or get held back a year. The only silver lining, the thing that gave me hope for Ridge, was that he'd owned up to cheating and claimed the girl who helped him knew nothing about it. He said he'd stolen her notebook from the locker and had copied her essays. Even though I knew that wasn't how it happened, I didn't call him out on the lie. He lied to protect someone and in my book that was the right thing to do.

"Who does schoolwork on a Friday night?" he complained when the front doorbell rang.

"People who don't want to fail the eleventh grade." I pointed my finger at him. "Make sure you're here when I get home."

"Chill, dude. You're starting to sound like your uncle Patrick."

How times had changed. I used to be lawless. A rule breaker. A cocky asshole who had gotten into more fights than I could count and had believed that fucking the bad shit out of my system was actually going to be my salvation.

But the birth of my son had changed me. Not to say I didn't still have a wild streak, but I was a rebel with a cause now. If anyone ever messed with my boy, I would kill the motherfucker with my bare hands then dance on his grave. Noah would never *ever* have to suffer the way I had. And if Ridge ever needed me, I'd be there for him too.

CHAPTER EIGHT

Brody

I STOOD outside the screen door and listened to Shiloh singing along to "Whole Lotta Love." Fuck, that voice. Even if I never kissed her lips or knew the feel of her body, the sound of her voice was enough to make me hard.

"Shiloh!" I shouted through the screen door to be heard over the music. The windows were open, ceiling fans whirring.

"Come in! It's not locked."

I let myself in and crossed the hardwood floor, stopping on the other side of the breakfast bar that separated the small kitchen from the living and dining area.

She looked up from the chopping board and smiled like she was happy to see me. She was wearing a loose black tank top over a thin white one, and I couldn't be sure, but I thought she was braless. Her green shorts were short, her feet bare, ink-black hair in one of those messy buns, a few loose strands framing her face, and it struck me that I was getting to know the girl, not the rock star who had thousands of fans screaming her name at sold-out concerts.

"Hi," she said finally after we'd been staring at each other for a few seconds, my mind going where it shouldn't because yep, she was sure as shit braless under those thin tank tops.

I laughed under my breath and scrubbed a hand over my face. "Hi."

"I hope you're not in a rush," she said. "I got a late start, so the jambalaya won't be ready for a while."

"How long is a while?"

"Are you starving?"

"Always. Need any help?"

"Nope." She grabbed an IPA from the fridge, flipped the lid and set it in front of me. "Just hang out and keep me company."

I took a long pull and watched her dice an onion. Tears streamed down her cheeks. "Onions always make me cry."

I studied the tattoo on her upper arm—a gnarled, twisted branch with delicate leaves—and pulled up a stool. She pushed the onions to the side with the blunt edge of her knife and hacked off the top of a pepper.

"What else makes you cry?"

"Sad songs. Minor notes. Movies that don't have happy endings. Poverty. Racism. Homophobia. Elevator music. It makes my ears bleed." She shuddered, the blade of her knife flashing as she expertly chopped peppers and celery stalks. I tried to make out the designs on her fingers—a music note, rosary beads and a cross on her ring finger, a crescent moon and three tiny stars on her index finger. A tiny flower inked in purple. A pansy, maybe.

"What makes you cry?" she asked.

"I don't cry."

"What makes you *want to* cry?"

"Country music." She laughed. "Animal cruelty. Child

abuse. Circuses. Fucking clowns. I hate clowns. Zoos. They're even sadder than circuses."

"Why?"

"I hate the idea of animals being taken out of their natural habitat and being forced to live behind bars with people gawking at them."

"Some zoos are nice. What about safaris? Do you have an issue with them?"

"Never been on one." I eyed her phone on the counter as it buzzed with an incoming call. "Do you need to get that?"

She glanced at it then reached over and silenced it. "It's my brother. He'll leave a message."

I watched her phone light up with incoming calls and messages. Her brother obviously didn't like being ignored. She flipped it over, so I couldn't see the screen.

"My manager is calling now too." She let out a weary sigh, her shoulders slumping. "I really needed this break, you know?"

"A break from what?"

She shook her head a little and gave me her back, turning on the gas ring under the pot. The oil sizzled when she added the chicken thighs and spicy sausage she'd cut up earlier. "I just finished the first two legs of my world tour. It started in Singapore. I was in Asia for the first leg and Australia and New Zealand for the second. After this break, I'm headed to Europe. Then South America before I come back to the States. And I just wanted some downtime to rest up. Touring takes a lot out of you. Mentally and physically."

I joined her by the stove and leaned my hip against the counter, drinking my cold beer while I watched her cook. "Did your Maw Maw teach you how to cook?"

"Yep. She always said that food is love." She smiled as she added the vegetables and the spices to her stew, guided by instinct instead of using measuring spoons. "I don't get to do it too often. I hardly ever go to the grocery store anymore. Sometimes I miss doing all the little, normal things I used to do. I wrote so many songs in the laundromat. There was just something about sitting in a laundromat and watching the clothes spin around in the washing machine that got my creative juices flowing."

"The price of fame. A girl can't even sit in the laundromat anymore. Add that to my list of things that make me wanna cry."

She laughed and added rice and chicken stock to the pot, stirring the ingredients with a wooden spoon. "I never wanted to be famous. I just wanted to make a living doing something I loved." She glanced at me. "You want to hear a secret?"

"Hit me."

"I'm petrified."

"Of what?"

"This tour. Every time I go out on the stage, I'm worried they'll figure out I'm a fraud. I'm not worth the money they spent on the tickets. I'm still that girl from the Louisiana Bayou. Sometimes I still wonder... why me? Why did I make it when there are thousands of great singers and musicians out there who will never get the opportunities I have?"

"I don't know a damn thing about the music industry, but I suspect it's like anything else. You got a lucky break, but I'm guessing you put in a shitload of hard work to get where you are."

She nodded. "We really did. Everyone called Acadian Storm an overnight success. Like we came out of nowhere and boom, we hit the big time with zero effort. They don't think about all the years when we were working crap jobs and begging for gigs. We were flat broke, living in roach-infested apartments and surviving on pot noodle. And now... well, now I don't have to worry about money."

"Ride it for all it's worth. When you stop enjoying the ride, then it's time to walk away."

"Walking away isn't so easy."

"Never is when it's something you love."

"You sound like you know something about that."

"I was a rodeo cowboy for years. A bareback bronc rider. I loved it but I hated that I loved it."

"Why?"

"It was a spectacle. Went against everything I believed in. Using horses for entertainment. I hated that I wore spurs. They're dull, not sharp but that's not the point. To get a good ride in, to score high, you have to mark out the horse as it leaves the chute. Dig your spurs into their shoulders," I explained.

"So why did you do it?"

"Money. The rush of adrenaline. The cheers of the crowd," I admitted. At the time, I'd needed that kind of validation, but it wasn't something I'd readily admit. "I walked away a couple years ago. Lost my appetite for it. Just couldn't do it anymore."

"But you still feel guilty that you loved it."

"A part of me does, yeah."

Her gaze roamed down my body before it returned to my face. "I bet you were good at it."

"One of the best."

"Humble too."

"There's nothing wrong with admitting when you're good at something."

She added more chicken stock to the pot and continued stirring the rice with her wooden spoon. If I'd been hungry before, I was practically salivating now.

"What made you walk away?"

I shrugged one shoulder. "I wasn't one of the best anymore."

"So you liked the glory?"

"Loved it. And I'm a bad loser."

She wiped the sweat off her forehead with the back of her arm, reminding me that this girl was slaving over a hot stove for me.

"Why don't you have the air con on?"

"I grew up in the deep South in a house with no air conditioning. I don't mind sweating. In fact, I kind of like it."

I tossed our empties in the recycling bin and grabbed two more cold beers from the fridge. Flipping the caps off on the edge of the counter, I pressed the cold bottle against her flushed cheek. She moaned, the sound shooting straight to my dick.

"That feels so good." She took the beer from my hand and held it to her forehead then clinked her bottle against mine. "Here's to new beginnings and knowing when it's time to walk away," she said, and I got the feeling she wasn't talking about her music career.

We drank to that and I watched her throat bob on a swallow, trying my damnedest not to think of all the things I wanted to do to her. When she lowered her bottle, her eyes locked onto mine. I moved closer and brushed the backs of my fingers along her jawline, noting the way her breath hitched at my touch.

"Brody," she whispered, looking up at me from beneath her lashes.

"Hmm?"

She leaned into me, her tits pressed against my chest and I set my beer on the counter and wrapped my hand around the back of her head. Her full lips parted on a sigh as my other hand coasted down her side and settled on her hip.

Her smoky grays were at half-mast and she exhaled a shuddering breath. "It's been so long."

"Since what?" My thumb brushed the soft skin just above the waistband of her shorts.

"Since someone made me feel like I would die if they didn't kiss me."

She tipped her face up to mine. She was so fucking beautiful, and I had that same feeling I did the night we met. Like I'd been waiting all my life for her without even realizing it. "You want me to kiss you, Shiloh?"

"Do you need an invitation? What are you waiting for, Cowboy?"

My eyes lowered to her full, pillow-soft lips. She tugged her bottom lip between her straight white teeth and I didn't know if it was a calculated move or not, but my dick got harder. "Whatever happened to being just friends?"

"We can still be friends," she breathed out, her arms circling my neck, her fingers tugging on the ends of my hair. She smelled like jasmine. Sexy. Exotic. Intoxicating. Like her. "*Good* friends."

"Yeah?" I framed her face in my hands and angled it up to mine.

"Yeah." She swallowed. "I mean... it's just a kiss, right?"

"Right."

I dipped my head and took my first taste of what felt like forbidden fruit. Sweet. Tempting. Completely off-limits. I would never be the kind of guy a girl like Shiloh Leroux would settle for. Our worlds were light years apart.

But it was *just* a kiss and neither of us had any interest in a relationship.

Her lips parted, and I slid my tongue into her mouth. She sucked on it, eliciting a groan from me as my hands roamed over her tight little body, exploring her dips and curves and her firm, round ass. She kissed me back with an urgency and intensity that made me think it had been too long since she'd been kissed.

I pulled back to catch my breath and gave her ass a little squeeze. "I like your idea of *just* friends."

"Shut up," she growled, fisting my T-shirt in her hands and pulling me closer, erasing the tiny space between us. I laughed, and she shut me up with a kiss then sunk her teeth into my bottom lip before placing a gentle kiss on my mouth. I loved pain mixed in with my pleasure.

Gripping the backs of her thighs, I lifted her off the ground and she wrapped her legs around my waist, grinding her body against my erection. I spun us around and propped her on the countertop, our lips fused, my tongue exploring the depths of her mouth, my dick straining against the confines of my jeans. But I had no intentions of fucking her tonight.

I lifted the hem of her black tank top, my eyes on hers. She licked her kiss-swollen lips, her chest heaving as I slid the material up her body and bit the fleshy underside of her breast through the thin fabric of her white tank top. She arched her back, her fingernails digging into my shoulders. I sucked one of her nipples into my mouth, kneading her other breast with my hand and her hands moved to the back of my head, her fingers tugging on my hair as I bit and sucked her nipple. Her legs cinched tighter around my waist and she rocked her hips.

I released her breast and kissed her lips then pulled back to look at her. "Brody..." she whispered.

"Where's that dinner you promised me?"

She stared at me for a moment then her eyes widened. "Oh shit. I forgot about the jambalaya." She shoved me out of the way, slid off the counter and flew to the stove, waving the wooden spoon at me. "If it's ruined, it's all your fault."

"How's it my fault you can't keep your hands off me?"

She snorted. "Oh please. You've got nothing on my big boy."

Oh. She was asking for it now. "Your big boy kisses you like that?"

"I slide my big boy into my mouth and then I suck on it. Nice and hard." She winked at me.

Fuck. She was teasing me, and it was working. My dick jumped in appreciation.

"What else do you do with your big boy?"

Without answering, she turned from the stove and shoved a plate of food at my chest. "Here's your dinner, Cowboy. Eat up."

"We're eating on the porch."

"Whatever you say." She did a little curtsy. "I'm at your beck and call."

How I'd love that. Somehow, I didn't think that would be the case. The girl had too much fire in her to be at anyone's beck and call. Fine by me. I loved a good challenge.

I carried my beer and my plate of food out to the porch. It was cooler out here than it was inside the house, the air scented with sweet pine and juniper, the last of the evening sun dipping into the lake. The lake was small, only took up two acres of land, but the water was cool and crystal clear bordered by cypress trees.

Fuck, I was hungry and not just for the food either. There was no table out here, so I set my beer on the arm of the Adirondack chair and without waiting for Shiloh, I took a bite of jambalaya. It was good. *Really* good.

R&B music piped from the portable speakers in the living room and the screen door slammed shut when she joined me on the porch and sat in the chair next to mine, tucking her legs underneath her.

"I forgot to add the shrimp," she said, guiding a forkful of jambalaya to her mouth. She'd put her hair up again, exposing the column of her neck, her high cheekbones more pronounced.

"Good thing. Would have ruined it. This is good as it is."

She smirked. "I gave you the burned rice from the bottom of the pot. It was the least I could do."

I laughed at her sass. Tasted just fine to me. We ate in silence, and she didn't try to fill it up with small talk which I appreciated. When we finished eating, I carried our plates and utensils to the kitchen, rejecting her offer to help. After I washed the dishes and stored the leftovers in the refrigerator, I grabbed two more beers and joined her on the porch. She moved her legs so I could pass then propped her bare feet on the banister again and thanked me for the beer.

When she caught me watching her, she wrapped her lips around her beer bottle and hollowed her cheeks. Jesus Christ. She laughed that dirty sexy laugh of hers which didn't help matters one bit. I adjusted myself in my jeans and that made her laugh harder.

"You're looking a little hot and bothered there, Cowboy."

"Nah. I'm chill." I took a swig of my beer and propped my booted feet next to hers on the banister. "Why? Are you hot and bothered?"

"Cool as a cuke." A few minutes passed in silence, but I could almost hear her brain ticking over. "I have a proposition for you."

I chuckled to myself. I had a feeling I knew what was coming. "Yeah? And what's that?"

"I've changed my mind. Maybe a casual hookup... no strings attached... is *exactly* what I need right now."

I eyed her. "So you want to use me for sex while you're here?" She nodded, a smile on her lips. "Looking to save on batteries?"

She laughed. "Maybe. But it sounds like a good plan, right? I can be yours for the rest of the time I'm here. You just have to promise not to be with anyone else because that shit don't fly with me. When it's time for me to leave, we'll go back to our regularly scheduled lives. No harm, no foul. How does that sound?"

"Too good to be true."

"Don't look a gift horse in the mouth."

I laughed. This girl. She had me up and down and sideways. I couldn't get a read on her. Which shouldn't be surprising. Horses, I could read. People confused the shit out of me. Too many mixed messages. Too many ulterior motives.

Shiloh wanted something from me, and it wasn't just sex. I hadn't figured out why she was here or what she wanted yet. But it was only a matter of time before the truth came out. It always did.

I patted my lap, testing how far she'd go to get what she wanted. "Come here."

She lifted her chin. "I don't take orders from any man."

Color me surprised. "And I don't chase after anyone." I finished my beer and set it on the porch then stood up. Time to go. "Thanks for dinner. See you around, Shy."

"Wait. You're leaving? Just like that?"

"You know where to find me," I called over my shoulder.

"Brody."

I stopped at the bottom of the porch stairs and turned around to face her. She was standing on the top step, the glow of the porch light behind her giving her a halo effect. Shiloh belonged in the spotlight, was born to be a star. Only a fool would have left her. I was a damn fool.

"Is that water safe for swimming?"

Not the question I'd expected. "Yeah, it's safe."

She looked over my shoulder at the line of trees. "And it's private, right?"

"Nobody's gonna come onto my property and take photos of you, if that's what you mean." She nodded. "Why? Thinking about taking a swim?"

She smiled and to me, it looked devious. "Yes, as a matter of fact, I am. The moon shines nice and bright here."

My eyes narrowed. "You wanna swim at night?"

"Mmmhmm." She turned off the music from her phone and silence descended. "Under the moon and stars. Night Brody."

I watched her ass as she sashayed away, the screen door slamming behind her with a ring of finality. Well, fuck. Now I was thinking I should stay and make sure she didn't drown in my damn lake.

"Go home, Brody. I'm a big girl. I can look out for myself," she called from inside. I debated for a moment before I finally walked away. She wasn't my problem and if she did decide to go for a swim, I doubted she'd get much further than dipping her toes in. That water stayed cool, even in the summer when the temperatures hit a hundred.

I was walking through the woods next to the guesthouse when I heard the guitar music and stopped to listen. I waited, hoping she would sing but after five or ten minutes of straining my ears for the sound of her voice, I gave up and went home to an empty house.

Fucking Ridge.

As if I hadn't suffered enough torture for one evening, I decided to torture myself further by listening to Shiloh's solo album. I listened to "Damage" on repeat. It told the story of a woman who had been abused by her lover and talked about the scars that faded but never healed. And I couldn't help but wonder if the song was autobiographical.

Had Dean the douche Bouchon abused her? I'd seen first-hand, with more than one person in my life, how drugs could change you. How they fucked with your brain, altered your perception, and made you do things you never dreamed you'd be capable of doing. I saw what drugs did to my mother, to the man I refused to call 'Dad', and then years later to my cousin Jude.

I had half a mind to go back over there and check on Shiloh. Just then I heard the front door open followed by something crashing to the floor and a decidedly feminine giggle.

Fuck my life. I scrubbed my hands over my face and stood up from the sofa. Now I had to go play bad cop.

CHAPTER NINE

Brody

THE NEXT MORNING, I showed up at Jude and Lila's stone and timber farmhouse, slightly worse for the wear. Thanks to Ridge, I was operating on four hours of sleep.

I banged on the front door again—a thick slab of solid oak with a brass knocker shaped like a lion's head—my limited patience being tested. When the door finally opened, I heard a screaming baby in the background and one look at Jude told me he wasn't faring much better than me this morning.

"Is Noah ready?"

"You're early. He's still eating his breakfast."

"You look like shit."

He looked down at his food-splattered T-shirt and raked a hand through his messy brown hair. "Levi's teething. He was up all night."

"Rub a little whiskey on his gums."

"The fuck?" Jude looked scandalized. "He's only ten months old."

"I heard that!" Noah yelled from the kitchen. "You sweared." His hearing was supersonic.

"I said fudge," Jude yelled back.

I heard a rattling sound and laughed. Noah had a swear jar, courtesy of Lila. By the time he hit his teens, he'd be a fucking millionaire.

"You didn't rub whiskey on Noah's gums, did you?" Jude asked as I followed him to the kitchen, passing by the family room, a cavernous space with a stone fireplace, vaulted ceilings and a wall of windows overlooking their five acres, most of which was dedicated to the flowers Lila grew for her floral arranging business.

"Nah. I poured it straight into his sippy cup."

He snorted. "You're such a shit."

"Pay up, Daddy Jude." Noah pointed at his swear jar on the marble countertop, and Jude transferred the change from his pockets to the jar.

"Hi Daddy." Noah gave me a big toothless smile from his spot on the stool at the island. Last week he'd lost his front tooth and every single time I saw him, it felt like he'd grown. Changed in the six days since I'd last seen him. He was still dressed in Dallas Cowboys pajamas.

"Hey little man." I ruffled his dirty blond hair and kissed the top of his head.

Noah was the spitting image of me. Not even biased when I say that my boy was the cutest kid on the planet. But truth be told, when he was born I had hoped he'd come out looking more like Lila. I'd always hated that I looked so different from the rest of the dark-haired blue-eyed McCallister boys. Hated it that I looked so much like *him*. Bad enough we shared the same DNA, I had to come out looking like my old man too. "How are you doing?"

"Better than Levi. All he does is cry." He shoved a forkful

of pancakes into his mouth and talked around them. "Can you fix him like you fix the horses?"

"I've got this, Noah." Jude held up his hands like he was the almighty savior. Half the time, I think he actually believed he was. "Leave it to me. It's all good."

God forbid Jude would ever say he needed help with anything. I poured myself a cup of coffee and leaned against the counter, watching in amusement as he took a screaming Levi out of his highchair and into his arms. He did everything he could to soothe Levi, but the baby was still screaming.

"Make him stop crying." Noah blocked his ears with his hands. "We should call Mommy. She'll know what to do."

"Your mommy is working. She's busy with all those weddings so we're not going to bother her," Jude said. Noah sighed but he nodded his head in agreement. "Finish your breakfast. I'll take care of Levi."

Noah pushed his plate away. He'd left half his pancakes, swimming in syrup which told me Jude was slipping and had left Noah to his own devices. "I can't eat anymore."

"Is your bag packed?" I asked him, eating the strip of bacon from his plate and a lone strawberry in a pool of syrup. He nodded. "Go get it. And put on some jeans and a T-shirt."

Not needing to be told twice, he jumped off the stool and ran out of the kitchen, eager to get away from the screaming baby.

When Noah was out of earshot, I turned to Jude. "Hand him over, you stubborn shit."

"You think you can do better?" he scoffed.

When we were kids, everything was a competition. Some things never changed. "Can't do much worse than what you're doing." He scowled at me. "You're so tightly wound I'm scared you might snap. Let me give it a try."

Reluctantly, Jude handed over Levi, and as if by magic, the baby stopped crying.

"How did you do that?" Jude asked incredulously.

Normally I'd fuck with him but not when it came to his parenting skills. As much as it pained me to admit it, Jude was a good dad and a good stepdad to my son. "He can feel how tense you are. Babies pick up on that shit."

He raked a hand through his hair and blew out a frustrated breath. Growing up, everything had come so easily to Jude. He'd been raised in a loving family, had excelled at school and sports, and everything he'd touched had turned to gold. Until it all turned to shit after he returned from five years of active duty in the Marines.

Jude had always believed he could control everything in his life. But he'd been brought to his knees. I'd taken no joy in his defeat. We used to be tight. There'd been a time when I called him my best friend and brother. The only person I'd ever truly confided in and trusted. So when I saw he was struggling, fucking everything up with Lila, I'd tried to help him. But he was so far gone there was only so much I could do. When he ran off and abandoned me and Lila without even so much as a phone call to let us know he was still alive and well, I washed my hands of him. Because fuck that. I saved his motherfucking life. I was there for him and for Lila when nobody else knew what to do to help.

"Were you like this with Noah?" he asked as I rocked Levi back and forth, gently rubbing his back to soothe him. The baby was wiped out, exhausted from screaming his head off.

Wish I could say I'd been able to do this every time Noah cried, but that hadn't always been the case.

I shook my head. "I used to think Kate was magic. She was able to do the same thing with Noah when me or Lila couldn't soothe him. Used to upset Lila. Made her feel like she was doing it all wrong. But she wasn't. That's just how it is with your own baby sometimes. You want to take away all their pain, but you can't always do that."

"He's asleep," he said quietly.

"Wore himself out crying."

Jude ran his hand through his hair. "Thanks."

I nodded, knowing it pained him to thank me for anything. "No problem. Where do you want him?"

Jude dragged the swing over and I set him inside, making sure his head was supported by the cushioned headrest. Jude turned the swing on and we both watched Levi sleeping as the swing gently rocked him, his face so peaceful and angelic you'd never know he'd been screaming like a lunatic only a short while ago.

"Maybe I can get some work done now."

"How's the storm chasing business?" I asked.

Years ago, Jude and his Marine buddy Tommy had started a veteran-led disaster relief non-profit. When Jude and Lila got back together two years ago, he cut back on his time in the field and focused on the leadership, training and fund-raising. Over the years, his organization had grown and now they had tens of thousands of volunteers across the country. It shouldn't have been a surprise that my silver-tongued cousin had found himself in the limelight once again when he was called upon to give motivational speeches and had even been featured in *Time* magazine for his innovative business plan and finding hope in the face of adversity. He was lauded as a hero and I guess that was the role he'd always played.

"Business is booming," he joked. "There's always a disaster somewhere."

"Ain't that the truth."

He poured himself a cup of coffee and sat at the island

facing me. "I hear you've got someone staying at the guesthouse."

"Uh huh."

"Talked to Ridge last night. He said you went over there for dinner."

"You were checking up on Ridge?" It was an attempt to change the subject, but I was also curious.

"He's family." He took a sip of coffee. "Why wouldn't I check up on him?" Like the answer was obvious.

"Was this before, during, or after he went out and got shitfaced?"

"Oh shit." Jude laughed. His gaze swung to Levi. "Not looking forward to the high school years. Especially if he's anything like us. Did you make him pay for it?"

I chuckled. "Got him mucking out stalls at six-thirty this morning."

"That'll teach him."

We both laughed, knowing full well it wouldn't stop him from going out and doing it again. Just like Patrick's early morning drills after our drunken nights out hadn't deterred us.

"So... your guest?" He folded his arms over his chest and gave me a knowing look. "Have you slept with her yet?"

Now I remembered why I sometimes hate my cousin. He was so fucking smug. "If I did, you'd be the last to know."

He smirked. Smug bastard. "This should be interesting."

I didn't even care to ask what he found so interesting. Noah came into the kitchen, all set to go, and I set my mug in the sink.

He smiled at his baby brother as I took the duffel bag off his shoulder and slid it onto mine. "He's cute. But 'specially when he's sleeping."

Jude and I shared a laugh.

"Have fun with your dad, slugger." Jude fist-bumped Noah

before he pulled him into a hug. "We'll see you at Grandma's tomorrow."

He nodded and smiled up at Jude. "Don't forget to bring the football so we can practice," Noah said.

"When have I ever forgotten?"

"Never. But Grandpa says you have to teach Uncle Ridge how to play so he can be on the team."

Jude groaned. I snorted. "This should be interesting. Can't wait to watch you work your magic, *Daddy Jude*."

He gave me the finger behind Noah's back then in typical Jude fashion, he smugly announced. "Piece of cake. I've got this."

Yeah, sure he did. Dumb shit.

I took my son and left without another word. Playing nice with Jude was something I tried to do for Noah. And for Lila. Because I promised her I would. But it sure as hell wasn't always easy.

I knew he still resented me for what I'd done. Had never truly forgiven me for getting Lila pregnant, even though he claimed he had. Shit like that couldn't be resolved with a few words over a beer. Not sure I'd forgiven him either. And I sure as hell hadn't forgotten the hell he'd put Lila through when he came home from Afghanistan. Or the way he'd abandoned her when the going got tough. Only to show up six years later and act like Lila had betrayed him. None of it had been her fault. It was all on me.

The night I'd been with Lila she was too drunk to know what she was saying or doing. Didn't matter that I was drunk too. A better man would have tucked her in and let her sleep it off. The next morning, I wished I'd done just that. In the harsh light of day, with the mother of all hangovers, I'd never felt like a bigger asshole than I did that morning.

I'd not only slept with my best friend, my cousin's jilted

fiancée and love of his life, I'd knocked her up. What were the chances the condom would break? What were the chances she'd get pregnant after only one try? One in a million. But here we were, one big happy fucked-up family, navigating parenthood the best way we could.

For the sake of everyone involved, Jude and I both lied and pretended we were good with the situation. I wasn't good with it, but I resigned to make the best of it. Just like I'd been doing for years. When I'd asked Lila to move in with me, she looked at me like I'd lost my everlovin' mind.

"Are you insane? I can't live with you."

"Why not? We're a family now."

She shook her head. *"We're not in love. I mean, yeah, we love each other but only as friends. I don't want Noah to get the wrong idea. Besides, you might meet someone special and I don't want to be standing in your way."*

"I'm not saying you have to sleep in my bed. Just live with me."

"I can't, Brody. You know I can't."

And that had been the end of it. We shared custody and Noah got shuttled between two houses but spent the lion's share of his time with his mom. Not what I would have wanted but you don't always get what you want.

I tuned into Noah who was chatting a mile a minute from the back seat as I drove.

"I'm working on my other tooth. It's kind of wobbly. Can we try the string trick?"

I stopped at a red light and adjusted the rearview mirror to see him better. "Why are you in such a hurry to lose your teeth?"

"Cause the tooth fairy comes and makes me rich. And Chase lost both of his front teeth already." He scowled at the mention of Chase's name and I stifled a laugh. His rivalry with

Chase went back to nursery school when he punched the little weasel for making his best friend Hayley cry.

Guess my boy was more like me than I'd like him to be sometimes.

When Noah and I walked through the front door, the sound of her throaty laughter greeted my ears. Noah looked up at me, eyes wide as we followed the sound of their voices—one male and one decidedly female. "Does Uncle Ridge have a girlfriend?"

I shook my head. "Nope."

"Lemme see." Noah ran to the kitchen, needing to find out for himself.

What was she doing here? In my house? Taking a deep breath, I ventured into the kitchen where Shiloh was sitting on the counter, a glass of something green in her hand. She was wearing skinny black jeans, a black cheetah print T-shirt and black leather high tops that were probably designer. Her hair was down, falling halfway down her back, shorter layers framing her face and in the light of day without makeup, she was fucking stunning.

"What are you doing here?" I asked, my voice gruff.

"Nice to see you too, Cowboy. I needed a blender for my breakfast smoothie." She lifted her glass to me. "Want one?"

"I'm Noah. I want a milkshake!"

He didn't want a milkshake. He just didn't want to be left out.

Shiloh smiled at him, giving him her full attention. If she was surprised that I had a son she didn't show it. "Hi Noah. It's nice to meet you. I'm... Sh... Viv," she said, catching herself. "Is that your artwork on the refrigerator?"

Noah nodded. "Yep. I drawed the horses for daddy's birthday." He ran over to the refrigerator and rearranged the Tabasco bottle magnets then pointed to the other drawing. "And that one's for Ridge. He likes fast girls and fast cars. So I drawed a girl runner. And a car."

Ridge snort-laughed. I shot him a look, having only just heard the inspiration for the drawing. He was shirtless and barefoot, his hair still damp from the shower, wearing nothing but a pair of basketball shorts slung low on his hips.

"Do you want to help me make the smoothie?" Shiloh asked Noah.

Never one to turn down an offer to help or show off, he nodded enthusiastically. "Yep. I'm good at chopping."

According to Noah, he was good at everything. Nobody had ever told him otherwise.

"Let's make a smoothie for your daddy too." She winked at him. "The kale will give him bigger muscles."

I pulled a face. Kale and apple and god knew what else went into that green drink. No way was I drinking it.

Noah's eyes widened. "Bigger? He already has big guns. My daddy is ten feet tall and bulletproof. He can fix all the horses and even my baby brother. Right, Daddy?"

I shrugged. Gotta keep the myth alive for as long as my kid believed it. Any day now he'd realize I was all too human and not a miracle worker. I dreaded that day. I dreaded the day he stopped looking at me like I was capable of making his world a better place. But for now, he was still a believer and far be it from me to dispute his claims.

"You know it, buddy." No mystery where my kid got his bragging rights. Ridge was laughing so hard he was doubled over. I scrubbed my hand over my face.

I'd never introduced Noah to any of my hook-ups. I'd always kept that part of my life separate. But Shiloh... she was different. We weren't even hooking up, but it already felt more intimate than sex with a random girl ever had. And now here she was, in my kitchen, peeling apples and talking with my son while my brother stared at her ass the same way I'd been doing last night.

"Wipe the drool off your mouth," I said, pulling up a stool at the island next to him.

Talk about a train wreck. Why was this girl barging into my life, taking over my kitchen and commanding the attention of all three males in the room?

"Not bad, huh?" Ridge smirked.

I ignored his smart-ass comment.

"You should invite your friends over more often."

"Didn't invite her."

"You're saying you don't want her here?" He was trying to goad me. I wasn't going to stoop to his teen combat tactics.

I wanted her here. I wanted her in my kitchen. In my bed. On the island. Underneath me. On top of me. I wanted her in every way imaginable.

"Hey Vivienne," Ridge said over the whirring of the blender, his phone in hand.

"Yeah?" she asked without turning around.

"What kind of music do you like?"

"All kinds."

"Huh. Okay." I side-eyed him as he scrolled through his playlists. Seconds later, he hit play, a smirk on his face as "The Ghost of You" by Acadian Storm blasted from the speakers. "This band is in my top ten. Might be inching its way up to number one."

"Stop being a dick," I said through clenched teeth. "Change the music."

"Nah. I like it. You like it, Viv?"

I wrestled the phone out of his hand and cut the music as

the blender stopped whirring. For a few seconds, there was total silence.

"I always wonder if bands listen to their own music," he pondered. The little shit. He was lucky I hadn't rearranged his face.

Shiloh turned from the counter and set a smoothie in front of me then focused her gaze on Ridge. "Can you do me a favor?"

"Sure."

"Can you keep this to yourself? I'm here for five and a half more weeks and if you want to hang with me, you totally can. But I don't want my whereabouts to be all over social media, okay?"

"I won't say shit to anyone. Swear on my life." He crossed his heart. "I'm good at keeping secrets. Been doing it all my life."

Shiloh gave him a smile. "Thanks."

"No problem."

"So you like Acadian Storm?" she asked, leaning her elbows on the counter and propping her chin in her hands. He nodded. "Is that song your favorite?"

"Yeah." He hung his head and rubbed the back of his neck. "It got me through some hard times. Used to listen to it on repeat."

Shiloh nudged my arm. "Play it again. For Ridge."

"Nah. It's okay," he mumbled. "Just forget it. I need some sleep." Shoulders slumped, he headed out of the kitchen and I watched his back until he was gone, somehow feeling like I'd been the one to fuck this up. I'd been trying to get through to him and he'd just shared more in the past five minutes than in all the months he'd been living with me.

"Hey." Shiloh placed her hand over mine and I dragged my eyes away from the doorway and to her face. "You should listen to the song sometime. It'll probably tell you more about Ridge than he could ever put into words."

"Is that what you do when you write your music? Do you share your truth?"

She studied my face before answering. "I slit a wrist and bleed onto the page." She laughed but I could tell she hadn't been joking.

I knew the song. But I'd never listened to it that closely. Now I would. It wouldn't only tell me what Ridge couldn't, it would also tell me a lot about Shiloh. And as much as I tried to deny it, I wanted to know everything about the woman standing in my kitchen.

"Uh oh," Noah said. "I missed."

I looked over at Noah who was using his hands to scoop up the smoothie that pooled on the counter and dripped onto the floor.

Shiloh burst out laughing. It was just another Saturday morning in my crazy life. I had a son who only stayed with me on the weekends. A brother who had a previous life I knew nothing about. And now I had a rock star looking for calm in the storm.

Funny. I'd always thought *I* was the storm.

A knock on the front door had Noah abandoning his efforts to clean up the mess. "Hayley's here. Yes!"

Shiloh cleared her throat. "Who's Hayley?"

"My best friend. We're getting married someday." Noah tugged on my hand with his sticky one. "Daddy, answer the door."

"Do you want me to leave?" Shiloh asked me.

"You can stay," Noah said. "Daddy wants you here. Right, Daddy?" I looked down at his upturned face then over at Shiloh.

"Stay. Go. It's your call."

CHAPTER TEN

Shiloh

My Nikes pounded the dirt trail, and I pushed myself harder, my thighs burning as I set a punishing pace on the hilly terrain. I hated running but it was good cardio, and I didn't have access to a gym or my personal trainer. Besides, as I'd demonstrated time and again, I was good at running.

It had been two days since I'd run away from Brody's house. From the kitchen, I'd heard Meredith's voice and started shaking uncontrollably. As if she'd take one look at me and somehow know I was the girl who had abandoned her own baby. As if she'd know I was Hayley's birth mother. Which was ridiculous. She had no idea who I was. No reason to think I'd come looking for my daughter six and a half years after I gave her up. Hayley didn't even look like me. She looked like Dean.

All I'd wanted was to spend time with Hayley and when the opportunity had presented itself, I panicked and blew it. When had I become such a coward?

Sweat poured down my face and my sports tank stuck to

my skin, but I forced myself to keep running. Like everything about Texas, the sky was bigger, and the sun was brighter here. Last night I watched the stars from the back porch, and I worked on the song I was writing. *Rolling Stone* had stated that the recurring themes in my music were heartbreak, loneliness, and disenchantment.

I didn't know if that was accurate. I just wrote whatever I was feeling at the time. Whatever moved me or grabbed hold of me and wouldn't let go until I put it into chords and lyrics. I always found it interesting to hear which songs spoke to someone. What did Ridge hear when he listened to "The Ghost of You?"

Dean and I wrote that song as a duet two years ago. It was the last one we ever wrote together. The song told the tale about the end of a relationship. About loving the idea of someone more than you loved the actual person. About trying to hold on to something, or someone, even when you knew they weren't good for you because you were too scared to let go. It was about addiction and toxic relationships and the toll they took on you and everyone around you. Heartache and loss—the emptiness that cracked your heart wide open. When we sat down to write the song, Dean had just come out of thirty days in rehab and was more vulnerable than he'd ever been.

The song was raw and gritty and honest, something Dean rarely was when he was jacked up on coke or drunk and belligerent. But when Dean was stone-cold sober, he was always sorry. He'd apologize and act repentant until I forgave him. It was a vicious cycle we'd repeated more times than I could count. When we released the single, Dean had second thoughts about putting it out in the world. Once it was out there, there was no going back. The music didn't belong to us anymore. It belonged to everyone who listened and felt a connection with it.

After the album dropped, we went on tour. Our last tour together. It was no small feat that we all made it out alive. All we did was fight and argue. The whole atmosphere had been so claustrophobic and so fraught with tension, it felt like I was suffocating the whole time. By then, Dean had asserted himself as the lead singer and I only sang on a few tracks. The rest of the time I was his backup singer and guitarist.

I hadn't been living the dream. I'd barely been making it through each day. The drugs and the drinking, the fame and the money and all the groupies and fangirls that found their way into bed with Dean and Landry and Gus, had been too much to handle. When I finally said I couldn't take it anymore, Landry chose Dean and the band over me, showing me exactly where his loyalties lay. The guys resented me for leaving and going solo but if I hadn't, that lifestyle would have destroyed me.

Now I was a solo artist, hoping and praying I'd live up to the hype surrounding my debut album. The bigger you got, the higher you climbed, the harder they fall. I *couldn't* fail. I *wouldn't*.

I crested a hill, having reached my destination, and dropped to the ground, panting from the exertion of running. When I caught my breath and my heart rate started to slow down, I unscrewed the lid of my water bottle and drank greedily. The Texas sun was no joke. After I drank my fill, I lifted a small pair of binoculars to my eyes that I'd bought the other day and searched for the wild mustangs. America's living legends.

I zoomed in on a rider on horseback. Brody. What the hell was he doing? He was leading another horse alongside him as he rode hell for leather. Crazy cowboy. I followed his progress as he rode across the valley, through the brush, and skirted around a limestone formation. The land he kept the wild horses on was more rugged than the rest of his land and parts of it looked like the desert. The way the sun hit him made him shimmer like gold. Like an apparition or a mirage. He and the horse he was leading rode right through a creek that meandered through the trees. After that, I lost sight of him and lowered the binoculars, wishing I could have captured that scene on a video and set it to music.

I sat under the shade of the tree and drank my water until the sweat dried on my skin and my flushed cheeks cooled. Then I stood up and I ran back the way I'd come. When I reached the end of the dirt trail, I looked over at the barn as Brody rode up with the other horse in tow and stopped in front of a tall, lanky man who appeared to be in his thirties or forties. After Brody dismounted, his eye caught mine and he tipped his chin in greeting. I gave him a little wave then turned left and headed back to the guesthouse.

Brody's life was here. Mine wasn't. It would be stupid to think we could ever mean anything to each other. What was the point in getting close to someone only to leave them in five weeks' time? But still. A big part of me hoped he'd seek me out. That he'd actually want to spend time with me without my having to chase after him or insinuate myself into his life.

I hadn't decided what I would do about Hayley yet but maybe next time, if there was a next time, I'd have the courage to face her.

I suffered from insomnia on and off, but lately, I was barely sleeping at night. I guess I'd always been a night owl. It went along with the job. After a performance, I was too keyed up to sleep. So I'd gotten in the habit of napping whenever I could. After I got back from my run, I took a shower, changed into cut-offs and a T-shirt and fell into bed. What felt like five minutes later, I was woken by a knock on the door. *Again.*

Without bothering to ask who it was, I swung the door open, expecting to see Brody. My smile slipped. A pretty brunette with green eyes gave me a smile.

"Hi. Sorry to barge in on you. I'm Lila. I just wanted to stop by and introduce myself. Ask if you needed anything..." Her voice trailed off.

I cleared my throat. "I'm good. Thanks. I'm... Viv."

"Viv," she repeated, nodding her head. "Right. Um... you met my son, Noah, the other day. He seems to think..." She stopped and laughed then shook her head. "Never mind. Six-year-olds have wild imaginations."

"You're Noah's mom?" She nodded. Oh wow. Okay. This just got interesting. Was Brody still in love with her? Was that why he only did casual hookups? "So... what did Noah think?"

She laughed. "Just forget I said anything." She lifted the bag in her hand. "I brought you a Welcome to Cypress Springs present."

I looked at the bag in her hand and the coral flowers she was holding in the other, a diamond and wedding band shimmering on her ring finger. "The peonies are from my garden. Coral charm," she said with a smile. "Not sure if Brody told you about this barbecue place yet but they have the best tacos you'll ever eat."

"Thank you." She handed me the bag and I peeked inside. The scent alone had me drooling. "Oh god, that smells so good. I love tacos. And now I'm starving."

She handed me the flowers tied with string. "Good. I hope you love them." She looked over her shoulder at her SUV. The back windows were open. "Well... my son is in the car, so I'd better get going. I just wanted to say hi."

"Okay. Thanks for the tacos."

"Anytime. See you around." She hesitated a moment but then turned and started walking away. I nearly had the door closed but stopped myself from shutting it.

"Hey. Lila."

"Yeah?"

"Have you eaten lunch yet?"

"No."

"There's enough here for both of us. Join me for lunch?"

She didn't even hesitate for a second. Her face lit up with a smile. "I would love to. Let me get Levi and I'll be right in."

I carried the food into the kitchen and set the breakfast bar for our cozy lunch, my mind going a mile a minute. What had happened between Brody and Lila? A few minutes later, after I'd swapped out the wildflowers in the mason jar for the fresh flowers she'd brought, she came in with her baby in the car seat and set it on the floor, dropping a diaper bag on the leather sofa.

"He's gorgeous." I leaned over for a better view of the sleeping baby with chubby cheeks, dark hair, and full pink lips that were pursed.

"Thank you. He looks so much like his daddy." She sighed. "Isn't that always the way?"

I laughed a little. "Yeah, I guess it is. Noah looks exactly like Brody."

"Yup. I'm hoping for a girl next time. Way too much testosterone in my life."

"I hear you. I've been surrounded by boys all my life."

"Same."

I poured two glasses of water and set them on the breakfast counter then pulled up a stool across from her. She slid one of the tacos in front of me and a plastic container of sauce. "Try this one. It's the brisket taco. Be liberal with the pico de gallo. It's amazing."

She watched me take my first bite. She wasn't joking. I

might have moaned. The taco was delicious, and I told her so. I'd eaten half of it when I caught her staring at me. I dabbed my mouth with a napkin, thinking I'd gotten sauce on it. Her cheeks flushed. She adjusted the sleeves of her blousy off-the-shoulder top then took a drink of water.

"Okay, look, I need to get this out of the way because I suck at keeping things to myself." She took a deep breath and let it out like she was gearing up to tell me the world was ending, and we only had twenty-four hours to live.

"I know who you are. Nobody told me. And don't worry, I won't fangirl all over you," she hastened to add. "Well, maybe just a little because I'm a huge fan. Huge. And I swear I'm not the type to fangirl over anyone. But I've been listening to your solo album non-stop. Just ask my husband. No offense, but he's sick of listening to it. I love every single song on it. I don't even think I could choose a favorite but if I had to, it would be 'Fragile.'" I can't believe I'm sitting across from Shiloh Leroux right now." She stopped and took a deep breath. "Phew. Okay. I've got that out of my system. I'm good now. Let's carry on like I never said anything." She picked up her taco and took a huge bite.

I sat back on my stool and laughed. I was laughing so hard I was snorting. Oh my god. This girl was the best. I already adored her and could understand why Brody would have loved her. When I finally pulled myself together, she gave me a rueful grin. "I sounded like a crazy woman, didn't I?"

I shook my head. "No. Not all. And thank you. It means a lot to me that you love that album." I hoped my words sounded sincere because I truly meant them. I'd poured my heart and soul, my blood, sweat, and tears into that album. It had been my therapy at one of the lowest points in my life. Everything had been broken, including me. Bastian told me to put it all into my music, every ounce of pain and heartache and anger and sadness.

"Fuck 'em. Rise from the ashes of the motherfucking house they burned down around you. This album is going to blow them the fuck away."

Beautiful Bastian. He'd been so right. And once again, music had saved me.

"So you and Brody..." I waved my hand in the air to erase the words. "Sorry. It's none of my business."

She chewed on her lower lip. "It's a crazy story, actually, and we don't really have that kind of time. But I'll give you the Cliff Notes. We've been best friends for most of our lives. Me, Brody, and Jude. Jude is Brody's cousin but they're more like brothers. And I've been in love with Jude since I was nine years old. He enlisted in the Marines right out of high school. Five years later, he came back a different man." She looked over at Levi who was still asleep then returned her gaze to me. "He was messed up when he got back from Afghanistan and we went through so much. And then one day he just up and left me. A year after he left, Brody and I got drunk. Drunker than I'd ever been in my life. And I ended up pregnant."

"Wow. I didn't see that coming."

"That's life. You never do."

"Are you married to Jude now?"

She smiled. "Yeah. He came back two years ago. It wasn't easy but we forgave each other."

"That must have been so hard. For both of you."

"So hard. But Jude is my one true love. Nobody could ever take his place."

"That's really amazing to find your one true love so young."

"It is, but it wasn't all smooth sailing. It took twenty years for us to get our acts together." She laughed a little and shook her head.

"And now you get to live happily ever after."

"Well, most days. We love each other but neither of us has changed much. He still thinks he knows everything, and I still fight him every step of the way." Her eyes sparkled. "Keeps him on his toes."

I laughed and wiped my hands on a paper napkin. "God, I'm so full."

She groaned and rubbed her flat stomach. "Me too."

We tossed the empty containers in the bag and Lila stuffed them in the garbage can while I rinsed the plates and stacked the dishwasher.

"What do you think of Brody?"

"I think Brody ..." I couldn't even put it into words. He was so many things. "Is pretty special."

She nodded, a small smile on her lips. "He's so special. Brody is a good man. But he'll try his best to convince you otherwise. The reason I mentioned Noah is because Brody has never introduced his son to any woman. Noah thought it was a pretty big deal that he got to meet you." The way she said it made it sound like a big deal.

"Just for the record, I showed up at his house uninvited. I needed to borrow his blender."

"But he didn't kick you out."

"If Noah hadn't been there, he probably would have."

Lila tapped her finger against her lips, a sly smile on her face. "I wouldn't be too sure about that."

We both looked over at Levi who was kicking his legs and waving his arms, making gurgling noises. By the time Lila took him out of the car seat, he was howling.

"Can I help?" I asked as she laid him on top of a plastic mat she pulled out of her diaper bag then deftly changed his diaper, undeterred that he was red-faced, kicking and crying.

"I've got it. But thanks."

Minutes later, peace was restored. Levi was greedily sucking on a bottle of formula while Lila held him in the crook of her arm. We'd moved to the back porch and were sitting on the Adirondack chairs facing the lake. Like two old friends instead of strangers who had just met a short while ago.

"What I wouldn't give to dive into that water right now," she said with a sigh.

"Go ahead. I'll look after Levi."

"Tempting. But I have to get going. I have a few errands to run before I pick up Noah from school. Sundays and Mondays are my only days off, so I always try to cram it all in."

"What do you do for a living?"

"My friend Christy and I opened a floral design studio right after we graduated from college. We mainly do weddings and special events."

"That sounds like a cool job."

"It is. I love it. But it's not as cool as your job. Ugh, if I could sing like you... I can't even imagine. I'm not just saying this, but your voice is incredible. Your vocal range... how do you hit those notes and hold them like that? I'd be gasping for breath."

I laughed. "I didn't used to be able to hold them that long. Before I released my solo album, I worked with a vocal coach. It made a huge difference. Before that, I didn't even realize I wasn't breathing properly. It also helped that I gave up smoking."

She nodded. "Don't ruin your voice or your health with cigarettes. They're far too precious."

"Yeah, I used to have a lot of bad habits. I'm working on becoming a better version of myself."

She stood up from her seat, holding the baby against her chest and I got to my feet. "I think that's what we all strive to do. Become the best versions of ourselves." She put Levi back in his car seat and clipped him in then slung the diaper bag over her shoulder and lifted the seat. "But some days I call it a success when I've managed to shower and look halfway presentable."

I laughed as I followed her to the door and held it open for her. Much like Brody, she refused my offer of help and told me she's got it. Must run in the family, even though they weren't related by blood.

"It was great meeting you," she said after she'd gotten Levi into the back seat and handed him a rubber ring he was gnawing on.

"You too. Thanks for stopping by."

"Why don't you take my number? If you need anything... tacos or visits from screaming babies... give me a call." I pulled my phone out of my pocket and entered the number she gave me then sent a quick text so she had mine too. I didn't usually give out my number so readily, but Lila was cool, and she seemed genuine. And even though we barely knew each other, I knew I could trust her.

After she was gone, I thought about the story she'd told me. It wasn't the craziest story I'd ever heard but it must have made for some interesting family dinners. I wondered if Brody was as cool with it as Lila seemed to be. Had he been in love with her? Was he *still* in love with her? That would explain a lot. But if Brody was in love with Lila, she was completely oblivious.

CHAPTER ELEVEN

Brody

I wasn't chasing after Shiloh. That's what I kept telling myself as my feet carried me to her door. It was ten o'clock at night. Too late for a social call. Yet here I was standing on her porch, calling her name through the screen door. Inside, the lights were blazing, so I didn't think she was asleep but after a few minutes of waiting for her to answer, I turned away, resigned to go back home. It was for the best, I told myself. As I walked down the back porch steps, I heard a twig snapping followed by a loud curse. I trained my phone flashlight on the trees. Shiloh was hopping around on one foot.

Chuckling under my breath, I moved closer for a better look. "Having some problems there, Shy?"

I aimed my phone flashlight at her. She spun around to face me and holy shit, she was wearing a black lacy bra and a matching thong, her tits spilling out of the bra, ample cleavage on display.

"My eyes are up here, Cowboy."

Slowly, my gaze moved up her body, over her taut, toned stomach and to her face. I leaned my shoulder against a cypress tree. "Just enjoying the view."

"Oh. So you enjoy it now?"

I grinned. "It'll do. It'll do just fine." I pushed off from the tree and moved closer until I was standing right in front of her. She didn't try to cover up her body or look embarrassed that my eyes were roaming again. "What are you doing out here?"

"I was about to take a swim in the lake." Her eyes roamed down my body, offering me the same courtesy I paid her and cocked a hip, putting her hand on it. "Care to join me?"

"You don't have a swimsuit?"

"Nope. Forgot to pack one. But I don't need one." She looked over her shoulder at the lake. "You said this is private, right?"

I nodded.

She grinned. "That's good. Because I'd hate for anyone to catch me swimming naked."

"You're going to swim naked?"

"It's the best way to swim." She turned her back to me and walked to the water's edge. Unclasping her bra with one hand, she slid it down one arm before removing it and dropping it to the ground. Then she hooked her fingers on the sides of her thong and slid it down over her thighs and calves. She lifted one foot and stepped out of them then kicked it off the other, the black lacy thong landing next to her bra.

Not gonna lie. Her naked body was fucking perfect. She looked at me over her shoulder, laughter on her lips before she faced forward and waded right the fuck into the water, gingerly stepping over the loose gravel and rocks at the bottom. Guess I should have mentioned there was a dock not far from here that would have made it a hell of a lot easier to get in. But nah, I kept my mouth shut, enjoying the view and her struggle. When the water reached mid-thigh, she dove all the way in as if the lake was bathwater warm.

Well, fuck. I couldn't just let her swim on her own now, could I?

Grabbing the lone towel and gathering up her clothes from the ground, I carried them to the dock hidden in the trees and turned on the portable camping lanterns I'd set up for Walt. He used to swim in this lake every night, regardless of the season, and claimed it was the fountain of youth. I toed off my high-tops, stripped naked and dove in.

Fuck. It was cold. Pretty sure my dick had shriveled to the size of a walnut.

Now where the hell was she?

I spun in a slow circle, searching for her in the light of the moon. I heard a splash followed by laughter. "Catch me if you can." Her voice echoed across the lake.

Guess who was doing the chasing now? Fully aware that I was playing right into her hands but not really caring enough to stop, I swam in the direction of her voice.

"Marco," she called out, laughing. I stopped swimming and spun around again. The witchy woman was outwitting me and had me going in circles. I could see her from here, her teeth so white in the darkness, her black hair slicked back and the moonlight glowing on her face. It looked like she was carved from marble.

"Polo," I said, playing her little game.

Neither of us made a move to bridge the distance. I could stay in this exact spot, treading water until my legs grew numb and I caught hypothermia, but I'd much rather have my arms wrapped around her and her legs wrapped around my waist. "Let's meet in the middle."

She hesitated, and you would think she was contemplating doing something crazy like jumping into a lake naked. Finally, she agreed and inched forward. At this rate, it would take all night to reach each other. But let's face it, the chase was the fun part. So, we moved closer and closer, neither of us giving an inch, until finally we were at arm's length.

"Hi," she said.

"Hi."

"You could have told me there was a dock."

"Where's the fun in that?"

She reached over and smacked my arm. I grabbed her hand and tugged her closer. "Cold?"

"Nope." Her teeth were chattering, and when I released her hand, she wrapped her arms around herself.

"Liar. Your lips are blue."

"You can't see that in the dark. We need to swim. Get our circulation going." I had a different plan. I wrapped my arms around her and pulled her against me. "And then the water won't seem as—"

I kissed her cold lips and she gasped as my tongue slid inside her warm mouth. She wrapped her arms around my neck and her legs around my waist and I held on to her, treading water while we kissed in a cold lake under a spring-time moon.

Were all her kisses this hungry or just the ones she reserved for me?

She was shivering in my arms, her naked breasts pressed against my chest. Skin to skin. And even though the water was ice cold, my dick was getting hard and prodding her stomach. Like the witchy woman she was, she rocked her hips, and rubbed her body against me just right, creating friction that zinged up my spine and made my balls tighten.

She pulled away and gave me a devious smile. "Race you back to the house."

"I moved your stuff to the dock."

"Perfect. When I win, I get the towel."

"This feels like old times," I said without thinking.

"Old times?" Her brows furrowed, and I realized my mistake. "With who? Lila?"

I'd never mentioned Lila to her. "How do you know about Lila?"

"She stopped by to visit me this afternoon. We had lunch together and it was highly informative." She smirked.

I could only imagine how that had gone down. Knowing Lila, she'd told Shiloh the whole story. "I'll bet it was."

Without another word, she started swimming toward the dock, her strokes strong and sure. I gave her a head start and waited a couple minutes before I set off. One thing was clear. She was a faster, more focused swimmer than Lila had ever been. Growing up, I'd always beaten Lila, but I'd never managed to beat Jude. Not a single fucking time. He'd always been better at every sport, but he steered clear of horses. The few times I'd seen him ride, he was total shit at it. Used to piss him off that the horse never did as he commanded.

I beat Shiloh to the dock but just barely. We were both hanging onto the ladder, neither of us making a move to get out of the water.

"Ladies first," I said.

"But I lost."

I shrugged. "You can have the towel."

"You sure?"

"I'm sure."

Still, she hesitated.

"I'm freezing my balls off so if you don't mind, I'd like to get out of here before they shrivel into raisins."

That made her laugh. "Okay. In the interest of protecting your manhood, move aside."

I moved aside, and she pulled herself out of the water. I

watched her climb the ladder, giving me the perfect view of her bare ass. She wrapped herself in the towel and then it was my turn to climb out. Not gonna lie. I would have loved to protect my manhood right now. But of course, her eyes lowered, and I couldn't tell her not to look or make excuses for how inadequate it looked after the equivalent of a cold shower.

"You're still pretty impressive. But not *quite* as impressive as my big boy."

I growled and stalked toward her. She let out a little yelp then turned and ran, her clothes clutched to her chest. I was buck naked, chasing after a girl and I wasn't even mad about it. I caught her around the waist, spun her around and tossed her over my shoulder. She weighed next to nothing and she was laughing so hard, her whole body was shaking.

I ran her up to the cabin, leaving a trail of water across the hardwood floors and into the small laundry room off the kitchen. Depositing her on top of the washing machine, I grabbed a towel from the shelf behind her.

"Helps to have local knowledge," she observed when I wrapped the towel around my waist because like a dumb shit, I'd left my clothes at the dock.

"You still cold?" I asked, rubbing her upper arms with my hands. She was still shivering, and goose bumps covered her skin.

"I'm warming up." She smiled when I grabbed another dry towel from the shelf, and wrapped it around her shoulders, putting a layer of cotton between her skin and dripping wet hair. "It's been so long since I've had so much fun doing stupid things. Didn't that make you feel so alive?"

I nodded and flattened a palm on either side of her. "Yeah, it did. You should have fun more often."

"I know. I really should." She traced a bead of water down my chest with her finger. "For the past few years... for a long time, really, it just feels like everything's gotten so heavy. And it feels like I haven't had time for anything but my music. Not that I'm complaining. I love what I do, and I know I'm incredibly fortunate but sometimes..."

"You just want to let your guard down and have some fun."

She nodded. "Yeah. That's exactly it." She leaned back on her hands and pinned me with a look. "Why didn't you mention you had a son?"

I straightened up and ran a hand through my wet hair. "Didn't really come up."

"That's such bullshit. You can do better than that."

I shrugged one shoulder. "I always try to keep that part of my life separate."

"Separate from what? You keep it a secret from your friends?" she teased, but she sounded hurt like I'd intentionally kept a big part of my life hidden from her.

"We're not friends, Shy. We barely know each other."

"Funny. I feel like we were becoming friends. And we do know each other." She hooked her legs around my waist and locked her ankles, slamming me up against the washing machine. *Feisty.* "I know what makes you want to cry."

"Well, now you know. I have a son. And my son's mother is married to my cousin."

"Are you still in love with her?"

I didn't want to talk about this with her. Or anyone. I shook my head. "It wasn't like that."

"Maybe not for her but what about for you?"

It wasn't something I'd ever told anyone. Not Lila. And not Jude when he questioned me. I'd lied to protect everyone involved. Whether I'd liked it or not, Lila had always belonged to Jude. He had staked his claim from the start, never questioning whether it was his right to do so. Maybe in another lifetime Lila could have fallen in love with me. But nah, I was too fucked up to be with Lila and she'd never had the same feelings for me.

Sometimes you had to accept your losses, know when you were beaten, and move on. Which was what I'd done a long time ago. Not just with Lila, but with so many other things in my life that I'd wanted but could never have. Add Shiloh to that list. Because this girl sure as hell wasn't going to stick around for long.

"Doesn't matter," I said, my hand coasting up her thigh. "It's ancient history."

"Okay."

I gave her thigh a little squeeze then unhooked her legs from my waist and backed away a few steps. She was studying my face a little too closely and even though the lights were out in the laundry room, I could see her just fine in the light coming in from the kitchen. "I need to go and get my clothes. Catch you later, Shy."

She opened her mouth as if to say something then shut it again and nodded.

"Hey Brody."

She always seemed to wait until I was walking away before she called my name. I stopped in the kitchen. "Yeah?"

"You're so much better than you think you are."

Where the hell had that come from? Maybe she really was a mind reader. *So are you, Shiloh. So are you.*

Once again, I left her when all I'd really wanted to do was stay. Typical Brody move. But in my experience, if something seemed too good to be true, it usually was.

CHAPTER TWELVE

Shiloh

On Tuesdays, Hayley took a gymnastics class in a small shopping complex a few miles from the elementary school. So I was parked in front of an ice cream parlor, sipping an iced coffee I'd gotten from the drive-thru while I watched her through my rearview mirror. Stalker central. It made me feel dirty. Hayley and her mom disappeared behind the plate glass door and I slumped in my seat. How many times was I going to put myself through this torture?

"Hi Viv!"

I jumped in my seat, my hand flying to my heart. Noah was standing outside my open window, an enormous ice cream cone in his hand. He grinned. "I told Daddy that was you."

I smiled. Brody's son was adorable, with thick wavy dirty blond hair to the nape of his neck and a smattering of freckles on his nose.

But even though I was wearing a ball cap and sunglasses, he'd noticed me right away. Which was kind of worrying. Kids were observant. "Hi Noah." I leaned out my open window. "How are you doing today?"

"Real good. I got two scoops." He held up his waffle cone to show me. It was so big he had to hold it with two hands.

"That's enough to make anyone smile."

Chocolate ice cream dripped down his hand and he let go of the cone with one hand to wipe it on his green T-shirt. I winced. He looked down at the chocolate ice cream smeared across the front of his shirt. "Oops." He shrugged one shoulder, unconcerned. "Oh well. Mommy can wash it."

Brody appeared next to him, took Noah's hand and wiped it with the napkins then tried to clean off his T-shirt. When he realized it was hopeless, he stuffed the napkins into his jeans pocket. "Viv. How's it going?"

"Yeah." I cleared my throat, trying to erase the image of Brody naked. "It's all good."

"What are you doing here?"

I lifted my iced coffee. "Just hanging out. Drinking my iced coffee."

He squinted at the shops I was parked in front of, then returned his gaze to me. "Not much of a view."

"I don't know." I took a moment to appreciate the sight of Brody in a white T-shirt and faded denim. Now I knew what he was hiding in those jeans and despite the cold water, he was more than ample. "From where I'm sitting, my view's pretty good."

He gave me that slow, lazy grin of his. "Mine's not so bad either. It was better last night though."

My cheeks heated. Wasn't I the one who claimed I didn't blush like a schoolgirl? I dragged my gaze away from Brody and focused on Noah which was far safer. "What are you guys up to today?"

"Daddy picked me up from school. He's gonna take me horse riding."

"That sounds like fun."

Noah took a few more licks of his ice cream. "Yep. It's a whole lotta fun. Daddy's the best rider in Texas. Probably the whole world." I stifled a laugh. "I'm really good too."

"I bet you are. I bet you're good at a lot of things. I saw what a good artist you are."

"Yep. I'm going to be an artist and a cowboy and a football player. And a motorcycle rider like Uncle Jesse. And I'm gonna be rich like Uncle Gideon."

"Wow. You're going to be busy."

"Mmhmm." He tilted his cone to lick it. Sure enough, the top scoop fell off and splattered on the blacktop at his feet. "Oh no." He face-palmed himself and groaned. "Not again." He looked up at Brody who shook his head and sighed.

"Now I remember why we don't get double scoops."

"It was my prize for the gold star at school," he reminded Brody. "Doesn't matter. I still have this one. Besides, I like the bubblegum one best. At the end, I get to chew the gum too."

"It's always good to look for the silver lining." I shared a laugh with Brody.

"Let's get you home." Brody put his hands on Noah's shoulders and steered him away from the truck. "See you around, Viv."

"See you Brody. Bye Noah."

"Bye. Wait, do you wanna ride horses with us?" Noah yelled back at me.

"I'm sure your daddy wants to spend time alone with you."

"Okay."

"But thanks for the offer." He was already gone, so he didn't hear me.

I watched them drive away in Brody's big black truck then

slunk down in my seat, feeling like an idiot. Five minutes later, I was still sitting there, thinking I should leave when a text came through from Brody.

If you want to ride with us, you're welcome to.

The corners of my lips lifted into a smile, and those stupid butterflies invaded my stomach. How ridiculous that a text from Brody made me feel this happy. Like, maybe he actually *wanted* to spend time with me.

You sure I won't be in your way?

I stared at my phone and two seconds later another text came through.

Meet us at the barn in half an hour.

Instead of waiting for Hayley to come out of her gymnastics class, I drove home. I had five weeks left in Cypress Springs and was coming to accept that maybe it would be better if I left her alone. I had seen as much as I needed to. She was a happy little girl and had obviously been adopted by a loving family who made her a priority. There must be a database for adopted kids where I could leave confidential information. That way it would be up to her. If she ever wanted to track down her birth mom, she could.

But even as I thought it, my blood ran cold. If she ever decided to look me up, how could I possibly explain what I'd done? I couldn't. Not even to myself. I was worse than my father. Maybe that was why I'd given him money when Landry refused. *Guilt.*

Rhett Holloway used the money to buy a bar in Nashville and named it after himself. Every night there was live music and singer/songwriter sessions. He performed on Friday nights and Sunday afternoons. Or at least that was what it said on the bar's website. As far as I knew, he hadn't released any new music and I hadn't heard from him since he opened the bar a few years ago. He'd sent me an invitation to the opening, but we were on tour. I emailed to let him know and that had been the end of it.

Did I forgive him for abandoning us? After Maw Maw died, Landry called him, asking for help. The house was falling down around us, and Maw Maw had exactly $177.56 in her bank account. Not even enough to cover the cost of a funeral. She'd never made a lot of money but whatever she'd made had gone into raising us. Rhett said he was sorry, but he was living in a one-bedroom apartment and money was tight. In other words, he didn't lift a finger to help us. So no, I couldn't forgive him.

I didn't know why I was thinking about this now as I walked over to the barn to meet Brody and Noah. I guess when you saw a good father in action, it made you realize all the more how shitty your own had been.

Brody was lifting Noah onto the saddle of the tan horse with a black mane. It was the first horse I'd led out of the pasture the other day and Brody had told me she was gentle, but still. That horse was big, and Noah looked so small sitting on its back.

"Wow. That's a big horse for a little guy."

Noah scoffed, taking offense to that. "I'm not little. I'm six." He made a muscle. "You see that? I've got big muscles."

I bit the inside of my cheek to stop myself from laughing. His arms were small and thin with no sign of a muscle, but I nodded seriously. "I can see that. Almost as big as your dad's."

He nodded, appeased by my words, and gathered up the reins. Not the least bit daunted that the horse underneath him was tossing its head, he leaned over the horse's neck and swatted away a fly then leaned back in the saddle, all chilled out and relaxed like he belonged up there on that big old horse.

"Can I go now?" he asked Brody.

"Hold on to your horses."

Noah cracked up over that one. He was laughing so hard I moved to his side, ready to catch him if he fell off the horse. "Get it? Hold your horses." He cracked up all over again and kept repeating it, trying to mimic Brody's deep voice, which had me laughing along with him.

"Ready, Viv?"

I wiped my sweaty palms on my jeans. "Um... I don't know."

"Come on." Noah waved his hand. "It's lots of fun. You'll see."

"Come here." Brody jerked his head toward a chestnut horse, and I went to stand by him.

"Just relax. I won't let anything happen to you." I nodded, believing him. He told me to stroke the horse so we could get acquainted which I did.

"What's her name?"

"Hail Mary."

"Oh Lord. Should I say my prayers?"

He laughed. "Come on. I'll give you a leg up." It only dawned on me then that he'd already had the horse saddled and waiting for me as if he knew I'd show up even though I hadn't texted back to say I'd be here. Maybe I should have been annoyed at his presumption, but I wasn't.

He gave me a leg up and instructed me to swing my right leg over the saddle. When I was sitting on the horse, he adjusted the length of the stirrups then wrapped his hand around my calf and looked up at me. "You good?"

I nodded then looked at the reins. "How do I hold them?"

He took the reins and positioned my hands to show me how to hold them. "We're just going to take it nice and easy." He glanced at Noah then lowered his voice. "Noah's not ready to do much more than walk and trot and these horses will follow me, okay?"

I nodded. "Okay. What else do I need to know?"

"Relax your hands, sit up straight, and go with the rhythm of the horse. You've got nothing to worry about. We're just taking a nice gentle trail ride. Smile and enjoy the scenery."

I smiled, and he returned it.

Two minutes later, he led us out of the barn, and I didn't have to do a thing. My horse followed Noah's horse. I took a few deep breaths and tried to relax. After about ten minutes, I got used to the rhythm of the horse—mostly—and started to enjoy the ride. Until Brody turned in his saddle and asked if we were ready to trot. No surprise that Noah punched the air, excited about the prospect. I wasn't the least bit excited.

Had I nodded? Had I given the impression that I was up for it? Looks like I had no choice because my horse broke into a trot and shit, that hurt. What could possibly be relaxing or enjoyable about bouncing around in a hard saddle while I held on to the saddle horn for dear life. Was this just a trot? It felt like my horse was running.

How did guys handle this? Didn't their dicks and balls take a beating?

Brody's laughter reached my ears. *Shit.* Had I said that out loud?

"Roll with it, Shy," he called back.

"Who's Shy?" Noah piped up.

Oh God. I hated lying to this little boy. My life was built on lies. "It's Viv's nickname," Brody said, saving me from having to answer.

Noah nodded, accepting it as a fact because his dad had said so and Brody had probably never lied to his son.

CHAPTER THIRTEEN

Shiloh

My BUTT WAS SORE, my thighs were burning, and I nearly fell on the ground at Brody's feet when he helped me out of the saddle. He caught my arms to steady me, barely suppressing his amusement. "Whoa there, girl."

"I'm good. Just have to find my sea legs."

He chuckled. "It's a good workout. Good practice," he added.

"Good practice for what?"

He leaned in close and whispered into my ear. "For riding a cowboy." He winked and gave my sore ass a smack. Great. Now he had me thinking about riding a cowboy. I bet he was good with ropes.

I looked over at Noah, worried that he'd overheard or could read my dirty thoughts. He was playing with Buster, rolling around on the ground with the dog and laughing, not paying any attention to the adults. Brody just grinned and pulled the saddle off my horse then carried it to the tack room.

After we'd groomed the horses, Brody led them into their stalls, and I wandered over to Cayenne to check on her.

She looked restless and was trying to scratch her stomach with her back hoof. Was that normal?

A few minutes later, Brody joined me. "Is she okay?" Now she was rubbing her backside against the side of the stall.

"She's fine. Pretty sure she's gonna drop her foal tonight."

"Tonight? Did you call the vet? Do you have to take her somewhere?"

"I've delivered a lot of foals. The only reason to call the vet is if something goes wrong. But this is her third foal. She'll be just fine."

"She has two other babies? Where are they?"

"They're not babies anymore. I sold them."

"You *sold* her babies? How could you do that to her?"

"I don't do this as a hobby, Shy. I need to make money at it."

"It just seems so mean to separate them."

"I don't kick them out as soon as they're born. I wait until they're weaned." I gave him a skeptical look.

"What's that look for?"

I shrugged and looked at Cayenne again. "It just sounds like it goes against everything you believe in."

"I've got my own moral compass and my own convictions. If you've got a problem with that, too bad. If I don't make money, I can't afford to rescue horses. I wouldn't expect you to give your music away for free. It might be your passion but it's still a job, and you've gotta accept the bad with the good, just like anything else."

I nodded, hearing the logic in his words. "I know. You're right. It's just... it's kind of sad." My gaze returned to Cayenne. I was taking this too personally and I knew it.

"It's the same as letting your kids go out in the world to find themselves once they get old enough to leave home. You can't hang onto them forever."

I turned my head to find him watching my face, searching for something. "I know." I forced a smile. "How else do you make your money?"

"Training horses. Starting colts and fillies. Gentling wild horses. And I work with a lot of 'problem' horses." He used air quotes for problem. "The horses are never the problem. It always goes back to the owners."

"Daddy Jude!" Noah's voice interrupted our conversation and I turned to look at the man who had just walked into the barn. Wow. So this was Lila's husband. These McCallister boys sure were easy on the eye. I'd expected him to look more like Brody, but they looked nothing alike.

"Hey buddy. Looks like you had some ice cream."

Brody left me by the stall and strode over to them. "I would have driven him home." He crossed his arms over his chest.

"Thought I'd save you the trip. You're always bitching and moaning about how busy you are."

"I don't bitch and moan."

I laughed. "Sure you don't."

Brody shot me a look as I joined them. Jude laughed. "Looks like she knows you already." His gaze landed on me and he smiled. Like Levi, his eyes were blue, and his hair was chestnut brown. He was a couple inches taller than Brody and had to be at least 6'3" with broad shoulders and sculpted muscles. "I'm Jude."

"Nice to meet you. I'm—"

"This is Shy Viv," Noah said.

We all laughed but Noah scowled, not catching the joke. "What's so funny?"

"Nothing." Brody lifted Noah off the ground and hugged him goodbye. "I'll see you on Sunday."

Why not Saturday?

"Okay. Love you Daddy."

"Love you more." He set Noah down and ruffled his hair. "Be good for your mommy."

I noticed he didn't mention *Daddy Jude*. Noah ran off with Buster and when he was out of earshot, Jude took me aside. "Listen. I know this is a shit thing to ask and I'd never normally do it. But for Lila, I'll suck up my pride and ask." He winced. "When the tickets went on sale for your concert in Austin, I tried to get tickets, but they sold out too fast." He ran his hand through his disheveled brown hair. "Fuck. I'm sorry but I'm prepared to drop to my knees and beg if I have to."

I laughed. "You don't have to beg. It's no problem. I'll hook you up."

He released a breath. "Yeah?"

"Yep. I can even get you backstage access." I winked at him. "I know a few people."

"You have no idea how happy this will make her. Won't hurt my cause either." He chuckled and rubbed hands together. "Pretty sure I'll win the best Christmas present contest this year."

"You're such a shit." Brody snorted with disgust. "She's trying to lay low. Not be hounded by assholes looking for handouts."

Jude held up his hands like he was innocent. "Hey. I did it in the name of love. The tickets are for Lila, not me. And there's *nothing* I wouldn't do to make her happy."

"History has proven otherwise," Brody said.

Jude's eyes narrowed. "Don't start."

"Not looking to start anything." Brody had a surly look on his face and despite his casual demeanor, leaning against the horse stall, arms and ankles crossed, I could feel the tension. "Just speaking the truth."

Jude pointed his finger at Brody. "You need to get the fuck over this. I apologized to you. I fucking thanked you for what you did for me. But why is it that every time I see you, I'm tempted to plant my fist in your face?"

"Feeling's mutual."

"Daddy Jude! Come on, I'm hungry. What's taking you so long?"

Jude rolled out his shoulders and took a deep breath before releasing it. "I'm coming." He turned his gaze on me. I felt like I shouldn't have been standing there, witnessing any of this. "Sorry about that. And thanks. I'm sure I'll be seeing you around."

I nodded once and gave him a smile then watched him stride away before I turned to look at Brody. His eyes were hooded, and he ran a hand through his hair. "Don't say it."

"What do you think I was going to say?"

"That I'm an asshole. And you'd be right."

"Brody..." I took a few steps closer to him. "I don't think you're an asshole. I mean, sometimes yeah..." He huffed out a laugh and looked down at his scuffed boots. "But that... what just happened with Jude... my brother Landry and I have done the same thing about a million times. Different set of issues, obviously, but that's how it is with family sometimes. You expect better from them. You hold them up to a higher standard because you care so damn much about each other. From where I'm standing, you and Jude are typical brothers. You love each other and would fight to the death for each other, but you don't always like each other very much."

He gripped my hips in his hands and walked me backward until my back hit the wall next to the barn door. I flattened my palms against the rough wood. "Where did you come from, Shiloh?" He moved his hand next to my head and used the other one to tuck a lock of hair behind my ear then kissed the sensitive spot just below it. "Why are you making excuses for me?"

"I don't know." My voice came out in a whisper. Lifting my hand to his face, I cupped his cheekbone and he leaned into my touch. "Maybe because I think you're too hard on yourself. You're only human, Brody."

He kissed the corner of my mouth. "Damn. I hate it that you figured that out."

I laughed a little, but my laughter got swallowed up by his kiss. It was different from our other kisses. Slow and easy, almost gentle, like he had all the time and the world, and his sole focus was on this kiss. He deepened the kiss and my body melted into his, my hands slowly exploring the hard muscles of his back and shoulders before sinking into his hair. He smelled like horses and leather and cedar and he tasted like a dream come true.

It's him, Maw Maw. I found him. I knew it as surely as I knew my own name.

I rocked my hips, angling them just right against his erection. He groaned, the sound deep and guttural, and it reached deep into my core. I rocked my hips again. He slid his hand down my thigh to the back of my knee and lifted my leg then wrapped it around his waist, so his hard length hit the spot between my thighs. My clit was throbbing, and I was so wet, my panties were soaked.

God, I wanted him. I wanted him so fucking much. I pulled his head down to mine, clawing his scalp as our slow, gentle kiss turned frenzied and wild. If he wanted to fuck me against the barn door right this very minute, I'd let him.

Someone cleared their throat. "Sorry to interrupt," a male voice said.

With a muttered curse, Brody released me and turned his back to me, blocking my view. "The hell do you want?"

The guy laughed. "Sorry to cockblock you..."

"No, you're not."

"You're right. I don't give a shit. You told me to come over at five. Guess you lost track of time, huh?"

"Shit," Brody said. "It's five already?"

"Yup. You gonna help me load 'em into the trailer or just leave me to my own devices?"

"I'll take care of it."

"Gonna introduce me to your friend, Bro-Bro?"

"Get the fuck out of here."

"Hey Austin, whassup?"

That sounded like Ridge. I was still standing behind Brody's back with his hand on my thigh.

"Hey man. How you been? Hear you and my nephew got lit the other night."

Ridge laughed. "Yeah. It was pretty sick."

"Have your fun now. When football practice starts, I'm gonna kick your asses into shape."

"Will I have to call you Coach?"

"Damn straight. Second thought, Sir will do."

Brody snort-laughed. "Whoever made you one of the coaches of a high school football team must be dumber than a box of rocks."

"I'm still a high school football legend."

"In your own mind."

I couldn't take it anymore. I needed to see who Brody was joking around with. I moved out from behind his protective stance and stood next to him. The guy standing in the stables was as big as Jude and built like a football player with dark brown hair cropped close to his head. His eyes nearly bugged out of his head. "Holy shit. You look a lot like that singer." He clicked his fingers, trying to come up with the name.

"Yeah, I get that all the time."

Brody's lips quirked in amusement. He looped an arm around my shoulders and pulled me close to his side. Austin's eyes widened. "Well, I'll be damned. When did this happen?"

"No idea what you're talking about."

"Yeah, okay. Brody Commitment-Phobe McCallister. I'm Austin Armacost." He extended his hand and I stepped forward to shake it.

"I'm ..." I looked over at Brody. He nodded, and I got the feeling he trusted this guy. "My name is Shiloh."

He released my hand. "Damn. That's it. Shiloh. It was on the tip of my tongue. Not sure what you see in this guy." He puffed out his chest. "My ranch is bigger than his."

"You inherited your ranch. Doesn't count."

"Still counts."

I laughed.

"Is she the reason you needed my pickup?" he asked Brody. Brody nodded.

"Glad to see it's in good hands."

"Thanks for lending it to me."

"Owed Brody a favor. It's no big deal. You gonna help me load these horses so you can get back to whatever the hell you were doing?"

"They're over in the pasture behind the round pen. Bring the trailer over to the gate."

Austin nodded and told me it was nice to meet me before he strode out of the barn. Ridge had disappeared a while ago, so it was just me and Brody now. "I've got a lot of people coming and going in my life."

"I can see that. They seem like good people."

"What I mean is that hanging out with me might mean a lot of people will find out who you are."

"I know what you meant. But you trust them, right?"

"As much as I trust anyone."

"That's good enough for me. Well..." I backed away toward the door. "I'll let you get to work. I have some calls I need to make."

Without waiting for a response, I turned and walked out the back door of the barn. I was hoping he'd visit me later.

After I made my calls to my manager, Marcus, then my publicist, I made an omelet and microwave popcorn for dinner, and worked on my music.

When I checked the time, it was already ten-thirty. Chances were I wouldn't be seeing Brody again. I picked up my phone and debated whether to call him or not. Maybe he was in bed already.

I set my phone down on the coffee table and turned on the TV, surfing through the channels until I got to a music documentary about Janis Joplin and settled in to watch it. She was strumming her guitar and singing "Me and Bobby McGee" with Jerry Garcia accompanying her on the guitar. Janis was so fucking cool. Why did all the best musicians have such tragic lives cut short?

My phone buzzed on the coffee table and I smiled when I saw Brody's name on the screen.

"You busy?"

"Just watching a music documentary. Wanna come over?"

"Can't. Was wondering if you wanted to see a foal being born."

I jumped off the sofa and stood up so quickly, I got a head rush. "I'll be right over."

CHAPTER FOURTEEN

Brody

"ADD this to the list of things that make me cry." She wiped the tears off her cheeks with the hem of one of my old flannels she'd found on a peg in the tack room. She was wearing it over a tank top, the sleeves rolled up, buttons undone, the hem longer than her cut-offs. "It's so beautiful, you know?"

I wrapped my arm around her shoulders, and she leaned into me. "I know."

Shiloh hadn't been the least bit squeamish when the foal was being born. She'd gotten right in the stall with me to help out in any way she could. Now the foal—a fine little filly that had come into the world an hour and a half ago—was on her feet and nursing while we stood a good distance away to observe so Cayenne and her newborn foal could do some bonding.

Exhausted from the birth, the filly lay down on the straw for a nap. Shiloh yawned again. I squeezed her shoulder. "Come on. I'll walk you home so you can get some sleep."

It was two in the morning and I'd only be getting a few hours' sleep. That's always how it went on foaling nights. With a final look at the mare and her foal, I grabbed a flashlight from the tack room and walked with Shiloh out of the barn and into the dark night with Buster close at my heels. She stumbled on the uneven ground and I caught her arm before she went down then clasped her hand in mine, training the flashlight ahead of us as we made our way in the dark. I couldn't remember the last time I'd held someone's hand. Had I ever? You would think at my age there wouldn't be any more firsts left to experience but being with Shiloh made everything feel new and different.

The joy and wonder on her face when that foal had come into the world. Her tears when she told me how beautiful it was, as if she'd never seen anything so wonderful before. Tonight, she'd told me about all the places she'd traveled and the sights she'd seen when she was touring. At twenty-five, she had seen the world, had frequented the hottest clubs and had dined in some of the finest restaurants. Yet to me she still seemed so genuine, casually shrugging off her fame and fortune as if it didn't impress her much.

She yawned again. "I might actually get some sleep tonight."

"You're not sleeping?"

She shrugged one shoulder. "I have insomnia. It's been this way for years. Late at night, my thoughts are always racing."

I was the opposite. As soon as my head hit the pillow, I was out for the count. "That's not good."

"It's just the way it is. Are you a good sleeper?"

"Like a fucking baby."

"I'm kind of jealous. How do you do it?"

"I kick all my problems out the bedroom door and slam it shut. Rest assured, they're always waiting for me the next morning."

She laughed. "Maybe I should try that."

"Dwelling on all the shit in your life has never solved a single problem. All you do is end up losing sleep and making your problems seem bigger than they really are."

"You're really smart."

"Never been accused of that before."

"Is it okay with you if I visit the foal tomorrow morning? Just to check and see how she's doing."

I glanced at her. "Fine by me. But just so you know, the vet will be coming by first thing in the morning. Glenn, one of the guys who works for me will be around and so will Chris."

"And what about you? Will you be around?"

"I'm leaving in the morning."

"You're going away?"

"Just for a few days. I'm doing a training clinic just outside of Abilene."

"You take your skills on the road?"

"When the money's right. I have a few training clinics lined up for the summer. Some are here. Some at other ranches."

"It's all about the hustle."

"Guess you'd know something about that."

"Yeah, I do." We stopped outside her door. "You were pretty impressive tonight, you know that?"

"Didn't do much of anything. The mare did all the work."

She placed her hand over my heart. "You got the filly breathing."

"You weren't too happy with my methods."

"I didn't know you were supposed to drop a baby on its head."

I laughed. "Not such a good idea for human babies but animals are different."

She smiled. "Well, good luck. Guess I'll see you in a few days." She put her hands on my shoulders and stood on her tiptoes to kiss me goodnight. It was just a sweet little kiss and ended all too quickly. Seconds later, she was inside, the door closed behind her. I headed back to the barn to check on Cayenne and her foal before I fell into bed, my alarm set to go off in four hours' time.

"I STILL DON'T GET why you won't let me stay home," Ridge muttered on the way to school the next morning.

"I want my house to still be standing when I get back, that's why."

"This blows. Walker said I could've stayed with him."

Walker was Austin's nephew, Ridge's partner in crime. Austin's sister was currently going through a nasty divorce so the last thing she needed was to look after Ridge. As it was, Austin was always having to step in to help out with Walker. "Patrick and Kate want to spend time with you."

He rolled his eyes. "Patrick just wants to lecture me. I won't hear the fucking end of it."

"I survived. You will too." He stared out the windshield the rest of the way to school and didn't say another word. When I pulled up outside the front doors, I reminded him that Kate would be picking him up from school.

"Whatever." He grabbed his bag and slammed the door of the truck then stalked away. I waited to make sure he actually walked through the front doors of the school. With Ridge, you could never be too sure. On top of his shitty grades, he'd been known to cut school and show up late for classes.

After I dropped Ridge off, I hit the road. I was supposed to meet with the ranch manager and the owner at noon and it was already twenty past eight. I couldn't afford to be late. Not when

I was being paid ten grand. I needed the money for a new roof and Noah's summer camp.

Fueled by coffee, I cranked up the volume on my music and listened to Shiloh Leroux all the way from Cypress Springs to Abilene. I'd never been one to get starstruck. I knew celebrities were just people, no better or worse than the rest of us. But I'm not gonna lie. It blew my mind that the bluesy rock voice blasting from my speakers came from the same girl who had helped me birth a foal last night. The same girl who I'd skinny-dipped with in the lake. And ate lunch with on the tailgate so she could see my wild horses in action.

I listened to Acadian Storm's music too. Whenever Dean the douche Bouchon was the lead singer on a track, it pissed me off. But I listened anyway. Even when Shiloh was singing the backing vocals, I could still hear her voice loud and clear. By the time I got to Abilene, I felt like I knew Shiloh on a more intimate level than I had before.

If her lyrics were a reflection of what she wanted and needed in her life, one thing was blindingly clear. Shiloh was looking for someone to love her.

CHAPTER FIFTEEN

Shiloh

It was eleven o'clock on Saturday night and I'd just gotten out of the shower when Brody called me. I answered the phone with a stupid smile on my face. He'd only been gone for a few days, so I shouldn't have missed him, but I had. It was weird that in such a short time I'd gotten used to having him around and when he wasn't here, this place felt emptier. "Hey Cowboy. How was Abilene?"

"It was all good. You still awake?"

"Well, if I wasn't before, I am now." Phone to my ear, I walked downstairs, liquid silk brushing my thighs, a warm breeze floating through the back screen door.

"What have you been up to?"

"Not much. Your cousin Jude stopped by yesterday."

"What did he want?" he asked gruffly. "More handouts?"

"No. He brought me his world-famous chili and some jalapeno cornbread."

Brody snorted with disgust. "My chili is better."

I stifled my laughter and plopped down on the sofa, my face tipped up to the cool breeze from the ceiling fan, my bare feet propped against the side of the coffee table. "Well, I don't know... his is *awfully* good. I'd say it's right up there with the best chili I've ever eaten."

"That's only because you haven't tried mine yet."

"There's a lot of things of yours I haven't tried." I rolled my eyes at myself. Could I be any more obvious? Might as well ask him to come over and fuck me while I was at it. Lana Del Rey was singing about drinking all day and talking all night, pleading with her lover not to leave, not to say goodbye.

"As luck would have it, I'm only two minutes away."

"If you're looking to have a chili cook-off, I've had my fill."

"I'm sure I can come up with something better than that."

"Ooh, I don't know. Competition is stiff. Austin gave me a truck. Jude gave me a week's worth of his prize-winning—"

"Answer the door." He cut the call and I started laughing.

When I opened the door, the laughter died on my lips. It had only been a few days since I'd last seen him, but it was almost like I'd forgotten what he looked like. I took a moment to drink him in, to appreciate the sight of Brody in a plain white tee and faded denim. His tall frame filled the doorway, longish dirty-blond hair disheveled like he'd been running his hands through it. He brought with him the familiar scent of leather and cedar and I inhaled, filling my lungs with it.

He graced me with one of his slow, lazy grins, his teeth so white against his tanned skin, and those little lines around his eyes crinkling. My stomach fluttered with anticipation, my nipples getting hard even though he hadn't made a move to touch me yet. This yearning. This longing to be touched. It was the best kind of foreplay.

"Is this what you wear to sit around the house on a Saturday night?" He looped his finger in the thin strap of my silky camisole and slid it up and down, sending delicious shivers up and down my spine as I stood in the open doorway, barely breathing.

"I was preparing to spend some quality time with my big boy. I wasn't expecting a booty call."

He put his hands on my hips and walked me backward, kicking the door shut behind him. "Good thing you're dressed for the occasion."

"Good thing."

My back hit the wall and he took my hands in his and raised them above my head, pinning them to the wall. Then he dipped his head and kissed the sensitive spot just below my ear. "Why's your hair wet?"

"Went for a swim in the lake and then I took a nice, long steamy shower." His lips coasted down my neck, brushing not kissing, as if he was breathing me in. He brushed his lips over my shoulder then my jawline and kissed the corner of my mouth. My heart raced and my breathing was shallow, almost scared that he was able to churn up so many emotions inside me with just a simple touch of his lips or his hands.

"Steamy, huh?" In the next beat, he said, "You went swimming without me?"

"Mmhmm. I floated on my back and sang to the moon." Jeff Buckley's version of "Hallelujah." Whenever I heard that song, I pictured him floating in the Mississippi River, fully dressed with his boots on, singing. I didn't think his death was an accident either.

"Lucky moon." Finally, Brody kissed my mouth. My eyes closed, and my lips parted, my nipples straining against the thin silk of my camisole. His tongue slipped into my mouth and his rough, calloused hands slid down my raised arms and down my sides before flattening his palms on either side of me. "Did you think about me when you were taking that steamy shower?"

"I was thinking about how I wanted to finish what we started." My hands were free to explore now so they found their way to the hem of his T-shirt and under it. I splayed my palms on his lower back and inched upwards over his hard muscles and warm, golden skin.

"Funny." He tugged my bottom lip between his teeth and sucked on it before releasing it. "I spent the whole drive home wondering what that sweet pussy of yours tastes like."

"You have a dirty mouth, Cowboy." I yanked his T-shirt up, wanting it off.

He acquiesced, reaching behind his neck to pull the T-shirt over his head then tossed it on the floor. "You love my dirty mouth."

Brody lowered his dirty mouth to my breasts and cupped the right one in his hand, teasing my nipple with his teeth. Biting it through the fabric. My chest heaved, and I held the back of his head to keep it there. "I love your dirty kisses."

"Then you're going to love the other things I can do with this dirty mouth."

"What are you waiting for?"

He lifted me up off the ground and my legs cinched around his waist, ankles locked as he carried me up the stairs. I held his face in my hands and kissed him hard as he blindly steered us to my bedroom, guided by the moonlight bathing the room in blue. Downstairs Lana Del Rey was singing "Born to Die", her falsetto voice effortlessly hitting the bright notes and dragging the listener to the depths of the dark ones. "Don't you just love Lana's sultry voice?"

"I love yours more."

"You're biased."

"I loved your voice before I ever met you."

I kissed him softly to thank him.

He tossed me on the bed and my back bounced off the

mattress and then his arms were braced on either side of me. I lifted my hands to touch his face and brushed my thumb over his lips.

"Tell me what you want, Shiloh."

I traced his jawline and his nose and the shape of his mouth with my fingertips, trying to commit them to memory. "I want you to ride me hard like I'm one of your bucking broncs."

He threw his head back and laughed. "Shit. How'd I get so lucky?"

"The stars aligned, and the universe is conspiring to make us happy. For a little while," I added. Because we both knew something like this could never last.

"If that's the case, we'd better make the most of it. We've already wasted too much time."

My thoughts exactly.

He didn't give me what I asked for. He gave me the opposite.

His hands skimmed up my sides, bringing the silk material with it and I sat up, so he could slide it off my body. He tossed it on the floor, his eyes roaming over my naked torso before he gently pushed my shoulders and my back hit the bed again. Slowly, so slowly, he slid my silky shorts down my thighs and over my calves, lifting one foot and then the other, planting them both flat on the mattress so I was spread out before him in all my naked glory. I pushed myself up on my elbows.

"Look at you," he said softly. "You're fucking perfect."

I was far from perfect, but I worked hard to keep my body strong and toned so I accepted the compliment. Using his hands, he spread my thighs and pressed them against the mattress and when he lowered his head between my legs and his mouth caressed my inner thigh, his tongue making lazy circles, I gasped.

His pace was maddening, a slow torture that had my clit

throbbing and my hands pulling his hair. He laughed, his lips against my skin, so close to where I wanted him, but not quite.

"I said hard and fast."

"I'm not your big boy," the charmer said. "I'll do whatever the fuck I want, and you'll thank me for it."

I squeezed my eyes shut and balled my fists in frustration. He stopped at the crease of my thigh, his soft breath teasing me and just when I thought I'd get what I wanted he bypassed my clit and paid the same careful attention to my other thigh. I growled, my legs clamping his head, making him laugh again, his fingers digging into my thighs to keep them spread for him.

He looked up at me, a wicked grin on his face, and with his eyes still pinned on mine, he licked me from slit to crack, making my hips buck off the mattress. He did it again. And again. And again. My hands fisted the sheets, and my legs wrapped around his neck, thighs trembling. "Mmm. Your pussy tastes even sweeter than I imagined."

Then he dove in, one hand cupping my breast and squeezing the nipple as he thoroughly fucked me with his mouth and teeth and hands. Speeding up. Slowing down. Biting my clit, mixing sweet pain with pleasure. Driving me out of my freaking mind.

When I came, temporarily blinded, he crawled up my body and kissed me hard, his tongue sliding into my mouth, so I could taste myself on him.

He rolled onto his back, bringing me with him, and I kissed his neck and bit his earlobe, his belt buckle digging into my hips. I moved down his body and unbuckled it, my fingers fighting with the top button of his jeans. He pushed my hand away and did it himself.

I rolled off him, and he kicked off his boots and pushed down his jeans and boxer briefs, his big, thick dick springing free. And as far as penises go, I thought his was beautiful.

Getting onto my knees on the mattress in front of him, I wrapped my hands around it, the skin velvety soft, and I guided it to my mouth, my tongue darting out for a taste. I licked the slit then wrapped my lips around the head.

His hand went to the back of my head, fingers tangling in my hair. I watched him from underneath my lashes as I licked the underside and felt the weight of his balls in my hand, gently rolling them. His eyes were hooded, chest rising and falling, his breathing getting quicker.

I took him into my mouth as far as I could take him and sucked on him, my cheeks hollowed.

"Fuck," he growled. "I don't want you like this."

I didn't listen. I kept sucking his dick, my hand squeezing his balls, waiting to see what he'd do.

He pulled away, reached for his jeans on the floor and came out with a strip of silver-foiled packets. Ripping one off, he tossed the others on the bed.

"How... ambitious of you. You're quite the optimist."

"I'm a realist."

I laughed and took the condom out of his hand then flung it across the room. "You don't need it. I'm on the shot and I'm clean."

"Yeah, I'm clean too. But I never go bare."

"All the more reason why you should. Live dangerously."

His eyes narrowed. "You sure?"

"Positive. And trust me when I say I'm not looking to get pregnant. I'd never trick you." I crossed my heart and scooted up the bed away from him, forcing him to chase after me. He crawled up the bed and I let out a yelp when he grabbed me and flipped me over, sliding his hand under my stomach and lifting me onto my hands and knees. I looked over my shoulder at him. "Is this how you want me, Cowboy?"

He pulled my back against his chest and skimmed his

hands down my arms then guided my hands to the headboard. "Hold on tight." He scraped his teeth across my shoulder. "It's going to be a wild ride."

I swiveled my hips and wiggled my butt. His hand met the flesh, and I felt the sting of the slap before he pushed my legs further apart and slid his hard cock between my slick folds, the head rubbing against my tight bundle of nerves as I angled my hips, so he would hit just right.

Oh God.

"You're so fucking wet. I could slip inside you so easily."

"Do it," I panted. My muscles clenched, and I gripped the wood of the headboard more tightly as he guided his tip to my entrance with one hand, and yanked my hair with the other, forcing my head back, my neck arched. God, I loved this.

He drove into me in one fluid motion until he was fully seated. Without giving me a chance to get used to the fullness, he thrust deeper. In. Out. In. Out. Fast and hard the way I said I wanted it. I white-knuckled the headboard, meeting him thrust for thrust, his hand fisting my hair, his other hand rubbing and squeezing my clit.

It was wild and frenzied, the headboard banging against the wall, sweat coating my skin. And with every thrust, he hit that magical spot that made me cry out.

"Oh God, I'm going to come."

He rubbed my clit harder and faster and I fell apart, my muscles clenching around him and my arms giving out. With my ass still in the air, my head collapsed to the pillow and I'd barely come down from my high when with one final thrust, I felt his body shudder and he let out a guttural sound, half groan, half growl.

"Fuuuck."

Which was exactly what we had just done. We'd fucked, and it had been glorious.

We collapsed on the bed and lay next to each other on our backs, catching our breath for a few seconds, his hand on my thigh. I turned my head to look at him and for reasons I couldn't explain, we both started laughing.

"Shit, that was fun."

I rolled onto my side and propped my head on my hand, trailing my fingers down his sweat-slick chest. "So much fun. I can't wait to do it again."

And then we both laughed again, and he pulled my head down to his for a kiss that tasted like cinnamon and me. For a brief moment I pretended we were a real couple, and this was my real life.

CHAPTER SIXTEEN

Brody

"I need to stop and buy something," Shiloh said from the passenger seat. I glanced at her as I drove the back roads. Whenever possible, I avoided the main roads. There were too many shitty drivers on the road and having to stop at red lights made me impatient, so I preferred to take the back roads where the scenery was better, and the air was cleaner without all the pollution from the exhaust fumes. Today Shiloh was wearing a faded black cotton tank dress with silver studded black sandals tied around her ankle. Even in casual clothes, she looked edgy. Rock n roll. But hot as hell in whatever she wore.

"Nobody expects you to bring anything." I was taking Shiloh to our Sunday family dinner. Another first for me. This morning, Kate had called and insisted I bring her so here we were. Meanwhile, I couldn't get the mental images of last night out of my head. If I could, I'd turn the truck around and take her back to bed. Hell, we didn't even need a bed. I'd fold her over the back of my truck and fuck her from behind.

"I can't show up empty-handed."

"You could draw a picture for Grandma," Noah piped up from the back seat. A vocal reminder of why I couldn't pull the truck over and fuck Shiloh in the field we were driving past. "She loves my drawings."

Shiloh smiled and turned around in her seat to look at Noah. "I should have thought of that sooner."

"You can do it for next week," he said confidently, as if this was going to be a weekly thing and Shiloh was a part of the family now.

"Brody. Stop!"

What the fuck? I checked my rearview mirror then pulled over and screeched to a halt. "What's wrong?"

She checked her side mirror. "There's a farm stand back there. Maybe we can buy some fruit or something. Oh, it looks like they have honey. How about some honey?"

Jesus Christ. The way she'd shouted at me to stop I thought it had been an emergency. "I told you not to worry about it."

She took a fifty-dollar bill out of her wallet and waved it under my nose. I crossed my arms over my chest, refusing to take it. "Please," she pleaded. "Just go buy some fruit and honey."

I ran my hand through my hair and exhaled a breath. "You don't need to bring anything."

"Fine. I'll go."

Before I could stop her, she was out of the truck and marching along the shoulder of the road. Goddammit. Stubborn woman. I backed up my truck and swung onto the shoulder, stopping in front of the farm stand. She was already talking to the elderly man and his wife who were selling fruit and honey products. Meanwhile, I was staring at her bare legs, remembering how they'd been wrapped around me when I'd pounded into her.

She held up a beeswax candle and sniffed it then turned around to face me, a big smile on her face. "It smells sooo good."

I shook my head and laughed then cut the engine and settled in for the long haul. I'd been around enough women to know that when it came to shopping, they could happily spend hours doing it. Didn't matter if it was a fancy boutique or the back of a truck alongside the road, they always managed to find something to spend their money on.

Noah was busy playing on his Nintendo DS, so I closed my eyes and took a nap. After round three last night, we drifted off to sleep for a few hours, only to be woken by my phone alarm. Life on a horse ranch started early so I left her sleeping before the sun had even come up. No use thinking about all the ways I wanted to fuck her from here to next Sunday when there wasn't a damn thing I could do about it. A case of blue balls wasn't on my agenda for the day.

"Daddy!"

I startled awake. "What's wrong?"

"Hayley's here!"

Oh shit. I checked my rearview mirror and sure enough, a silver SUV had pulled up behind me with Dale Peterson behind the wheel. Other than having kids in the same kinder-garten class, we had absolutely nothing in common. Yet he seemed to think we were buddies. He worked for a big accounting firm in Austin and commuted five days a week. On Saturdays he golfed. On Sundays, he took the family to church and spent the day with them. Now he got out of his SUV and walked up to my open window for a chat while his wife and daughter were at the farm stand. Dale was about ten years older than me, and on weekends he wore pressed chinos and polo shirts. Today he was wearing plaid shorts with his polo shirt, a side part in his sandy brown hair.

"Brody. Thought that was you. How's it going?"

"It's all good. How've you been?"

"Lemme out, Daddy." Noah had already unbuckled the straps of his booster seat and was trying to get out of the truck. I missed the days when he couldn't get out of his seat without help. "Stupid child locks," he complained, jiggling the handle and shoving his shoulder against the door as if that would magically open it. "I want to see Hayley."

Dale chuckled. "Boy's on a mission. Better let him out before he hurts himself."

Inwardly, I groaned then took another stab at trying to keep him from getting his own way. "Just wait in the car for Viv. She won't be long."

"But she's talking to Hayley." He stared out his closed window then climbed into the front passenger seat.

"Don't even think about opening that door."

"I can climb out the window."

It was a battle of wills. Guess who was going to win?

"Hurry, Daddy, I don't wanna miss her. I need to tell her something."

Sure, he did.

Dale took a couple steps back to give me room and I pushed open my door and rounded the hood to let Noah out. My kid was spoiled, used to getting his own way, and here I was giving in to his demands. The longer we stayed at this farm stand, the harder it would be to get away from the Petersons, but Shiloh was still talking to Meredith and Hayley.

As soon as Noah was free from the confines of the truck, he raced over to Hayley who gave him a big hug like it had been years instead of days since they'd last seen each other. I watched him with one eye while Dale joined me next to my truck to discuss the rising cost of real estate in the Hill Country. It was one of his favorite topics. Real estate, sports, and the weather. Thrilling.

"Your ears must have been ringing. I was just telling Meredith that you should turn your property into one of those luxury ranches. A farm-to-table restaurant. Some rustic luxury accommodations with all the amenities. Hell, you could even put in a spa. City folk pay top dollar to get away from it all. My firm is always looking for venues to host corporate retreats and team-building exercises. You could offer trail rides and hunting."

Yeah, no. Not fucking happening. Nothing about that sounded even remotely appealing but I took exception to the last part. "Hunting?"

He held up his hands. "It wouldn't have to be animals." He rubbed his jaw, considering. "Well, maybe duck or pheasant hunting."

"Ducks and pheasants are animals."

"Yeah, yeah, sure. Or you could do clay pigeon hunting."

I clenched my jaw and breathed through my nose to stop myself from telling him he could shove his plan up his ass. No need to be rude to the guy. Lila was always on my case, telling me I had to play nice with the other parents. And look where that had gotten me. As of four or five months ago, I was put in charge of Saturday morning 'playdates' for Noah and Hayley while Dale and Meredith played eighteen holes with another couple. Could have done without those, but it made Noah happy, so I soldiered through them.

"Appreciate your thinking of me, but I'm just fine keeping things the way they are."

As far as I was concerned, the subject was closed. But Dale kept talking. "It could be a real boost to the economy too. Think of how many more locals you can employ."

Think of all the money it would cost to turn my land into a luxury ranch I'd never in a million years consider. "I'll give it some thought," I said, to appease him.

My gaze wandered to Shiloh who was talking to Meredith. Her smile looked fake, and her laughter sounded forced. If I didn't know better, I'd say she looked nervous. I highly doubted that Dale and Meredith Peterson would know who she was but maybe she was worried they would recognize her.

Dale might have still been talking when I walked away from him and joined Shiloh. Without thinking, I wrapped my arm around her shoulders, feeling like she needed my protection.

Meredith smiled. "You two make a beautiful couple. Don't they, Dale?"

"Sure do."

"We're not—"

Shiloh cut me off. "Thank you."

Not sure what that was about but she leaned into me and put her hand on my chest as if to steady herself. "You good?"

She nodded, that same tight smile on her face. "I'm fine. I just... um..." She cleared her throat. Her eyes were hidden behind big black sunglasses, but I didn't need to see them to know she wasn't fine. "I have to pay for my things."

"You already paid, honey," the elderly woman said with a small laugh.

"Oh. Right." She gave the woman an apologetic smile and I stepped forward to take the bags from the woman's hands.

"You ready to go?"

Shiloh tucked her hair behind her ear with a shaky hand and nodded.

"Viv was just telling me she's staying in your guesthouse," Meredith said with a big smile.

"Yup." I kept my gaze on Shiloh. She was paler than normal.

"Make sure you show her all that the Hill Country has to offer."

"Will do. I'll show her *all* the best things." Meredith smiled and told Shiloh it was nice to meet her, and Shiloh echoed her words. With my arm still around her, I guided her away. "Noah, let's go."

"But I wanna play with Hayley."

"You'll see her at school. Say goodbye."

He exhaled loudly like I was ruining all his fun, but he was smart enough to know when he'd been beaten, so he said goodbye and climbed into the truck. When I pulled onto the road, Shiloh slumped in her seat and let out a weary sigh like the whole encounter had exhausted her.

I side-eyed her. Her face was averted, and she was still wearing sunglasses, so I couldn't see her expression. She was spinning the silver ring around her thumb. "Hey. You okay?"

"Yeah. I'm just..." She took a deep breath and let it out, shaking her head a little. "I'm fine."

Something felt off, but since I couldn't see her face and didn't *really* know her, I had to take her word for it. She was so quiet on the drive to Kate and Patrick's I thought she might have fallen asleep.

Ten minutes later, I pulled into the driveway of the stone farmhouse I'd grown up in and parked behind Lila's SUV. The first time I saw this house, I'd just turned ten and to me, it had looked like a mansion. Patrick had shown up at the foster home I'd been put in after social services had removed me from my home. The neighbors had reported a noise disturbance and when the police had come to investigate, they'd found me locked in the closet which was usually where I spent my time when my mother was hosting one of her ragers. As it turned out, living with my mother had seemed like a dream compared to the hell of foster care. When the social worker told me I was going to live with my aunt and uncle, my first thought had been, "Where the hell were you when I'd needed you?"

Kate used to take me to counseling every week, and every week it was the same. I kept my mouth shut and refused to speak about anything that had happened to me in the first ten years of my life. I still didn't talk about those things. There were only three people I'd ever told—Jude, Lila, and Walt. I had no recollection of telling Lila. It was the night Noah had been conceived and we'd been falling-down drunk. And of those three, only Walt knew the whole story.

His idea of therapy? A vision quest in the desert. And shit, that peyote had messed with my head for four of the weirdest, most fucked-up days of my life. But it had worked. I'd made my peace with all the shit that had happened and, for the most part, I let it go.

I opened the back door for Noah and he jumped out and took off running. Always in such a hurry to get to the next thing. He was right at home here and Kate spoiled him rotten.

"Hey Shy," I said as we crossed the front lawn, the bags clutched in her hand.

"Yeah?" She sounded distracted.

"I don't think the Petersons have any idea who you are."

She gave me a small smile. "I don't think they do either."

"People have a bad habit of being overly friendly in these parts. It's that damn Southern hospitality."

She laughed and bumped her shoulder against mine. "And how come you don't extend that same hospitality?"

When we reached the front porch, I pulled her into my arms. "Thought I was downright hospitable last night."

"Hmm..." She looped her arms around my neck and looked up at me. "I still think there's room for improvement."

I squeezed her ass. "Is that a challenge?"

"You need to up your game, Cowboy."

I pulled her closer and crushed my mouth against hers. "Takes two to play this game, Sugar Lips."

"Funny. Last night didn't feel like a game."

"Pretend I'm not here," came a voice through the front screen door. I released Shiloh and took a few steps back as Lila stepped onto the porch, a sly smile on her face. "Sorry to interrupt. I left Levi's favorite blanket in the car."

I groaned. "You're not starting that again. It took five years for Noah to give up that duckie blanket."

Shiloh burst out laughing and Lila joined her.

"Say it again," Shiloh prompted.

I shook my head.

"But it's so cute when you say duckie," Lila teased. I held up my middle finger. It only made them laugh harder. "Watch this," Lila told Shiloh, giving her an exaggerated wink.

Ever the subtle one, Lila lunged at me, her hands headed straight for my ribs. Oh hell no. I spun out of her reach and slammed the screen door in her face.

"Come back, duckie," Shiloh called.

The girls were still laughing on the porch as I headed toward the kitchen. Now Shiloh would know I was ticklish.

And I never got to ask her what last night had felt like to her, but it was for the best. It had felt like something real and good and true. But that wasn't our deal. Four more weeks. No strings attached. When it was over, we'd go our separate ways.

End of story.

CHAPTER SEVENTEEN

Shiloh

I WASN'T GOING to do it anymore. I was done.

I wasn't going to keep stalking Hayley or try to ingratiate myself into the Petersons' lives in the hopes of easing my troubled conscience. It would only create more problems. I'd have to keep spinning lies and fabricating stories and before I knew it, I'd get so tangled up in my web of lies I wouldn't be able to get out of it. So I'd made up my mind I was going to leave well enough alone.

I'd already seen Hayley. We'd spoken at the farm stand yesterday. She was cute and fun and adorable. She loved dancing and gymnastics and singing. Hayley had Dean's smile and his hazel eyes and my nose, but she was her own little person, separate from us, and that was how it should be. She had a mom and a dad who loved her, and a dog called Olaf named after the snowman in *Frozen*. I'd learned all of this in our brief conversation yesterday. She'd worn a black T-shirt with a purple sequined unicorn on it because she loved unicorns and had paired it with a rainbow skirt because she loved rainbows too.

Meredith told me Hayley sang all the time, mostly songs from Disney movies. "Let It Go" was her favorite song. I recognized the irony and took it as a sign. That's exactly what I needed to do. Let. It. Go.

"How do I look?" I asked Brody, striking a pose when I answered the door.

"You look like you're ready to ride a cowboy."

"Well, howdy pardner." I tipped my black cowboy hat at him. The hat had been Lila's idea of going incognito and when I told her how cool it was, she told me Brody had given it to her for her twenty-first birthday which she claimed was a million years ago. I was wearing the hat with the plaid flannel I'd borrowed from Brody, my only two clothing items stolen or borrowed. It hit mid-thigh, fit me like a mini dress and still smelled like Brody's cedar shower gel. "I hear you do a mean two-step."

He scowled. "Who told you that?"

"Lila."

"How does she know... second thought, never mind. I only do the two-step when I'm drunk."

I scrolled through my phone and hit play on a country song. I made the playlist for this specific purpose. He groaned. "What are you doing?"

"Pretend you're drunk and show me how it's done, Cowboy. Or better yet, maybe I should get you liquored up." I grabbed a bottle of his favorite bourbon from the kitchen and poured what I estimated to be the equivalent of two shots in tumbler glasses. Thanks to Lila, who I'd spent the day with, I knew quite a few more things about Brody now. I picked up my glass and handed one to him. "Drink up or I'll tickle you to death."

He scrubbed his hand over his face and shook his head then studied the contents in the glass before his gaze settled on the bottle on the counter. "You bought the bourbon I drink?"

He sounded surprised, like he couldn't believe anyone would do something like that for him. "Why wouldn't I? You're my main squeeze for a month." I gave him a wink, attempting to keep the mood light. He huffed out a laugh and raked his hand through his hair, not sure what to make of me.

We downed our shots and I poured two more. After we finished our second generous shot, he put his hand over the glass to indicate he'd had enough. "You really wanna dance?"

I nodded. "I really do. Just show me how it's done."

"I'll lead. You follow. It's that simple."

"Nothing about you is simple, Brody."

"Right back at you. But we don't have to make this complicated."

He wasn't talking about the Texas two-step, so I nodded, acknowledging I'd heard him and understood what he was saying. "I just want to have some fun while I'm here. So how about you show a Louisiana girl a good time, Texas-style?"

"Well, I happen to be pretty damn good at showing a girl a good time."

I didn't doubt that for a minute. He led, and I followed and we two-stepped right out the back door and onto the porch. When the third song ended, he dipped me so low to the ground, my hair touched the floorboards. His lips met mine briefly before he pulled away, his face so close to mine, shadowed in the moonlight. "That's how you two-step, darlin'."

I was laughing when he pulled me up off the floor and back into his arms.

Five minutes later, I was straddling him on the Adirondack chair, his jeans unbuttoned, boxer briefs shoved down by my hands to free him from the confines of denim and cotton. His hands spanned my waist and I lifted up and wrapped my hand around him, guiding him to my entrance. I dragged the tip through my slick folds as his hands cupped and kneaded my breasts, his mouth latching onto the right one and his tongue and teeth sucking and biting.

Slowly, ever so slowly, I sank down on him until he was buried to the hilt. I kissed my cowboy while I rode him hard, his fingers digging into the soft skin as his hands gripped my hips and I held onto the back of the chair.

Now, *that's* how you show a girl a good time.

THE NEXT AFTERNOON I was sitting on the back porch, working on my new music when Ridge appeared in my peripheral. He was wearing basketball shorts again but this time he wasn't shirtless. The sleeves of his Chicago Bulls T-shirt had been cut off and there was a rip in the collar. Unlike Brody, he didn't have a Texan drawl or even a Southern accent which made me wonder if he grew up in Chicago. If so, ending up here must have been a culture shock for him.

Ridge was young, only seventeen, but he already had all the makings of a heartbreaker. Beautiful. Cocky. Trouble with a capital T. Exactly the kind of guy I would have fallen for as a teen. I don't know exactly what it was but something about him reminded me of Dean.

I just hoped he'd stay away from drugs and out of the kind of trouble Dean had always found himself in. As a teen, anytime property was vandalized or there'd been a robbery, the cops in our town had always questioned Dean. It didn't matter if he'd been nowhere near the scene of the crime, they wanted to pin it on him. The Bouchon family had a reputation in our town and nothing said about them was ever good.

He stopped at the bottom of my porch steps and I looked up from my guitar and smiled.

"Hey Ridge. What's up?"

He chewed on his full bottom lip, not looking as confident or as cocky as he had when I'd first met him. It was that damn vulnerability that had always gotten me about Dean too. And why the hell was I thinking about Dean? Probably because today was his twenty-eighth birthday and he was spending it in rehab. Not the fancy, spa-like rehab either. More like a prison.

"I was wondering... if you're not busy sometime... do you think you could teach me a few chords?" He shrugged one shoulder like it was no big deal and my answer wouldn't matter to him one way or another. But I could tell it had taken a lot for him to come over here and ask me for a favor.

"I'm free right now. Is this a good time for you?"

His face broke into a smile and there was nothing cocky about it. It was bright, and it was genuine, and God help the girls if he ever bestowed that smile on them. They wouldn't stand a chance.

"Yeah. Works for me."

"Cool. Then come on up and let's get started."

CHAPTER EIGHTEEN

Brody

"If Ridge is bothering you, just say the word and I'll tell him to stop hanging around." Which was what he'd been doing every day after school for the past week. Now it was Friday evening and I'd been invited to dinner but so had Ridge. He was in the shower when I left him at the house to come over here.

"He's not bothering me at all. I love hanging out with him. He's picking up the guitar really fast too. You might have a budding rock star on your hands."

Just what I needed. Ridge already thought he was a rock star. "You didn't have to invite him to dinner."

She smacked my arm with the wooden spoon in her hand. The same spoon she was using to stir her 'world-famous gumbo.' "He's your brother. I didn't want him to have to eat alone. Besides, I made enough for an army."

"You obviously haven't seen how much Ridge eats."

"I've seen you eat. That's why I made enough for an army."

She turned down the heat under the pot and left it to simmer then turned to face me. I handed her the cold beer I'd opened for her and she took it from my hand with a smile. "Thanks, baby."

I was *baby* now. Okay. Not that I minded. Coming from those lush lips, I'd answer to just about anything. "After dinner, he's out of here."

"Not only are you a bad loser, you don't like sharing either?" she teased.

It hit a nerve, but I took a long pull of my beer to hide the expression on my face. I'd been sharing all my goddamn life and no, I didn't like it. I fucking hated it.

"Hey. I was just joking. I'm all yours. For three and a half more weeks."

She was always keeping a countdown, reminding me of how much time we had together. Didn't like that too much either. I pulled her against me and gave her a light smack on the ass. "And don't you forget it, *baby*." She laughed and I shut her up with a kiss that verged on becoming something more. "Let's go upstairs before—"

"Hey bro. Whassup?" With a loud sigh, I released Shiloh and she bit her lip to keep from laughing. I turned around to face my brother who had just walked in like he owned the damn place. His eyes lowered to my crotch. "Forget I asked. I can see what's up. What's for dinner?" He ran his hand over his washboard abs which were on display because somehow, not accidentally either, his shirt had conveniently ridden up. "I'm starving."

"You sound just like Brody."

"I'm better looking though." He winked at her. Fucking *winked* at her.

I exhaled loudly. Shiloh laughed like this whole thing was

hilarious. I'd love to know what these two got up to during these 'guitar lessons.' Second thought, I'd rather not know.

Since there were three of us instead of a cozy two, we ate at the table. And just when I thought Ridge couldn't possibly find another way to get under my skin, he did. "What time do you want to head out tomorrow?" he asked Shiloh.

My head swiveled in her direction. The fuck? "Where exactly are you headed?"

"I told Ridge I'd take him to buy a guitar."

"And I'm going to grab her those tacos she loves so she can stay in the truck and not be mobbed by any fans."

"Win-win." They high-fived like they were best buddies.

"Hold up." I held both hands up. "First of all, what the fuck are you talking about? Guitars cost money, Ridge."

"Yeah, I know. I've got some money saved up from my birthday."

His birthday was in February and everyone in the family had given him cash. I would have thought he'd have already blown it by now.

He took another bite of his food and grinned. "Good gumbo, Shy."

"Thanks Ridge."

"That's not enough money to buy a guitar."

"I'm more than happy to chip in," Shiloh said.

"You sure as hell are not going to chip in."

"Brody." Shiloh gave me a look I couldn't read. What the fuck was she trying to tell me?

"I'm not looking for handouts," Ridge said, his jaw clenched. "I've got the money for a decent guitar, maybe a used one. But you know what? Just forget it. Thanks for dinner, Shiloh."

He pushed back his chair, stood up from the table and strode to the door.

"Ridge, you don't have to go," Shiloh called after him.

"Nah, yeah, it's all good. And don't worry about the guitar. I'll figure something out."

"Meet me here at ten tomorrow morning. We're doing this. I'm not taking no for an answer, so you'd better be here, or I'll come find you."

"You sure?"

"I'm positive. Tomorrow we're going to buy you a guitar."

He glanced at me then at Shiloh and nodded. "Okay. See you tomorrow."

After he was gone, I sat back in my seat and looked over at Shiloh. Her eyes narrowed on me. I crossed my arms over my chest. "What?"

"He's found something he's excited about and you shot him down." She gathered up our plates and stomped into the kitchen. The dishes clattered in the sink and she turned to face me, her arms folded over her chest. "You said you wanted to find a way to get through to him. Well, maybe this is it. Music. And he's looking forward to being on the football team this year too."

I rubbed the back of my neck. "He told you that?"

She nodded. "Yeah, he did. He told me a lot of things."

"Like what?"

She shook her head. "He told me things in confidence. I'm not going to betray his trust in me."

"How did you do it? You've known him for a hot minute and suddenly he's opening up and telling you shit he never tells me." And I knew why he was hanging out with her. He had a massive crush on her. No doubt she hadn't even noticed but I had.

Shiloh gave me a little smile and came up behind me, wrapping her arms around me and resting her chin on my shoulder. "Because you're guys and guys are stupid sometimes. It's easier for him to talk to me. I'm not the one he looks up to. I'm not the one he doesn't want to disappoint."

I slid my wallet out of my back pocket and took out all the cash I'd gotten out to pay Chris tomorrow. I set three hundred bucks on the table. "Put that toward it. I don't want you to chip in. You're doing more than enough for him without giving him money too."

Shiloh smiled and kissed the side of my neck. "Okay."

I took her hand and pulled her into my lap. "Promise me you won't chip in."

"I promise."

Satisfied she was telling the truth, I nodded. She stood up and put her hands on my shoulders then straddled me on the kitchen chair, grabbed the back of my head and kissed me hard. "You're a good man, Brody."

"Not so sure about that. I'm fucking everything up with Ridge."

"No, you're not. If you were fucking it up, he'd be gone by now."

"He has nowhere else to go."

"That wouldn't stop him from leaving."

And I knew she was right. If Ridge hated it here and hated living with me, he would have been long gone, consequences be damned. At his age, I never would have stayed in a place I didn't want to be.

"He loves you and down deep he knows you only want the best for him."

I hoped that was true, but I didn't know if it was wishful thinking on her part or if he'd confided that in her. Pretty sure she was trying to make me feel better. "I think we've talked about Ridge enough for one night."

"What did you want to talk about?"

"How about let's not talk at all?"

"I feel like I should be offended."

"If you were offended you wouldn't be this wet for me."

ON SUNDAY AFTERNOON Noah and I were walking back to my house from Shiloh's when he dropped a bomb on me. The three of us had gone riding and thanks to our morning rides, Shiloh was improving. After the horse ride, Shiloh had invited Noah over for the fancy cupcakes she'd bought on her day out with Ridge. He'd come home looking like the cat who had swallowed the canary. I'd felt the need to remind him he was only seventeen but stopped short of telling him he didn't have a chance in hell with Shiloh. Pretty sure it was implied.

"Are you going to marry Shy Viv?" Noah asked out of the blue.

The fuck? "Nobody's getting married."

"But you kissed her, so you must love her. Daddy Jude kisses Mommy all the time and he's always saying how much he loves her. Like every single day."

No surprise there. Jude had always been demonstrative, and he'd always told Lila how much he loved her. "Yeah, well, you don't have to love someone to kiss them."

"Yes, you do. When you kiss someone, you have to get married."

"That's not how it works." Arguing with a six-year-old took the patience of a saint. "And I'm not going to marry Shy."

"If you want to, it's okay with me. I like her. She's real nice. And she's pretty too. Not as pretty as Mommy because she's the prettiest in the world. But Shy can be in second place."

"I'm sure she'd be thrilled to know she's runner-up in your beauty contest." Noah nodded, missing the sarcasm. "I'm gonna draw her a picture. She said she likes cupcakes and tacos and music and cowboys."

"She said she likes cowboys?"

"Yeah. She said she likes them even better than cupcakes and tacos."

"Huh."

"So that's a lot a lot." He gave me a sly look. "You're a cowboy. So she must like you more than cupcakes. I think you should marry her and have a baby."

I nearly choked. "I think you should stop thinking about marriage and babies."

"Make me." He dodged away and took off running, chanting *Daddy's getting married, Daddy's getting married.* Were other six-year-old boys as obsessed with marriage and kids as mine was? I caught up to him easily and tickled his ribs until he was laughing so hard he could barely breathe. He'd inherited the ticklish part from me. Then I threw him over my shoulder and jogged to the house while he pounded on my back and Buster chased after us, barking like this was a game he wanted to take part in.

"Let me down."

"Nah. I'm going to carry you around like this until you're eighteen."

That cracked him up and he slapped my back a few times. "You're so funny."

And you are the best thing that ever happened to me. My greatest gift.

Not something I'd ever say out loud, but it was the God's honest truth. Noah would never fully appreciate how much he meant to me or how much I loved him. How there was nothing in this world I wouldn't do for him. He'd never know that, in so many ways, he'd been the one to save me. To help me put my past behind me and truly believe there was good in the world.

Kids were so innocent. So trusting. And it was my privilege to call him mine and to be given the responsibility to help raise him.

I never wanted to fail him. Never wanted to give him false hopes or lie to him. I never had before, and I wasn't about to start now.

CHAPTER NINETEEN

Shiloh

"I WANT TO BUY THE FILLY," I told Brody after we came back from our morning ride. Ever since he'd come back from Abilene, we'd gone riding when the sun was barely up. He'd been teaching me how to handle the horse on my own without just sitting like a lump in the saddle and letting my horse follow his.

Now he opened his mouth to protest but I silenced him by placing my fingers over his lips. "Just hear me out. I'll pay however much you'd get for her and I'll pay all her expenses. I'll pay for her food and board and for your training costs. That way you can keep her. When she gets older, she can be Noah's horse."

"Nope." He pulled the saddle off my horse and I followed him to the tack room.

"What do you mean, nope?" I stood in the doorway and planted my hands on my hips. He brushed past me and strode over to his horse to unsaddle it.

"Don't come here and start flashing your money around, Shiloh. I'm not taking your money. So put that idea out of your head."

Once again, I trailed after him to the tack room. This guy was so damn stubborn. How could he not see that this was a good plan? If I really wanted to flash my money around, I'd buy him all the acres of land he needed for his wild horses. I'd looked at the cost of land here and it wouldn't even put a dent in my bank account, but I knew he was too proud to accept something like that, so I'd never suggest it. But this was something altogether different. "It would be like I'm adopting a horse." I winced at the word adopt but forged on. "I want to call her Phoenix. She's happy here, Brody. She can stay with her mom and—"

"No. Not happening." He came out of the tack room with a caddy filled with brushes to groom the horses. "I already have an interested buyer and as soon as she's weaned, I'm selling her."

"Who is it?" I asked, using the rubber curry comb to get up the dirt from Hail Mary's coat. "What will they do with her?"

"They'll turn her into a barrel racer. If she's not cut out for that, she'll help to round up the cattle."

"I just don't understand how you can get attached to these horses and then sell them."

"Horses are like people. They need a sense of purpose. I'm doing the best thing I can for her. I'd never sell any of my horses to bad owners. Trust me on that."

I exchanged the curry comb for a soft brush that made Hail Mary's coat shine. "I do trust you, but it doesn't mean I have to like it."

"No disrespect but you don't know the first thing about horses." I combed Hail Mary's mane and tail and we didn't say another word until the horses were groomed and we led them up the dirt path then turned them out in the pasture. I leaned against the fence and watched the horses join the others then walked back to the barn with Brody.

"This is my life, and you're just passing through on your way to something better," he said.

"I'm not sure I'd call it something better." I watched Buster running in circles, chasing his tail. "It's just... different."

"Call it what you want but it doesn't change the fact that this is just a pit stop for you. And while we're on the topic, I don't want Noah getting too attached to you either. It's my job to protect him and there's no sense in letting him get close when you'll be leaving soon. So I'd appreciate it if you stayed away from him."

I opened my mouth to protest then shut it again. It hurt that he would say that to me but he was trying to look out for his son so who was I to say he was wrong?

Hurt and defeated with nothing left to say, I walked out of the barn as Glenn pulled up in his truck and parked by the round pen. Brody was starting another colt this morning and as usual had a 'shitload of work.'

I'd just stay out of his way.

THE NEXT MORNING, instead of meeting Brody at the stables for our early morning horse ride, I went for a run. He hadn't called or come over last night and I told myself it was for the best. My real life was starting to catch up to me, my time for rest and relaxation was running out, and I was feeling the pressure.

"We've added more dates to the fifth leg of the tour," Marcus told me on the phone later that morning. The fifth leg of my tour felt like a million years from now. He reeled off the dates and cities and told me he'd email the schedule. The new dates meant this tour wouldn't finish until April of next year. The tour had started four months ago which would make it a fifteen-month tour by the time it ended.

"Sounds good." And it did. This was what I was meant to be focusing on. My music career. My own life. My future.

"Naomi set up a press junket in Europe." He talked about the radio shows and interviews my publicist had arranged for me when I arrived in the UK in June. At the end of our conversation, he reminded me to tweet more, then asked how I was doing.

"I'm doing great." I forced some cheer into my voice. He didn't need to know about my period cramps or my shitty mood, thanks to a certain cowboy. "Just relaxing and working on my new music."

"Good, good. That's what I want to hear. We'll have to discuss dates and make arrangements for getting you back into the recording studio for the next album."

My management team was the best in the business, and I trusted Marcus' ability to help shape and grow my career, but there was no room for slacking. I had to fight tooth and nail to convince him that I desperately needed six weeks of uninterrupted R&R before the next leg of the tour, without having to do promo or appearances or fundraisers to increase my media presence.

When a tour costs tens of millions of dollars and takes months and months of planning and logistics to put together, you couldn't afford to slack off. I had to go on that stage every night and perform, give my fans what they'd paid for no matter what was going on in my personal life. And I would. There was so much riding on this tour, and I would deliver. The alternative was unthinkable, and I never let my mind go there.

We wrapped up our call and two minutes later my phone

buzzed with another incoming call. I stared at the screen. I couldn't avoid him forever. Maybe talking to Landry was just what I needed. He was family. My *only* family. So I answered my phone.

"Hey Landry. How's it going?"

"Are you okay?"

I took a seat in the green Adirondack chair and stared at the lake through the trees. It was raining, a thin layer of mist shrouding the lake, and the air had cooled. "I'm fine."

He was quiet for a beat. "Why are you ignoring my calls?"

"I texted you back." I tucked my legs underneath me and absently chewed on my thumbnail.

"What's going on with you, Shy? And where the hell are you?"

"Nothing is going on with me. I told you already. I wanted to get out of L.A.. Lay low for a while."

"Right. Okay." He sounded hurt and I hated that. "You don't even want to tell me where you are."

"Landry. I'm not doing any of this to hurt you." I wanted to tell him where I was and why I was here. I wanted to tell him I saw Hayley and she was happy. But something stopped me from saying the words. It was sad to think I didn't trust my own brother. But if I told him about Hayley, it would go straight back to Dean and I didn't want him to know about this. "You made your choices and so did I."

"Oh. We're going there, are we?"

I squeezed my eyes shut. I wanted to kick myself for saying that. "No. We're not going there. I don't want to argue with you, okay? I'm tired of arguing."

"I didn't call to argue with you. I called to tell you I'm sorry for what I said before you left. I didn't mean it."

"Yeah, you did."

He'd called me selfish for leaving the band to start a solo

career. He'd accused me of sending Dean down into a spiral when I released "Damage." Had all but blamed me for Dean's most recent brush with the law. Had told me he wished I'd never been with Dean or had forced him to choose between his sister and the best friend he considered a brother. And I got why that had put him in a difficult position, I really did. He considered us both family. But still. A part of me had hoped he'd put me first.

He sighed. "It came out wrong, okay? I'm sorry."

"I know. Me too. I'm sorry everything is such a mess. I just wish... things had turned out differently."

"Yeah. Me too." He was quiet for a moment, and I waited for him to bring up Dean but thankfully he didn't. "Are you coming back to L.A. before you head to Europe?"

"I'll be back for two days. Just to pack up my things and get organized."

"Any chance you'll have an hour or two to hang out with your bonehead brother?"

I smiled. "I'm sure I can make time for you."

"Thanks. I'd like that. It's been too long since we hung out." He sniffed, and I bit the inside of my cheek to stop myself from asking if he'd been snorting lines. "And I miss you."

"I miss you too." My heart ached. How had we drifted so far apart? I felt a pang of homesickness. A longing and a sadness for the way things used to be when we were close, and my big brother was always there to look after me. When it was left to him to shoulder the responsibility of being my legal guardian, he'd just turned twenty. He always said he wouldn't have had it any other way and I loved him so much for that, but I couldn't help thinking how much easier his life would have been without the added burden of his grief-stricken little sister.

"Take care of yourself," he said. "Make sure you don't forget to eat. And get plenty of rest. Love you, boo."

I brushed away my tears, my throat clogged with emotion. Despite everything, I knew Landry still cared about me and I knew he loved me, the same way I loved him. "Love you too, bonehead. Be good and stay out of trouble." *Stay away from the drugs.*

THE FOLLOWING evening Brody showed up at my door. Rainwater dripped from his hair and his T-shirt was wet. I tried not to notice the way the soaked cotton clung to his body, accentuating his sculpted muscles. I tried not to notice how sexy he looked with wet hair and beads of water rolling down his face.

"Sorry, baby," I said, my voice cool and detached. "Can't be your beck and call girl tonight. I have my period. So... see ya." I tried to slam the door in his face, but he flattened his palm on the wood to stop it from closing.

"Let me in, Shy."

"I'm not in the mood to give you a blow job either so you're out of luck."

"For fuck's sake, just let me come in."

I heaved a sigh and returned to my spot in the corner of the leather sofa, my knees bent, feet planted on the cushion next to mine and arms folded. I'd just started watching a music documentary on Netflix and kept my gaze focused on the TV as Brody took a seat on the sofa. I gave him the evil eye, feeling like he deserved it for telling me to stay away from Noah and then ghosting me for the past few days.

"How do you know I didn't come over just to hang out with you?"

I shrugged. "I assumed you were here for sex and I'm currently unavailable."

He didn't comment. We watched the documentary in silence for a while.

A few minutes later, he lifted my feet and moved to the cushion next to mine then rearranged my legs, so they were draped over his and propped his booted feet on the distressed wood coffee table, making himself at home. I tried to pull my legs away, but he held them in place. "I came over to tell you Ridge passed all his final exams."

Despite myself, his words made me smile. Today had been Ridge's last day of school and he'd had finals all this week. "That's amazing."

"I took him out for barbecue to celebrate. I left him in his room, practicing the guitar."

"That's good. The more he practices, the better he'll get."

Brody nodded, and we lapsed into silence again, but I felt something was troubling him. I shouldn't care but I did and what I really wanted was an apology. "What is it, Brody?"

I nudged his thigh with my bare foot, and he ran his hands over his face. "I like hanging out with you. And I kind of miss you when you're not around." His voice sounded tortured like he was in agony for having to utter those words aloud. As if that was a huge confession.

I snickered. "How old are you? Seventeen?"

He scowled.

"Was that so hard to admit?"

He chuckled under his breath. "Yeah. It was."

"I like hanging out with you too. And I kind of miss you when you're not around."

"Not sure if that's good or bad."

"No idea. It's just how it is."

"What I said about Noah..."

"You're trying to look out for him. I get it."

"I don't think you do." I paused the documentary, sensing

he was going to tell me something important and that it was rare for him to open up.

He was rubbing my leg clad in black sweatpants, his gaze on the frozen TV screen while I stared at his profile and waited for him to speak. "I was raised by a junkie. Sometimes she'd get clean and make an effort. When I was around Noah's age, she met this guy. He wasn't like the other scumbags she usually brought home. He was half-decent and treated her right." He looked down at my legs draped over his lap. "He owned a few horses. He's the first one who ever took me riding. And I got this idea in my head that if my mom married this guy our lives would be better. But one night he came over to our apartment and I heard them fighting. Dishes were breaking and shit and my mom told him to get the hell out and never come back. I ran into the living room and I grabbed the guy's arm and I was begging him to stay, to take me with him. I don't know what the hell I wanted. A different life, I guess... But he just ruffled my hair then walked out the door and that was it."

"Brody..."

"Noah isn't me. His life is nothing like mine was. He likes you so there's no reason why you shouldn't hang out with him." He took the remote out of my hand and hit play, indicating that he was done talking.

"Brody, I'm so sorry that happened to you." I wanted to find the right words to console him, to say more on the topic, but he squeezed my thigh and jerked his chin toward the TV. "You're missing the show."

He was done talking, done sharing the secrets of his soul, so I went back to watching the documentary about the evolution of hip-hop. Halfway through it, I realized I was snuggled up against Brody, his arm wrapped around my shoulders and my cheek pressed against his chest, my hand over his heart. I didn't even know how I'd ended up here, but it felt right. I was thinking about the story he'd told me, and I had a feeling that so many worse things had happened in Brody's childhood. I'd seen for myself how drugs fucked up people's heads and turned them into different people, so I couldn't even imagine how horrible it would have been to be raised by an addict. And yet, out of all the stories he could have told, that one had made an impact on him. Maybe it was because, for a little while, someone had been kind to him and treated him like he mattered.

And while I was watching Tupac's beautiful face on the screen, something strange grabbed hold of me, a strong vibration I couldn't shake off.

I'd been too young to remember my mom or the shooting. But I used to go through the boxes of photos Maw Maw kept in the closet, sifting through my mother's memories. Of her as a girl holding her first guitar. Of her on the road with Rhett when she was his backup singer. She left home at eighteen and headed to Nashville with big dreams but all she'd ended up with was a lousy husband and two kids he never wanted. Maw Maw said they were in the midst of a divorce when she came back to Louisiana with me and Landry.

And on her way back, at just after midnight, she stopped for gas then ran into the convenience store to buy diapers and milk. Why had she been buying milk? I could see it splattered on the floor next to the pool of blood coming from my mother's bullet-ridden lifeless body.

Wrong place, wrong time. Landry and I had been asleep in the car, so she'd pulled up right in front of the store and thought she'd just run in real quick. Maybe she'd kept an eye on us to make sure we were okay, and that's why she hadn't noticed the man who walked in with a gun.

I could hear the sirens, the shots being fired, and the shouts into the radio that an officer was down.

The man came out of the convenience store and he looked straight at me then he lifted his gun and aimed it at me. *No. No, no, no. What are you doing, Brody?* My body jerked, and I tried to run but my legs were made of concrete.

"Hey. You're okay. You're okay."

I didn't know how long he'd been repeating the words or how long he'd been holding me in his arms but when my vision cleared, I went limp in his arms, exhausted.

"What happened?" he asked, stroking my hair so gently I nearly cried.

"I don't know. I just..." I shook my head, unable to explain it. How could I tell him I saw him with a gun in his hand, about to shoot me? How could I tell him I'd had a crazy vision that made zero sense? I always kept my visions to myself because if I told anyone the things I saw, they'd have me locked up.

"You went somewhere else. Where were you, Shiloh?"

I looked into his whiskey brown eyes and saw that he wasn't the person in my vision. It had just been someone who resembled him. Relief flooded my body. I touched his face and pushed back a lock of hair that had fallen over his forehead. "The past."

"Sometimes it's a dangerous place to visit."

I took a shuddering breath. "It is."

"Does this happen to you a lot?"

He knew this wasn't normal, and that I hadn't just been reminiscing or recalling a bad memory. That I'd actually felt like I was there, seeing it play out before my eyes. "Not a lot, no. Weirdly, the moon and my cycle affect it." Oh God, that sounded so crazy. Like I really was a witch.

"Like a lucid dream?" he asked, understanding it far better than I'd explained it.

"Yeah, it's like that. Have you ever had one?"

"I don't have the gift you do but I took a crazy trip once so I kind of get where you're coming from."

"What kind of crazy trip?"

"Peyote in the desert. I went on a vision quest."

"Holy shit. You tried that?"

"Yeah. Not sure I'd recommend it. It really fucks with your head."

"And you had visions?"

He nodded. "I wanted to escape them so in the beginning, I was fighting it tooth and nail which only made it worse. Until finally, I gave in and I went along for the journey."

"And did you come out in a better place?"

"I think so, yeah. Not that I have all the answers or that shit doesn't affect me when I let it get to me, but I started to learn how to let it go. And I've been trying to do it ever since. With varying degrees of success. Some things are harder to let go than others."

"Like when you're in love with someone who's not yours?"

I expected him to leave right then and there or to tell me to mind my own damn business. But he was still holding me, and he hadn't gone anywhere. "I let that go a long time ago. I think there's all different kinds of love and I don't love Lila the same way Jude does. Some people just aren't meant to be together. It would never have worked."

I looked at his face to see if that made him sad, but I didn't think it did. Then I thought about his words. "I should never have been with Dean. My ex-boyfriend," I added in case he didn't know.

"You loved him?"

"I did. Yes." There was no point in lying. I'd loved Dean. Even now, when he'd given me no reason to care, I still worried about him. I hoped he'd find a way to be happy, but I didn't know if Dean was even capable of that. "A part of me always will. But mostly because we have so much history."

"That's how it goes when you share a history with someone."

"I'm glad I met you, Brody. I'm glad it was you."

Before he could question the meaning of my words, I pulled his head down to mine for a kiss. I wanted to keep kissing him until I forgot the vision I'd had. I wanted to keep kissing him until the memory was imprinted on my brain, so I'd always remember this was a good time in my life. And long after I was gone, I could still carry the memory wherever I went.

When I'd asked Maw Maw to tell me who my one true love was, I hadn't bothered to ask if I'd be able to keep him or even how long he'd be in my life. I wasn't in love with Brody. Not yet anyway. But I thought he'd be so easy to love and so hard to let go.

Wrong place, wrong time.

CHAPTER TWENTY

Brody

Kᴀᴛᴇ's 60th birthday fell on the first Saturday in June and we all wanted to do something special for her. Lila had suggested we throw a party but when Patrick found out, he told us he had it all under control and appointed himself the man in charge. That was the first flaw in the plan.

Kate claimed that the only thing she wanted was to spend it with her family. So, Gideon flew in from New York. And Jesse, who was supposed to have been in a motocross race that weekend had injured his shoulder the week before. Since he wasn't able to ride, he made the trip home from California where he'd been living for the past two years.

On Friday evening, we were all summoned to the barn behind Patrick and Kate's house. Over the years, it had gone through many incarnations. Back in high school, I'd moved my horses to Austin's ranch and Patrick converted the barn into a gym. Now it was Patrick's man cave/workshop.

I'd arrived ten minutes ago, and along with the others had

carved my name onto the bottom of the oak farmhouse table Patrick had made for Kate. As far as I was concerned, this meeting was over, but Patrick asked us to stay and discuss logistics. For what? A surprise birthday dinner Kate was all too aware of?

It was already shaping up to be a typical family reunion. Everyone fell into their roles assigned during childhood. I was leaning against the wall next to the barn door trying to figure out why the hell this had merited a special meeting. Jude and Lila had claimed the old leather sofa and he had his arm around her. It was date night for them, so Kate had the kids and Lila was wearing one of her off-the-shoulder dresses, waves of glossy dark hair tumbling to her bare shoulders. Still as beautiful as ever.

Jesse was at the other end of the sofa, uploading selfies or whatever the hell he did on social media. He looked more like a California surfer dude than a motocross racer in his shorts, faded blue Quiksilver T-shirt and Vans. Growing up, everyone had always called him 'adorable' or worse, 'pretty', and even now in his mid-twenties, he still looked a lot younger than the rest of us. But I'd seen him ride and he was an animal, a competitive beast on a dirt bike. Since he'd gone pro at nineteen, he'd been inundated with sponsorships and endorsements who used his pretty face as the poster boy for motocross.

Gideon was sitting in Patrick's old recliner, perched at the very edge of the seat as if he didn't want the thread-bare fabric to sully his designer denim and tailored black button-up. It was hotter than balls in here, but I'd never seen Gideon so much as break a sweat. He always looked cool and composed, chronically bored, and made it abundantly clear he'd rather be getting a root canal than spending time in Bumfuck, Texas as he called it. But he loved his mother so here he was, in Bumfuck.

"Pretty much what I expected," Jude told Patrick after

tomorrow's plan had been revealed. "You're not winning any prizes for your grand romantic gestures, Dad."

Patrick speared him with a look. "Women don't want grand romantic gestures. They want someone reliable who they can depend on. I've been by that woman's side through thick and thin for thirty-five years. When you reach that milestone, be sure to let me know."

That was one way to shut up Jude. He clenched his jaw and said nothing. Gideon snickered at his father's words, eyes still glued to his phone.

"Don't worry," Lila assured Patrick, falling into her role as mediator. "It's going to be great. We'll make it special."

"It's already special," Patrick grumbled, taking offense. "I made her a table big enough to fit the whole family. What more could a woman want? And she loves that restaurant. It has an open barbecue pit."

"*You* love that restaurant," Gideon said. "Although calling that place a restaurant is like calling a McDonald's burger wagyu beef."

Patrick glared at him. Like always, Gideon ignored it and continued checking his emails or his big bank account or whatever he did on his phone 24/7.

"Your mother's just happy to have her whole family together," Patrick said, and that at least was true. It was the only thing Kate ever wanted for any holiday and it made her happy when we were all gathered in one place. Somehow, she was the only one who didn't notice the tension when we were all together. "She doesn't like those fancy Michelin-starred restaurants you frequent."

"She loved it when I took her to Nobu last year," Gideon said.

Jesse added, "She was pretty chill with the vegan cafe I took her to in SoCal. And you should really do a better job of eating heart-healthy food," he told Patrick then rolled out his shoulder and winced, not even noticing the glare Patrick threw his way.

I exhaled loudly, ready to get out of here. "Are we done now? Just tell me where and when and I'll be there." What the hell was so complicated about this?

"Brody has to get back to his lady love," Lila teased. "She's coming tomorrow, right?"

"Nah. Not her kind of thing." I realized my mistake too late. If I'd been smart, I would have denied even having a 'lady love.'

Lila's jaw dropped. "Are you kidding me? She would love it. Oh my god, you haven't even invited her, have you?"

"Hang on. Brody has a *girlfriend?*" Jesse asked. The way he said it you would think he'd just been informed there was a crop circle in the backfield and aliens were about to invade the planet.

"The fuck?" Gideon pocketed his phone and fixed his gaze on me, the discussion suddenly capturing his interest.

I raked my hand through my hair. "Thanks, L."

"Anytime, B."

Jude laughed. Figures he'd enjoy this.

"Who is she?" Jesse asked.

"I don't have a girlfriend."

"Keep telling yourself that," Jude said smugly. "From where I'm sitting it looks a hell of a lot like a relationship."

He'd seen us together at one family Sunday dinner and suddenly he was an expert. Typical Jude. "I've only known her for a month."

"That's completely irrelevant." His gaze settled on me. "You can know someone for over twenty years and *think* you're in love with them. Until you meet someone who makes you realize she was the one who was meant for you all along."

My eyes narrowed on him. That son of a bitch.

Lila laughed. "Jude, what are you talking about?"

"Brody knows exactly what I'm talking about. Don't you, *B*?"

For a few seconds, there was total silence. Nobody said a word. I should have denied it. Called him an asshole. Told him he didn't know jack shit. I should have walked away. I should have done a lot of things.

"This isn't awkward," Jesse said. "Maybe we should give them some privacy."

"Fuck that." Gideon leaned forward in his seat and rubbed his hands together. "I've been waiting for this day for ten years. Where's the popcorn?"

"Oh hell, here we go," Patrick muttered.

"Brody..." Lila's brow furrowed, trying to make sense of this. If I'd have laughed it off, the crisis could have been averted. But no, stupid me hadn't said a goddamn word. Why the hell was I still standing in this barn under everyone's scrutiny?

"You're not... you were never..." Lila let her words trail off then looked around at the others, the realization dawning on her that she was the last to know something that had been all too obvious to every person in this barn. Her eyes widened, and her hand went to her heart. "Oh my God."

My cue to leave. I strode to the door, but Lila jumped up from her seat and grabbed my arm to stop me.

"Brody," she whispered. Her dark brows furrowed, and she searched my face for an answer.

I studied her pretty heart-shaped face. Her eyes were vivid green, the same shade of green as the tall grass in the field. She still had a few freckles on her nose although they'd faded over the years. Same full lips and wide smile that lit up her whole damn face.

When we were kids, we rode horses together. Skipped rocks in the creek. Camped out in the backyard and told ghost stories. Me, Lila, and Jude had been inseparable. When we were in high school, I beat up Kyle Matthews for talking shit about her. When her mom died and she and Jude had a falling out, it was me she used to talk to about how much she missed her mom and what an asshole her stepdad was. When her stepdad skipped out and she moved in with us, her bedroom right down the hall from mine, I saw her every single day and I tried my best not to notice that the girl I'd grown up with had developed curves in all the right places and had a way of putting a smile on my face even on the worst days.

In our late teens and early twenties, when Jude was serving his five years of active duty in the Marines, we used to hang out a lot. She came to my rodeos and cheered louder than anyone. I took her to parties and football games at UT Austin so she wouldn't miss out on the college experience. I did it for Jude because he'd asked me to look out for her but that wasn't the only reason I did it. I loved spending time with Lila. I loved her laugh and her stubbornness and her resilience. I loved everything about her.

When Jude came home from Afghanistan and started self-medicating with drugs and booze, it was me who Lila confided in. It was me she called when she had a miscarriage and Jude was too stoned and high and drunk to get out of bed and drive her to the hospital. I was the one she called when Jude OD'd, and she was out of her mind with worry. By some miracle, I'd found him in a field, just in time.

When Noah was born, I insisted on being in the delivery room. I didn't give a shit if she wanted me there or not, I wasn't about to miss the birth of my son. She'd squeezed my hand so tightly I thought she'd broken some bones. But I didn't give a shit. The most important thing to me was that I'd been there for her through it all.

All of these memories raced through my head in the span of thirty seconds. Like a high-speed movie reel of Lila and Brody highlights over the years.

But I sure as hell wasn't going to admit any of this now. Not in front of my entire family. Not at all.

Jude won, I lost. But for the first time in longer than I could remember, it didn't feel like I had lost. I didn't feel any of the old bitterness or resentment. Now I could look into Lila's eyes without wondering what if...

Instead of seeing my future, I saw my past.

We were never meant to be and as much as it pained me to admit it, Jude was right. I wanted Shiloh in a way I'd never wanted Lila. And even if it would only be for another two weeks, and what I had with Shiloh could never be real, Shiloh already knew me in ways that Lila never had, never would. And I'd like to think she accepted me for exactly who I was. A rude, dirty-mouthed, asshole of a cowboy who had been known to get into too many fights, drink too much, and speak his own truth.

I opened the barn door and walked right the hell out of there, leaving Lila and my family behind. When I was halfway across the backyard, Lila caught up to me and grabbed my arm to stop me. "Brody... talk to me."

With a weary sigh, I turned to face her. Lila had never been one to let things go and I should have known she wouldn't do it now. "Why? What good would it do?"

"I just feel..." She gnawed on her bottom lip. "I'm so sorry I relied on you so much. I never meant to take advantage... I had no idea how you felt about me."

It was funny that Lila was the only one who had never seen it. But her love for Jude had made her blind. She never saw anyone but him. "You never took advantage. I've never done anything I didn't want to. I wanted to be there for you." And that was the damn truth. I'd been let down so many times in my life. Had been screwed over and fucked up beyond repair. So, a long time ago, I'd vowed that I would *never* fail the people I loved and cared about. "I wouldn't change a thing."

Her eyes welled up with tears. "I love you, Brody. You know that, right?"

I knew she loved me but like I'd told Shiloh there were all different kinds of love and the love Lila and I had for each other wasn't the romantic kind. You would have thought I'd have figured this out a long time ago but for far too long I'd stubbornly clung to an ideal of love that was never real. "Love you too. And don't worry your pretty head. I'm not in love with you."

"I can't believe I was so stupid."

"Yeah, well, I can think of plenty of times you did stupid things." She laughed a little and smacked my arm, still so physical.

"Most of the stupid things I did were with you."

"I always brought out the best in you."

"You did though. You really did. You were always there for me and I'll never ever forget everything you did for me over the years." She began crying and maybe she was remembering everything the way I just had.

"Am I dying? Have the doctors given me six months to live and I don't know about it?"

"Ugh. You're the worst." Catching me off guard, she threw her arms around me and held on tight. My arms wrapped around her and I took a deep breath. She still smelled like spring rain and honeysuckle. She was still, and always would be, the mother of my child and my best friend and the first girl I had a crush on. History couldn't be erased but that's all it was. History. Something to be left in the past where it belonged.

"I'm getting mascara on your clean T-shirt," she said, her voice muffled.

I laughed. "Not the first time a girl has cried on my T-shirt."

"I've cried on your T-shirt so many times."

We were still wrapped in an embrace when my eye caught Jude's. He was standing outside the barn watching me hold his wife. If this had happened five or ten years ago ... hell, even two years ago... we would have ended up in a fight. He would have thrown the first punch and we would have kept punching long after we'd both gone down. Now he just stood there, an expression on his face I couldn't read. Not smug, exactly. Secure in the knowledge that Lila belonged to him and nobody, not even his jackass cousin, could ever destroy that bond or the love they had for each other.

I released Lila and she smiled up at me through her tears. My first instinct was to wipe them away, but Jude appeared at her side and wrapped his arm around her shoulders. It was his job to take care of Lila. Message received. I wasn't even mad about it.

"Happy now? Did you get what you wanted?" I couldn't help myself, could I? But unlike in the past, there was no anger in my voice.

"You're such a dumb shit. I knew you were lying."

He was referring to the night two years ago when he asked me if I had ever been in love with Lila. "You weren't ready to handle the truth."

I'd lied to protect both of us. All three of us, really—myself, Lila, and Jude. The most fucked-up triangle that ever was.

"Thank you," he said, surprising the shit out of me.

Guess we were finally growing up, letting go of all the shit we'd both been holding onto for too long. I couldn't say it felt good, exactly, but it felt like a weight was lifted off my shoulders. After all these years, we'd cleared the air and I was finally free.

"Don't expect any more favors from me," I told him. "You're on your own now. If you fuck up, I won't be there to rescue you from your own stupidity."

He snorted. "Still an asshole."

"Takes one to know one." With that, I swaggered away like the cowboy I was.

"Bring Shiloh tomorrow," he called after me.

I kept right on walking as if I hadn't heard him.

"If you don't do it, I'm going to invite her," Lila shouted.

Oh Jesus. "Keep your nose out of my business," I called back, knowing damn well it would fall on deaf ears.

That was how I ended up taking a rock star to a family dinner at a BBQ joint.

"You don't have to do this," I insisted later that night while we were skinny dipping in the lake under the moon and stars. It was one of Shiloh's favorite things to do. By the time I'd come over, Shiloh had already been informed of the birthday dinner. Not by Lila. Kate had called to invite her. Everyone and their mother were conspiring to get us together.

"I love your family. Why wouldn't I want to be there? Unless you don't want me to be there... is that what this is about?" Her arms and legs were wrapped around me and we were spinning in a slow circle, my legs treading water, her body slippery wet against mine.

Normally, I would say, "Come. Don't come. Up to you." As if I didn't give a shit one way or the other. Which might have explained my shitty track record with relationships. But I was thirty-three fucking years old, and it was about time I started acknowledging what I *really* wanted.

"I want you there but it's not a private event," I warned her. "It's a roadside restaurant and you'll have to deal with other customers and my family."

"I know how restaurants work. Nobody will even notice me. It's not like I'm Carrie Underwood."

I laughed at that one.

"I've been here a month and nobody's so much as looked twice." She smiled like it made her happy to go unnoticed.

Too bad it wasn't true. Every male who laid eyes on her looked twice, if not three or four times. And tomorrow she would be surrounded by all the McCallister men. This should be interesting. I preferred it when it was just the two of us and I didn't have to share her with anyone. But you can't always get what you want.

And right now, I had her all to myself, in a cool lake on a warm June night under a sky reeling with stars. I kissed her lips and she kissed me back, her velvet tongue sliding against mine and her legs cinching tighter around my waist. And under her breath, she said, *Hallelujah.* I didn't even know what she meant by that. All I knew was that I wanted to get the hell out of this lake and get her into bed.

Right the fuck now.

WE NEVER MADE it to the bed.

We got as far as the back porch and dropped our towels. I fucked her against the wall, cedar shingles digging into her back, her moans muffled by Drake's "Fake Love" blasting from the speakers inside.

"This is going to mess you up," I said as I thrust into her. I was referring to the skin on her back getting scraped. She took it differently.

"It already has. I love the pain you give." She grabbed my face and held it in her hands, her chest heaving against mine, lush lips parted on a gasp as I stilled inside her. Buried so deep I wanted to stay there forever, her muscles clenching around my hard cock, the heels of her feet digging into my ass. I looked into her stormy grays, black hair slicked back from the swim in the lake, those high jagged cheekbones so prominent, and at that moment I knew that this was what falling in love really felt like.

It was fast and furious, and it hit you with the force of a fucking Mack truck. My breath seized in my lungs. *Shit.* This couldn't be good.

I didn't want her to look too closely, to read something on my face I wasn't willing to admit to, so I lowered my head to her left breast, my teeth teasing and biting her rosy nipple. Her back arched away from the wood and I squeezed her ass cheeks in my hands as I lifted her off me then drove back into her. She met me thrust for thrust, her fingers tugging the ends of my hair, digging into my shoulders, her teeth drawing blood when they sank into my lip.

And fuck I loved the pain she gave, too.

"But oh, what a beautiful mess," she said when she came, and I left all of me inside of her.

CHAPTER TWENTY-ONE

Shiloh

It was official. I loved Brody's family.

By the time the food arrived—racks of ribs, brisket, barbe-cued chicken, all made on the open pit and served family-style along with sides of mac and cheese, greens, coleslaw, beans—I'd already exchanged numbers with Jesse and Gideon. It was BYOB and Gideon had brought the wine, making sure to keep my glass, his mother's, and Lila's topped up.

"I'm doing a show at Madison Square Garden right before Christmas," I told Gideon as he poured more wine into my glass. Another gorgeous McCallister. His hair was the darkest, almost black, his features chiseled and cheekbones high, and his eyes were a cool Arctic blue. "If you want tickets, let me know."

I told Jesse the same thing, but in his case, it was for the Staples Center in L.A.. He forked some greens into his mouth then grinned. His hair was a lighter shade of brown and his eyes a deeper blue. So pretty. "Good to know the right people.

If you ever want to come and watch a motocross race, I'll hook you up."

I might have been a little tipsy, maybe even drunk which made me overly enthusiastic. I gushed, acting like motocross was my very favorite thing to watch. "I'd love to."

At that moment, I loved everyone. We were sitting on long benches, all nine adults, one child and a baby seated at a long wooden table topped with a red-and-white checkered plastic tablecloth. I was practically in Brody's lap. One of his arms was wrapped around me and he was forced to use his left hand to eat but he didn't complain or try to shove me off his lap.

"Just remember who you came with, *baby*," he growled in my ear after he caught me laughing at something Jesse said.

I turned my head to see his face better. Was Brody jealous? "Oh, I remember who I came with. Four times last night. Not that I was keeping count."

"It was five. And I was keeping count."

I laughed and fed him a bite of mac and cheese from my fork. "You're still my favorite McCallister."

"You're quickly becoming my favorite everything." His voice was low, so quiet I wasn't sure he'd actually said the words.

Before I could respond or ask him to repeat what he'd just said, he turned his head to talk to Ridge and left me wondering if I'd imagined it.

Kate smiled at me from across the table. She was at the other end, with Noah sitting between her and Patrick, a spot he'd claimed after stating that his grandma would want to sit next to her favorite boy on her birthday. For a minute I was worried she'd think I was a hussy, sitting in her nephew's lap for everyone to see, but I didn't see any judgment on her face. She nodded like she'd figured something out then lifted her glass to me in a silent toast and we both drank, although I wasn't entirely sure what we were drinking to.

Brody squeezed my thigh, drawing my attention back to him. I gave him a love-drunk smile. "What'd you need, baby?"

His arm around me tightened as my head swiveled in the direction of his gaze. Two teenage girls dressed in crop tops and cut-offs were standing at the foot of our table, cell phones in hand.

"It *is* her! Oh my god, it's Shiloh Leroux." The girl hadn't screamed it, but she'd spoken loudly enough to attract the attention of a few people at the other tables.

Shit. I loved my fans and normally I was happy to engage with them. Sign autographs and chat for a minute. But I always hated it when they interrupted a meal or barged into the middle of a family gathering.

They moved closer to where I was sitting. "Can we get a selfie with you?"

Before drunk me had a chance to catch up and say *sure what the hell*, Brody lifted me off him and deposited me on the seat then got to his feet and turned to face them. "Put your damn phones away," he growled. "We're trying to have a family dinner here."

Now he was causing a scene and attracting even more attention. "Brody. It's okay."

"I'll take care of this," Ridge announced, leaving his seat to join his brother. Now my view of the girls was obstructed by two sets of wide shoulders and the brothers' backs as they stood side by side, a united front attempting to protect me.

"Hey Ridge," one of the girls said, her voice saccharine sweet. "You never mentioned that you knew Shiloh Leroux."

"Listen, babe, I don't even know your damn name and I've never talked to either of you. Let's keep it that way, yeah? And if you think this is Shiloh Leroux, you must be fucking stoned.

So why don't you back the hell away from my family and go post some of those duck-faced selfies?"

I didn't catch their response. But they did as he said, and I stifled a laugh.

Ridge and Brody didn't budge until the girls were gone and only then did they return to their seats.

"If it wasn't for Ridge's accent, I would have sworn that was Brody talking," Jesse said.

Lila nodded. "It sounded exactly like something Brody would have said in high school."

"High school?" Jude snorted. "He'd say it now."

"Stop talking about me like I'm not sitting right here." Brody wrapped his arm around me, and I took another sip of wine I didn't need, a small smile on my lips.

Maybe Brody didn't notice it, but Ridge was a McCallister through and through, and his first loyalty was to his family. All the brothers were so different, had chosen their own paths in life, but you'd have to be blind not to see that every single one of them would drop everything to be there for each other. I was sure they had their share of disagreements in private, but they were fiercely loyal and quick to defend each other. I'd like to believe Landry would do the same for me, but history had proven otherwise, and it made me sad we'd grown so far apart.

"I'm not the one with the accent. That's all of y'all," Ridge said, mimicking a Texan accent that was so bad it made everyone laugh.

"Y'all owe me money for all the swear words," Noah piped up. "Except for Daddy. He needs to save his money. It costs a lot of money to get married." He tipped his face up to Patrick's. "Right, Grandpa?"

Patrick cleared his throat. "You got that right. Who's he marrying?"

Noah pointed his finger at me. "Shy Viv. They're gonna have a baby."

My eyes widened. Brody nearly choked on his beer.

Patrick crossed his arms over his chest and glared at Brody. "You knocked up another one?"

"Oh Jesus, here we go again," Brody muttered under his breath.

All I could do was laugh.

Before we all got into our cars to drive home, Kate hugged everyone goodbye. I was about to climb into the passenger seat of Brody's truck when she pulled me into a hug just like I was another one of her kids. "I'm so happy you and Brody found each other, honey."

I didn't have the heart to tell her we were only hooking up and this wasn't a real relationship.

"When a McCallister boy falls in love, it's for life." My heart stuttered. Could Brody be in love with me? Had Kate seen it on his face?

"You good?" Brody asked when I climbed into his truck, none the wiser about what Kate had said. If he'd heard her, he probably would have run scared.

I smiled. "Yeah, it's all good."

AND FOR THE next week and a half, everything was good. It was so good I had to pinch myself to make sure I wasn't dreaming.

Every morning Brody and I rode together at sunrise and every night he came over to the guest house. We talked, we fucked, we laughed so hard my stomach hurt. Sometimes he stayed the night but other times he went home, not wanting to leave Ridge on his own all the time. Ridge was working on a construction crew for the summer. Noah was in summer day camp from Monday to Friday. The same summer camp Hayley was enrolled in. On the Saturday after Kate's birthday dinner, Noah informed me that Hayley was away for the weekend and I felt equal parts relief and disappointment. I'd decided it was for the best, and I could leave here knowing that everything had worked out the way it was meant to. I'd gotten my music career and Hayley had ended up in a good family.

On Tuesday night, six days before I had to leave, Brody did something so unexpected and so sweet I added it to my list of things that made me want to cry.

"I can't see anything," I complained.

"That's usually what happens when you're blindfolded."

"Why am I blindfolded again? If you wanted kinky sex, you could have just said so." A twig snapped under my foot and his arm around me tightened, steadying me.

"Stop talking, woman. We're almost there."

"It feels like we've been walking for miles."

He snorted. "We can still see the guesthouse from here."

"Maybe you can but I can't see a thing."

"You don't need to. I'm guiding you." Just then he removed his arm that had been around me.

"Am I playing pin the tail on the donkey?" I asked. "Oh wait. Do you have a piñata out here?"

He chuckled. "Be quiet."

I couldn't tell what he was doing but a couple seconds later, he held my upper arms and guided me into a sitting position. Thankfully, there was a chair underneath to hold me up. When he took off the blindfold, my jaw dropped. "Oh my God."

Dumbfounded, I stared at the table in front of me set for two. Lanterns hung from the tree branches, casting a soft glow on the dark night. To my right was the lake and the guesthouse was behind us. The way the trees had grown here, it looked like a cathedral, a round clearing big enough for a table and two chairs. Next to our table was a camping stove with a pot sitting on it and next to that was a cooler full of beer and ice. It was those two things that made me laugh. They were so Brody. He didn't even bother with glasses, assuming we'd just drink them straight from the bottle. Which was exactly what we did after he popped the caps with his key and handed me a cold beer.

When he took a seat across from me, I stared at him for a few seconds in the flickering light from a candle in the center of our table. The candle was green, shaped like a cactus, and sat in a terracotta planter. The tablecloth was buffalo plaid, and I thought it might actually be a wool blanket doubling as a table covering.

Romance, cowboy-style.

He slid his phone out of his pocket, scrolled through his playlists and hit play. I laughed when The Rolling Stones' "Start Me Up" blasted from the portable speakers. The June night was warm, the stars were bright, and the man across from me was the most beautiful thing I'd ever seen. Not just on the outside. Through and through. This night couldn't get any more perfect than this.

"I can't believe you did all this for me."

"I did it for myself, not you."

"How so?"

"I wanted to take you out to dinner without having to punch anyone in the face or break someone's phone."

I sighed and put my hand over my heart. "What a charmer. How could I ever resist your sweet talk?"

He snorted.

If only he knew what it was like when I wasn't here, safe in this little bubble. Brody would hate it. He already told me he hated crowds and he hated cities and wasn't a big fan of flying or being stuck in traffic. Which was my entire life away from here. Yesterday I talked to Bastian. When I spoke to him, he was in Barcelona, headlining for a rock festival.

"So... did you find what you were looking for?" Bastian asked.

"I did. And I got so much more than I bargained for."

"You fell in love." I heard him take a drag of his cigarette.

"I did."

He was quiet for a beat. "Who is he?"

"Just... a guy. He owns the ranch I'm staying on."

"So you met a cowboy and you fell in love, but you have to leave him."

"That pretty much sums it up. When are you and Hayden finally going to admit your true love?"

"Never."

"Why not?"

"Because I would destroy him, and I love him too much to do that to him. Far better to love him from afar."

"So you do love him?"

"Was that ever a question? I love him as much as I'm capable of loving anyone. I'm a fickle, selfish, unholy mess of a lover. He would never be number one in my life. That spot is reserved for myself and my music. There's not a lot of room left over for anyone else."

"That sounds so lonely."

"You'll get used to it."

But I didn't think I ever would. I already missed Brody, and I was sitting right across from him.

Why couldn't we have the best of both worlds? Why couldn't we have it all?

I shook off my apprehensions and smiled at Brody. "What did you rustle up for dinner, Cowboy?"

"What do you think?"

I grinned. "I think I'm going to have to be the judge in a

chili cook-off."

"There's no contest. Mine is the best." He served the chili in two bowls, crushed a handful of Fritos over the top, a sprinkle of cilantro and a squeeze of lime.

"Fancy," I joked.

"It's the only way to go. Tortilla chips don't cut it." He watched me take the first bite. "Tell me this isn't better than Jude's."

Brody's chili was good. Delicious, even. But in all fairness, so was Jude's. In fact, if memory served, they tasted very similar. Jude and Brody were more alike than they'd care to admit. But for me, there was no contest.

Only one McCallister had captured my heart.

He held his hand up to block his face. "Enough with the photos."

I set my phone back on the table next to my bowl. "I love your face. I want to take it with me everywhere I go." The thought of leaving here, of leaving *him*, made my stomach sink.

He tipped the neck of his beer bottle at the portable speaker. The Goo Goo Dolls' "Iris" had just started playing. "You sang this the night I saw you in that bar in Lafayette." This song reminded me of Brody. Everything was starting to remind me of him. "I like your version better."

How crazy to think our paths had crossed nine years ago. What if they'd crossed many times in the past and neither of us had been the wiser? Maybe our paths had always been destined to cross. I stood up from my chair and walked around the table. He wrapped his hand around my wrist and tugged me into his lap, his arm encircling my waist. "You're biased."

"Just speaking the truth."

I kissed his jaw then buried my face in the crook of his neck and breathed him in. Leather and cedar with a hint of lime. I wanted to bottle his scent and carry it with me wherever I went. His arm around me was strong, heart beating under the palm of my hand, his muscles toned and taut, the cotton of his T-shirt so soft to the touch. His calloused hand on my thigh was warm, caressing my skin and sending delicious shivers up and down my spine. Being this close to Brody made me feel like I'd found a home after years of searching for a place—*or a person*—who could fill up the empty space inside me, heal my cracked heart and make it beat just for him.

Now that I've found you, how will I ever let you go? What will I do without you?

"Does it get lonely on the road?" he asked a few minutes later, once again surprising me with his keen sense of observation. In such a short amount of time, Brody could already read me better than anyone ever had.

"So lonely," I whispered, running my fingers through his thick, dirty blond hair. I kissed his face, the stubble on his jaw scraping my soft skin, and I kissed his lips. For a few seconds, we stayed like that, his lips soft yet firm against mine. Neither of us pushed for more. Yet somehow it felt more intimate than a kiss. When he exhaled, I inhaled, breathing the same air.

I pulled back to look at his face, my fingertips tracing the little crinkles next to his eyes. I wanted to capture this moment forever. "One more picture?"

His whiskey browns locked on mine and he squeezed my thigh. "Knock yourself out."

I reached across the table for my phone, but he got to it first and handed it to me. I angled the phone to capture us both in the photo. "Smile, Cowboy. Make it look like there's nowhere else you'd rather be."

"I don't have to pretend. It's the damn truth."

CHAPTER TWENTY-TWO

Shiloh

Two DAYS after our romantic dinner in the woods, Brody asked me if I wanted to go with him to pick up Noah from camp. It finished at four and he was planning to take Noah for tacos before he drove him home.

I said I'd love to. I was leaving in four days, and I wanted to spend as much time with him as possible. Ballcap and sunglasses firmly in place, we hit the road. The air was heavy, hot and humid, and it felt like a storm was on the way. We were three miles from his house when the music cut out and Lila's name showed up on Brody's phone screen. He pressed the button on his steering wheel to answer it, putting the call on speaker.

"What's up, L? I'm with Shy, so watch your dirty mouth."

She laughed. "Hi Shiloh."

"Hi Lila."

"I'm glad you're with him. We need to arrange a time to hang out before you leave."

"Definitely. I'm totally open, so whatever works—"

Brody grew impatient with our chit-chat and cut me off mid-sentence. "Did you need something, L?"

"I told Meredith I'd pick up Hayley today. She has a conference call she can't get out of. You're on the approved list for picking up Hayley. Are you okay with that?"

He muttered a curse under his breath. "Do I have a choice?"

"Nope."

Brody exhaled loudly like this was a huge inconvenience. I wiped my sweaty palms on my shorts and tried to regulate my breathing.

"We were planning to take Noah for tacos."

"Perfect. Take Hayley too. She'll love it. Meredith's meeting ends at six and I was planning to feed Hayley before I took her home. I'll message her and let her know there's been a change of plans."

"Fine. See you later."

"Bye guys. Have fun. See you soon."

I tried to reply but my voice wouldn't work.

Brody cut the call and I had half a mind to ask him to drop me off at the diner we were passing. Or turn the truck around and take me home before he picked up Noah. But I couldn't do that. I was trapped. I'd made my peace with the situation and had been all set to leave without seeing Hayley again. But now I'd have to spend two hours with her. And I didn't know how to deal with any of this.

I took a few deep breaths, trying to suck air into my lungs.

"I never know what the hell to say to Hayley," Brody said, running his hand through his hair.

His words surprised me. But it was also the tone of his voice. He sounded worried which pulled me out of my own panic attack. "What do you mean? You're great with Noah."

"Yeah, well, he's a boy and he's my kid. I'm always trying to be careful not to say the wrong thing around Hayley."

"Just be yourself." How ironic that I was giving him advice when I didn't have a clue what I would say to her or how to act around her. "I'm sure she thinks you're great."

He shrugged one shoulder. "I try to tone it down around her. I don't want to scare her."

"Is she sensitive?"

"She reminds me of those artsy girls from high school."

Despite my own fears, I laughed. "She's six, not a teenager."

He snorted. "Noah is six. Hayley is six going on sixteen. Girls are different from boys."

A laugh burst out of me. "How long did it take you to figure that one out?"

He snorted again, then side-eyed me before his eyes returned to the road. Two minutes later, he turned into a parking lot in front of a low brown building and put the truck in park but didn't get out right away. We were five minutes early. "What I mean is that girls are more emotional. I made her cry once and afterward I felt like shit."

I reached for his hand and gave it a squeeze. "I'm sure she's forgotten all about it."

"Maybe."

"What did you do to make her cry?"

"She fell and skinned her knee. I told her to cowboy up."

Not what I'd expected. I couldn't help it, I laughed. "What does that even mean?"

His lip ticked up at the corner. "It means that when you fall down, you pick yourself up, dust yourself off and act like a man about it."

"Kind of hard for a six-year-old girl to do."

"Yeah, well, let's just say I'm pretty damn happy I didn't

have a girl." He shoved open his car door. "Be right back."

I nodded and forced a smile. As soon as he was gone, I slumped in my seat and spun the sterling silver ring around my thumb. The ring was shaped like a feather, adjustable, and designed to fit on any finger. It had been on my mom's hand when she died. Maw Maw had waited until my sixteenth birthday to give it to me. Maybe she knew she'd be gone before I reached my next birthday. Maw Maw told me the feather was the wing of an angel, a reminder that there would always be someone watching over me and I'd never really be alone. She'd told me that my mother had loved me and Landry more than life itself. Despite my mom's unhappy marriage and a music career that had never taken off, we made her happy. I didn't know if it was true, but it was what I'd chosen to believe. We were loved.

How I wished my mom could be here now, in the flesh, so I could ask her how to handle this situation.

This was exactly what I had thought I wanted, to spend time with my baby girl, but now that it was happening, I was tempted to run away and hide. Something I'd been doing all too often lately.

WE ATE outside at a picnic table under a tree. My stomach was in knots and I couldn't have eaten a taco if my life depended on it so when Brody asked what I wanted, I said water and made the excuse that I'd eaten a late lunch.

Hayley was sitting directly across from me, and the kids had just finished telling us everything they'd done for the day. Volleyball, archery, a nature hike, play practice for the drama production they were putting on at the end of the summer, and an art project they said was top secret.

"Can we have peach cobbler now?" Noah asked as soon as they'd finished their tacos.

He had sauce all over his mouth and half the toppings from his taco had fallen into the basket when he'd taken his first bite. Whereas Hayley had taken smaller bites and kept refolding her taco so she wouldn't lose any of it.

"You both want cobbler?" Brody asked.

Hayley looked at Noah who nodded as if to reassure her it was okay to ask for what she wanted. "Yes, please."

She'd been taught manners and was quick to say please and thank you.

Brody gave my shoulder a little squeeze. "You okay to watch them?"

I took a deep breath and let it out, my voice breezy so I wouldn't let on that this was a big fucking deal. "Yeah. Sure. No problem."

"Be right back." Brody went inside to get their dessert, leaving me alone with the kids.

I tried not to stare at Hayley, but I couldn't help myself. Today her brown hair was in a French braid, the fine baby hairs around her face curling from the humidity. Like Noah she was wearing shorts with a bright yellow T-shirt that said: Happy Trails Summer Camp.

"I like the drawings on your arm and your fingers," Hayley said.

"Thank you."

"They're tattoos," Noah explained to her, repeating the words I'd told him when he asked if he could do that to his own arm with a Sharpie. "They *never* go away and never wash off."

Hayley's mouth formed a comical O that matched her wide eyes. "Not even if you scrub your skin with soap and water a million times?"

"Not even then," I said.

"Wow. I don't think my daddy would let me do that."

I smiled. "I don't think he would either. You're a bit too young for tattoos."

Her fingernails were painted with purple glitter nail polish and she was just so cute and so small that I wanted to wrap her up in my arms and breathe her in. But that would be too weird. To her, I was a total stranger so I couldn't hug her or kiss her or tell her that she'd been the sweetest, most precious little baby in the world.

"Your nails look pretty," I said, unable to come up with anything better. It was safe, at least, and not at all weird to compliment her nails.

She smiled, the dimples in her cheeks yet another reminder that she was Dean's daughter. "Thank you. My mommy took me for a manicure. Purple is my favorite color."

"It's my favorite color too."

"Oh. That's funny."

"Mine is green, like Daddy's," Noah said.

"Girls are like their mommies and boys are like their daddies," Hayley stated confidently. Noah nodded, accepting it as a fact. Little did Hayley know that she looked so much like her daddy. It seemed unfair she would have gotten so much from him and so little from me.

"I already know that Noah's a lot like his daddy. Are you..." I cleared my throat, preparing to venture into dangerous territory. "Are you like your mommy, Hayley?"

I held my breath and waited for her answer. She nodded. "My mommy loves Disney and so do I. We both love pepperoni pizza and mint chip ice cream. Oh, and here's a funny one. We both have crooked pinkies." She held up her hands to show me her crooked pinkies.

"Oh. I can see that. Wow."

"And you have brown hair like hers," Noah added.

She flipped the end of her braid over her shoulder and held it up to her eyes as if she needed to confirm that her hair was brown. "Yep. Same color. I looked just like her when I was a baby too." She jostled Noah's arm to get his attention. "I bet if you looked at our baby pictures you wouldn't be able to tell if it was me or my mommy."

"Probably not." He shrugged. "Babies all look the same."

Her eyes widened, offended by his words. "Do not. Levi is the cutest baby in the world."

"He's the loudest baby in the world, that's for sure." He shrugged one thin shoulder. "But he's cute sometimes, I guess."

"Do you look just like your mommy?" I asked Hayley. Why was I doing this to myself? Not to mention, it was wrong to pump a six-year-old for information.

She nodded. "My mommy and daddy picked me out of all the other babies."

My breath hitched. "They picked you?"

Shut up, Shiloh. Shut your fat mouth.

"They wanted a baby more than anything in the world. And one day they got a phone call that their baby was ready for them. And that was me." She smiled and held out her arms, like it was the best story ever. And I suppose it was. What could be better than to be chosen? To be wanted more than anything in the world? Nothing.

"That's amazing," I said when I found my voice. "They're so lucky to have found you."

"They said they were waiting for me for so long that they cried when they finally met me."

My throat was so clogged with emotion I had no idea how I got the words out. "I don't blame them," I said softly. "It would have made me cry too."

"What would have made you cry?" Brody asked, setting the cobbler and two plastic forks in front of the kids then taking his seat next to me. I'd been so focused on Hayley I hadn't even seen him coming.

Thankfully, Hayley saved me from having to answer his question.

"Thank you, Mr. McCallister."

"No problem. And it's just Brody."

"Okay. Mr. McCallister."

Noah and Hayley giggled then kept saying Mr. McCallister while they ate their cobbler. I was hoping the distraction would make him forget his question.

"Watch this," Noah said, elbowing Hayley. He grabbed the straw from her cup and his own and stuck one in each nostril. "I'm a walrus."

Hayley giggled. "Hello Silly Walrus."

She took the same two straws that had been in his nose and put them on top of her head, wiggling them around. "I'm an alien."

"Hello Silly Alien."

By the time we left the roadside taco joint, the kids were laughing their heads off.

"Can we go to the playground now?" Noah asked when we were all in the truck.

It was only five o'clock and we still had an hour left before we had to take Hayley home. "Do you want me to take you home first?" Brody asked me, waiting until my seat belt was fastened before he pulled out of his parking spot.

This was my chance to escape. All I had to do was tell him yes and I'd be home safe. But instead of saying yes, I shook my head no. "It's cool. I'll come along."

On the drive to the playground, Brody circled back to the question he'd asked earlier. "What would have made you cry?"

The kids were laughing and talking in the backseat, not paying us any mind so I lied and said the first thing that popped into my head. "I would have cried if someone tripped me while I was running."

Oh my God. I rolled my eyes at myself. That was so lame.

"Did someone trip Hayley or Noah?" His grip on the steering wheel tightened.

"No," I said quickly, sensing he was about to question them and if need be, deal with a situation that was totally fabricated. "We were talking about some other kids." His brow furrowed, trying to make sense of this. I waved my hand in the air. "Kids they don't even know. It had absolutely nothing to do with them. It happened on a TV show." The more I said, the worse I was making it.

Oh my God, shut up, Shiloh.

He gave me a funny look, but I pretended not to notice. I spun my thumb ring and stared out the windshield while I listened to Hayley's sweet voice. She and Noah were making up silly songs. The words didn't even make sense, but her voice was so pretty I couldn't resist. I turned in my seat to face her. She had an Elsa Band-Aid on her left knee. The inspiration for my stupid story.

"Your mom told me you like to sing "Let It Go." Is that your favorite song?"

"It's my second favorite now."

"What's your first favorite?"

"Do you want me to sing it?" she offered.

I nodded, my hand wrapping around my phone, so I had it ready. "I'd love to hear it."

Her face lit up at the prospect of singing for a captive audience. *Me.* "Okay."

Without preamble, she started singing The Beatles' "Here Comes the Sun." She knew every word and hit every note and I was thankful sunglasses hid my eyes so nobody could see the tears in them. When she was done singing, Noah said,

"Hayley's the best singer in Texas. Probably the world. Right?"

She gave him a big smile, but I could barely see through the blur of tears. "She's..." I cleared my throat. "... yes, she's the best singer I've ever heard."

I turned around to face forward as Brody pulled into a parking spot and cut the engine. My heart hurt so much, and I didn't know how I'd get through the rest of our time together. I wanted to curl into a ball and cry.

But with two kids clamoring to get to the playground, I didn't have that luxury, so with a heavy heart and heavy footsteps, I walked with Brody while the kids ran ahead. The playground was in a state park, a wood fence surrounding it, and shaded by trees but the heat was so oppressive, the air closed in on me. I peeled the tank top away from sweat-slick skin, trying to cool off. My heart was racing and the pressure building inside my head made it feel like it might explode.

"Why did you come to Cypress Springs, Shiloh?" Brody asked. As I'd already witnessed, he was observant, capable of reading my moods, so it shouldn't have surprised me that he chose now to ask the question again. Maybe he'd figured out the truth and was looking for confirmation. I wasn't ready to give him honesty. I didn't even know how I felt about spending time with Hayley, let alone try to explain any of this to him.

As an entertainer, I'd learned how to be a good actress. I had one face I showed the world and the other, the real one, that only a select few got to see. The whole time I'd been in Texas, Brody had gotten to see the real Shiloh. Not the entertainer who performed on a stage.

But now I turned on my dazzling smile, the one I used when I accepted my Grammy. "I came here looking for you, Cowboy." I lowered my sunglasses and winked at him. "And it's been a hell of a ride."

We stopped outside the fenced-in playground and he studied my face for a moment. "Yeah, okay. Message received." He raked his hand through his hair and laughed harshly. My flippant response obviously hadn't made him happy. "Fuck it. You don't owe me a damn thing."

With that, he strode away and left me standing outside the playground. I watched him from the other side of the fence while he stood guard, arms crossed over his chest, making sure the kids didn't fall and hurt themselves on the wood climbing frame. The kids were happily playing, oblivious to what was going on in the adults' lives. I watched Hayley climb the frame then she followed Noah across the rope ladder bridge, her feet moving from one rung to the next, her brow furrowed in concentration. So focused, one foot in front of the other, her sole purpose to get to the other side.

The air was so hot and muggy, and it felt like I was suffocating and couldn't draw enough air into my lungs. I was torn between wanting to join Brody and trying to make things right and walking away to get my head together. I needed time alone to think about this and to make my own peace.

His back was still turned to me, shoulders squared, legs slightly spread, eyes trained on the kids. And even though I couldn't see his face, I recognized his stance for what it was. He was putting up walls, trying to protect himself from the girl who refused to give him an honest answer to the only thing he had ever asked of her.

Like a coward, I turned and walked away, and I kept right on walking. Past the playground and the baseball diamond where a little league game was being played. I kept my eyes trained ahead of me, the brim of my ball cap pulled down low, and wiped away the tears as I walked away from Brody. Away from Hayley. Away from a life that would never be mine.

Last night, Dean had called me. Perfect timing, as always.

I'd let his calls go to voicemail and he'd left two messages I hadn't listened to yet. Maybe it was a sign. My old life was calling me back, a reminder of what was real and what was only a fantasy.

I was already feeling raw and vulnerable. Listening to Dean's voicemail now would be a mistake. Apparently, I was a masochist. I slid my phone out of my pocket and played back the first one, holding my phone to my ear so I could listen to his voice. Familiar. Raspy. The voice of a lead singer and a man who had done a lot of hard living in his twenty-eight years.

"Hey baby. I just got out of rehab. Landry says you've gone away for a while. I hope you're doing okay. I hope..." He paused to take a drag of his cigarette. Whenever he got clean, he chain-smoked. "Fuck. Here's the thing. I wrote a lot of music in the past sixty days. Like a shitload. And I think it's the best stuff I've ever written. But there's one song in particular... I wrote it for you. And it just fucking poured out of me. I know you don't want anything to do with me... I get it. But babe, I need you. I need you in my life. It's shit without you. Everything will be different. I'm clean and sober and I've been through hell and back ... I'm not going down that road again."

The voicemail ended and I pressed play on the next one. Why was I listening to my ex-boyfriend's bullshit explanations? I didn't have an answer, but I stood there under the shade of an oak tree and listened to the King of Excuses and Empty Promises, his voice dragging me back to another lifetime.

"Hey. It's me again. I know your answer will be no. But just think about it. When things were good, they were fucking awesome. It can be that way again. I want to send you this song I wrote. It's us, Shy. It's you and me, and nobody else can sing it. Even if you never come back to Acadian Storm or to me, just give me one more song. One more song, Shiloh. *Please.* Call me. I'll be waiting."

I slid my phone into my shorts pocket and lowered myself to the ground under the oak tree, the rough bark digging into my back as I leaned against it. It was too much. It was all too much. But that was so Dean. He always wanted just one more thing. The problem with Dean was that it never ended at one thing. He'd push and he'd push until he got exactly what he wanted. So I wasn't going to return his calls or record a duet with him. If he thought I could ever return to Acadian Storm or to him after all the shit he'd put me through, he must be crazier than I thought.

I hugged my knees to my chest and squeezed my eyes shut, assaulted by memories.

When I told Dean I was leaving him, I was in the swimming pool at our house in Malibu. A modern white box with a wall of windows overlooking the Pacific Ocean. A blank canvas we'd never bothered to decorate. Most of our things were still packed in boxes we hadn't bothered opening. I'd just finished swimming laps and he'd shown up after pulling an all-nighter. He'd smelled like a brothel and was so fucking high I didn't think he even knew where he was.

"You're never leaving me. When are you going to get that through your fucking head?"

"I'm done. I can't take this anymore."

When I'd gotten out of the pool, we had a fight. He'd shoved me, and I fell onto the limestone pool deck, bruising my hip in the fall. Instead of helping me up, he'd walked over to the outdoor bar—fully stocked, because he had to have alcohol within easy reach at all times—and had hurled the glasses and bottles at the glass doors and onto the patio. A river of alcohol poured from shattered bottles, shards of glass scattered across my only exit route.

"You want to leave?" He'd laughed like the maniac he was. "Try leaving now, baby."

In my bare feet, I'd walked across broken glass to get to that door, leaving a trail of blood in my wake. I'd called Bastian, not sure who else to turn to, and he said Hayden would be right over to pick me up. Then I'd tossed a few things in a bag and walked out the front door.

Dean had chased after me and grabbed my arm to stop me from leaving, his fingers leaving purple bruises on my skin. "Baby, don't go. I'm sorry. I'm so fucking sorry." He'd been crying, tugging on the ends of his hair like a little boy, his handsome face twisted and ugly. "I don't know why I do this. I love you."

"You call this love? You have no idea what love is, Dean."

Just then, Hayden had pulled up in the silver Aston Martin and stepped out of the car, arms crossed over his broad chest, ready to put a stop to yet another Dean and Shiloh shit show.

"You're leaving me for *him*, aren't you?" Dean had accused. "You bitch. You think I don't know you've been fucking Bastian Cox behind my back?"

Lies. The only one who had been fucking other people was Dean.

Hayden had stepped in and ushered me to the car. As we drove away, I watched Dean through my window. He'd looked so lost. So broken.

And the damn paparazzi had captured our finest moments. We were all over the tabloids.

Shiloh Leroux Left Dean Bouchon for British rock star, Bastian Cox

Shiloh Leroux's Split from Dean Bouchon Responsible for Breaking Up Acadian Storm

Will Losing Shiloh Send Dean into Another Downward Spiral?

And that was the last time I saw my ex-boyfriend. Fifteen

months ago. Two days later, Bastian and I wrote "Damage." Over the next couple months, I wrote enough music for an entire album. I cut off ties with my brother and Dean and I went to therapy and I cried a lot. And little by little, I got stronger and I started to heal. But now here I was, right back in that dark place again.

Dean and I had been chasing the music and the highs and had deluded ourselves into believing we were untouchable. Invincible.

But we weren't. We were all too human. We hurt each other, we fucked up, broke up and got back together, until one day I looked in the mirror and couldn't stand the person staring back at me. That night it came to me in a dream, my life and my own death playing out right before my eyes in technicolor. A stray bullet lodged itself into my heart and stopped it from beating. Dean was holding the gun, but I pulled the trigger. And I knew if I didn't get out right then and there, my life would have been cut tragically short. So I found the strength to leave him and swore I'd never look back.

If my years with Dean had taught me anything, it was that I had no clue how to be in a healthy relationship.

I took a few deep breaths and I texted Brody: **Hey, you guys can go on home without me. I'll run home from here**.

His response was immediate. **Suit yourself**.

Even though it was to be expected, my shoulders slumped.

This was how you broke your own heart.

I pressed play on my phone then I sat under the tree in a state park in Texas and I listened to the song I'd recorded earlier, Hayley's sweet voice singing, "Here Comes the Sun." My eyes drifted shut and tears streamed down my face.

Coming here had been a mistake.

CHAPTER TWENTY-THREE

Brody

I snatched my ringing phone off the coffee table and skipped the greeting. "Where the hell have you been?"

Outside thunder rumbled and lightning lit up the dark room. Our power had gone out earlier and the movie I'd been watching had gone off so now I was sitting in the darkness, staring at a blank screen, feet propped on the coffee table while I contemplated whether it would have been better had I never met Shiloh Leroux.

"Brody..." She sounded like she was crying.

"What's wrong?" And why the hell should I give a shit?

"I'm broken down on the side of the road. I had an accident..."

Shit. My feet hit the floor and I stood up from the sofa. "Are you hurt?"

"No. I'm okay..." She started crying again which made it hard to believe she was telling the truth. But I had a feeling Shiloh was good at lying. It made me question how much of what she'd told me was true. I hadn't seen her since she took off and left me in the park. That was eight hours ago. "Brody... I... something's happened... it's so bad..."

My head warred with my emotions, but I didn't have to think twice. "I'll come for you. Just tell me where you are." When she didn't respond, I prompted her. "Shy. Where are you? I'm coming to get you." I was already headed for the front door. Ridge came down the stairs, his phone flashlight guiding the way.

"Is that Shiloh?" he asked, his voice low. Earlier he'd gone over there to visit her, but she hadn't been there then, and he told me the truck was gone.

I nodded.

"I ... I'm not sure where I am," Shiloh said. "I don't even know why I'm calling you. I'm lost, Brody. I'm so fucking lost ..."

And I had the strange feeling she wasn't only talking about not knowing her geographical location. I wanted to know why she was crying, and why she'd disappeared, but this wasn't the time to ask. "I'm coming to get you, but you need to give me a landmark. Something. Anything to help me find you, okay?"

"Okay." She took a deep breath and let it out. "I was just driving. Not really paying any attention to where I was going. And I tried to call you earlier, but I couldn't get a signal. The GPS on my phone stopped working. I'm on that winding road that cuts through the hills... the one with the limestone formations..."

That didn't tell me jack shit. This was a rural area with hundreds of winding roads and limestone formations.

"Which direction were you headed? North, south, east, west?"

"I was headed home but I got lost and I ended up on that road that Ridge and I—"

The rest of her sentence was swallowed up by a clap of thunder. "Shiloh." Nothing. The line was dead. I fucking lost her.

I hit the call button, but it went straight to voicemail. Shit. Fuck. I ran my hand through my hair. Where the hell was she?

"Where is she?" Ridge asked.

"If I knew, I'd already be in my truck on my way to get her."

"Damn."

"She lost her signal and has no fucking idea where she is. But she mentioned your name."

I ignored the way his face lit up and repeated what little information Shiloh had given me. "Any idea where she could be?"

"Shit." He chewed on his lip, his brow furrowed, and it looked to me like he didn't have a fucking clue where she was.

I exhaled loudly, quickly losing patience. "North, south, east, west? Anything, Ridge?"

When no answer was forthcoming, I gave up waiting and scrolled through my phone, all set to swallow my pride and ask Jude for help. Just before I hit the call button, Ridge snapped his fingers like he'd suddenly had a brainstorm.

"Hang on. I think I know the road she's talking about. If I'm right, it's only about six or seven miles from here."

A hunch was better than nothing.

We made a dash for my truck, and drove down my winding drive, skirting around a fallen limb from an oak tree. When I got to the road, he instructed me to hang a right. Sheets of rain cascaded down my windshield, the wipers doing jack shit to help the situation, making visibility nearly impossible. I could only see as far as my headlights, a few feet in front of me. With our windows cracked, and the air vents blowing warm air to defog the windows, I drove as fast as the weather conditions allowed. Fucking sloth speed.

"That day we went to buy the guitar, we took a drive," Ridge said, filling me in as I drove, my eyes searching the road for any signs of a broken-down Chevy pickup. "Just talking and shit. And we passed these big-ass limestone formations. I asked her to pull over. Nobody was around, and I said it looked like an amphitheater and she should give me a mini-concert."

"And did she?" I asked, my curiosity piqued. I was hoping he'd say she didn't do it.

Ridge chuckled. "Yeah. We got out of the truck and hiked over to the rocks... I brought the tacos, so we could have a little picnic."

Jealousy reared its ugly head. He'd gotten the chance to be alone with her, having a 'little picnic' and listening to her sing just for him? She'd never sung just for me and while this was no time to get petty, I couldn't help myself. It felt like a sucker punch in the stomach. Just like earlier when she'd refused to give me an honest answer. This was what happened when you let someone get too close.

When you let someone in, you gave them the power to fuck with your head.

"What did she sing?"

"'The Ghost of You.'"

I side-eyed him. "She sang it for you."

"Yeah, she did." My grip tightened on the wheel. I was too old for this shit. Shouldn't be jealous of my own brother spending time with the girl who was never meant to be anything more than a casual hookup. She'd made that clear earlier when she refused to tell me why she was really here. Ridge was still talking, and I was straining my eyes to see through the river of rain while I listened to him.

"She's the real fucking deal. Her voice, you know... it just... gives me chills." He cleared his throat and turned his head, embarrassed by the admission. Her voice did the same thing to me, but she'd never given me a private concert or sang just for me. And I really fucking needed to stop dwelling on that.

"I thought it might be cool to be a roadie," he confided. He was obviously feeling talkative tonight, a rare occurrence for him. "Learn how to do the lighting or sound or some shit like that."

I was all set to shoot him down but then I remembered how Shiloh told me when he shared his dreams with me, I shouldn't immediately dismiss them as stupid. And hadn't I been the one to tell him that everyone needed a dream? So I kept my mouth shut. What good would it do to mock him for having that dream or tell him to dream bigger the way Patrick used to tell us when we were growing up?

My dreams had been my own and I'd never won those belt buckles for Patrick or because he pushed me to keep doing better, insisted that none of us settle for anything less than being number fucking one. Everything I'd done, every medal and trophy and cash prize I'd won, I'd done for myself. I had wanted to be world champion, and I had been. Twice. Where did you go from there? The higher you climb, the harder the fall. When you stopped being number one, it was harder than you'd think to pick yourself up, brush yourself off and walk away.

And maybe that was what this was all about. I wanted to be number fucking one in Shiloh's life, but there wasn't a chance in hell of that ever happening. Why settle for runner-up to music and world tours and platinum albums, and all the other shit that would always take precedence?

"There's the truck!" Ridge pointed up ahead and then in the next breath, "Holy shit."

Holy shit was right. My headlights illuminated the wrecked vehicle in the field. A small figure was on the shoulder of the road, and it looked like she was down on her knees, praying, her face tipped up to the sky while the rain poured down on her.

What the hell are you doing, woman?

I pulled over, left my truck running, and shoved open my door, my arms reaching for her as soon as I was close enough to hold her. I pulled her to her feet and into my arms. "What do you think you're doing?"

Sobs wracked her body, and I stroked her wet hair, holding her close against me as she clung to me, my eyes on the deer lying alongside the road.

"You found me. You came for me when I called..."

"I told you I would. I told you I'd come for you." Had she expected me to leave her out here in the middle of a thunderstorm? What kind of jackass would do something like that?

"But after the way I left you... you still came."

Yeah, well, I was a dumbass. Couldn't stop myself from caring about her even if I tried.

"The deer came out of nowhere. I didn't see her until she was right in front of my headlights and I tried to swerve but it was too late." She took a shuddering breath. "I killed her."

"It was an accident."

"She had a baby. I killed the baby's mother."

"Shh." I pulled her closer and kept stroking her wet hair, the rain beating down on us and the thunder rumbling in the distance. "It's okay. You couldn't help it. It happens. It was an accident."

Standing outside in the middle of a violent thunderstorm wasn't going to bring the deer back or do Shiloh any good. She was soaked to the bone, shivering uncontrollably. Lifting her into my arms, I carried her to my truck. Ridge shoved open the passenger door and climbed into the back. I set Shiloh in the seat and put two fingers under her chin, turning her face toward mine. Then I used both hands to gently push the wet hair off her face, so I could see it better in the light from the cab. Blood trickled down her forehead from a gash just below her hairline. She must have rammed it into the steering wheel. "Ridge. Give me your flannel shirt."

He took it off, leaving him in a T-shirt and handed it to me. I used it to dab off the blood on Shiloh's forehead and even though my touch was gentle, she winced. "Do you have any other injuries? Where else does it hurt?"

She shook her head a little and wrapped her hand around my wrist, pulling it away. "I'm fine."

Stormy grays locked on to mine and I saw a world of pain and sadness that seemed to go deeper than tonight's accident. "Brody," she whispered, her eyes welling up with tears again.

"Hey. It's okay. Everything is going to be okay. We need to get you to the hospital."

"No. I'm fine. Just... take me home, okay? Please."

Her whole body was trembling from the shock and the longer we stayed in my parked truck, the worse it would be for her.

"Get in the truck," she said. "You're getting soaked."

I almost laughed at that. I was drenched and so was she. "A little rain won't hurt me. Everything is going to be fine. Let's get you home."

"What about the deer?" She wrung her hands in her lap and gnawed on her bottom lip. "We can't just leave her on the road."

"I'll move her into the field and come back in the morning to take care of everything."

"I'm the one who hit her... I should be the one to—"

"You don't have to worry about anything," I assured her. "I'll take care of it."

"Why are you so good to me?"

"I'm just doing what anyone would do."

She shook her head. "No. Not all men are like you, Brody."

Then you've been with the wrong men. What kind of jackass wouldn't reassure her and tell her everything was going to be fine?

"Need help, bro?" Ridge asked from the back seat.

"Nah. I got it." I tossed his flannel shirt in the truck. I'd wash it later. "Just stay in the truck with Shiloh."

He nodded, probably relieved. Ridge wasn't a country boy, he'd grown up in a city, so he wasn't all that comfortable around animals, let alone dead ones. I closed Shiloh's door then walked over to the doe and crouched in front of it, my back to the truck. Just to make sure there was no hope, I felt for a pulse, but she was gone, eyes still open and staring blankly at the sky. Even in the pouring rain, coat wet and matted with blood, the white-tailed deer was a thing of beauty.

Animals were so pure and innocent. They didn't stab you in the back or break your heart or spread rumors. They weren't greedy, taking only what they needed to survive, and they only fought to protect their young or their territory or when they felt threatened.

I stood up, grabbed the doe by the hind legs and dragged her into the field. She was dead weight, weighing as much as I did, so it was slow going but I kept dragging her until she was in the tall grass where I left her to rest. Tomorrow I'd call the games warden and have it dealt with *after* I had Austin's truck towed. No need to alert the media that Shiloh Leroux had hit a deer in a borrowed truck.

Catching some rainwater on my hands, I scrubbed them together then wiped them on my soaking wet T-shirt. A bolt of lightning lit up the sky. In the distance stood three deer, one of which was a fawn, a stark relief to the dark landscape.

I turned away and walked back to the truck with the doe's blood still on my hands.

Before I could climb into the driver's seat, one of the county sheriff's black SUVs pulled up in front of my truck. *Fuck.*

He stepped out of the SUV, his black cowboy hat coming into view and then his ruddy face as he came to stand in front of me. Double fuck. I reached inside my truck and took my keys out of the ignition. "I'll take care of this," I told Shiloh, my voice low. She opened her mouth to protest. "Just stay quiet. It's all gonna be fine."

I turned to face Silas Barnes. I hated the fucker.

"Brody McCallister. It's been a while."

Not long enough. "How's it going, Sherriff?"

"That your truck?" He jerked his chin at the blue Chevy.

"Nope. Belongs to a friend."

He stroked his jaw. "Anyone hurt?"

"Nope. It's all good."

His eyes darted to my truck then back to me. Ready to accuse me of committing a crime or breaking the law. It felt like old times. "There a reason you got blood on your hands?"

When I was a teenager, Silas called me a juvenile delinquent and told me if I didn't straighten up, I'd turn out to be exactly like my no-good father. I couldn't think of a worse thing you could say to a sixteen-year-old. I'd told him to go fuck himself. After that, I'd gotten picked up a few times for minor infractions and had spent a few nights behind bars.

"I hit a deer," I said, opting for a half-truth. "Damn shame too. She was a beauty."

"You hit a deer?"

"That's what I said."

"So you were driving a friend's truck and you hit a deer?"

"Yup."

"That's not what happened," Shiloh said. "It was—"

"Me. I hit the deer," Ridge said, coming to stand next to me.

"It was me. I freaked out. Called Brody. He came out and took care of it."

Silas' eyes narrowed on Ridge. "You're the kid who stole the trucker's wallet, ain't ya?"

Ridge gave him a surly look. "Yup."

"Doesn't surprise me. Shelby McCallister was always trouble. The apples don't fall far from the tree."

My jaw clenched. Ridge opened his mouth about to say what I was sure would land him in more trouble. Before he could get a word out, I elbowed him in the ribs hard enough that he grunted. "Now, if you don't mind, we'll be on our way. I'll get the truck towed tomorrow."

He held up his hand like a traffic cop. "Not so fast. Show me the deer you hit. And I'm gonna need to see your license and the registration for that truck," he told Ridge.

"Ridge. Brody. You don't have to—"

I slammed the door shut, stopping the rest of Shiloh's words and beeped the locks so she couldn't get out of the truck. No need to get her involved in Silas Barnes' bullshit. Ridge and I would handle it.

Turns out, Ridge was a hell of a lot like me. I was so damn proud to call him my brother.

I STEPPED into the steaming hot shower behind Shiloh and turned her around to face me, the water pouring down over her head, mascara tracks on her cheeks and her smudged eyeliner giving her raccoon eyes. Only Shiloh could manage to make smeared eyeliner look so fucking sexy. I soaped every inch of her body, mindful of the bruises and welts on her skin from the seat belt digging into her and the injuries she'd sustained from whiplash. She let me do it without saying a word or putting up a fight. I squeezed shampoo into my hand and washed her hair then wiped the mascara off her cheekbones with the pads of my thumbs.

After we'd dealt with the sheriff who had a hard-on for the McCallisters from the wrong side of the tracks—not to be confused with Patrick's sons—I'd brought her back to my house and stripped off her clothes then threw them in the wash with mine. She'd been in the shower for twenty minutes, just standing under the water before I joined her. I'd already taken a quick shower in the one I'd installed next to the laundry room.

"What were you doing in here?" I asked her as the soap suds rinsed from her hair and circled the drain. Thankfully, the cut on her forehead wasn't too deep and I didn't think she needed stitches, but she'd taken the two Tylenol I'd given her because I thought the crying and the blow to her head would give her a headache.

She mustered a smile, and it was so sad, I'd have to add it to my list of things that made me want to cry. "I was letting it go."

"What do you have to let go, Shy?"

She lifted her hands to my face and cradled it. For a moment, I thought she was talking about us, but I knew it was something more. Something that went a lot deeper. She kissed my lips and it felt like goodbye. I wrapped my arm around her waist, her slippery-wet body flush with mine and it didn't seem like the time to think about sex but damn if my dick didn't get hard, like it had a mind of its own. She reached between us, her hand wrapping around my cock and squeezing, sliding up and down, applying just the right amount of pressure.

My mouth found hers and I kissed her softly then deepened the kiss, my tongue tangling with hers as she continued to stroke me, my dick getting impossibly hard in her hand.

She pulled back from our kiss, her lips still on mine and

murmured, "I want you. I need you. Right now." As if to drive home her point, she stroked me harder and faster, her chest heaving and her eyes at half-mast while the water cascaded over us and the steam filled the bathroom, making this look like a dreamscape.

My hands coasted over her ass and to the backs of her thighs and I lifted her up, her arms and legs wrapped around me as I pushed her against the tiles and drove into her.

"Fuck me," she said. "Fuck me hard."

I squeezed my eyes shut, thrusting in and out of her, my balls tightening and the base of my spine tingling. Her short nails dug into my shoulders and I wouldn't be surprised if she drew blood. My eyes opened and she threw back her head, exposing the column of her neck as she met me thrust for thrust. There was zero finesse in this, and no rhythm to speak of. She was pulling, and I was pushing, our breathing ragged as I pounded into her, needing more and more and more. Of fucking everything.

"Oh my God. Brody!" she screamed, her voice echoing off the tiles. I didn't let up, I kept the punishing pace until her legs clamped tighter around me and her head fell to my shoulder, her body trembling with the release. Seconds later, I came so hard my legs felt like they might give out. I flattened my palm on the tiles behind her to steady myself and catch my breath. For a few seconds, neither of us moved. My face was buried in the crook of her neck and she was still holding on so tightly like she was afraid that if she loosened her hold, I'd disappear.

"Don't leave me," she whispered, and I didn't know if she was talking about right this moment or four days from now.

I lifted my head and pushed the wet hair off her face, my thumb stroking her cheekbone, my dick still inside her. "I'm not going anywhere, Shiloh."

She was the one who would be doing the leaving, not me.

CHAPTER TWENTY-FOUR

Shiloh

Dressed in Brody's T-shirt and sweatpants, I crawled into bed next to him. He was wearing boxer briefs and lying on top of the covers, his back leaning against the headboard. It was strange that this was the first time I'd ever been in his bedroom, sleeping in his bed. His room was simply furnished with a tall oak dresser, two bedside tables that looked as if they'd been carved from a single piece of wood and off-white painted walls like the rest of the house. Everything was neat and tidy, no clothes strewn on the floor or dirty piles heaped in the corners of the room like Dean had always done.

The air smelled fresh and clean, like his cedar soap and the outdoors. Cream linen blinds covered the windows, open to let the fresh air in.

His bedding was forest green and a few framed black and white horse photos hung on the opposite wall. Horses were his first love, so I guess it was fitting that he kept photos of them in his bedroom.

He slid his arm around my shoulders, and I leaned into him, resting my hand on his heart, one of my legs draped across his lap. He wrapped his hand around my leg, just above my knee and asked me how I was feeling.

"I'm okay. Just a little stiff and shaken up."

"You'll be sore for a day or two." His thumb made lazy circles on my skin and I thought those hands of his held magic in them. They were made for healing, not for breaking things.

"I owe you and Ridge so much."

"You don't owe us a damn thing." But I did. They'd both stood up to take the blame for something I'd done. "You wanna tell me what's going on with you, Shy?"

Earlier, I'd made the decision that I wanted to tell him everything. "You remember when you asked me why I was here, and I told you I had my reasons, but they were personal?"

"I remember."

He waited for me to go on, his thumb still making lazy circles, his arm still wrapped around me. Not pushing me to hurry up and tell him what the hell was going on in my head. He'd come to find me tonight, no questions asked, and in some ways, he was part of the reason I'd broken down and cried so hard. Because real men, good men, showed up and tried to fix what was broken. They didn't call you an idiot for driving through a thunderstorm. Didn't try to make you feel shittier than you already did for wrecking a truck and killing that poor doe who had been unlucky enough to be in the wrong place at the wrong time. Real men carried your burdens along with their own, and I thought Brody's shoulders were broad enough to carry the weight of the world.

I took a deep breath in preparation to tell my story. Brody's arm tightened around me as if he alone could hold me together and keep me from losing it again. I wouldn't lose it though. I'd cried all my tears and it was time to let it go. "When I was eighteen, I got pregnant. But I didn't even realize it until I was four months gone and had just graduated high school." When I'd walked onto the stage to accept my diploma, Landry, Dean, and Gus had cheered louder than anyone else in that audience. It had been a good day. One of my best memories.

"The guys and I had been making plans to hit the road as soon as I graduated. Dean bought... or stole... I don't even know which... but he got this old van, big enough to fit all of us and all our equipment. The guys had been working on that thing for months. We all wanted to get away, especially Dean. His family was... still is... total shit. If his dad wasn't beating the shit out of him, his older brothers were. Anyway, I found out I was pregnant and that put a wrench in our plans... we were barely scraping by as it was..." I took a deep breath and let it out. Brody was massaging my upper arm with his hand and stayed quiet.

"Dean drove me to a clinic but when we got inside, I just couldn't do it. He said he'd take care of it. He said he'd find the money somehow and we wouldn't have to give up the baby or our dreams. I believed him because he can be very convincing, especially when he's telling you what you want to hear. Unfortunately, Dean's idea of taking care of things was to set up a chop shop in a garage he rented. A few months later, he got busted and ended up in jail. I had the baby at home. We couldn't afford to go to a hospital, so this elderly woman... one of Maw Maw's friends... delivered the baby. And it was love at first sight."

I shifted my position so I could see Brody's face. He tipped his chin down and his eyes met mine. "Hayley," he said. Not a question. A statement.

I nodded. "Yeah. Hayley was mine. But now she's not."

"You gave her up for adoption?"

I would have loved to lie and say yes. But I couldn't lie to him. Not when I'd set out to be open and honest and tell the whole truth. "No. I wanted to keep her but my brother... he said I had to give her up, that we couldn't take care of a baby. That I wasn't ready to be a fit mother. We had no money. Dean was in prison. And I knew he was right. I knew he was doing what was best for everyone. But it was so hard to do. He drove me to the hospital and walked me in and I handed my baby over to a nurse, and I said ... I said I was exercising the Safe Baby Haven law. I had to answer some questions... I don't even remember. But I didn't even have to give my name."

"And when I walked out of that hospital without my baby girl, I felt so empty. Like I'd lost a big piece of myself and I'd never get it back. Never be able to fill that hole in my heart." I rubbed my thumb over the rosary tattoo on my ring finger. "The strangest thing happened. This old woman chased after me in the parking lot and when I turned to look at her, she smiled and pressed a rosary into my hands. And she said, "The good Lord hears your prayers and always listens. Sometimes you don't get the answers you want, but the good Lord knows us better than we know ourselves, so we always get the answers we need." And I've never forgotten her words on what had to be one of the worst days of my life. But I still feel like a horrible person for what I did. I turned over my own baby like she was... an item of clothing that didn't fit quite right."

I stopped talking, and we were silent for a few seconds. Now that I'd told the story, I couldn't even look at Brody's face. What must he think of me?

"Listen to me... you were only eighteen and you weren't ready to be a mother. There's no shame in that. You did the best thing you could at the time. The best thing for her and the best thing for you."

"That's what I keep trying to tell myself. She's happy. And

that's all that really matters, so I need to leave her alone and stay out of her life. That's the best thing I can do for her."

"Is it though? And what about your feelings? You think they don't matter?"

I pulled back to look at him. "I thought you agreed with me. There's nothing I can do about it. What's done is done. And I'd love nothing more than to spend time with her, for her to know I'm her birth mother. But I can't take the risk that the media will get hold of it and spread the news all over the tabloids. I don't want that for her. I don't want to mess up her life, you know?"

"I know that. But don't you think *she* has the right to know you?"

"What good would that do, Brody? She's only six. Too young to understand. How would you feel if Noah had been adopted and his birth mother showed up at your door unannounced?"

"I don't know," he answered honestly.

"Because it's not something you can imagine. You would have never given up your son, just turned him over to some random nurse in a hospital without even knowing his fate, and neither would Lila."

"We were in a different place in our lives. We were in our twenties, making decent money and we had family to help out. But even with all those resources, it was hard. Raising a kid is a full-time job and babies are expensive. You have to change your whole life to accommodate one tiny little baby. Unlike animals, human babies are helpless, completely relying on their parents to take care of all their needs."

"And that's my point. Dale and Meredith did all that for her. They raised her, took care of her when she was sick, they were there for her every step of the way. I forfeited my right to call myself a mother... and Brody?"

"What?"

I was going to admit my worst sin of all. Like he was the priest, and I was the sinner sitting in the confessional, trying to ease my guilty conscience. "While I was driving, I realized that I really wasn't ready to be a mother. Not then and not now. I feel like that old woman was right. Raising a daughter wasn't part of the greater plan for my life. God knew that better than I did."

"You believe in God?" He sounded surprised.

Not the question I'd expected after my confession. "Yes. Don't you?"

"Nope."

"Do you believe in anything?"

"I believe in a lot of things."

"But not God?"

"Not God, no. I believe in reincarnation."

"Maybe we've come back in this life to find each other. Maybe we knew each other in a former life."

"Wouldn't surprise me."

Oh Brody. My heart felt like it might burst. Sometimes he said the sweetest, most unexpected things.

"Is this what you were doing today... is that why you took off on your own?"

I nodded. "I was trying to work through all my mixed-up feelings and when I hit that deer, I lost it. It was like..." I took a shuddering breath, remembering the horror when I'd discovered that deer was dead. Brody was going to think I was crazy for what I was about to say but I'd come this far, and he hadn't judged me once, so I might as well finish what I'd started. "It felt really symbolic, in the most horrific way imaginable. Like I'd killed off that fawn's mother..."

"And killed off the part of you that was bound to Hayley."

I sat back and stared at him. "How did you get that?"

He laughed and scrubbed his hand over his face. "Shit. I think I've been hanging out with you for too long. I'm starting to say all kinds of messed-up shit. Maybe I really can read your mind."

"Well, that would be scary."

"Doesn't scare me. Not even a little bit. I love your mind and your crazy ideas, and I love the way you speak your truth even when it's not pretty. I love all that about you, Shi-loh."

And I loved him. I was in love with him and I think I'd known it from the start. That I would fall for him. That he'd get under my skin and into my heart and I'd hear his voice in my head and conjure up the image of him no matter how far away I traveled or how long we were apart. I would always carry him with me.

But I didn't say the words and neither did he. I was free to go now, I'd done what I set out to do. I'd made my peace with what I'd done at eighteen. I could close this chapter of my life now. And if it weren't for Brody, I would leave tomorrow and return to L.A. But we still had four more days together and I didn't want to waste a single moment of the precious time I had left with him.

"Four more days," he said, reading my mind.

"Four more days," I echoed. "No regrets."

"Not a single one." He side-eyed me. "What do you want to do for the next four days?"

"How about we fuck like rock stars?"

He threw back his head and laughed and when he was done laughing, we fucked like rock stars. Somehow, we managed to break the bed and that had us laughing again, the two of us naked and slick with sweat, our bodies tangled together on the floor.

It was good and it was true and it was honest, all these feel-ings I had for Brody. My one true love who I'd found by accident but would be leaving behind in Texas. And now more than ever I had to believe all the things I'd sacrificed would be worth it in the end.

People came and went, but music... it would always be there for me. That was what I had to keep reminding myself.

CHAPTER TWENTY-FIVE

Shiloh

THE NEXT AFTERNOON, the sun was trying to come out from behind the clouds, the air was warm, and you'd never know it had stormed the night before. I was sitting on Brody's back porch, my body sore and my head throbbing, eyes shielded by sunglasses. From here, I had a view of the barn and the round pen where Brody was working with a yearling. But he was far enough away that he wouldn't be able to hear me. I scrolled through the contacts on my phone and pressed call. He answered on the second ring.

"Hey Gideon. It's Shiloh. I was hoping you could help me with something."

"I'll do my best, but you should know... Brody's always been a redneck. Not much I can do to change that."

I laughed. His Texan accent was barely detectable, and I suspected he'd worked hard to lose it. "I happen to like rednecks. Especially the charming ones."

"Are we talking about the same guy? Brody McCallister?"

I smiled. "The one and only."

"What can I do for you?"

"I heard you helped him get a grant." Brody hadn't told me. Lila had.

"I did."

I watched Brody doing his thing. Maybe he didn't like the term, but from where I was sitting, horse whisperer was the only way to describe the way he handled horses. "Wouldn't it be great if he could get an even bigger donation?"

He was silent for a moment. "If he ever finds out, he won't be happy. And that's putting it mildly."

"I know. That's why it will have to be our little secret."

"Tell me what you have in mind."

We talked for twenty minutes and when we cut the call, my headache was all but gone and I had a smile on my face.

Sometimes dreams come true, Brody. I couldn't give him everything I wanted to without raising suspicion, but I could help. Just a little.

"Hey Shy. How's it going?"

Ridge plopped down on the wicker chair next to me and planted his work boots on the banister.

"Hey Ridge. I'm so sorry about last night. And I never got the chance to thank you."

He laughed. "You thanked me about a million times last night. We're good. It's cool."

"How was work?"

"It sucked. Like always. Me and my uncle don't see eye to eye. On anything."

"That's hard."

"He's a hard-ass. I'm not a fan. I get why my mom never wanted to ask him for help. He would have made her feel like shit."

I side-eyed him. "Do you miss her?"

He shrugged one shoulder. "She wasn't the best mom in the world, but she was the only one I had. So yeah, sometimes I think about her. Pisses me off that she went back to drugs. She was doing so good for a while. I really thought she had her shit together."

I knew how that was, wanting to believe in someone when they told you they were clean and sober and never going back to drugs and alcohol. They'd lie and promise and swear up and down that everything was going to be different. Dean was doing it again now.

"If you could do anything... be anything you want... what would it be? What's your dream, Ridge?"

"What's the point in thinking like that? Dreams don't come true."

"Sometimes they do. Just tell me. It'll be our little secret."

"I guess..." He narrowed his eyes, thinking about it. "I'd do something in the music industry. Like... I don't know... I told Brody I wanted to be a roadie. But I want to do something with sound. Like mixing. Or a DJ or some shit like that."

"I could see you as a DJ."

"Yeah?"

"Yeah. Totally." What I could envision was him working at a hot club and all the women going crazy over him. But I didn't say that.

Ridge chuckled under his breath. I followed his gaze. Brody was walking across the backyard toward us. "He's so fucking jealous, it cracks me up. What a dumb shit."

Brody stopped in front of us, his eyes narrowed on Ridge. "She needs to rest."

"Which is why we're just hanging out and chillin', bro."

"Is he bothering you?" Brody asked me.

I shook my head. "Not at all. I love hanging out with Ridge."

Ridge snickered and moved his chair right next to mine then wrapped his arm around my shoulders. "I'm her favorite McCallister. Get at the back of the line, dude."

Brody scowled. "Get your fucking hands off her."

I tried to suppress my laughter but failed.

"What's so funny?" he asked me.

"You."

He rolled his eyes. It made him look like a teenager. Jealous Brody was kind of adorable.

THE NIGHT BEFORE I LEFT, Brody stayed with me at the guesthouse. That morning, I stood by the round pen and watched him start a colt. I was there when he put the saddle on its back and rode it for the first time. I had said goodbye to Phoenix, the filly Brody brought into this world, who was running in the pasture with the other horses. And I'd ridden Rebel, the black horse with the white star named after Lila. I'd found out Rebel was Jude's nickname for Lila which explained why Brody had laughed when he told me the horse's name.

Earlier that evening we'd gone to watch the wild horses, this time from the truck as we drove across the land they lived on, leaving a swath of salt in our wake for the horses. It had been the golden hour and once again Brody had shimmered like gold. So strong and true and beautiful.

Later, we watched the sun set over the hills from the back of the truck, the land bathed in hues of purple and pink, Brody's arms wrapped around me, my back leaning against his broad chest, and I thought about how much I'd changed and how much had happened in only six weeks. And how quickly Brody had become someone so special to me. I didn't want to leave him. I didn't want this to be the end, but neither of us had the power to stop time.

I'd already said my goodbyes to the McCallisters yesterday so now it was just me and Brody, sitting on the back porch steps watching the stars. They really did burn brighter here in Texas. This night was so bittersweet, and I couldn't believe it was our last one together.

I'd come here looking for one thing and had found something completely different.

"I hate goodbyes," I said. "There's something so sad and so final about them."

I was hoping and praying he'd say this didn't have to be goodbye. But he didn't. He just took my hand, laced his fingers in mine and led me up the stairs.

Then he undressed me in the soft light of the moon and caressed my skin with his rough, calloused hands before he lifted me up and laid me on the bed. So tender, so gentle I nearly cried. I watched him take off his clothes and then he climbed onto the bed and crawled up my body, his lips trailing his hands up my thighs, over my hips and ribcage. He palmed my breasts and sucked one nipple into his mouth. I grabbed his head and held it to my chest, digging my fingers into his hair. My legs wrapped around his back, and I angled my hips just right, cradling his hard length between my slick folds.

He moved to my mouth, his forearms braced on either side of me and for a few moments, he stared at my face as if he was trying to memorize it. A lock of hair fell over his forehead and I lifted my hand to brush it away then held his face in both of my hands.

"Brody," I whispered.

He dipped his head and slanted his mouth over mine. When our lips touched, my eyes drifted shut and my legs cinched more tightly around his back. Brody kissed me like this would be the last time he would ever kiss my lips.

I lifted my hips, and he nudged his tip against my entrance. Then he glided inside me, and ever so slowly thrust in and out, like we had all night, and he was in no hurry.

He kissed my lips. My jaw. The sensitive spot just below my ear.

This wasn't fucking. He was making love to me. This gentleness was the cruelest form of torture.

What felt like hours later, we both hurtled into shared orgasms. Afterward, he held me in his arms, and we talked until the sun came up.

***

"I'LL MISS YOU, COWBOY." We were standing near the security check at the Austin airport and even though we were standing close, facing each other, it felt like he was already gone. Like his mind was elsewhere and he was putting distance between us.

"Nah. You'll be just fine. Give it a day or two and you won't even remember my name. Brody who?" He mimicked my voice.

I tried to laugh but it came out sounding hollow. "Why is it so hard to leave?" And by that I meant, why is it so hard to leave *you?*

"You're gonna be just fine. You're Shiloh Leroux. You're a supernova. You shine so bright, baby. So fucking bright." He grasped my chin in his hand and gave me a soft kiss then released me. "You should go now. You'll miss your flight."

"Brody. We can make this work. I know we can."

"That wasn't our deal, Shy. Your life is out there, mine is here. We knew that from the start. We agreed. Six weeks. No regrets."

"Things change."

He took a step back, putting even more distance between us, and shook his head. "Don't make it harder than it already is. Just turn around and walk away."

I swallowed down the lump in my throat. He was right. Why prolong our goodbye? But I didn't want to leave him like this. I wanted him to tell me there was another way and that we had a future and he'd do everything in his power to make it happen, but he didn't say one single word.

"What if..."

"There's no what-if for us. You're a rock star. I'm just an asshole cowboy trying to keep a roof over my head. I've got nothing to offer you."

"How can you even say that?"

"We've had our fun and now it's over."

"So that's it?"

"That's it." He gave me his charming Brody McCallister grin and fed me my own words. "But it's been a hell of a ride, baby." He punctuated his words with a sexy wink, and I hated that he did that.

In my heart, I knew he wanted this as much as I did. I opened my mouth to call him out on his cavalier response. He pressed two fingers against my lips to stop the words.

"Go and do what you were born to do. Set the world on fire. Make your sacrifices matter."

Then he turned and he walked away, leaving me at airport security with an ache in my heart the size of Texas.

Come back. Come back. Come back.

But he didn't even turn around to look at me. Not once. He

kept on walking, and waltzed right out the door, taking a huge piece of my heart with him.

What a fool I'd been to think we could ever stay in the shallow end.

Once again, I'd taken a plunge into the deep end and found myself alone.

CHAPTER TWENTY-SIX

Shiloh

THE NEXT MORNING, I met Landry at a coffee shop on Melrose Place. I hadn't wanted to go to the house he shared with Dean and since Bastian was in Europe, it didn't feel right to invite my brother to a house that wasn't mine. When I arrived at the white stucco Mediterranean style cafe with ivy climbing the walls, Landry was waiting for me at a sidewalk table under a black and white umbrella. When he saw me, he stood up and waited for me to reach him then pulled me into a hug. "I missed you." I squeezed my eyes shut to keep the tears at bay.

"Missed you too."

He released me and we took our seats across from each other at the small wrought-iron table. Landry's hair was dark but not black like mine and his eyes were more blue than gray, hidden behind Ray-Ban Wayfarers. We looked a lot alike, enough to tell we were siblings. His dark hair was cut in short layers, kind of spikey on top, and we had the same smile. We both looked more like our mom and nothing like Rhett.

"You look great," he told me.

"So do you. Really good." He wore a floral-patterned button-up he wouldn't have been caught dead in as a teenager, untucked over frayed khaki shorts. I hadn't seen him since January when I'd asked him to be my date for the Grammy Awards. Big mistake. Bastian had been the one to pluck Acadian Storm out of obscurity and give us our big break, and when we opened for him on his world tour five years ago, Landry had worshiped the ground Bastian walked on. Now he resented Bastian. So rather than being a joyous occasion, it had been fraught with tension and animosity.

Landry drummed his fingers on the table, probably tapping out whatever beat was playing in his head. For as long as I could remember, that had been Landry's tell sign when he was nervous. I checked under the table and sure enough, his leg was bouncing up and down. Which made me think this wasn't just a friendly coffee date or a chance to catch up after five months of not seeing each other.

Before I could question him, a server turned up at our table. Landry ordered a breakfast burrito and a cold brew, and I ordered a sparkling espresso with orange zest and an egg white omelet. I wasn't in Texas anymore. And I was trying my best not to think about it or wonder what Brody was doing right this very minute.

"All set to conquer Europe?" Landry asked with a smile after the server left.

"Pretty sure it's already been conquered. I'm nervous but excited." Which was accurate. I'd missed performing and was looking forward to getting back on the stage.

"You have nothing to be nervous about. They're going to love you."

I loved him for saying that. We made small talk until our food arrived, neither of us saying much of anything important.

"Gus left the band."

I stared at him, thinking I'd misheard. "What? But Gus... why would he leave?"

"It all got too much for him."

"God. I'm sorry, Landry. Are you okay?"

"It wasn't a shock. It was a long time coming. But yeah, it hurt. We replaced him. And Noel said he'd stay."

Noel was a keyboard player who had joined us for my final tour with Acadian Storm.

"We need you, Shy."

I opened my mouth to protest. He held up his hand. "Just hear me out. I'm not here to ask you to come back to the band. But Dean... he needs a break, man. He's good. You know how good he is."

I knew how good he was, but I also knew how bad he could get and how toxic he'd made everything. His talent had taken a back seat to his volatile personality.

"One of us had to go, Landry. You know that. I mean... you know I'd do anything to help you but as long as you're in a band with Dean, I don't see how that's possible."

"You don't have anyone to open for you on the final leg of your tour yet."

I stared at him, not completely grasping what he was getting at.

"Let us open for you."

Oh my God. No. No fucking way. "Landry... I would do it for you, you know I would but..." I shook my head. "No. I can't do it."

"Shy, you broke up the band and now we're scrambling to pick up the pieces. You owe us."

My jaw dropped. I couldn't fucking believe he'd just said that. "*I owe you?* Wow. You sound exactly like Rhett."

"Fuck that. I'm nothing like him. I was there for you. I was there for you through it all."

"And I've always been so grateful to you but what you're asking me..." I shook my head. "... it's too much."

"Do it for me. Do it for the band."

"I can't just... this isn't even up to me. My management team would fight me on this."

"Bullshit. You're a Grammy winner. Your album went platinum. You're their cash cow, Shiloh. They work for you, not the other way around. If you say this is what you want, they'll bend over backward to make sure you're happy."

I wasn't so sure about that. Not to mention I didn't like his tone or what he was asking me to do. "I've been trying so hard to get to a good place, Landry. I've had to work so hard to get over all the shit Dean put me through. Not just me either. What about everything he did to you and Gus? Why are you still defending everything he's done?"

"Because I owe him. And so do you."

Oh my God. Unbelievable. "We paid our dues. We both tried to help him but what did he do? He's trouble, Landry. Always has been. And he's going to drag you down with him. It's what he does. How can you be so blind that you can't see that? You don't owe him anything."

"You don't get it, do you? You have no idea what he did for us."

I huffed out a laugh. "Oh, I know exactly what he did for us. None of it was good either."

"It was me. I was the one was cooking the meth. It was all my idea and I started doing it when you were still in high school. We had no money, Shy. Not a fucking cent. Do you really think my minimum wage jobs bought you that Fender guitar for your seventeenth birthday? Do you think it paid for our food and all the bills Maw Maw left me with? All you ever talked about was going out to L.A. And I wanted to make that happen for you. So did Dean. He always knew you had what it took to become a star. Everyone did. Why do you think Bastian Cox gave us our big break? It was because of *you*."

"You..." I shook my head. "I don't believe you. I would have known about this. It couldn't have been you. You were working two jobs..."

"No. I wasn't. In the beginning, I was, yeah. But they didn't pay enough. Dean took the fall. He served time when it should have been me."

I shook my head. "No. No way. You can't actually think I'm going to believe that?"

"It's the goddamn truth," he gritted out. "Dean knew if he got involved, they'd pin it on him, so he tried to stay out of it."

"If it's the truth, then why hasn't anyone ever mentioned it before? You've had *years* to tell me this. Why now? Why are you telling me this now, Landry?"

"Hey babe."

I clenched my jaw at the sound of his voice, steeling myself before I turned my head to look at Dean. He looked good. His hazel eyes were clear, not bloodshot or glossy. His brown hair was messy and disheveled, deconstructed, perfectly styled to look that way. He was wearing a clean white T-shirt, ripped black jeans and motorcycle boots. He looked like a rock star. He looked like a guy who had been to hell and back. His smile was sad, hopeful, like he was worried I'd kick him to the curb. I used to fall for that damn smile every time. "What are you doing here?"

I should have known they'd ambush me like this. I should have known better than to think my brother wanted to meet up for a friendly chat.

Without waiting for an invitation, Dean pulled up a chair next to mine.

"You didn't return my calls."

"I don't have anything left to say to you."

He nodded. "Can't say I blame you. You look beautiful."

"And you look like trouble."

"Because I am. But I'm not looking to cause you any more trouble."

"You're just looking for a favor. A really big one."

The server turned up and we fell into silence, not wanting to be overheard. He cleared our plates and took Dean's order—a double espresso. After the waiter was gone, Dean leaned in close to me and said, "But it's within your power to grant it. I'm begging you. Just do us this one solid."

Acadian Storm used to do headliner tours and now they were asking for a chance to open for me. "If this new music is so great, why don't you get into the recording studio and put out a new album? Line up some promo and a tour. You don't need me for that."

"Did you tell her about Gus?" he asked Landry, who nodded. "I fucked everything up. I know that. I've burned so many bridges. Pissed off the wrong people. Now we have to start from the ground up and try to do it the right way."

It reminded me of Brody when he was talking about the abused horses he worked with, how he started from the ground up and how you couldn't rush that kind of thing or you'd undo all your hard work.

"I know we're broken," Dean said. "I know there's not a chance in hell you'd ever take me back. But this is about the music. And once upon a time, you believed in me. I need this, Shy. Landry needs this. If you can't do it for me, do it for him. Please."

He sounded so sincere. I was tempted to tell him that his

daughter looked so much like him. That she sang all the time, and she had his changeable hazel eyes and dimpled smile. But the part of me who had been burned by him one too many times stopped me from saying anything.

"Will you at least think about it?" he pleaded.

I knew Dean. He only begged when he was in danger of losing everything. It would have taken a lot for him to ask this of me. I looked at my brother, the guy who had taken on the responsibility of watching over me after Maw Maw died. He'd worked two crap jobs just to keep a roof over our heads and food on the table. I didn't know if I believed him about the drugs or if he was trying to paint Dean in a better light. But Landry had given up a lot to support me and had never asked me for anything in return.

Had Dean really gone to prison for Landry?

I thought he probably would have. Dean was tougher than Landry. He was street smart and he would have done it to protect Landry. God, why was life so complicated? Why couldn't this be black and white, right and wrong? Why couldn't my ex-boyfriend be a heartless villain? But I guess if he had been, I never would have fallen in love with him in the first place.

But if I agreed to this, it would be for my brother, not for Dean. "I'll think about it."

Dean breathed a sigh of relief like it was already a done deal. "Thank you. You won't regret this."

I already did. "I'm not making any promises. This isn't just up to me."

"We'll sign whatever contract they put in front of us. No drugs, no booze, no trouble from me... I swear on my life."

Guilt was a powerful bargaining chip, and Dean had never been afraid to use every tool at his disposal. Once upon a time, I had fallen in love with the boy whose father and brothers had abused him. I'd tried to fix him. Save him. Fill up the emptiness inside him. I had fallen in love with the musician whose guitar skills were some of the best in the industry. I'd never be the guitar player Dean was. He had music in his soul, and I used to believe it would be enough to save him. But nothing had ever been enough for Dean. Not my love. Not the music. Not his friend's loyalty. Not fame or success or all the fans who screamed his name and proclaimed their undying love for him. The worse Dean's behavior was, the more his fans adored him.

For some people, you could give them the whole world and it still wouldn't be enough.

TEN MINUTES LATER, the three of us walked out of the cafe together. By the time I boarded my overnight flight to London later that same evening, our photos were all over social media along with a few headlines proclaiming: Acadian Storm is Getting Back Together. Dean and Shiloh Back Together. In one photo, Dean had his arm around the back of my chair, and it looked like he was about to kiss me. That wasn't what was happening but that was how it looked. And sometimes appearances were the only thing that mattered.

All I could think about on my flight was whether Brody had seen the photos or read the captions. And if he had, would he have even cared?

Would it have been better if I'd never even met him?

For six weeks, I'd been living in a bubble. Now the bubble had burst, and I was being thrown back into the real world. My world. My life. It wasn't in Texas. Never had been. It was probably for the best that Brody hadn't told me he loved me. Why offer false hope? Better to cut the ties now before either of us got in too deep. Before he got dragged into my world.

But my God, I missed him so much.

"Shiloh. Shiloh. Shiloh." The crowd chanted my name, raising goose bumps on my skin and sending shivers up and down my spine. This feeling never got old. I looked out at the sea of people, shoulder to shoulder in a field in Somerset, England. How had I gotten here? Headlining at Glastonbury. Standing under the spotlights of the Pyramid Stage. Flags from different countries waved in the light breeze and even though the sky was overcast, I was lit up from within.

The energy was palpable. Electrifying. Adrenaline zinged and fizzed through my veins. I sparked to life, feeling invincible. Like I could conquer the world.

"Hello Glastonbury! Are you ready to rock and roll?"

My question was met with cheers from the crowd.

I was on top of the world. Untouchable.

I forgot about everything except for the music. My guitar screamed and shivered in my hands, like an extension of my body, the music coming from somewhere deep inside my soul.

This was the high I chased. This was why I could never give this up. Today, I was adored. If only for a little while.

CHAPTER TWENTY-SEVEN

Brody

As soon as I walked into The Roadhouse, Colleen set a bottle of Bud on the bar and poured a shot of whiskey. This bar hadn't changed a bit in the twelve years we'd been coming here. The music was country, the memories weren't all good, and the women were easy. Over the years, I'd gone home with too many of them and had almost always regretted it the next day. Beer goggles. That's all I've got to say on that.

"The drinks are on Austin." Colleen winked at me and I thanked her before pulling up a stool next to Austin.

"Who died?" I asked him. Austin was notorious for being a cheapskate. Whenever it was his turn to buy a round, he vanished.

"Drink up. Might be the last time I buy you a drink. Second thought, wait for Jude."

I looked over my shoulder as Jude strode in, to the tune of Johnny Cash's "I Walk the Line" blasting from the speakers. Knowing him, he probably thought that was his theme song.

Colleen set a beer and a shot on the bar for him too. He gave her a smile and leaned across the bar to give her a hug. Colleen's son, Reese had enlisted in the Marines with Jude but hadn't been as lucky. He'd died in combat, and Jude had been right there with him, so he and Colleen shared a special bond.

"What's the big news?" he asked Austin.

Austin lifted his shot glass, and we did the same, waiting to hear what we were drinking to. The last time he'd called us to celebrate at The Roadhouse, it was to tell us he was getting a divorce.

"You're looking at the newest member of Texas A&M's coaching team."

"Holy shit. Who did you have to sleep with to get that job?" I asked.

Jude laughed and we congratulated Austin then downed our shots. Only then did it really sink in. He wouldn't be here to coach the high school team this year. And Texas A&M was a two-and-a-half-hour drive from here. Doubtful he'd be commuting. "What about Walker? Is he cool with it?" *And what about Ridge?*

"I wouldn't say he's thrilled but he understands. I never wanted to work on the ranch. The only reason I came back home was to help out my old man. After he died, I felt like it was my duty to keep things running. But it's not the life I want. And now that my dad's gone, my mom's talking about selling."

I took a pull of my beer, thinking about his words. "You're looking to sell the ranch?"

He nodded. "It's a shitload of work. I don't gotta tell you that. She'd love nothing more than to sell it to you."

"Yeah, well, I don't have the money."

"I know, man. Just wish you did."

So did I. The Armacosts owned a couple hundred acres of beautiful land and it was practically in my backyard.

"I'd lend you the money if I had it," Jude said. And I knew he would. Same as I would for him. But neither of us would ever accept the offer. "Why don't you give Gideon a call. He might be able to figure something out."

"Nah. I've already asked him for too many favors."

"If... *when*... we decide to sell, I'll let you know before it goes on the market," Austin said. "You never know. Your fortune might change by then. You might win the lottery."

"I'd have to buy a ticket to win."

"When are you leaving?" Jude asked Austin.

"Beginning of August. When this opportunity came up, it was too good to pass up."

"You have to do what's right for you. The ranch was your old man's dream, never yours," Jude said.

Austin nodded. "Damn leg."

"Fucking lousy break." Jude shook his head and took a swig of his beer.

"Very punny." Austin laughed. At least he could joke about it now.

In college, Austin had been the wide receiver for Texas A&M. He was supposed to get drafted into the NFL but at the start of his final season, a fractured tibia and fibula ended his football career. That was how he ended up back on the ranch he'd wanted to get away from.

"So... how's your girl doing?" Austin asked me.

I took a pull of my beer. "I'm sure she's doing just fine."

"What the hell does that mean?" Jude asked, his eyes narrowing on me.

"You don't understand English now? You need me to translate?"

"I don't understand Brody talk. Because it sounded like you don't have a fucking clue how she's doing."

I shrugged one shoulder. It had been four days since I

dropped Shiloh off at the airport and walked away from her. Since then, I'd kept myself busy—always plenty of work to be done on a horse ranch, thank fuck—and hadn't discussed this with anyone. Which was how I wanted it to stay. "Why would I? She's gone."

Brody and Austin exchanged a look. Then Austin rubbed his hands together. "Hell yeah. Does this mean my wingman is back in action?"

I snorted. "I've never been your wingman."

"Whatever you say." His eyes wandered to the other end of the bar. "Check out the two blondes over there. Since I'm feeling generous, I'll let you have the first pick."

I looked over at the blondes. Big boobs and bigger smiles. Had this been a couple months ago, I might have been up for it. But now, neither of these girls did anything for me. I turned my head away and took another pull of my beer. "They're all yours."

"Well, shit. This sounds serious. But far be it from me to argue with you." Jude and I watched Austin swagger over to the two blondes and introduce himself.

"Hello ladies, this must be your lucky day."

"What a douche," Jude and I said in unison and then we both shook our heads and laughed.

I finished my beer and set the empty bottle on the bar. "I'm out of here."

"Me too. I told Lila I was just stopping by for one."

It was a miracle he could stop at one drink now. Just went to show how far he'd come.

On the way out we said goodbye to Austin. He was holding court, flirting with both girls, and it hit me all over again that this had been my life. Meaningless hook-ups with random girls I'd met in a bar. Now it struck me as so fucking sad.

Jude and I stopped next to my truck which was parked next

to his white one. On the side, it said Team Phoenix, with the logo for his not-for-profit organization.

"I don't get it." He stared me down.

"What don't you get?"

"You finally found someone you love... who loves you... and you just let her go? Just like that?"

My jaw clenched. "What the fuck else was I supposed to do? She's in the middle of a world tour. I have no place in her life."

"Did she tell you this or did you just assume that?"

"She didn't need to spell out something that was clear as day."

"You didn't even discuss it with her, did you?"

"You're a pain in the ass." I yanked open my truck door and climbed into the driver's seat. He grabbed hold of the door to prevent me from closing it. "Let go of my fucking door."

"For once in your life, would you listen to me, you stubborn bastard?"

I crossed my arms over my chest and exhaled loudly. "Be quick. I've got somewhere I need to be."

"Bullshit. You don't have anywhere you need to be. It's a Friday night. Ridge is probably hanging out with his friends and Noah is at our house. So you're going home to an empty house. You know why you thought you were in love with Lila?"

"Fucking hell. Not this again. Move your fucking hand before I smash it with my door." He released his grip, and I yanked the door shut and turned my key in the ignition. Now he was hanging onto the frame of my open window. I exhaled loudly, communicating my impatience. "Let it go, Jude."

"You were scared. And you still are. That's why you clung to this notion that Lila was the girl for you. Because in your heart, you knew damn well she would never be yours. It was safe. You couldn't get hurt if you never put yourself on the line.

If you'd wanted Lila so badly you would have fought for her, the same way you fought for every other thing in your life that truly mattered to you. You've always been a fighter. It's who you are. So why do you think it is that you never fought for Lila?"

"Here we go. You never could resist the urge to play Dr. Phil. Too bad you don't know what the fuck you're talking about."

He huffed out a laugh. "I know you. I've known you for most of my life. Where do you think I'd be right now if I hadn't fought for Lila? I'd be a sad, miserable fuck still clinging to my wounded pride and not much else. Is it because you don't believe you deserve love? Is it because that asshole fucked you up so badly—"

"Don't fucking say it," I said through clenched teeth.

"Okay. Okay." He held up both hands. "Forget I said that. It was out of line. You deserve to be happy. And from what I've seen, Shiloh is worth fighting for."

Having said his piece, he backed away from my truck, and I drove away before he had a chance to say another word. Nothing good ever came of going to The Roadhouse. But his words had hit too close to home. I fucking hated it when he was right.

I WALKED into my empty house, grabbed a beer from the fridge and turned on the TV. After flipping through the channels and not finding anything I wanted to watch, I turned it off and went to visit my horses in the last of the evening sun.

Last week, I'd moved Dakota into a pasture with Cayenne and her filly, Phoenix and she seemed to enjoy the company. But even so, as soon as she sensed my presence, she turned her head to look at me then slowly made her way over to the fence. She hung her head over it, and I rubbed her forehead and behind her ears. It had taken months for Dakota to trust me enough to touch her like this. Now she loved the massages I gave her.

"Why would a girl like Shiloh, with the world at her feet, want a guy like me?" I asked Dakota, stroking her neck in long fluid motions, my mind drifting back to another time and place.

"Jesus don't love you, boy. Ain't nobody here gonna help you or hear your prayers. So you best do what I tell you to and keep your mouth shut about it."

I kicked and I screamed, and I punched. The leather of his belt left welts on my skin, and he stuffed a dirty rag in my mouth to stop my screams.

"I like 'em feisty. Makes it more fun."

Nobody heard my prayers.

"Hey bro."

Ridge's voice snapped me out of my reverie. Why the hell was I thinking about that now? I scrubbed my hand over my face, trying to erase the memories. Then I turned my head to look at him, my eyes narrowing on his split lip and bruised cheekbone.

"You've been fighting?"

He shrugged one shoulder. "No big deal."

"Who'd you get in a fight with and why?"

"Doesn't matter."

"Matters to me. Someone giving you a hard time?"

"Don't worry about it. I can hold my own in a fight. Been doing it all my life."

Ridge and I were born and raised fighters. You could take someone out of a shitty environment and give them a good home, do everything in your power to make their lives better, but you could never erase the past or change history no matter how much you wanted to. "You wanna talk about it?"

"Nope."

His gaze was trained on the horses in the pasture. "I think she needs you, man." At first, I thought he was talking about Dakota. But she looked okay to me. "I don't know what the deal was with you two but for what it's worth, I could tell she made you happy. That's gotta count for something, right?"

With that, he turned and walked away. When he was a few feet away from me, he turned and walked backward. I thought he was going to say more about Shiloh, which seemed to be a hot topic this evening. "You'll probably be getting a call from Patrick soon."

"Why?"

"I quit my job." He turned around and kept walking away with his back to me.

I pinched the bridge of my nose then strode after him. "What the hell happened?"

"Don't worry about it. I'll find another job. I never wanted to work for him anyway. And I'm not gonna be on the goddamn football team either. Team sports aren't my thing. As soon as I graduate, I'm getting out of this two-horse town. Texas sucks balls."

I grabbed his arm and spun him around to face me. "You wanna tell me what the hell happened to change your mind about everything?"

He stared at me with a stony expression. "Guilty until proven innocent, right?"

"What the hell are you talking about?"

"Ridge." I looked over at Patrick as he strode toward us. "You wanna tell me why the hell you took off like that?"

"You wanna tell me why the first one who gets blamed is the white trash kid from the wrong side of the tracks?"

Patrick planted his hands on his hips. "I had to question everyone."

Ridge huffed out a laugh. "But you didn't, did you? You automatically assumed it was me. You accused me in front of *everyone* on that building site. So fuck that. I'm done with you." He stalked away, his shoulders squared.

"Hold up." Patrick grabbed his arm to stop him. "You mind telling me where you got the money to buy all that sound equipment you had delivered this morning?"

Sound equipment? This was news to me. Patrick picked up Ridge for work every morning, so that must have been when he saw it.

Ridge shook off his hold. "Yeah, I do mind. None of your goddamn business. I told you I didn't steal anything, that I'd never steal a goddamn thing from my own family. You should have taken my word for it. That should have been good enough. But you're just like all the rest of them."

Ridge strode away and I didn't try to stop him. This time, he had every right to walk away. I glared at Patrick. My jaw was clenched so tight my molars felt like they might crack. "Why the hell would you do that to him?" I gritted out.

He crossed his arms over his chest. "Do you know where he got the money?"

"No." Although I had some idea. "But you should have taken him at his word. You should have put your faith in him."

"He's been known to steal in the past. And he's Shelby's boy, through and through. Looks just like her."

As if that justified his actions. I shook my head, disgusted with this conversation. "Now I remember what it was like growing up under your roof. Funny how Kate had never made me feel like I was my mother's son, but you always did."

"Hey now. That's not fair. I raised you the same as I did my three sons."

"Keep telling yourself that. I was *never* treated the same. And the only reason you took me in was because Kate insisted on it."

"That's a goddamn lie. As soon as I got the call, I drove out to Odessa to get you."

"When I was ten years old. What about all the times before that? When Shelby called you asking for help but you told her to sort herself out? Where the fuck were you then?"

"You were too young to remember any of that."

"I heard and saw a lot of shit when I was a kid. I wasn't too young to remember. I remember it all. But this isn't about me. It's about Ridge." I pointed my finger at him. "You owe him an apology and I want you to do it in front of all the people you accused him in front of. Until you make this right, you're not welcome on my land or anywhere near my house or Ridge."

I strode away.

"Who do you think you're talking to?" he called after me.

His words stopped me in my tracks. I could have kept walking. Could have kept my mouth shut. But fuck it. I had plenty to say and I'd been holding my tongue for far too long. Growing up, I was scared that if I confronted him, he'd kick me to the curb so I'd kept my mouth shut, harboring a resentment I'd thought was long gone by now. But nope, still there.

I wasn't a kid anymore and this was as good a time as any to get this off my chest. Slowly, I turned to face him. "I'm talking to my Uncle Patrick. My mother's brother who never lifted a finger to help until the social worker called and forced his hand. I'm talking to the man who brought his Marine buddy home for a visit and introduced him to his younger sister. My mother and Ridge's mother. She was only fifteen. You want to talk about that? You want to talk about how nobody in your family called it what it was? *Rape*. You think that might be the reason Shelby turned to drugs? You think that might have had something to do with how fucked up she was?"

For a few seconds, he stared at me. Too shocked to speak. Until he pulled himself together. "How do you even know about that?"

He couldn't even deny it because he knew it was the goddamn truth. This would have been laughable if it wasn't so fucking sad. "Like I said, I heard a lot of shit when I was a kid."

"I never wanted anything like that to happen to Shelby."

"But it did. And you and your asshole Marine father covered it up so your asshole Marine buddy wouldn't get in trouble. Oorah fucking rah."

"I didn't know."

"Bullshit."

Patrick shook his head. "I didn't find out about that until years later."

"It doesn't matter. You could have done something to help her. She was your sister. You were always preaching the importance of family and yet... you turned your back on her."

He stroked his jaw, considering my words. "You've never forgiven me for that."

Whenever I thought about the hell he could have saved me from by coming to my rescue sooner, and maybe even Shelby, no. I'd never forgiven him for that. "If you were in my shoes, would you have forgiven and forgotten?"

He lifted his chin and squared his shoulders, his gaze never wavering. "No. I've never been one to let things go so easily."

At least he was honest about it. "Well, there you go. You raised us to be the same as you. Make things right with Ridge." I walked away, leaving him to stew on his actions. It was too late for me, but it wasn't too late to make things right for Ridge.

Did I hate Patrick? No. He'd raised me and had tried to do the best he could. But he'd failed my mother who had been eight years younger than him. According to my mother, she'd been kicked out of the house when she was seventeen. At nineteen, she became a mother. My father never married her. Always called me Shelby's bastard. Unfortunately, he and my mother couldn't seem to stay away from each other. Which was how we ended up living in Lafayette, Louisiana off and on until I was eight years old.

When I'd told Shiloh there was no shame in giving up her baby, I'd meant it. I used to wish my mother would have done the same.

But Shiloh was nothing like Shelby.

With me, Shiloh had been good and true and honest. Besides Noah, she was the best thing that had ever happened to me.

Shiloh made me happy, and I'd like to think I'd made her happy too. And fuck, I missed her more than I should have. More than I'd ever care to admit.

I CLIMBED the stairs to the back porch of the guesthouse and sat on an Adirondack chair, my feet propped on the banister, my eyes on the lake. The guesthouse had been booked for most of the summer. New guests were arriving tomorrow but tonight it was empty. I slid my phone out of my pocket and did something I'd promised myself I wouldn't. I Googled Shiloh's name and scrolled through photos of her at Glastonbury earlier today. She was wearing a tiny black dress, thigh-high boots, and winged eyeliner, lips painted dark purple. The sky was overcast, the crowd shoulder to shoulder, and anyone could see she was in her element. She felt right at home on that stage in front of all those screaming fans. Bastian Cox joined her for the encore, and they sang "Damage" together. He looked like

Johnny Depp a la "Pirates of the Caribbean." His black eyeliner was almost as thick as hers and he wore a black fedora, a ripped T-shirt and silver rings on every finger. The fact I'd noticed all those details just went to show how closely I'd studied those damn photos.

A glutton for punishment, I kept scrolling, kept searching for clues to her life away from here, *away from me*. I stopped at a photo of her with Dean the douche Bouchon. It looked like they were having coffee at an outdoor café. His arm was around her and they were deep in conversation. I stared at the photo for a good five minutes. Had she gotten back together with Dean?

Fuck. I shut it down and pocketed my phone then stared at the lake through the trees. The stars were shining, and the moonlight glowed on the water. If Shiloh were here, we'd be naked and swimming in the lake. But she wasn't here. She was five thousand miles away. She might as well have been living on a different stratosphere.

Come back to me, Shiloh.

The problem was I hadn't fallen in love with the rock star. I'd fallen in love with the girl from the Louisiana Bayou. I'd fallen in love with the girl I'd skinny-dipped with in a cool lake and went horseback riding with at sunrise. I didn't know how to reconcile those two very different people.

But if I didn't try, if I didn't take the risk, I'd never know.

CHAPTER TWENTY-EIGHT

Shiloh

MY CELL BUZZED, dragging me out of my dream. Dammit. I rolled over and tried to fall back to sleep. I wanted to return to my dream. The one where Brody was walking through a sunlit field of wheat the same color as his hair. He'd been smiling. I'd called over my shoulder, *Catch me if you can.*

But the dream was lost, and he hadn't chased me like I'd hoped.

A few minutes later, when sleep wouldn't return, a thought infiltrated my foggy brain.

What if that had been Brody calling me?

I bolted upright in bed and flicked on the light then swiped my phone off the bedside table.

Brody.

My heart ricocheted off the walls of my chest. It had been one week since he left me in the airport. I took a few deep breaths and tried to contain my excitement. He'd changed his mind about us. He must have. Why else would he be calling? With shaky hands, I pressed call and lifted the phone to my ear.

"Hey Shy."

"Hey Cowboy." My voice sounded scratchy like it always did the morning after a performance. I cleared my throat and propped the pillows against the headboard then leaned against them and waited to hear why he was calling me at eight in the morning.

"I've been thinking... what if—"

"Yes." I cut him off, not waiting to hear what he was going to say. "Yes, yes, yes."

He laughed, a low rumble that reached deep inside me and made me feel all warm and tingly. It was so good to hear his laughter and his voice again. It felt like a million years ago since I'd last heard it. "You don't even know what I was going to say."

"I read your mind."

"And what was I thinking, Shiloh?"

I drew my legs to my chest and told him what *I* was thinking. "You were thinking that you missed me. That your life is emptier without me. You were thinking that our six weeks together was one of the best times in your life and you don't want it to end. You were thinking... what if we called and texted? What if you were to fly to the ends of the earth just to spend a day or two or ten with me? What if you met me in London and New York and L.A. and all the other towns and cities in between? And what if every song I sang was just for you? What if... what if... what if..." I let my voice trail off.

My words were met with silence. I squeezed my eyes shut and held my breath, waiting for his response.

After a few agonizing seconds, he finally said, "I guess you really are a mind reader."

Relief washed over me. I released my breath and the

tension in my body. "I miss you, Brody. It's so good to hear your voice."

"Right back at you. Where are you waking up today?"

"It's Monday. This must be Dublin." I walked over to the windows and drew the curtains, letting some light into the room—a modern space with blond wood, white Egyptian cotton bedding, and plush gray carpeting. Dublin was overcast, the sky hazy gray and cloudy.

"What are you doing right now?" I asked him. I threw open the doors, letting the fresh air into the temperature-controlled room and stepped onto my private balcony. The temperature was cooler here than it had been in Texas.

"Right now? I'm picturing you in bed wearing one of those silky numbers."

I looked down at Brody's T-shirt. I'd stolen two of them and the flannel shirt I took from the tack room the night Phoenix was born. "Turns out I'm wearing an old T-shirt. Sorry to burst your bubble."

"Yeah, well, that's the thing about having a good imagination. I can picture you any way I want."

I took a seat on a mint green cushioned lounger. Tucking my legs underneath me, I watched a ferry churning up the water of the River Liffey while I listened to his voice in my ear. I pictured him on the ranch with his horses, the sky so big and blue, the rolling hills so green, the sun shining on his dirty blond hair and suntanned skin.

"Like, right now I'm picturing you naked with my head between your legs," he said. "Fucking you with my hands and mouth and tongue. Biting your swollen clit. Licking you from slit to crack and everywhere in between. Mmm... I can taste you on my tongue. Sweeter than honey. Smoother than whiskey. My very favorite dessert."

His words had me squirming in my seat and clenching my

thighs. Damn you, Brody. "Did you call me for phone sex?"

He chuckled softly. "Nah. I called to thank you. But you shouldn't have spent all that money on sound equipment for Ridge."

Brody didn't sound angry, probably because I'd done it for Ridge. And Brody cared about his brother's happiness. "It was my way of saying thank you after what he did for me."

"You didn't owe him anything."

"I wanted to do it. I had to talk him into keeping it."

"You talked to Ridge?"

"He texted me."

He was quiet for a beat. "He's thinking he wants to be a DJ now."

"Ridge can be anything he wants."

"Yeah, he can. Are you doing okay, Shy?"

"Better now that I'm talking to you."

"What happened with Dean the douche?"

Dean the douche. Accurate. "Did you Google me?"

"Shouldn't have but yeah, I did."

My shoulders sagged in disappointment. I wouldn't have expected Brody to resort to those measures. "So instead of calling me to ask how I was... instead of getting the story first-hand, you thought you'd search the internet for answers?" I couldn't hide the hurt and anger in my voice.

"Like I said, I never claimed to be all that smart."

"I'll tell you everything you want to know. But just do me a favor and don't look me up again. Everything gets twisted, you know?"

"Yeah, I know. I was a dumb shit for getting my information from the internet. Won't do it again. Now tell me what happened." He paused. "Unless you're busy... didn't even think to ask if this is a good time."

"It's a perfect time." I was meeting my personal trainer at

nine, so I had an hour to myself. "I had to stop myself from calling you at least a hundred times," I admitted, spinning my thumb ring around with my index finger. "Maybe more."

"What would you have said if you'd called me?"

"I would have said that you're a bonehead for letting me go."

"And you would have been right."

I smirked. "I usually am."

He laughed at that one.

Curiosity prompted me to ask, "What made you change your mind?"

"I came to the conclusion that you're worth fighting for. And what we had was never *just* sex."

I leaned back against the cushion, my lips tugging into a smile, my stomach flipping. God, he had no idea how happy those words made me. "Took you long enough. I could have told you that from the start."

"Nobody likes a smart-ass," he growled. I laughed. "Now tell me about Dean the douche."

"I'll tell you about Dean if you promise to set a date for when I can see you next," I countered.

"Deal."

My brows shot up in surprise. He'd answered without a moment's hesitation. "Wow. That was easy," I couldn't resist saying. "What's the catch?"

"No catch. I already made up my mind before I called."

"What exactly did you make up your mind about?"

"That I was going to spend as much time as I could with you. And try to figure out a way to make this work."

My heart stuttered and I held my hand over it. Why couldn't he have said that in the airport and spared me a week of heartache?

"Now start talking," he prompted.

I sighed. Brody was protective, so I already knew he wasn't going to like this. But I told him the whole truth, repeating most of the conversation I'd had with Dean and Landry at the café in L.A. When I finished telling my story, I waited for him to gather his thoughts and speak.

"Let me get this straight. You're going to be on tour for three months with your *ex-boyfriend?*"

I heard the accusation in his tone and didn't appreciate it. "Yes. But Dean and I are over. Our relationship ended long before I left him. This is just about the music."

"Uh huh. Keep telling yourself that."

I bit my tongue and refrained from reminding him that he'd left me in the airport with no hope for a future together. That wasn't the point. My relationship with Brody had nothing to do with my decision to help out Landry. "I'm not doing this for Dean. I'm doing it for Landry. He's my only family. He's my *brother.*" Surely that was something Brody should understand. He would do anything for Ridge. "And I owe him so much," I added.

He was quiet for a few seconds. "Yeah, I get that he's family. But if he's making you feel like you owe him for being a half-decent brother and doing what *any* older brother would do—"

"He doesn't," I cut him off, immediately jumping to Landry's defense. "It's not like that. This is just me saying that I owe him a lot."

"Well, good. Glad to hear it." Although he made it sound like he was the opposite of glad, his tone brusque like he'd already made up his mind about Landry without ever having met him.

"You don't feel like Ridge owes you anything for taking him in?" As soon as the words were out, I wanted to retract the question.

"Hell no. He doesn't owe me a damn thing. Does he feel that way? Did he say anything to you?"

"No," I said quickly, trying to reassure him. Clearly, this was my issue, and had nothing to do with him and Ridge. "He never said anything like that to me. And I know you'd never make him feel that way. Ridge thinks you're pretty great."

Brody chuckled. "Pretty sure he never said that. You're just putting words in his mouth now."

I smiled a little. "I'm good at reading between the lines. It's what he wants to say but guys aren't so great at sharing their feelings with each other."

"Thank fuck for that."

I laughed. "Can't handle all those pesky emotions, huh?"

"Yeah, yeah. Enough about me. Tell me what your day looks like."

"Hmm, let's see. I'll eat breakfast. Oatmeal, fresh fruit, tea with lemon and honey."

"Tea?"

"Decaf."

"A rock star diet."

I laughed. "Exactly. Then I'll work out with my personal trainer. After that, I'll probably have a healthy smoothie followed by a massage. This afternoon I'm flying to Glasgow. Then I have a soundcheck. I'll eat a light meal. Protein and carbs, no dairy. Then it's on to hair, makeup and wardrobe, and I'll get so nervous I'll think I'm going to throw up..."

"And will you?" He sounded so genuinely interested, like he wanted to know every detail of my day and how I spent my time. Which was so sweet. But I guess I had the advantage here. I'd been introduced to his world, but he'd never spent any time in mine.

"Not usually, no. It's just nervous jitters. Then it's show time."

"And how will that feel?"

"Like I'm ten feet tall and bulletproof." I smiled at the memory of Noah saying that to Brody the morning I showed up to make smoothies.

"I bet when you're up on that stage, you really are ten feet tall and bulletproof. I bet you shine so bright. You always did. Even when you were here in Texas without the stage lights."

God, sometimes he was so damn sweet. I didn't think most people got to see this charming side of Brody. A wave of longing washed over me, and I rubbed my hand over my heart. Now that he'd called me, saying all these sweet words, I missed him even more than I'd been missing him for the past week. "Wish you were here, Cowboy," I said softly.

"Me too."

We talked for another twenty minutes about everything and nothing until I had to say goodbye and get started with my day. Thankfully, he didn't circle back to the conversation about Dean and Landry.

Before we hung up, we decided to meet in London in August for the final week of my European leg of the tour. Two months seemed like a long way off, but it was the soonest he could get away and it would work out in our favor. I'd have him for an entire week, and even better, for the last four days we'd be in the south of France for a mini-vacation at the villa Bastian had rented while he was on tour in Europe. From there, I'd head to Rio and Brody would return to Texas.

Funny how I was already feeling sad about leaving him before we'd even had a chance to be together again. But as it turned out, our relationship would be a long series of hellos and goodbyes. It was one of the many things we had to learn to deal with if we wanted to be together. And we did. We both wanted it so much.

CHAPTER TWENTY-NINE

Brody

August - London

THE SILVER MERCEDES pulled up in front of the hotel and I stared at the imposing red brick façade complete with fucking turrets. According to the driver, we were in Knightsbridge. Might as well have been Buckingham Palace. A bellhop in red tails and a black top hat stood on the hotel steps in front of a hanging basket of geraniums. I felt like I was going to meet the Queen for tea.

"Good luck, mate."

I was starting to think I'd need it. I thanked the driver who'd been sent to pick me up at Heathrow after my overnight flight and grabbed my duffel bag from the seat next to me. It held everything I needed and fit the requirements for carry-on luggage. During my rodeo days, I'd traveled a lot, but I'd never been to London and never in my fucking life had I set foot in a place as fancy as this.

As per Shiloh's instructions, I'd texted her when I landed, and I'd texted her when we were five minutes from the hotel, so she knew to expect me. Here goes nothing.

A duffel bag slung over my shoulder, I walked through the front door, feeling every bit like the guy in that Garth Brooks song "I've Got Friends in Low Places."

Instead of my usual boots, I was wearing black leather high tops, but I still felt like I'd brought the dirt and grit of my Texas horse ranch with me. I stopped in the marble lobby under a funky chandelier, and searched for Shiloh, unsure what the fuck I was supposed to do next. A few guests were milling around near the reception desk, and a well-dressed older couple passed me on their way to the front door. The woman lifted her nose in the air like she'd smelled something bad.

"May I help you, sir?" a man at the reception desk asked in his prim and proper British accent. One look at me and I was pretty sure he'd already figured out I didn't belong in this gilt and marble lobby that reeked of money and breeding.

Before I had a chance to answer, a guy built like a tank, with a shaved head wearing a black T-shirt, made a beeline for me. "You must be Brody." I nodded. "I'm James." He lowered his voice and spoke in hushed tones so as not to be overheard by the other guests. "I'm on Miss Leroux's security detail. She asked me to escort you to her room."

A flash of annoyance crossed my face. Why hadn't Shiloh come down to greet me herself? *James* handed me a cardboard envelope containing a card key to the room. "Right this way." He ushered me up a marble staircase with a brass railing and we stopped in front of the elevators. James pressed the button and I stared at the doors, waiting for them to open.

"I'm sure I can find it on my own."

"I'm sure you can but I'll accompany you."

He stepped into the elevator with me and we rode up in silence. When the elevator stopped, we stepped out and I followed him down the carpeted hallway. Two men were in the hallway, and I assumed they were more security detail for *Miss Leroux.*

Before I had a chance to knock on the door, it flew open. "Cowboy!" She threw herself into my arms, damn near knocking me over.

From behind me, I heard someone chuckle. I lifted Shiloh off the ground and her legs wrapped around my waist as I carried her further into the room, my duffel bag hitting the floor with a thud.

"Thanks, James," she called over my shoulder.

"No prob—"

I kicked the door shut before he'd even gotten the words out and slammed her against the wall next to the door. She let out a little gasp. I crushed my lips against hers and slid my tongue inside her mouth, kissing her like I was starving and half-crazed from missing her. Both accurate. Fuck, she felt so good in my arms, her tits pressed against my chest, my dick getting hard as she rolled her hips and I ground against her sweet little body, my tongue stroking the most sensitive parts of her mouth. Diving in and exploring, reminding myself of the taste of her. Her jasmine scent washed over me, every bit as intoxicating as I remembered.

She pulled back from our kiss and cradled my face in her hands, both of us taking a few moments to catch our breath and take in any changes since the last time we'd set eyes on each other. I consoled myself with the knowledge that even though her surroundings were more luxurious, she looked the same as I remembered. Stormy grays fringed by thick black lashes, high cheekbones, and full lips lifted into a smile.

No, that's a goddamn lie. She looked even more beautiful than I remembered. I gave her a soft kiss on the lips. "Hi."

She laughed. "Hi." She touched my face, and I dipped my head to kiss the side of her neck and brush my lips over her jaw.

"I can't believe you're really here." Her voice was hushed.

Neither could I. Still holding her in my arms, I turned us around and advanced into the room, taking it all in for the first time since I'd arrived. It looked like a rich person's living room. A funky chandelier hung over the purple velvet sofa and gray velvet chairs arranged around a marble coffee table, and a gilt-framed mirror hung above a brown marble fireplace. Directly across from us, French doors opened onto a balcony with a white balustrade and the only view I could see from here was blue skies and a lot of green.

"Slumming it, huh?"

She laughed, her legs cinching more tightly around my waist and her arms wrapped around my neck. "Don't be fooled by my surroundings. I'm still the same girl you met in Texas. Nothing has changed."

But she wasn't the same girl I met. She was different here. And London... Paris... the South of France... it changed everything.

"I ordered room service."

The round table on the balcony was set for two, covered with silver lidded dishes. It looked as if she'd ordered every-thing on the menu. "Were you expecting an army?"

"I know how much you eat."

"I'm not hungry for food."

"What are you hungry for?"

"You." I dipped my head and kissed the corner of her mouth then tugged her bottom lip between mine and sucked on it.

"God, I've missed you so much. You have no idea."

But I did have an idea. I'd missed her so much in the two months we'd been apart that I didn't know how I'd lived without her for the past thirty-three years. "Why don't you show me how much you've missed me?"

In long strides, I carried her into the bedroom and tossed her onto the bed. When she hit the mattress, she bounced and grabbed my hands, pulling me down on top of her. Bracing my weight on one forearm, I slid my finger under the thin strap of her silk and black lace camisole. Today it was forest green, my favorite color. "Did you wear this for me?"

She gave me a coy smile. "Maybe."

"Well, as pretty as it is, it's gotta go."

She sat up and I ripped it over her head and tossed it to the floor then pushed her back against the mattress. Hooking my fingers in the sides of her silky shorts, I pulled them down her legs, freeing her of them. I sat back on my heels, taking a moment to drink her in, my gaze roaming over every inch of her bare skin.

"Are you just going to stare at me all day?" she sassed, her hands reaching for the fly of my jeans. I swatted her hand away.

"Told you I was hungry." Kneeling between her legs, I lifted her left foot and planted it on the bed then did the same with the right one and used my forearms to pin her thighs flat to the mattress.

"You're hungry. I'm offering you a whole buffet. Eat up." She motioned with her hand across her naked body.

"Mmm. So accommodating. Let's skip to dessert."

With my eyes locked on hers, I dipped down and took a small taste. My tongue brushed her clit, and she bucked her hips against my face, letting out a moan that shot straight to my cock. I flattened my tongue and licked her from slit to crack. "Fuck, you taste so sweet," I murmured.

She dug her fingers into my shoulders, her thighs shaking as I used my tongue and fingers and mouth to fuck her.

"Oh my God, Brody," she panted, her fingers pulling my hair, her body convulsing as I drove my tongue deep inside her walls, her muscles clenching around it.

"Yes! Fuck. Shit. Holy Mother of God."

My body shook with laughter at the words flying out of her mouth. Her thighs clamped around my head and I pried them apart again. With the flat of my tongue, I gave her a few shallow licks to bring her down from the orgasm. Then I kissed the crease in her leg and moved up her body, my hands following my lips over her curves and silky soft skin. Her hip bones. Stomach. Ribs. I cupped her full tits in my hands and guided one rosy nipple into my mouth then sucked on it.

"It's too much." But even as she said it, her hands slid into my hair and she held me against her chest.

I released her nipple and moved to the other one then up to her mouth, kissing her long and hard so she could taste herself on my tongue. "Too much. But never enough."

Her legs wrapped around my waist and she rocked her hips. "Why aren't you naked yet, Cowboy?"

Good question. I sat up and pulled off my T-shirt while she unzipped my jeans, her hand wrapping around my dick and squeezing, making it impossibly hard. I pushed her hand away and stood up then stripped off my clothes and settled between her thighs, fucking desperate to be back in my favorite place. Buried deep inside her.

In one sharp thrust, I drove into her, causing her to cry out. Fuck yeah. Her back arched off the mattress and she met me thrust for thrust while I pounded into her, relentless, my pace punishing. Her nails scored my back as I pulled out then drove into her again. Bringing my hand down to where we were joined, I rubbed her clit.

I pulled back to watch her face. Lips parted, eyes at half-mast, ink-black hair tumbling over her bare shoulders. "Come for me, Shy. Come all over my cock." Her muscles clenched around me and I rubbed her clit harder and faster. "That's it. Clench my cock with that sweet little pussy of yours."

"Oh my God." Her chest was heaving, our bodies slick with sweat in all the places where our skin touched. I pinched her clit and she cried out. Her legs, wrapped around my back, shook as I drove into her one more time, buried to the hilt, so deep I wanted to live there forever. I came on a roar that didn't sound human, and she milked an orgasm out of me that seemed like it would never end.

With a shudder, I collapsed on top of her and buried my face in the crook of her neck.

"God, I missed you," she said. "My big boy's got nothing on you."

I growled and bit her earlobe. She laughed and I rolled us both over so she was on top of me and not bearing the brunt of my weight. She pushed herself up on one elbow and peered down at my face then brushed my hair off my forehead with her fingertips. I grabbed her fingers and guided them to my mouth, sucking on them.

"Still hungry?" she teased.

"When I'm with you? Always. I can never get my fill."

I WAS LOUNGING on the bed, arms tucked behind my head, watching her get ready for our day out. Since I'd arrived two hours ago, we'd fucked twice and had taken a shower together in the marble bathroom as big as my bedroom. "I'd be happy to spend the day here. In bed."

"It's your first time in London. I want to show you the sights."

She was insistent on playing tour guide. But most likely that would mean I wouldn't have her to myself. Shiloh Leroux didn't just walk out the front door of the hotel and wander the streets. That had been impressed upon me earlier when I'd met her manager, Marcus. He'd stopped by when we were eating our breakfast on the balcony and had given me the distinct impression that he was less than thrilled I was here, taking up Shiloh's precious time. Within two seconds of meeting her slick manager in his designer clothes, I'd concluded that I wasn't a big fan of his either. He was a cog in the wheel of a big money machine, and Shiloh was the jewel in his crown. He couldn't afford to lose her.

"You've already given me a full tour." I pulled her into my lap and kissed the side of her neck. "And it was even better than memory served. I don't need to see anything outside this hotel room."

"We have until three o'clock," she said, ignoring my words as she scrolled through her phone, checking out all the hot London tourist spots. None of which I had any intention of dragging her to. The sun was shining, it was summertime in London, and all those tourist spots would be mobbed. "How about the Tower of London? Or the London Dungeon? Ooh... Camden Market is fun. We could do a Thames River cruise. Or we could—"

I took the phone out of her hand and tossed it aside. "How about we take a walk?" I figured it would be more low-key and easier for her to remain anonymous. Although how I'd ever thought that was possible was fucking beyond me. My hand coasted up her thigh and under the hem of her short cotton dress. It was white with colorful embroidery around the collar and the three-quarter length sleeves. She was so fucking perfect, her suntanned legs draped over my lap and her lips so lush and pink.

When my hand ventured farther up, dragging the material of her dress with it and landed between her legs, she shoved it aside. "Don't start or we'll be stuck in this room all day."

"I can think of worse things than being stuck in a room with you."

She jumped off the bed and offered me her hand with a smile. "Let's go for a walk, Cowboy."

She put on a straw fedora and sunglasses and away we went, breezing right past the security guys in the hallway and into the elevator that miraculously opened the moment I pressed the down button. As soon as the doors closed, I pulled her into my arms and kissed her lips, my hands roaming down her back and cupping her ass as her arms looped around my neck, our lips locked until the doors slid open. Then we cruised right through the swanky hotel lobby and out the front door, hand in hand.

Shiloh had a big smile on her face, like a kid on Christmas morning. She loved London. Loved cities. Loved the people and black cabs and the red double-decker buses, she told me.

We cruised past Harrod's and checked out the window displays as we passed them. Designer dresses and shoes that probably cost more than my truck. And it struck me that Shiloh could afford to buy anything in that window. And everything in all the other fancy stores we passed as we walked down Sloane Street. A shiny red Ferrari cruised past and Shiloh said, "Sugar Daddy anyone?"

I laughed. The dude behind the wheel had a combover and had to be at least fifty. The woman next to him appeared to be in her twenties. An unlikely couple. Which was exactly what I thought when I caught our reflection in the Tiffany's window. Shiloh looked like she belonged here. Even though her clothes were casual, and she was wearing ankle boots with a little dress that was deceptively simple, I wasn't fooled. They were designer items. As was the leather fringed handbag over her shoulder.

We were waiting at the crosswalk for the light to change when it happened. The fuck? I stared at a passing bus. Unlike the other red ones, this one was painted white and the billboard on the side of it featured Shiloh's face advertising the "Wrecked and Damaged" Tour. Her fucking face stared back at me from a bus in London.

She tugged on my arm to get my attention. My gaze swung from the bus to the girl next to me. A hat and sunglasses did nothing to disguise her, but I guess she felt safer with them on when she was out in public. Less exposed. But even if she wasn't famous, she gave off the aura of someone who was special. Someone who would make you do a double-take.

"We can cross now."

We crossed the street and walked in silence. She told me this was Sloane Square which meant jack shit to me. I glanced at the red brick facades around a small leafy square, the traffic circling it, the sun shining and the sky so blue but all I could see was her face on that billboard. I could feel her watching me, her hand still clasped in mine and she gave it a squeeze, trying to get my attention.

"Don't let it freak you out. I'm still just me. Your Shiloh."

My Shiloh. Was that what she was? Mine? "I'm not freaked out," I scoffed. It was a lie, but she didn't call me out on it.

She smiled. "Good. I don't want this to change anything. I don't want anything to get in the way of us being us, okay?" She chewed on her bottom lip, the worry setting in.

I tugged on her hand and pulled her aside to let people pass then leaned down and kissed her. "Don't worry about me. I'm not so easily scared off."

"You're made of tougher stuff."

"You know it, baby."

I looped my arm around her shoulder, and we continued wandering the streets of London. Past fancy boutiques and little shops that sold handmade chocolates, designer shoes, hats so fanciful I couldn't imagine where the fuck anyone would wear them.

She guided us down streets in Belgravia with big wedding cake houses from another century that looked like they came with a butler and staff. Then we walked down a cobblestone alley that she said was the Mews. "This is where the horses lived. Behind the big house." She gestured with her hand, playing tour guide.

The houses were small, painted in pastels, with hanging flower baskets outside their doors. Earlier, I'd glanced at a real estate agent's window and fuck me, even these tiny houses cost millions.

"I can't imagine any horse being happy to live in a house. Where's the pasture? Where's the open spaces?"

She shrugged one shoulder. "They were obviously city horses."

I checked my phone for the time. "We'd better head back."

She nodded and we made our way back to the hotel, down a different cobblestoned alley, another Mews.

From what little I'd seen, London was a beautiful city and unlike New York, the cab drivers weren't maniacs and didn't lay on their horns every five minutes. But never in a million years could I live in a place like this. To me, it still felt claustrophobic. Even though they had Hyde Park on their doorstep and green squares fenced in behind wrought iron, the air wasn't sweet and fresh, and everyone lived right on top of each other.

When we got back to the main street near the hotel, we

were ambushed by three girls carrying shopping bags. One blonde and two brunettes.

"I'm sorry but would it be okay if we took a photo with you?" the spokesperson of the group asked in her polite British accent. The girls looked to be in their late teens or early twenties, wearing skimpy dresses and sunglasses. They were young and pretty and Ridge would have been having a field day.

Shiloh flashed them a smile, but it wasn't the same one she used with me. It was bigger and brighter, and I wouldn't call it fake, exactly, but it was more wary. "Of course."

I stood back while Shiloh posed for photos with the girls.

"'Damage' changed my life," the blonde said. "I had this wanker for a boyfriend, yeah? And after I heard your song, I found the strength to break up with him. Best decision ever."

"He was a tosser," one of the brunettes said.

"I know." The blonde sighed. "But I loved that tosser."

"Someone better will come along," Shiloh said with a smile. "Someone who treats you right and appreciates you for exactly who you are." She aimed her smile at me and squeezed my arm, making it clear the words were intended for me. My first thought was, how the fuck had I gotten so lucky? My second thought was nobody had ever thought of me as someone better. But I wanted to be that guy in her life, the one who put her first and never took her for granted.

Shiloh was special, I'd known that from the start, and not because she was *Shiloh Leroux*. She was tough and resilient with a vulnerability that made me want to protect her from the big bad world. No matter how many times life knocked her down, she got right back up again and proved how strong she was. I don't know what I did to deserve her, but now that I'd found her, I wasn't going to let her go.

CHAPTER THIRTY

Brody

"WHAT THE HELL?" I stared at the paparazzi across the street. They were waiting outside the Mandarin Oriental and one guess who they were waiting for.

"Dammit. Who tipped them off?" she muttered. "I need to call James."

I took the phone out of her hand. "You don't need him. You've got me." I looked across the street at the assholes, my hands clenched into fists.

"Brody..." She looked up at me from beneath the brim of her hat.

"What?"

She took a deep breath and released it. "Okay, listen... we should have talked about this before. This is my world. You showed me yours and now I'm showing you mine. And you have to trust that I know what I'm talking about. You have to keep a cool head, okay? Ignore anything they say, tune it out, and keep walking."

How was this her fucking life?

As if she'd read my mind, she said, "You have to take the bad with the good, remember?"

I nodded once. I remembered. Didn't mean I had to like it.

"Let's go." I grabbed her hand, and we strode across the street. No use putting it off. Wouldn't make them go away.

"Remember what I said. Promise me…"

I squeezed her hand. "I promise." She ducked her head and we kept walking, ignoring the questions being thrown at us and the flashes of the cameras going off all around us. They were pushy fuckers and if she hadn't made me promise to keep my mouth shut, I would have been tempted to tell them all to fuck off. But I didn't want to cause her any trouble.

"How do you feel about Acadian Storm's newest member? Is it true that you and Ari Bell were sleeping together on your last tour?"

"What's your name, mate? Are you her new bodyguard?"

"Hey Shiloh. Over here. Are you and Dean trying to reconcile?"

My arm around her tightened like a steel band. When we finally made it inside, I grabbed her hand and we hurried to the elevator. It was only when the elevator doors closed, and we were safely inside that I took a deep breath.

"Are you okay?" I looked down at her upturned face.

"I'm fine. You can loosen your hold now." I loosened my grip on her hand, but I didn't let go. "Everything is fine. It wasn't a big deal."

But nothing about what had just happened felt okay. They were fucking vultures, preying on her, trying to get stories and photos. I had no idea how she lived like this but for the past five years, this had been her life. Her private life wasn't even her own.

"You get used to it. You can't let it get to you. You wouldn't believe the things I've been accused of." She laughed, trying to lighten the mood.

I'd fallen for a girl whose life was delved into for public consumption. A girl who lived in the spotlight. Who posed for photos with her fans and stopped to sign autographs. I'd fallen for a girl whose face was plastered on fucking billboards. Few things were sacred when you lived in the public eye. And that was what she'd been trying to protect Hayley from. The public scrutiny. The media. The gossips and newshounds all vying for a piece of juicy news that would sell their magazines and tabloids.

Guarding your privacy was a luxury Shiloh didn't have. For me, it was a necessity. I had too many skeletons rattling around in my closet. Too many things I never wanted anyone to know about me.

"If you want to be with me," she said when I swiped the keycard and opened the door for her. "You'll have to find a way to block it out. Please don't let this scare you away."

I heard the worry in her tone. When we got inside the room, I wrapped my arms around her and pulled her close, feeling like she needed my reassurance and protection. "It doesn't scare me away. But I hate that they feel like they have a right to hound you like that. It's fucked up."

She shrugged one shoulder. "The first time I came to London, it was different. I was a nobody, so I walked the streets without anyone recognizing me."

I kissed her lips. "You've never been a nobody, Shiloh."

"If you want to skip the soundcheck and the meet and greet, I won't be offended. You can hang out in the room and come for the show."

Was she out of her fucking mind? "Listen to me. I'm here for you. Not for the sights or the fancy hotel room. Just you." I wanted her to hear me and understand. "If you want me there..."

"I do but—"

"No buts. Where you go, I go. Show me your world, Shiloh. That's why I'm here."

She smiled, the worried crease in her forehead smoothing out at my words. "Well then, you'd better hang on tight. It's going to be a wild ride."

———

AND SHIT, she hadn't been joking. It was crazy to witness how much went into one concert. Shiloh Leroux had an entire crew who took care of everything from the lighting to the sound to the stage set. She had a catering crew, wardrobe and makeup, a PA, her manager and tons of other people running around making sure everything ran smoothly for tonight's performance.

Later that night, I stood backstage and I watched Shiloh perform magic. Because that was what it was. Pure fucking magic. You'd never guess she had been nervous earlier. As soon as she'd stepped onto the stage and the lights had come up, she'd transformed before my eyes. I wasn't watching the girl I'd gotten to know in Texas. I was watching a rock star who had thousands of fans eating out of the palm of her hand as she strutted across the stage like she owned it, her voice soaring, reaching the ears of every person at this sold-out concert, her image projected from a big-ass screen so everyone could see her.

"Are you starting to get it?" Marcus asked as I stood, trans-fixed, listening to her voice as she sang, her voice sultry and sexy like the lyrics. "... late night drives with his hand on my thigh and the cherry glow of his cigarette burning brighter than the midnight moon." And I fucking hated it that she was most likely singing about the douche. I was imagining them driving around L.A. with his fucking hand on her thigh and I wanted to break his fingers for ever having dared to touch her.

I was a sick, jealous fuck.

"Get what?" I asked finally, turning to look at Marcus after the last note of the song played out.

"Do you see the transformation?" He waved his hand at the stage. He looked like your typical L.A. smooth-talking slickster with his black V-neck T-shirt, slicked-back hair and an expensive watch on his wrist.

I saw the transformation, it was impossible not to, but I had no intention of admitting it to him.

"You had your fun in Texas. But that wasn't her real life. This is who she is. So I suggest you disabuse yourself of the notion that she'd ever be happy to settle down in a small town with a rancher and have a bunch of kids."

Just as I'd suspected, Marcus saw me as a threat. I glanced at his wedding band and pitied the woman who had said yes to him. He didn't look like the type of guy to keep a woman satisfied in or out of bed. "Never crossed my mind. But I bet it scares the shit out of you, doesn't it? I bet you lose sleep at night worrying that she'll wake up and leave you."

"I'm good at my job, Brody. I do whatever I can to make sure she reaches her potential. She has everything it takes to get to the top and stay there. But I think you're missing the point. Can you honestly imagine her ever walking away from this?"

"Wasn't aware that was ever in question. She has no intention of giving this up and I'd never expect it."

"Huh. So where do you fit into her life?" He stroked his jaw, like he was giving this serious thought even though it was none of his goddamn business. "You're here for what... a week? And then you're on a plane back home? I give your relationship three months and that's being generous."

"Next time I want your opinion, I'll ask for it. In the meantime, kindly get the fuck away from me so I can listen to Shiloh without having to deal with your bullshit."

He did as I asked and put some distance between us. But my jaw was clenched so tight I couldn't enjoy the show. I rolled out my shoulders and tried to loosen up so I could focus on Shiloh. And I tried my damnedest not to let his words get under my skin. But try as I might, I couldn't stop thinking about it. I knew there was some truth in his words. I'd have to be an idiot not to notice that we lived in different worlds.

Where *did* I fit into Shiloh Leroux's life? And how the fuck were we going to make this work?

CHAPTER THIRTY-ONE

Shiloh

THREE DAYS, two cities, and three sold-out concerts later, we arrived in Saint-Jean-Cap-Ferrat for our mini-vacation. I was tired but chilled, looking forward to four days of sun and relaxation. The sky was deep blue and cloudless, the Mediterranean glittering turquoise in the sunshine. All the colors were saturated and sun-drenched, the sea air fresh, and the music piping from the speakers was summertime breezy. We'd picked up a rental car at the Nice Airport and Brody had navigated the winding curves and narrow roads along the coast with expertise.

"Jesus," Brody said under his breath when the pink villa came into view. It was at the end of a narrow private drive that hugged the sea, tucked away behind pines and palm trees.

I had no idea why Bastian had rented a villa on the Cote d'Azur when he claimed to hate the sunshine. But that was Bastian for you. An enigma. You never knew which version of Bastian you'd get on any given day. When he was laid low, he barricaded himself inside a dark room and sometimes didn't come out for days. When he was flying high, he was the life of the party.

Today he greeted us at the front door, barefoot and shirtless in swim trunks, and ushered us inside the red damask-papered foyer with a sweeping gesture of his hand. A black chandelier hung from the ceiling and potted palms flanked an ornately carved sideboard.

Bastian embraced me and kissed me on each cheek. He smelled like tobacco and sunscreen, his olive skin a few shades darker than the last time I'd seen him at Glastonbury. "You've been getting some sun. I'm so proud of you," I teased, giving him a little slug on the shoulder. He was lean but cut, thanks to the workouts Hayden forced him to do.

He waved his hand in the air theatrically then plucked a thin brown rollie from behind his ear and lit it. Took a drag and blew smoke into the air. It smelled like black licorice. "When in the south of France."

He turned his attention to Brody, his gaze roaming over him from head to toe, not even trying to hide the fact he was checking him out. I'd already warned Brody that Bastian might get flirtatious with him, but it didn't mean anything. Hopefully Brody would be cool with it and not get freaked out. This was uncharted territory, not a test exactly, but Bastian was my closest friend and I really wanted them to like each other. I didn't know how Brody would react to Bastian who had a flair for the dramatic.

I hung onto Brody's arm and gave it a little squeeze as if he needed my support.

"So this is your cowboy?" He narrowed his eyes as he took a drag of his cigarette. "I can see why you'd be tempted to ride him hard. But mate, you look more like a beach bum than a cowboy." Bastian's mouth turned down in disappointment. "I was hoping for tight Wranglers and a Stetson at the very least."

"Sorry to disappoint. Left my boots and spurs at home."

"Next time bring them with you. And the ropes and chaps too while you're at it." Bastian winked.

Brody snorted, and ran his hand through his hair, not quite sure what to make of Bastian. A lot of people felt that way, but Bastian's heart was in the right place, he'd been a good friend to me over the years, and that was all that mattered to me.

He extended his hand to Brody and they shook. "How's it going, mate?"

"Yeah, it's all good." Brody looked down at me then back at Bastian. "Thanks for having me."

I caught the wicked gleam in Bastian's eye. "I haven't had you—"

"Stop," I said, laughing. "Ease him in gently."

Bastian flashed us a smile. He was in a good mood today. "And it looks like I never will." He held his hand over his heart. "I wouldn't want to break my little chanteuse's heart."

"No fucking clue what a little chanteuse is but glad to hear it," Brody said gruffly.

"Another one that got away." Bastian sighed dramatically and waved his cigarette in the air, indicating we should follow him. Brody grabbed both of our bags and Bastian led us through the house, pointing out the chef's kitchen, the living area decorated with Oriental rugs, red sofas, antiques and tapestries, all of which he declared hideous. But the view of the Med from the French doors that opened onto a terracotta courtyard and lush gardens more than made up for the décor.

He told us there was a wine cellar and a cinema room downstairs. Then led us up a staircase, with floral wallpaper and oil paintings on the walls. Whoever decorated this house obviously wasn't going for a beachy theme. We followed him down a long Oriental carpeted hallway with more oil paintings and antique gold wall sconces.

At the end of the hallway, Bastian opened the door to a huge bedroom decorated in muted browns, sienna, and ivory, an ornately carved canopy bed taking center stage, the French doors affording another spectacular sea view. The first thing I did was cross the room and throw open the doors to let the sea air in. I knew how much Brody craved fresh air and open spaces. He joined me by the French doors and stepped onto the wrought-iron balcony, surveying the scenery. Down below, a few people were on loungers by the kidney-shaped pool, sipping cocktails. Hayden was talking to Cato, Bastian's drummer, and a stick-thin brunette who worked for the record label. She was topless. When in the south of France.

"Make yourselves at home, yeah?"

I turned from the French doors and thanked Bastian. He was standing in the open doorway, leaning against the door-frame, the thin cigarette dangling from his lips. "How many people are staying here besides us?"

"Depends on the day. Today it's six. Or ten." He ran his hand through his longish dark hair. He was wearing silver skull rings on every finger. "Fuck if I know. I'll leave you to it. The fridges are fully stocked and if you're hungry, Kristoff will sort you out."

Kristoff was Bastian's private chef. He always took him on tour with him, so he didn't have to eat 'shit food.'

The door closed behind Bastian, and I joined Brody on the balcony and wrapped my arm around his waist. "Are you okay?"

He slung his arm over my shoulders and pulled me close to his side. "Right as rain."

His eyes were on the sea, and I searched his profile, not sure if he was telling the truth. "Are you sure?"

He turned his head then and gave me a soft smile. "Stop looking so worried." He touched my nose with his index finger. "I can hold my own."

"I know. I just..." I gnawed on my lower lip, not sure what I was so worried about. Except that I wanted him to be happy, I guess.

"Hey. Listen to me." His tone was serious, and he held my gaze, wanting me to hear his words and believe him. "I'm just happy to be here with you. It doesn't matter to me if we're in a swanky villa in the south of France or in the middle of Bumfuck. I want *you* to be happy. I want you to spend time with your friends and chill out and relax. I've seen how grueling your schedule is. You work so fucking hard and you barely have a minute to yourself. Stop worrying about me. Just relax and enjoy yourself. Okay?"

I smiled. "Okay. Beach or swimming pool?"

"Let's try out the bed first."

Before I had a chance to reply, he lifted me off the ground and tossed me over his shoulder. I was laughing when my back hit the mattress. He dove on top of me and rolled us over, so I was on top, straddling him.

"Ride me hard, baby. Like I'm your bucking bronc."

That made me laugh harder. He grabbed the back of my head and pulled me down for a kiss that tasted like the cinnamon gum he was chewing earlier.

I wanted to tell him that I loved him, because I did, but maybe it was too soon to say the words. So I didn't.

THAT NIGHT there were eight of us for dinner. A round table had been set up on the rock cliff above the sea and we ate under the stars. Kristoff served us silver platters of fresh seafood on a bed of shaved ice. Lobster, prawns, crabs, clams, raw oysters. I looked up from the langoustine I'd just de-shelled and found all eyes on me.

"Holy shit," Brody said with a laugh.

"What?" I looked around the table.

Cato laughed. He was stunning. Dark skin stretched over high cheekbones, his smile so white. His girlfriend Anya was on his right, a cool Nordic blonde with ice blue eyes who had just landed her first big role in a sci-fi movie set to start filming this fall. Next to her was her sister, Astrid, equally beautiful and seated on Bastian's right, commanding his attention.

Bastian loved to surround himself with beautiful people. In the past, I would have been uptight. So busy watching Dean that I wouldn't have been able to fully enjoy myself. I'd be worried about how much he was drinking and how many trips to the bathroom he made to get his fix.

Unlike Dean, Brody's eyes never strayed to the other women, and he didn't make me feel like I had to worry he'd end up fucking someone else's girlfriend, one of Dean's specialty moves.

"How long did it take her to clean that shellfish?" Cato asked Brody.

"Two seconds. Tops."

"She's got hidden talents," Hayden said.

Brody grinned and took a swig of his beer. "Don't I know it."

I sucked the juices from the tail of the langoustine while Brody watched me, an amused look on his face. "There's plenty of food. No need to eat the tail."

"I grew up on the bayou. Do you have any idea how many crawfish I've cleaned in my life? Besides, you have to suck out the juices. That's where all the flavor is."

He dipped his head and whispered into my ear. "You did a

damn fine job of sucking my *juices* earlier. Pretty sure my fingers are still coated with yours."

My cheeks flushed with heat. Must have been from all the sun I caught this afternoon. It had nothing to do with the blow job I gave Brody on the private beach. We'd found a little secluded spot behind some rocks, although I couldn't help wondering if the yachts and boats passing by had caught some of the action. That had been part of the fun though.

Now, I fed Brody the white fleshy part of my langoustine dipped in aioli and he licked my fingers when he was done, a groan escaping his lips and shooting straight to my core. Nobody at the table so much as blinked. In the world of rock and roll, anything goes.

BRODY'S HAND was on my thigh, under the skirt of my short cotton dress, and I was buzzed from the chilled white wine, my belly full of fresh seafood. Drunk on life and high on Brody's nearness. I was talking to Jocelyn, the stick-thin brunette seated on my left. "Your cowboy is hot," she said, lifting her wineglass to her lips, her eyes on Brody as she took a sip. "And he's crazy about you."

I smiled. "I got lucky."

"Tell me about it. I meet all the assholes. But then, I guess you'd know a little something about assholes."

I didn't comment. Brody's hand was under my dress, his fingers stroking the cotton between my legs. When his fingers brushed my clit, I squirmed in my seat, my thighs clenching.

"How are you going to deal with being on tour with your ex? And how does *he* feel about it?" She jerked her chin toward Brody who was talking to Hayden, all chilled and casual, as if his hand wasn't performing magic under the table.

His thumb pressed against my clit and my breath hitched. Oh my God.

"Umm..." Jocelyn had asked me a question and now she was waiting for an answer, but it was hard to think straight when I was about to detonate. "He's cool with it." I cleared my throat and hoped that was true. "And Dean and I... we'll just keep it professional."

She arched her brows. "Won't that be difficult?"

"Not for me. I'm not in love with him anymore."

I didn't know how Brody could have possibly overheard us while he was talking to the others, but he chose that very moment to move my panties aside and slide his fingers through my wet heat. I squeezed my legs together, my chest heaving as he rubbed my clit. Seconds later, the orgasm crashed over me and my body jerked, my legs shaking.

Oh my God. Job done, he removed his hand and I tried to regulate my breathing then picked up my wine glass with a shaky hand and took a fortifying sip. Nothing to see here. Cool as a cuke.

I took a deep breath. *Wow.* Who needed dessert?

The sound of Brody's laughter reached my ears, and I turned my head to look at him. I hadn't been sure if he would get along with Bastian and Hayden, the only two people at this dinner who *truly* mattered to me. But any fears I'd had vanished earlier when Brody and Bastian struck up a conversation. A little while later, Bastian had given Brody his seal of approval. *"He's not a wanker."*

Brody caught me watching him and turned his smile on me, his voice low and intimate, his eyes locked on mine. "All good?"

I smiled, half-drunk, still in a state of post-orgasmic bliss. "Couldn't be better."

And it was true. I couldn't remember a time when I'd been so happy. All my worries that Brody would hate my life, or that he'd feel like he didn't fit in, or that he wouldn't know how to handle Bastian and the paparazzi and the chaos of a world tour, had vanished. I guess I should have given Brody more credit. But Marcus had put a lot of doubts in my head. Had made me question whether it was a smart move to invite Brody to join me for a week.

"This tour is a big deal, Shiloh. You can't afford to screw up," Marcus had said, as if I needed a reminder. It was my career, my tour, my responsibility to give the best damn show I could every single night. "I don't want you to be distracted. You have a lot on your plate without having to cater to a guy who knows nothing about the music industry."

Even my publicist, Naomi, had called from L.A. to discuss it with me. As if Brody's arrival needed security clearance. "I don't want to be blindsided. Is there anything I need to know about him?"

That had pissed me off. Like she fully expected me to dish the dirt and share all the intimate details of Brody's private life. "Only that I care about him and he's a good man." I'd answered. "That's all you need to know."

The funny part? When I'd told my management team that I wanted Acadian Storm to open for me in North America, nobody had even questioned it.

"I thought you would have put up a fight," I'd told Marcus.

"Acadian Storm is a good draw. Your fans will love it. And that's what it's all about, Shiloh. Keeping the fans happy."

It was a funny thing in the music industry. Short of murder and rape, everyone loved to watch rock stars behaving badly. As long as they gave the fans what they wanted, they were golden. And Dean... he knew exactly how to please a crowd. He was, after all, the master of deception. And I knew why Naomi and Marcus were thrilled at the prospect of having Acadian Storm open for me. It created the type of controversy that sold tickets and got everyone talking about us. While I was with Acadian Storm, some of our best concerts were on the nights when we were all at odds with each other. Our fights and anger had fueled our music and critics had declared our performances 'electrifying.'

But I didn't want to think about Dean or Acadian Storm or the rest of my tour. I wanted to enjoy my time with Brody while I had him right here next to me. It made me so happy to see his smile and listen to his laughter.

When someone is important to you, their happiness is a priority. And Brody was so important to me. I never wanted him to feel like he didn't have a place in my life. I could handle our time apart as long as we were on the same page, striving for the same thing.

CHAPTER THIRTY-TWO

Brody

It was day three in the big-ass villa on the Mediterranean. For the most part, it had been chilled and relaxed. I got along fine with Bastian and Hayden. Bastian was what I'd call your quintessential rock star. He claimed to be a recluse, yet he surrounded himself with people. He loved Shiloh but not in a romantic way, thank fuck. And Shiloh had assured me they'd never slept together. Now that I was here, I could tell they hadn't and that they really were 'just friends.'

This afternoon, it was just me and Shiloh poolside. A few of the others went out on a boat and Hayden had informed us that Bastian was hiding out in the cinema room and didn't want to be disturbed. I thought I was bad, but the dude was moody as fuck.

"You thirsty?" I asked Shiloh.

"Mmm." She nodded, her eyes hidden behind dark sunglasses, a sheen of sweat on her skin as she baked under the

French sun. She was wearing a tiny black bikini held together with strings I'd untied with my teeth earlier.

She lowered her sunglasses, and her grays met my browns. In the sunshine, her eyes looked clear, not stormy. For a brief moment, I felt like she could see straight into my soul and see every dirty secret I kept buried inside.

Had we met before? In another lifetime?

I shuddered, trying to shake off that weird deja vu feeling I got around her sometimes. Nobody had ever gotten under my skin like she did. Nobody had ever made me feel like I'd found the one thing I'd been searching for all my life. Sometimes, I didn't know what the hell to think about that.

"Is there any water out here?" She glanced at our empty bottles on the table.

"I'll go inside and get some."

"Thanks, babe."

I chuckled. "Anytime, *babe*."

I grabbed my phone from the table under the umbrella and left her lounging by the pool. The house was quiet, no signs of life, as I strode across the terracotta tiles, swiping my thumb over my phone. Lila's face appeared on the screen, her smile big and wide. It was four o'clock my time and nine o'clock their time. Since it was a Sunday morning, the whole family was together. "Hey B. Just in time. You have to see this."

She flipped the camera and I watched Levi take a few steps toward Noah who was kneeling on the living room floor with outstretched arms. I smiled at Levi's attempts to walk. He looked like a drunken sailor. Jude was off to the side, phone in hand, no doubt taking a video.

"Come on, Levi," Noah said. "You can do it." Noah kept moving back, widening the space as Levi lurched toward his big brother, a big gummy smile on his face. He fell down, his knees hitting the rug and for a minute it looked like he was about to burst into tears.

"Cowboy up, Levi," Noah said, making me chuckle. That's my boy. "You can do it."

After a second, Levi pulled himself to his feet and practically ran the rest of the way into Noah's arms. "You did it! You'll be playing football and riding horses with me in no time." Noah pulled him into his arms and carried him around, hooting and hollering, "Yeah, you did it!" The way he was carrying that poor kid, with Levi's face smashed against Noah's stomach and his legs dangling, it couldn't have been comfortable.

Jude and Lila were laughing, celebrating a milestone in their son's life. Jude took Levi from Noah and held him up in the air above his head. The picture returned to Lila who was still smiling like a proud mother.

"Did you tell him the news yet?" Jude said in the background.

Lila's smile grew wider and it didn't take a rocket scientist to figure out the good news she was about to deliver. "We're having another baby."

"Well, damn. That's a shocker." She rolled her eyes. "When are you due?"

"February."

I did the math. She'd waited until she was three months to announce the news to me. It shouldn't have mattered to me one way or the other, but I couldn't help feeling hurt that she'd waited so long. Should have been used to it by now. She'd done the same thing when she was pregnant with Levi.

"Congratulations."

Her smile dimmed. "Thanks. I would have told you sooner but..."

"I get it. You wanted to wait to make sure everything was okay."

She nodded and changed the subject. "How's it going? Are you having a great time?"

"Yeah, it's all good." I leaned against the granite counter in the big-ass kitchen, the stainless-steel gleaming and the air scented with freshly baked bread compliments of Chef Kristoff. A massive bowl of fresh fruit sat on the island. Next to it was a cheeseboard with at least twelve different cheeses, French baguettes and hand-dipped chocolate-covered strawberries the size of my fist. This was how the other one percent lived. "Is Ridge doing okay? Not giving you any trouble, is he?"

"He's been great. We love having him here. He's still asleep. But he's working this afternoon."

Ridge was staying with Jude and Lila for the week. He and Patrick still hadn't mended the rift, and back in June after their falling out, Ridge had gotten a job at the barbecue joint we took Kate to for her sixtieth birthday. "Does Noah wanna talk?"

"To his daddy? Always," Lila said with a soft smile as if she felt I needed the reassurance that my boy hadn't forgotten about me.

She called his name and within seconds his face appeared on the screen. I held the phone in front of me and listened to his voice as he chatted a mile a minute, filling me in on every little thing that had happened in his world in the three days since we'd last spoken.

"... and Mommy took me shopping for back-to-school clothes. Oh, and I got a new pencil case and a Spiderman back-pack. It's black and red with a big, gigantic black spider on it." His eyes widened and I smiled. He'd gotten into Marvel movies this summer and Spiderman was his favorite. "I'm gonna be in the first grade."

"What a big shot."

That cracked him up. But all I could think was, *where the hell had the time gone?* How could he be going into the first grade already? I still remembered him as a baby, taking his first steps like Levi just had. I rubbed my hand over my chest. Whenever I was away from him, I missed him like hell.

We talked for another five minutes and then he said he had to go get ready because they were taking Levi on a bear hunt. And they were having a big picnic at the lake. So we said our goodbyes and I told him I'd see him the day after tomorrow. Kids were always eager to get on to the next thing, so saying goodbye was never hard for Noah like it was for me.

I slid my phone into the pocket of my boardshorts and walked over to the glass refrigerator that held the drinks. It was filled with imported beers, soda and exotic juice drinks. Champagne, white wine, rose. I grabbed a bottle of beer and a couple waters from the bottom shelf then straightened up.

"Oh yeah."

No sooner were the words out of his mouth when two hands groped my ass and squeezed. The bottles dropped to the ground. I spun around, grabbed the asshole by the collar and slammed him against the wall next to the doorway. My fist smashed into his face and I kept on punching, so fucking blind with rage, I couldn't see straight, let alone stop to consider what I was doing.

"Brody! Stop. What are you doing?" She grabbed my arm, trying to pull me away from the guy. "Let him go, Brody."

Her voice finally reached my ears and she yanked on my arm and dragged me off the guy.

"The fuck was that?" the guy snarled, wiping his bloody lip on the back of his arm. "He a friend of yours?" he asked Shiloh.

"Yes. He's... my boyfriend," she replied, her voice faint, unsure like she had no fucking clue how this could be true. "God, Kevin, I'm so sorry. Are you okay?"

"What are you sorry about? You weren't the one punching the shit out of me." His eyes narrowed on me. "Looks like your boyfriend is homophobic."

My jaw clenched and I tried to breathe through my nose, but I couldn't get enough air into my lungs. My stomach was churning and if I didn't get out of this kitchen right the fuck now, I was going to lose my shit. I brushed past Shiloh, not even sparing a glance for the asshole, and strode out of the kitchen.

Shiloh chased after me and grabbed my arm to stop me. "Brody... what happened?"

I shook my head and shook off her hold, striding away. I needed some space. The walls were closing in on me. Once I got outside, I grabbed my keys from the table next to the lounger and strode back the way I'd come, right past Shiloh and out the front door. She chased after me and grabbed my arm. I shook off her hold on me.

"For fuck's sake. I need some space," I gritted out.

"Just help me understand what happened."

Fuck that. I couldn't even begin to help her understand. I couldn't even look at her face, not wanting to see her hurt and disappointment.

I climbed into the car and slammed the door shut. Then I took off and left her standing there.

I drove as fast as I could, trying to outrun my memories. Windows rolled down, music blasting, I tried to drown out the noise in my head. Too bad it didn't work.

IT WAS ALMOST midnight when I let myself into the room. Shiloh was sitting on the balcony, silhouetted in the moonlight, a glass of wine in her hand. I stood in the open French doors and stared at the moonlit sea.

"Where did you go?"

"Doesn't matter." I raked a hand through my hair. "I was just driving."

"For eight hours?"

I moved around her and leaned against the banister, facing her. Even in the moonlight, I could see that she'd been crying. "Why have you been crying?"

She sniffed and wiped away the tears with the palm of her hand. "I've been crying for you."

"For me? Why would you cry for me?"

She shook her head a little, not willing to tell me why. "What happened?"

I cleared my throat. I couldn't tell her the truth. I didn't want her to look at me differently. But I owed her something. "I'm not homophobic."

She nodded. "I know you're not. Otherwise, I could never be with you. I just wanted us to enjoy our time together. I should have never brought you here. It would have been better if it had only been the two of us, spending time alone."

"That's not how real life works. And none of this is your fault. You had this trip planned before you ever met me. I didn't mean to fuck everything up for you." Fuck, it was the last thing I'd wanted.

"You hate this life, don't you?" Her voice sounded so small and so sad.

"No. I don't hate it."

She laughed. "Sure you don't. We're so different here. I want things to be the way they were..."

"That's not how it works."

"I know. I guess I'm greedy. I want my cake and I want to eat it too."

"And I want you to have your cake with whipped cream and a fucking cherry on top. Shy, I don't want to screw everything up for you. I want you to have everything you've ever wanted."

"Does that mean I can have you too?"

"You still want me? Even after the stunt I pulled today?"

"You think I'm going to stop wanting you just because you drove away and left me for a while? That's not how it works."

"No?"

"No."

"Why did you beat up Kevin?"

His name was Kevin. Fucker. "He grabbed my ass." I shrugged one shoulder like it was no big deal. "Caught me by surprise. Guess I overreacted."

"No, you didn't. Nobody should have their ass groped by a random stranger. You felt violated."

"Is that how it felt for you that night when you were sixteen?"

"Yeah. But I didn't want to let on how much it had freaked me out." She set down her wineglass and stood up from her chair then came to stand in front of me. She took both of my hands in hers and gave them a squeeze.

"Do you feel that?" she asked quietly.

I looked down at our joined hands. How could I not feel it? There was an electric current running between us. "What is it?"

"It's me. And you. Just... don't freak out when I tell you this, okay?"

I huffed out a laugh. "If you're going to tell me you're a witchy woman, I already know that."

She let out a breath. "I can feel your vibrations, Brody. And I know... I know that something bad happened to you. I can feel it, but I can't see it clearly... I..."

I yanked my hands away from hers. "Just fucking stop doing that."

"I can't help it." She began crying again. I knew she was crying for me and I fucking hated that. I pulled her against me so she couldn't see my face, and she wrapped her arms around my middle, resting her cheek against my shoulder. I held the back of her head, my hand sliding into her hair and rested my chin on the top of her head. We stayed like that for a few long moments, her hot tears soaking the cotton of my T-shirt.

"Don't cry for me, baby. Please don't."

"I can't help it. I love you, Brody." She pulled back and lifted her face to mine. "I love you," she whispered.

It seemed like a strange time to say those three little words. I loved her too, I knew I did. But I wasn't ready to say it. Today I'd felt like I was still that same fucked-up kid I'd been all those years ago. I'd relived a memory that I thought I'd dealt with a long time ago. All because some asshole grabbed my ass. But this time I was bigger, and I was stronger, and I didn't have to take shit from anyone. Nobody got to touch me without my fucking permission.

"Are you in love with me?" she asked.

"What do you think? You're the mind reader."

She laughed a little. "Will you fight for me, Brody? Will you still be here when the going gets tough?"

"I'm right here."

"But you walked away from me earlier. I wanted to be with you."

"I came back. And I'm right here."

Too many people in Shiloh's life had let her down, and I didn't want to be another one of those people. I didn't want to fail her.

"What happened to you, Brody?" she pressed. She wasn't about to give up on this.

"Nothing. I just went for a drive..."

"Not tonight. What happened to you when you were

young?" I tried to pull away, but she grabbed my hand. "Brody. Please. I need to know."

"No, you don't."

"I trusted you with my secrets."

"This is different."

"How?"

I hung my head and rubbed the back of my neck. "I don't want you to look at me differently. I don't want you to..." Pity me. Cry for me. Think of me as weak or a victim. None of which I had ever wanted to be.

"Treat you like a victim? Feel sorry for you because you had a shitty childhood?"

There she went, reading my fucking mind again.

"I want to know you. I want to know everything about you. You're the one, Brody. My Maw Maw did a reading for me on my thirteenth birthday. And I asked her if I'd find my one true love. She said our paths would cross many times... you saved me in that bar when I was sixteen. You did that for me before we'd even met. And you rescued me again when I hit that deer and felt so lost. You were there. Let me in, Brody. Let me be the one you confide in and share your secrets and dreams with."

"You think I'm your one true love?"

"I know you are. I've known it from the start."

I took her hand and led her inside. "Come to bed."

"Why?"

"So I can talk to you in the dark."

CHAPTER THIRTY-THREE

Shiloh

We were lying on the bed in the dark, his face shadowed from the moonlight. Him on his back and me on my side facing him, our hands clasped, fingers entwined while he told his story, his gaze directed at the ceiling.

"When I was nine, I was put in foster care. The couple that took me in were really religious. They had crucifixes all over the house, always said their prayers before meals. Church every Sunday. They had two kids of their own. Both special needs. And the mother... she spent all her time looking after her kids. Both parents did volunteer work at the church. The father... he was a youth leader." Brody huffed out a laugh. "When I was a kid, I was scared of the dark. If I didn't have a nightlight, I couldn't sleep. I kept picturing myself in a closet, suffocating in the dark and it freaked me the fuck out. The first time the man came into my room, I'd been living there for about a month. It was the middle of the night and I woke up and it was dark. I was freaking out, screaming and sweating and shit. And he came into my room and locked the door and said everything would be okay. That he'd protect me. It was so fucked up."

I took a deep breath and kept silent, waiting for him to go on. I had an idea of what was coming. I'd seen it in a vision. But even so, it was impossible to prepare yourself to hear something so horrible. His voice was low, and the room was quiet and while he talked, I got the sense he'd mentally removed himself from the words he was saying.

"That night, he laid down with me on the bed and he held me. It felt wrong. But I didn't say anything. After that night, he started visiting me more often. Always at night. In the dark. When the rest of the house was asleep. And it started small. Just a touch. As time went on, he got bolder and his hand ventured inside my pajama pants. And he always told me not to tell anyone. Until one night he pulled down my pajama pants and I knew... I fucking knew what he was going to do."

I felt like I was going to vomit. I wanted to run away and block out the words, but I couldn't do that. I'd asked Brody for the truth and he was giving it to me. It was a gift and a burden. There was nothing I could do to change what happened to him, and I felt so helpless, but I needed to hear it all.

I squeezed his hand, letting him know that I was right next to him, that I was here for him.

"And he did it. He molested me when I was nine years old. Not just once either. I used to lie in bed, wondering if tonight was the night he'd come to my room. I tried locking the door. Barricading it. I did everything I could think of, but nothing stopped him."

My cheeks were wet with my tears and my heart hurt so fucking much to think there were such horrible people in this world who would do that to an innocent nine-year-old. To *my* Brody who despite it all, had grown up to become a good, true, honest man. How had he survived that? I couldn't even begin to imagine it.

I pushed myself up on my elbow and touched his face.

"Don't cry for me, Shiloh."

"I can't help it. I want to kill that fucker." He gave me a small smile. "Please tell me you got revenge."

"You don't think I'd let something like that go, do you?"

"No, I don't. Is he dead?"

He laughed, although I didn't see anything funny about this or what I'd said.

"If it had been left up to me, he would be. Right after high school graduation, I decided to go and exact my revenge. Damn Jude. He was waiting in my truck that morning and refused to let me do it on my own. He was scared I was going to kill the guy and end up in prison. I don't know what I'd planned to do when I got there. All I knew was that I wanted to fuck him up. Make him pay for what he did to me. I had no proof. Nothing that could put him away. It had happened ten years before and had never been reported. I knew I wouldn't have a leg to stand on. Who were they going to believe? Me or a guy who volunteered at the church and took in foster kids and showed the world that he was a good father to his two special needs kids? But at the time, I didn't give fuck. I would have rotted in prison rather than letting him get away with it.

"But Jude... he was thinking more rationally. He came up with a plan. Put the guy's photo on a flyer and alert everyone to the danger lurking right there in their own neighborhood. We made thousands of copies and distributed them everywhere. All over the neighborhood where he lived. The churches. Schools. Grocery stores. Parks. The places that mothers with young children went."

"So you didn't fuck him up? You didn't hurt him?"

He scrubbed a hand over his face. "I didn't say that."

"Good. I want to hear that you cut off his dick and fed it to him. That man doesn't deserve to walk the streets."

"You have a violent streak, you know that?"

"I know. I just... I want justice for you. What did you do?"

He stroked his jaw. "We delivered all those flyers. But we did it *after* we tied him to a kitchen chair, and I carved his chest up like a Halloween pumpkin."

"You did?"

"Yeah, I did. I used Jude's Swiss Army knife and I made sure if he ever took off his shirt, everyone could read the words. Child Molester."

"And whatever happened to him?"

"His wife turned him in. When she found out, she was so disgusted she called the cops on him. A few years later, she wrote me a letter. Tracked me down at one of my rodeos to give it to me. Guess she was too busy taking care of her kids to realize what a monster she'd married."

We were quiet for a few moments and I thought about his story, about the way that disgusting, vile man had abused him. And how the woman had been married to a monster without even knowing about it. Although I questioned how that could be true. Wouldn't you know the man you were married to? Maybe not. People were fucked up. You never truly knew what they were capable of.

"Thank you for trusting me with your truth. It means so much to me, Brody. And I don't look at you any differently now than I did yesterday. I don't see you as a victim. I think you're the strongest man I've ever known. You're ten feet tall and bulletproof."

"Yeah, well, it fucked me up for a long time. But after that crazy peyote trip, I decided it needed to stay in the past where it belonged. Like Walt said, if you give something the power to destroy you, it will. The mind is a dangerous place. You have to stop dwelling on the things you can't change and just keep pushing forward. Some days it's easier than others."

How could I have ever thought Brody was closed off? He was the most honest person I'd ever met. And I'd been right about him from the start. He'd made it through the storm, through all the horrible things in his life, and he'd come out on the other side of it. A little worse for the wear, damaged, but not broken. And I thought it said a lot about his character that he'd found the strength from within to ride out that storm and not let it destroy him.

I kissed his mouth, and he held the back of my head, parting the seam of my lips with his tongue and sliding inside, exploring the deepest recesses. That night I fell a little bit harder for the man who fixed broken horses and for the boy who had been forced to see the ugly side of life too young. When he made love to me, our bodies moving in perfect rhythm, my heart beating in sync with his, his strokes powerful and his muscles taut under my fingertips, I wondered if he felt the same as I did. Like we'd found our way home.

UNTITLED

"Stay away from those Brazilian cowboys." He had pushed me up against the side of the car for a goodbye kiss that was on the verge of turning into something more. I wanted to grab his hand and drag him back inside with me. My flight wasn't until tomorrow but his was today.

"There's only one cowboy for me."

He gave me one more kiss before he released me. "See you soon."

"Six weeks." God, it felt like an eternity.

"Nah. I'll see you on my phone screen. I'll have to use my left hand. Keep my right hand free."

I played coy like I didn't know what he was talking about. "And why would you need to keep your right hand free?"

He leaned in close and pulled me flush against him, his voice low. "So I can stroke my rock-hard cock while I watch you on your hands and knees, fucking your pussy with that big boy that doesn't even come close to doing what I can do. But when in Rio…"

With that, he gave me a sexy wink and released me. I sighed as I watched him drive away, already missing him. Dammit. And he'd left me aching for more.

———

He texted me from Paris, pissed off that I'd upgraded him to First Class.

Don't pull that shit again.

I'm a rock star. I'd do whatever the fuck I want, and you'll thank me for it. I punctuated it with a wink emoji.

Next time I see you, you're going to get a good spanking.

Promises, promises. You're all talk.

CHAPTER THIRTY-FOUR

Brody

Six weeks later, Shiloh flew to Austin to spend four days with me. Since I'd last seen her, she'd FaceTimed me from every capital city in South America, Mexico City, and L.A. where she'd been for the past few days.

Unfortunately, she arrived on a Sunday afternoon and as soon as everyone got wind of her arrival, they all wanted to spend time with her.

"I promised Lila I'd come to Sunday dinner," Shiloh said when I picked her up at the airport, our kiss more chaste than I'd have liked but Noah was with me. He drew a picture especially for her, a girl with black hair and a guitar. He also drew a cowboy that was supposed to me, cupcakes and tacos. Shiloh had given him a big hug and brushed the tears from her eyes.

I groaned. "Let's skip the family dinner."

"I love your family and I want to see them."

"Did you bring me a present?" Noah piped up from the back seat.

I scowled at him in the rearview mirror. "People don't need to give you a present every time they see you."

"Not every time. Just when they go away. Like when you were a rodeo man, remember? And after you got back from being with Shy Viv, remember?"

"Yeah, I remember." I didn't mention that my gift-giving had been fueled by guilt. Every time I left him, I felt like shit about it, so I never came home empty-handed. It had gotten to the point where he expected it, and since I never wanted to disappoint him, I always delivered. "But Shy doesn't need to bring gifts."

"Of course I brought you a present," Shy said. "I'll give it to you when we get to your grandma's, okay?"

"Okay. Did you bring Daddy a present too?"

"Okay, little man. That's enough from you. It's not cool to ask for presents."

Shiloh laughed. "I brought extra special presents for your daddy." She lowered her voice for my ears only. "You'll be getting yours later tonight."

"Yeah? Well, as it turns out, I've got a nice *big, juicy* something special just for you."

She laughed. "Juicy, huh?"

"Mmhmm. It's the gift that keeps on giving. All night long. Never quits. No batteries needed." I side-eyed her. "Not too late to change your mind about Sunday dinner."

"Tempting. But we're going. I want to see everyone."

Of course, she did.

Twenty minutes later, I pulled into the driveway at my aunt's and uncle's house. The porch was decorated with pumpkins and cobwebs and the old scarecrow was hanging in the front yard.

I opened Noah's door and he raced across the lawn. The air was crisp and cool, and it smelled like woodsmoke, the gold and orange and red fallen leaves raked into a big pile. I met Shiloh next to the passenger door. She was wearing a black hoodie and ripped black jeans with her Army boots, like the first time I'd picked her up at the airport.

"How's Jesse?" she asked as we crossed the front lawn.

Noah got a running start and threw himself right into the middle of the giant pile of leaves. I picked him up and tossed him in the leaves again.

"He's been better."

Jesse wasn't doing great, and that was putting it mildly. I'd never seen my youngest cousin like this before. The weekend after I flew back from France, he crashed his bike and broke his back. The surgery had gone well and physically, he was healing fine. He had to wear a back brace for another month or two and then he was starting physical therapy.

But his spirit was broken, and that was sad as fuck to see, especially when it was Jesse who had always been the charmer, the one most likely to put a positive spin on any situation. Now he was having to face the fact that his career might be over. Not to mention, the other shit he'd gone through when he found out his girlfriend had been cheating on him. Two weeks ago, he'd moved back to Texas and the few times I'd seen him he'd barely spoken a word let alone cracked a smile.

So yeah, Jesse was not in the best place right now. Hopefully, with time and distractions, he'd make it through to the other side.

EVERYONE WAS happy to see Shiloh again and peppered her with questions all through dinner. Steaks on the grill, corn on the cob, cheesy potatoes, and apple pie. We sat at the long farmhouse table Patrick had given Kate for her birthday and Shiloh regaled them with tales of the road. A natural storyteller, she had everyone at the table charmed, including Levi who was sitting in her lap, grabbing fistfuls of her hair and yanking on it. She laughed and kissed his chubby cheeks like it was the most adorable thing ever.

Jesse didn't even join us for dinner which said a lot. He was family-oriented and usually loved spending time with everyone. Ridge wasn't there either. He made it a point to work every Sunday so he could skip the family dinners. But he'd ended up joining the football team, and Patrick never missed a single Friday night game. None of us did if we could help it. We all showed up to cheer him on and even though he claimed to hate football, he was pretty damn good at it. He was big, he was strong, and he was fast. All raw power and brute strength.

By the time we left, it had gotten dark already, the days getting shorter.

"I've missed this place so much," Shiloh said when we walked through my front door. Buster was there to greet us, wagging his tail as Shiloh kneeled down to rub behind his ears. "Can we go see the horses?"

"That's the first thing you want to do?"

She smiled but it wasn't her genuine smile. "We have four days. And um, there's something I need to talk to you about."

I didn't like the way that sounded. "What is it?"

"Let's go see Phoenix."

My eyes narrowed on her. She smiled again and looped her arms around my neck, giving me a kiss, a promise of more to come. She was hedging, which was unlike her, so I knew it had to be something big. Something I wouldn't like. I grabbed a flashlight from the kitchen, and we walked to the barn, my arm around her shoulders, Buster trotting along beside us. Earlier, I'd brought Phoenix in from the pasture and put her into a stall, knowing Shiloh would want to see her. She whinnied in greeting as if she remembered Shiloh and was happy to see her.

I kept meaning to sell Phoenix, but something always stopped me. And that something—*someone*—was standing right next to me, stroking Phoenix's neck.

"What did you need to tell me?" What if she was pregnant? Wouldn't be the worst thing in the world, but I knew it wasn't something she wanted, so that might explain why she was gnawing on her lip, like she was scared to say the words. "Whatever it is... we'll deal with it."

She closed her eyes briefly then turned to face me. "When I was in L.A., I did something..."

My body tensed. Fuck. No. I took a step back. "Did you sleep with your ex-boyfriend?"

Her eyes widened. "What? No. God, I'd never do that." My momentary relief disappeared as soon as she uttered the next words. "I... told Dean I'd record a duet with him."

"*You what?*"

"I agreed to record a duet with Dean," she repeated as if I needed to hear the words again. "In December, I have six weeks free and I... I said we'd do it then."

Un-fucking-believable. I couldn't wrap my head around this. I reared back like I'd been sucker-punched which was how it felt. "Why the hell would you do that? Why would you give him what he wants?" I needed some explanation as to why she would have thought this was okay.

She closed her eyes and blew out a breath then raised her eyes to mine. "I'm sorry, okay? I just... the song is... it's amazing, Brody."

I huffed out a laugh. I didn't give a shit if it was Grammy-worthy. "*Your* songs are amazing. Why the fuck would you go into a recording studio with *him*? You don't need him, Shy." *You've got me.* But I wasn't a musician, and I couldn't write *amazing* songs or play a guitar or do jack shit when it came to music.

"It'll be good for my music career."

"Who the fuck told you that?" I grasped her chin in my hand and lifted her face to mine. "Is someone forcing you to do it? Your management team? Your publicist? The record label?"

"Would it make you feel better if I said yes?"

"I don't know, Shy. Is it the truth? Because that's all I want from you. The fucking truth."

She took a couple steps back, putting distance between us and folded her arms over her chest. "You want the truth? I love you. How's that for a truth?"

"What does that have to do with this conversation?"

"Why can't you say the words?"

The fuck? "Oh, hold on." My eyes narrowed on her. "Are you saying you agreed to record a duet with the douche because I haven't said three little words yet?"

Her shoulders sagged. "No. I'm going to record a duet with Dean because the song is good, and I don't want..." She released a breath and shook her head a little.

"You don't want what? What don't you want, Shy? Fucking say it."

She lifted her head, her eyes defiant. "I don't want Ari Bell to sing that duet with him."

I stared at her for a long moment, letting the words sink in and trying to make sense of them. I knew who Ari Bell was. The newest member of Acadian Storm, the one the paparazzi were asking about in London. "Why? Are you jealous of her? Do you wish you were back with Dean?"

"No. God, no. It's nothing like that. I told you, I'm not in love with Dean. I don't care if he fucks her from here to Sunday. I don't want her to sing a song that's so personal to me.

Please... try to understand where I'm coming from." She was pleading with me to understand, but I didn't. I couldn't.

I raked my hand through my hair and blew out a frustrated breath. "Nothing about this is okay."

"I know. And I'm sorry."

I looked over at Phoenix. Shiloh moved closer to me and put her hand on my chest right over my heart. "I don't want to hurt you, I swear."

Yeah, well, it fucking hurt. But right now, I was more pissed off than hurt. "Let's just get this straight. Every time Dean comes up with an amazing song, you'll drop everything to record it with him? Every time Dean asks you for something, like opening for you at a concert, you'll roll over and say yes? What more will you give him when he asks for it, Shiloh? Will you spread your legs because he asked you to?"

"That's not fair and no. It's not like that."

"You sure about that? Because from where I'm standing, it's *exactly* like that."

"If Lila asked for your help, you would drop everything and run to her side. I know you would."

How could she even compare them? "That's different. She's been my best friend since I was ten. And she's the mother of my child."

"I've known Dean since I was seven years old. He's the *father* of my child. And he's my brother's best friend. So how is this any different to what you have with Lila?"

"I was never Lila's boyfriend. And I never abused her... not mentally or physically or emotionally. *That's* how it's different. Worlds apart." I strode away, leaving her behind.

"Brody," she called after me. "You think I don't know you're in love with her?"

I stopped in my tracks. "I'm not in love with her."

"But you were. When did that change?"

"When I met you."

Without turning back to look at her or see the impact of my words, I strode out of the barn, across my backyard and into my house.

Fuck love. I rubbed my hand over my chest to ease the ache. I would never be enough. She'd made that clear when she agreed to record a song with Dean. I didn't have to meet Dean to understand what he was doing to her. He was trying to win her back, using every weapon in his arsenal to draw her in. Today it was one song. In three months, it was a world tour. They'd be seeing each other every day. In each other's space.

And where would that leave me? I grabbed a bottle of whiskey and a glass from the kitchen and carried them into the living room then sank down on the sofa. Pouring myself a glass of whiskey, I flipped through the channels. I stopped at a documentary about African elephants being hunted for their ivory. It fucking killed me that people were so corrupt and greedy, caring more about money than the lives of these majestic animals. Buster rested his head in my lap, and I stroked his thick fur.

About twenty minutes into the show, I was on my second glass of whiskey when Shiloh joined me. I lifted the glass to my lips and took a swig, not even turning my head to look at her. She took off her boots and tucked her legs underneath her in the corner of the sofa. I could feel her eyes on me, not on the TV. I had four days with her, and this wasn't how I wanted it to go. But you can't always get what you want. We sat in silence as I drank my whiskey and watched the show all while she watched my face.

"Will you come with me on tour? If you do, you'll see there's nothing between me and Dean."

My jaw clenched. "Can't."

She sighed loudly. "I know. But if there was a way—"

I turned up the volume, effectively drowning out her voice. She moved next to me, grabbed the remote from my hand, and muted the volume. "Brody. Talk to me."

"I've got nothing left to say. Why don't you read my fucking mind?"

She took the glass out of my hand and helped herself to my whiskey. What next? Just cut off my balls while you're at it. I reached for the bottle. I didn't need a glass.

"I've missed you so much. I dream about you. I've been counting down the days until I could see you again. I don't want to lose you, Brody. It would break my heart."

I huffed out a laugh then took a swig of whiskey from the bottle like the classy bastard I was. "Maybe you should have thought about that before you agreed to sing a duet with the douche. Because as far as I'm concerned, it's the same as cheating on me. Probably worse. Because that music... it will always be out there. It will live longer than you and me. A constant reminder that you don't give a shit about my feelings. It's all about the money. When will it ever be enough?"

"It's not all about the money. I don't care about the money."

"Let me ask you something. If you were me, how would you feel?"

She took a few seconds to think about her answer. "Jealous. Angry. Hurt. Worried."

"Well, there you go. So no, I don't have a fucking thing to say to you right now." There was only one thing that could fix this. She had to tell him she wasn't going to do it, that it was out of the fucking question. And even then, it would be more like a Band-Aid on a gaping wound.

The words had to come from her, it had to be what she wanted, not because I was forcing her to choose. But she didn't say a goddamn word.

A few minutes later, the front door opened, and Ridge

appeared in the living room in a hoodie and jeans, a backward baseball cap on his head. He read the tension in the air and raised his brows at me, but it didn't stop him from pulling Shiloh off the sofa into a big hug.

I left them together and strode out of the room without saying a word. Was I being unreasonable? Fuck if I know. This was my first real relationship, and I didn't have a clue how to navigate this uncharted territory.

All I knew was that what she'd done went against my moral code. Where was the loyalty? Shouldn't she have put me first? Instead, she'd gone behind my back and made a deal with the devil.

CHAPTER THIRTY-FIVE

Shiloh

"WHAT HAPPENED?" Ridge asked.

It had only been four months since I'd last seen him, but he'd gotten more muscular, bigger somehow, and he seemed more mature. Or maybe that was what I told myself because I was about to confide in a seventeen-year-old boy. I told him about Dean and how I'd promised to record a duet with him.

"Shit," Ridge said, pushing his hand through his hair and replacing his ball cap. "I get why he's pissed."

"I know. I screwed up. I never meant to hurt him..."

"But you're doing it anyway," he said, cutting right to the heart of it. "Why?"

It was so hard to explain but I tried. "To me, music is sacred. And Dean wrote a song that nobody else could sing except for us. I think, maybe, if Brody heard the song, he might be able to understand it better. It's not a sweet song. No hearts and flowers. It's..." I stopped to think about it for a moment, trying to find the best words to help him understand. "I wrote a song called 'Damage.' It was about me and Dean. And the song he wrote was almost like an apology letter."

"Why couldn't he have sung it himself?"

Good question.

"He's an addict, right?"

I nodded.

"Yeah, well, he's manipulating you. It's what they do. It came through loud and clear in all your music. I've been there. So has Brody. We know how an addict can twist the truth and lie and make excuses and make you feel like shit. They make you feel guilty for just being alive, for not doing enough to make their shitty life better."

God. Ridge was so smart. And he and Brody had been through so much in their lives.

"And you fell for it again. So yeah, I get why Brody's pissed. And I think you're great but if you go through with this, you'll be fucking up. Big time." He stood up from the sofa. "Make it right or you're gonna lose him. Catch you later."

I watched Ridge's back as he walked away from me. Then I sank back into the sofa cushions and tried to figure out how to fix what I'd broken. Brody's trust. Maybe his heart. I'd put my music and my career first. In his eyes, he probably thought I'd put Dean first too. And I really couldn't blame him.

Was it really worth it? If we recorded that duet and the song climbed the charts, would it be worth what I'd sacrificed to achieve that?

Dean had played me. Again. God, I was such an idiot. He'd brought Ari Bell in on purpose, knowing my ego would never allow me to let her sing a song written for me. She was the new lead guitarist and backup singer for Acadian Storm. She'd taken my place. And not for the first time either.

The first time I met Ari Bell, she had Dean's dick in her mouth. She'd been the guitarist in a band that opened for us on our third and final world tour together. And now I'd agreed to let Acadian Storm open for me in North America.

Why did I keep allowing myself to be manipulated by Dean? But he wasn't acting alone. My brother had played his part. I didn't want to acknowledge the truth about Landry. I wanted to believe he was better than that and wouldn't stoop to this level. But every time I spoke to him, it was getting harder to do. He kept reminding me that I owed him and I owed Dean.

When would it end? When would my debt be paid?

I didn't know who to trust anymore. No, that was a lie. I trusted Brody. I trusted every single person in his family. But I didn't trust my own family.

It had to stop. I called Landry first. He answered on the second ring. "Landry. We need to talk."

He laughed. "Whoa. That sounds serious. I just saw you yesterday."

"Yeah, I know. And you and Dean... you did it again, Landry. You made me feel guilty for saying no to him."

"If that's how you feel, I don't know what to tell you."

"Just tell me the truth. Who asked Ari Bell to join the band?"

"Why?"

I knew the answer. Dean couldn't have done it because he was in rehab at the time. "Why did Gus really leave?"

"Shy..."

"I know it was you, Landry. What I don't get is why you would do this."

"Are you fucking serious right now? You left the band. You destroyed us..."

"I didn't destroy the band. I left because I couldn't take it anymore. We always said it was about the music but little by little it stopped being about the music, Landry. When did everything change? When did you start caring more about making headlines than putting out good music?"

"Now you're saying our music is no good?"

"It's good. You know it is. But music took a back seat to all the other shit. You were chasing after the fame and money. I'm not going to record this duet with Dean. And when we're on tour, I'm going to keep my distance. I don't want to get sucked into that world again."

"You're blowing everything out of proportion. Just like you always did."

I gritted my teeth. "For once, I wish you would put me first. I wish you would have stood up for me and fought for me. But you never did. You always took Dean's side. And it took me a long time to figure out that I have to fight for myself because nobody else is going to do it for me. I love you, I really do, but I hate the things you do and the way you make me feel like I owe you. So I think it's better if we don't talk for a while."

"Shiloh... Jesus Christ. Where is all this coming from? You were fine yesterday."

"I've had some time to think about things. And I hate how much success has changed you, Landry."

He barked out a laugh. "Are you shitting me? You're the one who changed. You're the one who got all high and mighty and started acting like we weren't good enough for you anymore. Why do you think Dean fucked around? You made him feel like he was never good enough."

I squeezed my eyes shut and took a few deep breaths, trying to center myself. I'd spoken about all this with my therapist after I left Dean and she'd given me good advice, but I hadn't wanted to hear it at the time. I hadn't wanted to face the fact that my own brother was trying to sabotage me. To bring me down to a level where he could control me like he did when we were kids and I followed him wherever he went, always believing he knew best.

Instead of arguing with him, I said goodbye and I hung up. Then I sent a quick text to Dean and told him he could do whatever he wanted with the song, but I wasn't going to sing it with him.

My eyes drifted shut and I leaned my head against the sofa cushion, a crushing weight on my heart.

The cushion dipped under his weight and he pulled me into his arms and stroked my hair. I hadn't even heard him come in.

"How much did you hear?"

"Enough."

We were quiet for a while and he kept stroking my hair, his touch so soothing it made the tears well up in my eyes and my heart ache.

"I'm not going to do it. I'm not going to record the duet. I'm sorry I put you through that. I'm sorry I ever—"

"Stop beating yourself up."

I forced a laugh. "You're singing a new tune."

"Nah. I got my feelings hurt. I was jealous and angry and yeah, worried that you'd rather be with the douche."

I pulled back to see his face. "He's not half the man you are. After being with you, how could I ever go back to the life I had before?"

"I can't be with you the whole time. But I'll try to arrange my schedule so I can see you as much as possible. A few days at a time..." He shrugged one shoulder. "Better than nothing, right?"

"It's everything. And so are you. I wasn't thinking straight, Brody. I... God, how could I have ever agreed to that?"

"Easy. The people you love and care about don't always have your best interests at heart. And it's hard to accept that.

You don't want to believe it so you make excuses for them. Try to justify it."

"He's my only family and I just feel so betrayed, you know?"

"I know. But you've got me now. And the McCallisters. Like it or not, they're not gonna let you go. They're big on family and already consider you a part of it."

I could barely see him through the blur of tears. "I'm so lucky I found you."

"Damn straight. And don't you forget it, baby."

I smiled through my tears.

"Next time, talk to me first."

"There won't be a next time. But I will. I promise. Why isn't love ever easy?"

"In my experience, love has never been easy. It's messy and complicated. Like people. Like life. Nothing worth having ever comes easy. You have to fight for the things that matter."

"Am I worth fighting for?"

"If you have to ask, I'm thinking you'd better get naked."

"And why's that, Brody?"

"Because I obviously did a shit job of showing you that you're worth fighting for."

"And you need me naked for that?"

"Uh huh. I find that my words sink in better when I'm buried deep inside you."

"How convenient."

CHAPTER THIRTY-SIX

Brody

THE WEEK BEFORE CHRISTMAS, I flew to New York to see Shiloh. It was her last concert for this leg of the tour, and after this she had a six-week break before she hit the road with Acadian Storm. So she was spending the holidays with me.

"Holy shit," Gideon said. He sounded impressed. Which was rare for him. But how could you not be impressed when you were watching Shiloh perform on a stage in Madison Square Garden?

It was the first time I'd ever sat in the audience for one of her concerts, and she'd hooked us up with floor seats. We were four rows from center stage, surrounded by her most avid fans. The view was different from here. When I'd watched her from backstage in London and Paris, I'd been impressed. In awe of her talent. But that feeling was amplified a thousand-fold when I was surrounded by twenty thousand screaming fans who knew every single word to every single song she performed.

"How in the hell did Brody McCallister end up with a rock

star?" he mused, his eyes still on the stage, Shiloh holding his rapt attention just like every other person in this stadium.

"That's the question for the ages. It's a goddamn mystery." I didn't mention Shiloh's belief that we were each other's destiny. I didn't tell him about her grandmother, who had supposedly predicted that we would find each other. Gideon was too logical, too cold and cynical to believe in the mystical or unexplained phenomena.

When she finished the last song of her setlist, the lights went down, and she was gone. The crowd chanted for two minutes straight and I knew what would happen next. Time for an encore. That was all part of the show business of a rock concert. She always gave her fans more, never held back, and left it all on that stage no matter how exhausted she was or how much it strained her voice.

Tonight, though, when the lights came up again, she was sitting on a stool, cradling her acoustic guitar. She was dressed in black. Her skirt was short, her bustier was leather, and her stockings were fishnet. I didn't have a fucking clue how she'd strutted across the stage in those sky-high heels of her ankle boots, but she'd done it for ninety minutes. By now, she must have been exhausted but her smile was bright.

"I want to sing a song that's very special to me. It's not one of mine. But back when I was a teenager, playing in dive bars or anywhere that would give us a gig, I always finished the night with this song. So tonight, I'm going to sing 'Iris' by The Goo Goo Dolls." She waited for the cheering to stop and her eyes found mine. "This song is for a man who speaks his own truth and always fights for the things he believes in. My life would be so much emptier without him in it."

"Well, damn," Gideon said.

Well, damn was right. I sat back in my seat and I listened to the girl I loved singing "Iris" for twenty thousand people.

But she held my gaze and it felt like she was singing just for me.

"What if every song I sang was for you..."

What if... what if...

It had been almost ten years since the first time I saw her perform this. Her voice had changed, improved, was more mature, but it hadn't lost any of its magic.

Her voice was my favorite sound, and I didn't think I'd ever tire of listening to it. It still reached deep inside and rattled my bones. Made my heart ache in a way I couldn't explain. Nobody had ever touched me the way she had. Not even Lila had ever had this kind of power over me. There was nothing I wouldn't do for Shiloh.

Sometimes I still couldn't believe she'd chosen me. She could have had her pick of any guy she wanted. But still. She'd chosen me. Was I worthy of her love? Hell if I knew. But I'd fight for her and I'd do everything in my power not to fail her. I'd prove to her that I was nothing like her father who had abandoned her. Or her brother, who had betrayed and manipulated her. Or Dean, the fucking douche who had tried to break her.

Maybe we shouldn't have made sense. Maybe there was no world in which we ever should have gotten together. But somehow, we were two imperfect, flawed people who fit together perfectly and made each other's worlds a better place.

Shiloh and I belonged together. It was just that fucking simple. And I'd do whatever it took to hang on to the good thing I found.

WHAT THE HELL *had she done now?* I looked down at the papers in my hand then around at my family. Nobody looked surprised by Shiloh's grand gesture. They'd all been in on this.

Every single last one of them had known about it before she'd sprung this surprise on me. My gaze returned to Shiloh. "I told you not to come here and start flashing your money around. Remember when I told you that?"

She nodded. "I remember," she said calmly.

I grabbed her arm, pulled her off the sofa, and dragged her away from my family who were all gathered in the living room at Patrick and Kate's house. We stopped by the staircase in the hallway, out of earshot, and I crossed my arms over my chest.

"Then do you mind telling me why you handed me the deed to the Armacost ranch?" Wrapped in a fucking bow, might I add.

"Merry Christmas." She gave me a big smile, still not understanding that I didn't see this as a good thing. Then she hastened to add, "It's not what you think."

I threw my hands in the air. "Oh, here we go again. That's what you said when you were planning to record a duet with the douche."

She planted her hands on her hips and stared me down "Do you remember when you told me you wished you could rescue all the horses? But you didn't have enough land?"

"That wasn't an invitation for you to go out and buy it for me," I said through clenched teeth. "Are you trying to rub it in my face that you have more money than me? I don't want your fucking charity."

"Well, as a matter of fact, it *is* a charity."

My eyes narrowed on her. "What are you talking about?"

"Gideon helped me set it up. Actually, he did all the work. Submitted all the paperwork and... well, it's all set up as a not-for-profit horse rescue. And Jude said he can help with the volunteers. We did the research and working with horses is really good therapy for veterans with PTSD. Don't you see? You can make your dreams come true and you can help so many horses and people and... I have the resources, Brody. How could I *not* do this?"

I didn't have an answer for her. On the one hand, I couldn't believe she'd done all this for me. On the other hand, I hated feeling like a charity case. I hated it that she had the money and the resources I didn't. "I'm supposed to be the one taking care of you."

She laughed like that was a great big joke then slugged me on the shoulder. "What century do you live in, Cowboy?"

"Doesn't matter what century it is. Some things haven't changed. I'm the man. You're the woman."

"Wow. You're still so good at figuring out the different genders, Tarzan," she teased. "But I don't see your point."

I blew out a frustrated breath. "What part don't you get?"

"The part where you won't accept that money is not what I need from you."

"Put it in your own name. I want no part of it."

"Seriously? Do you know how ridiculous you sound right now?"

I glared at her. "Now I'm ridiculous?"

"You're acting ridiculous. I don't know the first thing about horses."

"I want your name on that fucking deed. I'll work for the non-for-profit or whatever the hell you set up. But that land doesn't belong to me." I pointed my finger at her. "It belongs to you. You shouldn't have done this."

"Well, I did. And I don't regret it. Not even a little bit. It's a good thing, Brody. You're just looking at it all wrong."

"Dad?" a voice from behind me said.

Who the hell was Dad?

I turned to look at Noah. "*Dad?*"

He nodded. "It's cooler. I'm not a baby anymore."

"Next thing you'll be asking to borrow the car," I muttered. *Slow down. Don't grow up so damn fast.*

His brow furrowed. "You have a truck, not a car."

Kids were so literal. "What'd you need?"

He crossed his arms over his small chest and scowled at me. "You shouldn't be mad at Shy."

"And why's that?"

"Because she wants you to be happy. And she wants you to fix all the broken horses." His gaze swung to Shiloh. "Right, Shy?"

She smiled. "That's right, Noah."

"You should tell her you're sorry for hurting her feelings."

I wanted to ask who sent him out here to deliver that message. Or had it been his idea? My boy didn't miss a trick. "Thanks for the advice."

He tilted his head and studied my face. "Are you gonna do as I say?"

"I'm the dad. You're the kid. So you do as I say, not the other way around." He frowned, not appreciating that I'd pointed it out.

"You're not allowed to fight on Christmas. It's a family rule."

"We're not fighting. We're just talking," Shiloh said. "Would it be okay with you if we had a few minutes alone to talk some more?"

He considered her question for a minute as if it was up to him. "I guess so. But don't take too long."

I waited until he was out of earshot before I returned my gaze to Shiloh. This morning I'd given her the filly, Phoenix. And now she'd given me two hundred and twenty acres of land. How could I ever compete with that?

"It's not a competition, Brody. I wasn't trying to flash my

money around. I'm not trying to make you feel bad. I want you to have this so badly."

"Stop reading my mind."

She shrugged one shoulder, her lips tugging into a small smile. "I can't help it. I'm so attuned to you and your moods and this big heart of yours." She placed her hand on my chest. "Look at this way. I'm not doing this for you. I'm doing it for all those horses that need a good home. And for the veterans with PTSD. And anyone who is lucky enough to see the work you do. Don't let your stubborn pride get in the way of all the good you can do."

With that, she walked away and left me standing in the hallway, trying to figure out how I should feel about this. Goddamn this woman. She'd already changed me so much, had me doing and saying things I'd never in a million years expected I'd be doing and saying.

Voices and laughter came from the family room and even among my loud, rowdy family, her voice and her laugh were all I heard. I walked out the front door and stood on the porch, taking deep breaths of frosty air. Christmas lights framed all the windows and Santa's sleigh and reindeer were parked in the front yard.

Ten or fifteen minutes later, I was still standing on the front porch, the cold seeping into my bones, hands in my pockets, when the front door opened and closed. Kate came to stand next to me. She was wearing a red and green Christmas sweater and a beaded Jingle ball necklace Noah had made her at school. She'd always made a big deal out of the holidays, especially Christmas. "We're about to play Charades. It's not the same without you."

"I hate Charades," I muttered.

She laughed. "I know. That's what makes it so much fun.

It's not about whether you like it or not, it's about having the whole family together. Nobody wants to play without you."

I felt like a sulky teen, having to be coaxed into doing something I didn't want to do.

"But you know... you always said you didn't like Charades. You all pretended to hate it. But that never stopped y'all from having fun. You were all so competitive."

"Still are."

"I know." She smiled. "Just like I know you all have your share of issues and arguments, but the love is always there. Sometimes you have to be willing to lose something in order to be the winner."

"What are you saying?"

She patted my arm. "I think you know exactly what I'm saying. Your pride won't keep you warm at night and it won't be there when you need a shoulder to lean on. You boys were all raised to be such macho men."

A laugh burst out of me at her choice of words. "Macho men?"

She waved her hand in the air. "Whatever they call it these days. But let me tell you something, Brody McCallister." She wagged her finger at me, her voice stern. I stifled my laughter. Kate was all of five-foot nothing and the nicest person you'd ever have the privilege of meeting. Growing up, whenever she'd reprimanded me, it had cracked me up. Still did.

"It's high time you let go of all that outdated thinking about what it means to be a man. And if you let that girl go, you'll be making the biggest mistake of your life. Sit on that thought for a minute." She lifted her chin in the air and walked away. "But don't take too long," she called over her shoulder. "We'll be expecting you in the family room for Charades."

After she was gone, I laughed and scrubbed my hands over my face. Where would I have been without Kate McCallister?

Patrick liked to think he was the boss around here, but growing up, I'd always known it was Kate who had the real strength. She'd kept us all in line, had made sure we always knew we were loved, and somehow handled Patrick without him ever realizing she was doing it.

So I returned to the family room, and I took in the scene. The floor was littered with wrapping paper, the tree decorated with all the ornaments we'd made when we were kids, strung with popcorn ball garland and gingerbread men Kate and Noah had made, the multicolored lights twinkling. Everyone was talking over each other, as per usual. Levi was having more fun playing with an empty box than with all the toys scattered around the floor. Now he was in the box and Noah was whipping him around the carpet, probably giving the poor kid whiplash. Jude and Gideon were on the floor, battling it out with Avengers superheroes on the LEGO Helicarrier. Ridge and Jesse were shooting each other with Nerf blasters. Patrick was on his recliner, reading the instruction manual for Noah's new Nintendo gaming system.

I took my seat on the sectional next to Shiloh who was talking to Lila and Kate about baby names. Jude and Lila were having a girl, and everyone was thrilled. A few days ago, Shiloh and I had been invited to dinner at Jude and Lila's and they'd announced the news. On the drive home, Shiloh and I had talked about Hayley. She told me she had entered her name in a database, giving Hayley the option to look her up when she got older, if she chose to.

"I've made my peace with it," she'd said. "I can't go back in time and change what I did. And now that I've seen her, I know I did the best thing I could for her."

Now, she gave me a little smile then slipped her warm hand into my cold one and laced our fingers together.

"Don't ever pull a stunt like that again," I said, my voice low. "I don't want you spending your money on me."

She smirked. "You can punish me later."

"Witchy woman."

"Stubborn cowboy. I'm on Lila and Kate's team for Charades. Girls against boys. We're gonna kick your asses. I happen to be a champion Charader."

A laugh burst out of me. "Charader?"

"Uh huh."

"You're crazy."

"About you."

I still wasn't happy about what she'd done for me, but I'd have to find a way to swallow my pride and make peace with the fact that my girlfriend was richer than I'd ever be in this lifetime. But fuck, it was a tough pill to swallow.

"Happy New Year."

"Happy New Year." Shiloh clinked her glass of whiskey against mine and we drank to the new year.

It was just the two of us, celebrating New Year's Eve, a holiday we both claimed to hate. Too many expectations and hopes pinned on one night. We were lounging on the sofa, her legs draped over my lap, her black hair all messy and disheveled from my hands running through it when I'd fucked her from behind. She was wearing my flannel shirt over a pair of sweats with thick cotton socks on her feet. Every item of clothing on her body belonged to me. I found it ridiculously sexy. Especially when I'd slipped my hand inside the sweats earlier and realized she wasn't wearing any underwear.

Supposedly, we were having a movie marathon. How very rock and roll of us. But neither of us had really been watching the movie. The coffee table was littered with cartons from our Chinese takeout and neither of us had made a move to clean it up when we'd finished eating.

And I thought this was what it was all about. Finding that one person you could just hang out with, in all your messy fucked-up glory and they didn't judge you for it or expect you to behave a certain way.

This was what love looked like.

So I just came right out and said the words I'd never said to anyone. I wasn't even looking at her. I was staring at the TV screen. "I love you, Shiloh."

She was quiet for a moment then she leaned over and wrapped her arms around you. "I love you too, Brody."

And that was how we rang in the new year. Best fucking New Year's Eve I'd ever had.

CHAPTER THIRTY-SEVEN

Shiloh

BRODY PROMISED to meet me in Miami at the end of February. We'd be in Miami for three nights, the first of which was a night off. It had been three and a half weeks since I'd left Cypress Springs. Three and a half weeks of touring with Acadian Storm. I'd gone out of my way to avoid Dean and Landry as much as possible. The few times our paths had crossed, when I was finishing a soundcheck and they were waiting for their turn, Landry had looked sheepish and Dean had looked straight through me as if I didn't exist.

The day before Brody arrived, I was in Tampa and I'd just finished my soundcheck. I had a few hours to myself before the concert, so I was heading back to the hotel to get some rest before the show.

On my way out of the arena, I ran into Ari Bell in the hallway. Her chin-length hair was dyed platinum blonde, her big brown eyes were kohl-rimmed. When she spoke, her voice sounded breathy. But when she sang, she was a vocal chameleon. Dark and sensual. Bright and angelic. Mesmerizing.

"How's it going, Shiloh?"

"Great. Couldn't be better." I had zero interest in hanging around to chat with her. I brushed past her. "Catch you later."

"Wait. Just a second. I just... I needed to talk to you." With a sigh, I turned around to face her. Her eyes darted up and down the hallway. A few members of the road crew were hanging out talking and James was waiting at the end of the corridor to take me back to the hotel.

"Landry feels really bad about everything."

I had no idea why she was telling me this. And I didn't think Landry felt bad. Since our phone call back in October, he hadn't called me or tried to apologize. "Why are you telling me this?"

She lowered her eyes, and I knew. Landry and Ari were sleeping together. "Wow. How long have you two been together?"

"It's kind of new," she hedged. And I didn't know what to believe. Had they gotten together before or after Landry asked Ari to join Acadian Storm? And why should it even matter? "It's not public knowledge so..."

"Right. Well, don't worry about it. My lips are sealed."

"He loves you. And he misses you."

"He has a funny way of showing it." The words had just slipped out. I didn't know why I was having this conversation with her.

"I'm sorry. I thought you knew about us."

"There's a lot of things I don't know about Landry." She gave me a sad little smile and I walked away before she could apologize again. My problem wasn't with her, it was with Landry. And yeah sure, Ari had given Dean a blowjob but by then my relationship with Dean was all but over. Oddly, that had hurt less than finding out, once again, that my brother had been lying and keeping secrets from me.

On the drive to the hotel, I tried to shake it off. I tried to tell myself it didn't matter who Landry slept with or what he did in his private life. Hadn't I been equally guilty by not telling him the real reason I'd gone to Texas back in May?

Now I regretted confiding in Landry. Back in October, when I saw him in L.A., I'd told him about Brody. I wish I'd kept it to myself. How many lies had he been feeding me all these years? God, he really was so much like Rhett. Our dad was the biggest liar. And he'd had no problem taking money from me. As if he'd earned it. As if I owed him just because I'd made something of myself. Like father, like son.

Try as I might, I couldn't shake off this feeling of betrayal. The more I learned about Landry, the less respect I had for him. And that made me so sad. My own brother was using me for his personal gain.

I pushed it out of my mind. I didn't want any of these bad feelings to ruin my time with Brody. Not when I only had him for three days. God, I'd missed him so much. The last time I'd left him was the hardest. Probably because we'd spent six weeks together and I'd gotten to see him every single day. Sleeping with him every night and waking up with him at the crack of dawn every morning to go horse riding. And every time he'd told me he loved me my heart felt like it might burst. Because I knew it was a huge deal for him to say those words.

The only cloud in our silver lining, if you could call it that, was that our relationship wasn't a secret anymore. We'd been caught together when we were in New York City before Christmas and the photos were everywhere. And it hadn't taken people long to figure out that he was the same guy I'd been with in London and Paris. The same guy I sang for at Madison Square Garden. Let them talk. Let them speculate. I wasn't about to announce it to the world. I would do the best I could to protect Brody's privacy, something I knew he valued.

BRODY ARRIVED LATE on Thursday afternoon. I'd left a keycard at the front desk for him and he'd texted to say he was on his way up to the room. I'd opened the glass doors to the balcony of my ocean-front suite. The air was warm and salt-scented, the room modern and decorated in all white. The only hints of color came from the bowl of green apples on the round white lacquer table in front of the sofa and the potted palms on the balcony.

When the room door opened, I tossed aside the magazine I was reading and stood up from the sofa. For a moment, I just stood in the middle of the room and drank him in. He was wearing faded denim and a plain white T-shirt, his dirty blond hair all messy and disheveled, reaching the collar of his T-shirt. Even in the winter, his skin was suntanned from being outdoors all day, his muscles threatening to burst the seams of his T-shirt. His broad shoulders and tall frame filled up all the available space.

Brody was all man, and that man was all mine.

He dropped his duffel bag to the floor and in a few long strides, he erased the distance between us. Pulling me into his arms, he fisted my hair in his hand and tugged on it so my face was tipped up to his. "Fuck, I missed you."

"Missed you more."

He crushed his mouth against mine and kissed me hard.

We'd become one of those sickening couples, but I didn't care. He swept me off my feet and I clung to his shoulders, my legs cinching his waist as he carried me to the bedroom. Our mouths collided and we said hello with a kiss that stole the breath from my lungs and made me dizzy. I never wanted to let him go.

I had no idea how I'd make it to the end of April with only a few stolen hours and days at a time with him. After a short break, I'd be going into the studio to record my next album. But I didn't want to think about any of that now. I didn't want to think about how I hadn't even gotten a chance to meet Gracie McCallister yet. Jude and Lila's baby was born three weeks ago. Two days before that, Ridge had celebrated his eighteenth birthday. In two weeks, Brody and Lila were throwing a seventh birthday party for Noah. I'd be missing that too. But I shoved it out of my mind and enjoyed the feel of his hard body under my fingertips, his lips on mine, soft but demanding.

He was here now, and that was all that mattered.

"ARE YOU SURE ABOUT THIS?" Brody had asked when I was getting ready for our night out.

"I'm positive." I'd given him a big smile. "It'll be fun."

Now I was tipsy on Mojitos and pleasantly sated from the Cubanos we'd eaten, my body moving to the Latin beat of the live music playing. We were sitting in a round red-upholstered booth at the back of the room near the small dance area, his arm slung over the back of my seat, my thigh pressed against his. The small club was dark and intimate, decorated in dark red and glossy black with ceiling fans and candles in red glass holders on each table.

My lips loosened by alcohol, I confided in Brody how betrayed I felt by Landry. Brody was more than just my lover, he was my best friend, and I'd made up my mind when we were in the South of France that I wouldn't keep anything from him. I needed to get this off my chest so I could move on and try to put it behind me.

"Do you think I'm overreacting?" I asked him when I finished telling him about the encounter with Ari Bell and how I suspected Landry had been with her even before he invited her to be the newest member of Acadian Storm. "It made me feel like he was the one manipulating me... I mean, I always knew Dean was capable of this. But my own brother?" I heard the hurt and disappointment in my voice and Brody must have heard it too.

"Yeah, I get it. You don't know what to believe anymore. He had a chance to discuss this with you, but he chose to keep it a secret. He destroyed your trust in him. And his first loyalty should have been to you. Not the band. Not Dean. But his own blood."

That was exactly it. Brody understood where I was coming from and hadn't tried to downplay my feelings which I appreciated more than he could ever know. I lifted my Mojito. "Let's make a toast."

He lifted his beer bottle and raised his brows, waiting to hear what we were toasting to. "To honesty. Let's always be open and honest with each other. No secrets, no lies." I turned in my seat for a better view of his face. He was staring straight ahead, not at me, his face in shadows from the glow of the candlelight. "Brody?"

"Yeah?" He turned his head and his eyes flitted over my face, searching for something although I didn't know what. He opened his mouth to speak then shut it again.

"Can we drink to that?"

He hesitated a beat then his eyes locked onto mine and he nodded. "Sure."

Maybe I should have noticed the hesitation, the troubled look on his face. But I didn't. He clinked his bottle against my glass and we both drank to honesty. No secrets, no lies, no with-held information. While I was in Texas over the Christmas holidays, we'd confided so many things to each other. I'd told him about Rhett Holloway and the money I'd given him to open a bar and how I hadn't heard from him since. Brody had said that Rhett didn't deserve to call himself a father and he wouldn't have given him a dime. That was when I figured out that Brody held grudges and didn't forgive easily.

When he'd probed me for more information about Dean, and asked if I'd been abused, I answered him honestly. I hadn't given him every little detail of my relationship with Dean, but enough that he got the picture. Our relationship had been toxic, fueled by alcohol and drugs, and by the time I left Dean I'd been in a bad place. But when I met Brody, he'd revived my faith in men. Had made me see there were good men out there who were honest and true and strong without making you feel like they needed to control you.

I didn't want to waste any more time dwelling on Landry or Dean or Rhett. Maybe, by the end of this tour, I'd find a way to talk to Landry and we'd clear the air. But tonight, I wanted to devote all my attention to Brody.

"Let's dance."

"You wanna dance?"

"Scared? Is the two-step the extent of your dancing reper-toire?" I teased.

He gave me that charming Brody McCallister grin, his teeth so white and the little lines around his eyes crinkling. "I'm not a one-trick pony, baby."

"Prove it."

And he did. He led, and I followed, our bodies moving in perfect sync to the rhythm of the sexy, sensuous beat. One hand on the small of my back, the other one clasping mine, our eyes locked, we danced in a small club in Miami. And everything about it was so perfect.

Being with Brody was almost too good to be true.

"Do you think it's possible for us to have it all?" I asked him.

Without hesitation he said, "We already do."

I'd found my one true love and I was going to prove everyone wrong. Brody and I would have it all.

CHAPTER THIRTY-EIGHT

Brody

On Friday morning I had a few hours to myself. Earlier, Shiloh had been chauffeured to a morning radio show appearance and afterward she had an interview. I sure as hell didn't want to spend my morning in this hotel room. Everything, and I mean *everything*, was white. The upholstered wall behind the white bed, the glossy white floor, the fucking marble in the bathroom, and all the furniture. It reminded me of a padded cell. A very expensive padded cell, no doubt.

After I worked out in the hotel gym, I took a shower in the room then strode out of the hotel, past the infinity pool with white cabanas and a few women who looked like fashion models. I didn't even look twice. I walked to the closest coffee shop, a hipster haven like most of South Beach and ordered a large coffee and a breakfast burrito then carried them to a sidewalk table.

After I ate the burrito, I sat back with my coffee and called Glenn to ask how everything was going at the ranch. What

Shiloh had failed to realize was that by giving me a not-for-profit horse rescue, my already limited free time was now virtually non-existent. It took a hell of a lot of work and resources to operate a horse ranch that size and even three days away from it was difficult to swing.

"Jude and his buddy Tommy are coming by later," Glenn told me.

My eyes narrowed. "What for?"

"Said they've recruited some volunteers."

"And why in the hell would Jude bring them over on a day I'm not there?"

"Can't answer for Jude. Best ask him yourself."

I sighed. "Everything else okay?"

"Yup. If I need you, I'll be sure to call you. No need to keep checking in." A man of few words, Glenn cut the call and I called my cousin.

"Why the hell can't you wait until I get home?" I asked, skipping the greeting.

"Good morning to you too," Jude said.

I rolled my eyes. "Answer the question."

"I might have fucked up the dates."

I could almost hear him wince. My brows shot up to my hairline. Then I smirked. "That's not like you."

"Lila says baby brain is a thing."

I chuckled. "Guess it is." I leaned back in my seat and took a sip of coffee. "How's Gracie?"

"I don't know, man. Having a girl is different. I've been losing sleep over the thought of her... fuck, there's so many douches out there. *We* were douches."

"She's three weeks old. Pretty sure she doesn't have sex on the brain yet."

"Jesus. Don't mention sex and my daughter in the same

sentence. I'm keeping her locked in the house until she's twenty-one. Even that seems too soon to let her out."

A laugh burst out of me. "You're such a dumb shit."

"Fatherhood is making me question my lack of teenage morals. How's Shiloh?"

"She's good." Although I wasn't so sure about that. Her brother was an asshole. Every time I thought about him, it made my blood boil. The girl was surrounded by users. No wonder she wasn't sure who she could trust. And last night I'd promised her to always be honest. No secrets, no lies.

Tonight I should tell her the truth and pray that she didn't look at me like I was some kind of monster by association.

"Have you met the ex yet?"

"Nope." My hand curled into a fist at the mere thought of meeting Dean the douche.

"Just do me a favor. When you do meet him, refrain from planting your fist in his face."

"As much as I would love to do just that, I won't. I don't want to cause a scene or upset Shy."

He was quiet for a couple seconds. "She's changed you."

Didn't I know it. And I wasn't even mad about it. "Yeah, yeah. Next time you recruit volunteers, run it by me first." I paused a moment then grudgingly said, "And thanks."

"That hurt, didn't it?"

I huffed out a laugh and we said goodbye. Then I hung out at a trendy coffee shop in South Beach, with the sun on my face, and watched the beautiful people go by. Sitting around doing jack shit didn't come easy to me. Two coffees later, I was bored and restless, so I went for a walk on the beach. About twenty minutes later, I'd had enough of that too, so I headed back to the hotel. By now, Shiloh should be done with her radio show.

I WAS CROSSING the hotel lobby, also white with a big-ass chandelier hanging from the high ceiling and gauzy white curtains hanging between the pillars, when a guy stepped out in front of me. It took me a second to realize who it was.

"You're the new boyfriend, right?"

"I'm the *only* boyfriend."

"Huh. Not what I expected."

"Funny. You're exactly what I expected." His eyes were hidden behind dark sunglasses, his dark hair spiky like he'd used a lot of styling products, and he was wearing skinny jeans with a dark gray button-up shirt untucked, an expensive-looking chunky silver watch on his wrist.

I was going to leave it at that. I had every intention of walking away from Landry Leroux and not saying another goddamn word.

But then he had to go and question me. "What's that supposed to mean?" He punctuated his question with a sniff. Jesus. The fucker was coked up at eleven-thirty in the morning.

"If it looks like a weasel and acts like a weasel, it is a goddamn weasel. You should clean your nose. You've left some nose candy in the left nostril." *Asshole.*

He swiped his hand over his nose. "I don't know what my sister told you, but she has a habit of twisting the truth. Blows everything out of proportion."

"Are you calling your sister a liar?"

"I'm just saying that you shouldn't be so quick to believe everything she says."

"Where the fuck do you get off badmouthing your own sister?" It was the drugs talking, I knew it. People got braver and stupider and said shit they regretted later. But right now this asshole was in my face, spouting shit about his own sister, and I couldn't just let that go. "You don't know me. Why are you telling me this?"

"Just thought you should know what you're getting yourself into. As soon as she gets tired of you, she'll toss you aside and move on. Maybe you think you've won this round..."

I stared at him. "What the fuck are you talking about?"

"I know you're the one who talked her out of singing that duet. I don't know what else you've been putting into her head, but she'll soon figure out that her loyalties lie with the people who really know her and care about her best interests."

This guy was fucking unbelievable. I laughed harshly. "And I guess you think that's you." I stabbed my finger at his chest. "If you cared about her so much, you should have given her your unquestioning loyalty instead of stabbing her in the back every time she turned around."

Let it be known for the record that he shoved me first.

We were equally matched in height but that was where the similarities ended. His muscles came from working out in a gym, and he wasn't a fighter. So why the fuck was he picking a fight with a guy who could lay him out in two seconds flat? It was a mystery to me.

I shoved him back. Just a shove. Not a punch. Not a kick in the balls like he deserved. Just a warning not to mess with me. His back slammed against the pillar behind him. I would have thought that would be the end of it.

I turned and started walking away. He grabbed my shoulder, spun me around, and punched me right below the ribs. Motherfucker. I returned the favor. One punch. Two punches, and he doubled over. I hauled him up by the shirt collar and got right into his face. "Don't you fucking mess with me. I will defend her until my dying day. And until you're ready to act like a decent brother and make amends for all the shit you've put her through, stay away from Shiloh."

I released him and he staggered back. Then I turned and walked away, avoiding the stares of everyone in the lobby who had stopped to take in the show. As I was leaving, security showed up. A little late for that, boys.

I stabbed the elevator button and tried to regulate my breathing.

"Brody."

Great. Just what I needed. Marcus. "We need to have a word."

"If it's all the same with you, I'd like to get back to Shiloh."

I should have known that wouldn't be the end of it. "This will only take two minutes." He was texting on his phone as he led me to an empty room next to one of the hotel restaurants. It must have been a conference room.

I leaned against the wall next to the door and crossed my arms over my chest, waiting for him to speak.

"What happened?"

"He was talking shit about Shiloh and I wasn't about to put up with that." There was no apology in my voice. I wasn't the least bit sorry.

"So you thought you'd punch him to shut him up. In a public space where anyone could see you?"

I shrugged one shoulder, not bothering to defend myself. Although I did add, "Nobody knows who I am."

He laughed. "You really are stupid, aren't you? Luckily, Naomi is here. She'll deal with the damage control."

Damage control.

Marcus pocketed his phone and held my gaze. "Shiloh doesn't need to know about this right now," he said. "I don't want any of this to affect her performance tonight."

My eyes narrowed on him. "You want me to lie to her?"

"I want you to keep it to yourself for now. Shiloh is my number one priority. If you really care about her, you'll do what's best for her right now and keep your mouth shut. She's under a lot of pressure. There's a lot of stress between her and Landry and if she hears about this, it will only add to it."

I considered his words. It was hard to tell if he cared about Shiloh or if she was just his meal ticket. I rubbed the back of my neck. "It doesn't sit right with me to withhold the truth from her."

"But it sits just fine with you to punch her brother."

I held his gaze. "He had it coming." He had no idea how much I could have fucked up Landry if I hadn't been holding back.

"Maybe he did, maybe he didn't. That's not for me to say. But I'll tell you one thing. At the end of the day, he's still her brother and they still have to get through this tour together. Don't make it any more difficult than it already is."

"What if he tells her first?" Then I'd lose her trust and look like the liar that I was.

"Trust me, he won't breathe a word of it."

I believed him. Marcus or Naomi or someone else on the management team would make sure of it. They were all shady as fuck.

But he was waiting for my answer, so I nodded once in silent agreement, and I justified my actions by telling myself I was doing the best thing I could for her.

Shiloh

Later that night after the concert, when I was starting to come down from the adrenaline rush of the crowd, the music still vibrating through my body, Brody pulled me against him in the elevator. With my back arched against his chest, his teeth grazed the side of my neck and my eyes drifted shut.

"There are cameras in here." I could feel his warm breath on my neck, his hard length pressed against my ass. I didn't really care about the cameras.

"Let them watch." His hand cupped my breast, his fingers pinching my nipple through the fabric of my silky shirt, his other hand coasting up my thigh and under my short black skirt. When he reached the spot between my thighs, he reared back.

"Jesus Christ. You're not wearing any underwear."

I almost laughed at how scandalized he sounded. "Oops. Must have lost them somewhere along the way."

"Fucking hell." His fingers glided between my slick folds. I was always so wet for him. So needy and ready. "Don't tell me you were up there tonight without underwear."

"Okay. I won't." I'd changed after the show, but he didn't need to know that. I liked that he got jealous. I gasped when two thick fingers slid inside me, curling and reaching for a spot he knew so well. Lifting my arms above my head, I looped them around the back of his neck. When he added a third finger, I ground my ass against his erection as he fucked me with his fingers, his thumb rubbing my swollen clit.

"Oh God." My chest was heaving, and I was chasing this high, nearly there but not quite. I barely noticed when the elevator stopped, and the doors slid open. But I did notice when he slid his fingers out.

"Brody." My frustration had me whimpering.

He grabbed my hand and strode down the hallway, his strides so long I had to jog to keep up with him.

Once we were inside the room, he dragged me over to the sofa.

Standing behind me, he slid his hands down my arms and

clasped my hands in one of his, pressing his other hand against my back and folding my body over the arm of the sofa. He extended my arms in front of me and pushed my hands onto the sofa cushion. "Don't move," he commanded in a rough voice.

Then he pulled up my skirt so it was bunched around my hips and he kicked my legs apart. Behind me, I could hear him unzipping his jeans. I looked over my shoulder as he fisted his hard length. I was soaked, my clit throbbing, my nipples straining as I writhed against the sofa cushion, seeking the friction. I couldn't take it anymore.

"Brody. I need you. Now," I said through clenched teeth.

That earned me a slap on the ass, causing me to cry out. Grabbing my ass cheeks in both hands, he squeezed them and glided his dick between them, so hard and thick and swollen. "One of these days I'm gonna fuck this sweet ass."

"Why not today?" I asked boldly.

He growled. "We don't have that kind of time. One day soon. That's a promise."

I didn't have time to think about that promise. With my cheek pressed against the sofa cushion, my hands clawing the fabric, he finally gave me what I wanted. Brody slammed into me from behind and sweet baby Jesus, he filled me so completely I nearly wept at how good it felt. He pulled out of me then drove into me again, breeching my tight walls, so hard and so deep, it hurt. Thrust after thrust, our moans and heavy breaths and the sound of his balls slapping against my ass, filled the silence.

"Is that enough for you?" he growled, his hands gripping my hips, his fingers biting into the soft flesh.

"Too much. But never enough." My chest was heaving, and I was panting as he pulled out, leaving just the tip inside me. "I want more," I gritted out.

I loved the pain he gave. I wanted more of it. I wanted everything he had to give me.

He fisted my hair and pulled my head up off the sofa cushion, sinking his teeth into my shoulder while his thumb rimmed my ass and he pounded into me from behind. Punishing. Relentless. Pure fucking heaven. I pushed back against his finger, wanting to feel him everywhere. He pushed his thumb all the way inside me and I clenched around his cock, eliciting a deep guttural groan from him that reverberated in my core.

I was floating, I was flying, chasing a high that no drug could ever give me.

My whole body was quivering, shaking uncontrollably and I didn't even know how I was still standing.

Just when I thought I couldn't take anymore, he brought his hand down to my clit and pinched it between his fingers as he rammed into me, stealing the breath from my lungs. The orgasm crashed over me, and came in waves. Weightless. Floating. Soaring. Light splintered behind my closed eyelids, a slew of curse words flying from my lips as he slammed into me one last time, our orgasms so powerful he collapsed against my back, covering my body with his. My cheek was pressed against the sofa cushion again, and he buried his face in the crook of my neck, lacing his fingers in mine.

After a few moments of silence, our breathing ragged as we came down from the high, he said, "Fuck. If this was my last night on Earth, I would die a happy man."

Much later, I would remember those words. That was the trouble with flying high. When you crashed, you burned.

CHAPTER THIRTY-NINE

Shiloh

ON SATURDAY AFTERNOON before my final show in Miami, Brody and I ordered room service and ate a late lunch on the balcony.

"Cat's out of the bag. They know your name," I said, scrolling through my phone. There were a few photos of us on social media. Yesterday afternoon Brody and I had gone jet skiing. What struck me about the photos was that I was smiling in every single one of them.

He took the phone out of my hand and set it on the table, screen down. "Stop searching the Internet for information about me." His tone was light and teasing. But there was a tightness in his jaw that made me think he wasn't as cool about it as he was letting on.

"I'm sorry, Brody."

"Not your fault. It goes with the territory. Finish your salad," he said gruffly.

I took a few more bites of grilled chicken and mango then

pushed my plate away and closed my eyes, basking in the sun for a while. Chilled out. Relaxed. My bare feet propped in his lap while he kneaded them in his big, strong, healing hands.

"You're cool with Dean, right?" I asked, eyes still closed against the sun, my face tipped up to it.

"I'm cool with it." I cracked one lid open. He squeezed my foot. "Stop worrying about every little thing."

"Okay. But if he gives you any trouble, you'll tell me, right?"

"Don't worry about me. I can handle your ex or anything else thrown my way."

His tone of voice, so confident and certain, reassured me that it wasn't a big deal, so I stopped worrying about it. As far as I knew, Dean and Brody had stayed out of each other's way. There hadn't been any drama, and for once Dean was sticking to his word. He was clean and sober, and focused on the music. Whatever he got up to before and after the show was of no concern to me.

LATER THAT NIGHT after the show, Brody had given me four orgasms and now we were lying on top of the white Egyptian cotton sheets, the warm sea breeze floating through the open windows. I kissed his lips and placed my hand over his beating heart. "I love you, Cowboy."

He placed his hand over mine and tipped his chin down to look at me. "You've infiltrated the cracks in my heart, and I'll be damned if I know how to get you out."

"Don't even try. I want to live there forever." He pulled me closer and I draped my leg over his. Brody's heart was beating sure and steady under the palm of my hand, his chest rising and falling, each breath he inhaled and exhaled in sync with mine, lulling me into a sense of peace and security.

"How do you do it?" I asked while his hand coasted down my side and over the curve of my hip, settling there.

"Do what?"

"Make me feel so calm and peaceful, even in the midst of a chaotic world tour."

"Guess I've always had a knack for handling wild things."

I smiled a little and lifted my hand to his face, tracing his squared jaw, the stubble rough under my fingertips. "You think I'm wild?"

"In all the very best ways."

A few moments later, he looked over at the bedside table. "You're popular tonight."

I glanced at my phone. I'd silenced it earlier, but it was lighting up with messages. "Turn it over so we can't see it." I was pleasantly drowsy and too lazy to move.

He flipped my phone over and stroked my hair. My eyelids were too heavy to keep open and moments later I drifted off to sleep.

I WAS WOKEN by pounding on the door. "What the hell?" Brody muttered.

I snuggled against him, my back against his chest, my body fitting into the curve of his. "Just ignore it," I mumbled. "Security will deal with it."

I was starting to drift off again when the pounding on the door grew louder. "Shiloh! Open the door."

That was Landry's voice. "It's my brother."

"Shit," Brody said, sitting up in bed and taking the warmth of his body away from me.

"What time is it?"

"Three in the morning."

"What the hell could he possibly want?" I sat up and scrubbed my hands over my face.

"I'll take care of it," Brody said. "Be right back."

"He's my brother. I should—"

"Just stay here. I've got this." He pulled on his jeans from the floor and closed the bedroom door behind him. I sat up in bed and pulled the sheets higher to cover my body.

A few seconds later, I heard Landry's voice. "You son of a bitch. I knew you were trouble," Landry spewed.

"What the hell are you doing here at three in the morning?"

After that, their voices were muffled, too low for me to hear no matter how hard I strained my ears. What could they possibly be talking about?

I heard a scuffle, it sounded like they were fighting followed by the sound of something shattering. Yanking the top sheet off the bed, I wrapped it around my body and stood up, ready to intervene. Just then the bedroom door burst open, a crazed-looking Landry filling the doorframe, his chest heaving, fists balled at his sides.

"What are you doing, Landry? Are you high?" Why was he standing in my bedroom at three in the morning looking like he was ready to murder someone?

"Shy..." Landry's face crumpled and for a minute I saw the boy, not the man. I thought he was going to cry. His voice was soft, his face so sad. "Get dressed, boo. There's something..." He stopped and took a deep breath. "We need to talk."

Boo. It was that term of endearment, spoken so tenderly, and the expression on his face that made me start shaking. He had that same look on his face when he came into my bedroom all those years ago to tell me Maw Maw was gone. He'd been the one to find her and it had been left up to him to break the news to me. I never wanted to see that look on his face for as long as I lived, yet here he was again, the bearer of bad news. "Landry? What's happened?"

"Just get dressed."

The door closed and I quickly threw on a tank top and cut-offs, my hands trembling. Something bad was headed my way. I could feel it in my bones. I closed my eyes and took a deep breath, gearing up for whatever shit storm was headed toward me.

Please God, don't let it be anything I can't handle.

When I walked into the living area on shaky legs, my gaze darted to the door of my suite. Marcus stepped inside, James right behind me. James stood by the door, although I had no idea what he was guarding me against.

"Does she know yet?" Marcus asked Landry. He shook his head no.

My gaze found Brody. He was leaning against the wall, arms crossed, head down. "Brody," I whispered. I wanted to go to him, wrap my arms around him and hang on tight. I wanted him to tell me everything was going to be okay, even though I knew it wouldn't be. But something stopped me from doing it.

He lifted his head, the expression on his face so bleak, I lost it. I began crying without even knowing why. But a part of me, the part I'd inherited from Maw Maw that turned out to be a curse not a blessing, *knew*. He made no move to erase the distance between us or to comfort me and wipe away my tears like he normally would.

"I'm sorry." His voice was no louder than a whisper. "You have no idea how fucking sorry I am."

"Come and sit down, honey," Marcus said, patting the sofa

cushion next to him. Marcus never called me honey. His face was serious, and not even he could spin this into something better. Because whatever I was about to hear, I knew it was bad.

My legs carried me across the room, and I took a seat on the sofa, perched on the edge of it, my fingers spinning the silver feather ring around and around. Landy took a seat on the other side of me. Brody was across from us, still leaning against the wall, looking like a man about to face a firing squad. I kept my eyes on him. Shirtless and barefoot, wearing faded denim. His hair messy and disheveled, made worse from running his hands through it. He didn't say a single word. He couldn't even look at me.

Landry held his phone in front of me, and I dragged my eyes away from Brody and took the phone from Landry's hand. In the first photo, Brody was punching Landry. It looked as if they were in the hotel lobby. The headline read: *Shiloh Leroux's Boyfriend Has a History of Violence.*

"You punched my brother?" I asked Brody.

He stared at the floor and didn't respond.

"Landry," Marcus said, and it sounded like a reprimand.

Before I could even react to this, Landry told me to keep scrolling. So I did. Although I wished I hadn't. My breath got trapped in my lungs. I stared at the photo of a man who looked so much like Brody that for a second, I thought it was him.

"Your boyfriend over there. His father killed our mom," Landry said. "He shot her in cold blood and left her there to die while we sat in a car outside, waiting for her to come back. Only she never did."

"I... how..." My eyes sought out Brody again. Only this time, instead of seeing the man I loved, I saw a murderer. I saw the man who had taken away our mother. I'd never even gotten the chance to know her. I'd never heard her voice singing me to sleep. Reading bedtime stories. Tucking me in and telling me she loved me. I'd been robbed of all that because of an addict who had been trying to rob a convenience store. He'd shot three people. A cop. The convenience store manager. And my mother. The cop lived. The store manager died instantly. My mother died in the hospital twenty-four hours later.

Anger bubbled up inside me, red hot and blinding. I stood up from my seat and hurled the phone at Brody. He didn't even try to duck out of the way. It hit him square in the chest and fell to the floor at his feet. I flew across the room and then I was on him. I struck. My fists pummeling him, my hands smacking and shoving his chest and his torso and shoulders—everywhere and anywhere I could reach.

I was blinded by my fury, fueled by rage. *Why did it have to be him?*

"You knew about this, didn't you? You were trying to hide it from me." My voice was a whisper, scared to say the words louder in fear that would make them real. I smacked his chest with the heels of my hands. My wrath knew no bounds.

His hands wrapped around my wrists and he tried to pull me against him, but I resisted.

"Don't touch me!"

"Get your filthy hands off my sister," Landry roared.

Brody released me and I took a step back, my chest heaving, tears streaming down my cheeks. "How could you keep this from me? How could you not tell me that your father killed my mother?"

"I didn't know. I swear on my life, I had no idea—"

"Bullshit! I *told* you. I told you my mother's name. How could you not know the names of your father's victims?"

"I didn't know," he repeated. "Do you think I would have kept something like this from you?"

I laughed harshly. "You told me your parents were dead. Is that true?"

"My mother is dead. The man who—"

"Your father," I seethed. "Are you going to deny that he's your father?"

He rubbed the back of his neck and exhaled a breath. "He's in prison for life. Louisiana State Penitentiary."

"That's not the same as dead, Brody. Being in prison is not the same as being dead." My voice sounded shrill, beyond hysterical. "My mother is dead, and your piece of shit father is still alive. How is that fair?"

"It's not."

"I hope he lives to be a hundred so he can spend every single day of his life being reminded of what he did."

Brody's eyes met mine. "You think I don't want the same thing? You think..." His voice cracked on the words and through the blur of my own tears, I saw that he was crying. "Fuck, Shy, I never... I didn't know."

"I don't believe you. I think you knew it all along. You were there, Brody. You were there, weren't you?"

He wiped his hand over his face and nodded yes.

I wrapped my arms around my body and tried to stop the shaking. My stomach was churning, and I felt like I was going to throw up. None of this seemed real. "Where were you when my mother was shot?"

"In the car. He told me... to wait in the car. Fuck, Shy. I never... I'm not him," he gritted out. His eyes were red-rimmed from crying but I couldn't feel any sympathy for him.

He would have been eight and a half at the time. He had to have known. How could he not have? Nothing made any sense.

And in that moment, I knew there was no coming back from this. We were over.

I lifted my chin and looked into the eyes of a murderer's son. "I never want to see your face again. It's just a reminder of everything me and Landry lost." My voice sounded so cold, so unlike me that for a moment I wasn't even sure those words had come out of my mouth. But they had.

His eyes drifted shut and then he nodded. I turned my back to him as he walked away. My brother pulled me into his arms and held me, the two of us hanging onto each other, a reminder that all we had in this world was each other. We were family. Nothing would ever change that. My brother had been there for me when Maw Maw died. Had tried his best to look after me when we were kids.

All I wanted was to get back to the way it used to be when we were close, and he was the big brother I looked up to and adored.

A few minutes later, I heard the door close behind Brody. Sobs wracked my body, and I could barely breathe. This time he hadn't even put up a fight. He did as I asked, leaving me in an all-white ocean suite in Miami, my tears soaking my brother's shirt, a gaping hole in my heart that used to be filled by Brody.

"If you need anything, I'll be right down the hall," Marcus said on his way out. I'd forgotten he was even here.

"Thank you," I said. But Marcus couldn't give me what I needed. Nobody could.

CHAPTER FORTY

Brody

RIDGE WRESTLED the bottle of whiskey out of my hand.

"Give it back." I stood up from my chair and lunged at him. He darted out of the way and I lunged for him again. Fuck. My hand reached for the banister to hold myself up. It slipped out of my grasp. I tumbled down the porch steps and landed on the ground. I didn't feel a goddamn thing.

I started laughing. I was laughing so hard tears sprang to my eyes. Then I rolled onto my back and stared up at the dark sky, trying to bring the stars into focus. Everything was blurry. The world was spinning.

"Come on, bro. Let's get you inside." He tried to lift me, but I smacked his hands away.

"Leave me the fuck alone," I mumbled.

He crouched next to me and peered into my face. "You can't keep doing this to yourself."

"Wanna bet?" I closed one eye, trying to bring him into

focus. He had a black eye and a split lip. "I'll do whatever the fuck I want. You shouldn't have gotten in that fight."

"Nobody is gonna talk shit about my brother and get away with it."

"My honor's not worth fighting for. I don't have any. I'm the son of a monster. I have his blood running through my veins. Same DNA."

"You're not him. You didn't kill Shiloh's mom."

"Might as well have pulled the trigger..." My eyes drifted shut. I wanted to sleep on the ground. Maybe when I woke up tomorrow, I'd realize this had all been a bad dream.

Ten days. That was how long it had been since I'd last seen Shiloh. Ten days since she told me she never wanted to see my face again. Couldn't blame her. If I were here, I would have felt the same way.

When I woke up, I flinched at the light. Too bright. I closed my eyes again. My head felt like there was a jackhammer working inside it and my mouth was so dry I could barely swallow.

"'Morning, sunshine."

I groaned. Just what I needed. My smug cousin. "What are you doing here?"

"Someone needed to haul your ass off the back lawn last night. Drink this water and take these aspirin. Doctor's orders."

I forced my eyes open, knowing damn well that nothing I said would make Jude leave, so I sat up. I was on the living room sofa, fully dressed except for my boots, a blanket covering me. I took the aspirin from his hand and washed them down with water. I felt like a fucking baby.

"This needs to stop," he said. "Drinking your sorrows away

never works. Take it from me, the dumb shit who tried to do it for an entire year. You'll only make things worse."

I huffed out a laugh and winced at the pain that shot through my head. "Really can't see how it could possibly get worse. Might as well be drunk while I sit back and watch my whole fucking world fall apart."

He sighed. "I know it feels like that now, but it won't always—"

I held up my hand to stop him. "Save the speech, Dr. Phil."

"Yeah, okay. So what are you going to do about it?"

I scrubbed my hands over my face. "There's not a damn thing I can do. If I could go into that first-grade classroom and kick every kid's ass who talks shit around my kid, I'd fucking do it. But something tells me, folks wouldn't take too kindly to that. Noah's suffering because of this. Ridge is having to deal with it... everyone around me is dealing with the shit storm that *I* caused."

"You didn't cause it. None of this is your fault."

"My name is mud around here. I wouldn't give a shit what anyone said if this was only affecting me. But it's not."

He was sitting on the coffee table across from me and leaned his forearms on his thighs. "Fuck. There must be some way to fix this."

"Not everything can be fixed, Jude. You know that as well as I do."

He nodded. "Have you heard from Shiloh?"

I shook my head. "No. And I won't. She's done with me." I rubbed my chest. Fuck, it hurt. All of it. I'd lost the only girl I'd ever truly loved. There would never be another Shiloh for me.

"What time is it?" I thought to ask.

"Eight."

"Fuck." My day usually started at six-thirty. Jude stood up

at the same time I got to my feet. "I need to get to work. Did Ridge—"

"He was just leaving for school when I got here. He's worried about you."

"I don't want anyone worrying about me."

"It's what we do. We're family. I need to get going but I'm only a phone call away."

I nodded once, acknowledging that I'd heard him.

"You're going to get through this, Brody. You'll come out the other side."

"And then what?" I'd be alone. A lonely, miserable bastard.

He shrugged one shoulder. "Time to start rebuilding. Time to figure out how to get her back."

"Not happening." He opened his mouth to protest, but I held up my hand again to stop him. "It's over, Jude. Save your breath."

He nodded once, then turned and walked out the front door.

After I took a quick shower, I poured coffee into a travel mug and carried it out to the barn. My only saving grace right now were my horses.

Four days later, we celebrated my son's seventh birthday. Instead of the party we'd planned, it was just a family affair at Jude and Lila's house.

As soon as Noah answered the door with Lila standing behind him, the baby in her arms, I handed him his gift. "Hey, little man. Happy Birthday."

He shoved it back at me and crossed his arms over his chest. "Keep it. I don't want it."

"Noah," Lila said, her voice sharp. "Tell your daddy thank you."

"It's okay," I said. "He's not too happy with me right now, are you, buddy?"

He shook his head, his eyes not meeting mine. "I didn't want any of my stupid friends to come today. But I wanted Hayley..." He raised his eyes to mine and the look on his face, the devastation, his eyes swimming with tears, nearly made me cry like a fucking baby. I'd hurt the most precious thing in my life, and I had no idea how to make this better.

"What happened with Hayley?" Obviously, Lila hadn't been telling me the whole truth about what was going on in Noah's life. Last weekend, he hadn't even wanted to see me, and I'd said it was fine, not wanting to force him to spend time with me if he didn't want to.

"Her mom and dad said you're a bad man. Because you beat people up. And they don't want her around you anymore."

My eyes closed briefly. Then I crouched in front of him. I'd been so caught up in my own shit that I hadn't really sat down to talk to him or tried to explain things. I'd left it up to Lila, thinking it would be better coming from her. He was confused, and I couldn't blame him. "I'm sorry. I'm sorry for everything. I never..." I stopped talking and ran my hand through my hair. Fuck, I hated myself right now. The shame was eating me up inside. Making it hard to breathe. And I didn't know what to say or do to make his world a better place.

"I made a lot of mistakes in my life, Noah. And I've done a lot of things I'm not proud of. But there's nothing in this world I wouldn't do to make your life better. What do you need from me? What can I do to make this better for you? Name it and I'll do it." There was probably something in the parenting manual that said this was the wrong approach. I was asking my own kid to tell me how to fix this, and there was something so fucked up about that. But I didn't have the answers. I'd disappointed my boy. Had failed him miserably. Had done everything I always promised I wouldn't. And guess what? Parenting didn't come with a manual. When you fucked up, you had to figure out how to fix it on your own.

"If you go away, Hayley can come over," he said.

I rose to my feet and staggered back like I'd been struck. That would have hurt a hell of a lot less.

"Noah. You don't want that," Lila said. "Your daddy loves you and he would do anything in the world for you. You know that." She'd never had to play mediator between me and Noah before and I hated that she was having to do it now. I didn't want that either.

"It's okay. Let him speak his own truth," I told Lila, my gaze returning to Noah. "Is that what you want? You want me to leave?"

Noah considered my question, not answering right away. Then he asked, "Was he a bad guy?"

"Who?" I didn't know if he was talking about my sperm donor or someone else.

"The guy you punched on the video. Was he a bad guy?"

"He... said some things about Shiloh that weren't very nice."

Noah gave that a moment's thought. "You were standing up for her?"

Not sure I deserved to be let off the hook, but it was the damn truth, so I nodded. "But fighting isn't the best way to settle a disagreement."

"I know. Mommy always tells me that."

"I'm sorry, Noah." *I'm sorry that I'm human and flawed and a total fuck-up.*

He looked at Lila then back at me. "It's okay. You can come to my party. And maybe... I *might* want that present."

I laughed a little, relief flooding my body. "You think so?"

He nodded vigorously. "I really do want it."

I handed him the present and he clutched it to his chest and granted me a smile before he ran into the family room to open his gift. Lila gave me a sad little smile. "How are you holding up?"

"I've been better. But shit happens, right?"

"God, this is just... so unreal. I can't believe..." She didn't finish her sentence, but I knew what she was referring to. "What were the chances?"

One in a million. About the same odds that a cowboy would end up with a rock star.

"Right now, I'm more worried about Noah than anything else."

"He's going to be okay," she said as we walked into the family room. Everyone was already gathered. It wasn't the party we'd planned but they'd tried to make it festive, the room decorated with Spider-Man-themed streamers and balloons, a Spider-Man cake on the sideboard next to a bowl of red punch with black candy spiders floating in it.

"Brody," Lila said, sucking in a sharp breath when Noah lifted the cowboy boots out of the box then flashed around the photo of a horse so everyone in the room could see it. "What did you do?"

I bought my kid a goddamn horse. That was what I'd done. Was I trying to buy his love? Was it guilt? I didn't know. But I'd gone ahead and done it. As long as I had that horse in my stables, Noah would want to come over and see it, ride it, spend time at the ranch. Yeah, I was pathetic.

Noah ran over to me with the photo, his eyes wide. "Is he mine?"

"He's all yours."

"What's his name?"

"Thought I'd leave that up to you."

"I'm gonna call him Spider-Man."

I laughed. "You think he looks like a Spider-Man?"

He looked down at the framed photo in his hand. "He looks like he could use a best friend. I'll be his best friend."

And my fucking heart cracked just a little bit more. I scrubbed my hand over my face to hide my emotions. Lila squeezed my arm. Kate gave me a little smile and nodded as if to say that everything was going to work out just fine. But I had no idea how that could possibly be true when everything was broken beyond repair.

ONE WEEK LATER, on a Sunday evening, I showed up at the Petersons' front door. I'd just dropped Noah off after having spent the weekend with him, and I wanted to try to make things right.

Dale answered the door, looking wary as if he was nervous that I'd plant my fist in his face. "What did you need, Brody?"

He didn't open the door all the way nor did he invite me into his home. That said it all, didn't it? But fuck it, I was here for Noah, so I'd say my piece despite the chilly reception. "You can think whatever you want about me..." I refrained from adding that I didn't give a shit what he thought of me. "But my boy deserves better. Don't punish him for the sins of his father." The irony wasn't lost on me.

He rocked back on his heels and tucked his hands in the pockets of his pressed khakis. "We just don't feel comfortable letting Hayley spend time with you. As a father, I'm sure you can understand where we're coming from."

I wanted to argue that I was the same man who had hosted all those playdates for Hayley and Noah. I hadn't changed, but the media had painted me to look like a villain. A man with a history of violence just like his 'father'. In the days following that first story, they'd dredged up more shit about me and unleashed a media storm. My mother was a junkie, my father was a murderer. I was the spawn of the devil.

People came out of the woodwork, speaking up about Brody McCallister's 'character' or lack thereof. The asshole sheriff had confirmed that I'd been a juvenile delinquent and as far as he could tell, I was still a brawler and a rule breaker with a bad attitude. Hell, there were even guys from my rodeo days who claimed I had a quick temper and was always the first one to throw a punch. A woman I'd supposedly slept with claimed that I'd 'roughed her up.' That was a goddamn lie. I'd never laid a hand on any woman. Everyone wanted their twenty seconds of fame. The truth got twisted, the stories were sensationalized and that video of me punching Landry had gone viral. Interestingly, Landry came out looking like the victim, my 'attack' unprovoked according to him. Fucking weasel.

By now, my story was yesterday's news, taking a backseat to all the other scandals going on in the world of celebrity gossip. But once that shit was on the Internet, you couldn't do a damn thing about it and you couldn't make it go away. It was out there for everyone to Google and read about.

"Hayley is Noah's best friend, and I don't want him to lose her because of me," I told Dale.

He nodded. "I can understand that. They're still friends. Noah's a good kid. Meredith and I are happy to let them play together. But like I said, we're not too comfortable leaving our baby girl with you. We've decided that would be best for now. For our own peace of mind."

How could I fault them for wanting to protect their daughter? I couldn't. Having no choice but to accept it, I nodded. "Thanks for your time. Sorry to interrupt your Sunday."

"Thanks for stopping by."

My eye caught on Hayley who had come to stand next to her dad. He put his hand on her shoulder as if to stop her from taking a step closer to the bad guy. She smiled at me, the dimples in her cheeks making an appearance and I returned her smile. Then the door closed in my face, blocking my view of Shiloh's little girl. It felt like I'd lost the very last piece of Shiloh. Like there was nothing left of our relationship except for the memories. And I had a shitload of them.

Some days I wished I could shut them off. Whenever I closed my eyes, I saw her face. I heard her voice in my head. And I remembered all the good times we'd had. The smiles and laughter, the sex and intimate moments, and all our conversations when we opened up and shared pieces of our soul with each other. Even though she was gone and there was no hope in hell she'd ever come back, I couldn't stop loving her or missing her or hoping she was okay. All I'd ever wanted was to be the man who never failed her. The one man in her life who would be there for her through thick and thin, the one person she could rely on when she didn't know who to trust. But that wasn't how it worked out.

I was there the night Michael Jenkins shot and killed Shiloh's mom. I stayed in the car like he'd told me to do. Scared shitless that if I didn't do as he said he'd punish me for it. What kind of a monster would bring an eight-year-old kid to an armed robbery? I'd hidden in the back seat. It was dark and I was scared, and I heard the screams, and sirens from the police car. But I'd stayed hidden. By the time the cops had found me, I'd peed my pants. I'd been so ashamed for peeing my pants that I'd refused to answer any of their questions. After that night, I'd blocked the memory, never to be revisited.

Until the night Landry had shown up at Shiloh's hotel room and flashed his phone in front of my face, forcing me to confront a sick and twisted turn of events I'd never in a million years have thought possible.

What were the chances that my path would have crossed Shiloh's on that fateful night? One in a million.

LATER THAT EVENING, I went to visit Phoenix in the pasture. She came right over to me when I whistled, like she knew it was her I'd come to see.

"Look at you. You're a beauty, aren't you?" I rubbed behind her ears and she nudged her nose against my side. "Yeah, I brought you something. Don't tell the others. They'll get jealous."

I fished the apple wedges out of my pocket and fed them to her. "What am I going to do with you now? You were born to do better things than hang out in a pasture all day."

Phoenix didn't have an answer for me.

"Talking to your horses now?" Ridge asked, joining me next to the fence.

I'd always talked to my horses, but I didn't usually have an audience. I side-eyed him. He'd just come home from work and smelled like smoke from the barbecue. The bruises on his face had faded but I still remembered his words, that he wouldn't let anyone talk shit about his brother. Ridge and I had come a long way over the past year. "You doing okay?"

"Better than you."

"That's not saying much."

"It's all good." He squinted into the distance. "So... I was thinking... maybe I'll give college a try."

My brows shot up. "No shit." I turned to face him. "You wanna go to college?"

He shrugged one shoulder. "I didn't do so bad on my SATs.

Even the guidance counselor was shocked." He huffed out a laugh.

"I didn't even know you took the SATs."

"You were away. I didn't want to say anything. Just in case I fucked them up. If I get in anywhere, I'll be able to get student loans and shit."

"Sounds like a good plan. As long as it's something you want," I added.

"Yeah. It is. Me and Walker have been talking about going together. We could be roommates."

"You want to stay in Texas?"

He shrugged. "There are worse places to be than Texas. Guess I don't hate it as much as I thought. And I kind of... I don't want to be too far from family. I mean, I might not even get in anywhere..."

Ridge wasn't used to getting what he wanted in life, so he was knocking himself down, trying to prepare himself for the inevitable disappointment. "Hey. You listen to me. Stop talking like you're not good enough. Like you don't deserve good things. You do, Ridge. You've worked hard for everything you have. Nothing's been handed to you. Be proud of what you've achieved. Don't put yourself down."

He averted his face so I couldn't see it. Then he laughed.

"What's so funny?"

"You. Sometimes you're so cheesy."

I rolled my eyes.

He clapped me on the shoulder. "Maybe you should take some of your own advice while you're at it, bro. You're better than you think you are."

With that, he walked away. The little shit. I scrubbed my hand over my face and laughed. Then I thought about his words.

"You're better than you think you are."

Shiloh had once told me that very same thing. Too bad she didn't believe it anymore. A few days after all the shit went down in Miami, I'd left her a voicemail, apologizing for every fucking thing. I never heard back from her and I guess I shouldn't be surprised. I'd promised to always be honest with her. No secrets, no lies. I'd broken that promise, and she probably didn't know what to believe anymore.

CHAPTER FORTY-ONE

Shiloh

THREE WEEKS after I lost Brody, Dean quit the band.

Still reeling from the shock of the last bomb that had been dropped on me, I wasn't prepared for another one to blow up in my face. But as bad luck would have it, I had a front-row seat. After I'd finished my soundcheck, I decided to hang around and watch Acadian Storm rehearse. Ever since the media shit storm had been unleashed, Landry and I had gotten closer. He'd been my rock, by my side through it all, our bond stronger than ever.

Whenever I found myself missing Brody, which was every single day, I had to stop and remind myself that he wasn't the man I thought he was. But still, I longed for him. Missed him so much it was physically painful.

Everyone was in place, instruments at the ready except Dean hadn't shown up yet.

Landry checked his phone again. "Where the hell is he?"

In the past, Dean had been unreliable but for this entire

tour, he'd been playing it by the book, showing up on time and behaving in a professional manner. No drama. No crazy parties or trashed hotel rooms. He'd kept his word, and had stayed clean and sober, not causing any trouble. I should have known it wouldn't last.

He showed up fifteen minutes later. I knew Dean, and it wasn't hard to see he was furious, his rage simmering below the surface, about to blow.

I held my breath, wondering what had set him off. He strode across the stage and ripped Landry from his seat behind the drum kit. "I'm so fucking tired of your bullshit," Dean said between clenched teeth, his voice low but ominous. "I'm done. You fucked me over so many times, but this is an all-time low. Even for you."

I got to my feet, ready to defend Landry.

"What are you talking about?" Landry tried to laugh it off.

Dean released Landry and fished something out of his pocket then sprinkled white powder on the floor. "I'm trying to stay clean and sober, you fucker. Do you want me to fail? Is that it? You want to bring me down to your level?"

Oh my God. My jaw dropped.

"Hey man, I don't know where you got that but it's not mine..."

"You're such a fucking liar. I know it's yours. You think I haven't noticed you've been coked up this whole tour?"

From the corner of my eye, I saw Marcus appear from backstage.

"No, man. You've got it all wrong."

"Hey Ari. Have I got it all wrong?" Dean asked her.

She looked at Landry then back at Dean and shook her head no.

Landry grabbed her arm. "Did you do this? Are you sleeping with Dean?"

She wrenched her arm out of his hold. "No. You did this." Her eyes darted to me.

"You've always wanted everything I ever had," Dean accused, his voice shaking with anger. "You're jealous of me. You're jealous of your own sister." His gaze swung to me and now everyone's eyes were on me.

"Landry... what's he talking about?"

"You know Dean. He's just talking shit. Trying to get under your skin." But Landry couldn't even meet my eyes, and I knew he was lying.

"What did you do, Landry?"

"Nothing. I didn't do jack shit."

"What did you do?" I shouted, my hands clenched into fists, my chest heaving.

"You've always been so fucking jealous of your sister," Dean seethed. "Because you know she has more talent in her pinkie than you do in your whole damn body. You've spent years trying to sabotage her. Bring her down to your level so you can control her."

"Don't listen to him, Shy. You know it's not true. We're family. I'd never—"

"Stop lying to me." I flew up to the stage and stood in front of my brother. "Look me in the eye and tell me what you did." At that moment, I knew. He had leaked the information about Brody.

"Shy... don't..."

Dean got behind Landry, grabbed his arm and twisted it behind his back, shoving his hand between his shoulder blades. "Tell her or I'll break your fucking arm, drummer boy."

Landry's face contorted in pain. "Fuck. Let up."

Dean twisted harder. "Okay. Okay. But I did it for you. I knew that guy was trouble. He wasn't good enough for you, so I did some digging. Turns out I did you a favor."

A sound escaped my lips that sounded like a growl. I launched myself at Landry, shoving him and smacking my palms against his chest the same way I'd done to Brody a few weeks ago. "How could you?" I smacked his shoulder. "Why don't you want me to be happy, Landry? Why?"

My heart hurt so fucking much. I took a step back from Landry and looked at him through the blur of tears in my eyes. It seemed like every time I turned around there was something new to cry over.

"You've broken my heart, Landry," I whispered. "And for what? What did you get out of it?"

Dean released Landry and gave him a shove.

"I'm done with you, man. You fucking disgust me." With a final glance at me, Dean strode away. Without him, there would be no Acadian Storm.

"Shiloh... I swear on my life I never wanted to hurt you. We're family."

I laughed harshly. "*Family?* I don't believe anything you say anymore, Landry. You're a liar and a user. You've just lost the only family you had."

I turned and I walked away, my heart heavy, my throat so clogged with emotion I couldn't swallow.

Marcus stepped forward, having watched the entire exchange. He put his hands on each of my shoulders and looked me in the eyes. "You've been through a lot in the past few weeks. If you need me to cancel tonight's show, say the word."

That he would even consider doing that for me made me tear up again. I shook my head. "But you might need to find another band to open for me. I know it's short notice..."

"You leave that to me. I'll take care of everything. James is waiting to drive you back to the hotel. I'll stop by later to check on you."

I mustered a smile for him. "Thank you."

THE NEXT FIVE weeks were the longest five weeks of my life. I didn't cancel a single show. I tried to give the best performance I could. And in the end, the tour was deemed a success. Financially, anyway.

Three days after my final show in L.A. I agreed to meet Dean for dinner. He was renting a place in Malibu. He loved the beach, loved to watch the ocean and back when we'd first moved to L.A., he'd taken up surfing.

"I'm still a shit surfer," he joked as we sat at the round patio table on his deck and ate cheeseburgers, fries, and shakes. The sun was setting over the Pacific, the sky painted apricot and lilac, the air salt-scented and warm with a light breeze coming off the ocean.

"How are you doing, Shy? How are you *really* doing?"

I looked up from my burger and met his gaze. "I don't think you've ever asked me that." I'm sure he had but what I'd meant was that it had been a long time since he asked it in a way that sounded like he actually cared.

"There are a lot of things I never asked you."

This was Dean, showing his vulnerable side. The breeze lifted his brown hair and this evening those hazel eyes were more green than brown. His skin was sun-tanned and he was wearing an old ripped T-shirt and board shorts, his feet bare. He looked more relaxed than I'd ever seen him, and I wanted to confide in him. Tell him all the things I should have told him a long time ago.

"Ask me now," I said.

He toyed with a fry then dropped it onto the burger wrapper and leaned back in his seat. "Okay. What the hell.

When I was in prison, why did you give up our baby?" I heard the hurt and the anger in his voice.

All the breath got knocked out of my lungs. Not the question I'd expected. "You... you never wanted that baby, Dean. You never even asked about her."

"Are you shitting me? I wanted that baby. I told you I did. I told you I'd do whatever it took to look after both of you. I went to prison so you and the baby would be looked after so don't fucking tell me I didn't want her."

I stared at him. "So it is true. You really did take the fall for Landry. Why would you do that?"

"Because I thought he'd do a better job of looking after you than I could. Everyone knew I was trouble. I never pretended to be a choirboy. And I wanted that kid, but I was scared shitless I'd fuck it all up. Because that's what I always did."

"You didn't fuck everything up. We had some good years. I loved you so much."

"I was crazy in love with you," he said with a small laugh. "Still am, if I'm being honest. But I always knew you deserved better."

"So you went out of your way to fuck everything up." Dean had always been so self-destructive.

"Did a damn good job of it too."

"You know what we were good at?" He lifted his chin, prompting me to tell him. "Music. We made magic together."

"Fuck yeah we did." He smiled at the thought of it.

"And we made a beautiful baby together, Dean. She looks so much like you." I smiled. "She has your dimples and your eyes. And she loves to sing and dance. She's happy."

His eyes searched mine. "You saw her?"

I nodded. "Yes. I went to see her. While you were in rehab. I just... I wanted to make sure she was okay and..." I stopped talking, my gaze on the ocean, my longing for Brody so painful it felt like I'd been stabbed in the chest. So much had been lost. My brother. Hayley. My relationship with Dean. Was it possible that Brody and I could find our way back to each other? After everything I said and the way I kicked him to the curb, I didn't think he'd ever forgive me. I returned my gaze to Dean, my first love. "I've made such a mess of everything, Dean."

He studied my face for a minute and somehow, he understood what I was talking about without my having to tell him. "I learned a few things from this last stint in rehab. Might help you too. You've got to be honest. With yourself. And with the other person. If you hurt someone, you need to own up to whatever you did and apologize. Try to fix it. The only thing within your control is the way you deal with all the shit that gets thrown at you. Make a plan and do the best you can. One day at a time."

"Wow. That was... really... that's really smart, Dean. I'm so proud of you."

He shrugged one shoulder. "I'm trying. I always said I didn't want to end up like my Pops..."

"You're not him. You're nothing like him."

He snorted. "That's bullshit and you of all people know that's not true. I put you through hell. And I'm sorry."

"I'm sorry too. We were so young and stupid."

He grinned, the dimples in his cheeks making an appearance. "We had some fun times though. We lived like fucking rock stars."

I laughed. "Yeah, we did."

He lit a cigarette and we sat in silence for a while, our eyes on the ocean as the last of the sun dipped into it. Before I left, he told me he was going solo and I was happy for him. Happy that he hadn't given up on the music. It had always been his salvation. I played Hayley's voice for him and he listened to her singing "Here Comes the Sun" at least ten times. I hoped Dean would stay clean and sober and that he'd find someone who made him happy in a way that I never had. We were different people now. Life changed us. And even though a part of me would always love him, my feelings for Dean didn't even come close to the way I loved Brody. The way I *love* Brody.

My life was so much emptier without him in it.

CHAPTER FORTY-TWO

Brody

RIDGE SLAMMED the refrigerator shut as I hobbled into the kitchen and filled a glass of water from the tap. He grabbed a green apple from the bowl on the counter and sat at the island, texting with one hand, eating an apple with the other, and somehow managing to keep one eye trained on me.

"What'd you do to your leg?" he asked.

"Nothing." I guzzled the water and refilled the glass then leaned against the counter to drink it. My hair was matted down with sweat, my T-shirt and jeans were covered in dirt, and I was weary to the bone.

"Why are you limping?"

"I'm not limping."

Ridge snorted. "Yeah, okay, whatever you say. You're a stubborn son of a bitch, you know that?"

"Not telling me anything I don't know."

He set his phone on the counter and stared at me for a minute. Had to admit my brother was a good-looking bastard.

In the evening sun, his eyes looked bluer, his skin bronzed and his longish brown hair streaked with blond. Tomorrow was his high school graduation and in a few months he'd be off to college. The thought of that made me sad. Happy for him, of course, but this house would be so much emptier when he was gone.

"It's been three months," he said finally. "You should call her. You're miserable without her."

"I'm just fine. Don't worry about me," I said gruffly, rubbing my hand over my chest. I couldn't decide what hurt more right now. My damn leg or my heart. My heart. Definitely my heart. It still hurt like a motherfucker any time I thought about her. Which was all the damn time. "I've moved on."

He laughed like that was a joke. "Yeah, sure you have. By the way, my English teacher said hi. She got engaged."

"Good for her." My 'relationship' with Chloe Whitman, if you could even call it that, felt like a million years ago. I hadn't seen her since that meeting about Ridge last year and could barely remember what she looked like.

"You slept with her, didn't you?"

I shrugged one shoulder. What did it matter?

"Walker and some of the guys are coming over before the party at the lake. We're gonna order pizza. You in?"

"Sure."

"Pepperoni?"

"Whatever."

He shook his head and sighed. "You need to—"

"Don't tell me what I need," I gritted out. I rubbed the back of my neck and took a few deep breaths then threw a few twenties on the counter. "Save me a few slices."

I tried my best not to limp as I walked out of the kitchen. "Good try, bro. But you're definitely limping." I held up my middle finger. His laughter followed me into the living room. It had been a while since I'd been thrown from a horse. But today I'd been thrown by a wild mustang I was trying to gentle. I'd rushed it. He wasn't ready. Another lesson learned the hard way.

After a quick shower, I changed into a clean gray T-shirt and black running shorts and collapsed on my bed. Every muscle in my body ached, a reminder that I wasn't eighteen anymore. Back in my rodeo days, I'd gotten thrown from horses plenty of times. Had broken so many bones and endured so many injuries, I'd lost count. But I'd always bounced right back. One time I'd broken my leg and had walked right out of the arena on my own two feet. Stubborn bastard.

Now it was all catching up to me, and it wasn't as easy to rebound from an injury. I tucked my arms under my head and stared at the bedroom ceiling. Over the past few months, I'd been tempted to call Shiloh a million times. Everyone had been on my case about it. Especially Jude who kept insisting that anything worth having was worth fighting for. But fighting for the things I believed in was partially to blame for getting us into this mess. And every single time I picked up the phone to call her, I was reminded of her parting words.

"I never want to see your face again. It's a reminder of every-thing me and Landry lost."

Her voice had been so cold. So hard. Her face twisted with grief and hurt and anger. And how could I blame her for never wanting to see my face again? I looked just like the man who had killed her mother. It had been hard enough trying to navigate our two very different worlds and find time to be together. But now... there was no chance in hell we could ever make it work. There were too many obstacles standing in our way.

At the end of the day, what was the point in calling her? There was nothing left to say. No world in which we could ever

—should have ever—been together. So yeah, you had to know when it was time to cut your losses and walk away.

My phone buzzed and I checked the screen. Kate.

"Hey. You good?"

"Hi honey. I just got a call from your new guest who checked in earlier. She said there's a problem with the water pressure."

I groaned.

"Would you mind stopping by and checking on it?"

Yeah, I minded but I wasn't about to bitch and moan about it. I swung my legs over the side of the bed and scrubbed my hand over my face. "Fine. I'll go now."

"Thank you."

She didn't need to thank me. It was my guesthouse but she did all the bookings and took care of everything.

"Catch you later."

I stood up from the bed, favoring my left leg and grabbed my Nikes from the closet. Might as well get this over with.

I DECIDED TO DRIVE, justifying it by telling myself it would be quicker. Bullshit. Five minutes later, I pulled up behind an SUV parked in front of the guesthouse. Then I hobbled up to the front door feeling like I was about a hundred years old and rapped my knuckles against the wood.

The door swung open and my breath hitched. For a long moment, neither of us said a word. She was wearing cut-offs and a black tank top over a thin white one. Braless. Barefoot. Long black hair falling halfway down her back. I stared at the tattoo on her arm as if it was the first time I'd ever seen it. Then my eyes moved to her lush lips and up to her eyes where they locked and held. Those goddamn eyes... stormy and gray, fringed by long dark lashes. They haunted my dreams and now that she was here, standing right in front of me, I didn't know what to do or say.

"Hi Cowboy." Her bottom lip quivered. "I... God, it's so good to see you."

My eyes narrowed on her. Dry tears streaked her cheeks. "Why were you crying?" *Who did I have to beat up?*

"I was chopping onions." She wiped her cheeks. "You know how that always makes me cry."

"Yeah. I remember." I stared at her face, half-expecting her to vanish into thin air. "What are you doing here?"

"Cooking dinner. For you. Jambalaya. I know you liked it so... have you eaten yet?"

I looked over my shoulder at the SUV parked in front of the guesthouse then back at her. Yep, she was still there. Not my imagination. "What are you really doing here?"

"I'm here for you. I..." She swallowed hard and I watched her throat bob. "I wanted to call you. So many times. But I never knew what to say or how to tell you how sorry I was. It didn't seem right to do it on the phone." She held out her arms and forced a smile. "So here I am."

"Here you are." I was still standing on the front porch, trying to make sense of this.

"I didn't even stop to think you might already have plans." She gnawed on her bottom lip. I'd kissed those lips hundreds of times. They'd been wrapped around my cock and... shit, I had to stop thinking about it.

"Are you free tonight? Have you eaten dinner yet?"

She spun the silver ring around her thumb, a nervous habit. I knew the significance of the ring now. The feather of an angel's wing, according to her Maw Maw. And the angel was her mother. Ophelia. Ophelia Leroux Holloway. Wife of Rhett

Holloway. Mother of Shiloh and Landry. Killed in a random shooting.

"Will you have dinner with me, Brody?"

My eyes narrowed on her. "You want me to have dinner with you?"

She nodded. "I want more than dinner, but it seemed like a good place to start." She opened the door wider and I hesitated before stepping inside. Her eyes lowered. "What happened to your leg?"

I shrugged one shoulder and cursed myself for not changing into jeans before I came over. But then, I hadn't expected her to be here. "It's nothing."

She inspected the side of my leg. It looked like road burn. Then my knee. It was red and swollen, and had blown up like a damn balloon. Somehow, I'd twisted it in the fall. "Jesus, Brody. Get in here. You need ice on that knee."

She came to stand next to me and grabbed my arm, pulling it over her shoulders. I looked down at her and scowled. "The hell do you think you're doing?"

"Lean on me."

"You can't carry my weight. You'd snap like a twig."

She glared at me. "I'm stronger than I look."

"I know you are," I said, my voice softer. "But I can walk on my own two feet and I'm not going to lean on you."

Shiloh rolled her eyes. "Still so stubborn."

I tried my damnedest to walk without limping but once again I failed miserably. I lowered myself onto a stool. She pulled up a stool across from me. "Prop up your leg, Cowboy. I'll get you an ice pack."

I did as she said, mostly because I had no choice. It hurt too much to bend my knee so I propped it up on the stool and she came back with a bag of frozen peas. "Frozen peas?"

"I don't have an ice pack." She planted her hands on her hips, her voice filled with accusation. "How did you do this?"

"Was trying to do the Texas two-step. Guess I've lost my touch."

She laughed, her gaze moving from my knee to my face. "You're crazy," she said softly.

"I know." She was standing so close I could smell her scent.

"Brody." Her voice was a mere whisper. I lifted my hand to her face and brushed my thumb over her soft, full lips. Her eyes drifted shut. "I've missed you so much."

"Missed you more." I dropped my hand to my side and cleared my throat. "How's that jambalaya coming along?"

"Oh shit." She flew to the stove and I chuckled as she stirred the pot, mumbling under her breath. "Every single time. You're too distracting."

I stared at her perfect ass. The curve of her hips. Her slender, toned legs that had been wrapped around my back more times than I could count. Talk about distracting. My knee might be fucked but my dick was working just fine. It stirred in my shorts, obviously appreciating the view.

"All is not lost," she said, sounding relieved as she lowered the heat under the pot and turned from the stove. I didn't know if she was talking about the dinner or us.

She grabbed two beers from the fridge and flipped the caps then handed one to me across the breakfast bar. I took it from her and thanked her.

"Let's make a toast."

Those words reminded me of that little club in Miami, and the last time we made a toast. Of the promises I'd made and broken. "Let's not." Without waiting to hear what she wanted to toast to, I took a swig of the cold beer.

Undeterred, she held up her beer. "How about we drink to new beginnings?"

"Is that what this is? A new beginning?"

She nodded. "I hope so. Now that I've found you, I don't know how to live without you. I don't want to live without you." She stopped and sucked in a breath. "And I was kind of hoping you felt the same way."

"We were never meant to be, Shy." I averted my head, unable to see the disappointment on her face, and took another swig of beer. Music was piping from her portable speakers—Cigarettes After Sex's "Nothing's Gonna Hurt You Baby." She'd played this for me once. We were in New York, staying at Bastian's loft in Tribeca and she'd been dancing, almost trance-like, her eyes painted smoky and her lips red, dressed in a loose black tank top and lacy black underwear. It was the sexiest thing I'd ever seen. She'd straddled me on the living room sofa and when she fucked me, she threw back her head, exposing the column of her neck that begged to be marked by my mouth and teeth.

"Don't say that," she said. "It's not true. We're perfect for each other."

"What about your mom?" My gaze swung to her, my eyes narrowed. "Do you think she'd feel the same way? How do you think she'd feel if she knew that her daughter was in love with the enemy?"

"My mom is gone. And you're not the enemy. It wasn't your fault and I was wrong to act like it was. It was the initial shock. But you were just a kid, Brody. An innocent kid who wasn't responsible for what that man did."

I shook my head, disputing that. "I look just like him. Every time you look at me, it will be a reminder of what you lost. I can't expect you to live with something like that."

"When I look at you, I don't see him. I see Brody McCallister. A good man. An amazing father. A man who speaks his own truth and is always there for the people he loves and cares about. You never let me down, Brody. I trusted you—*trust* you —with my life."

I rubbed my hand over my chest. "I lied to you."

"No. You didn't lie. You just... you didn't want to be associated with that monster. And I get it now. He's dead to you. What he did has nothing to do with us. You deserve good things, Brody. You are the best man I've ever known. The most honest and true and strong. And I shouldn't have reacted the way I did."

"You had every right to act that way."

"I love you, Brody. I don't want to lose you again. Please tell me there's still a chance for us. Tell me you're still willing to fight for me. To be by my side when I need someone to lean on. Tell me you're still that man."

"I fucked everything up for you. How can you still want me?" It shocked me that she could still think she wanted me, despite everything that had come out about me. Despite all the pain I'd caused her, she still wanted me.

She rounded the island and came to stand next to me. "How could I not?" She cradled my face in her hands and her grays locked on my browns. Unshed tears glittered in her eyes. "You're my one true love. We were always destined to be together. Our paths were always meant to cross."

I wrapped my hands around her wrists and lowered her hands, clasping them in mine. "Shy... our lives are too different. Even if we're able to get past what happened that night, there's no way to make this work."

She yanked her hands out of mine and crossed her arms over her chest. "I never took you for a coward."

"I'm being realistic."

"That's such bullshit. Where's the man who promised to fight for me, regardless of the odds?" She threw up her hands.

"This is just like that day at the airport. You're letting me go without a fight."

She stomped away, her movements jerky as she turned off the heat under the pot then spun around to face me, her eyes narrowed. She pointed her finger at me. "You are a big fat coward."

I couldn't help it. I burst out laughing. She glared at me. That made me laugh harder. She was so small and angry, and reminded me of one of those cartoon characters with the smoke coming out of their ears.

"What are you laughing at?"

I shook my head and tried to control my laughter. Didn't think she'd appreciate the cartoon reference. "You."

"I wasn't being funny."

I stopped and took a breath. "I know."

"What are you so scared of, Brody?"

I tugged my bottom lip between my teeth then I gave her an honest answer. "Losing you again. Not sure my heart could handle that."

"Oh Brody," she breathed. And then she began crying. There were no onions to blame her tears on this time.

I tossed the bag of frozen peas aside and went to stand in front of her. Then I gathered her into my arms and she clung to me like she was afraid I'd disappear if she didn't hold on tight enough.

"Don't let me go," she said, her voice muffled.

She pulled back a little and lifted her face to mine. I wiped away the tears with the pads of my thumbs. She was so fucking beautiful. Strong and true and fierce. But our love made us vulnerable. True bravery had nothing to do with looking your opponent in the eye before you knocked him to the ground and pummeled him with your fists. True bravery was looking into the eyes of the woman you loved and promising them forever. Despite the odds stacked against you, you'd be willing to risk it all for one more day, one more year, or if you got really lucky, an entire lifetime.

"I won't. I'm not going anywhere. We'll make it work. I promise, we'll figure it out."

"Maw Maw said there'd be a lot of storms in our way. The journey won't always be easy." She was testing me now, wanting to see if I had what it took to be the man for her.

"We'll ride out the storms." I tucked a lock of hair behind her ear, the backs of my fingers brushing over her jaw. "Come out on the other side."

She rewarded me with a smile that was so fucking glorious it knocked the air out of my lungs. "I love you so much, Cowboy."

"Pretty sure I love you more."

She laughed through her tears. "It's not a contest. But okay, if you want to turn it into one... game on."

I laughed and when I stopped laughing, I dipped my head and took the first taste of something I'd been denied for too long. Her arms looped around my neck, her tits pressed against my chest, and I forgot all about the pain in my leg and the long months of separation. Her lips were soft and her tongue lashed against mine, my heart beating at the same tempo as hers. We kissed until her lips were swollen and bruised, pouring all our love and pain and hope into this one kiss.

When we pulled away to catch our breath, she said, "It's so good to be home again."

And that was how it felt. Like our long search was over and we were back where we belonged. Home.

EPILOGUE

Shiloh

ONE YEAR Later

SOME GIRLS DREAM about their wedding day. Not me. I only ever dreamt about two things. Finding my one true love and having a music career. I was lucky enough to make both of those dreams come true.

"Let's do this," Brody said one morning about a week before I was leaving to go on tour for my second solo album. This tour would only be for five months, mostly in North America with a few weeks in Europe. We'd arranged it so that Brody and I would never be apart for more than two weeks at a time. It wasn't ideal, compromises had to be made, but it was our way of having it all. He said he wouldn't have it any other way and I believed him. He'd never expect or want me to give up my career any more than I'd expect him to give up his. The paths we'd chosen made us who we were and neither of us was looking to change the other. I loved him just as he was.

"Do what?" We'd just come back from a morning ride and I was grooming Phoenix, making her coat shine. Last year, when she'd turned one, Brody had trained her and I'd been riding her ever since. She was my special girl and I lavished so much attention on her that sometimes Brody got jealous. It was hilarious.

"Get married."

I turned to look at him, half-expecting him to laugh and say he was joking. But he looked dead serious. "You want to get married? You don't even believe in the institution of marriage." We'd had this conversation before. "We both agreed we weren't interested in getting married. And we have Noah so..." I gnawed on my lip, the worry setting in. What if he'd changed his mind about everything we'd discussed? "Wait. You're still cool with not having more kids, right? At least, not right now..."

"Stop your worrying." He squeezed my shoulder. "None of that's changed. And I'm not talking about a big wedding with all the hoopla."

"Hoopla?" I laughed. "So what are you saying?"

"Just you and me. Making a promise. Speaking our own truth." He shrugged one shoulder, trying to pass it off as if this was a casual conversation and he had no skin in the game. But I could tell by the look on his face that this meant a lot to him. "That's what it's all about, right? You and me making a vow to each other."

And I guess it was. Now here we are, just the two of us in the woods. It's close to midnight, and lanterns and tea lights in mason jars light up the darkness. Above us is a sky full of stars and a sliver of moon. The air is warm and smells like juniper and pine and the promise of summertime. Brody's wearing a white button-up, the sleeves rolled up to expose his tanned forearms, vein porn at its finest, his legs clad in faded denim. I'm wearing a silky gray slip dress trimmed in black lace. We look like us. The cowboy and the rock star. His hair is as light as the sun, mine is dark as midnight. He loves open spaces and guards his privacy, never goes on the Internet, nor does he have any social media accounts. I spend months at a time in cities, waking up in different hotel rooms, my photos splashed across the front page of tabloids and I have millions of followers on social media. Two opposites, living in different worlds, who never should have found each other but by some miracle, we did.

We're not perfect. We argue. We fight about stupid things and sometimes we drive each other crazy. He's still the most stubborn man I've ever met. He's still too proud to ask for anyone's help, always insisting that he can handle everything on his own. Spoiler alert: That's not always the case but try telling him that.

But no man could ever love me the way he does. And I have never loved anyone the way I love him. We're both a little crazy, with a wild streak and a temper. It makes for interesting times.

Now we're standing in the middle of this cathedral of trees, facing each other when he takes my hands in his.

"You go first," I tell him, stopping short of reminding him that it was his idea.

He nods solemnly, like he's taking this seriously, and I love that about him. I love that you never know exactly what to expect. Brody is always surprising me with the things he says and does. His outlook on life and love is so unique, and I can't wait to hear what he's going to say now.

Without any fanfare or hesitation, he starts speaking. "Before you came into my life two years ago, I thought I was exactly where I was meant to be. I didn't even know I was searching for you. But then, there you were. And I had no idea how I'd gotten through life without you. You make my world a better place. You love me for exactly who I am and never try to change me or turn me into your ideal version of a man. Despite my flaws and weaknesses, you still love me. And that fucking amazes me. I never thought I'd find a love like that. Every single day I ask myself, why me? How did I get so damn lucky?

"I'd consider it my greatest privilege to walk through this life with you. To be by your side through all the highs and lows, through every storm that life throws our way. As long as we're together, I have faith that we'll come through it just fine. It's been a hell of a ride already and we've only just begun." My heart is hammering against my ribcage, so full I think it might burst. "I love you, Shiloh. And now that I've found you, I'll do my damnedest to make sure you never regret choosing me. I promise to be true to you and only you and to fight for you and defend you until my dying day."

Tears are streaming down my cheeks. For a long moment, I just stare at his face, the face I love above all others, so overcome with emotion that I'm speechless. Then I throw my arms around his neck, nearly knocking him over, and I kiss him hard. "God, I love you."

"That's all you've got to say?" Brody snorts. "And they call you a poet."

I roll my eyes. "I wrote a whole album for you, Cowboy."

It's true too. Every song on my new album was written for him. There are two things I hold sacred. My music and my love for Brody. And not necessarily in that order.

"Yeah, you did." He pulls back and reaches into his pocket. Then he takes my left hand in his and slides a cool piece of metal on to my ring finger. I hold it up to my face and inspect the silver ring etched with designs I can't quite make out in this lighting. But the ring fits perfectly, and it's exactly something I would have chosen. I've never been big on diamonds or gemstones, and he knows this about me. "This is so beautiful," I whisper, holding my hand over my heart. "I love it."

"Thank fuck for that." He wipes imaginary sweat off his brow. Or maybe he really is sweating. "Otherwise, I'd be shit out of luck. Can't take it back. I had it made for you."

"You did that for me?"

"I'd do anything for you," he says simply. Then adds, "It's just a ring. No need to cry over it."

As if it was the ring I was crying over. It was his words and the thought of him going to a jeweler and giving them specifications for how he wanted this ring to turn out. "I can't help it. Sometimes you're just so sweet."

"There's nothing sweet about me," he says gruffly, even though we both know that's not true.

Then he gives me that charming Brody McCallister grin, mischief dancing in his whiskey brown eyes completely disarming me. I have no defense against Charming Brody. Before I even have a chance to process what's happening, he lifts me up off the ground and throws me over his shoulder. I'm laughing and pounding his back as he jogs to the dock. I've been living with this man every day for an entire year so I should have seen it coming but I didn't. Seconds later, he tosses me into the lake then dives in after me. When my head emerges from the water, he pulls my shivering body against him and I wrap my arms and legs around him, using his body heat to keep me warm.

"You're crazy," I say, laughing.

"About you."

We're fully dressed, swimming in a cool lake under the moon and stars two years to the day that I first came to stay in the guesthouse at Brody McCallister's ranch. It's an anniversary and a new beginning all rolled into one.

"Let me say my words." I cradle his face in my hands while he treads water to keep both of us afloat. "From the moment I saw you at the airport two years ago, I knew you were going to change my life. I had that feeling, you know?" He nods. He knows all about my freaky psychic powers that may or may not be a real thing. I don't even think it matters.

"When I'm with you, I know it's exactly where I belong. You are, quite literally, the man of my dreams. You still make me weak in the knees and your smile still makes my stomach flutter. I trust you with my life, my secrets, my hopes and dreams, my truths that aren't always pretty but they're real. Like you. Like us. You're my every dream come true. My ideal man. Strong and true and brave with a side of wild and crazy that I love." He smiles and I run my fingertips over the little crinkles next to his eyes. "It feels like I have loved you from the beginning of time and I will love you to the end. I have no doubt that we will weather every storm. Because this love of ours is one for the ages. I love you, Brody. Forever and ever. Amen."

"Hallelujah."

And then he kisses me, gentle but demanding, sealing the vows we made while he somehow manages to keep us both afloat. I say a silent little prayer to Maw Maw, thanking her for sending Brody to me. I'd like to believe that my mom and Maw Maw are up above looking down at us from the stars, giving us their blessing.

I have found my home in the arms of the man I love. I made my peace with giving up my daughter. I lost my brother. But the McCallisters have welcomed me into their family, and they treat me as one of their own.

I am loved. And I guess that's what I was searching for all

along. I was lucky enough to find a man who is willing to put up with the life of a rock star, to support and encourage me every step of the way, and I'll never take that for granted. Sometimes you really can have it all. And I do. I don't think it could get much better than this.

The End

ABOUT THE AUTHOR

Emery Rose has been known to indulge in good red wine, strong coffee, and a healthy dose of sarcasm. She loves writing about sexy alpha heroes, strong heroines, artists, beautiful souls, and flawed but redeemable characters who need to work for their happily ever after.

When she's not writing, you can find her binge-watching Netflix, trotting the globe in search of sunshine, or immersed in a good book. A former New Yorker, she currently lives in London with her two beautiful daughters.

Stay in touch!
> Facebook
> Facebook Group
> Instagram
> Twitter
> Newsletter
> BookBub
> Amazon
> Goodreads
> Pinterest

ACKNOWLEDGMENTS

Acknowledgements

As always, I have so many people to thank for helping me bring this book to life.

A huge thank you to Jen Mirabelli. Once again, I could not have done this without you. Thank you for believing in me and this story. Thank you for the daily chats, for taking my calls when I 'lost the plot' and for organizing all the promo and marketing. You do so much for me and I'm so grateful. xoxo

To Aliana Milano. Thank you for beta reading, for kicking my ass when I need it, and for all the midnight chats when we put the world to rights. Love you, boo.

Carol Radcliffe, thank you for friendship and your support. I'm so happy we found each other. Emily Meador, thank you for all you do for Emery's Rambling Roses and for doing such an amazing job of keeping the group going. I truly appreciate it.

Thank you, Ellie McLove for always fitting me into your schedule at the very last minute.

Najla Qamber, thank you for creating this gorgeous cover.

You are such a joy to work with. Thank you to Michelle Lancaster for taking this gorgeous cover photo. It's a true work of art.

To all the book bloggers and bookstagrammers who took the time to read and review and share, thank you so much! I appreciate you and everything you do for the indie community.

A big thank you to my daughters who are so supportive and understanding, even when I disappear for hours and days at a time and get lost in the world of my fictional characters. Love you to the moon and back. Forever and always.

And last but certainly not least, a huge thank you to the readers. Writing is a dream come true and I couldn't do this without you. Thank you so much for reading my words. Please consider taking a few seconds to leave an honest review. They mean so much to indie authors.

Thank you so very much.

Emery Rose xoxo

ALSO BY EMERY ROSE

The Beautiful Series

Beneath Your Beautiful

Beautiful Lies

Beautiful Rush

Love and Chaos Series

Wilder Love

Sweet Chaos

Lost Stars Series

When The Stars Fall

Made in the USA
Las Vegas, NV
06 November 2023

80320644R00256

Why is Elisha writing this Foreword?

I, the author of *Untouchable*, first met Elisha in 2009. In the 13 years since, and throughout the most demanding of tasks researching this work, I have relied countless times on Elisha for insight and understanding. As a westerner from Australia, many times I have floundered in the need to shed light on the enormity of the most deplorable apartheid regimes this planet has ever known.

Although *Untouchable* is a work of fiction, much of the content of this novel has been lifted directly from the life-and-death experiences of Elisha's world.

Since 2006, and against all odds, he has established, maintained, and exponentially expanded "Son-Shine," a unique, life-saving orphanage and school for deprived, poverty-stricken Dalits.

In a nation of over 1.3 billion, Elisha emerges as a man like few others. In the 13 years since our first meeting, Elisha has selflessly rescued, protected, housed, educated, and inspired many thousands of Dalit children. In doing so, he has equipped them to grasp a future far beyond their dreams.

It is my honor and my privilege to call him "friend."

FOREWORD

What can I say about our brother Richard's wonderful masterpiece ... ! This book is a window into the world of our Dalit children and people's lives. He wonderfully portrayed our lives in a very detailed way in which it looks as though he lived through it. The detail that Richard has gone into to showcase the life of Naggya and all the people in this book is amazing.

Untouchable amazingly portrays the hardships, suffering, pain, discrimination, and inhumane treatment that our people are experiencing every day. This is a window into the world of over 300 million Dalits! We are THE most and longest discriminated people on planet Earth, the Dalits of India.

The saying goes, "out of sight, out of mind," but this book will open your eyes to see the Dalit people's lives and what they go through daily. While this book shows the pain and suffering of the young boy Naggya, it also showcases the story of triumph against all odds, and of finding hope.

I feel privileged that my story is also part of this book.

Once you start reading it, you will never want to stop. Richard has a wonderful way of putting the story together without losing context.

I sincerely thank Richard for taking up the monumental task of making the lives of our Dalit people known to the world. I sincerely applaud him for it.

From the bottom of my heart, I encourage and challenge you to not just read this as you would read another book, but to read it as you would a life . . . not just a story, because it is about the lives of Naggya and other Dalit children and people.

Through this book, may your eyes be open to see the other side of the world of the Untouchable Dalits.

May God speak to you through this book.

Elisha
Founder & President, Son-Shine
India
www.lightkids.org

INSPIRED

BY

REAL EVENTS

Da·lit /ˈdälit/
noun

A member of the lowest class in the traditional Hindu social hierarchy having in traditional Hindu belief the quality of defiling by contact a member of a higher caste.*

In the traditional Indian caste system, those at the bottom of the hierarchy who fall outside the four main categories of Brahmins (priests and teachers), Kshatriyas (warriors and rulers), Vaishyas (traders and merchants), and the Shudras (laborers), are considered "untouchables" or Dalits.**

In 2023, India is home to 280 million Dalits.***

---

*Merriam-Webster Dictionary, s.v. "Definition word (Dalit)," Accessed February 23, 2023. https://www.merriam-webster.com/dictionary/Dalit.

**Sur, Priyali. "Under India's Caste System, Dalits Are Considered Untouchable. The Coronavirus is Intensifying That Slur." CNN. April 16, 2020. https://www.cnn.com/2020/04/15/asia/india-coronavirus-lower-castes-hnk-intl/index.html.

***Majumdar, Suprakash. "How India's Caste System Keeps Dalits From Accessing Disaster Relief." The New Humanitarian. November 29, 2022. https://www.thenewhumanitarian.org/news-feature/2022/11/29/India-Dalits-disaster-relief-aid.

CHAPTER
one

"Run, Naggya, run!"

At five, Naggya had already learned to run, to run fast. If not, he'd cop another beating, and there'd been too many already. "This way, Mummy, quick, he's coming!"

Arud had been drinking all through the day and most of the night, and had only returned when he'd run out of money. Arud's only hope of laying his hands on more drinking money was to forcibly extract whatever his wife may have hidden in their makeshift hut.

Punea could barely run; her exhaustion from staying awake fearing his return, coupled with his countless beatings and the many years spent slaving in the fields, had left her legs scarcely able to walk, let alone run.

"He can't find us in the jungle, Mummy! Quick!"

Most Dalits were forced to live outside the village and almost always on the poorest of land. Formerly a laborer in the quarry, Arud had been a drunk since a teenager and had remained addicted to alcohol for the bulk of their married life. He'd long since concluded it was far better for his wife to work in the rice fields than for him to rise early each day to work in the blazing sun, his rightful place in life was to sit among the local Dalit men.

"Naggya, you run ahead! I will catch up!"

"But, Mummy, he will find you! Run faster!"

In the haze of the morning's first light, Punea could see her husband staggering past the other Dalit huts. She could hear his repeated threats of another thrashing if she kept running. "Stop, filthy bitch! Run away and I will catch you! You know I will catch you! Where is it?! Where did you hide it?"

"Help us, please, help my son!" Punea screamed, knowing no one would interfere with a man's right to punish his own wife. Punea steeled herself for what was coming. Closer now, Arud picked up a rock and hurled it at his wife, striking her on the shoulder and sending her sprawling to the ground.

"Mummy!"

❖❖❖❖❖

The funeral was short, and the unmarked grave served only to echo her suffering. Punea; merely the latest, and the line was long. Naggya still had a father, of sorts, yet at five, he instinctively knew he'd become the latest orphan with nowhere to turn.

Naggya had visited his only living relative once, and all he could remember was his mother's sister lived somewhere on the far side of the big village. She was known to him only as "Aunty."

Being a five-year-old orphan presented mixed blessings; he could beg, and in doing so, might possibly receive a few morsels to sustain him, yet more likely he'd become fresh fodder for the depraved.

For three days and three long, lonely nights he wandered in

what he hoped was the direction toward Aunty's. "Where can I get some water?"

Clean drinking water was a constant struggle in rural Andhra Pradesh. For Naggya, that struggle was dwarfed by his fears that all the big people were following him. Early on the fourth day, he silently repeated his mother's words: "*Son, you must be strong!*"

Doesn't Aunty have a limp the same as Mummy?

A police van motored slowly by. Naggya's first inclination was to make his way towards the two officers, but he recalled his mother's warning and ran behind a buffalo, pretending to be caring for the animal. He remained there until the police had driven off and the buffalo shepherd had shooed him off with threats of violence.

In every clump of huts there would be at least one lady with a limp, and as the young pilgrim peered into their eyes, nothing at all reminded him of his mother's sister. *Help me please, Mummy,* and the need to cry was stifled by an even greater need to survive.

Naggya approached a stand of straggly trees that no shepherd deemed worthy as shelter for their cattle. He covered himself with rice husk and settled for a few hours' sleep. It had been just over a week since he'd fled his father's temper, and in that time, he'd slept perhaps twenty hours and consumed scarcely sufficient food to sustain a child for one day. Naggya was starving and exhausted, though nothing matched the terror that coursed through his emaciated little body.

At first light the ladies of the field set about tending the crops. They would work either bent over or would squat, causing painful debilitating pressures upon their knees.

Naggya struggled to his feet and brushed the rice husks from his threadbare shirt. The itch from the husks was almost unbearable as he yawned and stretched, making his way from the trees to cross the fields in search of food.

From the far side of the field a voice called out, "Naggya?! Is that you?"

A feeble lady in her 30s, who'd easily pass for double that age, limped slowly toward him. She squinted in the early light, "Naggya? It is you! Quick, get out of the fields. If the landowner sees you, he will beat us both!"

Rastard ushered Naggya out of sight and sat him down behind an old dray. She carefully scanned the roadway for signs of her employer, then turned to focus on her nephew. "Look at you, Naggya. You look terrible! What are you doing here?" She again glanced around then threw her bony arms around him and looked deeply into his terrified eyes, "Where is your mother?"

❖❖❖❖❖

Naggya endured ten hot, hungry, thirsty hours hidden behind the trees waiting for Aunty to finish work. Together, they walked three miles to the single-room hovel that Rastard called home.

"Sit there while I prepare a meal." She scrounged from her tiny stash of rice, curry, and potatoes, and as Naggya slipped into a slumber, Rastard fetched a pitcher of water from the village well. As she carried the heavy clay pitcher her burden shifted to the tormented thoughts of how she could possibly break the news to her only nephew.

CHAPTER
two

Naggya slept for eleven hours, yet still needed waking when Rastard left for work. "Stay here and keep as quiet as you can. There is water in the jug, but I am sorry there is no more food. The landowner should pay me today, and if he does, I can bring some rice home tonight. I will have to walk to the market after I finish in the fields, so please be very careful. Most importantly, you stay away from the men drinking. Naggya, please, you need to stay here," and she threw her arms around him as they both trembled. *How can I tell him?*

Rastard was a childless widow. Her husband had suffered from a dysentery condition common in that region. He'd had no medical treatment nor any medication, and for them to make ends meet, Rastard had continued working in the fields. After months of watching her husband of almost twenty years slip further toward the inevitable, she'd arrived home to discover he'd taken his own life.

Today, as she toiled in the fields, her unmistakable symptoms of the same condition seemed more intolerable than ever. Rastard had no one else to turn to, yet instinctively knew that her own time was short. *How much longer can I work in the fields? I can't earn enough to feed myself so how can I raise Naggya? And what if I pass my disease onto him? He's only five! The longer he stays with me the more he risks the sickness. God, help us, please!!*

Elijah was twenty when he first began the contemplation of life's bigger issues. From the humblest of beginnings, the young *untouchable* had gained entry to one of the poorest of the province's universities. Although rare for one of India's lowest castes to be granted admission to a university, their urgent need for cashflow during the latest economic downturn and, following, the miraculous provision of his entrance fee, Elijah had beaten the odds.

A budding communist, Elijah spent much of his time spruiking the philosophies of Lenin or Marx or Mao, yet deep within, he wrestled with the sincerity of his convictions. Elijah was convinced that surely the future of his populous nation depended upon the caste system not only being contested but utterly demolished. The young student had convinced himself that in place of the most discriminatory of social systems, the equitable sharing of wealth and opportunity would doubtless rise as the key to his nation's success. Elijah postulated that, surely, being born an ostracized Dalit was not only grossly unjust but was, in fact, in stark and absolute contrast to the teachings of the true masters.

Elijah's Christian roots were an anathema to him. During his first two decades, his own protesting eyes had seen not a thing to diminish the struggles of his parents, or their parents before them. Everywhere Elijah looked, he'd see evidence of the sufferings of the so-called chosen of God. *They've got it all wrong and I need to find the truth! I refuse to waste my life suffering like they have. When I show them a better way, they will follow. They must, and life will be better!*

Three years into his altruistic journey to enlightenment,

Elijah had been forced to accept the folly and the futility of his adopted belief system. *The job is just too big!*

During a rare home visit, one unexpected encounter, one Word, had miraculously set him free from his inner philosophical torment. From deep within the eyes of a homeless six-year-old orphan, Elijah's heart had been seared by one inescapable realization, *if my parents had died like so many others, this boy could so easily be me.*

An indescribable glow filled Elijah and, as he stared incredulously into the orphan boy's eyes, Elijah saw and felt a dimension of life he'd never known. Something from the very depths of his being shifted as a torrent of unfathomable compassion flooded his soul.

In stark contrast to his former rebellious rants, Elijah returned home from university, the unintended prodigal, embraced by the outstretched arms of his faithful father.

Elijah was gloriously *home,* and the shallow insincerity of his former belief systems had been irretrievably cast aside, replaced by an unshakable conviction, far greater, far more noble. Within his heaving heart, a determination took hold to start a revolution, not to the masses, but merely to one.

The humblest of beginnings formed under the veranda of his parents' two-room house. Within weeks, nestled safely against their external wall, sheltered the six-year-old orphan; his own past life one of abject tragedy. On the other side of the wall within the fifteen-foot-by-eight-foot mud home resided twenty-three-year-old Elijah and his faithful parents. Son-Shine had been launched; humbly, modestly, purposefully.

Within the first year, the number of orphans ballooned to twenty-nine. There'd been a necessary relocation to a bare patch of land that had no electricity supply. It did, however, boast a small run-down toilet block, though it lacked any running water.

During the following year, Son-Shine's numbers had swollen to around one hundred, along with four full-time caregivers and teachers, and a full-time cook. Within the same timeframe, concrete foundations had been poured for a new school block and the purchase of a thirty-year-old generator that constantly spewed plumes of black soot causing the cook-tent to temporarily disappear. A permanent water supply had miraculously been connected.

Each new day delivered the latest tragic story of orphans or poverty-stricken children, each one without any hope of survival or a future in life. Elijah felt powerless to turn them away. Every time he took in another homeless child, Son-Shine's running costs grew faster than his faith.

From within the local community, opposition to Son-Shine steadily mounted. Objections flooded in from government schools and from local and state government departments, on top of the ever-present menace of corruption. "We can't have these animals running schools!" would be protested loud and often. Elijah would regularly be the recipient of letters of demand, threats of closure, bewildering legislative interventions, and the ever-present risks of violence and intimidation. Despite all the opposition, a determination grew within the fledgling leader to not only endure but to expand Son-Shine.

We must meet the need, no matter how big.

❖❖❖❖❖

Rastard trusted no one. She was painfully aware that those who lived close by would swoop and take possession of her hut if anything prevented her from paying her way. She also knew that the ladies she worked with wouldn't hesitate to sell her out if she failed to fulfill her daily work requirements. Despite having worked for the same landowner for ten years, every worker in his fields had at least one family member ready, willing, and better able to take her place at a moment's notice. From the lofty heights of his higher caste, the landowner felt nothing by way of loyalty towards his Dalit employees, and knew that the supply of replacements was endless.

Forever mindful of her vulnerability, Rastard would conceal her limp as best she could and every day the proof of her dysentery would be concealed by whatever means possible.

How am I going to tell Naggya?

CHAPTER
three

"There are two sets of keys and the taxes are paid."

The shiny yellow bus was licensed to carry eighteen passengers, plus the driver. Just five years old and with sixty-thousand miles on the clock, the bus was in excellent condition. The bequest had come from an unlikely source. Kristen had only been given sixteen years in this life yet, despite her tender age, she'd seen things that many much older would scarcely comprehend. The provision of a school bus had been Kristen's dying wish after she and her parents had become the very first foreign supporters of Son-Shine. Kristen had fallen instantly in love with the children, and her bequest would mean that her many adopted Dalit brothers and sisters would no longer have to endure the six-mile walk from village to high school in the stifling heat or the monsoon rains.

"We are all so happy," Elijah beamed, as he wrapped his hands around the keys, though he did so in the knowledge of the considerable emotional and personal costs to Kristen's parents.

Being the proud and appreciative trustee of this latest blessing, the irony was that, not only did Elijah lack a license to drive such a vehicle, but he hadn't the vaguest clue of how to even start the engine. Elijah glanced sideways just long enough for a commemorative photograph to be taken. The previous owner, a man from a higher caste, was perfectly willing to overlook cultural taboos for the sake of money yet was visibly uncomfortable at doing so in full view of the passing motorists, and even more so while posing for photographs.

Punji was the new school bus driver, another Dalit with two children attending the school. Punji had offset the school fees by working as an unpaid laborer for several months prior to and since the commencement of the Son-Shine Junior School. Being in possession of the only bus driver's license within his nearby village, Punji worked a grueling six-days-a-week at Son-Shine. To feed his family of four, he also worked for his brother driving trucks at the local quarry.

Thrust unexpectedly into the role of official photographer, Punji peered into Elijah's phone and hoped he was somehow keeping the most relevant subject matters in shot.

"Did you get that, Punji?" asked Elijah while his right hand was being hurriedly extricated from that of the former bus owner.

From this day forward the Dalit orphanage and lower school now boasted the rarity of genuine transport. "The children will be so thrilled," declared Elijah, though it was unlikely the former owner would have heard his comment as he hastily placed the money into his pocket and departed to wash his hands.

When Punji drove the bus into the grassless school yard, and with Elijah following in his dilapidated 1988 Ambassador sedan, the children had already been lined up for two hours on either side of the track. At first sight of their sparkling miracle-on-wheels, the children jumped and shouted for joy, and as Punji eased the vehicle to a halt, a hundred sets of eyes jostled and jockeyed at the front door.

There is no way we'll deprive these children the joy of this day.

One by one they climbed aboard what, for many, was the first bus they had been in. One by one, the Son-Shine children from five to thirteen years of age pretended to be the driver, shuffling through the imaginary gears, and thrusting their tiny feet on imaginary brake pedals and tooting an imaginary horn. This was ecstasy; this was the most expensive toy they had ever dreamed of, yet following months of anticipation, discussion, and prayer, each knew it was to become so much more.

"Keep taking photos, Punji. Lots and lots of photos."

The celebrations lasted right up until evening prayer time, and for some, well beyond. Next morning their miracle-on-wheels began its new working life as thirty-five ninth grade students climbed aboard for their first bus trip to high school.

❖❖❖❖❖

A cousin of one of the Son-Shine teachers lived in a tiny Dalit village on the far side of Vijayawada. She had very recently become a widow after her husband's body had been found at the edge of one of the canals. The only plausible explanation pointed suspiciously to caste persecution. After a week of grieving, his widow's plea for help to take care of her eight-year-old daughter had reached the ears of Elijah. The following day, he'd arranged for the bus to set off on its latest rescue mission.

Roads into the village had been eroded during the latest monsoon, and as the bus slowly made its way into the village, Punji could feel the rear wheels slip, slide, and then spin. They were bogged. Only a few hundred yards from their destination, Punji and Elijah climbed out, and as they did, they acknowledged a number of Dalit men reclining on the porches of their huts. As one of them wandered toward the stricken vehicle to offer assistance, Elijah asked the man in the local tongue, Telugu, "Where is the little girl and her mother?"

Naggya hadn't eaten for three days, though the monsoon ensured plenty of water. Even more frail than when he'd been taken in by Aunty, his desperation for food had forced a willingness to risk his safety. The little boy ventured outside after hearing the sounds of a vehicle's spinning wheels and peered out from behind the palm tree fronds placed against the doorway to keep out the weather.

Beyond the shiny yellow bus stood a man dressed in a manner dissimilar to most of the men of the village; he wore clean clothes, relatively new shoes, and wore a watch on his wrist. When the man's eyes fell upon Naggya, he smiled. Reflexively, Naggya withdrew to the recesses of the hut and cowered behind Aunty's assortment of old cooking pots and her pottery jug. Elijah had witnessed such terror many times and, as Punji and the local Dalit stuffed branches under the rear wheels for traction, Elijah tentatively closed in on the hut and gently called out in his native tongue. Naggya trembled at the thought of a stranger entering the hut and as his panic-stricken eyes caught sight of the stranger's, he instinctively cried out for help.

"It's alright, little man. I am not here to hurt you. Please don't be afraid. You are safe. I am from a school on the other side of the city and my name is Elijah. What is your name?"

Naggya had been warned not to divulge anything to a stranger. His mother and Aunty had schooled him well and when Elijah entered the spartan hut with his hands raised as a gesture of peace, Naggya seized the opportunity to escape.

Despite his frailty and weakness from lack of food, Naggya side-stepped Elijah's grasp and fled down the path towards the edge of the jungle. The man assisting Punji appeared to smile as he watched Elijah's futile attempt to chase him. In Telugu he commented, "He is a very scared little boy since his mother died. I believe he came to live with his aunty as he had no one else, and he knows it can be very dangerous around here. It's not safe for most of the children unless they have a father to protect them. That little boy doesn't." The villager lowered his voice, "He doesn't get much to eat."

"Where is his aunty?"

"She works every day in the fields like most of the women of this village. Some of the men have jobs but there isn't a lot of work here. His aunty gets home just after dark every day but that's all I know."

With the bus again mobile, Elijah walked the remaining distance as Punji carefully followed, pulling up close to the hut without risking another bogging. The little girl's mother walked slowly towards Elijah with her head lowered and her hand tentatively outstretched. As he took hold of her hand and wrapped his other arm around her heaving shoulder she sobbed softly and pulled away. The little girl was a mix of fear and curiosity as she remained in the background staring at the bus.

"We brought food. Would you care to share some with us?"

During the next hour the lady gradually relaxed and became willing to convey a little of the family's background, while Elijah and Punji encouraged the little girl to join the conversation.

If this takes all day for them to be ready to say goodbye, then that's what we will do.

Two hours beyond dusk, Punji was gently easing the yellow bus through and around the potholes that the locals called a road. Onboard were not three but four; the little girl's name was Mary and sitting beside her was a wide-eyed terrified little boy. Naggya had become Son-Shine's latest rescue mission.

CHAPTER
four

For two days Naggya barely spoke; his inner challenge was still a mountain way too high. In time, his guard would likely come down and he'd join the other children, but for now, Elijah must wait.

On his third day Naggya was observed watching a game of Kabaddi, a game he'd never seen before. Though this game intrigued him, and as the children fought hard to win, Naggya was still fighting his own inner fears. From somewhere deep, his adventurous spirit yearned to be doing exactly what those bigger kids were doing, yet all the frightened little boy wanted was to run as far from Son-Shine as his tiny legs would carry him. In a bizarre twist, the thing he feared most seemed to be reeling him in, and try as he might, he simply couldn't look away.

Despite all the torment he'd endured while with his aunt, the terror of Aunty's village still represented a world so much more familiar. The daily cacophony of a hundred noisy children and the suffocating closeness of over thirty boys sleeping side-by-side on a classroom floor was an encounter that filled him with dread. Life for Naggya was tough. Life for Naggya was bewildering. *Why wouldn't Aunty let me stay with her? Why did she make me come here?*

For seven torturous days and seven almost sleepless nights Naggya resisted the efforts of Elijah and the teachers to help him assimilate.

Learning the most fundamental aspects of mathematics and reading amidst a classroom of twenty-five boys and girls of the same age, seemingly intent on him becoming their friend, only served to send Naggya into a downward spiral. On two occasions and on consecutive days, Naggya had tried to abscond, reaching the entrance gate the first day and the busy crossroads beyond, the next. *I shouldn't be in this horrible place!*

The boys' ablution block represented Naggya's most confronting challenge. During class, he could hide out of harm's way at the back; at playtime he could do the same, and so too could he at mealtimes, but showering naked and exposed left this little five-year-old shuddering with fear.

I have to run away. Mummy, please help me! I can't stay here. Please, Mummy!

Most nights one of the caregivers or a live-in teacher would be summoned as Naggya would cry out in his fitful sleep or sob so loudly the other boys couldn't settle. Something needed to change, and for everyone's sake, something needed to change quickly.

Thursdays were dance instruction days and, with the rapidly approaching fifth-year anniversary of Son-Shine, excitement was building. Though still the only Dalit orphanage and school in the region, a selection of local government officials had once again been invited, and following years of official invitations, a local government official had finally agreed to attend. Elijah was elated, though his elations remained shrouded in suspicion.

❖❖❖❖❖

With the anniversary celebration now only three weeks away, dance practice had become a twice-daily event, and the more the children practiced their dances, the more they loved them. Traditional native dancing had been tinged with a sprinkling of contemporary influences.

During the ensuing week, Naggya was observed watching kabaddi less, and the dances more. Throughout one of the practice sessions, one of the teachers, Yessuma, had noticed little Naggya's hands and feet tapping in time with the music though when she had approached, he immediately ceased.

"Have you ever danced before, Naggya?" she'd asked with an encouraging smile. Naggya turned and ran.

Since the foundation of Son-Shine, Elijah had scheduled nightly staff meetings straight after the children had gone to bed, and that night Yessuma asked if she could offer some thoughts on Naggya. "Of course you can, Yessuma. We are all aware and a little concerned that he has struggled to fit in."

The young teacher looked directly at her mentor. "Today, for the very first time, I saw Naggya begin to express himself. It was only brief, but he was definitely wanting to—"

"To what, Yessuma?"

"To dance. I believe Naggya wanted to dance. Considering his fears, I would have thought dancing would be the very last thing he would want to do, but he began to tap his hands and feet and for just a moment I saw him smile. Naggya has a beautiful smile, and his rhythm, his rhythm and timing are something I have not seen before in one so young, especially without any training. His rhythm fascinated me. But when I spoke to him, he ran away so how can we get him to—?"

"Yessuma, when all we have known is misery it can be so hard to receive joy. That is a challenge for us all."

CHAPTER
five

With only three weeks before the anniversary celebrations, Naggya was often seen to spin and twirl when he thought no one was looking. He would jump in the air and hold a perfect pose until the music ceased. Naggya's timing was indeed a gift. The dance teachers were becoming increasingly amazed that this little boy was not merely following the lead of the other children but was interpreting dance like one born within its mystery. During these moments of innocent abandon, Naggya shone. If this little boy needed an escape, the joy of dance could be his vessel.

The day before the anniversary ceremony, a game of kabaddi had been scheduled on the dusty playground for the last hour of daylight. A hastily prepared court had been scratched out using a broomstick dragged through the dirt.

Despite their physically demanding school days, the children's spirits always skyrocketed whenever the game was about to begin. Today's game was for the younger children and, from as early as the age of eight, kabaddi had already become enshrined in the psyche of every child. Each boy and girl would eagerly await their opportunity to compete in the predominantly older children's domain. A child's very first game of kabaddi was one of their rites of passage.

In the failing light, the teacher called "time" to howls of respectful protests for just one more play. "OK, but then we have to quickly finish and get ready for dinner."

Vivek was tall for his age and an emerging leader among the eight-year-olds. He'd stood out during the game and was considered one of the biggest threats to the opposing team. As he sprinted toward home base, he attempted to side-step his opposite number and as he did, he tripped and landed on the point of his elbow. Vivek shrieked as his right shoulder dislocated, and as the teacher rushed to his side, he shouted for one of the children to call for Elijah. Within minutes Vivek had been gently loaded into Elijah's old Ambassador en route to one of the few hospitals willing to treat Dalits. Seven hours later the blaze of the Ambassador's headlights bounced off the Son-Shine walls as Elijah pulled on the handbrake. "Come on, young man, you have been so brave. Let's get you off to bed."

Vivek looked up into his leader's eyes and pleaded, "But how can I dance?"

❖❖❖❖❖

As word spread on the extent of Vivek's injury and the impact it would have on the anniversary celebrations, Yessuma hadn't the slightest hesitation on how to replace him as lead dancer. Vivek was scheduled to feature prominently in seven dances and as she approached Elijah she was beaming. "There is only one child who can step-up and who knows every single step of every dance. He can do it, if he is willing."

"Who, Yessuma? Who else knows all the steps?"

"Naggya!"

Elijah paused then smiled, "That's one mighty step-up. He's never even danced in a group before, or on a stage, let alone in front of six hundred visitors. He's still only five years old and he's still petrified. If he did agree and it went badly it could set him back months. I don't want to risk putting any more pressure upon him. Do you really believe he'd be willing?"

Yessuma didn't flinch, "You are always telling us that we serve a miracle-working God. Please let me try."

Naggya was in his usual place at the rear of the classroom and as his name was called, his little body tensed and fear overtook his tiny face. He lowered his head and paused as he summoned the courage to speak, "I haven't done anything wrong! I haven't!"

Yessuma kneeled beside him and placed a comforting arm around his shoulder, "No, you haven't done anything wrong." Naggya flinched regardless. "In fact, you have done something very, very good. Can we go outside? I have something exciting to talk to you about."

Of all the Son-Shine teachers, Naggya trusted Yessuma the most.

Tentatively, he looked towards his classroom teacher who nodded her encouragement. His little mind raced, and he shook his hand free of Yessuma's and walked head down a few paces behind her as all the other children looked on in wonder.

Naggya wanted to run, and Yessuma could see his grief mounting as she looked across the schoolyard where Elijah was watching. She steeled herself and crouched down beside the frightened little boy and silently prayed for wisdom. Peering into Naggya's glistening eyes, she whispered, "Naggya, you have a gift."

He glanced up fleetingly at such an unexpected comment. Furtively, Yessuma looked across at Elijah and saw him smile before she continued.

"You have a God-given gift, and it is to dance. I have seen that gift in you, and so too have some of the other teachers. The other children have as well." Naggya turned away and tried to break free. "It's okay. Perhaps you may never have heard anyone say this to you before, but it is true. Something else that is true is that never before have you been in such a safe place. Naggya, this is now your home, and everyone here is wanting you to be happy. We all love you."

Little Naggya's shoulders began to tighten and tears began to drip from the tip of his nose. He quickly wiped his hand across his face but couldn't stem the flow. Yessuma again wrapped her arms around his shoulders and spoke softly into his ear, "It's time to let it out, Naggya. It's your time to let go."

Thirty minutes and a thousand healing tears miraculously passed, and all the while Elijah stood and prayed from a short distance. He, too, cried.

CHAPTER
six

The dusty playground had been transformed in the space of three hours; standing in its place was a makeshift stage adorned with so many vibrant colors, an assortment of objects of Son-Shine significance, and a selection of hastily decorated folding chairs for the honored guests. In front of the stage was a spread of old, worn carpet pieces on which a gathering of one hundred children would soon be seated. In a few hours, groups of the children would be ferried back and forth as their respective moments to shine upon the big stage would come and go.

Spread out behind the carpet were seemingly endless rows of begged or borrowed stacker chairs in various colors, styles, and conditions.

As dusk settled, the arena was almost devoid of humanity, yet with the first twinklings in the night sky, a sea of bewildered humanity had walked, ridden, or driven to Son-Shine to bear personal witness to this region's evolving enigma.

Following a guided tour of Son-Shine, Elijah escorted the VIPs to their places of honor upon the stage: three government officials, one senior police officer, and his wife, the pastors of Elijah's church, Kristen's parents all the way from Australia, and the latest couple of Son-Shine supporters from the West, who just happened to time their visit to coincide with the celebration.

In his native Telugu and resplendent in his best attire provided by the visitors from the West, Elijah invited his pastor to pray for the evening's success. He then welcomed the honored guests and invited each in turn to come to the borrowed church podium and speak into the borrowed microphone. Tribute after tribute blared out to more than seven hundred silent listeners. As the visitors from other nations watched on in wonder, not a single child budged from their seated positions on the carpet until urged to do so by a teacher.

Each of the speakers was draped in pooladandas of orange and yellow marigolds, and when the final guest had concluded speaking, an unmistakable buzz settled upon the crowd. On center stage, the first of many children's song-and-dance presentations was about to begin.

Befitting the occasion, the first of the presentations featured twelve children who, five years ago, had all begun their new lives at Son-Shine in its first year of operation. Their ages now ranged from nine to fourteen, and the joy that accompanied them onto that stage spoke far more than any speech.

Marshaling at the back of the stage and excitedly waiting their turn were ten five- and six-year-olds. So many months of practice and preparation had finally come down to this moment.

As the older children finished their first presentation to rapturous applause, with radiant smiles they made their exit from the far end of the stage. The next piped music heralded the youngest group as they jostled forward from the far end of the platform. The lead dancer looked about, fear and focus etched in equal measure across his handsome young face, and as Yessuma beckoned, and while the music lifted in volume, Naggya took his first fearful, tentative steps onto a terrifying stage.

A silent and magical switch flicked somewhere deep within him, and with his first dance step a stony face transformed before a cloud of witnesses; joy entered and giftedness prevailed.

By the end of the night's celebration, Naggya had graced center stage no less than seven times, and had yet to put a foot wrong.

Upon that humble stage, something was breathed, exquisite, exhilarating, exciting.

Five hours beyond and as the children were being shepherded toward their classrooms for bed, a far greater miracle unfolded. For the very first time, Naggya had allowed love to enter.

CHAPTER
seven

The visitors from the West had spent most of their lives in Chicago, however, six years ago they'd moved to New York to expand a manufacturing company they had formed a decade earlier. Impressions Costuming specialized in the design and production of costumes for the performing arts. Their sights were now firmly set upon the large and lucrative Broadway market. Broadway was considered the biggest fish in the worldwide theater pond, and despite their costume company having peaked in the Midwest, the lure of the world's juiciest market was a temptation much too tantalizing to resist.

On a trip to India five years ago to research a reliable supplier of traditional Indian costume materials, Chad and Lois had been introduced to Elijah through a mutual connection. Known affectionately to the children as Mummy and Daddy, Chad and Lois had been instrumental in raising significant amounts of money to not only keep Son-Shine's doors open but to see the diversity of curricular opportunities literally explode. Not for the first time, Mummy and Daddy had elected to delay their departure for another few days as they once again marveled at the hand of the Almighty doing astonishing things in young, impressionable lives.

Rambabu had joined Son-Shine just prior to the anniversary celebrations. Not yet six, he was willing to attend classes and activities with the other children, yet his expressionless, dark eyes still hinted of deep hardship and pain.

The bed rolls had been meticulously stowed away for the day, and by 7 a.m. the children had already visited the toilet block and put on their only set of school clothes after they'd been hand-washed and hung out to dry overnight.

Morning devotions always started precisely at 7 a.m., and the children settled into their places on the floor as Chad entered the classroom, just as he had every morning since arriving ten days earlier. As a mark of honor, Chad had been ushered to the front of the class and invited to sit upon a seat that had been borrowed from the staff room. Perched upon the wooden seat, Chad looked out across the group of thirty and marveled at the immediate silence. One of the nine-year-olds stood and walked purposefully to the front of the class, smiled proudly at Daddy Chad, then turned to face the other boys. He lifted his hands and his eyes and began to sing songs of praise in Telugu while the others joined in. For several weeks, this nine-year-old had been awaiting his turn to lead devotions, and as he began, his little hands trembled. Every child was expressing his own personal thanks; a thanks for the life each had been given, and the rescue each had received. Every child except one.

Rambabu sat cross-legged in the front row, his eyes neither raised or lowered. He searched about the room, scanned each face in turn, and silently hoped for a clue. He watched, he listened, and he wished for understanding, yet most of all he wondered how on earth these boys could possibly be emptying their hearts to an invisible god who'd been willing to let them all struggle and suffer. *So, how can they be happy?*

Chad watched as the little boy with the broken shirt button, and a heart to match, struggled to make sense of a world that just refused to even remotely add up. His lips moved in unison with the others yet his desperate cry to fit in tipped precariously upon the fact that he didn't have another life to go back to. He wanted desperately what these other boys had, yet nothing made sense, and nothing gave him the slightest clue.

Watching the little boy intently, Chad's focus fell upon Rambabu's broken shirt button, and his professional instinct went immediately to putting that right, although he knew the cry within this little boy's heart went way deeper than any outward appearance. *Lord, help him see you on the inside.*

Sitting right beside the little boy was Naggya, singing, shouting, and hands raised in majestic surrender, tears streaming down his glistening cheeks.

CHAPTER
eight

The morning was hot again, and at this time of the year cloud cover was rare. The mercury had already reached thirty-four as Yessuma peered into the combined grades one and two classroom. Naggya was seated with the others on the floor nearest the door, not because of any feeling of disengagement or thoughts of him being unwanted, but simply so he could be first out of the door at the end of class. Gone were his expressions of despair and betrayal, but in their place were reflections that still perplexed the teachers. Unlike most of the others of a similar age, Naggya would often be seen gazing off into a distant and private world while smiling to himself, until his teacher would prompt his reluctant return.

India was a nation of well over one billion people. In excess of three-hundred million were Dalits, all competing for a tiny slice of an ever-decreasing pie. Son-Shine's biggest challenge was to see its children emerge from their schooling effectively prepared to grab every opportunity, to see themselves not as victims but instead as part of a peaceful cultural revolution.

Yessuma smiled broadly as one of her favorite children filed out of the classroom and began to gain pace. Undoubtedly, he would have sprinted off in the direction of dance practice had Yessuma not gently wrapped an arm around his shoulder and pulled him in close for a cuddle. "How was your day, Naggya?"

He looked up and returned her soft, caring smile, resting his hand respectfully upon her arm, "Very fine, thanks, Miss."

"That's so good to hear. You have come so far in the past few weeks. Are you enjoying your classes?"

Naggya looked away and rubbed his hand over the back of his dark brown neck. "Yes, Miss."

"I know you have dance practice in a few minutes, but I would like to talk with you if that is OK."

Naggya squirmed. It'd only been a few short weeks since his life had turned around, and a few of his former predispositions hadn't fully disappeared.

"It's OK; you're not in any sort of trouble. I just wanted to check with you as I do with all the other children. A lot has happened for you in such a short time, and I want you to know I will always be here for you whenever you need to talk."

"But Miss—"

Yessuma wrapped her arm tighter around his bony little shoulder and gave it a squeeze. Gently, she whispered, "We all love you very much, Naggya. You do know that, don't you?"

The little boy looked up and peered deeply into his teacher's eyes, "Yes, Miss. Yes, I do," and he smiled. Yessuma returned his smile as he tentatively turned away before skipping off in the direction of dance practice.

It was after evening prayer before Yessuma beckoned Naggya to come, sit, and talk, and she could see that he was still reluctant. She sat on the step beside him and took him by the hand. "You love to dance, don't you?"

Instantly his little face brightened, and he could barely withhold his joy. "Yes, of course you do. It's truly as though you were born to dance. We can all see that, and we are so proud of you. Naggya, may I ask you a question?"

The thought of grown-ups noticing his skills and taking the time to acknowledge what they had seen had lifted his confidence, and he looked into Yessuma's eyes and slowly nodded.

His teacher shifted a little awkwardly and considered her words carefully, "Naggya, when you are in class and you gaze out of the window and you appear to not be listening, what are you thinking about?"

Naggya tightened a little and broke her gaze. "Please, Naggya, it's OK to have a dream. In fact, we want every child to have a dream and we will do everything we can to help you and every other child achieve your dreams. That is why we are here. Please, Naggya, tell me about your dream."

Tentatively at first, Naggya summoned the courage to share with one he had come to trust. His biggest obstacle in seeing his dream come to pass was his acutely ingrained awareness of the massive cultural limitations upon Dalits. The limitations of not possessing a birth certificate, or of knowing his own birthday, therefore remaining ineligible to obtain a passport had yet to have any genuine relevance. From a young age, Naggya had been indoctrinated into the belief that Dalits had no future. Anything beyond survival was tantamount to the most hideous of delusions.

Hesitantly, he drew breath and searched deep into Yessuma's gaze, "My dream is to be a dancer."

Naggya's words had confirmed Yessuma's beliefs, and her rehearsed response seemed to take Naggya by surprise. "Naggya, do you know what three-hundred million looks like?" Suddenly an exercise in his least favorite subject forced him to focus. Naggya's expression instantly transformed from sheer and unrestrained delight to one of disinterest and frustration as his little shoulders slumped. "Sorry, of course you don't. OK, so I am going to help you to get a picture of what that number looks like, so please, I want you to use your imagination. In our country, there are over one-hundred-and-twenty-million Dalits, but in our country, for every one of those Dalits there are many times that number from higher castes. For now, let's not think about the other castes but let us just concentrate on Dalits. That is what you are and that is what you always will be, OK?"

He was struggling with the prospect of a mathematics lesson at any time of the day, but to have one out of class time seemed even more unfair, especially this late in the evening. Yessuma could see that her young charge was struggling, but she pressed on. "To help you understand what I am trying to share, let's imagine there were only five-hundred guests at our anniversary celebrations and let us imagine they were all dancers, OK? If we can imagine another school next door with the same number of children and another one beside it with the same number, and then another one and another one all the way into the city and every one of those schools was filled with the same number of Dalit children and they all wanted to follow their dream of becoming dancers, OK?"

Naggya looked blankly into his teacher's eyes and wrestled with the notion of why this was so important. "Do you know how many schools side by side it would take to equal three-hundred million?" The little boy's eyes slowly began to fill with tears and he shrugged his shoulders and looked down at the ground.

"Naggya, please look at me," and she gripped his tiny shoulders and gently lifted his chin. "It's this many," and she held up her hands before him with fingers outstretched and opened and closed her hands over and over again. Naggya fell limply and pathetically into her arms and sobbed. As he did, he could still feel Yessuma's hands continuing to open and close behind his back as he heaved his lungs and emptied his heart. When his sobs eased, she pulled him clear and stared deeply into his reddened eyes. "Do you understand what I am saying to you?"

"But what about my dream? You said we all have a dream and you told me to tell you my dream!" Naggya sobbed again and tried to push Yessuma away. She held on tight and waited till his sobs subsided. A young Dalit life was now hanging lifelessly in her arms and her heart was breaking. *Lord, please help me.*

Much of India was a wasteland of shattered Dalit dreams, yet a hope that seemed impossible was still the very bedrock on which this school was founded. *How can it stand for Naggya right here, right now?*

Tentatively, Yessuma peeled him back from her tear-soaked dress and held him firmly at arm's length. She whispered, "Naggya, you can have your dream! When we give up on our dream we die here inside," and gently she tapped her chest.

"I am not trying to kill your dream, please believe me. It is so important that you know what it will take to see your dream come true. We will never rob you of your dream, and we will always do our very best to see your dream fulfilled. But, and this is a big but, you must know how things are if you are to achieve your dream. You *can* achieve your dream regardless of what stands against you. There is a scripture that says, 'If my God be for me then who can stand against me?' and on that we and our God stand for you now."

Naggya was confused and his exhaustion came like a flood. "Tomorrow, Elijah and I will talk more with you, OK? But for now, I am going to take you in with the other boys so you can sleep. It's late now," and she lovingly lifted him by his arms and carried the wilting little boy to the classroom as one of the older boys rushed to help. "I can carry him for you, Miss."

"Thank you, but it's OK, he's not heavy," and she peered into his troubled eyes and whispered, "Naggya, rest well tonight, but please know that this story ends well."

Naggya didn't utter a sound; his confusion had given way to exhaustion and the closer Yessuma walked to his tiny bedroll laid out upon the stone floor, the limper he felt in her arms. *God, give your young son rest and comfort him now in his sleep.*

❖❖❖❖❖

The morning arrived with its usual sunshine, yet Naggya was especially slow to receive its glorious rays. For a dancer, to be dragging one's feet is rarely a thing of beauty, and today, Naggya was feeling drained of life and devoid of all hope.

The first to see his heavy burden when he emerged from morning's devotions was Elijah; last night he'd spent an hour with Yessuma talking and praying about the way to proceed. "Hello, young man. It's such a magnificent day."

For Naggya, it wasn't. His shattered dream as a dancer hung heavy; his heart sat so very weighty in his chest. The other children buzzed about, laughing, joking, and playing games, but for Naggya, the jokes weren't funny, their games like poison, and their laughter just a horrible reminder that he was right back where he'd started. The door to Naggya's bright and limitless future had been slammed shut, bolted, and dead-locked. As Elijah moved closer, the prospect of a hug from the man who had instilled such great hope was now as repulsive as the memory of his father beating his mother, or his vivid recollection of abandonment when Aunty had told him to leave. Nothing could erase those memories and nothing would erase the depth of this terrifying new pain. *It's not fair! Why do I have to be a Dalit?*

Yessuma watched and waited, and silently she prayed. She remained at a distance, at least until Elijah beckoned. *Lord, please heal this little man's broken heart.*

Elijah crouched beside Naggya and tried to encourage him to look up, though his stifled sobs spoke of his pain. His mission had always been to build big dreams in the children, and now to see this fragile little boy's obliterated heart was tearing at his own.

"Naggya, your dream is still alive."

Naggya pulled away as hard as he could, and for the first time in many weeks he ran; he ran so fast, and he ran so hard. Little did he care that through his flood of tears and his heaving heart he was seeing nothing, nor did it matter the direction of his escape.

Elijah signaled toward Yessuma to stay where she was and to leave Naggya in his care. *Lord, what can I do? What can I say to ease Naggya's pain?*

CHAPTER
nine

It was three hundred yards to the first intersection and the road was as potholed as it had ever been. The unrelenting grind from the school bus, the heavy drays that daily hauled their produce to and fro, and the inevitable disintegration since the monsoon rains, forced Elijah to travel slowly in the old Ambassador. There were so many places to hide, yet Elijah's only hope was that Naggya would simply run along the road and keep running.

On either side of the road were row after row of paddy fields being irrigated from the monsoon run-off. The water streamed into the canals and worked its way into the underlying aquifers. Ever since the school opened, the canals had long been a safety threat, especially prior to the acquisition of the bus. Elijah's concerns began to mount as he reached the intersection and failed to find any trace of him. *Where would he go?*

Elijah reefed the gear stick into reverse and spun the vehicle around as the morning sun still bounced off the murky waters of each canal. Elijah strained for a sign, any sign. On his second sweep he caught a glimpse of a boy crouched near the edge of one of the shallow canals, and he quickly brought the car to a halt. As Elijah climbed out, he could see that the little boy was wearing a Son-Shine uniform and as he raced towards him, he called out. Naggya suddenly looked up and once again began to run.

"Stop, Naggya! I need to talk to you. Everything will be alright, but we need to talk."

In his long pants and wearing his best shoes in readiness for a meeting later in the morning, clambering up and over the uneven ground left Elijah no match for the bare-footed youngster. These fields were a haven for deadly snakes, and since the rains the snakes had become active and ravenous.

Typically, the canals ran in straight parallel lines, but at the boundary of a plot the canals would often change directions, and as Elijah reached one of the turns he searched along it and caught sight of Naggya attempting to cross over a canal to the far side. Too often the depth of the murky waters would change unexpectedly, and as Naggya turned to look behind him he could see that Elijah was closing in. With only fifteen yards before the canal ended, Naggya needed to choose another escape route or risk capture. Fear turned into rage over the man who had filled his head with such false hopes. *Elijah lied to me! He is the enemy!*

Naggya scrambled over a mound of soil beside the canal and tripped. He almost somersaulted then cracked his head on the sunbaked ground. Limply, Naggya slid headlong into the water without making a sound as Elijah clambered toward the spot where the boy had disappeared. He jumped feet-first into the waist-deep water and groped and thrashed about, yet he could feel nothing apart from mud, slush, and a few decomposing branches. *How long can he survive under the water?*

Elijah could barely swim. At no time during his twenty-eight years had he ever summoned the courage to have his head below the water, especially water as dark and treacherous as this. *He must be here! He must!*

A tiny ankle clutched by a despairing outstretched hand. Elijah gripped as tightly as he could and hauled the lifeless little body to the surface. As he struggled to steady himself in the mud, and with an almighty heave, he shoved the boy up and onto the ground beside the canal then dragged himself, arm-over-arm, out onto dry ground. Elijah turned Naggya onto his side to help drain the dirty water from his mouth. *What do I do, Lord?*

Tentatively, Elijah began to thrust his palm into the middle of Naggya's back. *Breathe, Naggya, breathe. Please, just breathe!*

When his attempts failed again and again, Elijah began to hit the lifeless little body harder and harder. As his own strength waned, Elijah cried out in a long, loud, pitiful wail.

Naggya coughed and sputtered, then spewed a torrent of filthy water from his heaving lungs.

Had this been an accident or . . .?

For two days Naggya didn't speak. He refused all food and water and remained determined to look away every time anyone spoke. Everyone tried but no one could reach him. If Naggya couldn't die, he'd make life within his own private prison as unbearable as he could. Life was once again nothing more than a relentless field of pain.

❖❖❖❖❖

Rambabu had been missing his best friend and walked in to see why Naggya was again absent from class. As he drew nearer, Naggya turned away and muttered something under his breath.

"Why aren't you coming to class, Naggya?" Rambabu put his little hand on Naggya's shoulder and felt him flinch and pull away. "Our teacher said you are sick, but you don't look sick, so why won't you come to class or play with us?"

Naggya no longer trusted anyone. His only dream had been ripped out of his chest, and his tormented heart had no room left for talking. Without turning, Naggya's frail little body stiffened and he scowled, "Go away!"

Rambabu didn't. "I didn't want to be here but now I do. You helped me, and now I want to help you. Naggya?"

"Go away!!"

Rambabu didn't. "I haven't got anywhere else to go, and neither do you." Rambabu gently placed his hand on Naggya's shoulder and when his hand was pushed away, he gently put it back. Silently, Rambabu remained beside his terrified friend for the next hour, and from just outside the room, Yessuma watched, and Yessuma prayed.

CHAPTER
ten

For the past two years, an international supporter of Son-Shine had begun funding the children on annual all-expenses-paid swimming trips to the far side of the city. Miraculously, after the money had been assured, the reluctant proprietors of the swimming pool were suddenly willing to allow Dalit children to use their facility, but only on the basis that the entire facility was booked. Mixing cultures, even within a large and antiquated swimming pool, was neither acceptable nor good for business.

In the weeks leading up to the trip, the children spoke of little else. The two-hour drive would prove a logistical challenge, and to ferry over a hundred excited kids in a fleet of borrowed or hired vehicles of varying sizes and conditions through the very center of the city would once again test Elijah's resourcefulness.

The odds of getting Naggya to join the children on a full day out were steep enough already. The notion of him being in or around a large parcel of water so soon after his near-death experience was a gamble Elijah was loath to take. His challenge also hinged on whether he should leave a teacher behind for the day knowing that supervision numbers for the trip were already stretched to the limit.

Elijah and his wife, Vani, had two young children, Bujji and Yakobu. Both would be attending Son-Shine once old enough, although Vani was reluctant to over-expose her children to school prematurely. Every time they visited Son-Shine, Vani would battle to get them to leave.

He wrestled with his decision concerning the pool visit for days and ultimately concluded that the only workable solution was to have Vani and their two children come in for the day to watch over him.

❖❖❖❖❖

It was a bright and seasonally warm morning and the buzz within Son-Shine was even greater than normal as the children hurried to be ready for their trip.

"Miss, I don't feel well."

His teacher bent forward and felt Rambabu's forehead. "You're not hot. Where do you feel sick?"

Despite his troubled start to life, Rambabu had become a healthy child and rarely experienced illness. "Just all over," and as he spoke, he turned away and vaguely ran his little hand across his upper body.

The teacher gently turned his chin and prompted Rambabu to make eye contact. "How about we come and sit down and you can tell me more about how you're feeling?"

Martha was a young teacher, not long out of high school, yet in her twelve months at Son-Shine she'd already won over most of the younger children and had forged a growing respect from among the other teachers. Rambabu was one of her keenest students, not least because she was like the big sister he'd always wanted but never had.

Martha led him by the hand away from the rest of the children and into the teachers' room where she sat him down and again peered into his eyes. "You're not really sick, little man, are you?"

Rambabu again tried to turn away but Martha gently held his shoulders and urged him to speak. "Not really sick, Miss."

"Are you frightened about going to the pool?" For many of the students, today would be their first time in deep water, and for some, the first time in anything wetter than a monsoon downpour or the school's hand-held showers. On the strength of a few embellished stories about previous years' trips by some of the older children, it wasn't unheard of for the younger children to become apprehensive. Martha suspected otherwise.

The little boy summoned the courage to shake his head. "Then what is it, Rambabu? What is troubling you?"

His eyes scanned the room and he fidgeted, not knowing how, or even if, he should disclose his secret. "Come on, young man, you've been so brave since coming to Son-Shine. How about you tell me what the problem is?"

As Rambabu continued to fidget, Martha leaned slightly forward and whispered, "Might this have something to do with Naggya?"

Rambabu's eyes flashed, and he stared back into his teacher's eyes in bewilderment. "But how . . . ?"

"Because I know how much you care for him. All the teachers can see that, and we are so proud of you."

Confusion and uncertainty dashed across the little boy's face. "Last night!"

"Yes, what about last night?"

He threw his little arms around the young teacher's neck and began to sob, "It was horrible!"

"What was horrible?"

"The dream! It was horrible!"

Martha waited and when Rambabu had exhausted his tears she again lifted his chin to look deeply into his bloodshot eyes. "Do you feel you are ready to tell me about the dream?"

"I must stay here today, Miss. Something horrible might happen to Naggya! Please don't let something happen to Naggya! Please, Miss!"

"Naggya will be safe here; you know that. Why are you so . . . ?"

"The nasty men!" and with his outburst Rambabu buried his head into Martha's chest and screamed.

From outside the room and despite the buzz of the morning, Elijah and Yessuma both heard his cries, and both hurried into the teachers' room. Rambabu was still crying, and Martha looked to her mentors for guidance as she mouthed the words, "bad dream."

Elijah eased in closer and hung an arm over Rambabu's tense shoulders. "Dreams can be scary, but they can also tell us things if we can describe them. Do you think you can remember anything that might help?"

Rambabu squirmed in Martha's embrace and briefly looked up into her eyes for assurance. As Martha nodded, Rambabu turned slightly to look at Elijah. "The men were very nasty!" and he clutched Martha tighter and again buried his head into her chest.

"And what did these men look like?" Once more, Rambabu looked towards Martha, "They were big men and they shouted," and as he stared up at his teacher, he blurted, "I have to stay with Naggya today. Naggya is very scared, and the nasty men will make him cry! Naggya would be too scared!"

Martha patted his back and gently stroked his hair. She could feel waves of tension coursing through his slender body.

Elijah moved in even closer, "You are a brave little man to want to stay with Naggya today. If you really want to stay behind, I am sure Naggya will be happy to have you beside him. Naggya trusts you like no one else, and it shows how grown up you have become." Elijah smiled towards Martha and briefly ran his hand through Rambabu's hair. "We will miss you today, but we will have lots of stories to tell when we get back, OK?"

Rambabu tried to smile, but the closest he managed was a momentary crease in his cheeks and the briefest glimpse of his front teeth.

❖❖❖❖❖

An hour later and Son-Shine fell eerily silent as the assorted convoy of vehicles rattled out of the gate and disappeared down the dusty road. Vani and her two children had waved them off from the front door of the main building, and before the dust settled she had led her children towards the boys' bedroom to check on Naggya and Rambabu. Naggya was lying on his mat facing away from the door and Rambabu was beside him, his little face grim, and his hand upon Naggya's side. Vani's children wanted to play with the two boys and protested loudly when she led them away, "Come, children, I have some games we can play."

One hundred pairs of coverall swimsuits were donned and excitedly dunked within minutes of arriving at the pool. A playground like nothing these children had ever seen; their joy, infectious, their excitement, immeasurable, and their energy, beyond bounds. The clock was already ticking. With four pools to choose from and three giant slides beckoning, each child's greatest dilemma was which adrenalin rush to tackle first. The complex became swathed in squeals of delight and laughter, and as their excitement peaked, Elijah smiled towards the other teachers and began to softly praise his God.

❖❖❖❖❖

Vani had just put her two-year-old son down for a nap and wandered out from her husband's tiny office to check on her daughter playing outside. Vani hadn't heard the vehicle approach and only with the slamming of the truck doors did she bother to look up. It was hours before she'd expected any of the vehicles to be returning, so the sight of three strangers alighting from an unfamiliar truck caused her to halt.

"Take whatever is valuable! Look for computers, jewelry, telephones, their generator . . . anything of value!"

The men paid scant regard to Vani as she backed away and quickly scanned the grounds for her daughter. "Where is the office, dog?!" Vani didn't answer. She spotted her daughter playing near the far fence line and realized that to reach her she would need to leave her sleeping son and the two boys unprotected. Vani watched as the three men stormed into the building and shouted loudly as they looked for items of value. Vani raced toward her daughter and, despite the little girl's protests, scooped her up and hurried back into the building, stopping only when confronted by one of the men. "We know you have laptops, dog! Where are they?" The man raised his fist as an act of hostility, yet culturally it was unlikely he would risk contamination by touching her. This was terrorism, and for the cowering Vani, the threat was paralyzing.

Rambabu peered out from behind the classroom door. Being played out before him was his dream. He recognized instantly the menace and the peril, and he turned and raced back to Naggya, planting himself beside the terrified little boy and he began to pray. Never before had he known such fear; never before had his life and that of his best friend been so brutally under threat. These men saw nothing of the slightest value in the life of a Dalit and would kill them all without a second thought. Deep down, Rambabu knew it. He and Naggya cringed against the classroom wall as Naggya began to tremble and to weep.

In the office, Vani had pressed Bujji down behind her and, acting as a human shield, she crouched in front of her sleeping son and braced herself for the inevitable. Many times, she'd been made aware of the atrocities meted out by men from higher castes, especially upon defenseless women. Dalits were a despised and expendable breed, nothing more than a scourge, an ugly, useless commodity.

Room by room the three men tore through the building, reefing appliances from their sockets and turning over furniture as they went. As two of the men entered the office,

Bujji began to scream and they both spat at her mother as one of the men seized the laptop atop her husband's rickety desk. "Shut the child up, dog, or you all die! Your rings, take them off!"

The three men spent another twenty minutes scouring the buildings, then marched outside to load the old generator onto the truck. They ripped the schoolyard floodlights from the walls and flung them inside the cab. They then climbed aboard the truck and, as one final act of contempt and disgust, they each spat upon the dusty ground.

CHAPTER
eleven

It was just at dusk when the bus rolled into the schoolyard at the head of the convoy. Elijah pulled up behind and eased on the handbrake of the old Ambassador. *The power must be out again, but surely we can't be out of diesel.*

The cook should have arrived hours earlier to prepare for the evening meal, and with so many starving mouths to feed her absence was baffling. *Something's not right.*

Elijah motioned for Punji to keep the children onboard the bus and sent a message down the line for the other drivers to do likewise.

As he scanned the schoolyard, Elijah noticed that the generator wasn't in its usual place. He picked up his pace, entered the main building, and called out to Vani, but all he heard were muffled cries coming from the boys' classroom. Elijah raced to the doorway, then halted; still cowering and sobbing in the corner were Vani, their two children, the two boys and Kamala, the cook.

Vani was a pathetic sight; gone was her usual composure and all her self-confidence, and in their place, grief and wretched fear. Petrified that the men might return to carry out their death threats, no one had moved and scarcely had they spoken.

Elijah eased himself down beside her and wrapped his arms around his wife and two children, but he too couldn't bring himself to speak. He searched their eyes for a clue but saw only horror. Nothing made sense. *What has happened?*

Kamala scrambled across beside him and craned her face to his ear, "Three men came and stole things. They threatened to kill Vani and the children. She is terrified they will come back."

"Did you see the men?"

Kamala shook her head, "Only from a distance when I was walking here, but I could see our generator was in the back of their truck. When I arrived, I found Vani and the children sitting right here, crying. They haven't moved. Elijah, they are so frightened! I am so frightened!" She paused and looked at Elijah, "If I have to, I am willing to die for Son-Shine, but not these children. They need to be safe."

Elijah squeezed her arm and slowly nodded, "A safe place is what we are, Kamala. We must be a safe place; a place our children know the pains of the past can no longer control them. Didn't you try to call me?"

"All the phones are gone! Not even one is left. I couldn't leave Vani and the children to run to a phone because the men might return. Elijah, I didn't know what to do! All I could do was try to make the children feel safe, but I didn't know how! I am so sorry!"

"You did the best you could, Kamala. Please do not punish yourself. This will pass."

Elijah was aware that by now all the other children would be getting restless. Unless the power came back on there would be no meal tonight, and with complete darkness soon to be upon them, they would be without light until the morning. By far his biggest challenge was the risk of the children knowing what had happened during their time away. *Lord, what do I tell them? I can't lie to them! But I can't shatter their security by telling them the truth. What do I do?*

Elijah asked Kamala to go outside and quietly inform Punji what had happened and to have all the children assemble outside the girl's dorm for instructions. He gently urged Vani to her feet and ushered her and the children into his office where he lit two old tilley lamps, "Please, Vani, wait here for a few moments and I will take you home as soon as I can. Vani, you are safe now. I promise you, you are safe."

He returned to Naggya and Rambabu; Naggya still in his fetal position and Rambabu crouching beside him rubbing his back with a trembling hand.

It had been years since Elijah had felt so helpless, so utterly out of his depth. Silently, he prayed. *Please, you promised.*

The sounds of the approaching children's voices multiplied, and once inside he heard the familiar sounds of the shuffling of many feet across the tiled floor. As Elijah timidly bent to comfort the boys, the lights flickered. *Thank you, God.*

The meal that night consisted of nothing more than boiled rice and vegetable stock. After their epic day and having been spared the horror that had unfolded while away, over a hundred weary children soon settled in for the night. Naggya and Rambabu were not among them. Their mats had been relocated to the office floor with Martha and Yessuma sharing the task of easing the two through the most harrowing of nights.

By first light they would most likely be exhausted, yet for the teachers, another day's demands would beckon, and somehow their need for sleep would again have to wait.

Elijah spent much of the night comforting his grief-stricken wife and their children at their tiny home, though when his mother arrived to sit with them Elijah slipped quietly out the door to return to his other family at Son-Shine.

At 5:30 a.m., he hauled himself from the Ambassador, walked inside the building, and poked his head around the office door. Rambabu had drifted off into a fitful slumber, though Naggya had stoically resisted all the urges to sleep. Wide awake, he stared blankly at the wall. Martha dragged herself to her feet and motioned Elijah outside. "He hasn't slept at all, and honestly, I am afraid."

Elijah held the young lady at arm's length and tried to smile, "I don't know how, but somehow all will be well. Please go and rest now."

"But . . ."

"I will stay with the boys. There is still another hour before the children wake. Please, rest. We have a big day ahead." Reluctantly, Martha allowed herself to be gently shepherded toward her mat.

Creeping back into the office and in the dim light, Elijah peered down at Naggya who blinked hard and buried his head further into his hands. Settling down beside him, Elijah felt him flinch as Naggya withdrew further. Silently, Elijah prayed in his heavenly tongue and searched the heavens for wisdom.

It wasn't long before the first murmurings from outside heralded a new dawn, and as Elijah's eyes adjusted to the

61

morning's light he reached across and tentatively stroked Naggya's back. This time, he didn't flinch; instead, from deep within the troubled little boy came the rhythmic hum of surrender.

There was so much to be done that morning, yet Elijah accomplished none of it. Instinctively he knew that somehow the other teachers and staff would rally in his absence. Six hours after the first signs of surrender, Naggya stirred as his eyes began to focus on the unfamiliar surroundings. Tentatively, he looked up at the man who was cradling him in his arms and reflexively tensed and pulled away. Elijah smiled and stroked his arm as little Naggya's eyes filled with tears and he began to sob.

For another hour and without a word spoken, he emptied his heart till little remained. Elijah prayed, cradled in his arms was a broken, hopeless child, willing to quit on life before he'd barely had the chance to start. It had taken six tumultuous years to reach the bottom, yet like many before him, Naggya had arrived at a dark place that had no expectation of ever being better.

Naggya was a Dalit, and he wanted to die.

❖❖❖❖❖

How long can a little boy stay alive when he refuses to eat?

Rambabu had become like a second skin and he pleaded for his best friend to eat or drink something, yet for two more days and sleepless nights, Naggya refused. Food and water represented the prolonging of a life he no longer wanted, and the quicker the end came, the quicker his pain would cease.

Little more than skin and bone, Naggya's eyes had already begun to sink deeper into his skull.

Days earlier, the sounds of the children playing nearby had caused his curiosity to be aroused. Not now. Each day when the power suddenly cut out or turned back on, Naggya scarcely blinked, and now forgotten were his attempts to turn over on his mat or to make himself more comfortable. Naggya just lay there, locked away in his own private world of torment and devouring fear.

Outside a prayer chain had been set up with their single focus being that Naggya would find a reason to live. The chain extended beyond the perimeter of Son-Shine to the pastor of Elijah's church in the nearby Dalit village, and to the far reaches of the expanding Son-Shine network, the USA and Australia, South Africa, and Europe. At any hour of the day someone somewhere would be praying for little Naggya to be healed and to find a reason to live. This little boy's life hung by the feeblest of threads.

CHAPTER
twelve

In New York, it was the third hour on the third day when Chad sat bolt upright in bed. Although he'd had visions before, this was by far the clearest. He reached for his cell phone and scrolled quickly through the address book.

"Hello, Chad. How are . . . ?"

"Naggya will dance before kings and queens and heads of state. Elijah, I saw it and you need to tell him!"

"If you've heard from God then of course I will tell him, Chad, but right now I'm not sure anything is getting through."

"Oh, it will get through."

Elijah hurried into the office and glanced first at Rambabu, then Martha.

Naggya was severely dehydrated and had become dangerously malnourished. It had been almost a week since he'd eaten anything, and during the past twenty-four hours he'd been slipping in and out of consciousness.

"If I take him to hospital, they'll demand payment in advance, and then let him die. No, we will fight this battle right here." Elijah crouched down and spoke softly into Naggya's ear, unsure of how Rambabu might react. "Naggya, you will not die but live, and you will dance before royalty and heads of state.

God has a plan and a purpose for your life, and He will use you to reach others."

Naggya didn't move. After Elijah squeezed his frail little hand, he waited for a response. None came. Rambabu moved in a little closer and rested a palm on Naggya's forehead. Rambabu looked up into Elijah's eye to whisper, "I too believe."

Martha shuffled in closer and laid a hand on Naggya's back as Elijah repeated over and over the words of the vision, and the promise through Jeremiah thousands of years earlier. "Naggya, you have a future and a hope."

It was after dark when Elijah drove out of Son-Shine while Martha and Rambabu and a couple of the other staff stayed with the boys and continued to pray.

Elijah's children and Vani were still deeply traumatized from the death threats and the robbery, and although Elijah had promised to be home each evening before dark, that had yet to happen.

Did Naggya's eyelids flutter when we were praying?

❖❖❖❖❖

The next morning arrived with a miracle. Naggya was still alive!

During the night Rambabu had reluctantly accepted food and the need for sleep while a succession of willing intercessors remained beside Naggya to pray without ceasing. Today would be crucial.

❖❖❖❖❖

Chad kept himself busy in his office, but his mind refused to settle. Despite deadlines for customers and an exciting new venture needing urgent attention, his mind raced and his heart thumped wildly. *"Arise, shine, for your light has come"* kept ringing in his ears, pounding in his chest.

❖❖❖❖❖

On the far side of the planet, Naggya didn't move. His breath now shallow and his pulse much weaker; he'd stopped sweating a day earlier despite the searing heat and the absence of wind. Naggya was shutting down, fast, and for anyone who cared to look, all the signs showed clearly that today would be his last. Nine days without food was life-threatening for most, but for a frail little boy, brutal, insufferable.

Around the clock there would be four or five intercessors beside him, praying fervently. As each was replaced by another, an air of inevitability appeared to trudge wearily from the room. Elijah would frequently come and go, and with the passing of time and his own faith ebbing, the leader of Son-Shine struggled to rally his troops.

There had never been a death at Son-Shine; not a student, not a teacher, nor a helper, and while he considered the prospects, Elijah was becoming fearful of the ramifications should Naggya lose his fight.

The middle of the day predictably delivered more searing heat and at this time of year before the rains and their reprieve, the mercury would top forty-five most days. With no hydration in his system and his hair already an ominous orange from malnutrition, Naggya was about to leave Son-Shine for all time.

❖❖❖❖❖

From another world and another climate *Arise, Shine* rang out time and again. Added to Chad's unceasing supplications were those of his wife and a few of their supporters. Chad had accepted the futility of remaining at work and had joined his wife at home as they emptied their hearts and begged for mercy. *Arise, Shine!* For the next three hours, nothing else left their lips.

❖❖❖❖❖

Martha recoiled. She sat up from beside Naggya and looked into the faces of the others. "He squeezed my hand!"

A passing visitor from Northern Europe, trained in nursing, had joined the bedside vigil and she looked across at Martha. Softly she whispered, "As the body shuts down, sometimes the nerves cause parts of the body to flinch."

"No, he squeezed my hand," and as she spoke, Martha recoiled a second time, "There, he did it again!"

CHAPTER
thirteen

Three more days; three more miracles. Whatever was keeping Naggya alive was beyond all the realms of the natural. Though he still clung by a thread, that flimsiest of threads refused to snap. The prayer vigil for him continued around the boy, around the clock, around Son-Shine, and all around the world. As each day passed and updates crisscrossed the globe, the host of witnesses multiplied in faith and in number.

Day one; Naggya took water. Day two; he opened his eyes, briefly. Day three; Naggya reluctantly accepted his first solid food in almost a fortnight. Though his skin remained wrinkled and dry and his hair orange, Naggya's breathing was stronger and his eyes had assumed the palest of light.

The number of times Chad's vision had been declared over the young boy had, by now, reached immeasurable proportions. "Arise, Shine! Naggya will dance before kings and queens and heads of state!"

❖❖❖❖❖

Since the Son-Shine robbery, Vani had continued to grieve, and with each passing day her need for her husband to be by her side multiplied. Barely could he leave the room without Vani beginning to panic, and each time Elijah attempted to return to Son-Shine, his wife's fears would skyrocket. Although their two children had outwardly put the incident behind them, Vani had convinced herself that, if left alone, she'd become the latest in the long line of racial debauchery and, in her opinion, an unthinkable death. Despite assurances from her husband and her own parents, Vani's grip upon sanity was slipping.

Is she really so afraid, or does she still resent me for my time at Son-Shine?

"Vani, I promise I won't be long, and your mother and my parents are with you. I must go but I will be back soon."

"You always say that! If they are more important to you than your own family, then go!"

Elijah wrapped his arms around his wife and held her tightly. Right now, no words would dispel her torment and all he could do was hold on and pray. His cell phone rang and reflexively he reached into his pocket, but Vani's glare forced him to freeze.

❖❖❖❖❖

"I want to stand up."

Rambabu spun around and glanced first at his frail young friend, and then toward Martha. Tentatively she moved in closer and searched deep within Naggya's eyes. "Why not just sit up for a while? It's been weeks since you last stood."

A steely resolve overtook his little face. Without a hint of disrespect, he replied, "No, Miss, I need to stand."

Martha's hands trembled as she linked arms with Naggya and eased him slowly to his feet. Tears rolled down her cheeks as she, in a faltering voice, whispered, "Elijah will be *so* thrilled."

CHAPTER
fourteen

"Miss, I think I can dance." Yessuma was a little startled and peered across at Naggya. His cheeks had begun to fill out, and after four weeks of regular meals his eyes had regained some of their sparkle and his hair a degree of its former luster. There'd also been a steadily increasing flow of words working their way out of his mouth, yet Yessuma was still surprised by what she had just heard.

"Are you sure you're ready, Naggya? Why don't we just keep trying to walk for a few more days?"

Naggya flashed her an impish smile, "If I can dance, I can walk, but if I can only walk . . . "

Yessuma smiled back at him, "Yes, little man, I take your point," and she moved in closer, kneeled beside him, and took him by the hand. After he managed to get to his feet and steadied himself, Yessuma led him into the center of the room. "I read somewhere that the hardest place to skate on ice is out in the middle of the pond. So, are you game enough to try?"

"But we don't have any ice here, Miss." Yessuma chuckled then tightened her grip to steady him as they plotted an uneasy course out into the middle of their imaginary pond.

"And what sort would you like your first dance to be after all these weeks, kind sir?"

Naggya felt a warm glow gush from within. The notion of being called "sir" caught him by surprise, and to be spoken to as an adult felt surreal. "Ah, I don't know. I think I'll just start and see what happens," and he gently shook Yessuma's hand free and took his first tentative steps. As though an inner switch suddenly flicked, he began with a slow spin to the left and raised an unsteady arm. Though far from fluent, by the time his first spin was complete, his face had been swamped by the most astonished grin. The spin was followed by an equally tentative second, then a third, and a fourth, but halfway through the fifth, it all came to a shuddering halt. Naggya flopped onto the tiled floor as Yessuma rushed to his side. Still plastered across his handsome young face was the most beguiling of smiles, "I did it, Miss, I did it!"

"Yes, Naggya, you did, you certainly did."

"Miss, what did that man say about kings and queens?"

Standing just outside the door were Elijah and Martha; two more radiant smiles had now completed the set.

❖❖❖❖❖

As the morning unfolded, the word spread of Naggya's tentative return to dance, and a wave of spontaneous celebration swept throughout Son-Shine. By lunchtime, a throng of exuberant young Dalits jostled for position outside the room in which Naggya had spent the past few weeks, and in unison they shouted his name. Naggya's excitement and sense of self-worth skyrocketed.

Martha and Yessuma stood beside him and waited for the gravity of the children's repeated shouts to sink in. Martha knelt down and took his hand in hers, "Would you like to come out and see your friends?"

Naggya said nothing while he climbed up from his make-shift bed. His baffled expression accompanied him all the way to the door and as Martha opened it wide, he was greeted by a sea of exhilarated children who wanted nothing more than to hug him. Naggya didn't want to cry, but was powerless to prevent a torrent of tears as one-by-one each child wrapped an arm around him and whispered their love into his astonished ears. Naggya was home. Naggya finally belonged.

Rambabu leaned against the far wall as a tear trickled slowly down his cheek. The journey for him had been just as traumatic and had taken a huge toll. Now, to witness his only true friend back on his feet, surrounded by all the children, and being restored to his rightful place, was a joy unspeakable. Elijah walked slowly toward him and placed a protective arm around his tiny shoulder. Rambabu didn't resist.

CHAPTER
fifteen

There were often mixed emotions leading up to and during birthday celebrations. Many of the children looked forward to celebrating their birthdays with the opportunity to share a special cake and to sing those very personal songs, yet for just as many, that day of the year amounted to a confusing reminder of their past. Far too many Dalits came into the world without any form of government recognition, so they couldn't accurately know when they were born. As each child grew, their awareness of the need of a document that potentially paved a way into a university, or eventually to a passport, also grew.

Within two years of Naggya joining Son-Shine, Aunty had slipped away. She had most likely died of the same dysentery disease as her late husband, all alone and in the most horrifying of circumstances. Only the stench of death had alluded to those nearby that she had died. Within twenty-four hours, her putrid remains had been unceremoniously discarded and her home had become the residence of new tenants. Death, life, and daily survival seamlessly rolled on.

It had taken several months before Elijah had become aware of her passing, and only then because the school bus had been dispatched to pick up and transport a new member to Son-Shine. As the bus passed by Aunty's, Elijah could see that there were unfamiliar people living there, and after he'd stopped to inquire, it became evident that they knew virtually nothing of Aunty, or for that matter, her family.

As the bus pulled in that evening, Elijah was faced with the unenviable task of breaking the news to Naggya. Had it not been for his love of his new home and the ever-present support of Rambabu, Naggya would have struggled with the news. The final link to his past had now been broken forever. Naggya had no opportunity to grieve, nor did it seem he wanted or needed one. It was now only ten days to the regional traditional dance competition, and Naggya hadn't eyes, ears, or thoughts for anything else. For this young boy, grief would somehow be buried along with Aunty, and in its place, life would deliver the hope of a better tomorrow. *Kings and queens and heads of state.*

❖❖❖❖❖

Naggya was somewhere in the vicinity of eight years old when, in 2006, he took part in the first regional dance championships that allowed Son-Shine teams to enter. The Vijayawada Youth Regional Dance Championships, to be staged in the Imperial Cultural Centre in the middle of the city, had accepted the applications of seventy dance troupes, ranging in age from seven to fifteen. Ever since the announcement of the inclusion of the Son-Shine teams, a backlash had raged from within the higher caste schools, and they had vehemently voiced their disgust. "How can a school of animals be possibly granted permission to compete alongside ours?" The galling inclusion of the filthy Dalit school was an insult to their culture and was deemed utterly intolerable.

For decades, the exclusive upper caste schools battled for regional supremacy, and with such prestige at stake, anything that offered a competitive edge would be vigorously explored. The quality and distinctive styles of the costuming had long played a vital role in establishing favor among the judges, and accordingly, budgets for costumes in most schools continued to swell. Elijah was staggered to learn that the outlay for one child's dance costume from another school would often exceed ten times that of Son-Shine's entire team.

The higher-caste backlash also hinged upon the very notion that their children's garments would become polluted and worthless from having come in contact with a Dalit. This constituted not only an insult but an unacceptable disgrace. Dalits were filth; Dalits were not human; Dalits should not be allowed to compete. Dalits, particularly their children, were beasts of burden, and their primary purpose in life was to be cheap labor and never anything more. To consider their own children competing alongside Dalits and in doing so to risk being contaminated was an anathema of the most detestable order. Throughout India, each generation had been indoctrinated into the essential need for their caste's prominence and domination to be maintained without exception. Dalits did not belong within the caste system, a fact that must be maintained at all costs and forever enshrined within Indian culture.

Much of the caste system hatred toward all Dalits was withheld from the Son-Shine children for as long as possible, however, as each attempt was made to break down the barriers, the backlash from higher castes would invariably be brutal. As the children grew older, their awareness multiplied.

Despite this unfolding sense of abhorrence toward them, the Son-Shine children prepared for the regionals as though their futures depended upon it; in many respects, they did.

CHAPTER
sixteen

Naggya had grown three inches in height during the past two years, and although still slight in build, he was beginning to show signs of his future physique. It wasn't uncommon for Indian children to become six-footers by their late teens, and Naggya was giving the impression he'd likely join their ranks. His flowing rhythmic dance style and his instinctive balance seemed to leap from one impressive level to the next. Dancing, for Naggya, was his release into a world that transcended all other worlds; a place where nothing else in this contaminated world mattered, and a place where all things were possible. Naggya's deeply hidden dream of *kings and queens* was rarely spoken of, yet remained preciously etched just beneath the surface. Through dance, and only through dance, never again would he be without purpose, without identity, or indeed, without hope.

Solomon had joined Son-Shine at the start of the year as a teacher of mathematics and geography. He was, however, also a very proficient traditional dancer, having been tutored for most of his life by his late father and several of his uncles in the ancient art of expression in cultural dance.

Almost from day one, Solomon had recognized and been drawn to the emerging talents of his star pupil, Naggya.

Although conscious of not putting his young protege on a pedestal, the fact was obvious that Solomon and Naggya were a team to be reckoned with. Also, from day one and at almost every opportunity, Naggya would follow Solomon like his shadow and mimic his every move.

"But, Naggya, are you sure you want to be in every dance? You don't want to spoil your chances."

Naggya smiled up at Solomon and didn't need to utter a word. "OK, OK, but be sure to rest well. We only have one week before regionals, and you need to be ready." Naggya launched into a triple spin and when he'd finished in perfect position and posture, he punched the air in triumph. "Yes, my boy, I get it."

❖❖❖❖❖

The morning of the regionals was particularly steamy. During March, temperatures often hovered around forty degrees, and being inland, typically the humidity would be low. Not today. While the team of ten Son-Shine youth dancers boarded the bus, Solomon's shirt was already drenched in perspiration. Boarding behind him was Elijah who leaned forward and whispered into Solomon's ear, "Is that because of the temperature or your nerves?" and he glanced down at Solomon's shirt.

Solomon chuckled, "A bit of both, Brother."

It was a thirty-minute drive into the city and Punji maneuvered the freshly washed bus through the morning traffic as though born to the task. Each of the schools had been instructed to have their respective teams assembled in the Imperial Cultural Centre basement no later than 9 a.m. for a 10 a.m. start. The prospect of having seventy teams as well as their entourages fit into a relatively confined area would be a logistical challenge at the best of times, but as word spread that the team from Son-Shine was in fact a Dalit team, the mood within the basement turned sour. Nearby teams were urgently shepherded away from the Dalits out of a sense of safety and disgust. The rest of the teams then expressed their dissatisfaction over being squeezed ever tighter into the confined space. Elijah glanced at Solomon and then towards the children. He leaned forward and ushered the ten young dancers in close, "Children, we must always be prepared and willing to turn the other cheek. We might be Dalits, but above all, we are Christians, and we will always put our faith before our fears. No matter what happens today, please remember, 'If God be for us, who can be against us?' We will do nothing to jeopardize our chances of being invited back. Our behavior here today has everything to do with who we are, and it has nothing to do with how others behave. Children, keep your heads held high and try to smile, no matter what happens, OK?" Ten sets of eyes were glued to their leader as ten heads nodded in unison. Solomon and Punji did likewise.

The infuriated protests from other nearby schools stemmed mainly from the adults, yet as the more vocal from the upper castes voiced their repulsion, their children began to follow suit. At first, there was little more than sneers and pointing of fingers, but not long after, the shaking of a clenched fist or a spit in the Dalit direction, forced the Son-Shine children to question their own capacities not to react. Being among the youngest, Naggya and Rambabu remained toward the back of their team; their courage small and their resolve tested.

Two police officers appeared at the entry to the basement and spoke to a group of very vocal men from a higher caste. After a brief exchange, the officers looked across and pointed towards the Son-Shine team. They manfully made their way through the crowd and as they got within a few feet of Elijah and Solomon standing in front of the team, the senior officer paused and asked, "So, your team are Dalits?"

Elijah took a small step forward and immediately, the senior officer raised his hand, "That's close enough. If you're going to make trouble, you and your team will need to leave! Do you understand?"

The children shuffled in even tighter as Elijah also raised his hand, although he did so in a spirit of humble surrender "We do not want any trouble, Sir. We have come to dance in these championships as one of the official entries. This is our first time to compete, and as soon as the championships conclude we will leave, quietly and respectfully, and we will immediately return to our village. Again, Sir, we do not want any trouble. We just want to dance."

The second officer spat on the floor in front of Elijah. He glared at him before turning to his senior colleague, who leaned across and whispered something into his ear. The senior officer then directed his gaze at Elijah, "If there is any trouble, any trouble at all, you will be sent away, immediately! Do you understand?!"

At the end of a tense and exhausting day in which the Son-Shine team literally shone, the 2006 Vijayawada Regional Dance Championships results were read out over the microphone to a crowd of over 3,000. The Royal Vijayawada Brahman College was awarded the overall first prize. The announcement was met with rapturous applause from certain sections of the crowd, while other sections fell into silence.

Standing huddled at the back, all alone, was the team from Son-Shine as they waited for the remaining results to be made known. By way of the judges' verdict, Son-Shine had placed a distant last. They left quietly.

❖❖❖❖❖

The following morning directly after devotions, Elijah called the entire school together for an unscheduled assembly. "Children, today we are so proud. We do not see yesterday's result as a failure, despite the behavior of the other schools at the Regional Championships. Yesterday was not about you, children. Yesterday was not about how well you danced. The truth is, children, it was never going to be. Yesterday's championships were always going to be political. We need to see that for how it is. What we need to be thankful for is that we, for the very first time, were allowed to compete. Yesterday was a major breakthrough. Today, we need to recognize that we are far better off than we were yesterday. We need to be rejoicing. After we were judged as the lowest team, and after the way we were treated, they won't be expecting us to come back, ever. They would be wrong. We will reenter the next competition, and the one after, and the one after that. Every time we compete, we will take another step forward. One day, and I don't know when that may be, but one day the judges' scores will reflect the fact that the Son-Shine team was not only as good as the team that claimed yesterday's first prize, but in truth, is clearly better. Next time we compete, we will do better still, and every time we compete we will keep getting better and keep aiming higher. Our goal is to become so good that they can deny us no longer. If we give up now, they will have won, and we will have put the battle for Dalit acceptance and equality right back to square one. We cannot and will not do that. We will never give up."

Four hundred Dalits clapped. Many cheered; many cried.

CHAPTER
seventeen

Each time Chad and Lois set a date to return to India, and in particular to the Son-Shine children, departure time seemed to drag. So much of their heart, their lives, and their love for the nation of India revolved around their devotion to these children. Chad and Lois always tried to remain impartial, to love them all the same and to not have favorites, yet for Chad, his love for Rambabu, the boy with the broken button, and his best friend Naggya, the boy with the feet of angels, that love simply refused to be contained.

Whenever they arrived at Son-Shine, pooladandas of orange and yellow marigolds would be lovingly draped around their necks the instant they'd stepped from their vehicle. The Son-Shine children loved Mummy Lois and Daddy Chad; wherever they went and whatever they were doing, a horde of doting children would be buzzing alongside, out in front and behind, vying for an opportunity to hold a hand or to ask a question. Never before, in all their years, had this couple who now called New York home felt such love and connection. Son-Shine was as near to Heaven as they'd ever known.

Chad searched among the sea of faces, familiar faces, and faces of children who'd arrived since their last trip a year ago. Secretly though, he searched for the faces of Rambabu and

Naggya. His beaming smile stretched to another level when standing in the background, as was their way, were his beloved two boys. Never to put themselves forward at the expense of others, Rambabu and Naggya would simply wait their turn, no matter how long that took.

The entrance to the main building had been tiled since their last trip, the upper floor had been walled-in and roofed and long gone were the exposed lengths of steel-reinforcing rods pointing skywards, so prevalent throughout India, in readiness and hope that one day they'd see completion. The children were eager to show Mummy and Daddy all that had changed and ushered them upstairs to soak up the splendor of the view of the surrounding countryside, all viewed from a bare room without glass in the windows. The children were so proud. "This will be where we will sleep soon, Daddy," said one, "and this will be where we do our homework," excitedly said another.

Back down on ground level and under the shelter from the midday sun, Chad spotted Rambabu and Naggya leaning against the wall adjacent to the main entrance. Beside them was an old generator that spluttered to life several times each day when the power from the electricity grid once again failed. Power failures were commonplace throughout India, and multiple times each day the children allocated to that responsibility would sprint into position and kick the forty-year-old diesel generator into life, accompanied by vast plumes of sooty black smoke.

Chad briefly extricated himself from his adoring posse and took a few steps towards the two boys; he paused, dropped to one knee and opened his arms wide as Rambabu and Naggya rushed into his embrace. "My, how you've both grown! You'll both be shaving before we know it," as each boy glanced at the other and chuckled as only ten-year-olds can. "Boys, I can hardly wait to see you both dance. Elijah has told me how much you've improved, but I must see that for myself, OK?"

Though not enchanted with dance nearly as much as Naggya, Rambabu always enjoyed dancing. For him it was as much a sign of his inclusion and acceptance into Son-Shine as it was the art, the culture, or the self-expression. Naggya lived, breathed, and dreamed dance; his first thought every day, the last as he closed his eyes every night, and much of his time between. "Would you like to see a new move I've been practicing, Daddy?" Naggya asked with unrestrained joy.

From a distance, Elijah beckoned Chad inside following their long and wearying travels. As Chad walked off, he turned to Naggya, "I can hardly wait, my boy. Soon, OK?"

Naggya smiled, yet his smile scarcely concealed the fact that he'd wanted so much to dance before his Daddy Chad right there on the spot, and now he would have to wait. Chad could see the disappointment upon the young boy's face, so he softly repeated, "Soon."

During a private meal with Elijah, Chad and Lois were brought up to date on all the latest school news, including the fact that a provincial dance championship was to be held in Hyderabad in twelve days. Chad and Lois exchanged furtive glances, then both smiled. Over the years, Elijah had grown familiar with those smiles and knew precisely what they meant, "Ah, somehow I feel I should be trying to get you a couple of special visitor tickets?"

Despite being placed last in every regional dance championship for the past three years, Son-Shine had been miraculously granted permission to enter the Junior State Titles. The invitation had come via a large Christian church in Hyderabad. The church, Jesus The Rock, had been battling, and to some extent overcoming, the same obstacles that Son-Shine had.

The previous year, there had been a chance meeting in the transit lounge in Kuala Lumpur Airport between two men. These two men, one with connections to Jesus The Rock and the other to Son-Shine, had stop-overs at the same time despite traveling in opposite directions. They had struck up a conversation over a meal and from that conversation, introductions were exchanged, ultimately paving the way for Elijah to link by phone to the pastor of Jesus The Rock, the largest Christian church in the state of Andhra Pradesh. Almost one year later, an invitation had been extended for Son-Shine to enter a small dance team on a one-off basis. "The children are so excited!"

Chad again glanced at his wife, "And how many are in this small team?"

Elijah gazed across into Chad's eyes, "Five, Chad, just five."

Lois had picked up on the subtlety of her husband's question and tentatively asked, "And would we know each of these children?"

Elijah let out a soft chuckle, "Do you mean, are Naggya and Rambabu part of the team?"

It was Chad's turn to smile as Lois glanced at each man in turn. "I know you both have special places in your hearts for all of the children, but honestly, it's OK to have favorites, that is of course so long as the other children don't realize. Not surprisingly, Naggya is on the team. Rambabu isn't." Elijah waited for a response, but none came. "It's not that Rambabu couldn't have been chosen, he just didn't want to be. He's perfectly happy here, in fact, he's never been happier, and we are delighted. Rambabu has not only become an important part of this place, but has matured beyond his years. Soon, I feel he will be one of the leaders of his age group, and from where he has come, that is a miracle. His faith continues to grow every day and we are so proud of him. Besides, with all due respect to Rambabu," and he leaned forward and lowered his voice, "there are better dancers who are so in love with dance that they will make our team so much stronger."

CHAPTER
eighteen

The days leading up to the State Titles had literally flown, and in that time, Naggya had managed not one but many opportunities to show Daddy Chad his new moves. Every time Naggya performed, Chad would gasp at the majesty and fluency of this budding star. Solomon had clearly been a major influence upon the team's cutting-edge style, with its compelling blend of the old and the new. There was an unmistakable crossover into ballet, yet when Chad inquired of Solomon's training in that craft, all that came back was a blank expression and a nebulous head wobble. Chad turned to his wife and shrugged his shoulders, "No formal training yet take a look at the quality. It's extraordinary, and they're still only babies. How can this be?" Chad looked to his wife for understanding, yet she was just as bewildered as he. "I mean, emerging ballet dancers train under the masters for a decade to become this good, yet here's a ten-year-old doing these movements like he's been born to it."

Lois gave her husband a hug, "You and I both know that he has," and they remained wrapped in their glowing bubble until Naggya pirouetted and looked imploringly in their direction. Naggya wasn't looking for accolades; he simply wanted to be sure that he had pleased them. Two sets of glistening eyes confirmed he had.

❖❖❖❖❖

At 4 p.m. the afternoon before their departure for Hyderabad for the Junior State Titles the following morning, Punji and Elijah drove into Vijayawada to take delivery of a hired minibus. Son-Shine's own bus would be required for the twice-daily school runs, and the old Ambassador was far too small for ten people and their luggage. As they pulled up outside the bus-hire office, a man hurried toward them, but when he recognized them to be Dalits, he about-faced and retreated inside, shutting the door behind him. From his cell phone, Elijah called the number on the hoarding and after confirming he was there to pick-up a minibus, the office door opened and Elijah was beckoned inside. Punji waited in the car. The proprietor directed Elijah to place the agreed amount on his desk, plus a previously unmentioned security deposit, refundable only if the bus was returned undamaged. Elijah respectfully objected, however the proprietor was well aware that very few bus-hire companies would be willing to hire Dalits, and given the lateness of the day and the fact that Elijah had already informed him they were leaving for Hyderabad early the next morning, he had Elijah over a barrel. Elijah produced a credit card and the man nodded. Elijah counted out a pile of rupees onto the desk, and again the man nodded. Though not providing any documentation or a receipt, the proprietor pointed outside where a minibus had magically appeared, complete with a thick covering of dirt and interior rubbish to match. The driver climbed out of the bus and grunted towards Punji, indicating that the keys were in the ignition, and then walked back into the office, crossing paths with Elijah on the way. Elijah made way for him and smiled. None came back.

Being smaller than the other driver, Punji adjusted the driving position and began to check the indicators, the brakes, and the headlights. Everything seemed to be in working order, however, when Punji tried the all-important horn, nothing happened. As Elijah climbed into the passenger seat he glanced across at Punji who turned towards him with a troubled expression, "Elijah, we can't drive this bus to Hyderabad. The horn doesn't work."

Elijah alighted from the bus and as he approached the office, the "closed" sign suddenly appeared on the door. When Elijah tried to go inside, the proprietor forced the door shut and pointed menacingly to the sign.

As Elijah climbed back into the bus, he tapped Punji lightly on the thigh, "We're going to trust God, my friend."

A troubled expression remained on Punji's face as Elijah chuckled, "Yes, I know. You use the horn more than you use the accelerator and the brakes. We will manage," and again he chuckled softly.

"But all the way to Hyderabad and back?"

Returning to Son-Shine, Elijah couldn't resist his thoughts, *they'd have fixed the horn if we weren't Dalits. The proprietor would be thinking, if we crash the bus because we didn't sound the horn, the company will keep our money and our credit card. They would claim on the insurance and get a brand new bus. On top of that, if we die, they would be very thankful that India would have a few less Dalits.* Elijah chose not to share his thoughts, but as they drove into the school grounds, his mood suddenly lifted. Once again, Elijah patted Punji's thigh and was still grinning by the time he entered the dining room. Elijah muttered under his breath, "First thing tomorrow, I will ring the bus company and tell them that we have two American VIPs traveling with us. When they know that, they won't be so quick to put our lives at risk. Yes, our God is smart. God is with us. God will protect us."

❖❖❖❖❖

At 5:30 a.m. the bus spluttered into life. Onboard were Elijah, Solomon, Lois and Chad, and five exhilarated children. As Punji engaged first gear, he tried to blast the horn, however, when nothing happened, most of the adults laughed. The children didn't, but instead, craned their necks trying to fathom what was so funny.

Surrounding the bus were two-hundred children who cheered and waved excitedly at their team of heroes, refusing to stop until the bus had driven out the gates and out of view down the gravel road.

Lois and Chad sat in the first double seat behind the driver. The children were in the seats behind.

They'd always commuted between Vijayawada and Hyderabad by air, so to see the countryside up close and personal was a treat Lois and Chad didn't want to miss. As they settled in for the anticipated five-hour journey, Chad had a clear sight of the road ahead, while Lois had an uninterrupted view of the passing Andhra Pradesh landscape. After watching the unfolding phenomenon repeated three or four times, Chad suddenly laughed out loud. Lois gently elbowed him in the ribs and turned to look at her husband, "What?"

Chad lowered his head and encouraged his wife to do the same, "Only in India. Seriously, only in India would people walking along a main road suddenly spin around and shake their fists at a vehicle for *not* honking the horn! I mean..."

Lois stifled her own giggles, "Yes, I get it. I really do. Anywhere else in the world..."

"Exactly. That's what I still find so bizarre. Do you remember the first time we saw the horn thing, and you loudly demanded to know why the hotel shuttle bus driver had blasted the horn?"

"Yes, and he looked at you like you had two heads."

They both giggled a little louder than intended. "Shhh, we'll get ourselves into trouble."

"Oh, how I adore this country. I can't help but be captivated by all the amazing colors, and those indescribable aromas, and the wonder of the people." Chad gave his wife yet another hug, and whispered, "But will we ever work it out?"

Lois turned to gaze into her husband's eyes, "I hope not. That's the joy. We never know what's around the next corner."

Chad took her by the hand and once again smiled, "I just had another curious thought. You know how they say that you can see the Great Wall of China from outer space? Well, I reckon you could hear India from there as well," and one more time they stifled their chuckles and kept their heads bowed.

"Seriously, can you imagine what India would have sounded like before cars and buses and trucks and motorbikes started honking their horns?" They both stared blankly out the window. *Nah, it just wouldn't be India.*

❖❖❖❖❖

At 8:30 a.m., Elijah pulled his cell phone from his pocket and called the bus hire company. In Telugu, Elijah informed the proprietor that his two VIP Americans had become concerned by the numbers of near-misses that had already taken place in the first few hours traveling, all because the horn didn't work. Within an hour, the proprietor called back with a contact number in Hyderabad to have the problem repaired and charged to the hire company. Elijah thanked the man and added that he hoped there would be no accidents during the remainder of the trip to the capital, before adding, "I would think it probably wouldn't be good for business if anything terrible happened with two American VIPs onboard your bus," and again he thanked the man before politely ending the call.

CHAPTER
nineteen

Naggya stood beside Daddy Chad and hung an arm up on his shoulder. Lois turned to look at the handsome young boy and marveled at the totally natural and uninhibited way he would show his affection and respect for her husband. "Are you getting hungry, Naggya?"

The slightest crease of a smile crossed his face, "Not really, Mummy."

"How are your nerves?" His smile broadened briefly, but he said nothing. Chad eased Naggya onto his knee and wrapped his arms around his athletic young body. "May I ask you something?" and getting a tentative head-wobble, Chad continued, "Naggya, do you ever think about the vision the Lord gave me about you?" Naggya appeared a little troubled by the question and squirmed. "Oh, my son, we never need to feel awkward about the blessings God has for us. He loves us so much and He wants only the very best."

Naggya appeared to relax, although a cautious expression remained on his face. "Do you mean about kings and queens?" With a confirming nod, Naggya bowed his head, "Sometimes." Chad wrapped his arms around tighter and whispered into his ear, "We do too."

Elijah called out from the back row of the bus, "We will be arriving in Suryapet soon, so we will stop just long enough to have something to eat. Mary has made us some of her beautiful sweet potato dahl."

Suryapet was a dusty township of a mere few hundred-thousand. Unremarkable in many ways, though it served as a convenient half-way rest stop for travelers to the capital, Hyderabad. Everyone, especially Punji, needed to stretch their legs before tackling the final leg of their journey into the heart of the big city. None of the children had ever been there before, and already their imaginations were running wild from their studies on the city, including that of Hyderabad's twin city, Secunderabad. Over the next two days, Solomon's knowledge as a geography teacher would be invaluable, and the fact that both he and Elijah had studied in the capital city would hopefully afford them a crucial edge as they negotiated the relentless traffic without a horn.

An hour from their destination, every nerve jangled with each passing mile. So much had been fought for over the years; so many battles for equality; countless battles for cultural breakthroughs; endless battles for the chance to chase down dreams, and here today, opening before them was a door that at times had threatened to remain forever shut.

Elijah took the cell phone from his pocket and called the number provided by the bus hire proprietor. Elijah was given an address that was only three miles from where they would be staying as guests of Jesus The Rock, and a time was set for next morning to repair or replace the defective horn. He walked to the front of the bus, "Tomorrow, Punji, and your prayers are answered."

Punji smiled and tapped the faulty warning device twice and trumpeted the sound of a horn. This time, even the children laughed.

❖❖❖❖❖

As they picked their way through the mid-afternoon traffic, the children marveled at all the sites; the most captivating of them all, the massive Golconda Fort perched high on the impressive hill. Solomon reminded the children that the fortress had been built in the 16th Century and in the hundreds of years since had been owned and presided over by a series of powerful rulers from various parts of the world. The children remained bug-eyed as they tried to contemplate how such a massive and imposing structure could possibly have been built in such a difficult location.

Hyderabad appeared to stretch out forever, and around every corner another overwhelming edifice kept their mouths from closing. As they skirted Hussain Sagar Lake, Solomon was relishing his role as tour guide, announcing with a degree of pride, "Hyderabad, also known as The Pearl City, and its twin city, Secunderabad, have a population around ten times that of Vijayawada. But," he added, "they are both still tiny compared to Mumbai or Delhi, or for that matter, even Bangalore."

By 3:30 p.m., some nine hours into their five-hour journey, the mini bus pulled into the Jesus The Rock car park. As Punji wearily pulled on the handbrake, Elijah alighted in search of the office. "Can I help you, young man?" was heard coming from behind a closed door.

Elijah paused and inquired where he might possibly find Pastor Karl? "Ah, you must be Elijah. We were expecting you a few hours ago."

Extending his hand by way of apology, Elijah responded, "Sorry, Pastor, we had quite a slow trip. We came all this way from just outside Vijayawada without a horn."

The wizened old sage released a chuckle, "Then God is surely on your side, young man. Where are you parked? You and your team will be staying upstairs in the next building. Follow me and I will show you the way."

CHAPTER
twenty

By 5 p.m., the travelers had settled in, and Solomon gathered the dance team together downstairs in the church foyer for a final practice before tomorrow's championships. Solomon recognized the pressures of the moment and he shepherded them in close and laid hands upon them, one-by-one, as Pastor Karl watched from a distance, praying silently.

Solomon then called for the team to take their places, as a tangible calm settled upon the group. The time had arrived for them to worship in the manner they knew and loved best. Solomon pressed play on the sound system and gave one soft clap in readiness as five young champions-of-life melded into one glorious symphony, a thousand hours practice majestically giving birth. Scarcely a foot put wrong nor a step out of rhythm, Solomon nodded and prompted while his charges unfurled the very depths of their young hearts. Their expression stretched way beyond art; this was their reason to be alive. Every member of the team shone with a brilliance that words spoken or read from a page could never capture. Silently, Pastor Karl continued to pray, and he smiled inwardly as his aging foot began to tap in time with the dance.

After twice running through their routine, Solomon graciously bowed before them, barely able to contain his joy.

"Team, we are ready."

As Pastor Karl emerged from the semi-darkness behind them, he was joined by Elijah who had caught the final moments of the practice. Just before they reached the team, Pastor Karl whispered, "I have seen many dancers, and these are indeed gifted, a force to behold," and he nodded towards Naggya, "Particularly that one."

During the evening meal and after the children had been fed and retired to their sleeping quarters, each of the adults had the opportunity to share about their respective experiences and dreams. These championships were Jesus The Rock's third attempt at dance recognition. In the previous two state titles, their team had placed last. No explanation given, nor expected. "This is a process. It can be a very long process. We strive to break down walls, and we are willing to suffer to do so, yet when we advance the cause of the Dalits, even if only by an inch, we rejoice, and we are thankful. We need to be careful how we do things. Opposition is deep, opposition can be very nasty, and opposition appears strong. But our God is stronger." The old sage paused and wiped the corners of his mouth as he gathered his thoughts, "The Good Book declares in Matthew 10:16 that we are to be as shrewd as snakes and harmless as doves. I urge you all to remember that, and to apply it wherever you go. It has served me well in the heat of battle and it will do for you, also."

Lois was seated next to the pastor's elderly wife, Ashish. Dabbing a tear from the corner of her eye, Lois turned to the lady beside her, "Your husband is such an inspiration. You must feel so blessed," and as she spoke, the pastor's wife looked away. "Sorry, I hope I wasn't being disrespectful, it's just that I . . ."

Ashish raised her hand gently to allay Lois's concerns, then smiled, "Actually, my name means 'blessing' and I pray I am that for my husband, as he has been for me for so many years."

"It's such a beautiful name, Ashish. May I ask how long you've been married?"

Ashish again smiled and looked down to spin her simple, solitary wedding band. "My husband and I have been married for sixty-five years."

The two ladies gazed into each other's glistening eyes; words utterly unnecessary.

Pastor Karl turned to Elijah, "You are doing a wonderful thing with your orphanage and your school. If time ever allowed, I would love to see it, but we are always so busy, always so much to do."

Elijah could see the sincerity and depth of the old man's desire and smiled back at him, "It would be our honor and a privilege to show you the miracles God has done. Perhaps one of your people could visit and bring back a report?"

"Perhaps," replied the pastor, and again, "Perhaps. For now, why don't you paint a few pictures for me while we sit?"

Elijah beamed as he recalled the parallel journeys of the two men, "Well, sir, as you spoke of all the struggles and the troubles and the oppositions you've faced, it was as though you were telling our story. Every day is a struggle. Every day we battle to feed the children, to clothe them, to keep them safe, but most of all, to keep their dreams alive. In every child, there's a dream. It wasn't there when they came to us, but little by little, their dreams come out, and we are privileged to help their dreams become real. Our first children are soon to graduate high school and then begin university. They could never have even hoped to get an education before God called Son-Shine into being, yet right in front of our eyes, He is making it so. There is nothing better in life but to see another's dream unfold."

"It's a powerful message you speak, Elijah, and I am thankful you've come to us to share. Tell me, young man, you mentioned about keeping your children safe. Please tell me more of that struggle."

Elijah glanced around the table and hesitated as he tried to discern how much of his world's reality to share. Pastor Karl could see the consternation upon his new friend's face, however, it was Ashish who turned to her husband to seek his guidance to speak. With an affirming nod, she said, "Elijah, we all know the hardship of suffering. We have all lived through so much pain and so much injustice in our lifetimes that there isn't much left that would shock. Please feel free to share as you are led." She glanced towards Chad and Lois, who nodded in agreement.

Elijah cleared his voice as his bottom lip quivered, "At Son-Shine, we are reasonably removed from some of the worst of the atrocities against Dalits. We live and we conduct school in the poorer rural areas away from the city and away from the nearest large towns. We are far enough removed that most of the upper caste people wouldn't even bother to come near us. That is a blessing, but when we go into the towns and into Vijayawada, we are treated like dogs, just like you are here. The upper caste people spit on us, they hit us, they shake their fists at us, and they threaten us whenever we get too close. They refuse to do business with us, yet not so surprisingly, when some of them see that we have a little money, they forget that we are Dalits until our money is in their hands, and then we are Dalits again and they chase us out of their shops with sticks and knives." Elijah hesitated and glanced around the room before continuing. "A few months ago," and again he paused, "A few months ago, three teenage Dalit girls were returning home from working in the fields." Solomon knew the story and knew the pain of its telling. He reached across and patted Elijah on the forearm and nodded in support. "The girls were fifteen and had been working for the same landowner for five years. When they passed by a stand of trees, just as they did every day, a group of young men from another caste were waiting for them. The men tied up the girls, they pack-raped them, tortured them, strangled them, then hung them by their necks in the trees for the Dalits to find next morning when they came to work in the fields. The families came," and once again Elijah paused to draw breath and to steady his voice. "The families came to cut down their girls and to take them home for burial, but for three days the landowner hunted them away. By the time the girls were allowed to be cut down, their bodies had swollen up in the heat and were swarming with . . . " Elijah bit down hard upon his lip. He breathed in deeply then exhaled and blinked hard before he could continue, "with flies. " The landowner wanted everyone to know that more of these killings would happen every time there were acts of defiance or disrespect against anyone from an upper caste."

Pastor Karl cleared his voice and reached out to Elijah, "My son, the Lord hears your cry. We all must grieve. It's of some comfort that their sufferings are now gone. They are each in Glory and they will be there with Jesus forever. We that remain will carry on, yet we know that our time too will come."

Elijah lowered his head as his sobs overwhelmed him and his shoulders heaved. "One of the girls was my cousin."

CHAPTER
twenty-one

Ever since the terrorist attacks in Hyderabad a couple of years earlier, the carrying of all bags in community buildings had been restricted and routinely searched.

After changing into their costumes in the toilets of the Hyderabad International Community Centre in Jubilee Hills and knowing there would be no safe place to leave their belongings, Punji had laid them neatly across the rear seats of the bus. "We will meet you back here around 7 p.m., OK? Be careful on your own, Punji. We will be praying."

Punji head-wobbled and smiled, "You have many other things to be praying for. I will be just fine," and he flicked the indicator and pulled cautiously out into the morning traffic.

The atmosphere inside the venue was already electric, despite the fact that the Junior State Titles would not commence for another hour. Ashish informed Lois and Chad that during last year's championships, this venue, which is licensed to accommodate 6,000 guests, swelled to over eight. Today, it will probably exceed nine. "And this venue is way too small to accommodate the Senior Titles."

One of the major reasons for the growing excitement was the performance by the National Traditional Dance Company scheduled directly after the opening ceremony. To make herself heard, Ashish needed to raise her voice despite the fact that they were walking side by side. "It's been over five years since we've seen one of their performances, and the word is, they have since scaled amazing new heights. The whole city is excited and a few of the lead dancers are almost looked upon as gods. My husband has always loved dance but I'm afraid, these days, he just wouldn't cope being on his feet all day. Besides, he now spends more and more time in prayer."

Lois glanced at Ashish with a puzzled expression, "So, there are no seats?"

Ashish shook her head, "That's how they squeeze all the extra people in. Sorry, but we will be standing all day. It might be wise for us to pray there is no fire. If a fire started inside this place, there would be a stampede, for sure."

Lois had become quite taken with Ashish and she cupped her hand and leaned in closer to the remarkable old lady. "We are so thrilled you've been able to join us today, Ashish."

Ashish bowed her head in respect, "It is I who is thrilled."

"With Punji not being able to attend, the spare ticket gave us the opportunity to spend the day together, and for that I am so very thankful. But actually, you don't look anything like a Punji," and the two ladies shared a treasured smile.

Ashish chuckled, "With a crowd so big, the last thing they will be checking are the names," and again they exchanged smiles.

A few yards in front of them, the children, adorned in all their finery, were following the men in their attempts to locate the team marshaling area. The two ladies could see Elijah, Solomon, and Chad looking at the official documentation and pointing in various directions. Lois suddenly realized that although the crowd was becoming increasingly congested, a wide void had formed around the children. Lois took hold of Ashish by the elbow, "Will you look at that. The people are making way for the children. Is it because of their . . . ?"

"It's because they are Dalits."

As they watched, the children were clearly being avoided. Adults and children alike were subjecting the team from Son-Shine to taunts, to threats of violence, and to verbal abuse. A wave of leers, jeers, and sneers, assaulted each child as the three men gathered the children in closer and directed them towards the back of the stage while the crowd parted before them like the Red Sea.

"But, how do they know? I mean, dressed in their costumes they all look . . . They're all the same color, they walk the same, they aren't saying anything, so it can't be their . . . Ashish, I just don't understand. How can they possibly know?"

Ashish turned to face Lois and gave her a tender squeeze. "My dear, when I first saw you, I knew you to be a Christian. I could see His love resting upon you, and I immediately loved you because of you having Him in your life. In these children of ours we see that same love, but," and she circled the room with her finger, "all these people see Jesus in our children, but rather than love, they hate. They hate Christians with a venom, a ferocity that they are born into. They don't really know why, but they hate with a fire that burns deeply within their souls. That's how they know. From their first glance, they see the light of Jesus in the eyes of the children, and they know. The thing is, they just can't stand the light. It is our responsibility to not show them hatred in return. We are to love them, and we are to serve them, and to wish them well, even as they persecute us, even as they spit upon us, even as they try to kill us. We must love them, and the truth is, we do love them."

A tear formed in Lois's eye and gently rolled down her cheek as she squeezed Ashish in return. "I may never understand, but I pray that one day I will have the depth of compassion that you do. One day I hope to see such things more clearly. Please help me understand, Ashish. Right at this moment, I feel so utterly helpless." The two ladies remained locked in a knowing embrace until Lois pulled clear. "But you, Ashish, you are not being persecuted like the children."

A knowing expression flooded Ashish, "It's because I am with you. You are from the West and most Indians immediately conclude that you have money, that you are wealthy. They would not dare risk offending you, so they just pretend that I am not here. If you were not with me, they would spit on me and tell me to leave."

"But they wouldn't hit you?"

"In India, there is a certain respect for the elderly, but if I defied them, if I chose to remain here, yes, yes, they would. They have."

❖❖❖❖❖

Inside the marshaling area, Elijah managed to locate the team from Jesus The Rock. It hadn't been a difficult assignment. They also were being assaulted with leers, jeers, and sneers, the same threats of violence and the same demands to leave. Threats to boycott the titles by some of the

Hyderabad heavyweights were only averted by a prominent event manager calling for calm over a loud hailer, informing the protesters that the two Dalit teams were being segregated. He went on to assure that the Dalits would perform last after every other team had been given their opportunity to compete. His ploy was teetering on failure when members of the National Traditional Dance Company emerged through the furthest entrance and all else was instantly forgotten.

Elijah's phone rang as he was comforting the children; he glanced at the screen and mouthed "Punji" to Chad and Solomon. "Hello Punji. Is everything OK? You will have to shout, it's very noisy backstage."

"Sorry, Elijah, but the place we've been told would repair the horn wants payment up front or they won't start the job."

"But they agreed when I spoke to them yesterday, so why have they changed their mind?" Elijah forced his way to the back wall to minimize the surrounding noise and tried to think of a plan. "I will call Vijayawada. What is the name of the person you've been speaking to?"

"I don't know. He didn't say, and he just told me to go away until I have the money."

"OK, Punji, wait with the bus until I call you back." Elijah walked back to join the others and broke the news. "I could tell the bus-hire people that we will leave the bus here in Hyderabad and we could catch the train back to Vijayawada, but he has our credit card." Elijah retrieved the bus company's number and shielded his face from the noise. When a man answered, Elijah was informed that the proprietor was not in, and Elijah would need to call back later.

"But—" and the call ended. Throughout the morning Elijah tried six times and got the same response. On the seventh, Elijah was told the same thing, but after he informed the man that his American VIP guest was very close friends with the head of *The New York Times* in Mumbai, and that he would be none too pleased if his close friend was involved in any sort of accident, the proprietor miraculously returned and was able to take Elijah's call. "You and I had an agreement, but now the repairer is refusing to do the work unless we pay him first."

The proprietor became instantly hostile and shouted through the phone, "Then pay the account and we will refund when you get back tomorrow!"

Elijah knew that to be a lie, but replied calmly, "Sir, it is too dangerous to drive back without a horn so unless the bus is repaired, we won't be back tomorrow."

"Then your credit card will be charged double!"

Elijah allowed the man a moment to consider his next remark, "Sir, my American guest is standing next to me. He's the same man whose very close friend manages *The New York Times* and he would like a word with you. Would you like to talk with him?"

It took the proprietor twenty seconds to arrive at his conclusion. Keeping face with the outside world, especially in the eyes of the wealthy West, played heavily upon his decision. Suddenly, the proprietor's tone had changed, and he cleared his throat, "No. I will call the repairer. Ring me back later."

An hour later, work began on the bus, and although payment had been guaranteed, there was no certainty the bus would be finished prior to the close of business.

Punji was told, "You can come back to pick it up later or in the morning. Now, get out!"

❖❖❖❖❖

The National Traditional Dance Company performance was beyond all expectations; the costuming was indescribable, the technology, astounding, the music, exhilarating, and the choreography, mind-blowing. Lois and Ashish stood and clapped and cheered along with 9,000 others. They were all crammed into a confined space, although surrounding Ashish there remained a small yet conspicuous gap.

Two hundred junior dance teams were all competing for the coveted prize. Although the trophy adorning the center stage was impressive, the prestige and financial opportunity afforded the winners would likely set them up for a life of stardom and riches. Traditional dance was very big business.

Backstage, as the squeeze gradually diminished following the completion of each performance, Solomon seized the opportunity to settle the children's nerves by having an impromptu rehearsal. One minute into their practice, an event marshal shouted loudly at them to cease, despite the fact that other teams were rehearsing all around them. Solomon gathered them together and repeated the message that Pastor Karl had told them last night: 'Be as shrewd as snakes and harmless as doves.' "Children, although we don't have permission to rehearse the way the other teams do, they can't stop us dancing in here," and he tapped the middle of his chest and then the side of his forehead. "Whenever our turn comes, even if it's at midnight, we will be ready, and we will dance as though we were dancing before the Lord Himself. You all know, in truth, we will be."

❖❖❖❖❖

The processing of two-hundred teams, despite them being split across two stages, required an inordinate amount of logistical expertise. By mid-afternoon, despite an almost constant flow of refreshments delivered on stage, even the judges were beginning to wilt. Down upon the main floor, the young and the elderly alike were beginning to flag. Lois turned to Ashish and stooped a little to ask, "Are you, OK? I'm beginning to struggle and I'm a lot younger than—"

Ashish shot her an understanding look, "For as long as it takes, my dear, for as long as it takes. Just when we think we can stand no longer, we discover we can. It's always been that way," and again she smiled.

From deep within her soul, Lois declared, "I so adore this lady."

At 5 p.m. Elijah rang Punji and was told that the bus was being repaired, however, Punji dare not encroach any closer. At 6 p.m., he called Elijah to ask what he should do. "Are there any signs that the repairer is finished?"

"Sorry, none. I can wait if you think it best?"

"Punji, we may still be here for at least another hour. The children have yet to dance, nor has the team from Jesus The Rock. There are only—" and he paused to count the remaining teams, "Only six more teams before us, and then the judges will need time to make their decisions. I don't know how long we will be. Can I call you back?"

By 7 p.m., the moment finally arrived when the unannounced team from Son-Shine was ushered on stage while the elated team from Jesus The Rock was being ushered off. They'd performed a contemporary arrangement that, to the very few neutrals, had been the match of any team seen throughout the day. They had indeed danced before the King of Kings, yet not a solitary sound accompanied them off stage, apart of course for the rapturous applause of Lois and Ashish.

The team from Son-Shine surveyed the vast arena as they walked onstage. Many of the 9,000 tired yet expectant dance lovers had kept their backs turned away. Many chose to continue hurling abuse at the Dalit children as the crowd awaited the judges' verdict; a verdict that, deep down, the Son-Shine children already knew would not be coming their way. Despite trying to hand the stage coordinator their music CD, the man simply waved it away and pointed toward the center of the stage. Solomon gestured to his team to take their places, he took one step forward, smiled to the children, beckoned them to lift their gazes heavenward, and sounded one single clap loudly enough to be heard.

Last night's final rehearsal, although sufficiently impressive to move the heart of a veteran like Pastor Karl, paled by comparison to the glory of tonight's expression. From within the burble of this vast, repulsed expanse, a melody floated, a melody released its heavenly breath, a breath of life. That same breath knocked and knocked again upon the gates of empty, frozen hearts.

Several from the panel of judges interrupted their tallying to briefly marvel at the majesty and brilliance of the team that danced without music. The reminder that this was indeed a team of Dalit animals had them urgently resume their counting.

The triumphant young charges returned backstage where they were swamped by the enveloping arms of Chad and Elijah and one inconsolable dance teacher.

Within minutes, the head of judges strode to the central microphone, a piece of paper in his trembling hand.

"It is my greatest honor to present to you here tonight the winners of the 2008 Andhra Pradesh Junior State Traditional Dance Championships. To present the trophies to the winners, please be up-standing, and please welcome to the stage, his Excellency, the Right Honorable Mayor of Hyderabad, MS Hussain."

Nine-thousand weary revelers clapped as the elder statesman took the trophy carefully from its plinth and tried to raise the large and imposing trophy into the air.

The head of judges continued, "Distinguished guests, ladies and gentlemen, and the many children who have competed so admirably here today, may I announce to you all, that the winning team for this year is from Aligarh University Junior School."

The majority of the 9,000 revelers ecstatically applauded as the winning team appeared from left of stage to claim their third consecutive title. Others in the crowd lowered and shook their heads, while two ladies gazed resolutely upward and prayed.

The Mayor presented the trophy and shook each of the team members by the hand before the triumphant team paraded several times around the stage in front of their adoring supporters.

The head of judges then went on to announce the minor prizes, however, while he did, the major prize winners continued parading their trophy. When requested to stand to one side for the official photographs with the Honorable Mayor, the head of judges called for silence as he once again thanked those present for supporting such an outstandingly successful event. He then invited everyone to return for next year's competition. Before he vacated center stage, he added, "For the first time in the history of these championships, our illustrious judging panel has recorded a dead-heat. One exactly the same points, but in last place, are the teams from Jesus The Rock and the team from Vijayawada, Son-Shine. No doubt you are privileged to compete but will need to work much harder for next year. Good evening, ladies and gentlemen."

Nine-thousand dance revelers vented their disgust.

❖❖❖❖❖

Punji had a four-mile walk ahead of him to return to the church. He'd been instructed to be back in the morning to pick up the bus immediately after Moslem prayers. He'd also been told that if he was late, he would have to wait until lunchtime. The man then turned his back and walked off to lock the workshop door.

At this time of the evening, a Dalit walking alone along the city streets was a vulnerable Dalit. Punji walked quickly and kept his head down.

"Dinner will be ready by the time you all arrive back at church," announced Ashish as she and Lois climbed into an auto-rickshaw at Castle Hills. Their driver was a Dalit and he smiled broadly as soon as he recognized the pastor's wife.

Elijah, Solomon, and Chad shielded the children as they set off on their six-mile walk back to the church. Catching public transport while still wearing their costumes was considered a certainty to attract further abuse. The depth of that abuse might be slightly mitigated by the fact that they were in the company of a Westerner, however, after such a long exhausting day, further trouble was the very last thing the children needed. It was just after 9:30 p.m. when the group trudged the final mile to their accommodation.

CHAPTER
twenty-two

Since returning to the church, Ashish and Lois had begun preparing a meal in the kitchen. Ashish had protested over Lois's offer to help, however, after ten hours on her 80-year-old feet, her resistance quickly gave way. "Thank you, my dear. You are indeed a blessing to us."

For the next few minutes, Ashish spoke about her dream; a dream that gave Dalit children, born into poverty, the opportunity to break free, to escape the clutches of hopelessness.

"Lois, a very small number of the children manage to break those bondages, but most barely struggle through life without an education. Most can do nothing more than the types of work higher caste people refuse to even touch. And when you see and know how talented many of these children are, but they don't get an opportunity, it breaks my heart. Such giftedness that goes unrewarded, at least in this life." Lois stood agog; hanging upon the old lady's every word, bursting to speak but unable to offer a sound.

From behind them, Pastor Karl entered the small room and looked first to his wife and then to Lois. He leant against the back of his chair and raised an eyebrow, "And?"

Ashish chuckled softly, "My husband, you know very well, 'and.'"

"Yes, I do. But our Lord has been speaking and my ears and heart are made glad. Holy Spirit is painting a much bigger picture."

Lois hadn't been in the habit of such outward demonstrations of emotion towards comparative strangers, yet without thinking, she threw her arms around the old pastor's shoulders and began to sob. "Thank you, thank you so much. Your wonderful wife and I have just been saying the exact same thing. Thank you, pastor. This means the world to me, to us."

Pastor Karl pulled back the chair and motioned for the two ladies to sit. "But the children will be here soon and they will be so hungry."

He again gestured for them to sit, "Everything is in order. I have arranged for the meal to be brought in. It will be here soon, now please, sit and tell me of your discussions."

Looking to her husband, Ashish settled comfortably into her old chair. "In some ways, we've had a delightful day. We've shared much, and we've cried too many times. But rather than it be me to speak, Lois has something in her spirit that I feel she is burning to reveal."

The two ladies exchanged glances and Ashish gestured for Lois to share. Nervously, she adjusted her position in the chair and folded her hands in her lap. Taking in a deep breath, Lois looked up into the old pastor's eyes, "It would seem that Chad and I have been brought on this trip, unlike any other trip, to see what the Lord has in store for some of these amazing Dalit children." Lois paused, yet she did so fleetingly until the pastor nodded his agreement. "Over the past few years, Chad and I have been growing our business in New York. It's quite an amazing place, and Chad and I could never have imagined . . . " again she paused, realizing she had inadvertently been tempted to head off on a tangent, but more importantly, she'd become aware that she was about to verbalize something that, until this very moment, she'd never uttered out loud, not even to her husband. "It's just that, in our many years of manufacturing costumes for the performing arts, firstly in Chicago and more recently in New York, we've mixed professionally and socially with most of the industry heavyweights. We've built up a large circle of contacts in most of the major opera companies; we often find ourselves on Broadway for most of the live theater productions, and quite recently we've been commissioned by the producers of the biggest of them all. It's all happened so fast, and we can hardly keep up, and I've been asking myself 'Why'? And I've been asking God the same question. It's not as though many of these people are the sorts we usually identify with, or would tend to spend time with, but all I've been getting back is, 'It's for a reason bigger than yourself.' As we stood watching today while our beautiful, gifted children were giving their absolute all, they were being abused and ridiculed and threatened. But while all that was happening, I kept hearing His still, small voice speaking so clearly to me. Three words; that's all I heard, three words, over and over, 'This is why,' and I knew, straight away, I just knew. So, 'this is why,' 'this is why,' 'this is why' we've come." Lois was suddenly aware that her voice had started to tremble and that her body was beginning to shake. She sniffled a couple of times as she reached for a tissue but was surprised when Ashish reached across, gently rubbed her back and encouraged her to press on.

Lois straightened up and blinked hard. "Pastor, you said last night that changes happen slowly, inch by inch, and I agree. But—" and she looked again into his eyes, "Cultural changes can happen more quickly when pressures come from the outside as well as the inside. Tonight, the lives of those championship winners changed; they changed probably for the better, so why can't that be the case for Dalits? Why shouldn't Dalits have the same opportunities just because they are poor? Ashish has just told me her dream. Pastor, her dream is my dream. Together, I know that we can break down the walls for Dalits now, not only in India, but also in America. We have been given the same dream! I know we can do this! And I know Chad will believe we can too!" On our way back this evening, Ashish confirmed what I've been hearing, and now, not one hour later, you've done the same! You have confirmed! Pastor, I know why we are here. We've been called to build a bridge for the children that," and unintentionally she raised her voice, "that there is 'a much bigger picture!'" Once more she threw her arms around the elderly couple and sobbed. "With my own ears I heard you use those same words, and now I've told you, but my own husband doesn't even know!"

The kitchen door opened slowly, and a man entered. He looked lovingly at his wife, "Doesn't even know what?"

Lois jumped to her feet and rushed to her husband, "Oh, Chad, we really are here for a reason."

Pastor Karl stood to his feet and motioned for Chad to sit, "Your wife has much to share, my friend, and it is good."

CHAPTER
twenty-three

At 8 a.m., the wailing and the blaring ceased. Moments later, Chad, Elijah, and Punji walked through the opening doors to the mechanical workshop. When the manager first spotted Chad, he instinctively sensed money, however, the instant he saw Punji behind him, his hopes nosedived. Chad walked toward the man and extended his hand, shaking the manager's limp grip confidently as the manager tried to return Chad's smile. "Thank you, good man, for repairing the bus that my wife and I are traveling back to Vijayawada in this morning. My good friend here," and he pointed to Punji, "tells me that all the work is complete and that the horn is working perfectly. I'm also assured that the bus hire company has confirmed full payment. Now, we hope to make an early start so may I please have the keys so that we can be on our way?" The manager's eyes showed all the signs of capitulation, and he gestured to the Westerner that the keys were in the bus. Chad continued to smile. "Please be assured that if I, or any of my colleagues, are visiting your fine city and are ever in need of any mechanical work done in the future, this is the first place we will come," and he again shook the manager's hand and directed Punji to board the bus. "We will find our own way out, good man. Have a nice day."

❖❖❖❖❖

The mood of the children couldn't have been more somber as they boarded the bus outside the church. Though the setting was the same as when they'd arrived thirty-six hours earlier, all other parallels were hard to find. The children were courteous and thankful toward their hosts, but gone were the exhilaration and the expectations so evident on their arrival. In their place was fatigue, disappointment, and a single desire to be home. Each boy hugged Ashish and Pastor Karl as they entered the bus and made their weary way to their seats for the long haul back to Son-Shine.

Chad and Lois expressed their blossoming love and respect for the elderly couple, then followed the children onboard while Solomon expressed his gratitude. He then planted himself into his seat and tried to rally his young team.

As Elijah hugged and thanked their hosts, Ashish took hold of the young man by the shoulders and peered into his eyes, "Foundations are the first and most important stage of any building. They are often not visible for long, but unless they are strong, the building cannot stand. Our foundations are becoming solid, even if they don't seem so right now," and she again hugged her new friend as another wave of emotions washed over them both.

As Pastor Karl hugged Elijah, he slipped a small object into his pocket. "This arrived late last night. I had my technical man produce it. Please text me the email address of your head teacher and a copy of this will be sent to him before you get home today." He patted Elijah's pocket and whispered, "This will help restore the children. A safe journey, my friend. May we walk this road together, and may you listen and hear clearly from the Lord. There is much ahead, for you, for us, and for our children." He loosened his embrace and withdrew to stand beside his wife, briefly wiping the corner of his eye as he wrapped a frail old arm around his beloved.

As Punji pulled out from the curb, he blasted the horn and the adults chuckled. By the outskirts of Hyderabad, Telangana, all of the children were asleep, while each of the adults had slipped into quiet reflection on the events of the past two days. Elijah reached into his pocket to retrieve the small object; a single memory stick.

❖❖❖❖❖

As the bus pulled back onto the main road following a brief rest stop in Suryapet, Elijah's cell phone rang. He lowered his voice, "Probably around two o'clock if all goes well. Yes, I gave the pastor your email address, but sorry, no, I don't know anything about what he was sending." Elijah strained to hear before replying, "What do you mean, 'There's no sound'"?

❖❖❖❖❖

It was just before 3 p.m. when the mini bus pulled off the dusty gravel road and through the gates of Son-Shine. Elijah had updated his head teacher with a revised arrival time, so he wasn't surprised when hundreds of children were excitedly lining the driveway awaiting the return of their heroes. The young dance team looked to Solomon and then to Elijah for an explanation, and Naggya stood in front of his mentor imploring him to help them understand. "But we failed, teacher. We came last!"

As the team was welcomed off the bus ahead of the adults, hundreds of children jumped and shouted in the same manner as they had two days earlier. The head teacher waved his arms then shouted loudly, "One, two, three" and 400 children began the sweetest, most heart-rendering rendition of their school anthem. The words "no matter whatever, whatever may come, we already live, the battle is won" rang out across the schoolyard. The returning troop was ushered through the very vocal guard of honor that led all the way into the main hall where the dancers were ushered into a place of prominence facing the wall. Projected upon the large whitewashed wall was the video of the children performing at the championships. Every child crammed into the room applauded wildly as each of the five dancers crumpled into tears. Elijah's puzzled expression prompted the head teacher to yell into his ear above the commotion, "This is the surprise from Pastor Karl, but for some reason there is no music and no sound?"

A bewildered Elijah watched on in amazement; "I'll explain later. Wow, look at our dancers. They are heroes." Every child in the dance team was now being mobbed by a sea of ecstatic and adoring peers. Earlier during the day, the head teacher had chosen thirty of the senior students to quickly learn an anthem of another kind, and following his second "one, two, three," a slightly modified version of "We Are the Champions" was reverberating around the crowded room. At the rear of the crowd and singing for different reasons stood Rambabu. His best friend in all the world had returned. Though only gone for two days, for Rambabu, it was so much more.

Elijah battled through the crowd towards Chad and Lois and all three embraced. Lois was bawling uncontrollably and Chad, struggling to avoid doing the same, was also searching the crowd for another equally special little boy.

At the top of his voice, Elijah shouted, "Yes, our children! They are all true champions!"

Elijah leaned forward and spoke first to Lois, then ushered Chad outside. "It would be so good to stay and rejoice with the children, but there's still a bus to be returned. How would you feel about coming with me?"

Chad smiled, "Are you kidding? I've been practicing my lines for the past hour!"

As Elijah and Chad followed Punji into Vijayawada, Elijah handed Chad his cell phone, "Could you please call the Pastor?"

The instant the old man's voice was heard, the two men launched into their spontaneous appreciation over his unexpected gift. "You can't begin to imagine the looks on our children's faces, Pastor. They were all going crazy with excitement. Thank you, thank you, thank you!"

Pastor Karl chuckled over the phone, "That is my pleasure, gentlemen. I am so glad they liked it."

Chad was holding the phone on speaker in front of Elijah, but leaned across to respond, "Liked it? They loved it! But how did you manage it?"

"Oh, that wasn't so hard. The father of one of our dance team filmed them last year and I knew he would do so again.

I just asked him to film your team, as well, and my tech guy did the rest."

"But the sound?" asked Chad.

"As you know, the stage manager refused to play your dance music, and I decided that your children didn't need to hear the crowd's abuse one more time. We just left it out."

"Pastor, I seriously hope you never tire of hearing us say how much we love you."

❖❖❖❖❖

As the bus-hire manager looked up from his desk, Chad walked in with a newspaper tucked under his arm. Chad acknowledged the manager with a broad smile, and as Elijah entered the office, Chad nodded in Elijah's direction. "I will leave you to take care of my friend. If you need me for anything, I will be right here reading my newspaper," and slowly and deliberately he opened his copy of *The New York Times*. The manager quickly processed the bus-hire return documents, then handed Elijah his credit card and a copy of the hire agreement, including a receipt marked "Paid in full."

CHAPTER
twenty-four

The coming-of-age looks differently among various cultures, yet within the nation of India there is still something universally worthy of celebrating when a person enters their teens. Somehow turning thirteen delivers a new view on life, a ramped-up set of expectations, and some new but often unwanted responsibilities.

❖❖❖❖❖

For several years, Pastor Karl and a small team of pro bono lawyers had been working toward securing a ruling by the Andhra Pradesh Department of Births, Deaths and Marriages in favor of orphans who didn't possess a birth certificate. For those who effectively had no reasonable prospects of proving when, where, and to whom they were born, this ruling was intended to enable applicants to obtain one. For millions of Dalits whose expectation in life is merely to survive to an old age, a birth certificate meant little. However, for those who remained committed to the hope of more, of breaking down barriers, of entering higher institutions of learning in order to pursue careers as doctors, engineers, lawyers, and teachers, or to possibly one day travel to other nations on an Indian passport, the prospect of a birth certificate was monumental.

When the decision was announced, Pastor Karl and the team of lawyers were elated, and shortly after the State Parliament had passed this piece of legislation, the aging pastor called Elijah to break the news.

Three years had passed since the two men had first met; three years of struggles; three years of trying to make the prospects for Dalits somehow better; three years of swelling student numbers; three years of finding desks, computers, beds, clothing, transport, and food for the growing children; three years of scouring the planet for financial supporters to help keep the dream alive; three years of dance practice; three years of local, regional, and state championships where teams from Son-Shine and Jesus The Rock failed to place above last; three years of visits by Chad and Lois; three years of international phone calls from the New Yorkers who embraced every conceivable possibility of change on two contrasting continents; three years of the constant need to attract and retain appropriately trained, committed, and faithful teachers willing to work for an uncertain income; three years of intense scrutiny from bureaucracies; and on top of all that, three years of birthdays.

The Department of Births, Deaths and Marriages had ultimately settled on a common birthdate when an alternate date could not be legally established. Although right in the middle of the monsoon season, July first had been deemed most suitable, exactly midway between the start and the end of the calendar year.

On hearing the news, Elijah was instantly elated. He blurted through the phone, "Pastor, I don't care which date they chose, getting a birth certificate for our orphans means it opens up the world. This is such a momentous day! Thank you, my great friend, thank you so much. And besides, July first is during the season when the rains fall. When the rains fall, new life comes. I can't wait to break the news."

An hour later, every child present at Son-Shine was called to assembly. As Elijah stood at the make-shift podium, his joy could not be contained, "Children, I have some exciting news, some remarkable news. Just an hour ago I received word through Pastor Karl in Hyderabad that the State Parliament has just passed a law that enables every child and every adult who does not have a birth certificate to now get one."

Many of the younger children couldn't help but wonder over the importance of such an announcement, however almost every child nine years and older jumped for joy. As of this very day, one more obstacle to the futures of Dalits had been removed. Deep within the crowd, Naggya leapt and cheered as loud as the loudest. Beside him, Rambabu stood in reflective silence. *So, what does this really mean?*

In the middle of the night on another continent, the phone rang. Chad fumbled for his cell phone and squinted at the screen, "Yes, brother?"

Moments later, Chad and Lois stood in the darkness of their Manhattan apartment and hugged and sobbed and shouted their praises, "Another giant step!" Their eyes filled with the biggest, fattest tears as Lois looked up at her husband, "Please, Darling, can we call the boys?"

❖❖❖❖❖

Eight years earlier, Chad and Lois had purchased an old factory in Upper Manhattan. Following a month of research up and down the city and surroundings, a building in the former industrial area of Manhattanville, not far from West Harlem, had been chosen. The wide side-street access at ground level had exceeded their needs and fitted the profile perfectly in establishing and expanding their niche-market business after relocating from Chicago. The restored multi-story building was spacious, and on the back of their research, was competitively priced and still within striking distance of the city and its performing arts hubs. It was also close enough to a healthy selection of appealing and affordable apartment buildings.

During the past three years, Chad and Lois had been strategically putting out feelers for nearby premises to house small numbers of young Dalits where they might live, study, rehearse, and possibly work. Chelsea Markets were within range, making part-time and casual work a possibility, once Green Cards had been obtained.

Their inquiries also involved discussions with their performing arts contacts to establish recruitment pathways for Dalits to hopefully gain work, and one day, to break into the bigtime. The consensus was that the risk profile of bringing untried children plucked from relative obscurity and thrust into the bright lights of New York's glamor strip probably amounted to a gamble few were willing to take. "There are queues of hopefuls outside our doors already, so to make it worthwhile speculating, they'd really have to be something extraordinary."

"And if they were?"

CHAPTER
twenty-five

"So, we are teenagers." Rambabu looked at Naggya and waited for him to respond. In recent months, their shared pathway had been a little less shared. Though they were both each other's best friend, the bond had weakened just a little. Gone were the days when they each had to exclusively be the one to stand beside at assembly, to be seated next to on the bus, or while waiting in line for a meal.

"Yes, that's what they are now telling us. Does it make you feel any different?"

Naggya smiled an awkward smile and shook his head, "Not really, and you?"

"Same."

With dance, his studies, and his sporting interests, particularly in kabaddi, Naggya had fostered many close friendships, but if pressed, he would still rate Rambabu as his closest. Rambabu probed into his friend's eyes, "It's funny, we'll always share the same birthday, no matter where we end up."

Naggya paused and tried to fathom the intent of the remark. "What do you mean, 'wherever we end up?'"

Rambabu grabbed his towel and walked off toward the showers. It was a bright morning, despite the predicted heavy monsoon rains. Naggya hurried to catch up, "You didn't answer me, Rambabu. What did you mean?"

Rambabu dragged the bottom of his foot several times across the smooth floor then looked up to respond. "We're different, you and I. You know we're different, and we probably always will be. The older we get, the more we're different." Slowly, but deliberately, he turned away.

Gently grasping his shoulder, Naggya urged him to wait. "I don't understand. What's this all about?"

"Like I said, you and I, we're just different. We were going this way," and he gestured to his right, "but now we're not, and we're heading in very different directions" as his outstretched arm swung about in a wide arc. "And we both know it. We think differently and we want different things. It's just what has happened, so let's stop pretending, OK!"

Despite trying to remain calm, Naggya was becoming irritated, "But what's wrong with that? Why do we have to be the same? Why can't we want different things and do different things and still be friends?"

It was Rambabu's turn to be irritated, "I didn't say we can't be friends, it's just that ... "

Naggya rubbed his hand over the top of his head and exhaled loudly, "It's just what? You're not making any sense!"

"Don't you remember what Daddy Chad told you?" Rambabu didn't wait for a reply, "Of course you do! It's your whole world! It's your dream! The thing is, Naggya, we'll end up having really different lives because ... "

With venom coming from his nostrils, Naggya thrust

himself forward to within inches of his best friend's nose and demanded, "Because of what?!"

Rambabu stepped back and dropped his head, "Because some are called to dance before kings and queens and, well, some to just grow vegetables for the poor."

Naggya gasped and let his grip on his friend's shoulder drop away. His deep love of dance had never been seen as anything but his calling in life. Standing before him was his closest friend telling him that this same love was tearing their friendship apart. Naggya slumped against the wall, a sense of bewilderment washing over him. He couldn't look at his friend, and slowly, he turned away. When Rambabu tried to speak, Naggya raised a hand in wounded protest and walked sullenly inside the building.

Entering the hallway from the opposite direction was Martha. "Hello, Naggya. How are you?" She received no reply.

Solomon was sitting at his old desk in the staffroom and after she'd crossed the room, she stood beside him. "Have you spoken to Naggya this evening?"

He looked up from the laptop and shook his head before returning to his report. Martha waited beside him until he stopped typing and looked up. "Perhaps you should have a word. I just called out to him but he ignored me."

"Are you sure he heard you? That's not like Naggya."

"Exactly, but he was right in front of me so he must have heard."

Solomon leaned back in the chair and gave the matter some thought. "He was OK at dance practice an hour ago. As a matter of fact, he was in great spirits, so I'm a little surprised."

He stood up and shot Martha a puzzled expression, "I'll go and see him."

As Solomon walked out of the staffroom, Elijah called out, "Oh, Solomon, I have just received an email from Chad and Lois. They want to call tomorrow night to speak to Rambabu and Naggya. Could you please let them know?"

Solomon turned and paused, "Actually, I was just on my way to talk with Naggya. Can you join me?"

The two men knew each other well, and instantly, Elijah recognized the hint of concern in Solomon's voice.

Seated alone in the far corner of the boy's dormitory was Naggya, head down and his back to the room. In front of him, nothing, no window, nothing more than a blank wall. The men exchanged glances then walked closer until Elijah softly called his name. Naggya didn't turn around. It had been eight years since Naggya had been taken in by Son-Shine, and Elijah's thoughts raced back to those painful beginnings. Silently, he prayed, "We've all come too far to let ourselves be robbed now," and he bent forward and placed an arm upon the new teenager's shoulder. Softly, he repeated his name. Naggya flinched sufficiently enough to send the message that he didn't want to talk. Again, the two men swapped glances until Solomon also reached down and stroked the top of Naggya's head, "We are here when you are ready." The two men straightened up and retreated to the dormitory door. As they left the room, Rambabu was walking across the wide hallway and halted. The seriousness upon his face perfectly mirrored that of Naggya.

The two men continued walking towards Rambabu and as the distance between them diminished, the expression upon his face intensified. Elijah leaned forward to bring his face in line with Rambabu's and smiled. It was an awkward smile, and it drew no response. Elijah rubbed Rambabu's arm and tried again to evoke a response. Rambabu was drowning under the unwanted attention as Elijah gently changed tack, "I have a message for you both. Perhaps you could pass it along to Naggya. Daddy Chad and Mummy Lois are calling tomorrow night. They asked me to let you both know how much they are looking forward to hearing your voices. Oh, and it's a Skype."

CHAPTER
twenty-six

Not a word nor any visual exchange had passed between the boys through dinner and beyond evening devotions. The pair spent time in the same room, yet their gulf, their rift, only widened and deepened.

Elijah wandered into the boys' dorm, a large multi-purpose room that by day served as a meeting room and classroom; by night, the same space was a place of study, of occasional games, and ultimately, when all else had wound down, a place where forty mats were unrolled every night in readiness for sleep. Elijah moved from child to child, a practice he'd maintained since Son-Shine's very first night many years earlier. He knew each child by name, by circumstance, and most importantly by nature and dream. Every child's dream was embedded indelibly within the man that all the children revered and affectionately called "sir." He worked his way through the room, stopping to talk, to encourage, and to pray.

Since their arrival, but for slightly different reasons, Naggya and Rambabu had always rolled out their mats close to the far wall. Not too long after he arrived, Rambabu had confided in Elijah that if an evil person came into the room in the middle of the night, there would be forty other children to be taken before him. For whatever reason, his choice had never changed. Rambabu tried to smile as Elijah made eye contact and again when he had crouched down beside him. "Tomorrow night's Skype will be great."

Naggya had his back to Rambabu but knowing Elijah was near, half-turned and looked up.

In a hushed tone, Elijah said, "It's pretty clear that something has happened between you two and I accept that you're not ready to talk to me. Please know that I won't try to force you. What I will say is that both of you know as well as I that the scriptures tell us not to let the day end before making your peace. I will say no more."

No peace was made that night, nor was there any the following day, and many of the children and a growing number of the teachers could see it. Naggya and Rambabu couldn't look at each other.

By 5 p.m., the boys appeared fit to explode, and as Elijah passed Naggya in the corridor but got nothing remotely resembling a smile, he propped and looked at him, "You'll be right for the call?" An unconvincing nod came back before Elijah added, "Please let Rambabu know that I'll meet you both in the office. Don't be late, OK?"

The boys waited outside the office until Elijah beckoned; they entered separately and settled uneasily into the two chairs deliberately placed side by side. Elijah softly cleared his throat, "I don't need to tell you that Mummy Lois and Daddy Chad love you very much. They will be hurt, just as we are, to see two best friends not speaking to each other, especially as this has never happened before. But that will not stop them loving you, and I know they will want to help you sort out whatever is troubling you. Now, before the call comes through, is there anything either of you would like to say?" They both stared at the floor and said nothing.

Chad and Lois had received an email warning them that the two boys had seriously fallen out, though the two New Yorkers were still as much in the dark over the cause as anyone. As Elijah positioned the laptop in front of the boys and adjusted the screen, the familiar sound of an incoming Skype broke the silence. Elijah received them warmly, then soon after, he left the room. Two beaming Americans greeted the boys and although still uncharacteristically quiet, they each did their best to smile. Lois was the next to speak, "Oh, how we've missed you two. It seems so long since we were with you both and we can hardly wait to come back." Cautiously, she waited for a response, and although the boys were smiling, words refused to come. "And by the way, happy birthday to you both! So, now you're a pair of teenagers! How exciting! Chad and I have been thinking what we can get you both, you know, to mark such an important occasion, but apart from sending you both all our love tonight and as many hugs as we can squeeze into a Skype, we haven't really been able to . . . " Lois faltered; she could see that the boys were intensely uncomfortable, and she visibly trembled as she tried to continue. Lois quickly wiped away a tear as her husband leaned forward to speak.

"Can I tell you a little secret?" and he waited for a response but got nothing apart from two hesitant nods. "I've been sitting here listening to Mummy Lois and when neither of you could say a word, I was wanting to ask, 'what's the matter, boys?' but I didn't, and would you like to know why?" Once again, he waited, this time longer, before two more faint nods gave him their consent to proceed. "It's because you both are no longer boys." Chad repositioned himself in front of the camera and peered into the eyes of each in turn. "You are both no longer boys. In fact, as of now, as of turning 13, you are two young men. The reality is, according to your culture, much of your childhood has now passed and you are entering a period in your lives when, strange as this may seem, but you are approaching adulthood. That might sound uncomfortable to hear, but that's where things are up to, and it's fair to say that it is so often a difficult time. It's often a time when lots of things change, and it's a time when we can easily become not only confused but misunderstood. Rambabu, Naggya, though you may not feel different, you are, and now you are both young men." Chad was conscious of the fact that he'd been hammering the point, yet he felt compelled to ask, "Is what I am telling you making any sense?"

Chad was convinced the two wanted to talk but neither was willing to be the first to break their stalemate. Chad watched intently for a chink, and continued, "As young men, some of the old ways need to be left behind. In their place come grown-up ways, and grown-up ways include talking through differences and trying to solve problems." Chad shifted his weight in the chair, "So, the question is, who is going to be the first to be a grown-up?" and he settled back to wait.

Lois was tempted to speak, but at her husband's gentle touch, she refrained, as another fat glistening tear trickled down the runway.

Rambabu was the first to show any sign of response. He shifted awkwardly, then gestured for Naggya to explain. Naggya pulled away and scowled, "You tell them. You started all this!"

Lois reached out and touched the screen. She looked toward Rambabu and implored, "Started what, my son?"

When Rambabu refused to engage, Naggya scowled, "He believes that I think I'm more important than he is! But I don't!" There was a mixture of anger and concealed pain in his voice. Rambabu slowly shook his head but still refused to look up or to make eye contact.

"Rambabu?" Is that the way you feel?—Son?" The young man continued to shake his head. "Son, we have all night if that's what it takes."

A mixture of annoyance and pressure accompanied Rambabu's gaze from the floor to the camera. "That's *not* what I said and that's *not* what I believe."

Lois jumped in, her heart pounding for the love of their adopted sons. "Please, Rambabu, can you tell us what did you say, and what did you mean?"

All eyes were upon him, and he wanted to run. Slowly he drew breath, "Naggya is so good at dancing. I know that, and everyone knows that. One day, he will leave here and dance before kings and queens. Mummy, Daddy, you told us he will, and I am very happy that he will. Naggya doesn't believe me, but I am. He will go and live somewhere else, but I will remain here because I am not part of his dream." He paused and fleetingly glanced at Naggya but jerked his head back to look at the screen. "That's *his* dream. Elijah always tells us that there is a dream in every one of us, and that we must fight for our dream, and we must never give up." Rambabu began to sob, yet from some place deep, he fought the need to let it out. He was a teenager now, no longer a boy, and he knew what was expected; he knew he needed to be tough. He coughed once then suppressed another, before he found the courage to empty his heart and share his own dream. "If we all have a dream, then why isn't my dream just as important as his?" Rambabu could speak no more. His body trembled and his young hands shook. Slowly from beside him, a hand, then an arm, wrapped itself around his shoulder and pulled him into an embrace that melted hearts on either side of the globe. Four sat in deep silence while love found its way.

Chad ultimately broke the silence, "I am reminded in the Scriptures in Corinthians that there are many parts that must exist to make a body work. Without every part, the body can't work, not properly. The passage tells us that a foot isn't a hand nor can an ear do the seeing. Rambabu, if Lois and I have ever made you think that your dream is not as important as Naggya's, or anyone else's, we are so, so sorry. That has never been in our hearts." Two adults and one teenager began to cry while Naggya held his best friend in the entire world, he cradled him in his arms and rocked him back and forth.

Lois dabbed her eyes with yet another tissue and entreated Rambabu to speak, "Please, my son, as Daddy Chad has said, we are so very sorry, and we should have asked you a long time ago. Will you please tell us about your dream?"

The young man released himself from his adopted brother's embrace and wiped his eyes with the back of his hand. He sat upright and looked into the eyes of his only parents in this world, now fully convinced that whatever he was about to reveal would be accepted, would be supported, and above all, would be treated with absolute respect.

"Mummy and Daddy, my heart breaks every time our old people go hungry. I will never forget what that is like, and it scares me so much. It scares me that too many of our old people try to get to sleep every night and they have nothing in their stomachs, and they don't know when they will eat again." Rambabu choked on his words and struggled to continue.

"Elijah does his best, but it's never enough. He doesn't tell us when some of the old people die, but next time we go there to take them food and there aren't as many old people, I know. Elijah doesn't need to tell us, I just know."

Chad eased himself forward, "And your dream?"

"My dream is to buy land and grow food for the poor."

Naggya again slipped his arm around his best friend and turned to look into his eyes, "Then we have the same dream, Rambabu. You and I, we share the same dream, but we will do it differently."

Rambabu couldn't contain his enormous smile, "So, Daddy Chad is right. We are just different parts."

CHAPTER
twenty-seven

"Ballet."

"Ballet?"

"Yes, Naggya, that's what it is called." Solomon smiled to himself as he watched Naggya assessing and critiquing synchronized movements as they leapt tantalizingly off the screen. He watched his young charge as his facial contortions and his wide-eyed amazement spoke volumes without so much as a word. Naggya was enthralled by the grace, the elegance, and the effortless power of the performers, yet despite the fascination, his innocence unwittingly conveyed a completely contrasting message.

"But don't they wear any—" And mid-sentence, Naggya stopped as he imagined himself performing such an inspiring maneuver, complete with a ballerina gracefully and impressively balanced overhead. "But how, how do they do that? It looks so—they must be so strong!"

Solomon chuckled at the random yet innocuous remarks coming from a teenager who'd just stumbled upon another vast and captivating world. He turned to his mentor with an intrigued yet embarrassed expression, "But, if I did ballet, couldn't I wear some more clothes?"

Another chuckle slipped from Solomon's lips, "Naggya, you may never do ballet, however . . . "

Naggya interrupted his teacher and instantly felt obliged to apologize. Solomon waved away the apology and encouraged his charge to continue. "But I want to. I want to so much, it's just I would feel so—"

"So embarrassed?"

Naggya looked away and searched for a response to match his dilemma, "Yes, embarrassed. The ladies had almost nothing on, and the men, well, you could see all their . . . you know," and he shrugged his athletic young shoulders and searched his mentor's face for understanding.

It was Solomon's turn to feel embarrassed; modesty and gender respect played a crucial role within their immediate culture, and despite the smorgasbord of exposed, gyrating midriffs of dancers from other schools at the regionals and state championships, nakedness on such a blatant scale remained utterly foreign.

In recent months Solomon had become increasingly conscious of the fact that the males in the dance classes, Naggya included, were becoming more and more aware of the pull of the opposite sex. "Yes, young man, some time back when I first started studying ballet, all I wanted was to study the style and the movement. But I guess I was just like you are now, because I really didn't know where to look. The thing is, Naggya," and he paused to form his words sensitively, "The thing is, if you really want to follow your dream and to become a truly great dancer and to make a difference for our people, then I believe ballet can help you get there."

As though a light had just been flicked, Naggya smiled broadly and suddenly straightened up to his full height, "Yes, sir, I also believe that is true. I believe I can learn much from ballet, and I would like to learn more. Are there any more videos we can watch?"

The laughter erupting from his mentor caught Naggya by surprise. "Naggya, we could watch ballet videos all day every day for a year and still not run out. Around the world, ballet is huge!"

With his latest incredulous expression, Naggya asked, "Do they do ballet in America where Mummy and Daddy live?"

❖❖❖❖❖

Rambabu and Naggya sat outside the staff room and waited for Elijah. Their relationship and mutual trust had gone to a new level since the teenagers had resolved their differences. Ever since, they were rarely seen apart, except, of course, when Naggya was watching ballet videos.

Elijah threw his arms wide and embraced the pair, "When God puts things back together, He always makes them better," and he invited them to sit. Now 14 years old, those within their age group were becoming more focused on not just setting future goals but on formulating strategies to see them happen. Elijah's standard response to impossible situations had been indelibly imprinted upon the hearts and minds of the children, "I can do all things through Christ who gives me strength." He looked at them in turn and asked, "So, what can I do to help you today?"

Rambabu and Naggya glanced at each other and Naggya

gestured for his friend to begin. Rambabu looked up into his leader's eyes and stammered. He drew breath before asking, "If we wanted to buy some land to grow food for the poor, where would the best place be?"

Elijah beamed and slowly raised his hands. "It's so interesting that you ask because I have just been speaking to some of our supporters in Australia about doing exactly that. We have found a parcel of suitable land just off the Gannavaram Road and it has good water, and . . . " Elijah could see that Naggya was excited but that Rambabu had dropped his head. Elijah waited for him to re-engage before he asked, "What, Rambabu? What is the problem?"

Naggya observed his friend and knew instantly what was running through his mind. He turned to Rambabu and asked if he might speak on his behalf? With a nod, Naggya looked across at Elijah, "Rambabu has his own dream. He always does everything he can to help others with their dreams, but . . . "

Elijah smiled softly towards Rambabu and slowly nodded, "Oh, I see," and he stood from behind the desk and walked around to crouch before the young man, "You know that since its very first day, Son-Shine has been built on the foundation of helping our students achieve their own dreams. Let me assure you that for as long as I am here, that will never change. Dreams can sometimes take time, but other dreams can come quickly. I have learned many things during my lifetime and if you will allow me, I would like to share two of them with you?" Without any resistance, Elijah continued, "The first is, 'Lord, help me to master the art of walking, then teach me to run.' The next is, 'Sometimes my second dream arrives before the first completes.' These two things may not mean a lot to you today, but please go and write them down because one day they will mean much more. I can see that you are still unsure about all this, but may I ask if you have any questions?" The two shook their heads, "On Saturday, our head teacher and I are again going to look at this land, and I would be honored if you two would like to join us." Elijah's offer was met with a couple of radiant smiles before he concluded, "Oh, and I have just learned that there are several other very good plots of land nearby." Rambabu and Naggya floated out of the office and, despite the expected propriety of 14-year-olds on school grounds, the two sprinted down the corridor and out into the daylight. They raced towards the kabaddi courts and leaped into the air.

❖❖❖❖❖

Long after the usual bedtime, but under Solomon's supervision, Naggya watched video after video after video. If there was a limit to how much ballet anyone could watch, Naggya had yet to reach it. And by day at the completion of each exhausting dance practice, it was always Naggya begging for more. His insatiable appetite to improve drove him on, long after the others were ready to drop. "Just a little longer, please" and "Can we do another run through?" would be heard time and again, at times to howls of student protests.

During the recent local school dance competitions and with Solomon's approval and direction, Naggya had increased the ballet content into many of the Son-Shine dance team's presentations. Although mostly met with scornful and derisive responses from the higher caste schools, there were the occasional prolonged, fascinated appraisals coming the way of Son-Shine's star performer.

On the homeward journey following their most recent last placing, Naggya turned to Solomon and whispered, "Do you think we might be able to get a large mirror?"

Solomon was mildly amused. "A mirror?"

"Yes, on one of the videos last night a ballet master said that he would never have been successful if he didn't have a mirror."

CHAPTER
twenty-eight

"Hello, is that Crossover? It is? Excellent. May I speak to your manager, please? My name? Yes, my name is Lois McNeil from Impressions Design & Costuming, Manhattan. Yes, I will hold, thank you."

Within minutes, a meeting was scheduled for 9:30 a.m. the following Monday.

"Chad, I've been thinking about something." Chad looked up from his laptop and turned to face his wife. "This last year, we've spent so much time talking to one organization after another about launching a program for kids like Naggya, but what if that doesn't work out? Why can't we just bring him to New York and let him stay with us? It would be so much easier."

Her husband smiled, "Yes, it would, but you know as well as I that this isn't just about Naggya. There are so many Naggya's in India, and..." Chad hesitated and once again smiled. "OK, maybe not the same as Naggya, but this is so much bigger than one person. This is about freedom for Dalits and giving opportunity to every child who..."

Lois stood up, walked over to her husband and stood before him, "Yes, I know. Sorry, I guess I'm just a little tired."

Chad stood and hugged his wife, "Yeah, it has been a journey, hasn't it? Naggya has lived most of his life surrounded by kids his own age and he will need kids his own age around him here as well. They'll all have so many things in common and so many stories to tell." Chad drew his wife in closer, "And besides, my dear, he'd probably cramp our style. So, tell me, just how tired are you?"

❖❖❖❖❖

The Crossover head office in East Harlem was small and uninspiring. Yet within minutes of entering the premises and sharing time and space with Kate Roberts, the general manager, Lois and Chad felt instinctively that despite a year of unproductive searching, they may have finally found someone with a heart big enough to embrace their dream.

In her late 30s, Kate was noticeably graying, considerably overweight, moved rather awkwardly and, it would seem, wasted little time on makeup. She did, however, possess a smile as wide as the Hudson. "Please, make yourselves comfortable. I know it's a little cramped in here, but what we lack in space, we make up for in grace. Coffee?"

Lois grinned and wondered how many times Kate had trotted out that line, but with such an engaging warmth, it just didn't matter.

"So, Lois and Chad from Impressions Design and Costuming here in Manhattan," and she shot them each a smile and a nod, "do you know much about Crossover, and if so, how may we be of service to you?" Kate buzzed through to reception to request three coffees, then leaned both her forearms on the desk and waited for her visitors to speak. Though not particularly conscious of the reasons why, Lois was already taken with the charm and easy nature of this lady, and without a moment's hesitation, launched into her spiel in spite of the fact that sitting beside her, Chad was open-mouthed wanting to do the same. Kate laughed and tapped the desk. "Oh, I can see we're in for an entertaining time," and she settled in her chair to listen and marvel at the couple's intense love for the Indian children. Lois spoke passionately of the children's boundless, untapped potential, their captivating natural talents, and she gushed over the children's unquenchable determination to see their dreams fulfilled. The instant Lois paused for breath, Chad interjected with equal fervor. The pair continued to play brag'n'tag as the scheduled thirty-minute meeting swelled well beyond an hour.

Lois rested both hands upon the desk and peered into Kate's eyes, "Chad and I have spent the last twelve months talking with just about every welfare organization in New York City, and no one, not even one of them, has grabbed hold of our dream the way you have. I am so encouraged and whether we proceed with you or not, the fact that you have heard our hearts and listened to our dream is already such a great joy to my husband and I. Thank you."

Kate once again beamed, although for the first time in over an hour, a trickle of emotion leaked into her voice, "Actually, it's me who should be thanking you. What you have shared this morning," and she smiled and checked her watch to confirm that in fact it was still the morning, "is an amazingly inspiring dream. The challenge to bring talented children from a third-world country to New York to pursue opportunities in the performing arts, now that excites me. Your extensive contacts in that industry will be invaluable, of that I am certain. And for these kids to be able to study and work while they pursue their dreams, then return to India to inspire their own people and chase their dreams, let me tell you, that is a dream worth fighting for. Ah, may I ask you a question?"

"Of course."

"Why just India?"

Chad and Lois looked at each other incredulously. "Why indeed?" asked Chad as his wife's mouth refused to close.

"Because I know our organization will adore it, absolutely adore it."

Chad raised a hand and apologized for his interruption as he tried to suppress his emotions, "Actually, Kate, everything you just said is correct, but I'm so sorry, we have failed to make the most important aspect clear. These children aren't just from poor third-world countries."

A puzzled expression crossed Kate's face. "They're not?"

"No, they're not. Here's the thing; they're not just poor, they are persecuted. They are persecuted in their own country. Though Lois and I are only really familiar with how that devastates the Dalits, but . . . "

It was Kate's turn to interrupt, "The Dalits?"

Lois's hands trembled as she looked across to her husband and gestured for him to explain. His hands also trembled as he struggled for the right words. "In India, as is the case in some other countries, there is a very distinct and pervasive caste system. There are five separate cultural castes that ultimately make up what is referred to as 'the body' of their nation of

1.3 billion people. The top caste is considered the head of the body and the other castes work their way down to the feet of the same body. The lower the caste, the lower they sit in the body and the lesser they are of importance. Dalits are the very bottom of the caste system and, according to the higher castes, Dalits are not even part of that body. Dalits are considered to be entirely separate. Today there are approximately 300 million Dalits, or as they are often called, 'Untouchables.' In India, Dalits are not considered human. They are animals, and that's how they are treated. To all other castes, they are nothing more than putrid lepers, and that's why they are untouchable. To touch one is to risk being contaminated. You see, Kate, these Dalits are the children we desperately need to help; to rescue and to help restore hope. They deserve to be given their opportunity to shine. Right now, they can't, and they won't, at least not in their own country. They are not animals, not dogs, they are beautiful, and they are talented, and they are so loving. We just want to . . . "

Kate was showing signs of becoming increasingly confused, "But how can we help 300 million?"

Chad slowly shook his head, "We can't, but we can start with a few and we can build for the future. It was Mother Teresa who famously once said, 'If I look at the mass, I will never act. If I look at the one, I will.'"

"Yes, but what's really puzzling me is that I have never heard the name Dalits. How can that possibly be?"

Lois began to sob and reached for a tissue as Chad began to blink away the fat tears that had begun to trickle down his cheeks.

Kate's eyes bulged as she tried to grasp the enormity of what she had just heard. "But we hear about the persecution of people groups around the world all the time on the news, so how can we not know about 300 million people? I just don't understand."

Lois cleared her throat and looked at the lady sitting opposite, "That's exactly the point, Kate. How can this be? Chad and I have been to India many times and every time we return, we are more determined than ever to help these Dalits break free. If we told you some of the things we've seen, you probably wouldn't believe us, but they are all true, every shameful thing is all true. So, we have decided to devote the rest of our lives to making a difference. What Chad is saying is that we're not looking to set up or run yet another talent scout program, although that's how it will look, but it's far bigger. This is a double-edged sword. Talented children get their chance to shine, but in the process, their lives are spared and so are the lives of those who will come after them. Kate, the bottom line is, we are determined to save lives."

Kate's eyes were glistening, and she again leaned forward and lowered her voice, "So, this isn't just about rewarding gifted kids from poor countries, this is a fully blown rescue mission!?"

"That's about it, Kate. And please, just because we speak for the Dalits, please don't imagine for one second that we think the Dalit children are the only ones on the planet being persecuted. They just happen to be the ones we know. But can you picture what influences these kids can have after they've become stars and go back to their nations with a voice that cannot be ignored? That's our dream, Kate. That's what we're willing to fight for."

Lois and Chad had no more words, and no more words could have impacted Kate any more than the unrestrained flow of tears streaming down their faces. "Wow, I'm, um, wow. I don't know what to say." Kate stood up and then almost reflexively sat back down, "You know something?" and in an exaggerated manner, she nodded her head. "Actually, I am really starting to see this. Yes! Thank you. Thank you both. This can truly be a rescue mission like no other," and she paused and turned to look away, trying desperately to piece together how she could, or even if she should, respond. "Um, I'll be honest with you, this has come as a huge shock and definitely not what I imagined. Crossover has never done anything like this before, but, I'm starting to realize that, somehow, we must. Actually, we have to. Yes! Um, as I said earlier, Crossover has always been about changing lives, but this is next-level." Kate strummed her fingers loudly on the desk, then the hint of a smile appeared on her face, "Let me say this, and though it might sound a bit like a boast, the facts are that whatever we take on, we do well, and Crossover will only take on what we know we can deliver. But this one, wow, this one is different. This dream of yours, this mission, is way past exciting and it is so far beyond inspiring. But now that you've painted it so powerfully I feel I've caught enough of your mission to say this; and I need to stress that it's not my decision to make, but I'm starting to believe that, for Crossover, this is a mission we would absolutely buy into."

Lois and Chad had fallen conspicuously quiet. Lois could scarcely breathe. Kate blinked several times, then flipped open her iPad, "Ah, I don't mean to be forward, but may I ask if you would consider presenting your proposal at our next board meeting? We meet on the third Thursday evening of every month, and yes, I can hear your brains ticking, yes, that happens to be this Thursday."

Chad and Lois turned to face each other and shrugged their shoulders then nodded and grinned. "But are you sure you can fit us in at such short notice?"

Kate couldn't have suppressed her smile had her life depended on it, "Ah, I've just checked the itinerary and oddly enough, a spot just became available. Would 7 o'clock work for you?"

❖❖❖❖❖

The Crossover boardroom was only marginally bigger than Kate's office. The furniture was spartan at best, although the walls were adorned with many photographs, almost all of them of kids; black kids, brown kids, Hispanic kids, white kids. What struck Lois and Chad most was the unmissable common denominator: they were all smiling. Quite prominent among many of the photographs was a much younger, slimmer Kate and as Lois pointed and whispered to Chad, Kate began to chuckle. "Yeah, you're probably wondering what happened, right?" and again she laughed. "Trying to keep up with these kids as well as going to the gym just didn't fit," and she shrugged and called the meeting to attention and introduced Lois and Chad to each of those present. The board was made up of seven; three men, four women. From their outward appearances Lois estimated the youngest to be well into his 60s and the eldest, probably in her 80s. As Kate finished her introductions, Lois was instantly overtaken by a warm and comforting thought. *They all smile the same way Kate does.*

It was soon evident that the board members had been comprehensively briefed prior to the meeting, so by the time Lois was wrapping up her presentation the room had become a sea of almost constant nods of agreement. As she sat down, Lois was comforted by the reemergence of those beaming smiles. Chad shot his wife a nod of his own just as one of the board members suddenly spoke, "Quite infectious, isn't it?"

Lois turned to the lady to ask, "What is?"

The lady looked at Lois and then around the room. Her face radiated a dimension that Chad and Lois, for over a year, had sought yet hadn't found, had craved yet had so far been denied. The lady softly yet assuredly responded to Lois's question, "When I joined the board of Crossover forty years ago, it was already here, and I wouldn't have joined if it wasn't. It's still here and despite us facing a constant up-hill battle, we can only keep helping these kids for as long as it remains. But one thing I know for certain, with Kate in charge and with her amazing team, who, by the way, are a lot younger than we are," and again she beamed. "It will always remain. The love of people, that's it in a nutshell, especially with the kids we are entrusted with. The love of people is the only rock on which we can build, and the love of people gives us the strength to keep going. So, to accomplish your dream, we will all need plenty of love. Nowhere else have I seen such a love for kids so evident and so unwavering as it is here at Crossover. We only wish we could help more, but by the time the overseas kids get to us at age 16, our first challenge is to undo so many of the hurts that have already robbed these kids of their childhoods."

Chad reflexively exclaimed, "16?"

Kate turned to Chad and Lois, "Yes, 16. Sorry, I thought you knew?"

Chad and Lois shook their heads, their brows furrowed, and their eyes dimmed.

Kate reached across and rested her hand upon Chad's arm. "It's because unless we legally adopt children from overseas, or we manage to get a guardianship in place, no private welfare organization can bring children into this country unless they have turned 16. The government can do it, but when they do, the children are funneled directly into government-controlled institutions. We would love it to be otherwise, sorry."

"But all these photos?"

Kate turned to face the couple seated beside her, "Oh, I see. Most of these children are American citizens. Many of them are part of our day-programs and are either still living at home, or they've fled from domestic violence and are now part of our Living-In-Safety programs. With overseas children, it's different."

Lois and Chad's minds were racing. Why haven't we been told this before now? Naggya is still only 14 years old.

CHAPTER
twenty-nine

An elated Elijah blurted through the phone line, "They finally arrived! Well, at least some of them."

Chad rolled over in bed to check the time, "Sorry, buddy, it's 4:30 in the morning."

Elijah checked the time on his phone before sheepishly apologizing, "Oh, I keep forgetting about your daylight saving. Sorry."

Chad sat up and tried to focus, "What arrived?"

"The birth certificates! We paid for forty but only twenty-eight have arrived. They said that they would all arrive together, but..."

Knowing that Lois was still asleep, Chad stifled a weary chuckle. "You know as well as I do they play games," and again he glanced at Lois. "Hey, can I call you later?"

As Chad ended the call, he stared out into the New York darkness, *Hmmm, would Naggya's and Rambabu's be among the twenty-eight?*

Chad climbed out of bed and crept out into the lounge room, then gazed out of their tenth-floor apartment window at the New York night sky as it glittered and enthralled.

So, what does all this mean? Can we now apply for a passport, or will the Indian bureaucracy throw us another curve ball? If we can get Naggya here for a visit and introduce him to a few of the right people, perhaps we can gauge how ready he is? Dreams are one thing, but this is a big, big city. How would he cope? Would he want to stay, or would he become so overwhelmed that he'd turn tail and run? I probably would. Chad flicked the kettle on and again checked the time. *No point going back to bed now. And of course, if we get Naggya a passport and a visitor's visa, he'll need a chaperone. It'd have to be Elijah. Yeah, definitely. And if Elijah came, he'd be a great contact for Crossover. Their hearts all came out of the same mold.* The kettle began to whistle and Chad raced to switch it off before the noise pierced the room. He was busy pouring a cup of coffee when a faint voice sounded from behind him, "Did I hear the phone?"

Chad wrapped his arms around his wife and drew her in close. Mid-yawn, he whispered into her ear, "Seems we may have taken another step."

❖❖❖❖❖

In the two months since they had met and agreed terms with Crossover, much had unfolded. Although far more streamlined than in India, the bureaucratic application process in the State of New York was still daunting. On occasions, Kate had been heard to quip, "We need one of those ballet dancers to tip-toe through this lot," after the latest wave of compliance requirements had lobbed in her inbox. Kate had successfully negotiated the tightropes associated with new welfare structures in the past, but to add the myriad of international complications to an already intricate process had brought the application to a whole new level. "The big plus is that once we've jumped through all their preliminary hoops, it's hopefully a downhill run." On several occasions, Kate had highlighted to Chad and Lois the regulatory need for a minimum age. "Can you just imagine how much more difficult the process would have to be if we were advocating for minors?"

Within those same two months, Kate had received and responded to multiple inquiries-of-intent from a growing number of countries. Welfare agencies from Sudan, Haiti, Somalia, Ethiopia, Bangladesh, The Congo, Malawi, Zimbabwe, Mexico, Honduras, Ghana, and The Philippines had all responded favorably, and although India had naturally been included in Crossover discussions, an official invitation to any other Indian connections apart from Son-Shine and Pastor Karl at Jesus The Rock Church, was deemed unnecessary.

Not long into the project, Kate had announced, "In order for this to fly, it has to stand on its own two feet financially. We need a diversity of nations involved to capture the attention and imagination of potential backers." In order to attract financial backers, Kate had produced an extensive International Performing Arts Prospectus to share the vision of this fledgling venture and to impressively itemize its basic operational needs.

Comparatively high occupancy rates for suitable accommodation around East Harlem over the past six months had driven up rental prices, making the acquisition of a suitable property yet another challenge. "It's like trying to find a needle in a haystack," Kate had stated while peering out at the city skyline, "But, we will find one. There's one out there with our name on it."

Chad and Lois had continued to devote as much time and energy as possible to the process, but with the demands of their rapidly expanding business and the nurturing of interest from within their industry contacts, their own personal resources and stamina were continually being stretched. "We haven't bitten off more than we can handle, have we?" rang out around their breakfast table. All doubts were quickly battered into submission as a new wave of determination swept over them. Lois gripped her husband's hand and pulled his head close to hers, "I cried out to God for years for us to have children. I begged Him, ever since we got married, I begged him, but He didn't, we couldn't . . . " and she steadied herself as Chad placed his other hand on top of hers. "Well, we don't have our own and we both know we never will, but Chad, look at what we've been given! We have been given so many children! And now, my joy at being Mummy Lois just bubbles up from way down deep and fills me with . . . " As their tears flowed, her whole body heaved.

❖❖❖❖❖

Kabaddi had been an institution within Son-Shine since day one, much as it had been throughout many parts of India. Most children were introduced to the game at a young age and, therefore, kabaddi had asserted itself as a genuine rite of passage, a mark of bravery and of a willingness to take the big hits. Since their earliest days at Son-Shine, Naggya and Rambabu had been irresistibly drawn to the energy and power of the contest, and now approaching their mid-teens, kabaddi had remained an integral part of their lives. Both were determined to share and experience as much as they could together before their choices in life inevitably took them down diverging pathways. Naggya had the added burden of not wanting to be seen as just a talented dancer; he wanted to be accepted, and yet he was constantly confronted by the risk factors of contact sports. As young men grew in size and strength, their big hits became bigger, and the potential for injury multiplied. Solomon would often be heard shouting from the sidelines, "Young men will be young men," after yet another teenager had hit the deck and writhed around in pain. Secretly though, he would be relieved to see that Naggya had survived another game. Not uncommon in the nationwide sport were dislocated shoulders and elbows, broken arms, fractured skulls, and severely damaged knees, any of which could dent the prospects of a dancer, particularly a budding ballet dancer. The first time Naggya took a significant tumble and rolled several times on the ground, Solomon was there beside him almost before he'd finished rolling. Solomon had gently turned Naggya onto his back and crouched down close, "Are you OK, Naggya?"

Looking up at his mentor with a cheeky grin, Naggya asked, "Do we get a penalty for that, sir?"

❖❖❖❖❖

Thankfully, Naggya's had been among the first batch of birth certificates and with it, Chad, Lois, and Elijah finally had all the requirements to apply for a passport.

The Department of Births, Deaths and Marriages in Vijayawada had estimated that the six passport applications

Elijah lodged on the same day would take around six months to be processed. As soon as Elijah had paid the application fees, the man behind the counter scowled, "Now get outside! There are others to be served!" and he waved away Elijah's request for individual application receipts. "I said, get out!"

"Six months, they told me." When he heard the news, Chad breathed heavily into his phone, got up from his desk in the Impressions office and mouthed the same words to Lois. She walked up to Chad as he put Elijah's call on speaker phone. "Sorry, but the news isn't so good. They said six months, but it might be twelve. I was wondering how much I should tell Naggya?"

Chad scratched his head and looked to his wife before replying, "Well, Elijah, we've faced mountains before and told them to move, so this is just the latest. Naggya needs to know the truth. Please tell him that his dream is alive. Tell him that as soon as the passport arrives, we will apply for a visa for you both to come visit us in New York. The government has been wrong before, but yes, I feel we should be transparent with Naggya. He is a young man who deserves nothing less. Talk soon, my friend."

Lois and Chad looked at each other as they silently contemplated a host of unknowns. Lois broke the long silence, "Let's say, for the sake of planning, that it does take six months, and we know that a visa application, particularly a first-time visa, would take another three months, that would mean that by the time of Naggya's first visit, he'd be near enough to 15 years old, right?"

"But if it takes longer, and if our contacts like what they see, by the time Crossover is fully up and running, Naggya would be approaching . . . "

"Yes, but what if they don't like him straight off and they tell us to come back when he's older?" Lois threw her hands in the air, "Oh, Chad, we can hypothesize till we're blue in the face, it gets us nowhere. We've just gotta walk this through one day at a time!"

CHAPTER
thirty

The hour between end of classes and preparation for the evening's activities had long been set aside as free time for the children. Most would head for the sports areas, some would study, while others would simply sit and talk in the heat of the late afternoon. As though their fuse was on slow burn, Rambabu and Naggya had recently fallen into the habit of finding a quiet place to share some private time. With each passing month, the fuse kept burning and their time spent together had become more and more revealing. "Naggya, won't you be scared when you get into one of those jet airliners? I mean, they look amazing and they fly so high, but—"

"But what, Rambabu?"

"But sometimes they crash, and when they do, no-one survives!" Rambabu looked away and tried to conceal his own deep concerns, concerns that went far deeper than a trip in an airplane.

Naggya waited for his best friend to turn back and look at him. "Most of them don't crash. Most of them take off the way they are supposed to and arrive where they are meant to, safely. So, no, I'm not scared. Would you be?"

"For the very first time, you mean? It's not likely I'm going to be flying anyway so it doesn't matter how I'd be feeling. And don't look at me like that; you know it's true. Airplane flights aren't part of my dream and that's fine by me."

"But your dream might mean you need to fly, have you thought about that?"

"My dream is about being right here. Flying around the world would just keep me from my dream, and my dream is getting bigger. I want to grow lots of food for lots of Dalits." Rambabu was becoming agitated and quickly steered the conversation back to Naggya. "Anyway, your first airplane flight will be from Vijayawada to Hyderabad and Solomon said that it takes less than one hour, but it takes five hours to drive. Wow, that's amazing," and they both looked at each other and forced a smile. "But then you fly from Hyderabad all the way to New York!"

It was Naggya who broke eye contact, but he quickly shot Rambabu a cheeky grin, "And the ladies that work on the planes, they come to your seat and serve you food, and Elijah says that the food is so nice and you can get drinks as well, and it doesn't cost you anything! Can you believe that?"

Rambabu interrupted, "Sometimes it's men that serve the food."

"I don't think so. The men fly the planes."

"Not all the time. I've seen it on the internet that sometimes men serve the food. They have men there in case the people drink too much alcohol." Childhood memories of alcohol abuse still sat painfully in the memories of them both, and Rambabu was quick to move on. "But when you land in New York, that video we saw showed the airplanes flying right past those really tall buildings before they landed at the airport. I mean, they looked like the wings could almost touch the—what are they called?"

"Skyscrapers. They're called skyscrapers."

"Yeah, and sometimes the airplanes land at night and all the skyscrapers have their lights on. How can they fly so close?"

Naggya chuckled loudly, "Practice, I guess. I sure hope our pilots have had plenty of practice."

"So, you are scared?!"

Naggya's chuckle took on a different tone, "A bit."

Rambabu gave his friend a shove and threw back his head, "More than a bit!"

The two young men fell into silence as they each contemplated issues, diverse and deep. Rambabu looked at his friend and slowly formed his words, "And New York has almost as many people as Hyderabad, but they all live in a space like one quarter the size. That doesn't make any sense. The USA is a huge nation so why would they all want to live on top of each other?"

Naggya shook his head, "Beats me. It's a cold place so maybe to keep warm?" They both laughed at the absurdity of such high density living and Naggya's bizarre explanation. "Well, there must be a reason. Anyway, Daddy Chad says that New York is the city that never sleeps, and you could go out at three in the morning and everything is open! Why would you do that?"

"To keep warm?" Rambabu gave Naggya another shove as the pair again lapsed into silence. "Some of those skyscrapers are like one hundred stories high! Do you remember that study we did on those two buildings that the jet planes flew into and then they came crashing down? That was terrorism, and you want to go and maybe live there?"

"Rambabu, we have talked about this before. We had terrorism in Hyderabad, remember? New York is the place where my dream can start to come true. Unless we pay a price, we can't see our dreams. Anyway, Elijah and Daddy Chad said that my trip probably won't happen for months, so why are we even talking about it now?"

Rambabu climbed to his feet and began to walk away. Tentatively Naggya got up and followed. Though they walked together, the gulf between them had returned and no words would come. Naggya placed an arm around his best friend's shoulder and Rambabu gently brushed it off. Naggya waited a moment as they walked towards the kabaddi court and Naggya again placed his arm upon his friend's shoulder. Rambabu slowly put his hand upon Naggya's and patted it softly. "Just because."

"Yes, I know."

The two were invited to join in the next game, but both declined. They walked toward the Son-Shine front gate, a metaphor for both their past and their futures. When they halted at the gate, Rambabu turned to look at his friend, "Naggya, as Dalits, we are faced with threats of violence and persecution almost every day, but New York? New York, is, is way different. We have studied New York and we know about the terrorism and the guns and the violence and the fights that happen on the streets. What if you get caught up in all that? Who will keep you safe?"

Naggya could see his friend's deep pain and was touched by its depth. "Rambabu, we know that the Lord will protect His children, and I go there not just for me but for our people. Remember when we were just little and those men came to Son-Shine and we thought we were going to die?!"

An unwanted truth settled upon Rambabu's countenance as a tiny tear formed in the corner of his eye. "That's not the same!"

"Maybe it's not, but God protected us then, and He will again, you know that. And besides, I have Mummy Lois and Daddy Chad, and the people from Crossover—"

"But you don't even know the Crossover people, so how can you say that?"

Naggya took hold of his best friend's shoulder, "That's true, but I know Daddy Chad and I know Mummy Lois and if they say the people from Crossover are good, then I can trust them, and anyway, you're forgetting one thing."

"And what's that?"

A wide and beguiling smile spread across Naggya's face, "I can run really fast."

"Not as fast as me!" declared Rambabu, as they sprinted from the front gate and all the way to the front door of their dorm.

"And you're forgetting one other thing, Rambabu," said Naggya as he sucked hard to regain his breath.

"Oh, yeah, and what might that be?"

Naggya, still breathing hard, straightened up and stepped in close, "Unlike here in India, in New York I am not seen as a Dalit. I will be just another dark-skinned person but with the same rights as everyone else. We must always remember that the rest of the world isn't the same as India."

"Perhaps you are right, and I have to remind myself that your dream is much bigger than us. Your dream is for our people and we must be strong. But there's still one thing that—"

"One thing that, what?"

Rambabu looked up and down the corridor and leaned forward to whisper, "Are you really going to be wearing those ballet tights?"

Naggya could scarcely contain his laughter. He bit his bottom lip hard and finally lowered his voice. "Actually, that has been on my mind a lot lately. I really don't know. I mean, it looks so . . . so rude. But all the ballet dancers do it, so I'll just have to wait and see. If I ever have to wear tights, I'll just—"

"Just what?"

Naggya shrugged his shoulders as he drifted silently into his own space. He'd possibly have remained in that space had Rambabu not suddenly burst into his own bout of laughter. Naggya looked up and frowned, "What's so funny?"

The cheesiest grin was plastered across Rambabu's handsome young face, "I was just recalling our conversations this afternoon, that's all."

"And that's what's so funny?"

"Well, yes."

Naggya's mystified expression forced Rambabu to explain, "Well, it's just the way the whole thing went. We started out talking about the flights, then the New York lights, and their nights, and the building heights, and all the New York fights, then about your rights and finally you wearing tights. So, what's next, flying kites?"

Solomon glanced at his two chuckling students, "Something funny to share?"

The two young men swapped impish grins, "No, sir. Probably best left with us."

CHAPTER
thirty-one

At times, epiphanies arrive at the most unexpected times and the most unlikely places. Following a month of fruitless pursuits for suitable premises, Kate was in desperate need of a breakthrough. Many of the Big Apple realtors had told her that her modest budget would position her toward the very far side of Jersey, at best. Soon after her moment of inspiration, Kate was busting to share the brilliant news so she called Lois, however, where the epiphany took place and what she was doing at that time would remain her secret. When pressed by Lois, she merely chuckled, "Let's just say in that small room, there wouldn't have been room for anyone else" and promptly changed the course of the conversation. "Lois, we're going on air!"

One week later, Lois, Chad, and Kate sat nervously in the waiting room of one of the most palatial penthouses in Manhattan. Joey D'Angelo was a name to be reckoned with in the top end of town, and to be given private time with this no-nonsense, self-made billionaire was a coup in itself. His PA served coffee then busied herself behind a stunningly impressive mahogany and pearl inlay desk. "He won't be long; just winding up a deal and he's usually pretty quick once he gets that smell in his—anyway, he shouldn't keep you long."

The three visitors could barely resist the temptations to gaze around the vast room with its sweeping panoramic views of a large chunk of the CBD skyline and beyond to Central Park. Kate was the least reluctant to conceal her amazement, prompting Lois to lean sideways and whisper, "Best keep your bottom jaw closed, my dear, just in case you dribble," and she winked at Kate and gave her arm a playful squeeze.

The PA's intercom buzzed, and she immediately stood to her feet and beckoned the trio towards the ten-foot solid timber doorway leading into Joey's office. All three were anxious but upon entry into Joey's inner sanctum, their greatest fears evaporated. "Come on, come on, I don't bite, and besides, I've already eaten." Joey ushered them towards four Chesterfield armchairs and smiled his billion-dollar smile, "Take a load off, you guys look like you's are goin' to a morgue. Relax, OK!"

Kate cleared her voice and thanked Joey for responding so quickly to their radio appeal.

"Sweetheart, you can thank one of my grandkids, Stacey, for you bein' here. I ain't ever got time to listen to no radio jock! Stacey tells me you're bringin' in a bunch of kids from Africa for some new dance school and ya need a place. Is that about the sum of it?"

Lois was bursting to say something but nodded to Kate to continue, "Yes, Mr. D'Angelo, we—"

"Hey, Babe, do I look like my ol' man? Call me Joey coz I don't answer to no mister, OK? Everybody calls me Joey, OK."

"Sorry, Joey, yes, these kids, some are from Africa but some are from South America, Asia, the Pacific islands, lots of places, but they're all from third world countries and they are all very talented and . . . "

"OK, I get de picture." Joey glanced at his wristwatch and looked again at Kate. "Sorry, babe, but we don't have a lot of time. Anyhow, I just love ta see young kids gettin' their names up in lights. Me, I can't sell fish wit dis voice, but we all do what we gotta do, OK. I lobbed in the Big Apple as just a kid from Jersey wit nuttin' and now I own haf de joint," and he let rip with one of his impressive chuckles, before adding, "Well, maybe not haf, but de day's still young, right?"

Chad cleared his throat and motioned to speak. "Joey, these kids aren't just about getting their names up in lights, they are from . . . "

"Of course, they want their names up in lights. If ya good, ya want opportunity! All kids do, it's natural."

Lois could remain silent not a moment longer, "Actually, Joey, these kids aren't just from third world countries. Every one of these kids come to us from persecuted cultures. They face life-and-death situations nearly every day of their lives, yet they come to America with their own dreams; dreams to make a difference and to save lives back in their countries. But they can only do that after they have, as you say, had their names up in lights. These kids are the true champions and they'd be some of the finest kids you could ever hope to meet." Lois could feel the emotion rising in her voice and she struggled to regain her composure. "But, with all due respect, Joey, it would be a mistake to think they're doing this for themselves; they're not. Their dream is to help save the lives of kids just like them back in their own countries."

Joey D'Angelo was no fool and had made his considerable fortune from quickly picking the genuine from the phonies. He listened attentively to the requests of these three strangers before he began wrapping up their meeting. "D'ya remember dat movie when dat babe says, 'Ya had me at hello'? Well, ya did, but now you've told me more, well, I guess I understand you's a whole lot better. Yous ave made dis ol' timer a bit misty and dat ain't no easy ting ta do," and he rubbed his bald head and looked to Kate, "OK, sweetheart, what exactly d'ya need?"

Kate couldn't help but flash one of her best Hudson River smiles and replied with an air of confidence that surprised everyone, including herself, "Joey, we need an entire floor of a city building, ideally around East Harlem, because that's where—"

Joey again interrupted and encouraged her to stick to the details, "I don't need to know ya reasons, just what ya need, OK."

"The building needs enough bathrooms, cooking facilities, and admin areas to cater for up to thirty students plus seven staff. Ideally, the building would have an open area suitable for practice and, of course, it must have good security."

"Ground floor?"

"Ideally not. These kids are mostly teenagers and many don't speak English. They are vulnerable, so, no, not ground floor. Second or third, or even—"

"OK, I get da picture." Joey walked to his desk, opened the top drawer and pulled out a business card. "Here, dis is my main man's private number. Give him a call tomorrow. I'll have spoken to him already," and he shot each a telling smile, "I reckon you'll be in before Christmas, OK."

❖❖❖❖❖

Kate smiled when Stan introduced himself and she couldn't resist making the comment, "So, you're Stan the main man?" and he'd tipped his imaginary hat and gave Kate a nod and a toothy grin. The building Stan had taken them to was set on a large chunk of a comparatively small Upper East Side city block and boasted front and side access with four large underground parking levels, including five permanently reserved spaces. The location was perfect for their needs and three of the broadest smiles in all of New York City accompanied Joey's main man as blessing after blessing was rolled out before them. By the time Stan's guided tour was complete, the three visitors were ecstatic, confident that, at a stretch, they could meet their deadlines, and as they walked and talked, Kate was already planning color schemes, bedding, and furniture.

"The boss must of taken a real shine to you guys coz he could easy get three times the rent for this place for what you guys are paying. Oh yeah, the boss told me to tell ya that he owns a removal company so if you don't mind fitting in when they got a bit of spare time, we can get you guys moved in for, like gratis, OK."

Joey was true to his word and on December 19, 2013, Crossover took possession of the entire third floor of the building, only four blocks from the Crossover headquarters.

The removal people bade them farewell as they disappeared

into the elevator, firing off one last "Merry Christmas" as the doors closed. Nestled upon an assortment of cardboard boxes, while sipping a glass of bubbly, was a tired yet elated band of seven: Lois, Chad, Kate, and four of her invaluable staff. In two weeks, the first of the overseas students was due to arrive, and probationary agreements were in place with several dance and theater companies for at least twelve of the students to commence their studies during the month of January. Discussions were also well under way with three other performing arts academies to enroll the rest.

The seven grinned at each other as they raised their plastic cups in triumph, "Who'd have ever thought?"

❖❖❖❖❖

"Three passports turned up today!" Elijah tempered his excitement in the knowledge that what he was about to share would bring Chad little comfort. He and Lois loved all the Son-Shine children yet their desire to see Naggya installed in Crossover's Dance and Performing Arts Academy all hinged on the arrival of his passport. "But, even though Naggya's wasn't among them, his can't be far off."

Chad breathed heavily over the phone, "Yes, Elijah, I'm sure you're right. It must be close now, and I suppose there's an upside to the Hindus running things there."

A bemused Elijah paused a moment before he replied, "And what would that be?"

Chad let out a stifled chuckle, "At least they don't close for Christmas." He then added, "The kids who received their passports must be excited."

Elijah beamed as he formed his response, "You should see them, Chad, they are so happy. I don't think I have ever seen so many children gathered around three passports before. They clapped and cheered and all tried to touch them at once. Chad, it was such a sight to see. Naggya's will be soon. Don't you worry."

Chad rubbed the back of his neck and gazed out their apartment window. Lois was out with friends, but on form, she was most likely turning a social outing into an opportunity to promote the Crossover DAPA Program. Chad smiled at the notion, and momentarily forgot that Elijah was still on the end of the line, "Sorry, my friend, I was just thinking about Lois and how she has been such a rock through all of this. She'll be disappointed that Naggya's passport hasn't arrived with the others, but of course, she will be just as ecstatic for the kids who received theirs. What an amazing milestone for each of them." Chad turned and walked back to his home office to check his diary and to count the number of business days before the holidays. "Elijah, me worrying about when the rest of the passports are going to arrive will change nothing, so of course, you're right. Anyway, are all the kids excited for Christmas?"

"Oh, Chad, they're beside themselves with anticipation, especially the little ones. We will probably get four-hundred people coming for the nativity evening, and all the children have been practicing so hard every day. They never stop smiling."

"And how many of the children will be going home for Christmas?"

"Not many. We'll have almost every Son-Shine child here

with us." There was a sadness in his voice; a sadness for those who actually had a family to go home to but who couldn't afford an extra mouth to feed. For parents of children at Son-Shine, their bittersweet longing to see their children, yet knowing they were safe, properly fed, and gaining not only an education but a future. An uneducated Dalit faced the bleak, life-long prospect of hardship and exploitation. An uneducated Dalit was a life without hope. With an education, each child could potentially follow their dreams, and for their parents, that amounted to an offset that somehow made their sacrifice bearable. "Chad, you know how it is for the parents. They love their children, but they know they have nothing to give them. That's always the hardest part."

CHAPTER
thirty-two

The Lincoln Centre had been abuzz for the New York season's final ballet production for 2013. The now famous Swedish producer, Philippe Montans, from Montans Majesty Dance Company, had never previously staged any of his productions at the Centre. Many of the critics saw this as a bold risk, not only because of his inexperience on such a tricky new stage complex, but that he had chosen a radically choreographed depiction of the time-honored classic, *Swan Lake*. Chad and Lois were excited to see the comparatively young producer risk his reputation, and the fact that he had picked their company, Impressions, from among a group of well-credentialed rival costume designers meant that their reputation was also in the crosshairs.

The crowds and reviews for the first weeks had been modest, and as the season built to its festive crescendo, so too did the pressures upon the Swede and his troupe of relatively young dancers. "I need more lift and more air" he would shout, loudly and often. "We must see Melana fly, not flutter!"

Lois had almost become a fixture backstage; if a seam split or a tight suddenly laddered, she would be first on the scene to quickly put it right. Although Impressions was spared any of the finger-pointing for the production's mediocrity, the pressures on Philippe seemed to transfer by osmosis to all those around him. Philippe was struggling, and it showed, not only upon his face but on his decision-making and his overall demeanor.

"It's not about the strength, it's about the technique," he would bellow in his adopted language. "Look, I am well past my prime but watch and learn," as he would gracefully lift Melana, high above his head and swirl her elegantly through three seamless spins to touch down upon a single pointed toe. "If I can do it, you can do it. Like I keep telling you, watch and learn!"

As Lois and Chad walked toward the exit following final rehearsal, Philippe crossed paths with them backstage. "Your costumes are a joy to work with. Thank you. If only my dancers were at the same level, my hair would not be going gray," and he ran his fingers through his impressive locks but kept on walking. "See you in a few hours."

Final night pulled a full house and present in the second and third rows was an array of critics from most of New York's leading performing arts publications, as well as The Big Apple's most respected tabloids.

Lois had declined an offer to be seated among the crowd, although Chad hadn't; aware that they could give no more than they already had, he'd gratefully accepted Philippe's invitation of a ticket in one of the prestigious elevated boxes. Chad settled into his seat as he surveyed the scene below, instantly recognizing most of the celebrities and the well-to-do in the front row. Hovering just behind, the bevy of critics as they sharpened their swords; tomorrow's headlines, a mere poor performance away.

Backstage, Lois caught Philippe by the arm, "It will go well tonight, Philippe. You've worked hard and these dancers have learned much from you. We're all praying."

Not one to express his affections, Philippe reached across and hugged her. "I hope you are right," and with an unconvincing smile he hurried on to double- then triple-check every vital detail. Each of the dancers knew that their own futures were also on the chopping block, and one false move, one delayed or premature entry or departure, would most likely have the perpetrator queuing for a new job come January. The atmosphere behind the stage was suffocating.

Pressure: It brings out the best and it brings out the worst.

When the flowers rained down at the feet of the entire cast and bouquets presented to the producer amid a full-house standing ovation, Philippe stood proud and shone like a beacon. His chest had never been so full nor his eyes so bright. Philippe's troupe had pulled off the impossible, and as the house remained standing, wildly applauding, the critics were already filing out the door; headlines refuse to wait.

❖❖❖❖❖

A new season was on the horizon and Philippe 's success had given him the confidence to choreograph his own version of *Don Quixote*. Including understudies, a cast of forty had been selected from seventy hand-picked applicants, and the only remaining impediment to an early April launch was the venue.

Philippe sat confidently in the theater manager's waiting room, a man he'd worked with on a number of previous productions. As soon as Sebastian's door opened, Philippe jumped to his feet and smiled as he extended his hand, "Seb, it's so good to be seeing you again," and brushed past him into the office where he sat down without being asked. "We're all so excited about the new season," as the manager sat down behind his desk. "We'd like to extend to four weeks if that fits for you?"

Sebastian's expression and his puzzling disconnect forced Philippe's smile to freeze. "Is there something wrong? I thought you'd be pleased we want an extra week."

The manager shifted in his seat. "Philippe, it would seem your final night success with *Swan Lake* may have worked against you. That, and the fact that the earlier performances had drawn only moderate support."

"What do you mean, 'worked against me,' I don't understand?"

"As you will recall, ever since we announced our new stage system, there have been question marks hanging over it, but thankfully, your success on the final night put paid to all the doubters. So, to put it bluntly, you've actually contributed to your own . . . "

The lines on Philippe's face began to deepen, "My own what? Downfall?" Sebastian sank back in his chair and chose not to complete his sentence.

"Come on, Seb, so what are you saying?"

Sebastian leaned forward and paused before responding, "Well, I'm saying that we've had three other major production companies make application for the same period. They all have proven track records at filling theaters night-in and night-out. As you also know only too well, we are considerably more profitable when the full-house sign is shining bright than when the crowds are," and he regarded Philippe intently, "small."

Philippe's cheeks were beginning to redden, and he also leaned forward so that the two men's faces were only two feet apart. "So, what you're saying is that even though we finished last season on a high, you still doubt we can pull a crowd?"

"Philippe, we run a business and we respond to each application on its merits. Yes, your last production finished well, but you can't deny what the critics had to say, 'One night doesn't erase weeks of mediocrity'. I know that's somewhat harsh, but you know as well as I do that, by their comments, critics either put bums on seats or they send the crowds elsewhere."

"What would they know?! Not one of them has ever done a major production, and none of them has ever . . . "

Sebastian raised a hand to interrupt, "Yes, Philippe, you're right, but that really changes nothing. With one of our rival venues currently off-line undergoing a re-fit, the market has come to us, and we've responded accordingly. Sorry, Philippe, but when we hadn't heard from you and these attractive options came our way, we simply . . . "

Philippe jumped to his feet, "What do you mean, you hadn't heard from me? On our final night, I said to you, 'See you next year, Seb,' and here I am. In case you haven't noticed, we're still in the first week of January. What would you have had me do, spend New Year's with you? For goodness sake, man, I thought we had an understanding!"

"Will you please sit down and lower your voice? As I said, this is a business and we have only one stage to offer. We are honor-bound to look at all proposals and that is precisely what we've done. Now, we do have a vacancy in late June, and we'd be more than happy to discuss that possibility with you but, sorry, we have nothing until then. Is there any way you can possibly postpone?"

Philippe paced around the office then slapped the manager's desk, "And what do I do with forty dancers and our backroom staff in the meantime? Stick them in the deepfreeze?!" By now, Philippe's face was crimson and as he continued to pace, he muttered angrily under his breath and refused to look at Sebastian. "I'll tell you what you can do with your 'late June!'" Philippe aimed a single up-turned finger in the direction of the center manager, slammed the office door behind him, and stormed out of the building.

CHAPTER
thirty-three

All the boys were drenched in sweat as the afternoon's game of kabaddi was drawing to a close. Naggya and Rambabu had been pitted against each other, yet their long friendship and loyalty amounted to little when the day's bragging rights were up for grabs. During the past six months Naggya had grown another couple of inches in height and his muscle definition had become significantly more pronounced. Rambabu was short by comparison, yet what he lacked in height and weight, he made up for in determination and tenacity.

Elijah walked purposefully from the main building towards Solomon and stood beside him as the teacher yelled encouragement and instruction in equal measure. When play paused momentarily, Elijah slipped a parcel into Solomon's pocket and grinned as he whispered a single word, "Finally."

When full-time was called and the scores remained even, Solomon declared honors shared, which yielded choruses of disappointment and a salvo of requests for extra time. He dismissed their requests and called for attention, "Now, you all know I love to see a result but considering what we are about to see, we definitely won't have time." Both teams looked toward their teacher with puzzled expressions as Solomon glanced at a beaming Elijah, then pulled the package from his pocket and called for complete silence. "Today's mail has arrived, and someone is about to become very, very excited." Every eye followed Solomon as he walked the short distance across court and passed the package to a dazed Naggya. Personally addressed packages arriving by mail to the children of Son-Shine were a rarity and Naggya's hands trembled as he reached out to receive the package. Embossed upon the front was the official Indian Government emblem.

Elijah stepped forward and placed an arm around his shoulder, "Well, aren't you going to open it?"

As though the value and the significance of the contents might suddenly be lost by its undoing, Naggya prized the package gently open to reveal a covering letter and within a plastic sleeve, a brand-new dark blue Indian Passport. Naggya delicately opened its cover to reveal a photograph of himself and his name emblazoned upon the first page. Instinctively he clutched the precious delivery to his chest as his eyes began to glisten and every student moved in closer to gaze upon his miracle.

Elijah waited for the crush to ease then stood in front of Naggya, "After dinner, would you like us to call Mummy Lois and Daddy Chad? There is much we need to arrange."

❖❖❖❖❖

"Kate, his passport has arrived! Yes, Elijah just called, and they will apply for visas today! No, he didn't know how long it'll take but we can only do our best and trust God for the rest! Yes, it's so exciting! Yes, of course I will keep you posted. See you tomorrow. Bye, Kate."

By mid-January, DAPA, Crossover's brand new center for international performing artists, was welcoming a new member almost every day, and to date, their support structures had coped adequately. Unlike most of Crossover's other programs, DAPA's responsibilities required oversight in the areas of multilingual translators, visa administration, Green Card applications, medicals, clothing, transport to-and-from performing arts classes, job interviews, resumes, communications to their respective homelands, and inbound travel coordination.

From day one, the Crossover team had acknowledged that a manual for such a groundbreaking venture simply did not exist. In its stead grew a mindset built upon the need to be ad hoc, essential if they were to survive the first few months. Kate was often heard to say, "We'll just have to write the text book later," and to reinforce her point, she had installed above the entrance to the complex a large colorful billboard that read; "If you think you can't succeed, you're in the wrong place— *your* future is DAPA."

❖❖❖❖❖

As though they were the ones under the microscope, Lois and Chad sat nervously in Galant Scott's waiting room. Big Apple Ballet Company was currently the leading ballet producer in New York and, many would claim, the world. Back in the late 1970s and early 1980s, Galant had performed with distinction on the most celebrated stages worldwide until a spinal injury forced him into early retirement. Since his reemergence as one of the great innovators in artistic choreography, the world had indeed become Galant's creative oyster.

"Come in, come in," he smiled as he ushered them into his office, adorned with almost life-sized photographs of instantly recognizable smash hits from across the globe. Interestingly, most of the photographs featured Galant prominently. "Please, make yourselves comfortable. Would you care for a drink?"

Chad and Lois glanced uneasily at each other, smiled, and politely declined. It wasn't yet 11 a.m.

"On the phone you mentioned you've helped set up a new dance academy. Should I be worried?" and he threw a thinly veiled gesture at them that spoke more of his own ego than of any genuine concerns. Without bothering to wait for a reply, he got to his feet and walked to a filing cabinet, pulled out a thick folder, and purposely dropped it on his desk. "That's just my current file of prospects, young prospects, who have been highly recommended and who would happily give their left lung to join my academy," and he pointed to the smorgasbord of photographs on the wall and quipped, "And why wouldn't they? We are the world's best. I am the world's best and second-best is still light years behind me!" Galant searched the eyes of his two guests and waited for his point to sink in. "We run a revolving door here, a very slowly revolving door, if you get my drift. We need to be finding emerging talent, that is true, but I will turn the talent that I select into superstars, and they will stay with me. So, the question I would put to you, despite my respect for your standing among the leading costume designers in New York, is this: what might you bring to the talent table that I don't already have in spades?"

Chad and Lois hadn't been prepared for such an egotistical onslaught and looked to one another to take the lead. Chad turned to Galant and stammered slightly before he found his confidence, "Galant, as you know we are huge admirers of your work, as it seems, you are of ours. In coming here today, we presuppose nothing, however, this one thing we do know; talent, the sort of talent that you can turn into superstars, as you rightly point out, must come from somewhere. It just so happens that in our travels we have unearthed a talent that we believe can become one of your widely acclaimed superstars. Had we not believed that, we would not be sitting before you now, and all we respectfully ask, given our professional standing with you and your company, is for you to trust us sufficiently to taste and see."

Galant smiled in his own inimitable style, and nodded his head, "Well, I've heard such a pitch so many times before, but to your credit, rarely with such conviction. Bravo to you," and he paused to consider. "And so, just for argument's sake, if I did elect to audition this potential superstar of yours, and I'm assuming it's a young man, where is he?"

Lois felt an urge to contribute to the debate and breathed in deeply before speaking, "Yes, Galant, you would be right in your assumption. This young man is 15 years old, and he lives in a small orphanage in Andhra Pradesh, India."

Galant reeled off a series of derisive chuckles then rolled his eyes and stared at Lois, "In India? Are you serious? What on earth do Indians know about the majesty and the uniqueness of my ballet? And what hope does a 15-year-old from one of the poorest nations on earth have of coping with the pressures of my world? He wouldn't last ten minutes! Come on, please, out of respect for you and your fine work, I have given you my time but do you truly want to give me a 15-year-old from the cesspit of the world?"

Chad stood to his feet. "Galant, like I said, all we ask is that you taste and see, but if we've taken up your time, then please accept our apology," and he gestured to Lois for them to leave.

Galant also stood to his feet and took a pace forward, "Chad, Lois, although many would probably argue that I am ruthless, and I make no apologies for that, I am a fair man, and I can see that you've been willing to take a risk for this boy." He slowly rubbed his chin with forefinger and thumb then turned to look at Chad, "So, what do you have to show me, given that this boy isn't even in the country?"

Lois retrieved a memory stick from her handbag and passed it to Galant, "We humbly trust that you will glean enough from this to want to see him dance. If you do, you know how to reach us. We expect to have Naggya here in New York with us for a couple of weeks quite soon. Sorry, but we can't be any more specific than that."

Tentatively, Galant took the memory stick and lobbed it onto his desk. "Thanks for coming. Although I admire what you are trying to do, I make no promises. Have a good day."

CHAPTER
thirty-four

"Then let's make it late in the day? 4:30? Yes, that works for me, and I can meet you in your office. No, no, that will be just fine. See you there, bye!"

Under normal circumstances, Lois and Chad would be going to Philippe's office but these weren't normal circumstances. Philippe was facing up to some monumental decisions, and to date, none of them offered him the same degree of hope or satisfaction as his original plan. He could wait until June and hope his dancers were sufficiently loyal to stay with him; if not, he'd be forced to start from scratch and recruit all over again, compounded by the fact that he'd be doing so on the back of five months without any significant revenue. The perfect scenario had always been to complete one season, retain his nucleus of dancers, and launch almost immediately into rehearsing for the next. Now, his perfect scenario lay in tatters, and if he hoped to regain top billing in top venues, his decisions needed to be wise. When news of the postponement of his next production went public, several offers from his native Sweden had come in. Always in demand, the return of the conquering hero was assured of success, yet with that success came a bunch of logistical hurdles. Given the significantly smaller budgets on offer, Philippe would have to either personally bankroll his lead dancers until the Swedish season commenced, or he'd need to hire and train local talent and run an unacceptable risk of failure. Philippe had been long-removed from the local scene, and although the Swedish critics waxed lyrical over the home-grown dancers, Philippe remained far from convinced they were up to his expected standards. Three to four weeks with full houses each night equated to break-even, and for him to turn a profit, he would need at least two, and ideally three, back-to-back seasons. By his own reckoning, the local market might be hard pushed to deliver.

Should Philippe elect to stay Stateside, he'd need to drastically compromise on the quality of available New York venues, and his fears rested largely on the premise that a producer downsizing the venue was a producer downsizing his career. For a producer who was considered to be still on the rise, this was a gamble he was loath to take. Some other major U.S. cities had come into consideration, with prospects of Chicago and Los Angeles offering a degree of attraction, but deep down, Philippe knew that New York and London were the benchmarks for success, and at this stage of his career, London remained a bridge too far.

As he entered the elevator, he chuckled uneasily at the realization he'd been jangling his keys in his pocket ever since parking the car, "I never do that! Pull yourself together, man!" and the elevator doors opened, and he strode as confidently as he could manage into the Impressions Costume and Design office. The receptionist recognized Philippe instantly and smiled broadly, "Good afternoon, Mr. Montans, and welcome to Impressions. Would you care for a coffee?" Philippe returned the smile but declined the coffee. "Chad and Lois will be with you shortly. Would you like to make yourself comfortable?"

Scarcely had Philippe sat down when Lois appeared from behind a door at the back of reception and extended her hand, "So good to see you again, Philippe. Please, come through," and he followed her through a set of large swinging doors then turned down a short corridor into their office. Chad was winding up a call and encouraged Philippe to take a seat as Lois closed the door behind her.

"That will be fine. Yes, we'll expect to see delivery soon. Thanks for your call," and he returned the handpiece to its cradle and turned to Philippe, "Sorry about that. Suppliers, you know what they're like."

There was an awkward silence as the three looked at each other. Mostly because their meetings were nearly always in Philippe's office, or in the theater, but today in no small part they each were acutely aware of Philippe's predicament. Chad broke the ice, "Philippe, we've all been in tight spots before and Lois and I have no doubts that you will come through this one. Please know that we will stand with you. We haven't even begun work on the costumes for *Don Quixote* as yet, and the materials we've purchased can sit and wait until they are needed."

"But you've had to pay for all the material."

"There really wasn't that much," said Lois respectfully.

"Forty costumes! How is that not much? Let's be honest, I've left you in the lurch."

Chad reached forward and tapped Philippe gently on the shoulder, "Only if you go belly-up, and you're not, right?"

Philippe tried to muster a smile, but none came, "Not if I've got any say in the matter."

"That's the spirit. And besides, you've got other matters to focus on."

Philippe's head went down, and he gazed into his clenched hands then looked at both in turn, "Are you sure about this?"

Chad's hand was still on Philippe's shoulder, "We're on your side, my friend, and we've been praying for you."

Philippe's mind raced back to the final night of *Swan Lake* when Lois had said the same thing. He smiled and looked at her as she, too, recalled her words. "Then if that accounts for anything, I guess we're a chance. Thank you both. I'm not sure what the next few months have in store for me, but at least I know I still have some friends," and the slightest tremor appeared in his voice.

Lois wanted to release the tension in the room and she sat up a little taller in her seat and softly cleared her voice, "Actually, there is something we wanted to talk to you about, and although it might be the very furthest thing you'd want to be discussing right now, it just might be the perfect distraction."

"Now, there's an oxymoron if ever I've heard one."

Lois had never seen Philippe so personally vulnerable. They had seen him professionally stretched to the breaking point on numerous occasions, but this was different. Lois eased delicately into her pitch. "Oxymorons, yes, don't you just love them? When we're really under the pump we just want things kept as simple as they can possibly be, but that's not how it pans out, not in our experience," and Philippe's mouth fell slightly open as though Lois had somehow been privy to his self-talk on the way to their meeting. "You're aware that Chad and I have a close relationship with an orphanage in India, which is a big part of why we spend time there each year. Of course, we source a lot of our costume material from India, but over the years a remarkable thing has emerged, and if you've the time, we would like to tell you about it."

Philippe leaned back in his chair and folded his arms, "Lois, Chad, somehow I feel like I'm being set up here, but actually I am little intrigued, so . . . "

Lois smiled and glanced at Chad, "Actually, you're not being set up but what we want to share just might put a grin back on your face. Have you ever heard of Crossover?"

Philippe slowly shook his head, "No, should I?"

"Possibly not, but we hope you soon will. Chad and I approached a lot of the local welfare service providers some time back and out of all the providers we spoke to, Crossover was far and away the standout. Standout for what, I hear you say? Well, in conjunction with Crossover we have very recently initiated a program called DAPA, the Dance And Performing Arts Academy, and we have set it up right here in East Harlem. DAPA brings gifted teenagers from persecuted third-world countries to New York to be trained under the masters, such as yourself, and then to return to their own countries to instill hope and a future."

"Lois, that all sounds terribly noble and altruistic but I don't get it, why are you telling me? I mean, I am flattered that you might see me as one of the masters, but right now, being a mentor to a bunch of foreign kids would be the very last thing that—"

"Sorry, Philippe, that's not where I am going with this." Philippe raised one eyebrow and unfolded his arms. "Actually, there is one particular young man we would absolutely love you to meet, not just because he's such an inspiration but because he's one of the most gifted dancers we have ever seen."

Philippe's countenance, scarcely a smile, hardly a frown, yet from somewhere in between, the very slightest nod slowly found its way out. "That's it? You just want me to meet a young Indian boy?"

Chad chuckled softly, "You really did think we were setting you up, didn't you? To be honest, Philippe, we'd love you to meet Naggya, ah, sorry, that's his name. Naggya is a Dalit, an untouchable," and he waited for a response, yet all that came back from Philippe was a slow but undeniable continuation of that same nod. "Naggya and Elijah, the founder of the orphanage, are currently awaiting U.S. visas so that they can fly to New York for two weeks. Once the visas are granted, we will get them on a plane from Hyderabad. Philippe, if you would do us the honor of meeting with Naggya and to see him dance, we would be forever thankful."

For the first time since this new venture had been spelled out, Philippe smiled. It was brief and it was faint, but it was a smile, and he visibly relaxed. "Sure, there's no harm in that, provided of course that I'm still in New York."

Chad and Lois both shot him inquiring glances. "Sweden is possibly opening up. I've had several inquiries and since those inquiries, a couple of offers."

"Really? So, the famous Swede might be going home?" asked Chad tentatively.

"There's still a lot of water that needs to flow down the Hudson before that might happen, but yes, maybe. But if it does happen, it will be only for a few months, six tops. New York is my home and New York is my future, but sometimes we need to take some unexpected detours."

CHAPTER
thirty-five

"Sir, I would just like to see it, that's all." Naggya looked into Elijah's eyes and blinked away his tears. "I can't explain. I just need to see it."

Elijah hugged the young man then crossed the office floor and reached into his pocket for a set of keys. The lockbox was tightly chained deep within the bottom draw of the locked filing cabinet. It was hardly Fort Knox, but it was the best Son-Shine could afford. From within the lockbox Elijah retrieved Naggya's passport and handed it over with a fatherly smile, "Please bring it straight back after you've had your time, OK?"

"Yes, sir. Thank you, sir." Naggya held his passport in two hands, turned and left the office where Rambabu was waiting outside. The two walked upstairs and settled on the floor outside the dorm.

"It looks so important, Naggya. It's like something we see on TV but it's yours. Can you believe it?"

Naggya stared down at the dark blue cover with the embossed crest and ran his fingers several times over it, as though it had some sort of unspoken hold on him. "It's more than important. It's my, no, it's our future," and carefully he opened the cover and flipped through the pages ever-so slowly and respectfully. Even since the time his photograph had been taken, Naggya's appearance had changed; his face was now slightly fuller and his hair a little longer, while his top lip now sported the evidence of puberty passed, a dark growth that seemed to thicken almost weekly. Naggya scanned the document over and over as though somehow, he may have overlooked some vital entry, or perhaps discover that something, somehow, had been missed. The keys to the world lay in his trembling hands and he could scarcely hold in his emotions. Naggya used his sleeve to wipe a tear away then froze as if paralyzed; he clenched the passport much more tightly.

Rambabu raised his focus from upon the open page to search Naggya's troubled face, "What?"

Naggya did not speak, nor did his expression alter. He just stared at the typed entry adjacent to his photograph. Rambabu took hold of Naggya's arm and gave it a shake, "What is it?"

His face had tightened and his pupils contracted. Naggya did not speak; he couldn't. He remained transfixed until his hand trembled so much that Rambabu reached across and took hold of him, "Naggya, please tell me what's the matter?"

Drawing in his breath, Naggya tried to steady himself. He held onto his inhaled breath before slowly turning to look at his friend. "I've never seen it written before."

A puzzled expression washed over Rambabu, "You've never seen what written before?"

Naggya's breathing was now shallow and erratic and still he struggled to speak. "'Orphan,' I've never seen it written before," and he wiped away a fresh flood of tears and tried to subdue his sobs.

Rambabu wrapped his arm around his best friend's shoulder and waited for the moment to pass. Naggya glanced up and down the corridor then whispered, "It's stupid! I feel so stupid! Why am I feeling so stupid?"

Rambabu had no words to comfort his friend. He considered a host of responses, yet, in the end, he just sat there and allowed Naggya to grieve the loss that had taken over a decade to work its way to the surface. "This doesn't make any sense; none at all. I know I am an orphan. I even wrote 'orphan' on the application forms, but . . . "

"But what?"

Slowly, Naggya shook his head, "It's one thing for me to write that word, but some stranger somewhere in the government has typed on my passport that I don't have a father or a mother, and suddenly it hurts! It really hurts!" As a group of students walked slowly past, Naggya was utterly incapable of withholding his grief and as he sobbed, the students halted and looked to Rambabu for guidance. Rambabu simply gestured for them to continue walking and he gripped Naggya's shoulders and held him tight.

"Why should it make a difference when someone else writes a word? I should still feel the same, but I don't! It's like somehow, now it's official, and neither of my parents even get to be on my passport. Why, Rambabu, why?"

"Perhaps your father could be listed. I mean, you don't really know he's dead, at least not for sure."

Naggya turned and looked Rambabu squarely in the eyes, "I do know!"

"But—"

"Rambabu, I know, OK! I just know!" and fleetingly he glanced away. "I wouldn't want him on my passport anyway. He killed my mother; he killed her right in front of me, and now he's dead. He's been dead for a long time, but my mother, my mother should be here on my passport, but no, it just says, 'orphan' like she never even existed."

Solomon climbed the stairs and looked towards two of his star students. As their teacher, he desperately wanted to help; he wanted to ease this glaring pain, yet for him to watch as two friends cared for one another, helped convince him that all was as good as it could be, at least for now. He eased himself down onto the floor a few yards away, bowed his head and began to pray. Not until the dinner bell sounded did any of them move.

Naggya climbed to his feet, and as he did, he became aware that his teacher was sitting nearby. Solomon briefly acknowledged them both and also climbed to his feet. The three walked down the stairs to the front door where Naggya broke away and returned to the office. He knocked tentatively until Elijah opened the door and without a word, held out his passport and hesitantly pressed it into Elijah's hands. Within the next few weeks, he would be boarding an airliner for the very first time in his life to fly halfway around the world with the man standing in front of him. Together, the pair would be embarking on a journey that would shape the future direction of their lives and possibly the futures of so many others.

Elijah held the passport close to his chest, "Would you like to talk, young man?"

❖❖❖❖❖

Naggya's every spare moment was devoted to expanding and refining his repertoire of the great solo ballet performances of the past fifty years. Solomon had initiated the practice of throwing challenges his way without warning in anticipation of the contacts Lois and Chad were arranging would likely do the same. At any moment, Solomon would rattle off a performance and a scene and within minutes, Naggya was expected to carry off that performance to an exacting standard.

❖❖❖❖❖

Early on February 2, 2014, Elijah's visa application was approved online, and before close of business the same day, Naggya's also. By 10:00 the following morning, their flights from Vijayawada via Hyderabad to New York had been booked and paid for. This dream was about to get wings and Naggya, now 15 years and seven months, had suddenly morphed into an intoxicating mix of excitement and almost overwhelming trepidation. With the departure date set, the pressure had soared to a whole new level. Every sunrise represented one less day to prepare and one day closer to the biggest adventure of his life.

CHAPTER
thirty-six

"You can let go of the seat now, Naggya." Elijah smiled as he recalled his very first flight on a jetliner not too many years ago. "Did you love the power as we were taking off?"

Naggya was in a world all his own and his heart raced as the adrenaline coursed through his body. The plane was only half full, which enabled Naggya to score the prized window seat, and even though he was directly over the wing, he found it impossible to avert his gaze from the disappearing landscape below.

"Um, how high are we off the ground?" Naggya asked but didn't bother to look to Elijah for the answer. He gasped as some turbulence caused the aircraft to shudder and shake.

Elijah leaned slightly across him and scanned the agricultural tapestry below, "We'll probably hear from the captain soon and he will tell us how high we are and what time we'll arrive in Hyderabad. He'll probably also tell us what the weather is like there," and no sooner had Elijah uttered the words, the captain's voice came through the sound system to inform all those onboard precisely that.

"Sir, can I get something out of my suitcase in Hyderabad?" Once more, Elijah smiled and turned in his seat to look into Naggya's eyes, "Actually, no, you can't. We won't see our suitcases again until we get to New York."

A baffled expression jumped onto Naggya's face, "But how can that be? How does our luggage go from Vijayawada to New York unless we---"

Elijah chuckled loudly then lowered his voice, "That's still the mystery, Naggya, but most of the time it gets where it is supposed to."

"Most of the time?"

Again, Elijah chuckled, "I'm sure ours will be there so you've no need to worry."

Naggya's grip on the arm of the seat relaxed only for as long as they remained at cruising altitude. As soon as they began their descent and burst through the cloud-cover, his grip tightened and remained that way until the aircraft eased to a halt. Naggya tried to smile but that proved difficult with his mouth still hanging wide open. "So, what happens now, Sir? Do we just sit here until the plane takes off?"

"Only if we want to go to Mumbai," and once more, a muffled chuckle wiggled its way out. "No, we get off this plane and we wait in the international terminal for our New York flight. Before we get on that plane, we will go through customs where they will check our passports and our visas. Remember, we talked about that?"

Naggya turned from craning his neck out the window to exclaim, "So many airplanes! I could never imagine there to be so many, and they are all different and have different colors and names!" Finally, he turned to look at Elijah but was still deep in thought as he watched most of the passengers getting to their feet and retrieving their hand luggage from the overhead lockers. "Do I remember? Ah, yes, I think so. Do we need to get up now, sir?"

Elijah patted Naggya on the arm, "There's no rush. We can let the others off first," as a number of higher caste passengers shuffled past and sneered at the two Dalits, ensuring there was no physical contact with the "untouchables." Some muttered that the "animals" should not be allowed to share their space, and one was heard to say, "They should be in with the cargo," and pushed past them as fast as the departing shuffle would allow.

Elijah and Naggya were the last to alight, and as they did, the stewards who'd been thanking the departing passengers suddenly turned to check their manifests without another word.

Inside the domestic terminal, as they walked toward the electronic information boards, Elijah pointed to the one that gave directions to the International Terminal. He leaned closer as they walked and whispered, "After we get onto the flight to New York, we will be treated differently."

Naggya looked up to him to ask, "But why, sir?"

"We will be flying with Cathay Pacific Airlines and as far as they are concerned, all Indian passengers are the same. When we get to the International Terminal, we will have a two-hour wait for our connecting flight and I need to discuss something with you."

Passing through Indian Customs had proved daunting for Elijah in the past, but now for two departing Dalits, one with a brand new passport, the tension and the prejudice meted out was even more intimidating. "Just smile, Naggya. Once we are through those gates, we will be fine."

The Customs official waved them through after applying hand sanitizer and vigorously rubbing his hands together. The man scowled, "Don't come back, pigs," and beckoned those waiting next in line to approach his counter.

The pair settled into a couple of lounge chairs as Elijah scanned the departure board. After double-checking the flight number on his ticket, he pointed to the board and informed Naggya, "That's us. That one right there. When that column says 'Boarding,' it'll be time to fly out of India for your very first time. Are you excited?"

Naggya's mind was still awash; he'd experienced the buzz of Hyderabad's city streets several times in the past, yet even though he knew that they were in that same city, this was a completely different world. This was the most modern and sophisticated building he had ever been in, and to see people of all colors, shapes, and sizes, many dressed in garments he had only ever seen on television, caused him to gape and gawk as though his head was on a swivel. "Excited? I can hardly breathe, sir."

Elijah leaned forward in his lounge chair, "Actually, Naggya, that's the thing I need to discuss."

"Sorry, sir, what?"

Elijah smiled broadly, "That. It might sound strange to you but just for the time we are away, I would like to give you permission to not call me 'sir', OK?"

Naggya once again seemed baffled, "But why, sir?"

With a slight chuckle, Elijah explained, "In our culture, it is appropriate for children and students to call adults, 'sir', but in other cultures, that's not so common. I know it might seem a little strange at first, but because you are fast becoming an adult and because we will be in a totally different culture these next two weeks, I would like to give you permission, while we are in America, to call me Elijah. Is that OK?" Elijah waited for a response but Naggya's silence spelled confusion, so he dropped the subject and again pointed to the departure board. "Look, Naggya, the flight to London is now boarding."

"But what if someone gets on the wrong plane?"

Elijah pointed to the airport staff at the departure counters, and in particular to what they were doing, "See, they are checking the boarding passes to make sure each passenger gets onto the correct flight. No need to worry, we will get onto the right airplane and when we arrive in New York in about twenty-nine hours, Mummy Lois and Daddy Chad will be waiting for us at the airport."

Naggya thought for a moment, "So what do I call them while we are in America?"

Elijah again chuckled, "Now, that is a matter for discussion. Are you getting hungry?"

"No, sir. Sorry, no."

CHAPTER
thirty-seven

In-flight service was yet another opportunity for Naggya to be bewildered. To see how all that food and drink could be distributed to so many passengers from such a small trolley and not drop a thing, literally captivated him. Several hours later, the aircraft's approach to Hong Kong Airport, in such close proximity to the many towering and intimidating buildings, had him drawing breath and wide-eyed, long after the wheels had stopped turning. His knuckles were still white when Elijah attempted to restore a bit of relativity, "I used to feel exactly the same for the first few take-offs and landings, but you just get used to it after a while."

Naggya blinked hard and let go of the armrest, "Really?"

A two-hour layover in Hong Kong meant two hours in the transit lounge, and as they walked about, Naggya could scarcely keep his head from turning left and right while he soaked up every little detail and every intriguing passerby. "This is nothing like I imagined. It's like a dream, but it's really happening." He proceeded to add "sir" on the end of his comment but reeled it back from the tip of his tongue.

When they reboarded the aircraft, Elijah suggested, "Naggya, we still have a long flight ahead of us, so if you can manage a bit of sleep that would be wise."

Naggya shook his head, "I don't think I could sleep, sorry. I'll just watch out the window and try to imagine what's going on below."

Elijah smiled and gave his arm a squeeze. "Of course, Naggya, I understand. If you need anything just wake me," and he rolled the blanket into the shape of a pillow and placed it behind his head. Two hours later, the stewardess gave him a gentle nudge before handing Elijah his meal.

Twenty-nine hours is a long time for anyone to be sitting still, especially a teenager, and Naggya was beginning to feel restless. If not for there being two people between him and the aisle, he'd have gladly gone exploring as the giant bird chewed through the miles en route to The Big Apple.

Elijah folded down his tray and switched the monitor to the tracking option to show Naggya how far they had already traveled, although more so, to give him a visual indication of how far they still had to go. "Not too long now and we will be flying over America. Did you manage to close your eyes?"

Naggya simply shrugged his shoulders, "I tried, but they wouldn't stay closed for long."

One of the younger stewardesses had become aware of his restlessness and leaned across Elijah to ask Naggya if he would care to watch a movie.

"Is there a cinema on this airplane?" and the stewardess stifled her giggle by softly coughing into her hand. She smiled and handed Naggya a set of headphones and switched the monitor to the movie menu. "There are two-hundred cinemas on this airplane. Now, what sort of movies do you like? Action or romance?"

The young man hadn't experienced blushing before, but as she smiled he felt a rush of blood to his cheeks and stammered twice, however nothing emerged that resembled an actual word.

The stewardess chuckled again and winked at him, sending his blush to a whole new level, "I think you'd like this one; it's a musical with lots of singing and dancing. Do you like to dance?"

Naggya's mouth, not for the first time that day, fell wide open and his sole response amounted to a stuttered, "Aha."

During a one-hundred-and-twenty-minute feature film, the stewardess must have walked past Naggya's seat twenty times, and twenty times his blush returned with interest, as he mused, *and I'm supposed to sleep?*

❖❖❖❖❖

It was ninety minutes until touchdown when Elijah woke from his slumber and Naggya had wondered if the gentleman in the aisle seat next to him had been kept awake by his snoring. With almost twenty-eight flying-time hours under their belts since Hyderabad, and six hours before that since leaving Son-Shine, Naggya could feel himself beginning to wilt. When Elijah asked him how he was feeling, Naggya managed a half smile and gestured towards the monitor in front of Elijah, "Not long now. Would Mummy Lois and Daddy Chad be at the airport yet?"

"Soon, Naggya, soon." Local arrival time was 6:30 in the morning, and based on the captain's commentary, New York was waking to a freezing winter's morning with The Big Apple shrouded in fog. According to the announcement, the pea-souper was thick, however, not quite thick enough to enforce a flight redirection. Forty degrees Fahrenheit in New York was a far cry from Son-Shine's forty degrees Celsius, although the prospect of having to wear the overcoats and gloves Mummy Lois had spoken of on the phone was still a reality yet to register in Naggya's reckoning.

Half an hour before touchdown, the captain announced, "Ladies and gentlemen, we have commenced our descent into New York, and we expect to be landing at JFK Airport right on time. Once again, thank you for choosing to fly Cathay Pacific."

Shortly after the landing gear was heard being lowered, Naggya caught his first sight of America. Through the thick fog he was certain he saw lights and he wriggled in his seat, searching out the window high and low for more. The stewards were systematically working through the rows, collecting empty drink containers and wrappers and encouraging each passenger to return their seats to the upright position. When the young stewardess reached across to retrieve Naggya's cup, with a beaming smile, she asked, "And did you enjoy the movie, handsome young man?"

Naggya had been privately rehearsing his much improved and far more mature responses to members of the opposite sex, however, when the pressure unexpectedly hit, his best effort once again amounted to "aha," accompanied by yet another blush.

Elijah frowned and whispered, "Is there something I'm missing here?"

Ten minutes later amid glimpses of New York lights and a rush of pure exhilaration and unrestrained joy, Naggya heard the sounds of squealing rubber tires establishing contact with The United States of America. Not for the first time, he let out a gasp. Elijah grabbed him by the arm and peered expectantly out the window, "We made it, Naggya, we're in New York!"

❖❖❖❖❖

A grin as wide as Andhra Pradesh was plastered across his face as Naggya retrieved his small suitcase from the revolving carousel. He had convinced himself his most valuable possessions in all the world, tucked away within that case, would be lost along the way. Standing the case upright, he extended the handle and spotted Elijah doing the same beside another carousel. Naggya felt like launching into a dance and only managed to restrain himself after he'd noticed a pair of armed security guards on patrol, oddly, reminding him of home.

"What now?" he asked when they'd been reunited.

"Now, we go through Customs."

"But we already went through Customs."

Elijah placed an arm around his shoulder, "Well, yes, that's true, but each country has its own Customs. We will need to fill out some forms and then we pass through the Customs gates just like in Hyderabad but on the other side, we are officially in America. And the best part is that on the other side of Customs there will be two very excited people waiting for us. Are you ready?"

There was a massive crush on the other side. JFK was one of the busiest airports in the world, and it would seem that half the world's population had crammed into and around the concourse. "Just stay close. We will find Chad and Lois somehow."

Naggya did indeed stay close, and as they searched through the crowd, Naggya said to Elijah, "I thought it would be cold but it's not."

"Air conditioning, my friend. Just wait until we get outside." In his entire life, Naggya had never experienced cold weather, and as he searched through the crush, he suddenly spotted a pair of familiar faces, arms waving, and weaving their way toward them. Instinctively, he yelled out loudly, "Mummy! Daddy!" as two nearby passengers observed with amused expressions.

The embraces were long and loving. As one round of hugs released, another commenced; tears were shed and tissues exchanged until Chad lamented, "Well, unfortunately New York hasn't turned on a beautiful morning for you. This fog isn't expected to lift for a couple of hours so I'm afraid you won't see too much of our fine city."

Noticing Naggya trying to suppress a yawn, Elijah again placed an arm around his shoulder and said, "Actually, I think a few hours' sleep might help."

Naggya protested, "I'm fine, honestly, sir, Elijah," and for different reasons, all three adults laughed.

Chad gestured toward the exit and as the four worked their way through the crowd, he handed Naggya a large coat and a pair of fur-lined gloves. "We are parked in the car park and it's freezing out there."

Naggya shot Chad a confused expression, however, he

hung the winter clothing over his suitcase while the others watched and chuckled. As they walked toward the exit and Naggya soaked up all that was unfolding around him, Elijah whispered the relevance of the "Sir Elijah" comment to Lois and Chad as a second wave of chuckles were exchanged.

Chad pointed ahead, "Out through those doors, Naggya," and as the giant doors slid open a wall of cold air hit them. Naggya suddenly stopped and stood rooted to the spot. "Might be a good time to put these on." Chad grabbed the coat and gloves and tossed them to Naggya.

The commute from JFK via Grand Central Parkway to Central Harlem should have taken forty minutes, but in the peak hour crawl and the thick fog, it was another hour before the apartment door was unlocked. By now, Naggya was barely attempting to conceal his yawns despite his excitement, and after half an hour of catch-up time, Chad led him into the spare bedroom. Within ten minutes, Naggya was already asleep.

CHAPTER
thirty-eight

After ten hours, Elijah gently opened the door to check on Naggya and two hours later, he did the same. Naggya rolled over in bed and looked out the window at the symphony of lights as a puzzled expression washed over him. Elijah chuckled, "You've been asleep for twelve hours."

Naggya stretched as he stood and walked slowly out into the loungeroom where Lois and Chad were waiting. "Well, how was your first day in New York?" asked Chad as he grinned, then invited Naggya to join them at the table.

"We have an exciting day for you tomorrow, son. Do you think you'll be up for it?" asked Lois as she wrapped her arms around his shoulders and kissed him on the top of his head. "We can't begin to tell you how blessed we are that you're finally here. Would you like something to eat?" and without waiting for a reply, added, "Of course you would, you haven't eaten since the plane. How about some eggs on toast?"

The four chatted for another two hours then retired for the night, however, Naggya was last to settle. He stood at the window and tried to get his head around the fact that after spending thirty hours inside a metal tube, he was now on the opposite side of the world staring out upon one of the most famous cities on the planet; a place that was known as "the city that never sleeps," and sardonically he smiled at the irony.

❖❖❖❖❖

After breakfast, Naggya and Elijah were driven across town to meet Kate at the Crossover head office, and after an hour they drove the short distance to see DAPA in all its unfolding glory. By now, DAPA was almost at full capacity with twenty-five teenagers from across the globe already installed in the program. Naggya's eyes bulged as, one after another, he was introduced to young and gifted performers whose passion and determination shone through as brightly as his own. Naggya shook hands, exchanged hugs and kisses on the cheeks from kids from Somalia, Ethiopia, Chad, Botswana, Tanzania, South Sudan, Bangladesh, Honduras, Mexico, Haiti, and The Philippines. The first youngsters from India and Zimbabwe were due to arrive within a week. "So, Naggya, do you think you might like to spend some time here?" asked Kate, as she took him on a guided tour of the remainder of DAPA.

The grin upon his face spoke far more than words, yet still concealed the fact that Naggya was about as far from his comfort zone as he'd been since arriving at Son-Shine ten years prior. After being shown around the facility, Kate stopped and looked into his engaging eyes. "I know it's a lot to take in, Naggya, but every person who now calls DAPA home has been in your shoes and felt what you are feeling right now. It hasn't stopped astounding me how quickly we have become a family, and with Chad and Lois here alongside you, you will soon be part of us too, OK?" Kate pointed out the window,

"Naggya, there is an amazing world of opportunity out there, and our goal is to help you to conquer and to shine."

Chelsea Markets was another twenty-minute drive, and two hours into their shopping expedition, Naggya and Elijah were decked-out in new and winter-appropriate clothing. Naggya couldn't stop smiling; he'd politely protested after the first couple of purchases, but after Lois had exclaimed, "I haven't had so much fun in months," he quit resisting and tried on another two pairs of jeans. "Son, you can leave your winter clothes in New York with us. Somehow, I don't think you'll be needing them at Son-Shine. Oh look, this jacket will be so good on you. Or maybe this one. Try them both."

Yesterday's fog hadn't returned, so after a trolley-load of new clothing had been crammed into the back of Chad's SUV, they climbed aboard for a guided tour of the famous city. Up and down Manhattan, along Madison and Park Avenues, past Time Square and over the Brooklyn Bridge and back, the history and highlights of New York's Manhattan Island were rolled out to an enthralled first-time visitor. "When we get a sunny day, we'll go up to the top of the Empire State Building. The view of the city and across to the Statue of Liberty is quite stunning," declared Chad. "We took you up last time you were here, Elijah, remember?"

"How can I ever forget?" Elijah was keeping a close eye on Naggya and smiled as a bitterly cold blast of wind forced the young man to grit his teeth and turn his face away. "I'm just so glad it doesn't get cold here," declared Elijah, and he laughed as they both recalled Naggya's comment at the airport. "It might take a bit of getting used to, Naggya, but can you imagine what it's like when it snows?"

❖❖❖❖❖

Lois had scheduled two meetings for the following afternoon with a couple of New York's lower-profile ballet producers. Her strategy was to give Naggya two practice auditions with these lesser lights in order to better prepare him for the big guns later in the week. The plan also involved giving Naggya an insight into the performing arts culture in the Big Apple by an hour-long back-stage tour of the Metropolitan Opera House and The Apollo, the first scheduled for 9:00 in the morning.

Throughout the day, Chad and Lois waited for the right moment to broach the next subject, and while Naggya was washing down his first-ever New York hotdog with his first-ever New York milkshake in a quintessential New York diner, Chad winked at his wife then attracted Naggya's attention. "Son, today has been so special and it is such a blessing to finally have you here in New York. It is fair to say that tomorrow will be very different, a day we have all waited so long for, and now your big day is almost here. We can only imagine how you're feeling, but we believe with all our hearts that you are ready and that God has prepared you for what is ahead. Lois and I want you to know that whatever the outcome tomorrow and the days beyond bring, our love for you will always remain. Nothing can ever, or will ever, change that. We hope you know that you have always been our special son, and our love for you has grown beyond words ever since we first met you a decade ago, remember? We know God has made this way for you and that He will finish what He has started, OK?" As Chad was speaking, Naggya's expression began to shift; initially his face reflected a sense of surprise at Chad's sudden change of tone, but as the reality of his Mummy and Daddy's love and unconditional support began to sink further into his consciousness, his face started to quiver, his lips began to tremble, and he was awash with a flood of emotion. Naggya bowed his head and as the tears began to flow, he glanced around the packed diner as a sense of vulnerability and unexpected exposure tried to take hold. Lois handed him a tissue and as discreetly as he could, he wiped away his tears and lifted his gaze. His lips still quivered and his eyes glistened as Lois reached across the booth and instinctively interlocked her fingers with his.

"We know you are ready, son, and now that you are finally here, we just wanted to ask how you are feeling?"

Naggya sat in silence as he looked from one to the other and searched for the right words. Several times he glanced away and when his eyes again rested on his adopted parents, his faltering voice softly declared, "Mummy Lois, Daddy Chad, I'm scared." Naggya's fingers trembled within Lois's grip and his eyelids blinked away a fresh flood of tears, "But, I think it's OK to be scared. I've been praying and, and I think being scared tells me how important this is for me and for my people." Lois placed her other hand on top of his as Elijah slipped an arm around Naggya's shoulder. "Maybe I will always be scared, but being scared won't stop me."

Every eye within that busy diner turned upon their booth as three adults stood as one to lavish their love, their hopes, and their affections upon a young man who was ready to grasp his destiny; this was his time, his time to use what he'd been given for a cause beyond his own. Naggya lowered his head and began to weep for such a time as this.

CHAPTER
thirty-nine

The four were ushered into the Lincoln Center in Lincoln Square by the head of security, a man known to Chad and Lois following a string of performances in which Impressions Costumes had featured prominently. After introductions, he escorted them around the complex, informing Naggya that The Lincoln Center had been founded by John D. Rockefeller and opened back in 1969. For Naggya to be standing in a complex of this size with its iconic reputation was as intimidating as it was inspiring. Half an hour into the tour, Naggya wandered off to hover all alone in the wings, an image forming in his mind of nervous performers waiting for their cues to dance onto the stage in front of hundreds of enthralled ballet connoisseurs. Naggya's mind swam as the image gradually crystallized to reveal himself among them. His hands trembled.

❖❖❖❖❖

Baryshnikov Arts Center on West 37th St. was opened by Mikhail Baryshnikov in 2005. The contrast between this place and the Lincoln Centre was so vast, so evocative, that Naggya found himself tossing the two conflicting images around and around in his head. At the conclusion of the second tour, Naggya had slipped once again into his own private world.

He'd immersed his thoughts in a wildly fertile imagination so essential for any performing artist. Lost in that world, he'd almost resented the intrusions of those around him.

❖❖❖❖❖

"Naggya, our next appointment is at 1:30 and it's a twenty-minute drive. Do you feel like having an early lunch?"

Out in the cold, fresh air of a typical New York January day, Naggya was still withdrawn. He'd not spoken more than a few words during the previous hour, and his complexion had turned noticeably ashen. In the passing hours he'd become increasingly aware that very soon his individual ballet talents would be put under the microscope. Dancing in a troupe in his own country, even under the critical gaze of higher caste judges, was one thing, yet soon his capacity to stand alone and convince a ballet choreographer that he was worth a risk, began to weigh heavily.

Performance, pride, passion, and purpose: all suddenly on the line.

Elijah stepped a little closer and reached out to him, "We're right here with you, Naggya. You're never alone, OK?"

Naggya slowly shrugged and half turned to look at his long-time mentor, "I'll be fine, Elijah," and the tiniest of smiles appeared at the corner of his mouth at the realization he'd just deliberately called him by name; it felt good for the very first time. "I just need to gather my thoughts."

During the drive to The Kirkoff School of Dance, Naggya remained deep inside his own cocoon. The others were content to let Naggya walk this part of his journey all alone with his God. He prayed in his spiritual language all the way from the car to the reception area where Lois and Chad had arranged to meet Dominic Kirkoff, one of the new breed of creative choreographers making a name for himself among the bright lights of the city's best. Chad and Lois had specifically selected Dominic to be audition number one. Despite being in town for five years, Dominic was still regarded as a New York newcomer, his growing reputation for unearthing young talent considered a wise place for Naggya to begin.

He slung his kit bag over his shoulder and waited in the background as Chad, Lois, and Dominic exchanged greetings.

"And I take it, this is the young man you've been telling me about?" and he politely brushed past Chad and Lois and extended his hand to Naggya. "Young man, it's not so long ago I was the brand new boy on the block, so I know how you feel. Actually, I am quite normal when you get to know me. Would you like to bring your gear inside and we can talk?" Naggya mustered his faintest smile and after shaking Dominic's hand, he again slung his bag over his shoulder and tentatively followed Dominic inside. A couple of minutes later, Dominic emerged and beckoned Chad, Lois, and Elijah into the viewing area and invited them to sit. "Would you like some coffee?" an offer politely declined. "Naggya has a fine physique for my brand of dance, and the fact that he is obviously handsome helps. If he's as good as you've mentioned, he will do well here. I've asked him to start with a selection of dances using his own music. We'll see how he goes, and if all is well, I will throw him a challenge and see how he responds."

Following his warm-up and stretch, Naggya appeared to settle, and when he indicated that he was ready, the music was cued and he launched into a routine that he'd performed hundreds of times. Dominic's facial expression scarcely changed as he paced slowly back and forth to assess and view from different angles. Naggya was conscious of Dominic's movements but was equally conscious of his need to remain focused. Mid-performance, Dominic strode onto the floor and paused the music, "Naggya, you are doing well, despite your nerves, but I want you to try something different for me. When you do your final leap, I want you to not hold back. I want you to find an extra foot in height and I want you to extend your leading arm so that it remains perfectly straight. I don't want to see your arm bend at all, and I want you to keep your head up and proud, and your eyes must be fixed straight ahead, OK?"

Naggya re-ran the instructions in his mind then nodded. Dominic reset the music then gestured for Naggya to resume. At the critical moment, Naggya leapt higher and further than he had ever done before and as he landed, he did so with a grace and an elegance that triggered Dominic's slow yet deliberate hand-clap. Once again, Dominic walked onto the floor and raised a hand to interrupt, "Did you know you could leap that high?" The smile on Naggya's face indicated otherwise. "OK, young man, you have done particularly well, with your own music, but a true artist can perform even when he's put on the spot. From his pocket he retrieved a piece of his own music and loaded it into the sound system. "I'm going to play this two-minute piece through for you once, and then I will give you another two minutes to decide how you will dance it, OK? Just remember this, we're not looking for robots, so if you get this right, you're a long way to becoming a candidate for the Academy, but if you don't . . . " and he paused, "Just do your best, OK?"

❖❖❖❖❖

Back in the car, Naggya was still visibly shaken despite all the encouragement and reassurance from three of his biggest fans. Dominic had been suitably impressed and had instructed his office manager to furnish Chad and Lois with all the necessary enrollment forms. No sooner had Naggya wrapped-up his audition than another young hopeful was being invited into the warm-up area.

❖❖❖❖❖

At 3:00 p.m., the four entered the second-floor studio of The New York Contemporary Dance Academy, an impressive blend of the old and the new in 21st Century ballet. Like Dominic, David J. Zscech was also an emerging contender among New York's elite masters. Although he'd arrived on the local scene quite late, four successful seasons at the Lincoln had seen his brand name and his status reach dizzying heights. Chad and Lois had concluded that a change of personality after Dominic might help Naggya adapt to the constantly changing demands of the industry. Despite being considered slightly eccentric, David was deemed a man who could not only bring the best out in Naggya but potentially launch him onto the very grandest of stages.

From the outset, David appeared to be employing a similar assessment process as Dominic, and while Naggya worked his way through the thirty-minute evaluation, he was noticeably relaxing.

"I want to see your grace, Naggya, and I long to see the very depths of your soul. We are born to express what is within. We are the purveyors of passion, we are the deliverers of drama, and we are the laureates of love! Now, show me your spirit!"

Far from intimidated by the demands of this stranger, Naggya visibly lifted throughout the trial. As though David was uncorking a dimension that had been screaming for release, Naggya finished his piece with a radiance that reached every eye and a fury that tore at every heart. Breathless, he crouched on the floor, stunned, as the choreographer walked silently to his side and touched him briefly, gently, respectfully. Frozen for but a moment, David uttered one single whispered word, "Bravo."

Naggya uncoiled himself and stood to his feet. Slowly, he left the floor and disappeared behind the closed door to change into his winter clothing, emerging moments later with a glazed expression still etched upon his face. David, Chad, Lois, and Elijah turned from their huddle and watched the young man approach. David broke the silence, "Naggya, I need to ask you a question. It's a simple question, yet in truth, it isn't. I need to ask you: what do you want?"

Thoughtfully, Naggya lowered his kit bag to the floor as hesitation rolled vexingly through his mind. He'd asked himself the same question countless times yet never had he been required to voice his answer to anyone but Rambabu. David could see his anguish and recognized his pain. There was a dimension evident in this young man that, in David's world, separated a performer from a genuine artist. "It's a difficult thing I ask, but the answer is within you, of that I am sure. Your dance speaks loudly, but I want to hear your answer in words. Please don't be frightened to speak big dreams, for I will applaud you if you do. Please."

Naggya shifted awkwardly from one leg to the other. He drew heavily from the depths of his chest as he summoned the courage to speak, "I—I know I have been given a gift—and I know it is to bless others—my gift is not for me, but for my people. I don't really know much more, but Daddy Chad had a vision that I would dance before kings and queens, and that's what I want, not for me, but for my people who suffer and die, and—"

David reached forward and embraced Naggya, "Then, my young friend, this day you have shown me your heart, and from that heart, I also believe your vision. Chad and Lois have told me you will be auditioning with several other academies, but I want you to know that should you decide to join mine, I will move heaven and earth to see your vision fulfilled," and he hugged Naggya tightly then turned and walked away.

CHAPTER
forty

Next morning, a wintery sun poked through the clouds and, although Lois and Chad needed to be at their factory later in the day, they seized the opportunity to take Naggya and Elijah to the top of The Empire State Building, then on to Times Square and later to Madison Square Garden. As they fought their way from place to place amid the unrelenting chaos of the New York traffic, Naggya privately tried to reconcile the parallels and the differences between New York and Hyderabad. In their own unique ways, both cities were unrecognizable from life at Son-Shine, and the notion of why so many people had chosen to share such confined spaces remained a puzzle that kept his mind in a spin.

Chad and Lois dropped their visitors outside Crossover and arranged to pick them up after work. "We should be back by about 6 p.m. We can eat at one of our favorite restaurants a couple of blocks from home, OK? I just called and Kate is expecting you upstairs. See you later," and Chad accelerated from the curb into traffic to the sound of blaring car horns.

Elijah and Naggya spent the next three hours getting to know the other students, the members of staff on duty, and some more specifics of how the place functioned. The English-speaking students talked openly about their attempts to find work and how the staff had assisted them to settle, and the public transport challenges each faced commuting to and from their respective studies. Some of the students also spoke of their aspirations for the future and the reasons why they believed coming to New York would further their dreams. This was a time for Naggya to be soaking up the experiences of others as he attempted to rationalize their dreams and experiences to those of his own.

Elijah surreptitiously glanced in Naggya's direction in an attempt to gauge how he was coping with the flood of information. For as long as Elijah was there as back up, Naggya's need to recall every little detail wasn't critical. However, on his return in six months, he'd be flying solo, and in a big bustling city, that might be daunting.

Elijah was encouraged by the manner in which Naggya was willing to lay aside his natural shyness in order to learn from others. Every student had a tragic story to tell, a story that only made the whole transition from native war zones to the war zone known as the Big Apple all the more confounding.

By the time Chad and Lois arrived to take them out for dinner, Elijah was struggling to get Naggya to leave. Already, he had begun the process of grafting himself into the life and times of this new and vibrant way of life. Chad winked at Naggya and asked, "Would you prefer to stay the night, son?"

A smile crossed his lips before Naggya respectfully declined.

❖❖❖❖❖

"Good morning, son. Did you sleep well?" Chad drew back

the curtains to allow the weakest of morning light to filter into the room.

Naggya stretched and looked to Chad, "Yes, thank you Daddy. It took me a while to get off to sleep but . . . Ah, we have two auditions today?"

"Yes, now breakfast is almost ready so come on out and we'll fill you in on the details. If you'd like a shower first, you'll need to be quick."

After his shower, Naggya smiled broadly as he pondered which of his new clothes he should wear. So recently, he had only one set of clothes plus his school uniform, and now his biggest daily decision was to choose from among the many. "How amazing," he thought as he slipped on a pullover that still had the tags attached.

Lois had scheduled a 10 a.m. audition with Philippe Montans at Montans Majesty Dance Company's new premises. Philippe's decision to remain in New York rather than return to Sweden had necessitated downsizing his facilities until he'd recovered from the Lincoln Centre setback. Philippe had become fiercely determined to ride out the storm and to fight to forge his name. Time would tell if the fickle following of the elite ballet fraternity would welcome him back or churn him out as yet the latest in a long line of failed ballet masters.

Chad and Lois genuinely liked Philippe and wanted him to succeed. They saw his determination to claw his way back was admirable. His quite radical choreography and being younger than many of his peers might be a bonus for Naggya during his settling into a whole new way of life.

Just before 10 a.m., the four entered the modest premises and called out from the front room. In his former premises, a receptionist or a budding dancer looking to make some extra dollars would have greeted them; however, on this occasion, no one. Chad and Lois looked at each other puzzled. The rear door opened and Philippe walked in holding a cup of coffee and a croissant. "Good morning, folks, sorry to leave you on your own. Please, come on through."

Several times Chad and Lois sent each other quizzical glances but smiled politely at Philippe as he directed them towards some plastic chairs adjacent to a small dance floor.

"Now, this must be your protégé?" and he looked toward Naggya and smiled as he offered his hand. Naggya had picked up on Chad and Lois's awkwardness but accepted Philippe's handshake, and then placed his kit bag on one of the chairs. "This place is a little spartan, yes, but it's only temporary until we settle on a new season. It's certainly nothing grand, but, you know, it is a new start." Philippe invited them to sit and turned to Naggya, "Chad and Lois are big fans of yours and they are very fine people, so you're certainly in good hands," and he looked to Elijah who smiled in return and shook his hand. "And this is?"

"Sorry, Philippe, this is our amazing friend, Elijah. We've known Elijah for over ten years and he's the founder of the school and the orphanage Naggya is from. Remember, we told you about him? Elijah has accompanied Naggya as we look to find the best way forward for him."

Philippe and Elijah exchanged smiling glances until Philippe again spoke, "That must be some story, Elijah, to start an orphanage like you've done? Does your government pay you to do that?"

All eyes turned on Philippe as though he'd asked the most uninformed yet innocent of questions. "Actually, no," replied Elijah. "We get no government support. Everything we do, we do by faith."

"By faith? What do you mean? Does a church support you?"

Again, Elijah used the same words to reply, "Actually, no."

Five people in that room suddenly felt uncomfortable. Normally Elijah wouldn't miss a chance to speak of the goodness and the provision of his God, but pursuing the subject could easily have taken the focus from this morning's purpose. "Perhaps I could explain later? I don't want to keep you from your time with our . . . " and he nodded toward Naggya.

"Of course, of course. Naggya, please tell me, what style of ballet do you prefer?"

Naggya shifted his weight and looked uneasily at each of the others, "Style?"

Rather than trying to clarify his question, Philippe simply grinned and nodded, "So, you just like to dance? You like to feel? Is that what you're saying?"

Naggya looked deeply into this man's eyes and returned his nod with an innocent, "Yes."

"Perfect. I detest labels. Now, if you'd like to follow me, you can get changed and we'll get you doing what you love best. Is that OK?"

Several minutes later, Naggya returned and approached Philippe to hand him his music. "Ah, my good young man, your music isn't in your hand. Your music is in your heart," and he tapped his chest and smiled a long and knowing smile that reached deeply into Naggya in a way few would understand. "Just go where your heart leads. Take your time. Dance is art, and art is an unfolding mystery that you carry deep within to touch and to inspire. Please," and he gestured toward the dance floor, "When you are ready."

Naggya fought back tears as he recognized the knowing in this master; a knowing that he'd longed for; a knowing that failed to be translated; a knowing that intrinsically spelled *home*.

Stretching to his full height, Naggya froze in anticipation of a prompting; a prompting that he knew was about to be poured out as a type of drink offering. Chad, Lois, and Elijah looked on uncomfortably as if Naggya had lost his way, but Philippe gazed in amazement that one so young could be so unmoved by the silence and the still. The countenance upon the young man's face didn't shift, his piercing eyes lit the humble stage, and as though the deepest of art was being set free, his body began to grace the floor with a joy, a fluency, and a melody that transported the giver and the receiver in equal, unspeakable measure. Time and again, Naggya floated around that floor, he leapt and he landed and he flew as though gravity had ceased to be, and his heart had grown the most graceful of wings. Naggya had gone to the third Heaven and would remain there forever had it not been for the applause and the adoration of the master who'd willingly become the student.

Philippe had so little to offer, and yet, so much. The five gathered at the entrance to the humble Montans Majesty Dance Company, and as he embraced Naggya for perhaps the final time, whispered, "Think long and hard before deciding, my friend. All that glitters—you know?"

CHAPTER
forty-one

"Three down and one to go, Naggya. How are you feeling?" asked Lois as they pulled up outside BABC.

There was a growing emptiness in his expression and the young man was beginning to show the signs of pressure. Almost with each passing hour he was speaking less and frowning more. "I'm OK, I guess. I didn't think it would be this hard but—"

Galant Scott had taken a fair degree of persuading to audition Naggya. His ego was as jam-packed as his appointment book, and if an upside couldn't be immediately seen, the matter would be summarily terminated.

"I'll park the car and meet you inside, OK?" Chad could also see the weight of burden upon their adopted son. He and his wife had discussed canceling the final audition, but the ramifications of offending arguably New York's biggest ballet producer at short notice wasn't something they cared to risk.

BABC's entrance and reception area was worlds away from that of Philippe's. The back wall was impressively adorned with a splash of posters from their most recent seasons and, of course, Galant featured front-and-center.

"Sorry, but Mr. Scott is running a little behind schedule. Would you care to take a seat?" asked the pretty lady from behind her desk.

Chad arrived a little out of breath, "I had to park two blocks away. Have I missed anything?"

"Running late," whispered Lois.

Thirty minutes after the appointed time, Galant had yet to appear, and his receptionist hadn't said a word. Just on forty-five minutes late, a young dancer in tights walked into the room and beckoned them to follow, "Mr. Scott will see you now. This way."

A tall young male dancer appeared to be in deep discussion with Galant just off stage. Galant acknowledged Chad and Lois and gave Naggya and Elijah a quick once-over as he wound up his discussion and walked towards them. "Sorry, it's always bedlam around here. The price of success, I suppose. How have you both been?" and he first hugged Lois and then Chad. "How are the new costumes coming along?"

Lois smiled and assured Galant that the work was on schedule, and turned to introduce Naggya. Galant gave him another once-over, only this time his gaze lingered a fraction longer. "Well, young man, you've come a long way to see me, haven't you?" and without waiting for a reply, he added, "Yes, tall enough, I suppose. A bit skinny but we can take care of that, that's if we decide to take him on. How old is he?" and he turned his focus to Chad.

Chad motioned toward Naggya then smiled at Galant, "His English is quite extensive, so he's very capable of answering for himself. Naggya?"

"Sir, I will be 16 in July," and straight after speaking, he broke eye contact as the piercing stare of the master bore deep.

"And you want to be a star, I'm told. Well, if anyone can

turn you into a star, it's me. You can get changed backstage. Be back and ready in ten minutes and we'll see what you've got. Do you have music?"

Naggya glanced quickly at Lois as the impertinence of this man began to seep through his defenses. He reached into his kit bag and tried to hand his music to Galant. "Not to me! Give it to my sound man," and he turned and gestured for Chad, Lois, and Elijah to take a seat. "I'll be back soon," and walked toward the backstage area to resume his conversation with the young dancer who'd been waiting on his return.

Having changed into his tights and given his music to the sound technician just off stage, Naggya waited in the wings. He waited another ten minutes until Galant marched to the edge of the dance floor and clapped his hands loudly, "Right, what are you performing for me?"

Stammering that he would be doing a solo from *Giselle*, Naggya waited for Galant to give him further instructions.

"No, too easy. Give me something from *La Bayadere*! Can you do that?"

"Yes, but I don't have the music."

"Then do it without music! Can't you do that? Quickly, young man, time is money." Galant folded his arms and assumed an aggressive stance.

Naggya raced through his routine in his mind then walked to the center of the stage. "Why are you starting in the center?" barked Galant. "You wouldn't start there in a performance so why do it now?" Naggya retraced his steps and began from the edge of the wings. He completed three impressive spins and two leaps before turning to do a series of alternating lead-leg leaps across stage and was about to continue in the opposite direction when he fleetingly lost balance and almost toppled to the floor. "Stop, stop, stop! What on earth are you doing?" Galant stormed onto the dance floor and marched up to Naggya, "Look, young man, there is no room in my academy for dancers who cannot handle a bit of pressure. Do you understand?!"

This latest act of aggression caught Naggya off guard and he didn't respond.

"I said, do you understand?!"

After receiving a brief nod, Galant uttered an obscenity before informing Naggya, "Now, I have things to do. I am going backstage. I will return in ten minutes. If you ever hope to join my troupe of dancers, you'd best be getting your routine together before I return!" and he turned his back on Naggya and stomped off stage.

Visibly shaken, Naggya wrestled with what to do. He fleetingly looked to his supporters who urged him to keep going. Naggya knew he needed to revisit the place he'd been earlier in the day. He crouched low to summon his resolve to block out the rudeness, just as he had done so many times in India when a higher caste person had spat on him or threatened violence. Stretching tall, he reentered his most beautiful of places and left the natural world far behind. Within seconds, Naggya was once again flying; his grace and beauty had returned, and his glorious wings lifted him higher, longer; leaps became flights and his spins turned into orbits. Time after time he graced that stage with the unending elements of exquisite fluency and the most perfect of timing.

Lois, Chad, and Elijah were once again transported into another realm; one without sound; a dimension that lacked limits, and a joy that only the keenest of eye could attest. Naggya flew for several minutes yet would have remained for hours, had it not been for a subdued Galant Scott reentering the stage with both hands raised and mouth hanging open. "That is not *La Bayadere!*" Returning to planet Earth, Naggya panted and waited motionless before the master choreographer. "That is nothing like *La Bayadere!*"

Hanging his head low, he refused to look at Galant. Naggya would not be robbed, even by a man considered the best.

"Young man, I told you that I was going backstage, but I didn't. I stood in the wings and I watched what you would do. I needed to know if you would follow instructions. I needed to know if indeed you *could* follow instructions, and you didn't. In fact, you didn't even try, which is a massive problem for me as a teacher. Do you hear what I am saying to you?"

Softly, his answer came, "Yes, sir. Sorry, sir."

"What you gave me wasn't *La Bayadere*! What you gave me was nothing like *La Bayadere*! What you gave me was far, far better," and he moved closer and whispered, "Thank you. The truth is, I don't see your giftedness very often, and just now you took me to a place few others can. I tricked you into thinking I wasn't watching, but I did. I watched very, very closely and what you showed me was—was indeed priceless. Your gift is not of this world." Suddenly and without warning, Galant took a step backward as the businessman within him was restored to prominence. "Should I choose to bring you into my academy, I will channel and refine that gift, and, in

241

time, I will place that gift on the world's biggest stages. Under my guidance, you will become a star," and his face slowly contorted, "What is your name again?"

"Naggya, sir, my name is Naggya."

The other young dancer had been standing in the wings; he turned and hurried away.

Backstage, Naggya's heart was still pounding. One of the world's leading authorities in modern ballet had just paid him the highest compliment, and yet, his bizarre methods troubled the young man deeply. As he reentered the change room, he wrestled with his thoughts until someone entered the room behind him. As Naggya slipped off his tights, the lead dancer Galant had been speaking with earlier walked up to Naggya and stopped within inches of his face. The tall, athletic dancer glared into his eyes and took hold of Naggya's hands. He leaned in close and rubbed his fingertips provocatively up and down Naggya's inner thigh, feigned a kiss, then pulled back to stare again into Naggya's eyes before seductively whispering, "Pretty Indian flower, just waiting to be plucked."

CHAPTER
forty-two

"That was a very long sleep, son. Are you OK?"

Taking his place at the breakfast table, Naggya tried to camouflage his torment. He tried to smile and to reassure the three people who had given and risked so much that he was OK.

"We thought you'd be relieved to now have your four auditions behind you."

"I am. I guess I am, just a bit—"

"Drained?" asked Lois. "Yes, I can well imagine you would be. Hungry?"

Pushing his bacon and eggs around his plate hardly convinced the watching trio that his struggle was one of fatigue. The physical and emotional lift that was anticipated from the successful completion of four highly pressurized assessments, now seemed a million miles away. The three exchanged furtive glances as Elijah gently pushed his chair away from the table and looked at his young charge, "Naggya, if you're worried about which academy to choose, please talk to us. We watched the pressure on you build over the past few days and we can only begin to imagine how you must be feeling. We are so very proud of you, please know that there is nothing more you could have done. You have been extraordinary through this whole examination, and we are confident all four will be lining up to invite you into their programs, so—"

He pushed his plate away and lowered his gaze, deeply troubled. So many questions were spinning around inside his head, and last night all he'd wanted to do was sleep, but he couldn't; he just couldn't.

How could he risk telling Chad and Lois what had happened in that change room? How could he jeopardize their biggest customer? Naggya had lay awake most of the night, a night when his spirits should have been soaring, yet instead, his heart was breaking. Over and over, he'd thought through all the possible scenarios, and every time he would arrive at a conclusion, a haunting complication would jump into his thinking to shatter the plan, and he'd have to start all over again. *Who can I tell? Certainly not Daddy Chad or Mummy Lois. I could tell Elijah. Elijah would understand, but how could we be alone long enough to explain without suspicion? And what could Elijah do if he knew? He'd be in exactly the same predicament.* He'd considered telling Kate, but apart from being supportive, what could she possibly do without risking the same collateral damage? Did Galant know? Was his lead dancer propositioning others? Or was he the only one? Was he trying to seduce Naggya, or was he trying to intimidate him so that Naggya wouldn't join the academy and possibly displace him as lead dancer? If Galant knew, did he even care? If he knew, but didn't care, what might that mean to Naggya if he joined his academy? After what happened, could he even contemplate joining his academy? Could he cope with the bullying? And who was that other Galant who appeared for

244

a moment then disappeared behind the ruthless dictator? If Galant offers Naggya a contract but he turns him down, what does that do to Chad and Lois's business? Will accepting, or not accepting, really make any difference, or is Naggya just getting confused? What if he went to a different academy and the same thing happened? Does it happen everywhere in dance academies? Does it happen everywhere in New York? How would he know? Who could he ask? Should he even come to America? Should he stay home in India and not see this dream fulfilled? But then Chad and Lois would want to know why, and he would have to explain. Why did all this have to happen?

Climbing slowly to his feet, Naggya asked, "Ah, what are we doing today?"

Lois glanced at her husband, then to Elijah, "Naggya, we can do whatever you want. Do you have any suggestions?"

His face was ashen as he turned to walk away, "Would it be OK if I stayed in my room this morning? Sorry, I'm feeling a bit tired."

❖❖❖❖❖

When lunch was ready, Chad opened the door gently and peered into Naggya's room. A low rhythmic sound met him as he realized Naggya was sleeping. He eased the door closed and returned to the living room where Lois and Elijah were seated, "He's fast asleep, so, I don't know. What do you think?"

Elijah was the first to speak, "I watched Naggya yesterday when Galant was being so rude, and I could see how much he was hurting from the intimidation. I think he is just struggling with the fear of experiencing more of that if he joined Galant's team. It's the only thing that makes sense, apart from the fact that Naggya has been under so much pressure and now that it's over, he just can't switch off."

Lois slowly nodded in agreement, "Yes, that's pretty much how I see it, as well. He seemed to connect best with Philippe, but Galant can offer him so much more, so maybe that's in his thinking. If he joins Galant, he's almost assured of success, that's if he can somehow cope with the intimidation. And we both know his reputation for that, don't we Chad?"

"Yes, he's famous for it. And yet, he keeps churning out superstars, and we all know that Naggya could easily be his next. At present, Philippe can't offer Naggya anything remotely like that, and as we saw yesterday morning, he's battling to keep the doors open. I mean, what a contrast, right?"

All three fell into their own private contemplations until Chad's cell phone rang in the background. Within the space of sixty minutes, Naggya had been offered entry into David Zscech's New York Contemporary Dance Academy and Dominic Kirkoff's School of Dance. As he ended the second call, Chad turned to the others, "Well, I can only begin to wonder what tomorrow might bring?"

CHAPTER
forty-three

"So, it's official, you're definitely coming back in early July?"

His eyes lit up as Kate wrapped her arms around him and gave him a squeeze. A beaming Kate sat down at her desk and invited Naggya to sit. "All the kids have been asking, every single one of them."

"Really?" Naggya's eyes were now the size of dinner plates and his teeth literally shone at the realization that all the kids, kids who were all older than him, had at least shown enough interest to ask.

"Absolutely for real. There isn't one who hasn't asked me at least once if you've been accepted into an academy. And already you have the choice of two! We are all so very proud, Naggya. Have you decided which one yet, or are you still waiting on the others?"

As though all the air had just been sucked out of his balloon, Naggya's countenance plummeted and as she watched his head drop, Kate stood up and walked around the desk to stand beside him, "What, Naggya? What just happened?"

The emotional roller coaster kicked in and, for the thousandth time, his mind raced through the pros and the cons of whether to speak or remain silent.

"Whatever the issue, Naggya, I'll share two things with you; the first is that anything you say in this room, stays in this room, that is, unless you give me permission to share it, OK?" Naggya wanted to believe what he was hearing, yet his body language convinced Kate he didn't. "And the second is that the three people who have been through this with you, right from the very beginning, are three of the finest people I know," and as Naggya's eyes again dropped, she added, "I mean that, Naggya. I'm blessed with knowing some of the most amazing people in America, but none could be any better. If there is a problem, I would strongly encourage you to speak to them. And because they love you the way they do, they will understand. Naggya, please look at me," and slowly, painfully, Naggya restored eye contact but held it only briefly. "Is there anything, anything at all, that you would like to ask me, or tell me? And while you're thinking, no one is going to walk through that door to interrupt us, so please, take your time." Naggya sat with his face turned down for several minutes but said nothing. Kate climbed to her feet and ran her hand gently over the top of his head, "I'm going to get a coffee and I'll be back soon."

When Kate returned, Naggya waited until she had sat down before he reengaged, "There is something I'd like to tell you, but I can't tell you all of it. It's just too hard. If I tell you the whole thing, there is nothing you can do to fix it. Whatever I decide, people will suffer, and I don't want them to suffer because of me."

Kate's phone rang and before answering, she looked to Naggya. He nodded, and she lifted the receiver and heard Lois's voice. "Yes, he's with me. Yes, he's OK. An hour?" and Kate looked to Naggya, who again nodded. "Yes, Lois, that will be perfect. See you then."

"Kate, if I do something that could be good for me, but it causes problems, big problems, for people who are really important to me, should I do it?"

Kate drew breath, "Wow, what a question. I'm sensing you can't divulge much, but this would have to do with your decision about the academies?"

Naggya didn't need to utter a sound. Kate paused, "I see. OK, let's just play hypotheticals for a moment; let's say that your decision on which academy you select might possibly impact on Lois and Chad, and that makes you feel sad because you don't want them to possibly lose business because of your choice? Might I possibly be on the right track?" Once again, Naggya's silence spoke plenty. "If I was you, and I was thinking the same thing, I'm just wondering if Mummy and Daddy might not have already come to the same conclusion? They are both very intelligent people, Naggya, and I'd be very surprised if they hadn't already considered this possibility. Ah, would you mind if we talked it through with them?"

Getting closer to the crux of the problem caused Naggya to squirm in his chair. He rubbed the back of his neck and looked out the window, "I just want to dance. I didn't think it would be so hard to please everyone."

Kate smiled and leaned back in her chair, "Oh, I see. Actually, Naggya, trying to please everyone is a dangerous road to travel. If you make the right decision for the right reason, then that's all you can do. And trying to please everyone will never bring you peace. Naggya, would it be OK if you and I and Lois have a talk?"

His eyes blinked hard as he waited to reply, "It's not that easy."

"Have I missed something? Is there more to this problem?"

Tears filled Naggya's eyes and slowly, painfully, his head moved up and down and his fists clenched hard upon the chair.

Kate again stood to her feet. She wrapped her arms around him as he began to sob. Ten minutes later, neither had moved.

❖❖❖❖❖

"Great news! I've just signed to do a season at Saratoga starting at the end of May."

"Really? That sounds promising, Philippe. So, you've decided against returning to Sweden?" asked Chad.

"For the time being. We'll be doing four weeks, possibly five, and I'm really excited about bringing *Cinderella* back to life. Chad, out there at Saratoga can be the perfect blend, and if I get this right, it brings The Lincoln back into reckoning for later in the year. Chad, I'm feeling really good about this, and if you're willing to stay patient, just for a little longer, we can be all squared away on what I owe you, hopefully by June. Is that OK by you?"

"Naturally, I will need to speak to Lois, but yes, I think that might work for us. What will you need for *Cinderella*?"

"Ah, Chad, now there's the question. I've chosen *Cinderella* partly because, as you may recall, we did a season not too long ago and some of the costumes we can reuse. And if I may be so bold, might my slate extend to this new season? I mean, in for a penny? I can send you a copy of the contract if that helps?"

Chad paused before responding, "Ah, as I say, I will need to confer with Lois. Can I get back to you?"

"Of course, of course. Oh, and the other thing I would like to say to you is that, your young man, Naggya, is such a talent. I see true star quality in him. Tell me again, when is he returning to New York?"

"July. At his stage, he will be returning to New York in July as soon as he turns 16, provided, of course, that he has settled on an academy by then."

Philippe fairly bristled through the phone, "Chad, I would love to mentor Naggya. I know you are shopping him around, and I know that other academies might seem to have more to offer right now, but truly, Chad, truly, he will do well with me. With what is ahead for me now, this young man will have a place to shine. Some academies churn through dancers like a sausage machine, but as you know only too well—"

"Ah, sorry, Philippe, actually Lois has just popped into the office, and we need to go to Crossover and fetch Naggya. Lois and I will talk over what we've discussed and get back to you later, OK?"

❖❖❖❖❖

Following another day of Naggya bottling his feelings, it was felt Elijah should be the one to try and crack the cone of silence. Although a decision on which academy to choose was not imperative before returning home, it was preferable. Effectively, he had three definite options, although Galant Scott was still to declare his hand. With just under a week remaining, all Naggya outwardly appeared interested in was familiarizing himself with Crossroads and the day-to-day practicalities of living in New York. As these things became clearer, Elijah seized the opportunity to spend the day helping Naggya to find his way around the city using public transport. The subway was an experience unlike anything Naggya had encountered, and the first time he went underground to board a train, the color drained from his face.

"Now, when you become a student here, you will be issued a special pass that makes travel on the subway cheaper, but for now, we pay full price. Here's some money, so how about you work out how much it will cost for us to get to Chinatown, then buy the tickets and work out how to get there?"

Naggya's countenance lifted with the challenge but Elijah was convinced that, for this troubled young man, any distraction would be appealing.

Returning with two tickets, there was a hint of satisfaction on his face for the first time in days. "OK, show us the way." Twenty-five minutes later, they were walking up the stairs onto street level near Chinatown, "Wow, this place is so busy," he declared as his head seemed to be on a swivel. "And the smells; it's a bit like Vijayawada," then as he reconsidered his comment, he added, "Actually, no, it isn't at all," and he smiled at Elijah and peered into the front of a restaurant.

"Are you hungry?"

"I wasn't, but I am now," and he chuckled and walked to the next one.

"OK, you pick one and we'll have an early lunch, but straight after, your next challenge is to find your way to Wall Street. We can invest a few thousand dollars in shares, OK?"

Once more, Naggya chuckled at the absurdity of having a few thousand dollars, let alone to be investing in shares.

"So now you can choose what we eat, order it, and pay, got it?"

"Ah, what about the money?" and he looked at Elijah and again smiled, "I almost called you 'sir.'"

"Never mind, it's good practice for when we get home."

The word "home" appeared to catch Naggya by surprise, and he again fell silent. *So, where will my home be after all this?*

The food was delicious and after three servings Naggya shook his head at the offer of more. When the waitress had gone to make up the bill, Naggya declared, "Glad I don't have to dance after all that food. I wouldn't be able to get off the ground."

Sensing now might be a good time to broach the subject, Elijah leaned slightly forward and looked into Naggya's dark eyes, "You seem to be struggling with your decision. Would you like to talk?"

Kate's identical question jumped into his thoughts and he realized he couldn't keep dodging the issue. Those that mattered had a right to know, at least some of the issues.

He leaned forward and whispered, "I know I need to talk about this, but I really don't know what to do." Elijah remained silent but encouraged his young charge to continue. "If it was just a choice of which academy to pick, it wouldn't be so difficult, but—"

Elijah waited, then to prompt Naggya, he simply added, "But?"

"But it's become more than just picking, and I don't know if I can talk about it without causing problems."

"And what might those problems be?"

This was the bit that every time he practiced it in his head, always came out wrong. "The problems that—that will come to Mummy and Daddy after I've made my choice."

"But you can only choose one academy, so there must be losers. Ever since Lois and Chad decided to arrange more than one audition, they've known there would be consequences."

"I know!" Naggya raised his voice but immediately lowered it and apologized, "Sorry, I know, but that's not the problem."

"Then what is?"

Naggya looked around the room before he was willing to speak, "Something happened."

The waitress returned and held the bill out in front of her, "Who do I give this to?"

Elijah almost snatched the bill from her hand then sent the young lady an apologetic glance and mouthed the word "sorry" as she was walking away, "What happened, Naggya?"

"If I tell you, you will want to tell Mummy and Daddy, and if they know, then it becomes impossible."

"Naggya, clearly this is painful to talk about, but I can't help you if I don't understand."

"You can't help. That's the problem! No one can."

"But—"

"I don't want to talk about it! Can we go? Please?"

CHAPTER
forty-four

The countdown was well and truly on. With three days to go before the return flight to India, Naggya had yet to make a decision. He'd continued to spend his days at Crossover and had developed a healthy rapport with all the other students and staff, particularly Kate. All of the other twenty-eight students, including a young opera singer from Pastor Karl's Jesus The Rock Church in Hyderabad, had settled into their respective studies in a range of performing arts academies throughout Manhattan and its surrounds. There was a real buzz around Crossover as each new day brought new challenges and new opportunities. Many of the students had scored paid positions, mainly in hospitality, retail, and courier work, despite the fact that they had virtually no knowledge of the local geography. They were simply told, "If you have a smartphone, you can find anything or anyone. Just do the work and you'll get paid."

This was a rich and exciting time for all the kids, and the camaraderie and trust that was building within the group seemed to fill Naggya with a sense of belonging and of much-needed confidence. Kate watched from a distance as each teenager embraced their new challenges and she'd adopted a policy of laissez-faire within her staff. "What these kids can work out for themselves can often be far greater than what we might show them," Kate would often say.

As Kate was about to leave for the Crossover head office, she spotted Naggya talking with Samuel, the student from Hyderabad. The two young men appeared to be deep in conversation and as she passed by, they both looked up and immediately stopped talking. "Everything OK?" she asked.

Their uncomfortable responses convinced Kate that Naggya's unresolved dilemma was likely the subject of their discussions, and she walked a little closer. "If we can help, you know we will. That's what we're here for. I'll be back in the morning and my door is always open. You know that, right?"

As the two nodded their acknowledgements, Kate smiled and turned towards the exit, "See you tomorrow."

❖❖❖❖❖

"Chad, I've decided that your young man can have a spot. Have him come down and fill out the forms tomorrow morning."

Galant Scott hadn't spoken to Chad or Lois in a week, yet suddenly he was on the phone dishing out instructions. Chad mouthed his name to Lois who was working nearby and he put the phone on speaker. "Just a sec, Galant, I've got Lois here with me."

"Hello, Galant. How are you?"

"Fine thanks, Lois. I was just telling Chad I've decided to let your young dancer join my academy, so you can bring him down tomorrow and we can get all the formalities out of the way."

Chad and Lois frowned at each other before Chad replied, "Thanks, Galant, I'm sure Naggya will be thrilled to learn of your offer. He's not here right now but we'll be seeing him this afternoon so we can let him know."

"10 a.m. will work for me. Will you bring him, or that other Indian?"

Lois leaned in closer to the phone and said to Galant, "As Chad mentioned, we'll be seeing Naggya a little later. We'll tell him what you've said, and we will get back to you then."

"I have another busy day tomorrow and 10:00 is the only time slot. I'll need him for about twenty, and he will need to bring his passport. I'll be in rehearsals this afternoon so just confirm with my receptionist." Chad and Lois looked at each other as the phone went dead.

"Well, that's brought things to a head, I must say," said Chad as they again exchanged frowns.

Elijah, Chad, and Lois entered DAPA and found Naggya talking with two of the African students. When Naggya looked up and saw them, he interrupted his conversation and walked up to give each of the three a hug. "Those two ladies from Africa have both started work today," he announced excitedly.

The three adults smiled briefly before the conversation ceased awkwardly. "Is there something wrong?" asked Naggya.

Elijah moved in a little closer, "Chad had a call from Galant Scott a little earlier and," at the mention of his name, Naggya froze.

"And the good news is, he wants to offer you a place in his academy. So, that's four out of four! You must be so thrilled—" Naggya's face telegraphed the fact that he wasn't.

Lois also moved in closer, "Naggya, perhaps now might be a good time for us to find a quiet spot to talk? You now have four genuine offers and to be fair to them, it's probably best we discuss how you're feeling. Perhaps at home might be best?" and she wrapped her arms around Naggya and whispered, "We love you so much."

Scarcely a word was spoken until they reached their apartment and settled in around the table. Elijah was seated next to Naggya and he turned to look closely into his eyes, "I remember the first day I saw you when you were just this high," and he held his hand a couple of feet from the floor and smiled, "Do you remember?"

Although appreciative of all that Elijah was trying to do, the elephant in the room was trumpeting so loudly, and all Naggya could think about was the relentless impasse gnawing away inside. "We've all come a long way since those days, Naggya, and who would have thought, but here we are in New York, and four different academies all want you to join them. We would all love to help you make the best decision, but right now, we're not exactly sure how we can do that."

Lois placed her hand tenderly upon Naggya's and said, "We know you have been struggling with your decision for over a week now, and it is hard for us to see you in such pain and not be able to help."

Naggya blinked several times; he'd thrashed this thing out in his head so many times but still nothing made sense. He desperately wanted to make the right choice, for the right reasons, but his first choice would almost guarantee the greatest negative impact upon Lois and Chad's business. To say no to

Galant Scott meant having to explain why, and for Naggya to fully divulge his reasons would only make matters worse. Galant Scott was the biggest player in town, and everyone knew it. No matter how much he wanted to reveal the whole story, he just couldn't. In Naggya's world, being secretly propositioned and fondled by another male, especially Galant Scott's lead dancer, came at a price he just couldn't pay.

Lois again squeezed his hand, "Putting everything else aside, the most important thing is that you have to feel comfortable with your mentor. Nothing else matters."

Naggya placed his other hand on top of hers and continued to slowly nod, as Chad asked his burning question, "Son, is there one of the mentors that you feel most comfortable with?" Again, he nodded. "OK, good. May I ask, is there one of the mentors you don't feel comfortable with?"

He stopped nodding as tears began to well up, and he didn't try to contain them. A solitary tear trickled down his cheek and as it reached his chin, he raised one shoulder to wipe it away then looked down at the table.

Elijah swallowed hard and cleared his voice, "Naggya, we have watched you closely this past week and from what we have observed, you seemed to have been quite comfortable with the first two mentors, Dominic and David, but the one you seemed to best connect with, was Philippe," and at the sound of his name, Naggya lifted his head and tried to smile. Slowly and purposefully he looked at each of them and nodded his agreement.

Chad was next to speak, "Actually, Philippe rang me to say that he has signed a contract to do a season starting late spring just outside the city, and if that all goes well, he is hopeful of returning to The Lincoln later in the year. Philippe told me that he would be absolutely thrilled to have you involved, that's if you would like to?" An instant grin enveloped Naggya's face as the three adults exchanged knowing glances. "Then, it would appear that your decision has been made."

"But, what about Mr. Scott?"

Chad asked, "What about him?"

"I heard you say the other day that he doesn't like to be told no, so if I say 'no,' he won't be happy with me, and he won't be happy with you."

Lois wrapped an arm around him and looked at Naggya, "Ah, so that's what's been worrying you? Oh, son, we love you so much. If only you had spoken to us."

"I couldn't. I wanted to, but—"

Chad interjected, "Naggya, you leave Mr. Scott to us, OK? We're not meant to live under a spirit of fear, and we won't. We will deal with Mr. Scott, and I can assure you that no harm will come to us. So, are we agreed?"

A relieved young man climbed to his feet and all four entered into the most beautiful, spontaneous, and prolonged embrace.

Chad ultimately broke free, "Please excuse me," and he reached for his cell phone and walked to another room where he tapped open his address book and scrolled to Galant's number.

"Good afternoon, Big Apple Ballet Company, Tristen speaking."

"Good afternoon, Tristen, this is Chad from Impressions."

"Oh, hello, Chad, it's so nice to hear your voice again. Mr. Scott said you'd be calling to confirm. 10:00 in the morning, isn't it?"

"Sorry, Tristen, but we won't be coming."

"But Mr. Scott said—"

"Please tell Mr. Scott that I will call him tomorrow at 10:00."

"Yes, but—"

"Thanks, Tristen. Bye for now."

CHAPTER
forty-five

"Good morning, Galant."

"What's going on, Chad? I'm a busy man and you and your boy are supposed to be here!"

"Actually, that's why I am calling. Thank you so much for your very generous offer, but Naggya won't be joining BABC."

"And why would that be? I'm offering your boy the best break he's ever going to get!" Galant's volume was beginning to rise and his tone, vexed.

"Quite possibly so, Galant, but Naggya has come to his conclusion, and we need to respect his choice."

"So, what are you telling me? That the boy has decided to go with someone else?"

"Yes, Galant, that is what I am telling you."

"Oh, for pity's sake, man, who on earth can give him what I can? I know you took him to David and Dominic, but they're only second-tier at best!"

"Actually, Naggya has chosen Philippe."

"What! That pip-squeak! You must be kidding! I told your boy I would make him a star! I can put him on Broadway but all Montans could do is put him on the subway! Tell me you aren't serious! Montans isn't even fit to carry my bags, so why would your boy pick him? Why would the boy take the bottom of the barrel when he could have number one, or two, or even three? But to pick dead last! Montans is a complete loser. I hear he's just had to go out of town to even get a start. Chad, this is not only ridiculous, it's an insult!"

Chad battled to get a word in over the outpouring of Galant's rage. "Sorry, Galant, I can hear that you're not happy with the decision, but it is what it is. Thanks again for your offer and we will talk again soon." He waited for a response but all he could hear from the other end of the line was a series of long, deep breaths and what sounded like some sort of muffled hiss.

Finally, Galant spoke, "Well, we'll see about that!" and ended the call.

"How did Galant take the news?" asked Lois who had been praying in the other room.

"About as well as we expected."

"And?"

"Let's just say his temper was up, and he may possibly have just hinted at consequences."

"Oh," said Lois, "And do you have any idea what sort of consequences?"

"Half the time he's little more than a blow-hard. You know that as well as I do. Now, is Naggya up and about?"

"Actually, while you were on the phone, he and Elijah announced that they were going out for a walk, said they'd be back soon."

"Did they say where they were going?"

"No, and I didn't ask. Any particular reason?"

Chad smiled and gave his wife a hug, "Oh, nothing of importance."

Fifteen minutes later, Elijah walked through the apartment door along with Naggya carrying a huge bouquet of flowers and sporting the biggest grin he'd worn in days, "These are for you, Mummy," and he handed Lois the bouquet and wrapped his arms around her with a hug fit to burst. "I just needed to say, thank you."

❖❖❖❖❖

"Really?"

"Yes, really."

"Well, I don't quite know what to say. I felt certain that Naggya would choose Galant Scott, but he picked me?"

"Philippe, Naggya and Elijah fly back to India in a couple of days so I guess we should get some paperwork sorted?"

"Yes, yes, of course. Sorry, this has come as a bit of a shock. Um, we'll be in early rehearsal for a while but what about 5:00 this afternoon?"

"5:00 will work in just fine. And afterwards, why don't you join us for a meal?"

"That would be the perfect way to top off an amazing day. See you at 5:00."

❖❖❖❖❖

"American Airlines flight AA416 to Hong Kong, leaving from Gate 106, will soon be boarding. All passengers please make your way to Gate 106. This is your first announcement."

Lois clung to Naggya as the four made their way through

the departure terminal. "Can you believe two weeks have come and gone, Naggya?"

Scrunching the back of her jacket as though somehow he could prolong their time, Naggya was feeling an uneasy mix of excitement and deep sadness. In less than six months, he would return alone to begin a frightening new life, yet in the meantime the closest he would get to Lois and Chad would be by two-dimensional images on a computer screen. Six months would be the longest they would be apart in ten years, and the thought of such a separation stung. With their heavy workload running Impressions, and their involvement at DAPA, on top of preparing for Naggya's return, a trip to India seemed remote at best.

The walk to Gate 106 was a slow and painful one, and by the time they arrived, conversation had disintegrated and tears had taken center stage. For the two returning Indians, it seemed odd to no longer be draped in multiple layers of clothing, and despite their heritage, both Elijah and Naggya had dropped a shade or two in color following two weeks of freezing temperatures and minimal sunlight. Lois held Naggya tightly and pressed her face against his, "Oh, Naggya, we will miss you both so much. We would love to be going back with you, but—"

Looking into her eyes, the young man tried to stifle his tears and to offer a smile, "I know, but we can still talk."

"Yes, my son, we can, and you will be back here in no time. And it won't be nearly as cold! Oh, how we would love some of your hot days here in New York right now."

"This is the final announcement for American Airlines

flight AA416 to Hong Kong leaving from Gate 106. Please proceed to Gate 106 where your flight is now boarding, ready for departure."

Chad hugged Elijah and then Naggya, whose cheeks had become rivers. Naggya broke free and walked quickly through the gate and disappeared without looking back. "He'll be fine once we're in the air," announced Elijah. "A takeoff in one of those big birds and an in-flight movie, you know, he'll be OK. Thank you both so much. We certainly had our hurdles but I believe he has made the right decision. I will call you when we get home, OK?" With one final hug, Elijah picked up his carry-on luggage, showed his boarding pass and made his way through towards Customs.

Naggya was standing off to one side and had wiped away his tears as Elijah approached. "Are you OK?"

"Yes, Elijah," and he smiled weakly, "I suppose I better start getting used to calling you 'sir' again."

As they proceeded to a vacant counter to fill in their departure declarations, Elijah returned his smile and rested his arm on Naggya's shoulder. "Would you like to fill these in? Might be good practice."

"It's OK, would you mind doing it?"

Elijah reached for a pen as Naggya reflected on two of the most impactful weeks of his life. One haunting thought kept running rampant through his mind: *How long can I keep this secret?*

CHAPTER
forty-six

The first time Solomon's dance troupe arrived home following the state dance championships, Son-Shine hailed them as returning heroes. This time, there were just two. Pooladandas of orange and yellow marigolds were draped around their necks as the weary travelers strode the last few meters of their trek home. Naggya was hugged almost within an inch of his life, and as he bathed in the purest of love, deep down he wondered how he could ever manage to leave.

Five months, three weeks, and two days was all that remained before these, these most extraordinary of times, would come to an end.

❖❖❖❖❖

Remembering how he'd suffered jetlag following the outward flight, Elijah promised Naggya the luxury of the next day off, yet at 6:00 the following morning, the young man respectfully stood in line for the showers as he rattled off story upon story and adventure upon adventure with the adoring throng hanging on his every word. Solomon walked past and shot his star pupil the proudest of smiles.

Over the next days and weeks, Rambabu and Naggya were once again inseparable. Apart from dance practice, most other times would see the two playing kabaddi, walking, talking, eating, or sharing dreams together. Although the inevitable sat menacingly in the backs of their minds, rarely was it spoken of; in its place, an unspoken need to milk every waking moment.

❖❖❖❖❖

Philippe had emailed a series of video clips to Elijah, clips of his troupe's preparations for *Cinderella*. Solomon and Naggya studied the clips with an appetite that refused to quit. Philippe's war cry; "It's all about leaps, lifts, and landings!" would ring out time and again, and as each new standard in Naggya's athleticism was reached, Philippe's chilling, inspiring voice would lift him to another.

Solomon quipped one afternoon after one of Naggya's latest superhuman performances, "I'm going to have to get you a parachute!"

With his 16th birthday approaching, Naggya's physique was assuming the proportions of a fully developed adult; his shoulders were broadening at an impressive rate and his biceps and thighs were akin to those of an Olympian sprinter. "Naggya, that's your third helping of dinner," was oftentimes heard in the dining room.

As he and Rambabu were returning to the sports areas, Rambabu quietly asked, "What's the matter?"

"Nothing. Why?"

"Yes, there is. Since you got back from New York, there's been a—"

"A what?"

Rambabu looked at his best friend, "We are all so excited about what's been offered to you, but there's something, something else you're keeping to yourself. One minute, you're all excited but then, it's like you're somewhere else."

"And that surprises you?"

"No, but there's still something else."

"I don't know what you're talking about. Now, can we leave it? Kabaddi starts in fifteen minutes, and I don't want to be spending time on some crazy—"

"Crazy? I don't think so. Naggya, whatever it is and whenever you are ready, just say so, OK?"

Naggya didn't want to admit that something was eating away at him, but clearly his best friend could see it and wasn't being fooled by his attempts at a cover up. He kicked at the ground and muffled a coerced response, "OK."

❖❖❖❖❖

"Good morning, Lois."

"Hi Kate. How is everything shaping up today?"

"Yes, all is well here at DAPA, other than it being such a freezing day. All the kids apart from Samuel have left for the day, most are working, some, in classes. It's quiet here now, so that's a good thing. Samuel has an interview later today and, provided they feel his English is adequate, he should at least get a start. Now, we need to get Naggya's work visa application rolling. The applications have been flowing through the system fairly well of late, but now's not the time for us to get complacent, is it?"

"Just tell me what we need, Kate, and it's as good as yours."

For the next thirty minutes, Kate had gathered sufficient

info to lodge, "Oh, there's one other thing; you mentioned a while back that you were considering employing Naggya while he studied. Is that still the plan?"

"Actually, Kate, in all the cut-and-thrust of his academy applications, we really haven't discussed the matter lately. My thinking is that it makes perfect sense, at least until Naggya is offered a performing contract. Can I run it past Chad and get back to you?"

"Certainly, it's just that visa applications look more favorably upon requests if there's a paid position already lined up."

"Of course, yes, I see that. I'll get back to you ASAP, OK?"

Lois walked into Chad's office and sat waiting for him to end his call, a call that unbeknownst to her was with Galant Scott. When Chad indicated who he had on the line, he interrupted the caller to say, "Actually, Galant, Lois has just walked into my office. Would you please tell Lois what you've just told me?"

"Oh, for pity's sake, can't you tell her?!"

"I'd prefer it came from you, Galant, if you don't mind. After all, we have been your preferred supplier for a few years now."

"Hello, Galant."

"Hello, Lois. I was just telling Chad that one of your major competitors has been in touch to tell me they have completely reworked their pricing structure, so I'd be crazy not to take a good look, now wouldn't I?"

Lois glanced at her husband, then responded to Galant's unsubtle announcement, "Of course, Galant. That's business, right? And of course, price is one of the considerations in business, and so too are quality and reliability of supply. So, Galant, should you choose to go elsewhere for some, or all of your costumes, you will quickly remember why Impressions has been built on getting the balance right. There's an old saying that you'll long remember the quality, or lack of it, long after you've forgotten the price. Now, is there anything else we can help you with today?"

For a man unused to being spoken to the way he spoke to others, Galant spluttered, "Well, we'll see about that. Anyway, it's my business and I'd be crazy not to have a look."

Chad reentered the discussion, "Well, Galant, if there's nothing else we can do for you, we'd best be getting on with things, being as busy as we are. Thanks for the call and have a great day."

Chad turned to his wife, "Well, we didn't have to wait long."

Lois frowned, then added, "Do you think he's serious?"

"Lois, we know our competitors only too well, so if he is serious and we happen to lose Galant's business, we won't lose it for long."

CHAPTER
forty-seven

"Not just vegetables, but fruit and chickens and buffalo cows for milking, and pigs and ducks and flowers and ..."

"Wow, Rambabu, that really is a big dream."

"It must be big, Naggya. Our people starve, and many die and too many are murdered. While you were away, the teachers told us about a Dalit who was protesting about his daughter being pack-raped and killed. The man was attacked by higher castes and had his hands cut off and part of his leg! And we were told of a man our age who was killed for eating in front of some higher castes. Naggya, it must stop, and you and I are called to bring change! If we believe only for small, we deny the many, and we deny our God. He has been showing me many things while you have been away and to do these things, much land is required, and much water, and many to work the land. But, He has told me only to trust and to be ready."

"And I will be so far away and cannot be there to help you."

Rambabu looked at Naggya before he replied, softly, "You will be doing what you are called to do, and so will I. That's just how it is."

Since returning to Son-Shine, Naggya had been struggling with the notion of following his calling, and the many sacrifices it required. He'd been counting the costs, asking himself, "Am I willing?" And now, standing there before him, his answers were being poured out.

"The lesson I have been learning has made me stronger and much more determined, Naggya. God has been whispering to me, 'Rambabu, there are many paths up the mountain, yet each will lead to home,' and I believe that. You must do what you must do, and so it is with me."

"But I want to help you."

Rambabu's eyes were glistening as he looked into the face of his best friend, "You will. I don't know how, but you will. Knowing that gives me great comfort."

The pair stood to their feet and began to walk. "The land near Gannavaram is where we will start, but we will need so much more. We need to be producing food for our people far and wide. This is what He is showing me."

"And where will that be?"

"He told me that when I need to know, He will make it clear. And He told me that I am not to worry about the money."

"He told you that?"

"Yes, many times. God just keeps telling me to trust Him . . . that He is faithful . . . and He will provide. He just keeps saying, 'I shall supply all of your needs according to my riches.' I've been looking for that in my Bible, but I haven't found it yet."

"We could ask Elijah."

"Yes, but like I said, when I need to know, He will show me."

❖❖❖❖❖

A three-hour drive from New York or three-and-a-half on the train. Is it too far?" That's the question Philippe kept asking himself. *"Will they come? Or might there be enough support upstate these days to not need the New Yorkers? Don't be ridiculous, man, of course we need the New Yorkers! If we don't win back the New Yorkers, The Lincoln will never happen! And if The Lincoln doesn't happen, what's the point?*

Philippe's torment swirled around and around in his head. *What I do know is that, in the springtime, the critics will travel, there's nothing surer than that, even if it's just to ram their stinking knives into my back one more time! The first week, that's the key. That's what we need to get right. We can't afford another slow start. If we get the first week right, we'll be OK. But, if we don't—*

For weeks, his leaps, lifts, and landings rang out around their makeshift dance floor. Philippe was mindful of the risk of pushing his troupe too hard despite the entire cast being acutely aware that their own reputations and futures were as much on the line as Philippe's. "Each of us dance for today, but we are all dancing for our tomorrows. What is good today, must keep getting better every single day we dance. There is no time or room for anything but our absolute finest!"

Philippe's leading lady, his Cinderella, was beginning to shine. In the prime of her dance career, she'd experienced the highs and some of the lows of the industry's unforgiving spotlight. Melana Radwanska had star-quality, yet Philippe was still to be convinced she had what it takes to reach the heady heights of a ballet super-star. Etched upon her exquisite face each day, was a fierce determination to master the one-percenters that separated the best from the rest, and time and again, she would pause and look to her mentor to help set her apart.

"Melana, you are a joy to me. Keep on looking up and you will indeed reach to the stars, my sweet."

The jury was still out on Philippe's *Prince Charming*. Randolph Sezsharn had been head-hunted by the Montans' stable from another troupe a year ago, expressly for the Lincoln season. Now considered somewhat a veteran, he still hinted at the quality he'd once been famous for, though his willingness to go beyond the thresholds of pain had given rise to a sea of doubt, especially within his new mentor.

"Find that extra dimension, Randolph. Look deep within. It is still there waiting to be re-discovered. Dig deep! Find it, and we will be shouting your name and clamoring for more!"

CHAPTER
forty-eight

"I said I would, didn't I?"

"You did, Naggya, but it's still eating at you, and others can see it as well."

"You're imagining things, Rambabu."

Rambabu sat down next to Naggya and draped his arm over his best friend's shoulder, "OK, if you don't think anyone else has noticed, then are you brave enough to find out?" Naggya flipped Rambabu's arm away and stood up. "You can't just leave it alone, can you?"

"You're going back to New York in a couple of weeks, and whatever is bothering you, well, it seems to be..."

"Stop it! You're talking rubbish! Stop making things up!"

"Am I? You are training like you've never trained before, and dancing like you've never danced before, but your joy? Where is your joy?"

"It's where it's always been!"

"Then it's suddenly gone into hiding, because I can't see it. It's like you're doing a job and this thing is still holding on and troubling you. Why won't you talk to me about it?"

Naggya walked down the stairs and out into the yard. Solomon glanced across from the sports field as Rambabu followed his friend a few paces behind. When Rambabu caught up, his arm of friendship was again rejected. Solomon tossed his whistle to one of the other teachers and walked toward the pair as they settled near the front gates. When they noticed Solomon approaching, they both fell silent.

"Is everything OK?"

They each declined to reply and were reluctant to engage eye contact until Rambabu turned to face his friend, "Go on, ask him, if you're so sure no one has noticed."

Solomon crouched in front of the two young men, "Noticed what, Rambabu?"

Naggya's gaze remained fixed on the ground as he waited for his friend to speak. "Ah, it's not for me to say, sir."

"Naggya?"

Several minutes of stony silence passed before he could lift his eyes toward his teacher, "Rambabu believes that people have noticed something, but I don't agree."

"And what might 'these people' have noticed?"

Again, Rambabu shot his friend an imploring glance. Naggya coughed awkwardly then mumbled, "That something has been bothering me."

"And has there?"

"Sir, I don't feel ready to talk about it. Sorry."

Solomon could see the depth of his young charge's pain. He squeezed Naggya's arm and stood up. "What Rambabu is saying, there is some truth to it," and he paused, "But whenever you are ready, OK?"

Naggya didn't look up but nodded his agreement before his teacher slowly turned away to return to the sports field.

It was a silent walk as the pair made their way back to the dorm. As he settled on the floor, Naggya looked across at his friend, "Did you ask him to say that?"

"Naggya!"

"Sorry, but I had to ask."

◆◆◆◆◆

"Good morning, Kate. That's such great news about his work permit. Chad and I are so thrilled. And although we've assured Naggya of a job, if he wants to try and find work with some of the other kids, then we won't stand in his way."

"Yes, Lois, we are thrilled as well and perhaps you're right; he'll probably just want to fit in with the others as much as possible. Anyway, his room will be all set up and ready for him. It's funny, you know, this whole journey started with Naggya, yet he's the last one to arrive. All the kids are so looking forward to having him back, especially Samuel."

"Thirty gifted teenagers! Wow! We've really started something special here!"

Kate needed to catch her breath before she could respond, "Yes, we have. All the long hours and all the struggles and it's moments like these that, you know, that make it all worthwhile." Kate's voice still had a tremor in it when she continued, "Um, have you decided if you'll bring Naggya directly here when he arrives, or back to yours for a sleep?"

"Actually, Chad and I were just talking about that. When he arrived with Elijah, he was completely out of it for over half a day, so who knows what condition he'll be in this time, especially traveling all alone. I guess like so many things, we'll just have to wait and see. But from the way he's been speaking, Naggya will want to go straight to DAPA."

❖❖❖❖❖

"But I don't want a fuss. If some of the students start to cry, then I'll, you know—"

Solomon looked down at Naggya and smiled, "Yes, I know. But how will they feel if you just leave without giving them the opportunity to say goodbye?"

"It won't be goodbye. That's just it. When Mummy and Daddy come back here, maybe I can come with them, just for a visit, and I will see them."

"And if some of the students are no longer here?"

His head dropped as a sense of foreboding threatened to smother Naggya. "Why does it all have to be so hard?"

Solomon wrapped a protective arm around Naggya's shoulder, "Maybe *it all* seems so hard because *one* part of it seems so hard."

"What do you mean?"

Standing to his feet, Solomon gently rubbed the young man's back, then started to walk from the room, "I think you know what I mean."

❖❖❖❖❖

With less than a week before flying out to the States, Naggya still hadn't given light to his torment. The world he was about to enter was unrecognizable to that of his own. This new world was as ruthless as it was cutthroat; a creative new horizon was beckoning where pomp and pageantry danced side by side with dictators and thinly veiled debauchery; where finesse and vulgarity at times shared a common stage; and where expression and exploitation vied for preeminence. Was this new world a place where the young, the vulnerable, and the utterly naïve might thrive, or where each would be thrust into a cesspool of uncertainty?

So many questions. And amid them all was Naggya's constant dilemma; do I remain silent? Or do I speak? And if I speak, what might be the consequences?

For six months, day and night, Naggya kept asking himself the same questions, yet the most troubling of them all—what if it happens again?

CHAPTER
forty-nine

"It's your special dinner tonight and then you're gone early in the morning. How are you feeling?"

Being honest with Elijah had never been such a battle, yet now on the eve of his biggest adventure since searching for Auntie following his mother's brutal murder over a decade ago, being asked to give a truthful answer seemed incongruous. Yes, he was off to New York with the assured support of Lois and Chad, Kate, all the kids at DAPA and his mentor, Philippe Montans, but he'd also be sharing life with almost eight-and-a-half-million total strangers. And gnawing away inside was one of his biggest fears, "just how strange are they, really?"

Naggya had stalled as long as he could, and finally made eye contact. "I'd be lying if I said I wasn't nervous."

"Is 'nervous' all it is, or perhaps some second thoughts?"

Elijah's question could have been addressed on so many levels, yet instinctively he knew it demanded honesty. Right now, he honestly didn't know if he could.

"I don't have any second thoughts, not anymore. I have dreamed of this for as long as I can remember and now it's finally arrived, so, no, there are no second thoughts."

Elijah smiled an unconvincing smile as he waited for Naggya to once again make eye contact. "That's encouraging.

We never really know for certain what we'll find on the road ahead, but tomorrow, once you set foot on that plane, if there's anything you haven't said, you may never have the chance. If that is so, I urge you to put it right."

Have they all been talking behind my back?

Without another word, Naggya walked out of the staff office and climbed the stairs. Standing at the door to the boys' dorm, he paused and peered through the small window in the door in search of Rambabu. There, standing in his usual place was his best friend; *and tomorrow my chance will be gone.*

As though the creaking of the door had been amplified a thousand-fold, Rambabu spun around, knowing his friend had arrived, as had the moment. Rambabu stood motionless as the distance between the two diminished, step by painful step. With each but a heartbeat apart, Rambabu reached out and took his friend by the hand, "Here, or outside?" With nothing more than a nod over his shoulder, Naggya led him out of the room, down the stairs, and out into the late afternoon sun.

An hour later, when they each returned, gone was his burden and lighter was his step. Naggya had dared to trust, had risked the deepest of Dalit humiliation. He had ventured where he had never had the courage to go. No longer was his shame a secret, no longer did its disgrace hold sway. Naggya had come out of the second darkest tunnel of his life; the first, after he'd embraced his very own everlasting adoption; the second, his true identity restored.

Rambabu's words kept echoing in his head. My life: My right, or my opportunity?

❖❖❖❖❖

It was supposed to be a private departure, yet at 5:15 the following morning, Naggya ran the gauntlet past two-hundred Dalit students and thirty Dalit teaching staff as they lined the driveway to bid their courageous soldier farewell. Naggya was going where no Dalit had ventured before, to risk and to conquer a world so foreign and a mountain too impossible to climb. Sixteen-year-old Naggya was carrying the hopes, the dreams, and the prayers of his generation upon his young shoulders. He knew much of their hopes, yet deeper still, he knew much more: his calling.

Tears flooded his cheeks as he waved his last goodbyes from the rear window of the old Ambassador. Elijah sat in the front seat and spoke not a word until they'd reached the outskirts of Vijayawada, then glanced in the rearview mirror, "Ten minutes to the airport, my friend."

Together they checked in his small suitcase at departures. An upper caste official scanned the ticket and scoffed loudly, "New York?! You pig!" and hurled the suitcase onto the luggage trolley and waved them aside to allow passengers queuing behind to approach.

When the jet taxied away from the terminal, Naggya strained for a glimpse of Elijah. He saw nothing, and already, he knew he was on his own.

❖❖❖❖❖

For thirty hours, apart from airline stewards and airport personnel, Naggya spoke to no one. For thirty hours, Naggya prayed, and for thirty-hours, Naggya fought back tears. From Vijayawada to New York, he crossed paths with hundreds of travelers going in different directions, yet not one had the slightest inkling of what Naggya was doing, and not one seemed heading in his direction.

How can I be surrounded by so many people yet feel so alone?

❖❖❖❖❖

"Naggya! Naggya!" The first meaningful words in thirty hours filled his heart and saturated his spirit. Naggya fell into Lois and Chad's arms and clung tight, and while the three stood among the throng of hundreds of strangers, all three wept.

"Are you hungry? Are you tired? What would you like to do? Is there anything you need? Did you get some sleep?" So many questions, and yet all Lois really wanted was to hug this young man, the one who was the closest to being a son she would likely ever have. "Oh, Naggya, how much we have missed you!"

Traffic, as always, was heavy, but the dazzling summer sun seemed refreshing to Naggya, a far cry from the drab and the dreary of his previous mid-winter experiences in the Big Apple. Grand Central Parkway stuttered and stalled all the way into the city as an endless procession of daily commutes peeled off to who knows where. "We've turned on a pretty impressive sunshiny day for you, haven't we, son," beamed Chad from behind the wheel of their new Volkswagen. "When you're ready, all the DAPA kids are bursting to see you."

"Really?"

Lois reached forward from the back seat and rubbed Naggya's neck, "Oh, yes. They've all been counting down the days. There's such a buzz in that place, and all the kids have done so amazingly well. They've all added their own creative touches and now, well, now, it's more like a—"

"Like a home," added Chad.

"Yes, Naggya, that's exactly how it feels. It's a home."

Naggya smiled as he gazed out at the New York skyline. He wondered how a team of virtual strangers from many of the poorest parts of the world could possibly have created a home amid the intimidation of concrete and glass. His exhaustion mixed intoxicatingly with the rush of adrenalin as one yellow taxi after another weaved through the morning rush hour. He leaned against the window and marveled, *for as long as it takes, right here is my world.*

CHAPTER
fifty

Unlike his first time in New York, after five hours sleep, Naggya was up and raring to get to DAPA. As he entered the main entrance and spotted the "Welcome back, Naggya" banner draped across the foyer, he dropped his bag and ran into the outstretched arms of first, Kate, and then Samuel. Before he could catch his breath, a posse of students had surrounded and engulfed him in an outpouring of emotion. *Yes, this will be my home.*

Given the honor of helping Naggya settle into his small yet private room, Samuel prattled on about all that had unfolded since Naggya left six months earlier. "I have so many things to tell you, but soon I must leave for work."

"What work are you doing?"

"I work at the markets. It is hard work hauling all the vegetables but I find it rewarding and I can't believe the money they pay me. It's amazing! I am earning three times as much as my father in Hyderabad and I only have to work for six hours each day, and I don't have to work on Sundays!"

"Really? Do you think your employer might have some work for me?"

Samuel chuckled, "Of course! They keep telling me they can't get enough reliable workers. Some work for one day and we never see them again. Some turn up and spend all their time on the cell phones, and they drop some of the boxes on the floor and they spill out all over the place. If you're a good worker, I can talk to my boss."

Despite Lois and Chad's offer of twice the hourly rate, Naggya started work at the markets three days later. "Naggya, we want you to make your own way as much as possible, so if the markets don't work out, just remember that our offer of work is always there," said Lois as she threw her arms around him at the end of his first exhausting day.

"Thank you, Mummy. And besides, the work will keep me fit and strong. Those sacks of potatoes are heavy, so I just picture myself lifting one of the dancers and before I know it, it feels really great."

"Oh, Naggya, we love you so much," and she threw her arms around him one more time and squeezed him tight.

❖❖❖❖❖

The three-hour drive up to Saratoga Springs was the first time Naggya had been out of the city precinct. Immediately after his first Saturday's work, Chad and Lois picked him up, drove him to DAPA, and soon after, were heading north along Route 287 towards Albany; ETA in Saratoga Springs, 6 p.m. Chad had spoken to Philippe and arranged for three backstage passes to be left at the front counter at Saratoga Performing Arts Center. SPAC's 25,000-seat capacity had been stretched several times during Philippe's wildly successful *Cinderella* season. As a consequence, Philippe's initial four-week season from June 1 had been extended until late July following a contractual dispute that forced the cancellation of a series of sold-out rock concerts scheduled soon after *Cinderella*.

A few minutes after 6:00, Chad pulled into the carpark of their hotel and brought the Volkswagen to a halt just outside reception. The three climbed from the vehicle and chuckled as each began to stretch their bodies in unison. The air was clean and fresh and the temperature still a pleasant eighty degrees.

Inside, the concierge showed them to their rooms and within thirty minutes they were showered, changed, and seated in the hotel restaurant. With *Cinderella* due to commence at 8 p.m., now was the perfect time to relax and to reflect after a long drive.

As Chad and Lois scanned the menu, Naggya checked the clock on the far wall. Lois reached across and placed her hand on top of his, "Have you decided what you'd like to eat, Naggya?"

"Um, I'm not too hungry."

"What, after all that hard work today?" asked Chad before shooting his wife an inquiring glance.

Lois smiled, "Your sudden loss of appetite wouldn't have anything to do with tonight's concert, would it?"

It was Naggya's turn to smile, though his was brief and unconvincing. She patted the back of his hand and added, "Son, it's perfectly natural that you might feel a little anxious. After all, the troupe you'll be working with are just down the road," and she swept her other hand across the table and gestured toward the city. "And they'll be preparing for tonight's concert, and you're here, so close, but with us. You want to be there, don't you?"

Naggya bowed his head and didn't make a sound. "Lois is right, son. It is perfectly natural. The funny thing is, I thought I'd be hungry, but suddenly, I'm not."

Gently, Lois climbed to her feet and walked the short distance to speak to the maître de. "Ah, we need to be leaving sooner than expected. Do you do room service later?"

"But of course, madam. Until midnight."

The three walked out of the restaurant and down to the car. Within minutes, Chad was pulling on the handbrake in the SPAC car park while much of Naggya's color drained from his face. "Come on, son, this is going to be a night you will remember for the rest of your life."

The impressive foyer was abuzz as patrons gathered to chat, to purchase merchandise, and to excitedly flick through their programs. Naggya's foot tapped impatiently while Chad and Lois spoke with a young lady across the main counter. She turned to her supervisor, spoke briefly, and then reached behind the counter for a small lockbox. Smiling, she returned her attention to Lois and handed over three lanyards, apologizing, "Please excuse me, but I'm still getting used to this venue."

Lois was about to engage her in polite small talk when she noticed Naggya's facial expression, then thanked the young lady and handed one lanyard to Naggya and another to her husband. "Ah, if you ask any of the security staff, they will happily direct you backstage," declared the young lady as Naggya placed his lanyard around his neck, turned, and headed off in search of anyone wearing a security uniform.

Backstage, the atmosphere changed dramatically. Although the season was already into its fifth week, the air was thick with anticipation and heavy with nervous energy. Despite Chad and Lois being already quite familiar with most of the troupe following weeks of pre-season costume adjustments, they chose to hang back and allow Naggya to feel his own bewildered and fascinated way. None of the troupe had a clue who he was, and immersed in their own worlds, scarcely even noticed or cared that yet another stranger had infiltrated their midst.

"Naggya! My man!" reverberated around the assembly point deep inside the wings. Philippe Montans strutted toward him before also spotting Chad and Lois, "Oh, my goodness, my guests of honor," and he beckoned them forward and lavishly hugged each one in turn. "Please, please, come in. What a privilege to have you three with us!"

The greater the fuss Philippe made of Naggya, the more his presence was registering among the troupe. Though common for the costume designers to be backstage pre-performance, this was the first time Lois and Chad had been present during this season. The distance from New York to Saratoga and their current heavy workload necessitated Chad and Lois sending a staff member in their stead.

"My goodness, we've done well! Every night the house-full lights go up and the encores have been to die for. Naggya, get ready for a treat, and I can scarcely wait for you to be with us after we return to New York. Truly, you are joining an amazing team!" and several of the troupe shot inquiring expressions in Naggya's direction.

From the proceeds of just five weeks of full-house attendance, Philippe had exacted great pleasure from being able to square away his debt to Lois and Chad.

"Twenty-five minutes and counting," bellowed Philippe as the intensity of the atmosphere ratcheted up another couple of notches. "Naggya, you will watch with me from the wings?"

CHAPTER
fifty-one

"He kept saying it over and over."

"What, Naggya? What did he say?"

"Lifts, leaps, and landings! I know he said it a few times on the video clips, but last night—"

Lois and Chad smiled as they sat around the coffee table in their hotel room. "Sorry, but we couldn't hear him from where we were."

"I could. I was standing right next to him, and all the dancers could hear him."

"And tell me, Naggya, how did that make you feel?"

"You mean, him repeating it over and over? Well, I already wanted to be out there, but Philippe's saying it over and over made me want to even more."

"And?"

"OK, to leap even higher every time—OK, I get it."

Chad was the first to speak, "Let me ask you something, son. How many times have you heard us tell you we love you?"

Naggya slowly shook his head, "I couldn't tell you. Thousands?"

"And do you tire of hearing it?"

A huge smile flooded his face as Naggya reached for his cup. "Yes, I do get it."

Philippe arranged to meet Naggya, Lois, and Chad for morning tea the next day at his hotel. With five weeks of success under his belt, Philippe had vacated the two-star hotel on the outskirts of town for five-star luxury smack in the middle.

"Good morning, good morning! Isn't life just so grand!" he quipped, as he approached them in the foyer and held each in a tight embrace.

"Come, I've arranged for a table overlooking the water. This way," and he shepherded the trio out through the double glass doors and onto the terrace. "Sleep well, young man?"

Naggya looked down and gave a half-smile, "Not really."

"Let me guess. You were too excited! I know, I know! It gets you right in here," and he stabbed his middle finger deep into the pit of his stomach.

They spent the next two hours drooling over the prospects of the upcoming season at The Lincoln. Locked in for four weeks from late August, Philippe had allowed himself just over a month to prepare the troupe for his own mouth-watering depiction of *Giselle*. "I can scarcely wait," he gushed, as he sipped on his mocha decaf, before adding, "I've wanted to put my own spin on *Giselle* like forever! Oh, Naggya, we'll show those toffee-noses a thing or two, won't we!" and without the slightest need for a reply, he continued, "And I want you to understudy Randolph. He can be such a draft horse at times! But, when he's on-song, he's adequate, at least for now," and he patted Naggya's hand and took another sip from his cup. "This will be the perfect opportunity for you, and you're such a good fit for Melana." He looked away pensively before adding, "Randolph probably has only a couple more seasons in him, if I'm any sort of judge. Of course, modesty prevents me from saying I am," and he chuckled loudly and expressively tossed his head.

Lois, Chad, and Naggya watched on as the one-man self-promotion machine prattled incessantly, such a world away from the man down for the count only a few short months earlier.

❖❖❖❖❖

"Samuel, it was so amazing!"

The two young men settled down on a lounge in the DAPA common room to bring each other up-to-date on the events of the weekend. Before elaborating on the trip to Saratoga, Naggya sensed that Samuel had something on his mind. For the last month, to supplement his earnings from his job at the markets, Samuel had taken a position as a backing vocalist with a band regularly gigging in pubs and restaurants around Manhattan. His tenor voice was versatile enough to accommodate their soft-rock style, yet his biggest challenge had nothing to do with his competency as a singer, or in learning all the new lyrics, or even him fitting into the band. His greatest challenge was coping with the advances made by both genders during and after each gig. "They even follow us into the toilets," he confided, after discreetly lowering his voice.

Naggya fleetingly considered confiding details of his own painful experience but suppressed his thoughts when Conchita, a young South American dancer entered the room and skipped across to join them.

Quickly changing tack, Samuel urged Naggya to share

some more on his experiences in Saratoga. For the next few minutes, Naggya painted vivid and riveting pictures of their performance and the spellbinding impact they'd had upon the capacity crowd. Samuel and Conchita listened, enthralled, and nodded appreciatively, encouraging Naggya to tell them more. As he transported them into the final scene, his mood changed and without warning, he stared silently down into his hands. The two waited for Naggya to resume but could see that he'd been jolted from a sense of the incredulous into something far less appealing. Conchita slid in a little closer and wrapped her hands around his arm, "What, Naggya? What happened?"

He remained silent for a moment, then awkwardly lifted his gaze and shook his head. "Nothing happened, well, not that most would notice. But I did."

Samuel also moved in closer, "What did you notice?"

Once again, he was slow to respond. Naggya drew breath and whispered, "They had all been so confident, so sure of every step, every movement, but suddenly they all seemed to get scared."

"Scared?"

"Yes, scared. It was like they had built up to the climax without doing anything wrong, but at the most important part, they were afraid of failing and letting Philippe down. Except for the lady playing *Cinderella*, every one of them, right in the final scene, they all stole quick glances at Philippe. He was standing in the wings, and it was like they all had to take a quick look, just to get his—to get his—"

"Approval?"

"Yes, to get his approval. I was standing right next to him, and it was like he was loving it. They didn't even see me. They all looked at him, and he just smiled."

Conchita squeezed Naggya's arm a little tighter and peered long into his eyes. "I know that look, Naggya. I have seen it myself. It's like the master has all the power and the troupe performs not so much for the audience, but just to please the master."

Samuel lowered his head and took both his friends by their hands, "I, too, have seen that thing, many times."

Naggya's head again dropped, "I could never do that. I just couldn't. If we dance the way we should, he will be pleased. He must be," and he looked away before continuing. "I don't understand. Daddy and Mummy and I had a meal with Philippe today and it was like he wasn't even aware of what happened. Is that what they're all about? Is it all about pleasing the master?"

❖❖❖❖❖

With a little over a week remaining before joining Philippe and his troupe following their return to Manhattan, Naggya had been taking every opportunity to work as many shifts at the markets as he could. If he wasn't working, he was studying *Giselle*, or he'd be spending time with the kids at DAPA. With their own preparations for *Giselle*'s costuming, particularly within an unusually short lead-time, Chad and Lois were also under the pump. What work they had lost from Galant, they had more than made up for with Philippe and a couple of other masters as they geared up for the autumn season.

"Good morning, Lois."

"Oh, Kate, I've been meaning to call, sorry, we've just been so busy."

Kate didn't want to alarm Lois so she talked about the incredibly hot days New York had been experiencing of late, then tentatively asked, "Ah, have you seen much of Naggya lately?"

"We've been working most nights until 9:00, and Naggya has been working so much himself, there just hasn't been time. It would be so much easier if he was working with us, but . . . "

"Yes, true, but he's to be admired for wanting to forge his own way."

"Agreed, Kate, but we do miss him so much. Um, do you ask for a particular reason?"

The two ladies had grown to know and read each other well. Kate paused before answering, "It's just that he doesn't seem to be as excited as I imagined he would be."

"Do you mean he seems unhappy?"

Again, Kate paused, "No, I wouldn't call it being unhappy. If I was to describe his mood, I'd call it bottling things up a little."

"Yes, he does that at times. We've seen it several times in the past, and we must remember that he's just turned 16, he's in a foreign country away from his friends, and he's working, and he's about to start—oh, Kate, please excuse me. How insensitive of me. Here I am rattling on as though you wouldn't already know these things. You see and deal with them every day, and I've jumped in and—"

"Lois, it's OK, really. I take no offense, and I agree with you.

I just wondered if he'd said anything?"

"Like I say, we've not seen him since Saratoga, and now I'm feeling guilty, and—"

"Lois, please don't be hard on yourself. Um, how about we keep a close eye on him until he starts with Philippe, and if he still seems a bit, shall we say 'distant,' we might try a few things then. What do you think?"

"Yes, yes, of course, and I'll talk to Chad and if Naggya's still 'bottling' as you say, perhaps we might again broach the subject of him coming to work with us. We could certainly do with an extra pair of hands."

"And from what some of our young ladies tell me, he'd certainly make an impressive costume model," and she giggled into the phone.

"Lois, please don't overly concern yourself, I'm sure it's something that will pass once he's settled into the troupe."

"Thanks, Kate. Oh, and thanks for being such a tower of strength. We give thanks for you every day."

"Likewise. Oh, and mum's the word, OK?"

CHAPTER
fifty-two

It surprised not many that while away in Saratoga, Philippe had arranged for a huge banner to be erected in the entrance to their Manhattan studio. "Leaps, Lifts, and Landing'" emblazoned in vibrant color from one side of the wall to the other.

With his latest short yet successful season now tucked firmly into his belt, Philippe had commenced the search for a more impressive studio and had wasted little time in letting the industry-watchers know he was fast-tracking back to the top. "Philippe Montans . . . Grand Ballet Master," in his own modest opinion, had a certain savoir faire and an undeniable inevitability about it.

While 10 a.m. seemed an odd time to Naggya for rehearsal to begin, he was soon to learn that a late start generally translated into a late finish, and the thought had already embedded itself as to how he would fit working at the markets into Philippe's demanding schedule.

Despite the rigors of a busy season still within their nostrils, the troupe was cheerful and animated as they gathered together on day one leading up to *Giselle*. As each member was formally introduced to Naggya, they each embraced him with a sincerity that encouraged him. Though as animated as the rest, Randolph stole a slightly longer look at Naggya, and almost immediately after, at Philippe. His "welcome aboard" might have been genuine, yet an uneasy feeling washed over Naggya as the two briefly exchanged greetings.

"Right, we have much ahead and with barely a month to prepare for *Giselle*, there is no time to waste. I've been informed just this morning that The Lincoln is willing to forego their usual two-week interval straight after our contracted season to allow us to extend if the demand is there. Let me make this very, very clear; the demand will be there! If anyone has the slightest doubt about that, this folder is filled with hopefuls who would sell their soul to be in your shoes," and theatrically Philippe waved the folder above his head to reinforce his point. "Impressions Costuming will be here tomorrow to do their measuring, so no weight fluctuations between now and opening, or you'll be answering to me, understood?" Several muffled mumbles drifted his way. "Today I will walk everyone through how my *Giselle* will be presented, so make sure you have your devices ready to take plenty of notes. This is a *Giselle* like you've never seen before, and most likely, never will again. We are now the benchmark! And as you all should know only too well, we've set the mark so far above everyone else, the rest cease to be relevant!"

Naggya's mind raced as a flood of conflicting thoughts swished about in his head. *I don't have a device so how do I take notes? Is this the way we are to be treated? How do we dance to our best when Philippe is riding us all the time? And what's with Randolph?*

As the troupe made themselves comfortable around the stage, Philippe walked past Naggya and slipped a pen and notepad into his hand, "See, I can read you already," and smiled briefly before he marched to the center of the dance floor, ominously cleared his throat, and began to conduct court.

❖❖❖❖❖

"Keep it low-key, alright? I don't want this getting any airtime around New York!"

One of Philippe's industry cronies was well-versed at sniffing around behind the scenes, and since returning to New York, his crony had been given the task of looking for a leading man to replace Randolph. With big-money contracts very much the norm for male and female lead dancers, the likelihood of a top-quality dancer willing to switch camps at short notice was unlikely, except on the back of a falling out. Philippe was banking on that possibility. Somewhere out there within the heady and sometimes fickle world of ballet, was a disenchanted replacement desperate to switch camps.

With such a short time before the new season, for the crony to pull this off would require an almost immediate result. Following ten days of his dirtiest digging, he reported back that every dark nook he'd crawled down had delivered nothing but big fat zeros.

"Believe it or not, Philippe, every lead dancer worth his salt is either happy where he is, or not willing to risk—"

"To risk what?!"

The crony hesitated as Philippe began to explode, "What? Risk me?! Can't these imbeciles read?!"

"Sorry, but it would appear some believe the jury is still out on you, Philippe. Some of them say that it will take at least one full season in New York before they'll even begin to be convinced."

"Well, if they're that bloody blind, I don't want them! Any of them!" and he hurled his phone onto his desk and stormed outside.

❖❖❖❖❖

At the end of the first full week of rehearsals, on top of trying to fit in shifts at the markets, Naggya had not only failed to emerge from his emotional cave but seemed to have dug in deeper. During the week, Kate and Lois had exchanged numerous phone calls and by week's end, their concerns were compounding.

With a 5:30 a.m. start, Naggya had to be up and ready to leave for work by 5:00, work a short shift until 9:30, followed by a crazy dash to the studio to start rehearsal by 10:00.

Was it just fatigue and pressure or was there something else bothering him? The same questions kept circling like buzzards waiting to land.

Sundays for Lois and Chad were generally spent in church, and since he'd arrived, Naggya had been invited each week to join them. For reasons born of practicality and survival, their invitations had yet to be accepted. Naggya would sleep until almost lunchtime, and when finally out of bed, he'd do his washing then spend time with the other DAPA kids, many of whom, for similar reasons, had fallen into similar patterns.

❖❖❖❖❖

"Surprise!"

Samuel and Naggya spun around to see two familiar faces walking towards them, smiles upon their faces, and arms heavy-laden with bags of food.

"Mummy! Daddy! I have missed you so much!" Naggya threw his arms around his quasi parents and hugged them tightly. Samuel waited for the embrace to cease before doing the same, albeit a little less intensely.

"We wondered if you could do with some food?" asked Chad as he dangled a couple of the bags back and forth in front of them. "And this one is your favorite, chicken biryani," and he licked his lips and winked as the smiles on each broadened.

Over the next couple of hours, the four exchanged chitchat with some of the students and kept the conversations as light and free-flowing as possible. Chad and Lois couldn't help but see how tired Naggya looked, and as they plied each of the students with food, they waited patiently for the right moment to explore deeper issues.

Nine p.m. on a Sunday evening was an interesting time in the DAPA common room. Always a buzz in the place, yet with seemingly endless weeks ahead of them for the thirty creative arts students, many were showing unmistakable signs of winding down for the night.

"Another early start for you two in the morning?" probed Lois.

Samuel glanced at Naggya before replying, "Yes, but my classes don't start until the afternoon, so I get in a full shift, but Naggya—" and again he glanced at his friend who was mopping up the last of the biryani.

"I just do another short-shift," and Naggya's countenance dropped. "But that's OK. The shift flies by and before I know it, I'm racing off to the studio."

Lois looked toward Naggya, "Actually, I'll probably see you there tomorrow. A bit of a minor alteration to Melana's costume."

Naggya forced a smile and placed his empty plate on the coffee table in front of him. He stole a sneak peek at the clock then returned his attention to the group. It was now 9:45 and Lois and Chad could see that Naggya was beginning to feel uncomfortable.

"A bit of an early start for us as well, mind you, not quite as early as yours," declared Chad. "We best be getting along, but it's been such a delight to spend the evening with you both," and he stood to his feet and stretched his arms high above his head as he waited for the others to stand.

Lois wrapped her arms first around Samuel and then Naggya. As she pressed her body against his, she looked up into his eyes and searched for wisdom. "Son,—"

"Yes, Mummy?"

Lois hesitated before Naggya softly repeated his question. "Naggya, we are so busy at work. There just never seems to be enough hours in the day to spend time with you, and that's one of the reasons that—" and again she hesitated, as Naggya's own searching eyes began to glisten. "That's why we'd always hoped you'd work with us in the business." No sooner had the words left her lips, Lois lamented the possibility that Naggya may receive them as some sort of guilt trip. She wrapped her arms around him tighter and whispered into his ears, "Sorry, son, I didn't mean that to sound like—"

"It's OK, Mummy, really." He took Lois's head in his trembling hands and gazed into her eyes, "Um, I've been thinking about talking to you about work."

Lois went limp in his arms and rested upon his shoulder. "Really?

Naggya nodded as tears began cascading down their cheeks.

Chad walked behind the pair and placed his hands upon their heads, "Let not your hearts be troubled, neither let them be afraid."

CHAPTER
fifty-three

"It's only small, but the water supply is close by, and the soil is quite fertile, a bit sandy, but we can easily add some dung."

Rambabu looked across at Elijah and frowned. "But we will need so much more land than this, sir. We won't be able to feed many of our people from just one acre."

In the months since Naggya had been away, Elijah had attempted to step in to help fill the huge void. He peered wistfully at the young man who'd become so serious in the absence of his best friend. Rambabu had never been, nor had he aspired to be a top student, and Elijah harbored no expectations of him pursuing any further education beyond high school. Over the past year, Rambabu had not attempted to conceal that his calling in life was to be on the land and his greatest hope was to ensure his Dalit people were delivered from their ever-present struggles to avert starvation.

Several months ago, Chad and Lois had sent him a copy of *Faith Like Potatoes*, and over the following weeks, Rambabu had devoured the contents several times over. "If Angus could do it, so can I," he would declare whenever confronted with an obstacle. Chad, Lois, and Naggya had been encouraging him to complete his studies so that he would be better prepared for the academic aspects of his calling. Reluctantly, he'd agreed, although the countdown had already begun, and his eyes were never too far from the finish line. With the money Mummy Lois and Daddy Chad had sent, coupled with some from sponsors in Australia and the promise of more, plus the small but growing supplement from Naggya, Rambabu was confident of soon being able to purchase his first plot of land. Indian real estate ownership laws made the ownership of any land for someone so young onerous to say the least. "With God, nothing is impossible," Elijah would tell the young man, time and again.

As the pair walked across the plot, Elijah could see his young charge slipping further and further from the present day into the future. He chuckled softly before asking, "And what will be growing here, Rambabu?"

Proudly, and with a blaze of unrestrained excitement across his young face, Rambabu declared, "Our maize is already this high," and with both hands stretched above his head, he leapt into the air, "And over there will be rice and up on the higher ground will be tomatoes and carrots and onions, all kinds of onions!"

Elijah's pulse raced and his heart thumped as his own journey resonated with this young man's unquenchable dream. He reached across and grabbed Rambabu by the arm, "See that land beyond the old fence?"

"Yes, I see it."

"The man who owns it is old. His plot is very large, and his sons have moved to Mumbai."

"Yes, so?"

"They don't want to return." He squeezed the young man's arm tighter, "Dream big, Rambabu, dream very big."

❖❖❖❖❖

"We've always needed someone who understands the subtleties of costumes. And that's why you've done so well here, Naggya. You just know instinctively." *Giselle* was due to open in two days, and in the past few weeks, between rehearsals as Randolph's understudy, Naggya had become an invaluable cog within Impressions Costuming's perpetually turning wheels.

The intensity and frequency of his darker moods had decreased, though truth would be denied in concluding he was better. Being less fatigued from not having to rise so early and no longer having to throw sacks of potatoes around for hours on end was helping. Mostly though, working for weeks in an environment where his mind was at play, rather than his muscles, had been a major factor. Each morning, he would hear Samuel rise early and although a hint of uneasiness remained over abandoning his new friend, Naggya was relishing having an extra couple of hours in bed.

❖❖❖❖❖

"So, do you see yourself as lead dancer?"

Naggya had been dreading this interrogation and tried to offer his best banal response. "Shouldn't everyone aspire to lead?"

Randolph wasn't satisfied with the side-step, and again asked, "But you do want the role, don't you? Everyone can see it so why don't you just say so?"

It was evident to Naggya the veteran troupe leader wasn't

going to be content until his suspicions were confirmed. "Randolph, you're a very fine lead dancer and I have learned so much from you already. I am still very young, and no one would pass you over for me, so—"

Randolph's eyes blazed, "Who said anything about you taking over from me?! You crappy little opportunist! Who the hell do you think you are?!" and he swirled around and announced loudly to the rest of the troupe, "Naggya, the pride of India, has just told me he's about to replace me! Can you believe such absurd rot?!"

Today of all days, no one had anticipated such a vitriolic outburst, and yet few would have failed to recognize that this day would come. It was clear Naggya was being groomed for bigger things, but such a divisive outburst a day before commencement of a new season could hardly be helpful. The resultant deathly silence left Randolph looking foolish and Naggya visibly shaken.

、"What the hell is going on?" demanded Philippe as he strode into the middle of the floor in readiness for the afternoon session. When no-one answered and with Naggya's utter humiliation so obvious, Philippe repeated his question. The silence continued until Randolph took a half-step forward to attempt an explanation, "Ah, Naggya and I were just horsing around. It would seem we've somehow been misunderstood. We're fine now, aren't we, Naggya?"

"Naggya? You don't look fine," and he waited for the young man to reply.

With every eye upon him, Naggya attempted to speak but little sound managed to leave his lips. He gulped hard and raised both hands as an act of surrender. A tiny "fine" slipped out awkwardly.

Philippe snapped his fingers loudly, "We have much still to do, and a day out from opening, we don't need shit like this! Understood?" Once again, he snapped his fingers and ordered his troupe to take their places. "Last session is tonight and we're full dress rehearsal. Got it?!" and he stormed firstly past Randolph and then Naggya, scowling the same words to each; words that were fully intended to be heard by the entire troupe, "We'll sort this out privately! Now, I expect everyone to be in place and ready in five minutes!" and he strode out of the room. Seconds later, the walls shook as his office door was almost slammed off its hinges.

CHAPTER
fifty-four

"So, who's excited?" Philippe had his game face on, and nothing was about to stand in his way. "Uppermost in your minds tonight; as you all know only too well, *Giselle* is from the Romantic Era. The best way we can portray romance is from our upper bodies, and by the placement of our heads! Tonight, we unleash upon New York romance like they've never seen romance; never, ever, ever! They will see Montans romance. Every lingering kiss, so provocative, so incredibly intoxicating. Every tantalizing caress will arouse every person out there," and he pointed beyond the curtain, "the arousal will be greater, stronger, and last longer than even the most powerful opiate. Take every person in this jam-packed house on a journey that will burn deep in their memories! You have all worked tremendously hard, and you are ready!" Theatrically, Philippe strode among the members of his troupe and touched each in turn, whispering instructions and his own brand of encouragement. "Now, go out and do me proud!"

Naggya had hung enthralled upon his master's every word, until his final three. *Oh no, he's doing it again.*

❖❖❖❖❖

"What's that word?"

Lois looked up from her work and considered the expression upon his face, "It's narcissism."

"And that's why he did it again at the end of last night's performance?"

Lois put down her work and walked the short distance to stand beside Naggya. "Yes, son, it is, and if you watch closely, as we have over the years, you will see evidence of it in many other settings. Not that I am suggesting you keep looking, mind, but just for your understanding. And may I extremely and strongly emphasize, being narcissistic does not mean he isn't an excellent ballet teacher."

Naggya ran finger and thumb slowly across his chin, "No, I'm not worried about him being a great teacher. I know he is, it's just I don't understand this thing called narcissism. I've not heard of it before."

Lois smiled and ran her fingers through Naggya's lengthening locks, "And may you never see too much more of it, but—"

"But what?"

"But I'm afraid in our world today, it's not an uncommon thing, and in performing arts, it's—"

Naggya nodded as an awareness had just suddenly dropped into his understanding, "But where does it come from?"

Lois chuckled loudly, "Ah, now, that's a discussion for another day," and glancing at the clock, she turned, still smiling, and returned to her work.

Night one of the Montans Spring Season of *Giselle* at The Lincoln had proved a blockbusting success. The morning's entertainment pages in all the New York dailies had waxed lyrical over the reemergence of the self-titled Grand Ballet Master, Philippe Montans. Social media was running white-hot with rave reviews, all destined to make immediate appearances on either the studio walls, his own extensive marketing stream, his burgeoning CV, or most probably, all three. Yes, on the strength of last night's performance, Philippe was back in a big, big way. Throughout any season, Philippe's usual practice was to meet briefly with the troupe for a critique and a performance run-through at 3 p.m. at the theater, then have them back for makeup by 6:30 for an 8:15 start.

The much later start and his role as understudy meant extra hours for Naggya to work at Impressions and to get in some extra rehearsal time alone at the studio. Most of all, it gave him time to think.

❖❖❖❖❖

"One-point-nine-million IR?! Really?"

"Yes, Rambabu, and on top of that there's registration charges and the annual crop taxes."

"But, sir, that's so much money."

"It is, but our God is bigger. I've already let Chad and Lois know, and of course, they will tell Naggya. And our Australian sponsors will honor their pledges as soon as we send them details. It works out to be just over twenty-five-thousand dollars American. And then we must allow for electricity and maybe for digging more wells for water, and to build shelters for the animals, and a place to store seeds, and—"

Rambabu was briefly crestfallen then turned to Elijah, "But what did they say?"

His mentor and senior confidante smiled before replying, "You mean, Mummy Lois and Daddy Chad?"

"Yes, what did they say when you told them about the money?"

"Exactly what I just said, 'Our God is bigger.' Their work is being blessed like never before and, as you know, they share your vision, so you needn't be worrying. Remember what we studied in devotions the other day about worry?"

Rambabu dragged his foot across the floor and slowly shook his head, "Yes, I remember that it is not what God would have us do, but almost two-million rupee is too much money."

"All the gold and all the silver is His, young man. It's just us who sees it as too much. Now, have you drawn up any plans for the land?"

Rambabu's eyes lit up as he reached into his school bag to retrieve his drawings, "Would you like to see them?"

For the next thirty minutes, the pair pored over Rambabu's impressively detailed sketches, all drawn to scale, and together they deliberated the pros and cons of possibly moving things around.

"As well as rice, I'm going to plant tomatoes, eggplant, bananas, green chiles, beans, cucumber, and bottle gourd."

Chuckling softly, Elijah said, "Just remember that it's just over an acre. And what about animals?"

"Yes, sir, I haven't forgotten the animals. There will be three or four water buffalo to start with for milk, and chickens for eggs, and I want to get some sheep for the wool and for meat."

Barely able to contain his smile, Elijah again reminded his young charge of the plot's size before adding, "And where will these animals graze?"

"That's why the old man's farm is so important. It doesn't look like he's doing anything on it at present, so maybe I can graze the animals there?"

"That's smart thinking, Rambabu, and I would encourage you to pray about how you would approach him. The farmer is from a higher caste, so he won't be happy about being spoken to by a Dalit, especially a very young Dalit, unless of course, there's good money in it for him. If we approach him wisely, he might accept that what we offer him is his best option, and he'll quickly forget that we are Dalits."

"Yes, I see that. Maybe Mummy and Daddy might be here for a visit when we—"

Once more, Elijah smiled, "One thing at a time, Rambabu."

Elijah had obtained an aerial view of the property that incorporated the neighboring plots, including the larger plot owned by the elderly farmer. He placed an arm on Rambabu's shoulder and softly asked, "I think you can already see it in your mind's eye?"

As he held the aerial view, his hands began to tremble and he looked up to engage Elijah's gaze, "No, I see it in here," and he tapped the middle of his chest as tears welled up in his eyes.

CHAPTER
fifty-five

"Listen up everybody. The season looks like being extended, probably by two weeks. It seems the paying public can't get enough of us, so you should all be feeling very proud, very proud indeed. And of course, your bank accounts will all be swelling as a result," and Philippe glanced around the room to gauge his troupe's response. "I'm very mindful of the extra workload this places upon you so I will be watching closely in case the standard drops. Please be assured, I won't hesitate to bring in the understudies if it does," and he pointedly shot his two lead dancers, Randolph and Melana, a tilted nod.

Naggya could feel his blood pressure rising and instinctively, he looked down at his feet and shifted his weight uneasily.

"On the plus side of the ledger, the critics have continued to post positive reviews, and rightly so, but mark my words, give them just one slip-up and they'll turn on us like the vultures they are! We take nothing for granted! Our name is only as valuable as our next performance. Have we all got that?"

It was difficult to fathom if the mood within the room rested on his first or his last remark, or if indeed it was still reflecting the balance of their bank accounts.

❖❖❖❖❖

"Just one more week, and *Giselle* will slip gracefully into hibernation, at least for now." Philippe's swagger had never been more pronounced nor proud. A fabulously successful season had banished the days of lack and struggle, and in their place was an air of invincibility and an unhealthy level of extravagance. "If it enhances our performance, buy it, and don't spare the expense," he would scowl, time and again at his small team of technicians.

Philippe ushered Naggya toward his temporary office at The Lincoln. "Young man, Randolph isn't impressing me. Melana is, but not so the draft horse. He's been adequate up until now, but the bar needs to be raised higher, much higher. I've been watching him like a hawk, and he's at his limit. So, I'm all but ready to bring you in for a couple of the final performances." The master intently searched his young protege's face for signs of doubt; none came. "Naggya, the day will come when you will be ten times the dancer Randolph could ever be. My challenge is in deciding when you're ready. Sixteen is young, yet 16 is enough, if what's inside is enough. If you have any doubts, now is the time to say so."

A slight pause hung upon his lips before Naggya was willing to speak, "When?"

"You ask 'when' with a hesitation in your voice? If you ask 'when,' I am not convinced. If you ask 'when' I hear 'doubt.' Doubt is not what I need to hear! If you say 'when' then that speaks to me of an attempt to stall."

Purposefully, Naggya stood to his feet, "If it's tonight, I am ready."

A satisfied grin spread slowly across Philippe's face as he, too, climbed to his feet, "Now, that's precisely what I need to hear! Tonight it is. And not a word to Randolph. Leave him and Melana to me. I know Randolph, and he won't take this at all well, but I will handle him. My Melana, however, my precious Melana, she will be thrilled. Now, be off with you."

❖❖❖❖❖

Despite his jangling nerves, Naggya followed the script to perfection and as he stood hand-in-hand with Melana to a standing ovation, he resisted the sudden urge to glance toward the master. Philippe strode to center stage, bowed audaciously, then blew kisses to the adoring crowd. Absent from the evening was Randolph, who'd succumbed to a mysterious twenty-four-hour virus.

As the troupe took their second standing ovation, Naggya felt a tingling rush that filled him with a joy quite indescribable, yet as it did, he heard that still, small voice within, "Be careful, my son, be very careful." Naggya glanced heavenward and smiled as his spirit leapt.

Lois and Chad were backstage and swamped their adopted son with hugs and kisses that promised to last a lifetime, "We are so proud, Naggya, so incredibly proud."

❖❖❖❖❖

Whistling softly, Naggya arose early to share of the success of last night's performance before Samuel left for work. As he rushed out the door, Samuel hugged his friend, grinned and said, "You should be so happy."

As Naggya reflected upon Samuel's words his mind soon began to stray to things less happy. His thoughts turned to

Randolph and how best he should handle their next meeting. *He's bound to be angry, so what do I say to him?*

Lois offered to take Naggya with her to The Lincoln to do a few running repairs following five weeks of performances. As he climbed into her car, she kissed him on the cheek and pulled out into the early afternoon traffic. "Did you sleep well?" and before he'd a chance to reply, she added, "And how are you feeling?"

"Yes, to the first and OK to the second."

"Just OK? I thought you'd be in raptures."

Naggya's mind raced back to Son-Shine and a study Elijah had led earlier in the year. Silently, he mused, *that's not a word I'd have expected from you, Mummy.* He shifted in his seat before responding, "I guess it's a lot to take in. I don't really know how to feel at the moment. It's been a bit of a rush."

As they pulled into the restricted car park in The Lincoln basement, Lois took Naggya by the hand and looked into his dark eyes, "A rush? Now there's an understatement. But there's nothing else you want to talk about?"

Holding her gaze, Naggya felt suddenly awkward but he shook his head and turned to climb out of the car. "Nothing is too hard when we walk together, son, and we will always be here to walk with you, you know that, right?"

From somewhere deep inside, Naggya recalled his birth mother saying the same thing many years ago. Stifling his pain, he replied, "Yes, Mummy, I know."

Out of the corner of his eye, he spotted Philippe getting out of his vehicle. From a distance, Naggya heard, "Good morning, my new star," and he flinched and reflexively looked around to see if anyone else had heard him. Lois chuckled as she retrieved her sewing bag from the back seat.

When Philippe caught up to them, he swapped his briefcase into his other hand and threw an arm around Naggya, "We did quite well last night, didn't we!" And before a word was uttered in response, he added, "That applause is to die for, right?"

The three entered the elevator and exchanged comments about the success of last night's performance until Philippe asked the question, "So, young man, tell me how you think you did?"

Once again, Naggya flinched. "He looked first to Lois and then Philippe and shrugged his shoulders, "Everyone seemed to be pleased."

"That's not what I asked," retorted the master in a stern tone.

It was evident Naggya needed to respond candidly, and as he drew breath, he gathered up his determination, "I feel I performed the way you wanted me to perform and that Melana and I bonded well, so as far as my performance goes, I'm satisfied that we did a good job."

A chuckle worked its way from Philippe's ample lungs, before he continued, "And what does 'the way you wanted me to perform' mean, precisely?"

Naggya could feel his blood pressure rising and as Lois left them to begin the costume repairs, he suddenly felt alone and vulnerable, "Well, Naggya?"

He stammered a couple of times and tried to summon his thoughts and his courage. "Art is interpretation, and I performed according to your quite brilliant interpretation."

Scoffing loudly, Philippe bristled, "Don't go trying to butter me up, young man."

"I wasn't."

"Come on, Naggya, I've been sucked up to by experts. You don't hope to fool me, do you? Now, out with it!"

"Sir, your interpretation is as you see *Giselle* and how you view Count Albrecht. I meant what I said about it being brilliant. I would probably not have seen it that way, so I danced the way you see it."

Philippe slowly nodded his head as a wry smile appeared upon his face, "And tell me, how do you see Count Albrecht?"

He closed his office door and stood within inches of his new star. Naggya's Adam's apple bounced up and down within his throat, and for a brief second, he closed his eyes. "This morning I was up early to pray, and—"

"Come on, young man, don't go giving me that God stuff! I asked you a question."

"Yes, sir, you did, and I was trying to give you my reply."

A smirk crossed his face as the master impatiently gestured for his pupil to continue.

"While I was praying, I heard this—"

Philippe erupted into mock laughter, "So, this god of yours speaks to you, does he?"

A puzzled expression appeared on Naggya's face, "Not just to me, sir."

Philippe was fast losing patience with the conversation and glanced at his watch, "You've got two minutes, and then we have some serious work to be getting on with."

"As I was praying, He whispered to me after I asked Him,

'I've looked at that thing so many ways, yet might there be a limit to seeing?'"

"Oh really! And?"

"And He said, 'No, My son, there isn't.'"

CHAPTER
fifty-six

"And because of my higher pay, I'll be sending more money."

Rambabu gushed into the handpiece, "Oh, Naggya, it's almost too good to believe. And Elijah has just told me that a lot more money has just arrived from Australia!"

"Wow! That's amazing. So how much do you have now?"

Rambabu's hands began to tremble as he punched in some numbers on the calculator, then tried to form his words, "I now have more than half the money. Just over one million rupee. At this rate—"

Naggya excitedly interrupted, "Never mind 'at this rate,' Rambabu! Mummy and Daddy are about to send more than what you need, and with my money added you can buy the farm now!" Naggya stopped talking when the sound of his best friend weeping caused his own eyes to well up. From opposite sides of the globe, joy, relief, and the deepest gratitude morphed into astonished silence. Naggya could still hear his friend sobbing, so for as long as it took, he would wait. After he heard Rambabu cough and clear his voice, Naggya gently clarified, "Daddy told me that you will have the money by the end of this week, Rambabu, that's just a few days! Do you think you can ask Elijah to start the purchase?"

Elijah removed the receiver from Rambabu and in his own croaky voice said, "I can call the seller's people today, Naggya. They will be eager to get their hands on our money, so I wouldn't expect any delays. This is such wonderful news! All of our children and all of the staff will be so excited," and he pressed the button to put the phone on speaker, then turned to Rambabu, "At assembly this morning, would you like to make the announcement?"

Rambabu slowly shook his head and softly mouthed the words, "I can't speak."

"Sir, I think you'll have to do it."

"Yes, Naggya, it would seem so. Oh, and by the way, we have just been told that the adjoining farm has had a big fire."

"The large farm owned by the old man?"

"Yes, that one."

❖❖❖❖❖

The twenty-four-hour virus lasted forty-eight, and Philippe's patience was running out. "Front up tonight or your contract goes up in smoke! Got it?"

Randolph waited for the heat in his employer to subside before responding, "Yes, Philippe, I've got it, and today is the first day I'm feeling better, so—"

"Cut the crap, princess! There's nothing wrong with you apart from having one almighty sulk! Now, will you be coming in or not?!"

Once again, Randolph waited. "Yes, I will be in, but who will be leading?"

"For goodness sake, you spoiled brat, why don't you find

some balls and ask the real question? I know you're dying to ask it!"

"Which is?"

"Do you honestly think I came down in the last thunderstorm? What you really want to know is if I've given your job to Naggya!"

"And have you?"

With his patience all but spent, Philippe raised his voice even higher, "Well, if you'd been around instead of hiding away in your cave, you'd know the answer to your own question! You are such a pea-brain! He's 16! What were you actually ready for at 16?! No, don't bother to answer! Just be here early today, or you might as well turn up very, very late, and if I have to spell out what that means for you, then you're more stupid than even I give you credit for!" Philippe ended the call and slammed his cell phone down onto his desk.

In another part of the city, Randolph nervously climbed to his feet to begin cramming his personal item into his day-bag.

The next four hours would be long.

❖❖❖❖❖

"Did Philippe ring you?!"

Naggya hesitated before replying, "He didn't have to."

"You smart little shit! I ought to make a mess of your pretty brown—oh, hello Philippe. I was just saying hi to Naggya."

Philippe walked in close and breathed heavily into Randolph's bulging eyes, "Then you best learn to say hi a little more quietly, then, hadn't you! Now before I show you a bit of my own upper-body strength, get the hell changed

325

and show me why I'm still bothering to pay you so much money!"

As Randolph tried to regain his composure, he was assaulted with an even louder directive, "Now!" complete with an extended pointer finger and a violently stamped foot. He turned to Naggya and winked. "The wild bear needs to get out of his cage every now and then," and he much more sedately pointed in the same direction for Naggya to follow the lead dancer into the changing rooms. "Oh, and I don't expect another word on the subject from either of you," and for good measure he added another wink and a thoroughly self-satisfied smile.

❖❖❖❖❖

"It's going to be nice to have a week off, Mummy. Can we ring Rambabu tonight please?"

"Absolutely! Dad and I are so looking forward to finding out about settlement for the farm, aren't you?"

Naggya didn't need to speak. His grin extended inches either side of his cheeks, while his eyes sparkled.

"You miss your best friend, don't you?"

"He is doing what he needs to, Mummy, and our friendship can't get in the way."

Lois smiled widely, "That's funny."

Naggya shot his adopted Mummy a curious frown.

"It's funny because when I asked Rambabu the same question, he gave the exact same answer. Have you made some sort of secret pact?"

Naggya's frown deepened before Lois grabbed his hand,

"I'm just teasing, son, we know you both respect and admire each other deeply, so—"

"We're both called by the same God to do different things but to achieve the same goal, and we must give everything for that to happen, otherwise—"

Lois put down her work and threw her arms around his shoulders. She peered up into his amazing eyes and fought to rein in her emotions, "For us, Naggya, there is no otherwise; never has been, and never will," and she held him tighter as though holding onto one son somehow let her hold onto both.

When Chad walked into the room, he propped and asked softly, "Did I miss something?" and was greeted with two sets of wet cheeks.

"Son, I just got off a phone call from Philippe and he's asked me to ask you a question."

Wiping his moist cheeks, Naggya turned and asked, "Yes, Daddy, what is it?"

Chad cleared his throat and walked in a little closer, "He wants to know if Randolph has been giving you a hard time?"

Glancing first at Lois and then Chad, Naggya softly said, "No. He hasn't said much at all. We finished the season well."

Chad waited a moment before continuing, "Then why do I get the impression there's more to this?"

Naggya drew breath and lowered his head, "It's like he's buried it, but he knows exactly where it is, and he's just waiting to dig it up. Daddy, I really hope I'm wrong, but—"

CHAPTER
fifty-seven

"The lawyer says by Friday, Rambabu. So, in three days the farm is in your name!"

The young man hugged everyone and everything in sight. He leaped high off the ground and fist-punched the air! All he could shout, over and over again, was "Three days!"

"Mummy and Daddy will be beside themselves with joy. Would you like to call them straight away?"

"Thank you, sir," and he paused to consider, "Ah, what time is it in New York?"

Elijah chuckled loudly, "Do you really think it matters?" and before he'd allowed Rambabu time to respond, he added, "Actually, it's just after 6:00 in the morning, so I'm sure they won't mind. Come on, we can call from the office."

When the slightly groggy sound of Chad's voice could be heard over the speaker phone, Rambabu screamed, "Daddy, on Friday it's ours!"

Rubbing his eyes and sitting up in bed, Chad leaned over and gave his wife a gentle prod. They'd been up until midnight on a call with Philippe discussing the new season's costumes, and as a result, hadn't settled in bed before one. "That's extraordinary news, son. Mummy is here with me, and she's ecstatic, that is, she will be once she's properly awake."

A similarly groggy voice blurted, "Don't pay any attention to Daddy, I am awake, and yes, I am ecstatic!" She gave her husband a playful dig in the ribs and snuggled in closer. "Tell us, Rambabu, what is the first thing you're going to do?"

Rambabu giggled through the phone, "Well, seeing I won't be having school the next day, I was thinking about sleeping there," and sheepishly he glanced at Elijah to ask, "That's if it is OK with you, sir?"

Once again, Elijah chuckled, "Well, I don't see why not. Matter of fact, I haven't slept under the stars for a while myself, so I just might join you."

Lois excitedly interrupted, "The minute we get off the phone from you, Rambabu, we will call Naggya to give him the amazing news."

There was a momentary pause until Elijah intervened, "Um, I think Rambabu would prefer he was the one to do that, if you don't mind?"

"Of course, of course. What was I thinking? It's still early here, son, and with all this excitement, you know . . . "

"I love you, Mummy. And you too, Daddy. Thank you so much for all you've done. I won't let you down," and his voice faltered as his tone switched from elation to trepidation.

Chad replied, "We know you will never let anyone down, my son, and you must never forget that we will be forever proud of you," and as his own emotions began to peak, he tailed off with, "Now, Naggya won't mind being woken to hear from you. We'll talk again very soon, so off you go, OK."

As the call terminated, husband and wife locked in an

embrace that spoke so perfectly, so clearly, of endless thanks and of an uncontainable hope.

❖❖❖❖❖

Amid their euphoric exchanges, the intended ten-minute call stretched to thirty as Rambabu gushed over the plans for a glorious future. "And when I get it all set up, you must come home to see it, Naggya, you must."

Reluctantly, Naggya ended the call, and as he did, despite the volume of words shared, stuck painfully in his throat was just one: *home*.

Shortly after, Chad called to offer Naggya the day off to celebrate. Not surprisingly, the offer was declined.

❖❖❖❖❖

"Actually, Rambabu, it's not really a tent. It's more a square piece of canvas, but we can probably make it look like a tent. Anyway, it will help keep the insects away, and the rodents." Elijah may as well have said "elephants" as far as Rambabu was concerned.

Despite the piece of paper in his hand being a photocopy, he'd been staring at it ever since it was handed to him an hour earlier. With the original securely locked away, Rambabu's eyes jumped from the incredulous, to the intrigued, to the overwhelmed, and back again so many times, his mentor could only watch on in awe of one so blessed. Rambabu, still not 16-and-a-half years old, was the debt-free owner of one-point-two acres of farmland. *Thank you, Lord.*

"Where should we put the shelter, sir?"

"That depends on which direction the elephants come from."

"Pardon? Elephants!"

"Sorry, young man, just a silly joke. What about over there in the corner so we can tie onto the fence?"

"What's left of the fence."

Laughing loudly, Elijah began to walk toward the rickety old wooden structure that remotely resembled a fence. "Do I see it as it is, or how it will be? That's the question that you need to be asking yourself, young man."

Within half an hour the canvas had been securely tied to the fence, the bedrolls rolled out, the crude cooking implements unloaded, and a makeshift fireplace set up. They'd also brought with them a couple of shovels, an assortment of picks and axes, and Elijah had parked the old Ambassador as close as possible to serve as both a source of music and some added protection.

"You were just joking about the elephants, weren't you, sir?"

Elijah smiled at one of his all-time favorite students and said softly, "I promise to tell you, in the morning."

CHAPTER
fifty-eight

"If we breathe new life into it, the fact that we did or even planned to do the same ballet only recently doesn't matter a toss! The people out there long to feel something, to be deeply moved, and that's precisely what we will give them. There are millions of New Yorkers who are starved of inspiration right now, and mark my words, we will feed them! That is our challenge," and provocatively, he gestured back and forth between the three, "but this is my promise!" Philippe stared long and fierce into the eyes of Randolph and Melana; the first to blink or to turn away would lose. Philippe wouldn't. "Fine then, we do *Don Quixote*, and we do *Don Quixote* like no one has ever done *Don Quixote* before! With more heart than has ever been, we will put more bums on seats than The Palace Theatre has ever seen."

The two lead dancers walked silently from Philippe's office. When they reached the entrance to the dance floor, they went their separate ways without a word spoken.

Randolph walked into the changing room and sat down on one of the benches. He ran his hands over the top of his head and muttered, "But I don't want to do *Don Quixote*."

From the far side of the room came the sound of a familiar voice, "Why not?"

Randolph spun around, "I should have known it would be you! And I suppose you do want *Don Quixote*! Yes, of course you would. Your tongue is the same color as your skin!"

Naggya frowned as he tried to decipher the meaning, "Sorry, but I don't understand."

"Work it out for yourself, bum boy!" and he stood to his feet and stormed out of the room.

A few of the other dancers straggled in and immediately noticed the expression on Naggya's face. "Are you OK?" asked one.

"What's a bum boy?"

Another of the dancers responded, "Ah, did someone say that to you?"

Naggya did not answer. He climbed to his feet and gestured to leave, as the same dancer added, "I suggest you go and discuss that with Philippe."

❖❖❖❖❖

"Hello, Galant, it's Randolph."

❖❖❖❖❖

An hour later, Randolph knocked on Galant's office door. "Come in and sit down! Now, what's this all about?"

In the years they'd known each other, Galant had never been one to waste precious time, and instinctively Randolph knew to get straight to the point. "What do you have coming up?"

Galant briefly studied the veteran dancer before any sound came from his lips, "At the end of this current season we'll be going straight into rehearsing for *La Bayadere*. Why?"

"And you've cast?"

Galant exhaled loudly and leaned forward, "Listen, Randolph, I don't play games so spit it out. I'm a busy man and I won't be stuffed around."

"OK, OK, I want out!"

"Why? Has the pip-squeak tossed you aside?"

Randolph had practiced his lines, but under the blowtorch of Galant Scott, he'd already begun to fluff them. "Ah, not really, it's just that—"

Galant thumped the desk, "What?!"

"It's two things. He wants to do *Don Quixote*, again, and that little Indian!"

Galant leaned back in his seat, "Oh, I see. You're being squeezed out so that Philippe can bring in a cheaper option. Didn't take long, did it? Can't say I'm surprised! Cheapskate that he is!"

"Actually, no, he hasn't squeezed me out, well, not yet anyway."

An eruption of laughter filled his office before Galant again spoke, "Blind Freddy can see through that one, Randy!"

Randolph weakly raised a hand in protest, "You know I don't like to be called that, so if you don't mind—"

"In my office, Randy, I'll call you Gwenevere if I bloody well choose to! Now what do you want?"

"I just wanted to ask you if you might have a place?"

"What? For you?!" Galant rolled his eyes, then smirked. "Your best is history," and sarcastically he scowled as he emphasized the dancer's name, "Randolph, from what I hear it's already ancient history, so, no, I don't have a place! Try down the road! Now, be a good boy and shut the door on your way out!"

As Randolph was leaving, Galant added, "And the Indian boy? He's a fast learner?" From the disgusted expression that jumped across Randolph's face, clearly, he was. *Interesting. Very interesting.*

Galant picked up his cell phone. A few seconds later, he asked, "That young Indian, what's the word around town? Really? Then dig deeper!"

❖❖❖❖❖

Randolph needed to tread warily. The Big Apple was indeed big, yet the ballet fraternity not so, and nothing moved quicker than a bit of juicy gossip, particularly when a lead dancer was involved or one of the masters. Throw in both, and there was a headline frantically searching to land. Despite Galant's dire assessment, Randolph knew that if he could remain fit, healthy, and injury-free, two or three more years at, or even close to the top, would see him set for life. Randolph had accepted that his days of commanding multi-million-dollar-a-year contracts were behind him. *But, surely I can still pull at least half!*

CHAPTER
fifty-nine

"This weekend, sir?"

Elijah paused before speaking, "Ah, sorry, Rambabu, but I have promised our children we would visit my wife's parents tomorrow. Our children love their grandparents, and we haven't seen them for so long, and—"

"It's OK, sir, I understand."

"I can drive you there after school. You can't expect to carry all those tools on your own."

Rambabu smiled, "Not on my own, sir. Some of my friends have offered to help."

A concerned frown cut across his face as Elijah considered how to reply, "And, are you planning on staying the night?"

"I am, sir, but if the others get tired or scared, they might not. I've told them the elephants are away on vacation, so—"

The comment was intended to make his mentor smile. It didn't. "Do any of your friends have phones?" It was a dumb question and Elijah knew better. He was simply buying time to allow his thoughts to settle. He reached into the desk drawer and pulled out an old cell phone. "It will need charging, and I can do a pre-paid for it for the next week, and . . . "

"But, sir, how would I keep it charged? We have no power

at the farm, and anyway, as you will remember, the coverage out there isn't so good."

Rambabu's logic was operating on a higher level than his mentor's right now, "Yes, yes, you're of course right. I'm just trying to make sure you'll be OK, that's all. It's quite a walk out there."

Once again, Rambabu smiled. "We go further in a game of kabaddi, sir, and when we play, we are running." Elijah could see that Rambabu's mind was indeed made up. "And besides, sir, you taught us again yesterday that we are not to worry."

❖❖❖❖❖

Five 16-year-olds carrying an array of farm implements wound their way along the gravel road. The plan was to arrive well before dark and to be all set up and finished cooking before darkness fell.

❖❖❖❖❖

With their bellies full and their nerves still dancing over the prospects of a night under the stars, the young men sat around the fire and tried to appear brave. Apart from Rambabu, none of his school peers had slept under the stars since those who still had a family had gone home to visit. Although at home, the risks were just as high, but at least with family there might have been a village to help keep them safe. Out here, five 16-year-olds with picks and axes might do little beyond putting on a bold front.

At first light, Rambabu was on the end of a shovel as he fashioned a strategic course for the next heavy rain. The farm had lay fallow for a number of years, and with a slight fall towards an adjacent property, the higher-caste-owned farm had enjoyed the benefits of runoff, a luxury Rambabu was intent on bringing to an end. He had not met or even seen the neighboring farmer, though instinctively he knew it was wise to be on constant lookout.

By mid-morning, the five young men had finished redirecting most of the channels to ensure that as much of the water that fell on the property stayed on the property. "That's a great job, my friends. We can start planting some of the crops now, and then we pray for rain."

The other four were exchanging glances until Rambabu spotted them, "I know what you're thinking. We don't get rain at this time of the year, but Angus Buchan planted in a drought, and even though it didn't rain, he still got potatoes. Loads of potatoes. And I have as much faith as Angus!"

By dusk, ten long rows of seeds had been planted and a huge mound of weeds had been pulled, gathered, and burned. As the fire burned down, Rambabu noticed two men watching from behind a tree on the next property. Rambabu walked towards his school friends and beckoned them to gather around their makeshift campsite. "Don't look now, but two men are watching us. They haven't moved but I can't see any others, so we outnumber them. If anyone wants to leave, now would be the best time to go."

The others again exchanged glances and shuffled awkwardly. Ezekiel was the first to speak, "But, if we leave now, they can attack us on the road, and if any of us do leave, that means there's less of us here to stop the men."

Rambabu reached for the cell phone and strained to read the screen by the firelight. There was only one charge bar remaining and as he tilted the screen to get a better look, he could see, "no coverage" displayed at the top of the screen. He quickly slipped the phone into his pocket and said nothing, glancing from friend to friend, trying to gauge their mood.

Jacob, the biggest of the four, stepped slightly closer. "I say, we stay. We are all strong and fit, and if we stick together, we can overcome these men."

"And we have the farm tools. We can use them if we need to."

Rambabu was thankful that his friends were willing to remain. He knew only too well that the day would come when he'd be required to take a stand on his own, like a young King David, and dare to fight the lions, the bears, and all the angry giants. "Then, we are as one?"

Four young men summoned their courage, "Yes, we are one.

❖❖❖❖❖

It was just after 11 p.m. when fifteen higher-caste men slipped from behind that same tree. They were armed and ready to surround the Dalits. The leader brandished a large knife, while in the semi-darkness, the five friends could see the hatred etched upon their attackers' faces. In Telugu, the leader shouted for the band of raiders to attack, and fifteen grown men rushed headlong at the five teenagers.

Before the battle ended, not a planted seed remained in place, not a trough still intact, nor a teenage limb not beaten, bloodied, and bruised.

"Leave them to die slowly!" shouted the leader. "By morning

they will be food for the vultures, and it will serve to warn other Dalits not to come! Seize their tools and take anything of value. Now, we go to our homes to celebrate. Tonight, we rid the earth of five more bits of scum!"

❖❖❖❖❖

Vani rolled over in bed and searched the darkness. Pacing a few yards away, her husband turned at the sound of his wife stirring. "What's the matter?"

"I don't know. I have a deep prompting. I have a deep pain." Vani sat up and propped her back against the old cement wall in their bedroom. "Elijah, you must go to the doctor."

"It's not that sort of pain. I must go, but not to the doctor," and he kissed his wife and whispered, "Please pray."

"For what?"

As her husband left the room, he turned to add, "I don't know."

It was a two-mile drive from their home, and as Elijah drove along the gravel road and tried to avoid the potholes, he glanced at the dashboard. *Three o'clock. I should have known.*

Sobbing and crouched over the body of a young man destined not to see 17, Rambabu held him tight as three others lay close by, wounded, bleeding, and utterly afraid. One cried out at the approaching headlights. *Are they returning to finish their killing?*

Elijah drove close and scrambled clumsily from the old Ambassador as Rambabu held Ezekiel's lifeless body. Elijah hesitated at the sounds of Rambabu's pitiful shrieks; shrieks that thudded mercilessly into his chest. All Rambabu could scream, over and over, was one compelling word, "Why?"

The three others had fought the good fight. The product of big sticks and even bigger stones; at least one broken leg, three broken arms, deep cuts and lacerations, and who could know how much spilled blood? The price yet to be measured, nor even time to count. At 3:00 in the morning, the enemy's worst, on show. At 3:00 in the morning, Elijah and his courageous five were faltering on their knees. *Why!*

Chapter
sixty

There was only one place to turn; one place with the capacity and the heart to meet this urgent need. As he pulled up at the entrance to the only hospital in the region willing to accept Dalits, even viciously and unlawfully attacked Dalits, Elijah knew that even this hospital would deny treatment until payment had been assured.

Lois answered the phone. It was early evening in Manhattan and the day had been long. She glanced at the screen and recognized Elijah's number, "Well, hello, Elijah. Chad and I have just been talking about you. How is the planting going?"

A feeble whimpering choked him as he tried to form words, words that struggled to come, stuck horrid in his throat. "Elijah? Are you there?"

Lois could hear the sounds of fitful breathing, and she called for Chad to come to the phone. Lois looked to her husband, "It's Elijah, but there's no sound apart from someone breathing."

Chad took the phone, "Hello. Is anyone there?"

Elijah slowly turned back to see four twisted and beaten young men, each slumped in the front and back seats of his car. Ezekiel's disfigured corpse had been hidden in the trunk, "Yes, Chad, I am here."

"Elijah, what is going on?"

"Ezekiel—Ezekiel is dead, and—"

"Dead? How can Ezekiel be dead? Elijah, this is quite bizarre. You aren't making sense."

A massive lump lodged in his throat. Elijah swallowed hard, breathed as deeply as he could, and summoned the ability to speak, "During the night, all five were attacked out at the farm, and—" Elijah crumpled against the hospital wall, a wretched and pathetic string of moans and sniffles found their pitiful way to New York. "We need your help, Chad. The other boys will die if I, if we, can't get them into—"

Chad instinctively knew what was coming. "Elijah, now listen carefully. Where are you?"

"Outside the hospital."

"Right, get the boys inside and hand the phone to the manager!"

"The manager wouldn't speak to me, and he wouldn't touch my phone."

"Then get his number and I will call him."

Elijah's lips and hands were trembling, and he nodded, then realized the absurdity of the gesture. "Sorry, yes, yes I will." He entered through the main door, and covered in blood from the boys' injuries, was immediately prevented entry by a burly security officer who stood ominously in front of him. Elijah raised one hand and motioned toward the phone in the other, "I have four young men outside who have been badly beaten, and they need immediate treatment, and—"

"We don't treat Dalits!"

"And on this phone, I have a famous American who will

guarantee to make payment, so—"

The security officer sized Elijah up and down, then turned to walk away. "Wait there and don't move or you will be thrown out!"

Within fifteen minutes, the four young men had been loaded onto trolleys and admitted to the rear ward, just inside the doors to the incinerators. The same security officer marched up to Elijah, "Is that your car outside?"

"Yes."

"Move it! It's for our patients!"

"But—"

"Move it!"

The morning sun was climbing in the sky as Elijah trudged the half-mile back from the only parking spot he could find, Ezekiel's body still hidden in the trunk. Once again, he called Chad. "I'm so sorry, Chad, I didn't know what else to do. I still don't know what I'm to do with Ezekiel's—" He couldn't bring himself to say the word "body." He knew from past experience that, for the right money, some of the funeral parlors would prepare Dalit remains, but as an orphan, where respectfully should Ezekiel be buried?

Chad waited patiently as Elijah gathered his thoughts and formed his words. Elijah was in shock, and Chad and Lois could only begin to imagine how Rambabu and the others were feeling, assuming of course that they were still alive.

"Elijah, I know you won't want to, but this is murder, and you will need to report this to the police."

The very sound of the word sent shivers down Elijah's quivering spine. "But they won't care, and they won't do anything. They will probably be happy that another Dalit is—"

The mournful wails of one of Chad's most loved and respected tore deep, and all he wanted to do was reach through the line and comfort and console the inconsolable. Chad waited for Elijah's grief to ease, "Ah, can you get one of the teachers to come in and sit with the boys? If you can do that, we'll work out what's best to do with Ezekiel's remains, OK?"

Elijah crossed the carpark and was about to enter the main entrance to the hospital. He stopped and said, "I can call Solomon. He has a motorcycle so if I call him now, he could get here quite soon."

"Yes, do that, and I will call the hospital to get an update on the boys, OK?"

❖❖❖❖❖

"Mister Chad, two of your children have fractured skulls, and one has severe hemorrhaging on the brain. He may not make it."

Chad listened intently and asked, "And which boy is that?"

"Mister Chad, I am a very busy doctor. I don't have time to waste learning names, especially—"

"Especially what?"

The doctor considered his words carefully before responding, "Especially being so short-staffed as we are. Now, if you'll excuse me, I must return to the other patients."

❖❖❖❖❖

Elijah left Solomon to watch over three heavily sedated young men, each clinging to life. Rambabu was wide awake and sobbed, not just from the pain of his wounds or the grief of such devastating loss, but in the throes of his suffocating remorse. *This is all my fault! I should have gone alone.*

Two fractured skulls, four depressed eye sockets, one broken leg, three broken arms, numerous lost teeth, multiple deep cuts and contusions, and all four with life-threatening concussions.

During the next three critical hours, and despite the close scrutiny and attention the other patients in the ward received from the nursing staff, the four Dalits were given none, apart from an occasional glance from the doctor-on-duty.

Elijah pulled up outside the Gollanapalli police station and parked the Ambassador under the only shade on offer. Already the temperature was approaching thirty-five. His hands were still trembling as he pushed the station door open and tentatively stepped inside. From behind the counter, a uniformed officer leaped to his feet and thundered, "Get out of here, you stinking bloody animal!"

"Sorry, sir, I have come to report a murder, and four other—"

The officer glared at the unwelcome intruder, "Were they Dalits?!"

"Sir, they are Indians."

"If you've come to report the death of a Dalit, report it to the central station in Vijayawada! Now get out!"

Ezekiel had been one of the orphans recently granted a birth certificate, so having him on record as being born entitled him to be recorded at his time of death, at least in the eyes of the law.

"Sorry, sir, but if I drive him into the city, his remains will start to smell."

The officer walked menacingly a little closer, "Where is the body?!"

"In the trunk of my car, sir."

"He died in the trunk of your car?"

"No, sir, he was murdered out near Gannavaram, but I knew that you wouldn't come out to—"

"Someone has accidentally died, and then you've disturbed the accident scene by removing the body! You Dalits are so stupid! You are all a disgrace to India! Now get out of my station before you are the next accident!"

❖❖❖❖❖

The following afternoon, all four were simultaneously discharged from hospital, the 5,000-US-dollar account duly paid but not receipted.

Ezekiel's embalmed remains were picked up and transported to Son-Shine on Wednesday, following settlement of the unlicensed funeral parlor's account.

CHAPTER
sixty-one

Chad and Lois drove to DAPA to break the news to Naggya. As they entered the common room, suddenly all eyes were upon them; bad news has an expression all its own. Naggya thoughtfully placed his breakfast bowl on the counter and turned to meet their bloodshot gaze, "What?"

Lois wrapped him in her arms and kissed his cheek as Chad moved in close to speak. "Son, we have some news that's disturbing. There is no easy way to break this to you, so I'm just going to give it to you straight, OK?"

"Daddy, you're scaring me." He looked deep into his adopted father's eyes, "What is it?"

"I'm afraid to have to tell you, but Ezekiel has been killed, and—"

Before another sound passed Chad's lips, Naggya's body began to stiffen, then shake; a disconnect enveloped his body. Chad gripped his son tighter, and as softly as he could, added, "And Rambabu, Jacob, Noah, and Lemuel are all fighting for their lives. Sorry, son, but you need to know. They were attacked during the night out at the farm, and then left to die."

Chad and Lois lowered Naggya into a chair as the other DAPA students gathered around to attempt to somehow ease his torment. As Kate entered the room, ten students were weeping, praying, and searching to find comfort. They'd each faced and survived such torture and barbarity in their own nations, and somehow, in time, Naggya would once again do the same.

Kate joined the group of mourners, and even though she knew nothing of the source, she knew the need, and the need right now was immense.

Naggya forcibly stood to his feet, "Daddy, I need to know what happened, everything," as his imploring eyes burned deeply into Chad. He'd hoped to spare Naggya the depths of the detail, but, by the intensity of Naggya's pleading, that wasn't possible.

It took an hour to adequately sate his need. Naggya's fists clenched, then shook, then clenched time and again. What? Why? How? And where? All poured out with a rage with each and every asking. After that hour, Naggya turned to announce to his parents, "I need to go home!"

Chad's eyes raced to his wife's and then back to their son, "If that's what you want, Naggya, we will move mountains to get you there. For a visit, or for good?"

Grief speaks so many languages, and there, in Naggya's eyes, grief spoke. Naggya didn't have a clue.

Lois gripped Naggya's hand tighter, "I will go to see Philippe and tell him that you need some time, OK?" A single nod, his only response.

❖❖❖❖❖

"Oh, that's terrible, Lois."

"Yes, it is. In America we hear so little of these atrocities in

India, that is, until they are ones we know personally. These five are our children, Philippe, and it hurts beyond words. Naggya is torn. They are his only family."

"Of course, yes, of course. Tell Naggya to take some time off."

"He will need time to grieve. Chad is checking on flights now."

"What do you mean, flights?"

"Philippe, Naggya will need to be there for the funeral, at the very least."

Flipping open his planner, he mused for a moment then responded, "Ah, I can spare him for a week, tops."

Lois's eyes widened, "It'll take almost that long getting him there and back, that's assuming he's—"

"Assuming he's what? Coming back?!"

"He's hardly in any state to be making big decisions right now. One of his best friends has just been murdered, and as we speak, four of his closest friends are clinging to life! You can't expect him to be rational right now, surely?"

"It's a tragedy, Lois, I'll grant you that, but he will realize that life will go on and that his future is still the most important thing. In time, I'm sure he will—"

Lois jumped to her feet and as she turned to leave Philippe's office, she loudly interjected, "In time, yes, but how much time, we will tell you when we know," and she shut the door behind her and burst into tears.

❖❖❖❖❖

"Naggya, in order to book flights, and for your visa, it's better I know if it's one-way, or return?"

The depths and ramifications of that question were vast. How could he know? And how should he answer?

"I know this is very difficult for you, son, and if I could make it any easier, I'd—"

"It's OK, Daddy, but you can't," and he hugged Chad as another wave of grief coursed through him. There were so many unknowns and being so far away served only to multiply his confusion.

"Perhaps Rambabu will be awake when we ring. It would be so amazing to hear his voice, wouldn't it, son?"

Naggya's deepest fear was that he may never hear his closest friend's voice again. "He will pull through, Daddy, he must."

❖❖❖❖❖

Elijah walked into their makeshift Son-Shine recovery ward. Although the hospital had discharged the four, the hospital doctor had done so without any medication or prescriptions, leaving all four to battle the pain of internal bleeding and fractured bones and skulls with nothing more than over-the-counter pain relief, and a whole lot of prayer.

For several days, Rambabu, like the other three, slipped in and out of consciousness. On one occasion during a semi-comatose rant, he'd recounted a brief conversation with a doctor in the hospital as the doctor was applying the cast to Rambabu's broken leg. The doctor told him that normally he would be fitted with a much higher cast, but that he would just have to make do with a lower one. Rambabu had replied, "If it wasn't for higher caste, I wouldn't be needing any," or, had he only thought it?

The young man's eyes fluttered in response to Elijah's gentle touch. During his previous lucid moments, Elijah had urged him not to blame himself for what had happened. Yet, as the words left his lips, Elijah continued to wrestle with his own guilt over the exact same issue.

In his pocket, he felt the vibration of his phone. Rambabu's eyes were struggling to remain open as Elijah walked from the room to accept the call. "Sorry, Lois, there is no more news, apart from the fact that miraculously, all four are alive!"

"And the funeral?"

Elijah could hear the catch in her voice. This was far more than a question over dates and times. This had major issues attached, causing Elijah to hesitate before answering. "Um, we haven't really set a date. Ezekiel didn't have any family, but we want, we hope, that at least one of the boys will be well enough to be there. If we have the funeral without them, you know, it would just make things so much harder. We've decided to wait as long as we can."

"I understand, really I do, but Naggya doesn't know what he should do and he's wanting to get on a plane. Elijah, he's been through so much already, and we just don't know what to do."

"The next time one of the boys wakes up, I will call you, OK?"

"Day or night, Elijah, just call."

CHAPTER
sixty-two

"OK, ten days. The draft horse can cover in the meantime but with each passing month, Naggya becomes more crucial to our direction. I get his reasons to fly back at this time, and I understand his grief, but—"

"Do you, Philippe? Do you really?" asked Chad as he struggled with his own. "Grief, especially in such obscene circumstances, isn't something you can put time limits on. If you want the best out of Naggya, then you have to allow him sufficient time."

"I am, that's why I've extended to ten, maybe even fourteen at a squeeze, but that's it, Chad. I have millions of dollars tied up in this, and Naggya is a big part of the vision. He will deal with this, just like he's dealt with every other tragedy. Now, if you don't mind, I have a show to run."

❖❖❖❖❖

"Hello, Elijah?"

"Yes, this is Elijah. How can I help you?"

"My name is Adam Thomson, but everyone calls me Tommo."

Elijah would normally have smiled or chuckled to hear the

friendly sound of an Aussie, but these weren't normal times. "Yes, Tommo?"

"Actually, I'm friends with two of your Australian supporters, the ones who helped you buy the farm recently. Anyway, I'm in Andhra Pradesh, and was hoping to pay you a visit."

Elijah hesitated, trying to summon a polite way to decline, given the urgency and uncertainty at Son-Shine right now. "We love visitors from Australia but when were you thinking of coming?"

"Tomorrow, if that's convenient."

"Sorry, Tommo, but we are dealing with a very serious problem here at the moment. On the farm you spoke of, five of our students were attacked a few nights ago. One died, and four," and he paused, "they are fighting for life. I've been keeping all our supporters updated so I'm surprised you didn't already know."

"I'm so sorry, Elijah. I didn't know. My phone coverage has been a bit sketchy in some areas, and at times I've had no reception at all. Um, you said this took place only a few nights ago?"

"Yes."

"That is so tragic. I intended being there over a week ago. If only my plans hadn't changed."

"What do you mean, changed?"

"It's not important right now. Elijah, I realize I should have made contact earlier. Perhaps I'm too late, and that now is bad timing, so—"

Elijah could hear the concern in Tommo's voice. "It's not

that you couldn't come. It's more that I wouldn't have much time to spend with you. We have a funeral to arrange, and the needs of all the other students."

"If I make my own way to Son-Shine and have no expectations upon your time, would it still be OK to come? I wouldn't be a burden, I promise, it's just that I'm so close and have heard so much about Son-Shine."

From behind him, Elijah heard voices coming from the treatment room, "Sorry, Tommo, I must go! If you can make your own way, you are welcome. Sorry."

Rambabu had woken and was wanting to talk.

❖❖❖❖❖

"Is that really you?"

"Yes, Naggya, it really is me."

A pause might have separated, but for these two young men, knowing that each was on the end of the line, even a very long line, galvanized like nothing on earth. "Are you OK?"

"My head is still hurting but I will be better soon. I don't know when the funeral will be, but—"

"Oh, my best friend, it must have been so horrible. You must have been so—"

"Scared? It all happened so fast, so there wasn't time to be scared."

Rambabu craned his neck to see who was awake and which of the teachers might be nearby, "The others are asleep, but our wounds, they will heal. We must not let our problems defeat us, Naggya."

"But you almost died, and so did Lemuel and Jacob and Noah. And poor Ezekiel, he's—"

"He's in a much better place, and you must trust. We have traveled too far to be turning back now, Naggya. Remember Daddy Chad's dream for you?"

Naggya tried to interrupt but Rambabu wasn't having any of his protests, "Well, I have had a dream. It was the clearest dream I have ever had, and God has shown me things I couldn't have known. Naggya, though it's not a time when we feel weak, for when we are, He is made stronger, and He spoke to me."

"When did He speak?"

"Two nights ago. At least I think it was nighttime."

Naggya's mind raced and forced him to wonder, *was that*

God who spoke or his troubled mind, addled and twisted in the midst of such intolerable pain?

"Are you sure it was God who spoke, I mean—?"

"Naggya, it was God! And He told me not to worry, and that despite everything that is happening, all will be well. It was so clear, Naggya, and He told me that help is on the way."

"Help? What help?"

Rambabu shifted awkwardly and painfully upon his temporary bed, "I don't know. He didn't say."

"Daddy Chad is booking my flight home."

Before he'd had time to consider his response, a vehement "No!" leaped from his lips. "You must not come home, Naggya! Coming home now means that we are giving up! You must stay and continue the vision. Don't you see?"

Another long pause ensued before Naggya spoke, "No, I don't see, but you're telling me, you do?"

"Yes, Naggya, that's what I am telling you. I would love to see you, but not now. Not like this. You must stay where you are. We must not let the enemy win! Our dream can only be fulfilled if we stay strong." From the next bed came a stirring and a long, piercing moan. Rambabu lowered his voice, "Jacob is waking. I must go."

CHAPTER
sixty-three

"Good morning. You must be Elijah."

Elijah forced a smile and shook the outstretched hand of a tall, lean man in his 40s sporting an Akubra and wearing a pair of Billabong shorts, a t-shirt, and thongs. "And you must be Tommo."

"You got me in one. I'm so sorry for what has happened, and I can't begin to imagine how much this has hurt. If only I'd—"

"If only you'd what?"

Tommo scoured the schoolyard. Hundreds of children would normally be playing, joking, and having fun, but not today. "The kids, they all look so sad."

Elijah traced the gaze of the stranger, "Yes, they are right now, but God has not given them a spirit of fear, but—"

"But of love, and power and a sound mind. Yes, I can see that, despite their pain. I should have been here over a week ago, but I kept being held up on business in Mumbai. I felt so uneasy the whole time and I knew I should have left already, but—I know nothing can change what's happened."

"We are about to have assembly, so if you'd like to join us?"

The two men walked to the raised marble apron just outside the largest of the three school blocks. Gathered before them were 200 children ranging in age from 6 to

12, with most of the older children already having left for senior school for the day.

Grief took many shapes and sizes that day, but Elijah was determined it would not take hold for long. He raised his hands in surrender as the music began to bubble up from among the staff and the children. "Amazing grace, how sweet the sound" drifted on the morning, painfully at first, yet as surrender took hold, so too, the grace. Tears rolled down cheeks as hundreds worshiped; many entering into that great exchange, offering up their praise for what they were yet to comprehend. When, as one, they sang "When we've been there ten thousand years," hundreds thought of another one; one who had arrived in that place very recently, and who already was "bright, shining as the sun." Hundreds wept and hundreds still grieved for their unspeakable loss. Tommo sank to his knees as wave upon wave of guilt and remorse flooded his soul, *I should have been here. You told me to get here, so why didn't I listen?*

When the children headed off for classes, Tommo was still on his knees. Elijah left him to do his business with God and departed to his office to continue to pray. Moments later, he heard a soft tap at his door. "Yes, please come in."

Tommo hadn't bothered to wipe the tears from his face and tentatively entered the room, "I'm sorry, Elijah, I know you have much to take care of, it's just that I wanted to ask how I could get to the farm?"

"The farm? Why would you want to go there?"

Over the next few minutes, Tommo told of his business dealings in electronics back in Oz, and in particular, in security and CCTV. He informed Elijah that he and his brother's company had been importing components from China for over ten years, but they'd grown increasingly unsettled about continuing to do so. "Can't really put our fingers on the problem, so, recently we've been looking at India as an alternative. That's why I've spent the last weeks here talking with suppliers. While I was in Mumbai, I kept feeling a very strong prompting to come here, but no matter how hard I tried, I couldn't get away."

"Please don't go blaming yourself, Tommo, you couldn't possibly have known, nor could you have done much to prevent what happened."

"But that's what I'm saying, Elijah, God knew, and He was telling me to come, and if I'd listened I would have been here. Elijah, I feel so horrible!"

Elijah got up from his desk and placed an arm around the heaving shoulders of his visitor, "You must not try to take the blame. Our enemy has been trying to destroy us for so long. This is just the latest."

"But I need to help fight the fight. Ever since my friends told me about Son-Shine, I've been drawn to this place. Please, can I go to the farm? Can I walk there?"

"My friend, you would probably get lost. There are no road signs."

"But I have my GPS, surely that will be enough."

"As you have already discovered, your phone coverage is poor, and out there it is only poorer."

"Elijah, I know that Indians respect Westerners, and I understand how that works, and us Aussies, we know a thing or two about taking care of ourselves if we're attacked. So, if you're concerned about me, then you needn't worry. I'm more than capable of—"

"It's not that, but any Westerner on his own out there near the farm, against twenty attackers, what could you do? Anyway, on your own, you might only make yourself a target to be taken for ransom."

A sense of frustration washed over Tommo until Elijah continued, "How much time would you need there?"

Tommo tugged at his beard and shrugged his shoulders, "Not sure, maybe one, maybe two hours."

"Can you drive?"

"Are you kidding? Back home, we learn to drive before we learn to talk!"

Elijah reached into his pocket to retrieve the car keys. "I will give you directions to my parents' house. Take my car and pick up my father. The upper castes won't touch such an old Dalit, especially a poor one, even if he's with you. My father will go with you, but you will need to be back by 2 p.m., OK?"

❖❖❖❖❖

"That's an amazing old car, Elijah," declared Tommo as he climbed from the Ambassador at 1:45.

"Yes, it has served us well. Did you find what you were looking for?"

For the first time since arriving, Tommo smiled, "If you will allow me, the farm will be as safe as Fort Knox by the time the students are ready to—" and he paused to check his words, "By the time they are better."

A puzzled expression washed over Elijah until Tommo finished outlining his plan. "Um, two of the injured students are now awake. Would you care to meet them?"

Noah tried to sit up for the first time since the attack but grimaced from his multiple fractures and the residual swelling on his brain. He glanced at the visitor and attempted a brief smile, before shutting his eyes tight and slowly working his way back down into a horizontal position. Rambabu didn't try to smile, or move, his mind and spirit irresistibly drawn to the man standing in front of him.

"Rambabu, this is Tommo. He's visiting from Australia and he's just arrived back from your farm."

Tommo reached out his hand but instantly withdrew it when he noticed the cast on the young man's forearm, as well as the one on his leg. "You have a very fine piece of land, young man, very fine indeed."

A curious frown settled upon Rambabu and only lifted after Tommo had shared his thoughts on not only attack-proofing the farm, but on improving the fertility of the soil. "You see, Rambabu, before my brother and I left for Sydney, we grew up on our family farm, so we have a fair knowledge about making a farm produce to its best, that's if you'll allow me to help."

The frown suddenly returned, prompting Rambabu to ask, "But how much will all this cost?"

"How much do you have?"

Rambabu's head dropped, "I have nothing."

"Funny, but that's exactly the figure I had in mind."

Help is on its way, indeed.

❖❖❖❖❖

"Naggya! What are you doing here?"

"I've come to rehearse."

"But, what about your flight to India, and all your friends?"

"Philippe, God said I need to be here even more."

God said? Really? Then, who am I to argue with God?

CHAPTER
sixty-four

Six months had passed since Ezekiel's death. Though the grief had largely worked its way through those who called Son-Shine home, the mention of his name still delivered a sting.

At the entrance to the farm just inside the electrified gate, Ezekiel's memory was immortalized in the form of a sign that proudly identified the property as "Legacy."

Tommo had made two subsequent trips to supply and fit Legacy's new security gates, electrified fences, CCTV, and movement-sensitive lighting. Legacy had not only become fertile and productive, but also a much safer place for Dalits to work.

Scarcely noticeable was Rambabu's limp; his broken arm had healed, though it had lost its ability to fully straighten. A scar remained on the crown of his head, barely visible through his thick hair, and especially while wearing the Akubra Tommo left him at the end of his first trip.

As soon as I'm strong enough, I'm leaving school. Rambabu's declaration was accompanied almost around the clock by his two sidekicks, Philly and Pip; 12-month-old German Shepherd guard dogs, compliments of Tommo and his brother.

With all food and vet bills included in their gift, the brothers had taken great joy and a whole lot of comfort in naming the pair straight out of Philippians 3:2.

Elijah had undertaken to teach Rambabu to drive and had promised to pass on the old Ambassador to Rambabu after Tommo had offered to buy Son-Shine a much newer replacement.

Lemuel and Noah were two of Rambabu's most loyal weekend supporters, feeling a whole lot safer behind the security fences and with Philly and Pip forever nearby wagging their menacing tails. Jacob's wounds had not healed. Based on the experiences of others elsewhere, a crippled Dalit like Jacob would be destined for a life begging on the streets. Chad, Lois, Tommo, and all of Son-Shine begged to differ.

Chad had already instructed Elijah to initiate the process of hiring a contractor to drill for water on the farm, and they had deemed it only right and proper to name this perpetual water supply "Jacob's Well." No one in all of India was as proud to hear the news.

❖❖❖❖❖

Six months of performing and rehearsing had only served to cement Naggya's desires and his fierce determination, and even at the delicate and impressionable age of 17, Naggya was the heir-apparent. Philippe had taken his troupe on a ten-week, sold-out tour of the USA, performing *Romeo and Juliet* to rapturous nightly ovations and impressive reviews. Right now, many believed Philippe Montans to be sitting in pole position on the grid, with all the others lagging behind.

Naggya was fast forging his own name, seen among the premier lead dancers as their equal, and soon to overtake even the very best of the world of ballet. Philippe was ecstatic; his grooming now validated, and his stamp upon the young and emerging star, unquestionable, at least as far as Philippe saw it.

His relationship with Randolph, however, remained fractious at best. "Just remember, Philippe, I still have a year to run on my contract, and I will see you in court before ever allowing you to rob me of one penny," he'd threatened on more than one occasion.

Philippe had implemented a roster in which he would blood Naggya into the rigors and physical demands of nightly performances while simultaneously teasing Randolph towards his inevitable exit. Randolph and Naggya rarely spoke, and when forced to, their exchanges were as cold as they were brief.

Melana, despite the iciness from one of her lead dancers, had continued to shine. During rehearsals, as Randolph approached, her eyes would glaze over as she would fly to her own place, remaining until it was safe to return. Though when Naggya approached, she would soar, her eyes sparkling and dancing as sweetly as her feet.

"We have a break coming up directly after San Francisco, so everyone must continue to fizz. Then and only then we'll all enjoy a well-earned rest. Your reputations have skyrocketed and, as a result, your wallets are bulging. Next stop, Europe. You should all be very proud."

❖❖❖❖❖

"Are you happy playing second fiddle?"

Randolph glanced down at his screen and saw "ID unknown" illuminated. "Who is this?"

"Never mind, but a certain big player would like to send you a message, that's unless you're willing to see out your contract?"

"Listen, I don't play games with strangers, so why don't you just—"

"Funny, that's not what I've heard."

Randolph was becoming angrier by the second, "So, you work for Galant?"

"You don't need to know who I work for, and you never will! The only thing that's important is do you grab your one and only chance to get square with that clown?"

"So, you do work for Galant! Has Galant changed his mind about me joining his troupe?"

"You don't listen very well, do you? Now, I haven't got time to waste; are you interested in making some serious money or not?"

Randolph glanced around to ensure no one was within earshot, "What do you have in mind?"

"Meet me at Fisherman's Wharf at 11 p.m. And come alone."

"But how will I recognize you?"

"You won't, but I'll recognize you."

"And how do I know you can be trusted?"

After a momentary pause, "Well, that depends on how much you want the money. 11:00."

CHAPTER
sixty-five

"He took the bait."

"I knew he would. He's nowhere else to turn, and even the pip-squeak calls him draft horse! We just need to ensure we can't be traced."

"Way ahead of you, Boss. And besides, he ain't that bright."

❖ ❖ ❖ ❖ ❖

"So, I told him the word was none of the masters would be interested in touching him, especially with that dicky knee. He tried to deny it, but when I told him we knew where he was having treatment and have photos, he shut up quick-time. Anyway, when I waved half a million in one night under his nose, and the chance to destroy Montans, he suddenly got interested. I told him he'd be wise to skip the country with all his money afterwards and stay away till everything blows over."

"And?"

"And he didn't seem too bothered about leaving. He reckoned he's had enough of America anyway."

"So, you were with him a while?"

"Nah, I pretty much did all the talking and it was all

wrapped up in ten. I kept him in the dark so there's no way he'd recognize me. These new fake beards work a treat."

"They've five shows left in California, so I'm wondering when's best?"

"Boss, I'd say second-last night."

Galant chuckled down the phone, "Two minds thinking alike!"

"He wants half up front."

"And you can cover that?"

There was another loud chuckle, only this time, not from Galant. "That depends on how quick you send me the money, including mine."

"You'd better be sure. It'll be in your account tomorrow. But how can you be certain the account's not traceable?"

"Boss, it's not just the beard that's fake."

❖❖❖❖❖

Naggya had been looking forward to a break; the constant tension with Randolph and the demands of weeks of touring had taken a toll. Hours spent alone in a hotel room in unfamiliar cities wasn't his idea of paradise, and on top of all that, he was missing Mummy Lois and Daddy Chad. The extra three hours' time difference between the Western states and Son-Shine had added another dimension to keeping in touch by phone. *I just need to talk with Rambabu.*

❖❖❖❖❖

"I know getting cabs in San Francisco is different from New York, but please try to make rehearsal on time. We have two more shows, and then we fly back East. Please remember that the bums on seats tonight aren't the same bums as last night. These people are seeing us for the first time, and we won't be just recycling last night's performance! Tonight will be our best ever, but only until tomorrow night! Got it?"

A round of nods and agreements satisfied the grand master that his message had found its mark, except for one. "What's with you?"

Randolph raised a hand in an unconvincing protest, "I have no idea what you're talking about." Never before had Randolph stooped to sabotage. Never before had he risked so much, but never before had he found himself at life's crossroads.

"As you know only too well, Randolph, it's your turn to dance lead tonight, so if you're not up to it—?"

Suddenly, the prospect of his secret plan not having a landing strip kicked him into a higher gear. "I'm raring to go, Philippe. We will give them a show they will never forget."

"Now, that's more like it. Now off you go, get your tights on." Philippe gave his lead dancer a shove towards the changing rooms and walked over to Melana and Naggya. "Keep an eye on him. Something's not right."

❖❖❖❖❖

The house lights dimmed right on time and a hush quickly settled over the crowd. Every dancer was super-charged with adrenaline, as much to do with the house-full sign as the fact that vacation was now only two performances away. Naggya took his place alongside Melana's understudy, as he had done many times before. Philippe positioned himself even closer than usual, and whispered to Naggya, "Is it my imagination, or is Randolph behaving even stranger?" He scanned the wings and noticed Randolph again averting his gaze. "Don't bother, Naggya, just be ready!" Seconds after the orchestra ushered in the first scene, the troupe danced its most gracious and fluent way out onto the softly lit stage, transporting the enthralled audience magically back to fourteenth century Verona. Instantly, every imagination was thrust in the middle of a fierce family feud.

Randolph, as Romeo, a member of the Montague family, and Melana, as Juliet, a Capulet, were both in impeccable form; time and again, they'd individually or collectively elicit oohs and ahs from the audience. All through Acts One and Two, Philippe observed from the wings, drifting from deep concern to satisfied approval. *Yes, much more like it! Bravo!*

Act Three began with Romeo, who had just secretly wed Juliet, blissfully walking the streets of Verona to be confronted by Juliet's cousin, Tybalt, and some of his friends. An argument ensued, setting the perfect stage for Randolph to sabotage the entire production. Instead of Mercutio stepping in to defend the reluctant Romeo, totally contrary to script, Randolph lunged forward in an attempt to shove Tybalt headlong into the orchestra pit.

Philippe was apoplectic, the troupe froze and looked about in confused horror, as were those from within the crowd with knowledge of how the scene was meant to play out. Shrieks rang out throughout the theater as those who hadn't understood the deviation from script craned their necks to discover the reason for the unexpected commotion.

As forcefully as Romeo attempted to shove Tybalt into the orchestra pit, Tybalt resisted, until, from stage left, a second Romeo leapt from the wings. With the precision and power of a pillaging tiger, he broke the hold on Tybalt, spun Romeo number one around several times, then flung him head-first from the stage into the waiting arms of the security officers. Romeo number two gracefully pirouetted before completing the rescue of the disoriented Tybalt.

Contrary to the script, the curtain fell, as did Philippe.

❖❖❖❖❖

Act Three Scene Two unfolded in front of an unsettled and still vocal audience, while two burly security officers restrained Romeo number one deep within the bowels of the theater. Romeo number two and his new wife, the much-relieved Juliet, steered the script gloriously back on track, while Philippe remained almost comatose with rage. He'd most likely have remained that way had it not been for the ten-minute standing ovation and a shower of flowers.

CHAPTER
sixty-six

A number of the nation's dailies ran with a similar theme the next morning; "Bizarre sabotage almost kills off Romeo and Juliet!" while others zeroed in on the impulsive rescue that ushered in the most astounding of outcomes. "Naggya, the hero from India," was an overnight success, and by the end of the following night's rapturous finale, his name was already etched in ballet folklore. Philippe's smile widened and, so too would his bank account as offers came flooding in from around the globe. *So much for a holiday*, he thought as he packed for the flight home; *Naggya, the hero from India... hmmmm... I like the sound of that. I'd best get his new contract stitched up before the vultures come circling.*

In between phone inquiries, Philippe managed to call his lawyer, "You have had every legal and moral right to tear up Randolph's contract, however, although you may have moral grounds to sue him for damages, I don't see you winning. Quite simply, despite there being intent to cause harm, at this point in time, he's done you an enormous favor. I'd be letting sleeping dogs lie, if I were you."

Philippe thanked his lawyer, though he couldn't resist a parting remark, "Don't let him know that! I want the draft horse to suffer!"

"And I wouldn't be calling him that either or you might have a damages case against you. Oh, this Indian lad, seems he suddenly has a bit of a cult following if the papers are anything to go by. Have you considered locking him down to a new contract?"

"I've just been thinking the same thing. But isn't that what I pay you for?"

The lawyer chuckled, "Well, ever since you've been able to afford to pay me, but don't forget all the pro bono work I've done when you were, shall we say, a little less—"

"Wealthy? Quite. Just make sure it's a long contract!"

"And the dollar amount?"

Philippe almost choked on his reply, "Can we afford a mill?"

"I'm your lawyer, not your accountant. The thing you need to decide is how much will lock him in."

"Leave it with me, but now, I have another call to make." With great delight he contacted his former lead dancer, "Your contract is terminated as of now! Your services are no longer required, ever!" With the sound of another incoming call, Philippe quickly added, "And you'll be hearing from my lawyer over a claim for damages, loser!" The call ended abruptly.

❖❖❖❖❖

"Caller Unknown" lit up time and again. *How the hell do I track this con man? He still owes me a quarter of a million dollars! He must be working for Galant Scott! Who else would be splashing that sort of money?*

Galant sat in his New York office and stared blankly at the

newspaper headline. *So, how am I supposed to land Naggya now? That boy's just cost me a packet!*

❖❖❖❖❖

While the entire troupe gathered at their hotel before flying back to the Big Apple, Philippe's smile showed no signs of abating. Melana tentatively stepped forward to pose a question that had been on everyone's lips; "Naggya, it still astounds me, but how did you possibly stay so calm when we were all panicking?"

Clearly embarrassed, he averted their gaze until Philippe added, "Yes, Naggya, please, we'd all like to know."

The young dancer fidgeted and stared intently at the ground, "When I was five, I witnessed my father kill my mother. After that, nothing comes close."

CHAPTER
sixty-seven

"Hello, is that Information and Faults? It is? Thank you, I'm trying to contact a caller who has made several calls to my phone. Every time I try to return the call, it just tells me the caller is unknown, so what can I do?" Randolph listened carefully to the service operator's reply as his heart sank deeper. "So, there's no way I can trace the calls?" By now, his heart was pounding, and he could feel his blood pressure rising, "Thank you anyway." Randolph slid limply down to the floor and began to moan, softly at first, but by the time it had reached wail, he was a complete mess. *How could I be so stupid?!* Randolph finally accepted he'd been used. *I'll get you, Scott!* Randolph thrashed all manner of scenarios around for the next hour; he considered going to the police but knew he'd be only incriminating himself. *No, I'll have to outsmart him. I've got half the money, so I'm OK for now, and the rent is paid for a month. Think Randolph, just think!*

❖ ❖ ❖ ❖ ❖

"Offer the Indian 1.25 to start with, but if we have to go higher, we will. I can make that back in six months, but just get him away from that pip-squeak before he becomes a lost cause! You know where he lives?"

"Yes, I do. He's still at that halfway house for those foreign performers."

"Then get to it, man! Time is money!"

❖❖❖❖❖

Chad, Lois, Naggya, and Samuel found a quiet corner in their favorite Indian restaurant, Manhattan Makhani, where they settled in for the evening.

When the waitress finished taking their orders, she placed her pad in front of Naggya and asked him to sign, "It's just for confirmation," and she smiled sweetly and waited while a puzzled expression overtook him. When Lois encouraged Naggya to oblige, the young waitress clutched the pad to her chest and disappeared into the kitchen.

"You'd best be getting used to that, young man. Requests for autographs will come in all shapes and sizes."

As the second course was being placed in front of them by another equally attentive waitress, Chad turned in amusement to glance around the room. As he did, he noticed a gentleman sitting on his own nearby. When their eyes met, the man smiled and nodded. "He's somewhat of a celebrity," and waited to see if anyone responded.

By the time the dessert dishes and cups were being cleared away to howls of protests over the offer of more, Chad overheard an exchange between the waitress and the man who had requested his bill. Climbing to his feet, the man made his way towards them, "Sorry for my intrusion but, please, may I pay my respects to the nation's finest costume designers and the world's greatest emerging star?"

Chad stood to his feet, "So, you're a supporter of the arts, sir?"

The man extended his hand, "Oh, goodness me, yes. Ever since a youngster, and clearly that was a while ago." He pivoted to face Naggya, "Young man, you are indeed a prodigious talent. It's been my privilege to watch your rapid and rightful rise to prominence. Congratulations! And at such a young age. Impressive, very impressive."

The man gestured to leave, but paused, "Ah, with such a promising future ahead, I hope you're being taken care of to your satisfaction, because if you're not, a good friend of mine would be happy to—"

Chad reached across and took the man firmly by the arm, "Sorry, sir, but this is not the time or the place, nor is it appropriate to be discussing business, so if you don't mind?"

The man half bowed and gave a brief nod, "Of course, Mr. McNeil, how impertinent of me. Please forgive," and he reached into his jacket pocket and retrieved a business card. "May I at least leave my card? My friend is a great admirer of all of you, and he is extremely generous. Good evening all," and he tipped his imaginary hat and bid the four a good evening while placing his card directly in front of Naggya.

❖❖❖❖❖

"Mr. Scott is in rehearsal and cannot be disturbed. Sorry, but you will have to make an appointment."

"I will do nothing of the sort! Unless you'd prefer an ugly scene in front of all your visitors, I suggest you let him know I'm here, now!"

The receptionist picked up the phone and turned her back, "Um, sorry, but Randolph Sezsharn's here and he's causing a fuss. He's demanding to see you."

Galant strummed the mouthpiece of the phone as he considered his response, "Tell him to come back in an hour. Tell him if he causes any trouble, security will throw him out, and he'll certainly remember how that feels!"

❖❖❖❖❖

"Sit down and make this quick!"

"I know it was you, and I will prove it. You still owe me 250 thousand! That is unless you want to face charges!"

"Randy, you are all washed up and a sad bit of work! I have no idea what you're on about, so unless you'd like to be thrown out I strongly suggest you leave peaceably! That is, unless you have something worth hearing."

"We both know we'd be far better off with Philippe and the Indian off the scene, so my plan is we finish the job we started?"

"You amuse me, Randy, you really do. But, just for entertainment's sake, what sort of sinister plan have you dredged up?"

Randolph smiled at the prospect of having Galant Scott on the hook, "The Indian, he's gay."

"And that's your plan?! Half of the performing arts are gay!"

"Yes, but half aren't Indian and from the lowest caste. He's a Dalit!"

"A what?"

"He's a Dalit. He's from the lowest in the caste system! Dalits are seen as nothing more than animals, and—"

"Listen, Randolph, I don't care if he's a bleeding Southern Baptist! All I care about is his dancing!"

"But in his world—"

"I couldn't care a scrap about his world. I'm only interested in mine! Now, if he was in my stable instead of that pip-squeak's, I'd make him so famous, even the Indians would love him!"

"Ah, so you're suddenly a social reformer?!"

"Listen, I've had enough of your insolence! Unless you've got something better, we're done!"

"Are you saying you want him in your stable?"

"Who's in my stable is my business, not yours. The Indian is a rare talent, the likes of which only come along a couple of times in a career, but unless he's in my stable, he might as well pack his bags and go back to India."

"Galant, in their world, homosexuality is considered—"

"Listen, if that's where you want to go with this, then get out, because you're wasting my time!"

"Think about it, Galant, if we get to the Indian through a gay plant, we get to him through another plant."

"What?!"

Randolph leaned forward and lowered his voice, "Everyone knows about drugs in the arts. Where there's money, there's drugs, right? So, we get a gay dancer to get past his defenses, and we plant some drugs on the Indian and arrange a sting. We do it on Philippe's property and nab them both for possession and trafficking. The Indian goes down and he takes Montans with him. The scandal would be priceless! Virtually overnight, double barrel, they're both history. Best of all, you rule the roost again!"

"I already rule the roost, Sezsharn, and don't ever forget it!"

"Then why the sabotage in San Francisco?"

"Like I said, you amuse me. And what, pray tell, might you get out of it?"

"Apart from the satisfaction of destroying Montans and the Indian, in return for delivering you a very juicy monopoly, I get enough dollars to leave this place and set myself up in Europe. Oh, and don't forget, you still owe me for the other job."

Galant forced a chuckle, "According to the newspapers, it was you who made the stuff up of discrediting Montans!"

"Which is why we have to get it right this time!"

CHAPTER
sixty-eight

"Mr. McNeil, how did you enjoy your meal?"

"Sorry, who is calling?"

"We met the other night at the Makhani and I left you my card. It's Maurice Weaver. Have I caught you at a convenient time?"

Chad frowned towards his wife and shrugged his shoulders, "And what might we do for you, Mr. Weaver?"

"I was hoping to set a time to come and see you regarding your Naggya."

Chad shifted the phone to his other shoulder before replying, "Mr. Weaver, can you tell me why we would be doing that?"

"Please excuse the secrecy. As I mentioned the other night, my friend is a great admirer of Naggya, and as I also mentioned, is very generous and very well-connected. Your lad would do well to consider his—"

"And who might this mystery man be?"

"Ah, a very reasonable question, Mr. McNeil, and may I suggest that at our meeting, all the relevant and the very attractive matters would be detailed in full. Would during business hours or after-hours suit you best?"

This guy's really getting on my nerves. "Actually, neither, that is unless you identify who your friend is."

"Sorry, Mr. McNeil, but with so much money at stake, I'm sure you can appreciate the need for discretion."

Chad raised his voice, "Mr. Weaver, we haven't even mentioned money. As far as we're concerned, it is and would always be about the person, so if you're not willing to identify who this person is, then . . . "

"Mr. McNeil, the last thing I would want to do is upset you, and it would seem I have. With over a million-dollars-a-year on offer, I—"

"Mr. Weaver, the identity?!"

"Actually, the person involved is well known to you and you've done much fine work for him over many years, so it would possibly come as no surprise that a person of his caliber and unrivaled standing worldwide would take such an interest in Naggya's future. That person is, and can only be, Galant Scott."

"I thought as much. Mr. Weaver, Galant hasn't put one single order our way ever since Naggya chose to join Philippe, so we're hardly swayed by—"

"Actually, Mr. Scott has asked me to inquire if you'd be interested in becoming his exclusive supplier, on top of the work you do for other smaller studios, of course. I mean, it's a win for Naggya and very much a win for you."

"I will discuss the matter with my wife. We have your card, so I can call you after we've had a chance to consider your offer."

"Thank you, Mr. McNeil, and may I say that you've handled this matter extremely sensitively, just as Mr. Scott said you would. He speaks very highly of you and your work, and he has asked me to stress that the figures I have mentioned are flexible, very flexible. And may I also add, knowing how busy you are, if you've not had time to discuss this in, say, a few days, I will call to answer any queries you may have."

"I'll call you if we're interested. Now, if you don't mind."

"Talk soon, Mr. McNeil, and have a great day."

Weaver clicked open his address book and made another call, "They're nibbling. I'd like to be a fly on the wall at the McNeil's tonight."

"Good, but make this happen quick. The Indian either joins us or he suffers the consequences."

❖❖❖❖❖

"Naggya, how long would you like to keep dancing?"

The young man looked across at Philippe, "What do you mean?"

"I mean, how many years would you see yourself being lead dancer of my troupe? You're still not 18, so—"

"I need to keep dancing for as long as my people have needs."

"But you told me that there are over one billion people in India!"

"My Dalit people."

"And there are what, more than 300-million Dalits?"

"About that."

"Then you'll need to be dancing for a very long time."

Naggya's expression deepened, "Sorry, I don't understand why you're asking. Aren't you happy with my dancing?"

Philippe chuckled in a feeble attempt to conceal his true motives, "It's just that I've been looking at your contract, and now that you've been promoted to lead dancer, it's only fair you should be rewarded with some more money. And now that you've told me how long you need to dance, for your people's sake, it would be best to make the contract a long one. The longer, the better, wouldn't you agree?"

"I guess so. Daddy just called me and said he's had a phone call today about the same thing."

"Who from?"

"He didn't tell me, but said we'd be talking about it tonight. Do dancers really get that much?"

Philippe gulped awkwardly but tried to appear calm, "And how much is *that much*?"

"I don't know. He just said we could buy a whole lot of farming land with so much money, but that's all he said."

CHAPTER
sixty-nine

The first few days of his vacation were mostly spent resting. So much had unfolded since his last break, and with a European tour on the horizon there was so much to occupy his thinking. *Four whole months non-stop in new and exciting countries, and I will be lead dancer! Wow!*

DAPA had continued to grow and already Kate was looking to expand. Tentative plans were before the architect to redesign the entire floor to accommodate another ten students. With his significantly higher earnings, Naggya briefly considered getting a place of his own, but just as quickly dismissed the notion: *What, I'm suddenly better than the others just because my dancing pays more money!* He raised the matter of subsidizing the DAPA running costs with Kate one morning; "Why can't I pay some extra money? It'd help reduce the burden and I'd feel a whole lot better knowing I was contributing a bit more."

Kate looked at one of her favorite residents fondly and smiled, "You're one in a million! It's little wonder we all love you so much," and she wrapped her long plump arms around him and planted a big kiss on his forehead. "But I think it would need to be done on the quiet, you know, to avoid division."

With most of the students away either studying, performing, or working during the day, Naggya found himself with time on his hands and soon grew restless. For two hours each afternoon he would go to the studio to practice, often on his own, before calling into Impressions to speak with Mummy and Daddy.

By the end of the first week, he'd quickly slipped into a routine.

❖❖❖❖❖

"Ah, Mr. McNeil, how nice to hear your voice."

"Mr. Weaver, I thought we made it clear we would call you if we needed any further—"

"Quite so, quite so, and I wouldn't have bothered you, had it not been for an incredibly exciting development."

Chad beckoned his wife into the office and put the call on speaker. "And what might that be?"

"As you very well know, Mr. Scott is at the very forefront of world ballet, and due to his unparalleled world standing, he's about to announce the establishment of his very own junior pathway academy! It's so exciting! The academy will not only be set-up here in New York, but in Chicago, Los Angeles, Milan, New York, and quite possibly Paris. Everything's still top-secret, but very soon there will be major simultaneous worldwide announcements."

Chad and Lois exchanged glances as thoughts began to form in their minds, "That is exciting, Mr. Weaver, but why are you telling us?"

"This is where it gets very interesting for you. Mr. Scott has expressly asked me to let you know he would be delighted to offer your company, Impressions, the contract to become exclusive costume supplier, worldwide. As I said, it's so exciting and I'm sure this must be tantalizing music to your ears after so many years of your diligent work. Just imagine, you're one step away from an additional multi-multi-million-dollar-a-year turnover."

The exchanges between Chad and Lois deepened as their suspicions began to grow, "Mr. Weaver, it's Lois, and I'm wondering—"

"How delightful to be speaking again, and please, call me Maurice. We could easily be about to become friends."

"Mr. Weaver, might this proposal be possibly conditional upon Naggya switching camps?"

"A very interesting question, Lois. It is acceptable to be calling you by your first name, is it not?"

"Does it?" she repeated.

"Actually, Mr. Scott didn't say, not in so many words at least, but I imagine he would be delighted if we were all in this together, you know, one big happy family. May I pass on to Mr. Scott that you've received his amazing and very lucrative proposal favorably?"

"There is much to take into consideration, Mr. Weaver, but we will not only require far more detail, an appropriate amount of time to consider, and of course, the opportunity to discuss this offer with Naggya. So, unless you have anything further to add, my wife and I will bid you a good afternoon and thank you for your call."

"Quite so, Mr. McNeil. Enjoy your contemplations and I will keep you posted on developments. For now though, have a great day."

Chad stood to face his wife, "So, what do you make of all that?"

Lois reflexively straightened the creases in her skirt and turned to face her husband, "Ah, if only half of it was true, it would be an absolute Godsend for our business, but—"

"But what?"

"Naggya. We can't go putting any further pressure on him. He's had enough already, so I'm a bit—"

Chad peered past his wife at the slightly ajar office door; it slowly opened.

"Naggya!

❖❖❖❖❖

"Please, son, you must eat. You've hardly touched your dinner."

"Sorry, Mummy." Naggya pushed the food around his plate then pushed it away.

"Son, we know you're trying to please everyone, but you can't always do that." Listening to Chad usually came easily to Naggya, but not now. He knew how much of a blessing the extra business would mean to them, and Galant's offer amounted to almost double that of Philippe's, even allowing for the likelihood of both parties still willing to up the ante.

The possibility of changing camps brought with it a raft of considerations, most of which he could comfortably discuss with his adopted parents, but one, he could never bring out into the light of day. *It kills me even thinking about it.*

Lois took Naggya's hand in hers, "Son, we can see your torment, but in the end, you have to make a decision that works best for you."

"But the best for me isn't the best for you."

"Possibly so, but if you chose Galant, what do you think Philippe would likely do about our business?"

"Yes, he'd probably drop you, but Philippe's not going worldwide!"

Chad stood and walked around to Naggya's side of the table and leaned in close, "We only have the word of his messenger, and since we first met Mr. Weaver, I've had an uneasy feeling about him, not to mention the dubious reputation of Galant Scott. Lois is right, you need to decide what's best for you."

"It's just, I can't get my head around so much money. One-and-a-half-million a year. That's—too much."

CHAPTER
seventy

"Rambabu!"

"Oh, how I've needed to hear your voice!"

"Please tell me, how is your leg?"

Rambabu smiled as he imagined his best friend in the whole world on the other end of the line, "Ah, no one has invited me onto their kabaddi team lately."

A wry smile crossed Naggya's lips, "That's okay, you were never much good anyway," evoking a pair of transcontinental chuckles of the very best kind.

"And the farm?"

"We now have the best water supply in all of Krishna, and the maize is so tall, we need to buy a ladder!"

The tone deepened when Naggya asked his next question, "Um, speaking of the farm, has anything happened on the property next to you?"

"You mean the big one?"

"Yes."

"We haven't seen anyone on it for many weeks, and the weeds, they are nearly as tall as our banana trees. Why do you ask?"

"Can you ask Elijah how much it'd take to buy?"

"I don't have to ask him. He told me the other day."

"And?"

"He said if someone offered eighteen-million Rupee, the old man might sell. Why are you asking?"

"I will call you back soon."

❖❖❖❖❖

"Daddy, do you know how much eighteen-million Rupee is in U.S. dollars?"

Chad grinned as he began to see Naggya's plan taking shape. He quickly opened the currency converter on his laptop and punched in some numbers. "It's around a quarter-of-a-million U.S. But no matter which master you go with, neither will give you that much up front, son."

A sparkle leapt into Naggya's eyes, "But didn't our pastor say last Sunday, "We have not because we ask not'?"

Their embrace was long, and intense.

❖❖❖❖❖

"Look, Galant, if I push any harder it's just going to drive them away. Chad has made it very clear, they won't be hurried."

"Then give them a reason to make a decision!"

Maurice Weaver shifted awkwardly in his chair directly across from his employer, "Well, the biggest lever we have right now is the launch, so we could—"

"What launch?!"

"The world ballet academy's launch, of course."

"There is no launch! It's nothing more than an idea!"

"You and I know that, but they don't. If we hit them with a

juicy enough proposal and let them believe it's imperative to be onboard before our launch, they might swallow the bait. Once we've got a signed contract, we again hold all the aces. The big question is, how much are you willing to bid to land the Indian?"

Galant Scott didn't appreciate being played at his own game and squirmed as he contemplated vocalizing the biggest dollar figure he'd ever offered, especially to a dancer not yet 18. Galant rocked back in his chair, "Go to one-and-a-half, but only if he'll sign immediately!"

Weaver's eyes lit up as he salivated his commission. "I'll ring and set up an appointment. And Impressions?"

"I really couldn't care less! Offer them an exclusive, subject to six monthly performance reviews. That should shut them up, now, get the Indian signed!"

❖❖❖❖❖

"Mr. McNeil, no doubt you'll appreciate being kept up to date before everything goes public, so might I come to your office before the news breaks? Rest assured, you will be amazed."

"Mr. Weaver, we are very busy."

"Quite so. You'll recall I mentioned that the figures we recently discussed were flexible? I can confirm they are, and I have something irresistible to share. I'd need around ten minutes, so might we settle on 5 p.m.?"

Three hours later, Maurice Weaver confidently walked into the Impressions outer office, briefcase in hand. Fifteen minutes later, he strode out, leaving Chad in possession of a most impressive sham and a signed proposal for Naggya to countersign. The contract was for an annual retainer of one-point-five-million dollars plus two-point-five percent of net profits, however, the offer had an expiry date of seven days. Proposed on a separate contract was an offer for Impressions to become Galant Scott's exclusive costume supplier commencing three months from the date of the contract. The offer also had an expiry of seven days.

Maurice Weaver departed Impressions with a grin, "My number is available twenty-four-seven, but with the worldwide launch about to be made, it would be prudent to act speedily."

❖❖❖❖❖

"Yes, Philippe, he's here."

"I've been trying to call him. We need to get his contract settled."

Chad motioned for Lois to close the office door and put the call on speaker. "Naggya is in the cutting room at the moment. Can I help?"

"My lawyer sent a new contract to him days ago, but for some reason we seem to be dragging the chain. Is there a problem?"

"Actually, we're about to break for dinner and we'll be discussing the offers then."

"Offers?"

"Yes, Philippe, offers. Seems our Naggya is suddenly in high demand."

A prolonged silence ensued before Chad asked, "Are you still there, Philippe?"

"Yes, yes, I was just thinking. A number of exciting developments have taken place over the past few days, and so—"

"Yes, Philippe?"

"So, despite my very generous earlier offer, there might possibly be a little wiggle room."

"That's good to hear, because that might help make up the shortfall."

"How much shortfall?"

"Like I say, Philippe, we'll be discussing the matter tonight, but the extent of the shortfall will be determined by the scope of your wiggle room. Whichever way it goes, we'll be in touch in the morning."

"Just in case you need to ask anything, I'll keep my phone on."

Now where have I heard that before? Chad smiled and ended the call.

❖❖❖❖❖

The three gathered in the office and settled comfortably into recliners, "Here, Naggya, pass me your plate." Lois divided up their takeout dinner as they respectfully gave thanks to eat.

"Tell us, son, how are you feeling about this whole contract decision?"

He wiped the corner of his mouth with a napkin and forced a smile, "I'll just be glad when it's all settled and I can concentrate on dancing again. It's so much money! If I'm being honest, it's got me a little worried what Philippe will expect from me after spending so much."

"So, you're not considering Galant?"

Naggya's head dropped and he stopped chewing. Slowly, his head shook from side to side as he raised his glistening eyes, "I can't. I just can't."

Lois put her food down and moved in closer, "You know, as his lead dancer, Galant would probably treat you a whole lot differently than when you first met. He's offered a whole lot more money than Philippe, so it's in Galant's best interests to keep you happy."

Naggya's head again lowered and remained that way until Lois put her arm around him and gently stroked his hair, "Son?"

"It's not the money, Mummy."

Chad joined his wife and wrapped his arms around both, "Then, what is it?"

Waves of emotions coursed through the young man as the horror of Galant Scott's changing room played out time and again, assaulting the depths of his soul.

"I just can't!"

It was a long time before the crying ceased, yet only one would ever likely know why. He purposed his gaze upon his beloved parents, "I'm sorry."

"So, we're settled on Philippe. He rang earlier and wanted to know your decision. He told me that his offer might be improved, so should we ask him how much?"

Once again, Naggya dried his eyes and looked to his dad and nodded. As Chad reached for his phone, Naggya raised his hand and said, "Wait, please Daddy. Ask him if he'll go to one-point-one with two-hundred-and-fifty straight away?"

Chad smiled and winked at his wife, "I'm confident he'll agree, but might I suggest point-two and see what he says? After all, Galant's offer is considerably higher."

"If you think he'll agree, Daddy, but there's one more thing. Philippe needs to put in writing that Impressions gets all his work for the next five years."

The trio smiled, and ten minutes after the call, the amendments to Philippe's contract were added, initialed, and they were now set to make another call.

"Rambabu, make a cash offer of fifteen-million rupee! Ask Elijah to let the old man know we can settle in one month, and if he hesitates, remind him not many would want his farm with Dalits on the farm next door!"

CHAPTER
seventy-one

"Get Randolph on the phone! Chad just called and they've gone with the pip-squeak! If they think they can mess with me, I'll destroy the lot of them, especially that Indian ingrate!"

❖❖❖❖❖

"I've got just the boy for the job. He's new to the stable, he's a very promising dancer, and he's so, so gay! But we'll need a quantity of coke. Can you lay your hands on a kilo?"

"Listen, Randolph, I'm a ballet master not some petty drug mule! If I'm to be paying you a truck-load of greens, you'll have to find the stuff yourself!"

"And I'm a lead dancer, and I—"

"You mean, you were a lead dancer!"

"If I'm going to risk everything, then it's going to cost you big-time!"

Galant Scott could sense the desperation in Randolph's voice, and as his own pulse raced over the prospect of obliterating his major competitor, he mused, *If we get this right, I'm back on top and the opportunities will just keep rolling in. Number one, with no one else in sight.* "And just how much is big-time?"

"Half a mill up front and another half when we bring them down."

"Hah, you're dreaming!"

"Am I? Galant, I suggest you sleep on it, and when you've realized I'm your best shot, you know my number. In the meantime, I'll be talking with the boy. Oh, and by the way, the Indian already likes him."

❖❖❖❖❖

"Tommo, the man from Australia, just called and can make the whole ten acres secure and upgrade the pump so we can irrigate everything from the same well. And he's sending more money!"

"That's so great, Rambabu, but what did the old man say?"

"Elijah is calling him again today so we should know in a few hours. Has your money come through?"

"Just let me know what account to send it to and it will all be there within days. And Mummy and Daddy will be sending some more money as well. They've just signed a new contract with Philippe, so we're all very excited."

"Wow, Naggya, we have been so blessed. Soon we will have enough land to feed many more of our people. I too am so excited!"

"Aren't you going to ask how much money we'll be sending?"

There was a momentary silence before Naggya repeated his question.

"Whatever is sent will be enough. This is what I have learned."

Naggya smiled and a soft, knowing chuckle drifted down the line, "On top of the money for the land and the government charges, we will be sending another 35,000 dollars."

"And that's how much in our money?"

"That's about two-and-a-half-million rupee."

"And Tommo is sending two-million more! Naggya, we can plant straight away, and we can buy all the tools we will need, and build a storage shed, and—"

"Rambabu, the old man hasn't said yes yet."

"But he will, I know he will.

❖❖❖❖❖

Elijah drove to Legacy and climbed from the vehicle Tommo had purchased. He walked poker-faced towards Rambabu and said nothing. Within several paces Elijah threw his arms around his former-student and declared with a shout, "The old man said 'yes'! The big farm will soon be yours!"

Tears of joy rolled down their faces as the pair sang and they danced as wildly as Rambabu's twisted leg would allow. Their praises filled the early afternoon sunshine and floated majestically upon the softest of breezes. *Eleven amazing acres!*

CHAPTER
seventy-two

"No, he would love to help you. He's not a snob like a lot of dancers, and don't forget, not long ago he was just like you."

Winston shook his head and looked away, "He was never like me. He's in another galaxy. I'm just ordinary."

"I've watched you dance, Winston, and you're unquestionably not ordinary. And besides, I've watched the way Naggya looks at you."

"What do you mean?"

Randolph placed an arm on the young man's shoulder and smiled, "You know exactly what I mean."

❖❖❖❖❖

Official rehearsals weren't due to commence for another couple of days, however, Naggya hadn't missed a day's practice since shortly after returning from Frisco. "Metronomic" was his warm-up and his stretch routine, and never until he'd launch into self-expression would his routine ever vary.

From behind him, he sensed someone watching, and on landing from an impressive twisting leap, he caught sight of Winston, as a half-smile appeared on his handsome young face.

Naggya unleashed several of his most exhilarating sequences and in his exuberance, almost brushed the wall as his expression climaxed to the gasp of his onlooker. Frozen in time and space as he gathered his breath, the young Indian's gaze turned to the wings and beckoned Winston forward. "Are you here to see Philippe?"

"Actually, I wanted to see you."

"Oh, really?" and again, Naggya smiled. "And how can I help you?"

Winston stood within a foot of his hero and placed a hand on Naggya's still-heaving chest, "I'd like to study under you, if that's possible? I want to be just like you."

Gently, Naggya removed Winston's hand and peered into his eyes, "Don't try to be me. Discover who you are instead."

Winston broke eye contact and lowered his head, "If I'm being truly honest, I wouldn't even know where to start looking."

"That's the best place to start."

"What is?"

"Being truly honest. We can become just another clone, or we can choose to bury our real selves. Neither takes real honesty."

Winston's eyes were once again galvanized upon Naggya's.

"Do you think we might become friends?"

❖❖❖❖❖

"Tommo arrives in three days and he's planning on staying a week. He said all the components for the new security systems and the plumbing to irrigate the whole property should arrive before he gets here. He said he wants to get straight to work. Oh, and the lawyer said the money has cleared into the holding account and he has asked the old man to allow you access before settlement."

"And what did the old man say?" asked Rambabu.

"All the old man wants is his money. If the lawyer releases the full amount before settlement, then he's willing to allow you to start work."

"But, Elijah, if we give him all the money, can anything go wrong before the legal transfer?"

"The lawyer says it should be OK."

"Should be?"

❖ ❖ ❖ ❖ ❖

"Tommo, Tommo, how wonderful to see you!" yelled Rambabu as he hobbled to the vehicle.

"Wow, the crops look amazing!"

The pair embraced then gazed upon the fruits of their combined labors. "Guess what, young fella?"

Rambabu chuckled as his mind pondered how to respond, "Will I ever get used to your Aussie lingo? So, what do I need to guess?"

Tommo hammed up his ocker response, "Crikey, mate, most'a the gear's arrived 'n we can get crackin' at sparrow's tomorra!" Rambabu stood wide-eyed and shrugged his shoulders, inviting Tommo to translate. "It means, all the parts have arrived so we can get started at first light in the morning!"

❖ ❖ ❖ ❖ ❖

All their work was wrapped up in five long, grueling days. Six of his Son-Shine students added some extra muscle, and the small tractor Tommo had supplied a couple of months earlier had been fitted with a post-hole digger for the new fences. By dusk on the fifth day, the big farm was now fully fenced and electrified. Comprehensive CCTV coverage had been established and monitors set up in the main Legacy building, as well as a real-time satellite feed back to Son-Shine.

As the exhausted crew gathered, Tommo invited Rambabu to turn the tap, releasing fresh, clean water to flow from Jacob's Well to all parts of the big farm.

CHAPTER
seventy-three

"Getting back into full stride shouldn't take long, however, unearthing that extra dimension is always our greatest challenge." Philippe paraded across the dance floor and searched the faces of his troupe. "As you all know, Melana's new lead dance partner is our own Naggya," and he proceeded to steer the troupe into an impassioned round of applause. "My intention is to search within my troupe for a suitable understudy, however, if one isn't forthcoming in the very near future, mark my words, I am prepared to go beyond these four walls! We are now fully booked for the next year, much of which we will be based in Europe, so I trust you'll be ready and that all your passports are in order. Thankfully, we no longer have the millstone of that draft horse around our necks, so I'm counting on the atmosphere around here to remain positive!" Once again, Philippe scanned the room. "If you young bucks harbor aspirations of following in Naggya's footsteps and you'd like to be considered, then remember this, my door is open. Courage and determination are just as crucial to success as ability! So, work hard, aim high! You all have two extraordinary role models as proof that nothing can hold you back if you're sold out to success. We open in ten days, so waste not one single moment."

❖❖❖❖❖

"Ten days of rehearsals, a three-week season, and then they leave for Europe!"

"Yes, Randolph, I do read the papers."

"Well?"

"Well what?"

"Do we do this, or don't we? There's not a lot of time!"

"Oh, really, Sherlock! And what are you doing about actioning this plan of yours?"

"Listen, Galant, I may have plenty to gain from this, but you've got more! The word on the street is that Montans is numero uno and you're slipping fast, especially after you failed to tempt the Indian to switch camps!"

"No one knows anything about that!"

"Oh, really?"

"You low-life hustler, mess with me and—"

"And you'll what?! If you'd just stop using your dick and start using your brain, you'd realize we can both win out of this, but only if we work smart and we work quick. So, Mr. Scott, do we win, or do we lose? Your call."

Galant Scott slammed his phone on the desk and thumped his fist loud and hard. Five minutes later, he made a call.

"Twenty grand? And it's not traceable?"

"Gilt-edged, boss."

"And that's enough for trafficking?"

"Sure is."

"Set it up and I'll let you know the address, but don't let it get anywhere near me!"

Galant again reached for his phone.

"I thought I'd be hearing back from you. So, it's go?"

"You foul this up, Randolph, and you're history!"

"A mill in my pocket is a very good incentive not to, but just remember, the plan stays parked until half is safely in my hands."

❖❖❖❖❖

It was the eve before opening night and the inevitable buzz continued to build. The media had zeroed in on the question of whether the Montans Midas touch could outdo the standards set in California, especially with his relatively new lead dancer. For many, the Wild West was still considered second-tier, and until a new combination could cut it in the crucible of Broadway, they hadn't cut it at all. This was big-time and all eyes were upon the hero from India.

"Every time I turn around, you seem to be there."

"And that's a problem?"

"It surprises me."

"In a bad way?" smiled Winston, "Or in a good way?"

"Just 'surprised.' So, you've decided to try for understudy?"

"Naggya, I'd be a fool to not want to be under you, now wouldn't I?"

Returning his smile, Naggya responded, "I wouldn't call you a fool."

Melana's understudy had relished her handful of opportunities, and under the tutelage of Philippe, the young lady was being groomed for much more, particularly during the lengthy European tour. Philippe remained in a quandary, though, over who to fill the role of her male counterpart.

"Several of you are showing promising signs, but I'm still waiting for one of you to step up and really knock me out. There are those who believe it takes an extra one percent, but I demand more; much more. So, dig deep and find the je ne sais quoi, or you might easily remain little more than a troupe dancer. Already, there have been a number of impressive outsiders vying for the position, a position that could soon be yours."

Winston glanced across the room at Naggya and raised an eyebrow, then walked closer to whisper, "Are we still on for a bit extra after rehearsal?"

"It's the only way to grow."

"And you certainly know how to make me grow." Winston smiled and winked before wandering away to warm up.

❖❖❖❖❖

"And why would you consider being just his understudy?"

"What do you mean?"

"Listen, Winston, Naggya cannot last in our world. Sure, he's a novelty right now, and the paparazzi are lapping him up, but that won't last, and soon he'll be tossed aside without a second thought. He's a fad at best, and you need to be ready to take your chance."

"But I'm learning so much from him, and he's so, so sexy! I just want to eat him!"

"And does he want to eat you?"

"Ah, now that's the mystery. He's playing hard-to-get, but if I could just get him alone a bit longer—yummy!"

"Winston, don't forget, you're on a mission! Letting your

hormones take over will cost you not only your opportunity but a lot of money as well. Do yourself a favor and keep your concentration where it needs to be."

"But, can't I have both?"

"Listen, there will always be pretty young play-things floating around, but this is your chance in a lifetime, and the clock is ticking fast. When is your next private session?"

"Ahhh, you're such a killjoy. We're meeting at the studio three hours before the show every day this week. Naggya wants me to be his understudy, so he's keen to show me a few more of his tricks."

"I bet he is. All you have to do is slip the package into his bag then make an excuse to leave."

"And then what?"

"The less you know, the better. Just plant the package and get out! And remember, you've got a lot to gain from this. A year's salary for ten minutes' work. We don't have a lot of time, so be ready! I'll call as soon as everything is set."

CHAPTER
seventy-four

"Ooh, I'm so excited, Samuel! And we're right here in the third row! Wow!" Kate settled into her seat and encouraged the DAPA students to do likewise as the Lincoln continued to fill around them. Naggya had paid for all twenty-nine students from DAPA as well as three staff members to be his guests. While they picked their way to rows three and four, the buzz in the house multiplied with each passing minute.

"I'm so glad we didn't take a box," said Chad softly to his wife. "It's so much better down here among the kids."

Over a thousand patrons filled the magnificent theater, while backstage, the nerves of the troupe had already begun to jangle and twitch.

Resplendent in the orchestra pit just offstage, the musicians fine-tuned their instruments, adding another dimension to the mystique and magnetism of live theater. Showtime was now but a few quivering, panting breaths away.

Backstage, Naggya and Melana dazzled in their now-familiar roles of Romeo and Juliet. As they ran through their routines, the rest of the troupe nervously wound up their own preparations. Winston stole a glance toward Naggya. He tapped his chest and blew him a kiss, though the lead dancer saw none of it, immersed in a world few could conceive.

Hovering between backstage and the wings, Philippe's erratic contractions were now arriving mere seconds apart. The Grand Master was about to give birth, and no power on earth was about to stand in his way.

Despite the enormous pressures on the team, not a foot was placed in error, nor a cue missed, as the Grand Master's troupe, led faultlessly by Naggya and Melana, soared majestically through each pulsating scene. During Act Three, an audible groan followed by a collective sigh of relief resonated throughout the vast theater. The confrontation between Romeo and Tybalt's had run to script.

Was that a tiny smile on Naggya's face?

❖❖❖❖❖

"You were amazing tonight, Nag."

"Please, don't call me that."

"Sorry, it's just me showing affection."

"My name is Naggya. I don't call you Win, do I?"

"You can call me anything you like, so long as you don't stop calling," and he squeezed Naggya's bicep and purred provocatively. "Would you care for a nightcap? I know a quiet place."

Gently, Naggya removed Winston's hand and looked into his eyes, "I have promised my friends we will go for coffee, and they're waiting for me outside."

"Another time, perhaps? Um, are we still meeting at the studio tomorrow?"

As Naggya left his dressing room, he softly replied, "We have an agreement."

❖❖❖❖❖

At 10:00 next morning, Randolph's phone rang, "It's all set for tomorrow. That pip-squeak must be sorted out, now!"

"And the dough?"

"It'll be with the package. You'll get a call today. Be ready!"

"Just make sure the delivery boy waits while I count it. Not that you'd shortchange me now, would you?"

"Listen, Randolph, this is my absolute last involvement in this! If you know what's good for you, cooperate with my man, or else! And if anyone shortchanges anyone, it better not be you!"

❖❖❖❖❖

"This morning's papers are full of praise. This one asks, 'How does the Hero from India fly so high?' You should be very proud."

"Thank you, Philippe, but it's you who should be proud."

"We do what we must," and he smiled as he glanced at his watch. "Ah, why so early?"

"Winston has asked for some extra training."

Again, Philippe smiled, "Yes, I'm sure he has. Just be careful."

"Why?"

Philippe returned to his newspapers but couldn't resist adding a remark, "Sharp claws, that one. Where is he?"

"He should already be here. We're practicing every day this week for two hours and we're supposed to start at 3:00. Um, may I ask if he's in line for understudy?"

Philippe carefully put down his newspaper, "Would you

like him to be?"

"I just want what's best."

"For you, or for the show?"

"If it's best for the show, then it's best for me."

Philippe looked again at his newspaper and gazed upon the headline.

❖❖❖❖❖

"Starbucks, just off Wall Street. Tomorrow at 11:00."

"But that place will be teeming with people!"

"Exactly, and they're all so self-absorbed, no one will even notice or care. Be on time!"

"And the tip-off to the cops?"

"All under control."

"Galant's got the rest ready?"

"I told you before, no names! The boss is well away from all this, right! This is down to you, me, and your boy, and you don't know who I am. Just have your boy out of there by 5:00."

"Pip-squeak and the Indian will be the only ones still in the studio, so we get a nice, neat sting! They both go down, and their entire operation gets canned. This is a done deal."

❖❖❖❖❖

"Many of our people will have smiles on their faces today because of what you have done. And many will go to sleep tonight, not with the ache of emptiness, but with the joy of a full belly. God bless you, my son."

Rambabu rested his head upon the neck of his former teacher, and through his sobs and sniffles, whispered, "My heart leaps for what we can do for our people. Through all our years of suffering, this is what I was born for. Thank you, sir."

As the young man wiped the stream of tears from his cheeks, he stooped to drag more of the harvested crops upon the flimsy wooden tray on the back of the old truck. Elijah glanced down at its sagging springs and grinned, "I don't think we can fit much more on, Rambabu. We will return for more this afternoon."

Jacob hobbled to stand beside Rambabu, his best friend and now his employer, "We did well, brother."

"Yes, with God's help, we did well."

CHAPTER
seventy-five

"You're late, Winston."

"Sorry, the traffic was awful, plus I have a thumping headache.'"

Naggya paused his warm-up and drew closer, "Then perhaps you should rest until tonight."

Winston's heart pounded at the risk of missing his only opportunity. "No, I just took a pill," and he looked away at his clumsy reference to drugs. "Ah, I'll go and change and be straight back. Oh, and are they new tights? So yummy," and he smiled and dashed off to the changing rooms, waving nervously to Philippe as he passed by the office door.

An hour into their session, Winston executed the next phase of the plan, "Oh, this darn headache just won't quit."

"If it hasn't eased by now, it's probably unlikely to soon. You're not taking in anything I'm saying anyway, so—"

"Sorry, Naggya, I must apologize. It's this understudy thing, you know, the waiting and all." He glanced at the clock on the wall, *twenty minutes until the raid. If I leave now, there's just enough time to change my clothes and get out.* "Ah, I don't want to waste any more of your time and I know you never stop a session without properly warming down, so—"

"Warm down? I've hardly warmed up! No, I'll leave with you to make sure you're okay."

Panic surged through Winston as he searched for a plausible excuse to keep Naggya away from the changing rooms. "Actually, I'm a little embarrassed to admit this, but ever since we've been having our private sessions, when I see you getting changed, Naggya, I can't help it, but I get a bit, you know—" and he deliberately broke eye contact, "Sorry." Winston rushed from the dance floor and listened for following footsteps. There were none.

❖ ❖ ❖ ❖ ❖

"This's the place. According to the informer, there's only the one way in." The detective directed his uniformed officers to cover the doorway as he and two others crept past reception and quickly located the main office.

"What do you think you're doing barging in here?!"

"Sit down and place your hands on the desk!"

"But you can't—"

"I said, 'sit down'! This is a warrant to search these premises! Now, who are you?"

"I own this studio and I demand to know what's—"

"Cuff him!"

The officer in charge proceeded to the changing rooms and drew his service pistol. "Cover me. I'm heading in."

On the far side of the men's changing room sat a young dark-skinned man with his back turned. In his hands were two packages wrapped in shiny silver paper.

"Get on the ground! Keep your hands behind your back and don't move!"

An irate Philippe and a bewildered Naggya were led in handcuffs to two patrol cars, lights flashing in readiness to deliver two of the city's drug traffickers to the New York Police Department.

Hiding in the shadows at the front of a nearby building, Winston's body still quivered. His hands trembled as he scrolled through his phone for Randolph's number, then turned to walk away to deliver the good news. "They're both being led away now."

"How do you know?"

"Because I'm watching from next door."

"You're what?! You idiot, get the hell out of there!"

"Calm down, Randolph, everything's—"

"You there!"

As Winston swung around in response to the shout, he was confronted by a uniformed officer with his pistol drawn.

"Get off the phone and keep your hands in the air!"

❖❖❖❖❖

"A commercial quantity of methamphetamine has been found on your premises. What do you have to say about that, Mr. Montans?"

"I have no idea what you're talking about! I have a show starting at the Lincoln in two hours, so if you don't mind—"

"The only place you'll be in two hours is a holding cell, unless you start cooperating! Now sit back down and start talking!"

Philippe looked across at the arresting officer and slowly, defiantly shook his head, "I have nothing to say without my lawyer present. Now, if you insist on detaining me, may I please inform the Lincoln that you are holding me, and my lead dancer, so that there is no way tonight's performance can go ahead?!"

"Listen, Montans, we haul scum like you off the streets every day so more innocent people don't get killed or destroyed by your drugs, and all you want to do is give me a sob story about some poxy dance!"

❖❖❖❖❖

"I already told you, I went to get changed after a teaching session and when I reached into my bag, I found the two packages. That's all I know."

"You said you'd finished a teaching session, so if you were all alone, who were you teaching?"

"The dancer I was teaching is one of our troupe and he wanted some extra help, but he had a headache, so I—"

"How convenient, he had a headache! But you were all alone and in possession of over two kilos of meth. Seems a little odd, doesn't it, that no one is with you yet you've got a large quantity of a prohibited narcotic in your hands at the time of your arrest?"

"Like I said, all I know is I found the packages in my bag, and I have never seen them before. I don't know what meth is."

The detective threw his head back and laughed, "Yeah, they all say that. The rich and famous; they're all the same! They think they can do whatever they like, whenever and wherever they like, and they're all above the law! Well, mister, they're not! For this quantity of drugs in your sole possession, you've done your last dance for a long, long time! Charge him!"

CHAPTER
seventy-six

"Performance Canceled" was plastered across a hastily positioned sandwich board at the entrance to the Lincoln as a growing horde of patrons milled around and demanded answers.

The troupe gathered backstage, minus three conspicuous members. Melana, Chad, and Lois all repeatedly tried to make contact with Philippe and with Naggya, but all they managed was a series of increasingly desperate messages.

❖❖❖❖❖

"Oh, my God! Chad, these headlines, they're deplorable! 'Montans, the Grand Meth Master,' and this one, 'Indian Ecstasy.' They're so awful, but these two hurt the most, 'Christian dancer trades in drugs,' and 'This is how the Indian stays so high?' How can they write such lies?"

❖❖❖❖❖

"Right, I've delivered, now it's your turn. I need the other half, today!"

"Might your sudden need for cash have anything to do with your boy being in custody? Listen, you'll get the rest when the dust settles and the whole season gets canceled, not one minute before! You better hope your boy can keep his mouth shut!"

Randolph's mind was awash; *my entire future is resting on Winston. Shit, I've got to get out! I've got to get out of here now!*

❖❖❖❖❖

"So, Winston, what were you doing there last night?"

"Just waiting to see Naggya."

"But you're a dancer in the Montans troupe. You could just walk inside to see him, so why wait outside?"

Winston fidgeted and shifted his weight in the chair, "It's complicated."

"Were you waiting to buy drugs from him?"

"No, sir, I don't do drugs."

"Then you were waiting to buy from him to sell?"

"No, no, that's not how it is!"

"Then tell me, young man, just how is it?"

The simple, unsophisticated dancer was way out of his depth, and his head began to spin. "I wanted to see Naggya privately."

"But you've already told us you'd just spent over an hour with him, privately, so why the need to see him again, especially when you'd be seeing him at the Lincoln in just over an hour? Surely whatever was so important could wait until then?"

Despite the air-conditioning, Winston could feel his hands becoming clammy and tiny beads of sweat forming above his eyes. "It's personal."

"Are you having an affair with the accused?"

"The accused?"

"Yes, the accused!"

"Not really."

"What does 'not really' mean?"

Winston had painted himself into a corner, "Um, I'd like to, but I'm not sure he's—"

"Not sure he's what?"

There was a knock at the door and another officer entered the interview room and whispered to the detective.

"It would seem there has been a development, so we need to suspend the interview while further evidence is gathered. You will be taken to another department where some forensic tests will be conducted."

❖❖❖❖❖

"But, he's like a son to us. Please, can we see him?"

"Apart from legal representation, the accused is currently not permitted visitors."

"Yes, officer, we understand, but Naggya's no criminal. This is one huge mistake. He's just not like that."

"Mr. and Mrs. McNeil, the young man is facing serious charges and has been caught in possession of a significant quantity of illegal drugs."

"Then if we can't see him, can you please get a message to him? Please tell him that everything will be OK and remember that the truth always comes out. His lawyer will be here soon, and—"

"And?"

"And that we are praying for him, and we love him so much," Chad turned to his wife and comforted her as she tried to stifle her cries.

❖❖❖❖❖

"Winston, your fingerprints are a perfect match to those found on the narcotics taken from the crime scene. Can you please explain how they got there?"

"Um, I, ah—"

"Yes?!"

Winston glanced anxiously around the room, *this is nothing like how it was meant to be.*

"Winston, you are really starting to test my patience!"

"Ah, yes, I remember now. When I went into the changing rooms, I saw Naggya's bag open and I saw two strange packages and I wondered what they were, so I picked them up, and then I put them both back in his bag."

The detective smiled. "Winston, you are without doubt a very poor liar, and clearly not too smart. Nothing has been said about there being two packages. Only someone with personal involvement would know that fact."

"But I was only doing what I was told!"

"Really? By whom?"

Feeling the walls closing in, he again lowered his head, "I'm not supposed to say."

"From your admission, you will now be facing charges of trafficking a commercial quantity of drugs. We'll soon see how loyal you are. Do you understand?"

Winston's head remained hanging low as he slowly nodded.

"So, unless you choose to face all the charges on your own, I strongly suggest you tell us what you know, or the next dance you do will be in front of prison inmates, and they sure as hell will love a pretty, young dancer like you!"

Within thirty minutes, the detective had in his possession

a signed statement. Winston had not only squealed, but had done so loudly and very, very clearly.

❖❖❖❖❖

"'The flight to Brussels is now boarding."

Standing nervously in the departure queue, one of the travelers checked and rechecked his boarding pass. *What's taking them so long?* He reached into the lining of his coat to reposition the thick wads of hundred-dollar bills.

Everything's so dark with these sunglasses on. Just keep them on until I'm onboard the plane.

A hand seized his shoulder, "Randolph Sezsharn, you are under arrest. You do not need to say anything, but anything you do say may be used against you in a court of law. Do you understand?"

CHAPTER
seventy-seven

"Extortion is a serious enough crime on its own, Sezsharn, but when we add trafficking, you and your accomplice are looking at a very long stretch. Unlike young Winston, you were arrested with almost half-a-million in cash on you, so I would suggest now might be a very smart time to explain why."

"Not without my lawyer present."

"He's on his way, so I suggest you get your story straight because your boy has had plenty to say already, and most of it implicates you."

❖❖❖❖❖

"Mummy, they said they are pursuing a different line of inquiry and are releasing me on bail. What does that mean?"

"It means, son, they're finally realizing you're not the guilty one, and the bail, it's so you don't suddenly disappear."

"But we've got a show to do every night so how could I disappear?"

Lois threw her head back and laughed, "If everyone was as honorable as you, my son, this world would be a far brighter place. How much is the bail?"

"They said 100,000, but isn't that way too much if they think I'm innocent?"

"Oh, Naggya, may you be in our lives forever! Daddy and I will arrange bail and we'll come get you straight away. Have they said anything to you about Philippe?"

"Nothing."

❖❖❖❖❖

"Sezsharn, this is NYPD, not James Bond. Despite what people think, we're not in the habit of tapping everyone's phone calls."

"But surely the phone records will show how much we've been in touch with each other."

"And, under instruction, he'll say you were discussing the weather. Proof, mister, or you and the boy are facing this on your own."

Randolph Sezsharn's brief leaned across the desk and requested the interview be interrupted. The interview resumed a few minutes later. "Officer, my client would like to cooperate with you in exchange for a reduced charge."

"You want a plea bargain? And just what does your client have to offer?"

"Sufficient to convict."

"Oh, really, and to what charge might your client be willing to confess?"

Randolph sat silently as two professionals unemotionally haggled over his future. "With sufficient evidence to convict Galant Scott, my client is willing to confess to possession, not trafficking, and we drop the extortion."

"You must be joking! Why would we, when we can most likely bring them both down?"

"That's the offer. Now, if you have nothing further to offer, my client would like to exercise his right to remain silent."

"Possession and abetting. That's the best offer on the table, and it won't stay there long!"

The brief covered his mouth and whispered into Randolph's ear, "You're looking at one-to-two as opposed to ten-plus. With good behavior and your clean record, you could be out in one. I think it's fair, but it's your choice."

❖❖❖❖❖

"No, they're not willing to print a retraction. They told me to speak to my client and if we still feel sufficiently aggrieved, they reminded me of the legal avenues open to us for compensation."

"The nerve of these tabloids; they rely on hearsay and go to print without evidence."

"Actually, all they reported is that both you and Naggya had been detained for questioning after the drugs were found on your premises. We'd be hard-pushed to get a win, but, it's your reputation that's been slandered, and that's where we stand the greatest chance."

"You mean, a payout?"

"Well, as your lawyer, I wouldn't quite refer to it as such, but yes, a payout. We stand an excellent chance following the quick development regarding Randolph Sezsharn and young Winston. My advice is to focus on restoring your reputation in the eyes of the public and keep filling the Lincoln night after night. It's a bonus that the theater has seen fit to resume so soon after you've both been cleared of the charges."

"What, and let the papers get away with it?!"

"Did I say that? Listen, Philippe, just do what you do best and leave all the legalities to me, OK?"

❖❖❖❖❖

"We resume in two days. Will you be ready?"

"I can be ready today, Philippe."

"Good. I'll call Melana and tell her the good news. We will all need to meet in the studio at 3:00 this afternoon."

Naggya got off the phone and rushed into Lois's outstretched arms, "Oh, Mummy, we're back on!"

CHAPTER
seventy-eight

"All circumstantial, I'm afraid. The links between you and Scott are certainly indicative of intent, but they fall short of being legally conclusive. Even if his fingerprints were on some of the money, that's still only circumstantial. We've got a stronger case against his go-between, if only we could find him."

"But, where's his motive? He's just the middleman."

"Ah, but if we get him on charges, suddenly he's a songbird desperate to sing. Was he wearing gloves when he handed you the money and the drugs?"

A forlorn Randolph looked across the interview room at his lawyer and nodded slowly as an ominous silence settled. The lawyer thought for a moment, then snapped his fingers, "Yes, he'd be careful to wear gloves when he handed over the goodies, but I'm now wondering if he was quite so diligent when he parceled them up? Guard!"

❖❖❖❖❖

The news of Naggya and Philippe's release surged all around the planet, while the performing arts world was repulsed by the latest revelation of more superstars falling to the lure of the illegal. Reinstatement to their former glory, however, had yet to be accorded.

In India, a substantial disconnect had been quickly and predictably established, distancing the Indian upper castes from the Dalit community. In the media, Naggya was unceremoniously painted as nothing more than another filthy Dalit trying to extract money from those far worthier. Once his charges had been withdrawn and his name cleared of any wrongdoing, Naggya's standing as a world-leader in the eyes of the Indian public was left flapping in a ferocious storm.

After a call from Chad to Son-Shine, waves of spontaneous rejoicing broke out, and a day of celebration was declared; the orphanage's biggest financial contributor and one of its favorite sons had been exonerated.

❖❖❖❖❖

"A creature of habit, sir?" Relaxing in his favorite diner in the Bronx, Eddie was finishing his coffee when he glanced up at the two men standing before him.

"Who wants to know?"

One of the men produced his badge, "NYPD. I don't suppose you'd have any objections accompanying us down to headquarters?"

Eddie pushed his coffee cup away and looked directly at the man still holding his badge, "And why would I do that?"

"We have a number of serious matters to discuss. Now, sir, we can do this the easy way, or the hard. Either way, you will be accompanying us, sir. Now which way would you prefer?"

"I would like to call my—"

"Your lawyer, yes, of course. By chance, would you happen to use the same lawyer as Galant Scott? Oh, and by the way, don't forget your gloves."

❖❖❖❖❖

The detective slipped menacingly into the interview room chair. "You see, Eddie, it's being a creature of habit that's worked against you."

His lawyer glanced sideways and gestured for his client to say nothing.

"We have obtained extensive CCTV footage showing you meeting with Randolph Sezsharn at Starbucks on two occasions. On the second occasion, you handed him three packages, two of which are identical to those seized later the same day as part of a raid on a dance studio owned by Philippe Montans. As you know, Montans is a rival of a business acquaintance of yours, Galant Scott. We also have extensive evidence of phone calls made between you and Mr. Scott leading up to and subsequent to that raid. Although much of this information is circumstantial, as no doubt your lawyer will point out, where prosecution becomes compelling is that your fingerprints have shown up on some of the money. And, Eddie, where it gets even more compelling is we also have records of a quite large cash withdrawal made by Mr. Scott the day before the raid. Further CCTV footage will show you meeting with Mr. Scott outside the exact same Starbucks early on the morning of the raid. I would have thought it wise to choose somewhere else to do your handover, wouldn't you?"

Once again, the lawyer gestured to his client to say nothing.

"Under the Provisions of Crime Act, NYPD has obtained confirmation from the bank of several other vital pieces of evidence. Interestingly, the amount of that withdrawal is almost identical to the amount seized from Mr. Sezsharn as he tried to flee the country the very next day. And, we will prove in court, the money, all in 100-dollar bills, is the same money withdrawn by your Mr. Scott and not-so-secretly handed over to you. The bank has been most cooperative, even as far as to provide the serial numbers of the notes, so, taking all this evidence into account, I suggest it's now in your best interest to discuss your options with your brief. Interview suspended at 10:50."

❖❖❖❖❖

Philippe sat in his office with his feet up on the desk. Last night's performance, the first since the resumption of the season at the Lincoln, couldn't possibly have gone better. Yet something far juicier was causing his spirits to soar and causing a beaming smile to jump upon his face. Philippe spread the morning's papers in front of him and let loose a booming chuckle.

Splashed across the front page of one of New York's leading dailies, "Former Frisco Flop to Dealer to the Stars." And one of America's most influential publication's headlines read, "Great Scott not-so-Galant."

As he drooled over his latest, and perhaps greatest moment in the sun, Philippe mused, *I think I know where I can get Naggya's understudy,* and he followed up his thought with another booming chuckle.

CHAPTER
seventy-nine

"I've called you together for a particular reason, but before I get to that, I want to remind you of something. Though hard to believe, it's now been three years, three mind-blowing, unforgettable years, since that imbecile, Galant Scott and his band of idiots, tried to wipe us out! We've stood tall through that test and now we're enjoying the many spoils. I recall vividly, my lawyer argued that pursuing them for compensation was a waste of time, and with most of them still in prison and bankrupt, he was proven correct. He advised we single-mindedly focus on the ride, and be thankful it's all behind us. Again, he was correct. We've emerged better than ever, and today we are the undisputed dominant force in world ballet! To those who have been with me since those troubling times, I say to you, be proud, be very proud! Naggya and Melana are household names throughout the Western world and are fast becoming just as recognizable in much of the East."

Philippe paused in readiness for what he was about to announce. "On top of all that, I've just completed a series of phone calls with some of the most prominent business leaders in a part of the world we've never before performed in. So, it is with great pleasure that I announce to you today, we will be doing an eight-week season in Southern Africa. More details will be made known in due course, but I simply wanted to let you know. In the not-too-distant future, our amazing troupe will be performing in Johannesburg and Durban and Cape Town, and some place called Sun City. I suggest you all take a few moments to let that sink in. Imagine visiting all those glorious game parks, jungles, and nightspots . . . Anyhow, like I said, more about that later. As you all know only too well, we'll soon be finishing our European season performing yet again at the grandest performing arts theaters on the continent. Our sell-out seasons in Japan, Singapore, Hong Kong, New Zealand, and Australia were unprecedented successes, and as some of you already know, we've already locked in return seasons four years from now. The world has fallen in love with us, and you can all proudly take the credit. That's all for now." As they dispersed, a wave of pride and anticipation swept through the troupe.

❖❖❖❖❖

For several months, Naggya had been pushing Philippe for some time off. "Just a week. That's all I'm asking. I just need to go home and see my people. It's been so long, Philippe, surely my understudy can—"

"It's you they pay to see, Naggya. You and Melana have created something the world can't get enough of. Sorry, but not until the next break."

"But that's another six months away. Can't I just have one week?"

"Actually, it may be a little longer if the Southern Africa season fits. That'd be nice wouldn't it, all those glorious game parks and . . . "

Naggya barely heard the rest of the sentence as his mind raced to matters elsewhere. During the last three years, and several hefty salary increases, Naggya had overtaken Chad and Lois as DAPA's major financial supporters and had personally funded two more DAPA facilities in other U.S. cities. He'd also set up a school in Upper Harlem for underprivileged American kids to be taught a variety of dance styles at no charge.

I can't just keep on dancing. I'm getting tired, and all these temptations! They are starting to—I need to get away. I need to concentrate on other things. I need to be where I can put them out of my mind and where I can make a difference.

❖❖❖❖❖

"What sort of virus?" Philippe cradled his phone against his neck as he placed one of his suitcases onto a hotel trolley. "I've never heard of such a thing. You mean like SARS?" "So, what's that to do with us? We're not even touring China—" "Oh, that's rubbish!" "What do you mean cancel?! No, that's a complete over-reaction! Tell me you're not serious!"

❖❖❖❖❖

"One week straight after Vienna. I can rejoin in time for LA."

"And what if there are flight delays? You've read the papers as much as I have. This new virus thing is starting to really get inconvenient."

"Philippe, that's why I need to go. My people in India survive from day to day, and they will be the most affected.

Already, people are—"

"What?"

Naggya couldn't bring himself to say the word "dying." "They are—suffering, suffering really badly. I just need to go, that's all. Just for one week."

Philippe searched the young man's face. Standing before him was a giant in the world of ballet, yet standing before him was also a young man carrying the weight of the hopes of over 100-million Dalits on his sagging shoulders.

"Let me think about it, OK? I'll give you my answer tomorrow. Oh, and you'll be excited to know, it's just been confirmed, we'll be doing a Royal Command Gala Performance for the Queen of England at the Royal Opera House in London. It's a one-off, fly-in-fly-out and I know you wouldn't want to miss that."

CHAPTER
eighty

"We might be coming back to New York, Mummy. This Covid problem is getting really bad here in Europe."

"Yes, son, we've been following it closely. Far too many deaths."

"Philippe says that most of the tour has been canceled. He wanted us to go to South Africa but now he says that's not happening either."

"Naggya, it's really hard to know what and who to believe. We keep being told one thing, then the other. But, how are you?"

"Yes, I am fine, but one of our troupe has been put in quarantine, even though he told Philippe he wasn't feeling sick. I don't understand."

"No, I don't think many do understand. It's like everyone is panicking and—"

"Mummy, I can't get any news about home. Do you know anything?"

Lois hesitated before she could summon the courage and the sensitivity to break the news. "Son, there's no easy way to say this, but all of India is going into lockdown."

"But what does that mean?"

Lois could feel her throat tightening, knowing the dire consequences of what she was about to reveal. "It means, just like in many other countries, people are being forced to stay inside their homes. They aren't allowed to go to work, and like many other countries, none of the children can go to school." She paused to allow Naggya to absorb the enormity of this news.

"But Mummy, India isn't like other countries! If my people cannot go to work every day, they will starve. Mummy, don't they realize our people could starve to death?"

Lois listened as Naggya plummeted into waves of sobs and pitiful wails. She longed to be there to comfort her beloved son, but right now, she'd never felt so helpless.

"What are we going to do, Mummy? My people cannot survive if they cannot work!" Strings of saliva and snot streamed from his face, yet he could barely bring himself to wipe them away. "My people cannot be left to starve to death, Mummy! Something must be done! What can we do, Mummy? Please!"

❖❖❖❖❖

"Take your seats, everyone. I have some urgent news."

The world-famous Montans Troupe settled awkwardly into their Viennese hotel dining room as Philippe waited patiently to introduce the unknown spokesman. The dining room had been set aside for their exclusive use, however in twelve hours it was to be designated off-limits in preparation for total sterilization.

The spokesman wasted little time. "I have been instructed to inform you that we must act now. After conferring closely with the

U.S. Embassy over the past few days, I have been informed that you should make your way back to the States as soon as possible. At this stage, it is unknown how long you will be required to remain there, or when you might resume performing. You will all be issued facemasks. It is highly recommended you wear them. It's likely you will be flying Stateside tomorrow, but I'm told that is subject to change. I'm also told, you probably won't be allowed to fly into JFK. Most likely, you will fly into Washington, where you will be transferred to your preferred destinations, provided they are deemed safe. New York is going into lockdown of all non-essential services, and yes, that includes performing arts. I know this is disappointing news, but as of now, there are very few options. I suggest you all go back to your rooms immediately and pack. You are being transported by coach to the airport in two hours, so be quick about it. Wear your masks, and please keep your cell phones switched on at all times. Now, unless you've any questions, off you go." A sea of blank faces stared back at the man as Philippe watched on. *What a total disaster! Do these officials have any idea how disruptive this is?*

❖❖❖❖❖

Under lockdown, severe and unsustainable restrictions had been imposed in India to limit the spread of the virus. Without daily work, more were already suffering from starvation than from the effects of Covid. Punishment for non-essential travel was being meted out harshly, and some within the ranks of the poor were already questioning whether this was some sort of genocide to rid the nation of those incapable of fending for themselves. Morale among the Dalits was plunging to an all-time low.

If questioned while away from Son-Shine, Elijah would need to beg leniency in procuring food for the children and staff members who had remained, having no other family to return to. Thankfully, the remoteness of their village and the reluctance by police and armed forces to risk contamination from Dalits was working in his favor.

A month had already passed; a month of an ever-increasing reliance upon food from the big farm.

Elijah marveled as he drove up to Legacy. Tall and lush were all the plants and the bright, plump produce almost falling from the vines. There to meet him were Philly and Pip, tails wagging and tongues dripping from their mouths.

"Elijah, Elijah," yelled Jacob, as he hobbled to the gate. "It's so good to see you! We've missed you!"

With the gate fully open, Elijah drove in but waited close inside until it closed behind him.

"You look worried, sir. What's the matter?"

"Oh, nothing really. Where is Rambabu?"

"Unless my ears deceive, that's him coming on the tractor. You still look worried."

Elijah spotted the tractor as it emerged from behind the maize crop and waved to the driver. Rambabu drove the tractor within a few feet of him, knocked it out of gear, and switched off the engine. "This is a surprise. We weren't expecting you until Friday."

"I wanted to ask if you've had any more problems from the locals?"

"Do you mean, like attacks?"

"Yes, have you?"

Rambabu eased himself down from the driver's seat and walked towards his former school principal. Almost unnoticeable, these days, was his limp, however, Elijah often wondered if Rambabu was concealing his wounds in order to minimize concerns. "No, not since Tommo finished our latest security. Would you like to hear it?"

Elijah visibly relaxed in the knowledge two of his most vulnerable former students were faring well following their catastrophic beginnings on the property. "I would be delighted to hear it."

"You're going to love it! Tommo is such a wise man and clever, too. He can do accents. I'll turn the volume right down so the neighbors don't hear. We don't want them thinking it's not real, do we, sir?" Rambabu proceeded to initialize one of the attack response options before Elijah reeled back from the sudden sound of salvos of gunshots being fired into the air. The gunshots were immediately followed by a stern warning, first in Telugu, then in menacing American that sounded suspiciously like Tommo, announced, "Every move you make is being recorded. Facial recognition has already been used and the footage sent directly to Vijayawada Police as well as our security headquarters in New York. Unless you turn around and leave this property immediately, you will be shot, and our pack of hungry dogs released."

The warning was made to the terrifying accompaniment of a large pack of snarling, snapping, barking dogs, the sound of which caused Philly and Pip to instantly join in.

"And you say that's with the sound turned down? How loud is it turned up?"

"Do you really want to know?"

As Elijah placed a finger in each ear, he shook his head. "I guess not. How many of these warning signals do you have?"

"Twelve, but Tommo is sending more!"

"You look even more worried now, sir," declared Jacob with a wide grin.

The three walked inside and settled upon their makeshift seats. "Actually, I came out early because we need to talk. It's such a blessing for you both to be here doing what God has called you to. Our people are so thankful, and many would have perished without you." Elijah paused and looked at the two young men, both quite small in stature, both maimed from battles past, yet both as nailed to the cross of sacrifice as any other in today's world. "Being out here has shielded you from many of the things happening here in our nation and throughout the rest of the world. In all the earth, there is tragedy unfolding, and I feel it is time to tell you of them."

Rambabu reached out towards his mentor and tried to smile, "Sir, we have been through so much together, and through more we will yet pass. Please tell us the whole truth. We need to know," and he turned to Jacob who nodded his agreement.

For the next two hours, Elijah shared about the depths and the suffering of their fellow Dalits. "News reports say that already there have been over four million cases of this virus. Too many do not have hospitals or medicine for their pain. We do not know how the government has counted them because they don't come and ask, so how would they know? Every day we hear reports that hundreds of thousands have already died, and many are losing hope." Elijah's voice began to waver, and his hands trembled as he battled for the strength to continue, "Many are taking their own lives."

The three began to pray, though the blanket of heaviness caused their prayers to be labored and their cries loud and long. "Love among family members has been shaken. Many are at rock bottom. When a family member dies of Coronavirus, often the body is abandoned among all the other dead bodies, and the family members declare the dead person is not known or related to them. It is so sad. Our own people are turning away from faith and are turning to alcohol to numb their deep pain. Rambabu, Jacob, we are hearing more and more stories like these every day. A wife spent days with her dead husband's body in her house. No one came, as they feared that they also may get the disease."

Elijah took a piece of paper from his pocket and scanned for more details until Jacob held up his hands, "Sir, enough. We have heard enough," and his pathetic sobs took hold and his shoulders heaved. Far too familiar was the last story, too much a mirror to the horror of his own younger life.

How can we keep our people alive and restore their hope?

CHAPTER
eighty-one

Unlike any other, 2020 was fast becoming the year of far too many unanswered questions.

"But what if I do stay here? I can't do anything."

"Naggya, the borders to India are closed, period. There's no point in discussing going there, so let's not keep talking about it, OK?"

"Yes, but—"

"Yes, but nothing. Look, we are all in the same boat. We prepare as though the solution is just around the corner, and we make sure we can jump as soon as it is."

"That's fine for you, Philippe, but your people are much safer while mine are dying!"

"Yes, of course. Sorry, I honestly didn't mean to sound heartless. It's just that I don't have any answers, and I can't help but wonder what on earth you would have me do to make things any easier?"

Naggya strummed his fingers on his desk and stared out at the New York streets below. "It's just so hard being cooped up here when there is so much to be done."

"The authorities keep telling us we must be patient. It runs against the grain for me, too, but if we rush the process we risk going back to square one."

"That doesn't sound like something you'd normally say, Philippe."

"Normal? I'm already forgetting what normal is. This Covid thing is costing me a fortune!"

Now that sounds more like Philippe. "At least I have the kids from DAPA, and Mummy and Daddy have each other, but I feel for all those people stuck at home with no one to talk to. Philippe, how do you cope with being at home all alone?"

"The day you need to worry about me is a rare day indeed, young man!"

"But you're only human after all, Philippe. Aren't you getting lonely?"

The grandmaster chuckled into his phone, "Zoom, Zoom, oh talented one; Zoom, Zoom! Now be off with you, for I have many more calls to make." Philippe ended the call and stared blankly ahead. Slowly and purposefully, he rested his head in his pale hands. *If only it was that simple.*

❖❖❖❖❖

Zoom, Zoom indeed. As often as four times per week, Zoom was the only effective vessel for Naggya, Chad, Lois, and Elijah to keep in touch, yet every Zoom seemed to accomplish little more than deliver more horror stories and endless tales of woe.

❖❖❖❖❖

Naggya sat quietly, all alone in his room, yet in the night's stillness, a wildfire raged. *What's the point of doing all this if my people are suffering, dying? Should I even be here? Do I take the risk by going home, or do I stay in New York and wait? If I go home, when might I return? After so long away from my home, will I even want to come back here? And how long will all this take? I miss home so much! And I worry about my people, and all the starvation, all the suffering, and all the injustice.*

Naggya sat bolt-upright on his bed and blinked away his tears. *And every day there are more of these temptations. Why can't they leave me alone? I just want to dance! I didn't come here for all that! But they keep shoving their stuff in my face! All the time! It's just not right! Why do they try to make it OK? It's not! Oh, Lord, what must I do?*

❖❖❖❖❖

For much of 2020, the numbers of questions continued to far outweigh the answers. Lockdowns, border closings, then reopenings, and then closings yet again. Wave after wave of Covid hotspots and skyrocketing numbers of outbreaks, all with inevitable consequences. People across the globe were perishing in record numbers. Everyone seemed to be pushing their own personal solutions, yet few could deliver, while still more suffered and died.

A vaccine was widely touted as the answer, but when? Would it arrive in time? What would be the economic, social, and moral costs?

Questions—so many questions—

CHAPTER
eighty-two

"It's been eight months!"

"Actually, it's only seven," said his lawyer softly, as reassuringly as he could.

"Seven, eight! What difference does it make?! We need to be performing again, and we need to be performing in front of live audiences, live paying audiences!"

"Yes, Philippe, I know. You've told me, like, a thousand times already. As soon as I have news, I will let you know, OK?"

Philippe exhaled loudly through his flaring nostrils and gripped the edge of his desk as his lawyer looked on, conveying as much compassion as he could muster. "Philippe, I'm suffering as well, you know. Most of my clients have gone to ground, and the last thing on their minds is paying me. They're all battling to stay afloat just like you."

"It's a good thing you've got such deep pockets, then, isn't it? You Jews, you're all the same!"

"That's enough! I've taken about as much of your insults as I'm going to, and just remember, I could easily wipe your—"

"OK, OK. Sorry, I shouldn't have— It's just all this cabin fever! Seems, we're all going a bit loopy after all this—sorry."

Julien, his lawyer, paused before he felt it timely to continue, "Actually, it's encouraging about the Royal Command Performance. Seems the Queen wants her postponed birthday celebrations to coincide with the build up to Christmas. Sort of a ray of hope in a new festive season."

"Well, after two postponements already, this one better not fizzle and become a third. Is it definite?"

"Everything is subject to change, Philippe. You know that as well as I do, but at this stage, it's as definite as it can be. I don't think the British government will want to backflip again. They know their people are at a breaking point, especially after all that Brexit bullshit, and they know the world is watching! I'd be getting your troupe ready if I were in your shoes."

"Yes, Julien, I agree. But we can't just do a fly-in, fly-out with nothing before or following! It's just not economic sense."

"True, but what can I do? And don't forget, New York needs to be opening its doors for the same reasons."

"Ah, but last time I looked, we don't have a Queen!"

Chuckling at the screen, Julien said with a wry smile, "That's not what you keep saying about Trump!"

❖❖❖❖❖

"OK, everyone, listen up. I have some important news. I'm sorry it's been such a trying year for all of you, as it has for me. As you know, I was forced to take the regrettable but unavoidable step of laying you off earlier in the year. I know some of you sought and received some welfare assistance, but hopefully that's behind us now. It's been tough on everyone. OK, enough of the bad news. In light of recent developments, I have elected

to take the huge gamble of putting you all back on the payroll."
Once again, he scanned the room for a reaction and short of
a few fleeting smiles, he got little. "So, now, the good news.
It's been announced but not definitely confirmed that we will
finally be doing the Royal Command Performance in front of
the Queen of England in London. At the moment, it's planned
during the first week of December. It goes without saying, this
will be amazing and a massive honor! Then, two days later, we
hope to fly to Salzburg for a short season before coming home
to Manhattan for ten nights leading right up to Christmas.
With the cultural drought everyone's had to endure, we can be
absolutely certain of packed houses every night. The proceeds
will help replenish these past few months of lack, OK? Now, due
to the short lead-up, by necessity, we will again be performing
Romeo and Juliet on every occasion. But with the way they've all
been starved, the audiences wouldn't balk at paying top dollar to
see Mr. Magoo, so long as he was wearing tights and doing our
famous lifts, leaps, and landings!"

Philippe watched and waited for a response but apart from
a couple of stifled giggles, little bounced back his way. "At
this stage, it's looking likely we will have until early in January
back here in New York before possibly six-to-ten major cities
of the USA then back to Europe. But I need to stress, this is all
subject to change, and change can materialize at a moment's
notice. So, are we all clear?"

CHAPTER
eighty-three

Heathrow was abuzz with excited travelers. One of the world's busiest airports, even under strict Covid restrictions, was a hive of expectation. The first week of a winter like no other had been ushered in with a chilly bite forcing everyone to scurry indoors. "Apparently, it's just as cold as New York," exclaimed one of the newer troupe members as she grappled her luggage from the carousel.

"Yes, but it never stops raining," remarked another. "Last time we were here we didn't see the sun for two weeks!"

This was Naggya's fifth arrival at Heathrow, yet he couldn't help but make the comparison with the first time he flew into JFK. *So much has happened since then.*

A chartered coach, with engine running and heaters cranked to the max, sat adjacent to the arrivals' terminal. Following Customs' examinations, the troupe, proudly led by Philippe, Melana, and Naggya, picked their way past the questionably socially distanced gauntlet of waiting fans and the inevitable paparazzi.

Philippe stood to address his troupe as the coach driver eased to a halt. "We've all had a big day, so I suggest you take things easy. We've no need to rush at playing tourists. I'll buzz you all soon," and he hauled himself to his feet to retrieve his hand luggage.

Within the hour, each of the troupe was settled into their Knightsbridge hotel, awaiting further instructions from the Grand Master.

"That's Big Ben and the Houses of Parliament," announced one to his roommate as they peered through the early afternoon mist from their third-floor window.

"And all those bridges. Is one the London Bridge?"

"No, I don't think so. I read that it got sold and they moved it."

"Really? How do you move a bridge?"

❖❖❖❖❖

"What do you mean, 'get out,' we've only arrived yesterday!"

"I know, Philippe, but if what I've just been told proves correct, and the likelihood appears high, if we don't move now, you and all your troupe could be stranded in London indefinitely. Don't forget how long the last lockdown took!"

Philippe snapped at this unwanted complication and instantly shook with rage, "This Covid thing has already cost me an absolute fortune! It's ridiculous! Have these Brits any idea what they're doing?! Rule Britannia, my foot! They couldn't rule a . . . oh, never mind!"

"Philippe, we can protest as much as we like, but if we don't move now, the U.S. government might again shut our borders! It is a huge gamble, but that's just how it is," and he hesitated before pressing, "so, what's your decision?"

"And you expect me to decide with what, one moment's notice? We've had this planned for months!" Philippe could hear his business manager sigh through the phone. "Don't go getting uppity with me! And on top of all this inconvenience, what gets me so riled is who'll be paying for all this?"

"You know the answer to that perfectly well. I accept how difficult this must be for you but time is of the essence. We need your decision."

The grandmaster stalled and searched for an upside. There wasn't one. "Whichever way I look at this, it's an annoying intrusion and a very costly interruption to my plans!"

"Philippe, people are dying!"

"And you think I don't know that!" He paused and then asked, "How long do I have?"

"The quicker you move, the better your chances."

Pacing the floor of his hotel suite, Philippe's blood pressure soared, "Mark my words, someone *will* pay for all this, and it won't be me!" He rubbed the back of his neck and stared hard at the ceiling. "I don't have any choice, do I?! No, don't bother, you've made that abundantly clear. Send a text to everyone, like, immediately! How quickly can we get out?"

"We'll be in the air in four hours."

❖❖❖❖❖

As soon as the captain finished his announcement, Naggya unbuckled and removed his seatbelt, got up and walked the short distance to ease himself into the seat next to Philippe. "I suppose you've not had any updates?"

"What, you mean since we took off?" and he glanced sideways at his star performer before adding, "Sorry, Naggya, that was rude of me. No, I have nothing new to report, but as soon as I do, I'll let you know, OK?"

The young lead dancer patted the back of the grandmaster's hand and nodded slowly as they craned their necks to peer out the window. "I remember the first time I flew from Vijayawada to meet you, but how that world out there has changed."

CHAPTER
eighty-four

During the ensuing months, the world indeed changed, a whole lot.

"When will it all end? This is madness! All I want is a bit of normality! Is that too much to ask?" Philippe paced his office like a caged lion. Across his desk lay a bunch of printed bank statements and an array of printed emails. "And how am I supposed to turn out world-class performances when these complete idiots keep changing their minds?! One minute we're told everything is back on, and the next . . . " He paused and pored over the papers, then flung them across the room. "Don't they even care?!"

❖❖❖❖❖

"Mummy, I just can't stand it much longer. Our people are dying! Elijah told me there are more starving than dying from the virus! What can we do?"

The lockdowns had hit everyone. Although the lives of thousands of New Yorkers continued to be turned upside down, few were displaced and even fewer died. Perspective; it's a funny thing.

"Son, apart from what we're already doing by sending money for food to Elijah, and praying of course, I don't see what more we can do. We just have to trust and ride it out.

Sooner or later, seasons always come to an end. I'd love to be able to come over there and give you a hug."

Naggya sniffled into his phone. "Yes, Mummy, that would be so good. I miss you and Daddy so much. You're so close but . . . "

"Yes, Son, we know, and we feel exactly the same. I'm told this latest lockdown could soon end. How are all the kids at DAPA coping?"

"They are all waiting for their phones to ring, just like me. We all feel so helpless."

❖❖❖❖❖

"I've just heard it right from the top. It's all back on!"

"Are you certain? I mean, how many times have we been told that in the last year? For goodness sake, man, I won't stand for any more of these false alarms!"

Philippe's business manager had become well-versed at propping up the faltering grandmaster. To fill his head with unsubstantiated hopes served only to fuel a simmering fire, yet to withhold vital information on unfolding events was tantamount to commercial hari-kari. "As certain as I can be. We all want what you want, Philippe, and considering all that the world has been through, the doors can't afford to remain closed much longer. These are the strongest signs since . . . "

"You said that last time!"

"Yes, and based on the best advice available at the time, I did say that, and based on the latest best advice, I'm saying it again! Do you want me to keep you informed, or to merely wait like everyone else and miss being the first to jump? It's your call."

"Every time I've taken the risk, it costs me plenty."

"True, but if you don't take the risk and therefore aren't ready when the doors open, and rest assured they will open, who's the loser then? Every performing arts center worldwide will be clamoring to get bums back on seats. They're hurting too, so do you think they'll wait for you, or any other ballet company, to be getting ready?"

"Yes, I see your point, but just remember who's paying the bills!"

Philippe's business manager fairly bristled on the end of the line but restrained himself sufficiently to chuckle, "How could I forget? You tell me every five minutes. And besides, I do happen to know how healthy your bottom line's looking on the back of some very profitable years!" He paused just long enough for his point to sink in. "So, what do you want to do?"

The grandmaster strutted about his office and propped in front of one of his many life-sized posters. "Let me sleep on it," and abruptly he terminated the call.

For several minutes, Philippe stood and reflected upon his own image. He mused closer, longer, deeper. *Can anyone, anyone in all the world, hope to lead ballet from its slumber better than I? Philippe, you know better than all the rest, it can only be me.* He snatched his phone.

"That was a very short sleep."

"Contact the entire troupe. We're back in business!"

❖❖❖❖❖

Ever since December's aborted London Royal Command Performance, the United Kingdom had been anything but united. And with Europe continuing to suffer from enforced economic inactivity and the unspeakable traumas of the winter's discontent imprisoned in social isolation, an entire continent hung heavily in its hurting.

Two of Great Britain's major economic drivers were still faltering. Sport, in its many forms, particularly football, and the incomparable lure of the Royal Family, stuttered and spluttered towards a questionable finale. Could the showpiece of world sport, the FA Cup Final, surely be destined to be staged in front of an empty stadium, again? Could the world's most popular sport hope to survive week-in and week-out played in empty stadiums? Really?

Might the Royal Family possibly survive yet another scandal and hope to remain a tourist dollar drawcard? The aging Prince Philip took ill, and the world held its breath. And he died. And now? A century of memories poured out before so few, and a grieving Monarch sitting all alone.

What truly is this world right now?

Wedding anniversaries, especially landmark celebrations following seventy-three years in the world's spotlight, were meant to be monumental, yet how many could raise their spirits and strength with one so loved so recently departed?

No, it had to be the marking of the Queen's unprecedented reign and her unyielding accumulation of birthdays to carry the day. It must. It simply must.

A rescheduled Royal Command Performance; the perfect tonic to resuscitate the ailing nation, to put the Great back in Britain.

❖❖❖❖❖

"Because of Covid restrictions, we've been granted only two practice sessions at the Palladium before our performance two nights later. We're again booked in at Knightsbridge, so it turns out it's just the same as last time."

"It better not be the same as last time!" barked the rejuvenated Grand Master. "In an impossibly short time, I alone have rallied the troupe, and provided that no one screws up, they will be ready! No more last-minute complications, right?"

"Yes, yes, of course, Philippe."

CHAPTER
eighty-five

"Our first rehearsal is tomorrow morning at 10:00. Our transport will pick us up out front at 9:00 so be sure to be ready. It's a short drive to the theater, but London's traffic can be just as bad as New York's, so we've allowed extra travel time. Any questions?"

As usual, there were none. "As you know, we've set aside two days for sightseeing after the performance, so for now, I suggest you all rest up in your rooms. Dinner is at 7:00 sharp."

❖❖❖❖❖

The Palladium Theatre's usual capacity of 2,200 guests had been Covid-trimmed to 1,500 meticulously screened guests. The audience was a strategic blend of the under-privileged, the marginalized, a bevy of high achievers, as well as many from the upper echelon in the world of performing arts. In the wake of two Covid-driven false starts, the buzz inside the regal amphitheater was already tantalizing. Backstage, Philippe's own phobic attempts to prepare his troupe for the performance of their lives was fast becoming a threat to the night's success.

"Are you OK, Philippe?" asked Naggya as he again straightened his seams.

"Of course, I'm OK! Why wouldn't I be OK?"

"It's just, you're very pale, and you're breathing like—"

"Everyone is pale compared to you, now stop all the fussing. I've waited a lifetime for this opportunity, so it's no wonder I'm a little—" and he paused to peer out from behind the curtain one more time just in case something had unexpectedly changed since checking sixty seconds earlier, "— a little excited."

When the trumpets sounded, every eye turned expectantly toward the Royal Box. First to enter was Her Royal Highness, Queen Elizabeth II, followed by the heir to the throne, her son, Prince Charles, accompanied by his wife, Camilla, and next-in-line to the throne, Prince William and his wife, Catherine. Every other person remained transfixed while the Royal Family settled in their seats and the Queen nodded.

"I thought she'd be wearing her crown," whispered one of the troupe from behind the curtain.

"Only for Royal engagements," responded another.

"So, what's this then, a BBQ?" but before another word was uttered, an orchestral fanfare commenced, sending shivers down the spine of every person within earshot. Isaac Abrahams, the Master of Ceremony, then regally welcomed the royal guests and invited the distinguished members of the audience to take their seats.

Backstage, Philippe ceremoniously tapped his chest several times and mouthed the words, "Time to shine, peeps, time to shine!"

❖❖❖❖❖

When the final curtain fell to rapturous adulation, every patron in the house, bar one, stood to give praise to the gifts of the troupe. When the curtain raised, each member received their due, and as Melana strode center stage, the grandeur of the century-old theater almost shifted from its foundations. The troupe had risen beyond all wildest expectations; flawless, impeccable, indelible. With the euphoric applause showing little sign of abating, Melana gracefully stepped back to sweep her extended arm toward the back of the stage where a young man stood, waiting, patiently, gracefully, to emerge to a tribute beyond anything the Monarch had ever witnessed.

In the space of two hours, "the hero from India" had been etched forever into the hearts and minds of an adoring generation. His humble yet effusive charm, his incomparable precision, and his faultless fluidity had launched the star way beyond measure.

Naggya bowed slow and low, as streams of living waters cascaded down his cheeks, his humility to deflect the adoration toward his peers merely fueled a greater fire. Respectfully, he peered across toward the Royal Box to bear witness to the astonishing: the Monarch, Her Royal Highness, Queen Elizabeth II, slowly stood to her feet, and as tears flooded her own cheeks, she looked directly at Romeo, and simply, slowly, and purposefully, clapped.

The Master of Ceremony walked center stage, microphone in hand, and waited. Patiently, he waited, yet each time he raised the microphone to his mouth, the applause again lifted, and the MC beamed in bewilderment while the Queen slowly clapped.

One more time, the MC raised the microphone to his mouth and repeatedly motioned for the audience to take their seats. Above the clamor, he inquired, "Your Highness, have you enjoyed your birthday?" and the applause lifted, yet again, and the Queen slowly clapped.

❖❖❖❖❖

Someone in the third row began singing, and before reaching the fourth word, 1,500 joined in a stirring rendition of *Happy Birthday* to the smiling Queen of England. When another attempted to follow that impromptu rendition with a celebratory *Three Cheers*, MC Isaac Abraham vehemently intervened, steering their outpouring in another direction; a direction far-removed from the insensitive consideration of her husband's heritage and the origins of the Queen's own faith. Fifteen-hundred formed a chorus of "For she's a jolly good fellow," until ceremoniously, the curtain fell for the final time.

❖❖❖❖❖

A swarm of reporters and photographers jockeyed for position in the foyer. At their insistence, the Indian Ambassador had been summoned and waited awkwardly to have photos taken with Naggya. "Can you face each other and smile?" asked one. "Can you be shaking hands?" asked another. "What about a victory hug?" pleaded yet another.

Tentatively, Naggya reached out to take the right hand of the Ambassador, a man whose camera smile was fading fast.

To choruses of encouragement from among the swarm, and as camera flashes popped and fizzed, Naggya's grip tightened as his and the Ambassador's right hands moved uncomfortably up and down. Naggya could feel the Ambassador attempting to break free but to the encouragement of those watching, Naggya tightened his grip and peered into his eyes.

The Ambassador broke eye contact and turned to face the swarm, "We, the people of India, are delighted to continue to support the arts."

A brown-skinned reporter searching for a story, loudly quipped, "Don't you mean 'Dalited'?"

"Good shot," and "Great pic" rang out from their midst, until the repeated request for a hug pic caused the Ambassador to raise his left hand in mock surrender. "I must go now," and he shook his right free and secretly scowled at Naggya, "Dalit pig!" He then made a hasty retreat to the cloakroom.

From a short distance, embroiled in his own smaller posse of attention, Philippe kept a watchful eye on the attention lavished upon his superstar. The Grand Master extricated himself and a few seconds later, followed the Ambassador into the cloakroom.

Standing at the basins, a man vigorously scrubbed his hands as Philippe stood beside him to implore, "Why?"

"These things are not for you to comprehend," and continued to scrub.

CHAPTER
eighty-six

"The sightseeing bus will be leaving from the front of the hotel at 9:30. Please confirm your seat by immediately replying to this text with either 'yes' or 'no.'"

"I want to see Buckingham Palace."

"No, I'd rather go on the London Eye. They say you can see everywhere from up there!"

"But what about Madame Tussaud's. This time next year, Melana and Naggya will be their main attraction," joked her understudy as she giggled toward Melana.

"Come to think about it, where is Naggya?"

"Did he reply to the text?"

"Maybe he's asleep?"

"That'd be a first. Hey, there's the coach. Let's go. London, here we come!"

❖❖❖❖❖

"Naggya, where are you?! This is my fifth message. Call me the minute you get this!'"

As the elevator doors opened, Philippe peered out toward the front doors. It was getting dark outside and as he walked to speak to the concierge, the Grand Master had a gnawing feeling deep in the pit of his stomach. He smiled at the young lady and moved in as close as Covid protocols allowed. "Have you any messages for me from Naggya? He's the young Indian—"

The young lady smiled politely, "Sir, after all the news headlines today, we all know who Naggya is." She checked the messages then slowly shook her head. "Sorry, sir, nothing I'm afraid."

"Has anyone seen him?"

One of her colleagues overheard their exchange and walked closer, "Sorry, sir, no, nothing at all. Ah—"

"Yes?"

"Does he have long hair?"

"No, short. Why?"

She hesitated, "I started my shift early this morning, and I recall seeing a dark-skinned athletic young man leave through the front doors."

"And?"

"Well, sir, I thought it a little odd to be wearing sunglasses while it was still dark. It's probably nothing to do with your Naggya as this particular young man had quite long hair, so—"

The gnawing in Philippe's stomach intensified as his mind raced, "Ah, can you try his room?

"Certainly, sir."

After twenty rings, she turned to face Philippe. "Perhaps he's out with the others, or asleep, or—"

"Can we go and check his room?"

"That's not appropriate, Mr. Montans. Apart from cleaning,

it's against hotel policy, unless perhaps there's a compelling reason."

Philippe's mind continued to race, "Ah, it's possible he might have met with foul play. He had a bit of, shall we say, 'an incident' with an Indian Embassy official last night, and we haven't seen him all day. To be quite honest, I've been a little concerned."

The two staff members looked at each other before conferring in whispers. "Sir, we'll refer the matter to our duty manager. Would you mind waiting a moment?"

An impeccably dressed gentleman in his late thirties appeared from behind a partition wall and approached Philippe. "You have reason to suspect foul play, Mr. Montans?"

❖❖❖❖❖

After knocking firmly but without response, the duty manager turned to Philippe. "Sir, I'll ask you to please stand back. If what you are saying is correct, potentially, we are entering a crime scene. My assistant and I will go in, and provided there is nothing untoward, you might then enter. Is that to your satisfaction?"

With a nod from Philippe, the duty manager swiped his access card then heard the click of the latch. He glanced at his assistant and eased the door ajar to peer inside. Slowly, he shouldered the door open and ventured carefully along the hall. With his assistant right behind him, he entered the lounge room as the main door self-closed and locked ominously behind them.

Several minutes later, it reopened. The duty manager and

his assistant stood before the grandmaster and waited for him to make eye contact. "I'm afraid you're too late."

"Too late?" Philippe toppled back against the wall and slid down to the floor. "Do you think he suffered?"

"Suffered?"

Philippe's voice was already failing as he tried to form his words. "I mean, blood? Is there much blood?"

The two hotel staff members looked at each other before the "A letter? You mean a ransom letter? So, he's been kidnapped?"

"Sir, I really don't know. Perhaps you should just read the—"

Philippe's mind was awash with erratic, conflicting emotions while that gnawing feeling in his stomach now rampaged throughout his entire body. "But how would they get him out? There are cameras—and he'd have put up a fight—surely? Or, he was drugged—but then—this makes no sense!"

Calmly, the duty manager suggested, "Sir, if you'd like to go in and read the letter, you are welcome. I'll have the room cleared out in an hour, in case he's left anything."

"But—if it's a crime scene, surely—"

"Sir, it appears your man has simply checked out."

The Grand Master cautiously entered the suite and hesitated at the end of the hall. The lavish suite appeared in order. Nothing out of place, nothing broken, nothing overturned to indicate any sort of struggle.

"This is bizarre!"

The letter with his name handwritten upon the envelope

sat alongside a piece of cellophane wrapper on the coffee table. Philippe carefully picked up the envelope and gently prized it open, mindful not to smudge fingerprints.

A single-page letter rested in his trembling hands.

Dear Philippe,

This is the most difficult letter I have ever written, and it comes after many torments and sleepless nights. Please forgive me, but by the time you get this, I will be back in my homeland. Though the borders are closed I have found a way by putting money into the right hands. This should hopefully get me through Customs. As in other places, money talks.

Being away from my people has been unbearable, and without God's strength, I wouldn't have made it. Mummy and Daddy and my friends at DAPA have all helped ease the pain, but the truth is, my home is calling. I will write to them soon, but, no, they know nothing about my decision.

Being in your care for these years has been a great joy, and I owe you much. I will miss you all deeply. I had hoped to train Winston to replace me, but—

Philippe threw his hands in the air then flung the letter onto the coffee table, "Miss us all deeply, my ass!!! That ungrateful son-of-a-bitch has run out on me! I gave him everything, and this is how he repays me! You selfish black bastard!"

He sat shaking, trying to contemplate his next desperate move. "How could he do this to me?! I made him! And now, he just leaves! And the shit rubs his boyfriend Winston in my face! They almost ruined me! And now he's vanished and left me a letter, and," glancing at the bottom of the note on the coffee table, "And he leaves me in the lurch and didn't even have the decency to sign it! You gutless piece of shit!"

---but now you have a far better replacement, and I know he will step up in Salzburg and do you proud. He is indeed ready. Melana and he are a match made in heaven.

Speaking of a match made in heaven, for quite a while now, I have longed to be married—

"What!! But you can't! You know you can't! How can you ever get married to another man in your country?!" He scanned the single-page letter from top to bottom as his hands continued to tremble. "I made you, and I've turned you into the world's most famous dancer! I need you and you abandon me, for what? A boyfriend?!" At the bottom of the letter, he spotted a tiny "pto," and flipped it over to continue reading.

—and so I have asked the only person in India I trust enough to make the wisest decision for me. You have met Elijah, and I trust him as the father I never really had. He has made me the happiest man in the world by offering his daughter to be my wife.

"But you're gay! How can you—?"

I have known Elijah's daughter for most of my life, and soon she will become my wife.

One of the biggest struggles was with Winston. I wanted to see him shine as a great dancer, but he, and so many others like him wanted something from me I didn't have to give. I just couldn't.

Philippe, my people are suffering and dying in India. I only arrived at my difficult decision very recently, in fact, during this pandemic. The harder I tried to get home, the more impossible it became. That's when I realized there was no point getting paid so much doing what I love while my own people are starving. It has caused me such great pain. All the money you have paid me has been sent to feed our starving Dalits, but if my decision has hurt you financially, please tell me, and somehow, I will repay. Please forgive me. There was no other way.

God willing, I hope to return to dance for you. I will always spread the word of your wisdom and the faith you show in the young dancers. You have turned them into stars, just as you have me.

I can never say thank you enough.

Philippe, no matter what is ahead, I will always respect you and love you.

Naggya

Philippe sobbed and with trembling hands he placed the letter upon the coffee table. He turned the cellophane wrapper over to reveal its label: New York Wig Company.

The End

Luke 1:37: With God nothing is impossible.

UNTOUCHABLE

What's the greatest tragedy in this story?

Actually, the greatest tragedy in this story isn't, in fact, in this story.

Untouchable is a work of fiction, so in real life, the Naggya who inspired the story didn't actually become a world-famous dancer nor did he transfer millions of dollars to save his starving Dalits.

In real life, the greatest tragedy is that Naggya didn't get his chance! He was abundantly talented, yet like countless young Dalits like him, Naggya was denied his opportunity to shine! Poverty, persecution and deeply engrained corruption stood in his way.

The greatest tragedy is that in India today over three-hundred-million Dalits are kept hidden!

Why?

A Savior

All around, such crumbling I see
Questions from deep, how impacting me?
'Returning to normal' so often heard shout
But when might the hidden, finally, come out?

Declared 'we're too many
Our numbers must fall'
But what be the measure
Be it fair for us all?

What things do true matter?
What passes the test?
New hope I'm to find?
Or the future been set?

By the things I have done
By those battles I've won

Might my best behavior
Serve now as my savior?

Any point to me trying
Yet all done, still dying

By my best behavior
Never serve as my savior

Yet still, outstretched hand
Beckoning 'come', not demand
God whispers 'I love you'
In Me, you can stand

He asks, 'will you reach out
Receive Jesus, My Son?
Your battle's not over
New life has begun'

To stand in His presence
To be weighed as I must
Both now and forever
Where place I, my trust?

What serves all my efforts
What matters behavior
For now be my moment
"Yes Jesus, my Savior"

-RICHARD CONVERY

TRUSTING JESUS FOR SALVATION...

Dear Lord Jesus, I know that I am a sinner, and I ask for
Your forgiveness. I believe You died for my sins and rose
from the dead. I turn from my sins and invite You to come
into my heart and life. I choose to trust and follow You as my
Lord and Savior. In Your Name. Amen.

If you prayed this prayer, hallelujah! Tell someone and let
me know at: rich@spiritmedia.us.

RICHARD CONVERY

UNTOUCHABLE
author hails from
NSW, Australia

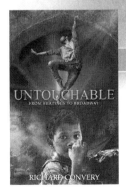

richardconvery.com

Made in the USA
Columbia, SC
02 May 2023

16053342R00286